The Collected
Supernatural and Weird
Fiction of
Edgar Allan Poe
Volume 1

The Collected Supernatural and Weird Fiction of Edgar Allan Poe
Volume 1

Including One Novel "The Narrative of Arthur Gordon Pym of Nantucket," One Novelette "The Unparalleled Adventures of One Hans Pfaal," and Nineteen Short Stories of the Strange and Unusual

Edgar Allan Poe

LEONAUR

The Collected
Supernatural and Weird
Fiction of
Edgar Allan Poe
Volume 1
Including One Novel "The Narrative of Arthur Gordon Pym of Nantucket,"
One Novelette "The Unparalleled Adventures of One Hans Pfaal," and Nineteen
Short Stories of the Strange and Unusual
by Edgar Allan Poe

FIRST EDITION

Leonaur is an imprint
of Oakpast Ltd

ISBN: 978-1-78282-178-6 (hardcover)
ISBN:978-1-78282-179-3 (softcover)

http://www.leonaur.com

Publisher's Notes

Contents

Introduction
By John Buchan

Last year a selection of Emerson's writings was issued in this series, and it seems desirable to follow it with a collection of the best work of that American writer who, morally and intellectually, was Emerson's extreme antitype. There could be no harsher contrast than between the careers of the two men. One came early to recognition, and lived his simple, blameless, prosperous life amid the plaudits of the world. The other died young after a career of bitter drudgery, and left little behind him but a legacy of hate. In Edgar Allan Poe genius burned with no "hard, gem-like flame," but with a murky intensity that scandalised his contemporaries. In the orderly *bourgeois* world of young America he moved like a panther among polar-bears. No nation least of all a young, self-satisfied nation likes to be told that it is "one vast perambulating humbug," and he spoke his opinions equally plainly of his colleagues in literature.

The natural result followed. Every species of literary vulture battened on his reputation, the scandals of his life were magnified, and his genius was hidden by a cloud of vulgar abuse. No man was less, fortunate in his epoch and his country. He found an America, middle-class, prosaic, still half Puritan and indomitably respectable, and he ran his head against the stone walls which hemmed him in. He wrote his great stories for starvation wages, since the taste which could value them had largely to be created. Had he lived today, we can well imagine that a more cosmopolitan America would have made him a hero almost beyond his deserts. Had he fared less hardly at the world's hands, there might have been no gall in his pen and fewer dark places in his life.

His posthumous reward has been great, for to no other American writer has it been given to exercise so profound an influence at once on English and French literature. For myself, I should rank him, in the hierarchy of American prose, below Hawthorne, who seems to me to have combined a profounder moral insight with an equal sense of form and an equal imaginative force; but certainly, save for Hawthorne, he has no rival.

The tragic story of his life has been often written: one of the best short biographies is that by Professor Harrison of Virginia, which is prefixed to the recent *Virginia Edition* of his works. He was born in 1809, the same year which gave to the world Tennyson, Gladstone, Lincoln, Darwin, Mendelssohn, and Chopin. It is part of the irony of his fate that Boston, the city which he hated like the plague, should have had the honour of giving him birth. He came of good stock, originally from Ulster; his parents were on the stage, and lived a roving, unhappy, impecunious life, both dying shortly after he was born. He was adopted by an elderly Scotsman called Allan, a merchant in Richmond, Virginia; and till his adopted father's second marriage regarded himself, and was regarded by others, as his heir. He spent some years at school in England, where he imbibed the romance of an older country, and then went at an early age to the University of Virginia.

He did not greatly distinguish himself there in scholarship, but became noted as a Ion vivant and an athlete. He next went to the famous West Point Academy, and afterwards, Allan having died without leaving him anything, turned to journalism as a profession. For the rest of his days he was tied to the drudgery of the pen, and wrote for his bread tales, poems, reviews, essays, any kind of work, much of it strangely bad, but some of an excellence which no contemporary could claim. He made many enemies, and his wild neurotic nature kept him always in a state of white-heat, a fury either of affection or dislike. He took to drink and drugs, though he was never an ordinary drunkard, seeking a stimulant or a narcotic to relieve the misery of his daily life. His end was as tragic and strange as his life. Passing through Baltimore, he seems to have been drinking in a tavern, where he was drugged by some electioneering roughs and carried round in their custody to the different voting-booths. He never recovered from the treatment, and a few days later died in hospital.

To most people Poe is best known as a poet, and the poems which have the widest vogue are unfortunately his worst productions. *The Raven* was, in his own words, to be composed of "equal proportions of Beauty and Quaintness intermingled with Melancholy." The result was a parody of his peculiar qualities, and the parody, as in the similar case of *The Bells*, has been accepted for the original. That sinister fowl has stood between him and the highest kind of poetic fame. "The vagueness of exaltation," he wrote, "aroused by a sweet air (which should be strictly indefinite and never too strongly suggestive) is precisely what we should aim at in poetry." It is a narrow definition, but in his small body of verse he repeatedly reaches the ideal. *To Helen, The City in the Sea, The Haunted Palace, To One in Paradise, The Sleeper, For Annie, Annabel Lee*, and even beautiful nonsense like *Ulalume*, have all the strange haunting sweetness of music.

On his own definition Poe is a master-singer, and on any definition he is a true lyric poet. But his real medium was prose, for, apart from gifts of style and melody, he had in the highest degree the constructive imagination which can reproduce a realm of fancy with the minute realism of everyday life. He reveals all around us the shadowy domain of the back-world, and behind our smug complacency the shrieking horror of the unknown. There is no humour in him, none of that wise detachment which makes *Wandering Willie's* Tale immortal, for every nerve, as he writes, quivers at the terrors he is conjuring. To this imaginative intensity he added a style of singular flexibility and grace. He has, to be sure, appalling lapses into the banal, but at his best he has a store of apt and jewelled words in which to clothe his recondite thoughts.

It is this combination which endeared him to Théophile

Gautier and his school, and gave him Baudelaire and Mallarmé as his translators. But style and imagination, if left alone, might have landed him in an unprofitable mysticism. What gives him his unique power is the mathematical accuracy of his mind. All his life he had a passion for cryptographs, and maintained that human ingenuity could create no cipher which human ingenuity could not unravel. His mind worked on data with the most logical precision, and he once startled Dickens by predicting the whole plot of *Barnaby Rudge* from the material furnished in the earlier chapters. Hence in all his tales there is a clear sequence of cause and effect which gives them an imaginative coherence and verisimilitude.

Without this gift his fancy would have lost itself in vague flights and barren splendours. The conjunction of such very different talents gives him a right to a high place among the masters of the short story, in his own genre perhaps to the highest place, for I know no French imitator who can produce the haunting sense of fate which we get from *The Fall of the House of Usher*, or the devilish horror of *The Cask of Amontillado*. How admirable, too, are his mystifications, *The Murders in the Rue Morgue* or *The Gold-Bug*. Sometimes, as in *Berenice*, his "mortuary turn of mind" carries him too far for serious art; but he makes amends in tales like *The Narrative of A. Gordon Pym*, where his imagination works soberly and convincingly among realities.

It is a fascinating but barren game which critics sometimes indulge in to discuss which is the best short story in the world. If I were put on oath I should decide for Scott's *Wandering Willie's Tale*, and give the second place to Mr. Kipling's *Man who would be King*. But such a classification, like the Cambridge Senior Wranglership, is captious and unintelligent. A more sensible form of the game is to create a small first-class, say of a dozen. Here it is possible to get something nearer a general agreement. Most people would give one place to Scott (*Wandering Willie's Tale*); one to Stevenson (*Thrawn Janet*, perhaps); one to Hawthorne (the choice is large); one place each to Tourgeniev, Balzac, Guy de Maupassant, Daudet, Anatole France, and Mr. Kipling. In the remaining three I should include Mr. Joseph Conrad's *Youth*, and the two other places I should leave to Poe. The truth seems to be that while Poe wrote nothing that wholly transcends his rivals in his own sphere, he wrote more stories that reach the level of the very best. He deserves two places in a roll of honour where the others have only one.

In an excellent recent essay Mr. Hamilton W. Mabie discusses Poe's place in American literature, and finds in his complete aloofness from vulgar ideals, his exquisite craftsmanship, and his devotion to an austere art for its own sake the example which was especially needed by his generation. He sought above all things distinction, and to a nation which was apt to content itself with the gods of the market-place he preached in his strange way a wholesome lesson. "The final justification of a democracy lies in its ability to clear the way for superiority." The democracy which suffered under his lash is at last beginning to realise the superiority of its critic. So far he is the one great surprise of American letters. A shrewd observer, after the Revolution, might have predicted Longfellow and Emerson and Holmes and Hawthorne, but it would have passed the wit of man to foretell Poe.

J. B.

The Narrative of Arthur Gordon Pym of Nantucket

PREFACE

Upon my return to the United States a few months ago, after the extraordinary series of adventure in the South Seas and elsewhere, of which an account is given in the following pages, accident threw me into the society of several gentlemen in Richmond, Va., who felt deep interest in all matters relating to the regions I had visited, and who were constantly urging it upon me, as a duty, to give my narrative to the public. I had several reasons, however, for declining to do so, some of which were of a nature altogether private, and concern no person but myself; others not so much so. One consideration which deterred me was, that, having kept no journal during a greater portion of the time in which I was absent, I feared I should not be able to write, from mere memory, a statement so minute and connected as to have the appearance of that truth it would really possess, barring only the natural and unavoidable exaggeration to which all of us are prone when detailing events which have had powerful influence in exciting the imaginative faculties.

Another reason was, that the incidents to be narrated were of a nature so positively marvellous, that, unsupported as my assertions must necessarily be (except by the evidence of a single individual, and he a half-breed Indian), I could only hope for belief among my family, and those of my friends who have had reason, through life, to put faith in my veracity—the probability being that the public at large would regard what I should put forth as merely an impudent and ingenious fiction. A distrust in my own abilities as a writer was, nevertheless, one of the principal causes which prevented me from complying with the suggestions of my advisers.

Among those gentlemen in Virginia who expressed the greatest interest in my statement, more particularly in regard to that portion of it which related to the Antarctic Ocean, was Mr. Poe, lately editor of the *Southern Literary Messenger*, a monthly magazine, published by Mr. Thomas W. White, in the city of Richmond. He strongly advised me, among others, to prepare at once a full account of what I had seen and undergone, and trust to the shrewdness and common sense of the public—insisting, with great plausibility, that how ever roughly, as regards mere authorship, my book should be got up, its very uncouthness, if there were any, would give it all the better chance of being received as truth.

Notwithstanding this representation, I did not make up my mind to do as he suggested. He afterward proposed (finding that I would not stir in the matter) that I should allow him to draw up, in his own words, a narrative of the earlier portion of my adventures, from facts afforded by myself, publishing it in the *Southern Messenger under the garb of fiction*. To this, perceiving no objection, I consented, stipulating only that my real name should be retained. Two numbers of the pretended fiction appeared, consequently, in the *Messenger* for January and February (1837), and, in order that it might certainly be regarded as fiction, the name of Mr. Poe was affixed to the articles in the table of contents of the magazine.

The manner in which this *ruse* was received has induced me at length to undertake a regular compilation and publication of the adventures in question; for I found that, in spite of the air of fable which had been so ingeniously thrown around that portion of my statement which appeared in the *Messenger* (without altering or distorting a single fact), the public were still not at all disposed to receive it as fable, and several letters were sent to Mr.

P.'s address distinctly expressing a conviction to the contrary. I thence concluded that the facts of my narrative would prove of such a nature as to carry with them sufficient evidence of their own authenticity, and that I had consequently little to fear on the score of popular incredulity.

This *exposé* being made, it will be seen at once how much of what follows I claim to be my own writing; and it will also be understood that no fact is misrepresented in the first few pages which were written by Mr. Poe. Even to those readers who have not seen the *Messenger*, it will be unnecessary to point out where his portion ends and my own commences; the difference in point of style will be readily perceived.

A. G. Pym.

New-York, July, 1838.

Chapter one

My name is Arthur Gordon Pym. My father was a respectable trader in sea-stores at Nantucket, where I was born. My maternal grandfather was an attorney in good practice. He was fortunate in everything, and had speculated very successfully in stocks of the Edgarton New-Bank, as it was formerly called. By these and other means he had managed to lay by a tolerable sum of money. He was more attached to myself, I believe, than to any other person in the world, and I expected to inherit the most of his property at his death. He sent me, at six years of age, to the school of old Mr. Ricketts, a gentleman with only one arm, and of eccentric manners—he is well known to almost every person who has visited New Bedford. I stayed at his school until I was sixteen, when I left him for Mr. E. Ronald's academy on the hill.

Here I became intimate with the son of Mr. Barnard, a sea captain, who generally sailed in the employ of Lloyd and Vredenburgh—Mr. Barnard is also very well known in New Bedford, and has many relations, I am certain, in Edgarton. His son was named Augustus, and he was nearly two years older than my self. He had been on a whaling voyage with his father in the

John Donaldson, and was always talking to me of his adventures in the South Pacific Ocean. I used frequently to go home with him, and remain all day, and sometimes all night. We occupied the same bed, and he would be sure to keep me awake until almost light, telling me stories of the natives of the Island of Tinian, and other places he had visited in his travels.

At last I could not help being interested in what he said, and by degrees I felt the greatest desire to go to sea. I owned a sailboat called the *Ariel*, and worth about seventy-five dollars. She had a half-deck or cuddy, and was rigged sloop-fashion—I forget her tonnage, but she would hold ten persons without much crowding. In this boat we were in the habit of going on some of the maddest freaks in the world; and, when I now think of them, it appears to me a thousand wonders that I am alive today, (1838).

I will relate one of these adventures by way of introduction to a longer and more momentous narrative. One night there was a party at Mr. Barnard's, and both Augustus and myself were not a little intoxicated towards the close of it. As usual, in such cases, I took part of his bed in preference to going home. He went to sleep, as I thought, very quietly (it being near one when the party broke up), and without saying a word on his favourite topic. It might have been half an hour from the time of our getting in bed, and I was just about falling into a doze, when he suddenly started up, and swore with a terrible oath that he would not go to sleep for any Arthur Pym in Christendom, when there was so glorious a breeze from the southwest. I never was so astonished in my life, not knowing what he intended, and thinking that the wines and liquors he had drunk had set him entirely beside himself. He proceeded to talk very coolly, however, saying he knew that I supposed him intoxicated, but that he was never more sober in his life.

He was only tired, he added, of lying in bed on such a fine night like a dog, and was determined to get up and dress, and go out on a frolic with the boat. I can hardly tell what possessed me, but the words were no sooner out of his mouth than I felt a thrill of the greatest excitement and pleasure, and thought his mad idea one of the most delightful and most reasonable things in the world. It was blowing almost a gale, and the weather was very cold—it being late in October. I sprang out of bed, nevertheless, in a kind of ecstasy, and told him I was quite as brave as himself, and quite as tired as he was of lying in bed like a dog, and quite as ready for any fun or frolic as any Augustus Barnard in Nantucket.

We lost no time in getting on our clothes and hurrying down to the boat. She was lying at the old decayed wharf by the lumber-yard of Pankey & Co., and almost thumping her sides out against the rough logs. Augustus got into her and bailed her, for she was nearly half full of water. This being done, we hoisted jib and main sail, kept full, and started boldly out to sea. The wind, as I before said, blew freshly from the southwest. The night was very clear and cold. Augustus had taken the helm, and I stationed myself by the mast, on the deck of the cuddy. We flew along at a great rate neither of us having said a word since casting loose from the wharf. I now asked my companion what course he intended to steer, and what time he thought it probable we should get back. He whistled for a few minutes, and then said crustily, "*I* am going to sea—*you* may go home if you think proper."

Turning my eyes upon him, I perceived at once that, in spite of his assumed *nonchalance*, he was greatly agitated. I could see him distinctly by the light of the moon—his face was paler than any marble, and his hand shook so excessively that he could scarcely retain hold of the tiller. I found that something had gone wrong, and be came seriously alarmed. At this period I knew little about the management of a boat, and was now depending entirely upon the nautical skill of my friend. The wind, too, had suddenly increased, as we were fast getting out of the lee of the land—still I was ashamed to betray any trepidation, and for almost half an hour maintained a resolute silence. I could stand it no longer, however, and spoke to Augustus about the propriety of turning back. As before, it was nearly a minute before he made answer, or took any notice of my suggestion. "By-

and-by," said he at length—"time enough—home by-and-by."

I had expected a similar reply, but there was something in the tone of these words which filled me with an indescribable feeling of dread. I again looked at the speaker attentively. His lips were perfectly livid, and his knees shook so violently together that he seemed scarcely able to stand. "For God's sake, Augustus," I screamed, now heartily frightened, "what ails you?—what is the matter?—what *are* you going to do?"

"Matter!" he stammered, in the greatest apparent surprise, letting go the tiller at the same moment, and falling forward into the bottom of the boat—"matter!—why, nothing is the—matter—going home—d—d—don't you see?"

The whole truth now flashed upon me. I flew to him and raised him up. He was drunk—beastly drunk—he could no longer either stand, speak, or see. His eyes were perfectly glazed; and as I let him go in the extremity of my despair, he rolled like a mere log into the bilge-water from which I had lifted him. It was evident that, during the evening, he had drunk far more than I suspected, and that his conduct in bed had been the result of a highly-concentrated state of intoxication—a state which, like madness, frequently enables the victim to imitate the outward demeanour of one in perfect possession of his senses. The coolness of the night air, however, had had its usual effect—the mental energy began to yield before its influence—and the confused perception which he no doubt then had of his perilous situation had assisted in hastening the catastrophe. He was now thoroughly insensible, and there was no probability that he would be otherwise for many hours.

It is hardly possible to conceive the extremity of my terror. The fumes of the wine lately taken had evaporated, leaving me doubly timid and irresolute. I knew that I was altogether incapable of managing the boat, and that a fierce wind and strong ebb tide were hurrying us to destruction. A storm was evidently gathering be hind us; we had neither compass nor provisions; and it was clear that, if we held our present course, we should be out of sight of land before daybreak. These thoughts, with a crowd of others equally fearful, flashed through my mind with a bewildering rapidity, and for some moments paralysed me beyond the possibility of making any exertion.

The boat was going through the water at a terrible rate—full before the wind—no reef in either jib or mainsail—running her bows completely under the foam. It was a thousand wonders she did not broach—to Augustus having let go the tiller, as I said before, and I being too much agitated to think of taking it my self. By good luck, however, she kept steady, and gradually I recovered some degree of presence of mind. Still the wind was increasing fearfully; and whenever we rose from a plunge forward, the sea behind fell combing over our counter, and deluged us with water. I was so utterly benumbed, too, in every limb, as to be nearly unconscious of sensation. At length I summoned up the resolution of despair, and rushing to the mainsail, let it go by the run.

As might have been expected, it flew over the bows, and, getting drenched with water, carried away the mast short off by the board. This latter accident alone saved me from instant destruction. Under the jib only, I now boomed along before the wind, shipping heavy seas occasionally over the counter, but relieved from the terror of immediate death. I took the helm, and breathed with greater freedom as I found that there yet remained to us a chance of ultimate escape. Augustus still lay senseless in the bottom of the boat; and as there was imminent danger of his drowning (the water being nearly a foot deep just where he fell), I contrived to raise him partially up, and keep him in a sitting position, by passing a rope round his waist, and lashing it to a ringbolt in the deck of the cuddy. Having thus arranged everything as well as I could in my chilled and agitated condition, I recommended myself to God, and made up my mind to bear what ever might happen with all the fortitude in my power.

Hardly had I come to this resolution, when, suddenly, a loud and long scream or yell, as if from the throats of a thousand demons, seemed to pervade the whole atmosphere around and above the boat. Never while I live shall I forget the intense agony of terror I experienced at that moment. My hair stood erect on my head—I felt the blood congealing in my veins—my heart ceased utterly to beat, and without having once raised my eyes to learn the source of my alarm, I tumbled headlong and insensible upon the body of my fallen companion.

I found myself, upon reviving, in the cabin of a large whaling-ship (the *Penguin*) bound to Nantucket. Several persons were standing over me, and Augustus, paler than death, was busily occupied in chafing my hands. Upon seeing me open my eyes, his exclamations of gratitude and joy excited alternate laughter and tears from the rough-looking personages who were present. The mystery of our being in existence was now soon explained. We had been run down by the whaling-ship, which was close hauled, beating up to Nantucket with every sail she could venture to set, and consequently running almost at right angles to our own course. Several men were on the look-out forward, but did not perceive our boat until it was an impossibility to avoid coming in contact their shouts of warning upon seeing us were what so terribly alarmed me. The huge ship, I was told, rode immediately over us with as much ease as our own little vessel would have passed over a feather, and without the least perceptible impediment to her progress.

Not a scream arose from the deck of the victim—there was a slight grating sound to be heard mingling with the roar of wind and water, as the frail bark which was swallowed up rubbed for a moment along the keel of her destroyer—but this was all. Thinking our boat (which it will be remembered was dismasted) some mere shell cut adrift as useless, the captain (Captain E. T.V. Block of New London) was for proceeding on his course without troubling himself further about the matter. Luckily, there were two of the look-out who swore positively to having seen some person at our helm, and represented the possibility of yet saving him. A discussion ensued, when Block grew angry, and, after a while, said that "it was no business of his to be eternally watching for eggshells; that the ship should *not* put about for any such nonsense; and if there was a man run down, it was nobody's fault but his own—he might drown and be d——d," or some language to that effect. Henderson, the first mate, now took the matter up, being justly indignant, as well as the whole ship's crew, at a speech evincing so base a degree of heartless atrocity.

He spoke plainly, seeing himself upheld by the men, told the captain he considered him a fit subject for the gallows, and that he would disobey his orders if he were hanged for it the moment he set his foot on shore. He strode aft, jostling Block (who turned very pale and made no answer) on one side, and seizing the helm, gave the word, in a firm voice, *Hard-a-lee!* The men flew to their posts, and the ship went cleverly about. All this had occupied nearly five minutes, and it was supposed to be hardly within the bounds of possibility that any individual could be saved—allowing any to have been on board the boat. Yet, as the reader has seen, both Augustus and myself were rescued; and our deliverance seemed to have been brought about by two of those almost inconceivable pieces of good fortune which are attributed by the wise and pious to the special interference of Providence.

While the ship was yet in stays, the mate lowered the jolly-boat and jumped into her with the very two men, I believe, who spoke up as having seen me at the helm. They had just left the lee of the vessel (the moon still shining brightly) when she made a long and heavy roll to windward, and Henderson, at the same moment, starting up in his seat, bawled out to his crew to *back water*. He would say nothing else—repeating his cry impatiently, *back water! back water!* The men put back as speedily as possible; but by this time the ship had gone round, and gotten fully under headway, although all hands on board were making great exertions to take in sail. In despite of the danger of the attempt, the mate clung to the main-chains as soon as they came within his reach.

Another huge lurch now brought the starboard side of the vessel out of water nearly as far as her keel, when the cause of his anxiety was rendered obvious enough. The body of a man was seen to be affixed in the most singular manner to the smooth and shining bottom (the *Penguin* was coppered and copper-fastened), and beating violently against it with every movement of the hull. After several ineffectual efforts, made during the lurches of the ship, and at the imminent risk of swamping the boat, I was finally disengaged from my perilous situation and taken on board—for the body proved to be my own.

It appeared that one of the timber-bolts having started and broken a passage through the copper, it had arrested my progress as I passed under the ship, and fastened me in so extraordinary a manner to her bottom. The head of the bolt had made its way through the collar of the green baize jacket I had on, and through the back part of my neck, forcing itself out between two sinews and just below the right ear. I was immediately put to bed—although life seemed to be totally extinct. There was no surgeon on board. The captain, however, treated me with every attention—to make amends, I presume, in the eyes of his crew, for his atrocious behaviour in the previous portion of the adventure.

In the meantime, Henderson had again put off from the ship, although the wind was now blowing almost a hurricane. He had not been gone many minutes when he fell in with some fragments of our boat, and shortly afterward one of the men with him asserted that he could distinguish a cry for help at intervals amid the roaring of the tempest. This induced the hardy seamen to persevere in their search for more than half an hour, although repeated signals to return were made them by Captain Block, and although every moment on the water in so frail a boat was fraught to them with the most imminent and deadly peril. Indeed, it is nearly impossible to conceive how the small jolly they were in could have escaped destruction for a single instant. She was built, however, for the whaling service, and was fitted, as I have since had reason to believe, with air-boxes, in the manner of some life-boats used on the coast of Wales.

After searching in vain for about the period of time just mentioned, it was determined to get back to the ship. They had scarcely made this resolve when a feeble cry arose from a dark object which floated rapidly by. They pursued and soon overtook it. It proved to be the entire deck of the *Ariel's* cuddy. Augustus was struggling near it, apparently in the last agonies. Upon getting hold of him it was found that he was attached by a rope to the floating timber.

This rope, it will be remembered, I had myself tied round his waist, and made fast to a ringbolt, for the purpose of keeping him in an upright position, and my so doing, it appeared, had been ultimately the means of preserving his life. The *Ariel* was slightly put together, and in going down her frame naturally went to pieces; the deck of the cuddy, as might be expected, was lifted, by the force of the water rushing in, entirely from the main timbers, and floated (with other fragments, no doubt) to the surface—Augustus was buoyed up with it, and thus escaped a terrible death.

It was more than an hour after being taken on board the *Penguin* before he could give any account of himself, or be made to comprehend the nature of the accident which had befallen our boat. At length he became thoroughly aroused, and spoke much of his sensations while in the water. Upon his first attaining any degree of consciousness, he found himself beneath the surface, whirling round and round with inconceivable rapidity, and with a rope wrapped in three or four folds tightly about his neck. In an instant afterward he felt himself going rapidly upward, when, his head striking violently against a hard substance, he again relapsed into insensibility. Upon once more reviving he was in fuller possession of his reason—this was still, however, in the greatest degree clouded and confused.

He now knew that some accident had occurred, and that he was in the water, although his mouth was above the surface, and he could breathe with some freedom. Possibly, at this period, the deck was drifting rapidly before the wind, and drawing him after it, as he floated upon his back. Of course, as long as he could have retained this position, it would have been nearly impossible that he should be drowned. Presently a surge threw him directly athwart the deck; and this post he endeavoured to maintain, screaming at intervals for help. Just before he was discovered by Mr. Henderson, he had been obliged to relax his hold through exhaustion, and, falling into the sea, had given himself up for lost. During the whole period of his struggles he had not the faintest recollection of the *Ariel*, nor of any matters in connexion with the source of his disaster.

A vague feeling of terror and despair had taken entire possession of his faculties. When he was finally picked up, every power of his mind had failed him; and, as before said, it was nearly an hour after getting on board the *Penguin* before he became fully aware of his condition. In regard to myself—I was resuscitated from a state bordering very nearly upon death (and after every other means had been tried in vain for three hours and a half) by vigorous friction with flannels bathed in hot oil—a proceeding suggested by Augustus. The wound in my neck, although of an ugly appearance, proved of little real consequence, and I soon recovered from its effects.

The *Penguin* got into port about nine o'clock in the morning, after encountering one of the severest gales ever experienced off Nantucket. Both Augustus and myself managed to appear at Mr. Barnard's in time for breakfast—which, luckily, was somewhat late, owing to the party over night. I suppose all at the table were too much fatigued themselves to notice our jaded appearance—of course, it would not have borne a very rigid scrutiny. Schoolboys, however, can accomplish wonders in the way of deception, and I verily believe not one of our friends in Nantucket had the slightest suspicion that the terrible story told by some sailors in town of their having run down a vessel at sea and drowned some thirty or forty poor devils, had reference either to the *Ariel*, my companion, or myself.

We two have since very frequently talked the matter over—but never without a shudder. In one of our conversations' Augustus frankly confessed to me, that in his whole life he had at no time experienced so excruciating a sense of dismay, as when on board our little boat he first discovered the extent of his intoxication, and felt himself sinking beneath its influence.

Chapter 2

In no affairs of mere prejudice, *pro* or *con*, do we deduce inferences with entire certainty even from the most simple data. It might be supposed that a catastrophe such as I have just related would have effectually cooled my incipient passion for the sea. On the contrary, I never experienced a more ardent longing for the wild adventures incident to the life of a navigator than within a week after our miraculous deliverance. This short period proved amply long enough to erase from my memory the shadows, and bring out in vivid light all the pleasurably exciting points of colour, all the picturesqueness of the late perilous accident. My conversations with Augustus grew daily more frequent and more intensely full of interest. He had a manner of relating his stories of the ocean (more than one half of which I now suspect to have been sheer fabrications) well adapted to have weight with one of my enthusiastic temperament, and somewhat gloomy, although glowing imagination.

It is strange, too, that he most strongly enlisted my feelings in behalf of the life of a seaman, when he depicted his more terrible moments of suffering and despair. For the bright side of the painting I had a limited sympathy. My visions were of shipwreck and famine; of death or captivity among barbarian hordes; of a lifetime dragged out in sorrow and tears, upon some gray and desolate rock, in an ocean unapproachable and unknown. Such visions or desires—for they amounted to desires are common, I have since been assured, to the whole numerous race of the melancholy among men—at the time of which I speak I regarded them only as prophetic glimpses of a destiny which I felt myself in a measure bound to fulfil. Augustus thoroughly entered into my state of mind. It is probable, indeed, that our intimate communion had resulted in a partial interchange of character.

About eighteen months after the period of the *Ariel's* disaster, the firm of Lloyd and Vredenburgh (a house connected in some manner with the Messieurs Enderby, I believe, of Liverpool) were engaged in repairing and fitting out the brig *Grampus* for a whaling voyage. She was an old hulk, and scarcely seaworthy when all was done to her that could be done. I hardly know why she was chosen in preference to other good vessels belonging to the same owners—but so it was. Mr. Barnard was appointed to command her, and Augustus was going with him.

While the brig was getting ready, he frequently urged upon me the excellency of the opportunity now offered for indulging my desire of travel. He found me by no means an unwilling listener—yet the matter could not be so easily arranged. My father made no direct opposition; but my mother went into hysterics at the bare mention of the design; and, more than all, my grandfather, from whom I expected much, vowed to cut me off with a shilling if I should ever broach the subject to him again. These difficulties, however, so far from abating my desire, only added fuel to the flame. I determined to go at all hazards; and, having made known my intention to Augustus, we set about arranging a plan by which it might be accomplished. In the meantime I forbore speaking to any of my relations in regard to the voyage, and, as I busied my self ostensibly with my usual studies, it was supposed that I had abandoned the design.

I have since frequently examined my conduct on this occasion with sentiments of displeasure as well as of surprise. The intense hypocrisy I made use of for the furtherance of my project—an hypocrisy pervading every word and action of my life for so long a period of time—could only have been rendered tolerable to myself by the wild and burning expectation with which I looked forward to the fulfilment of my long-cherished visions of travel.

In pursuance of my scheme of deception, I was necessarily obliged to leave much to the management of Augustus, who was employed for the greater part of every day on board the *Grampus*, attending to some arrangements for his father in the cabin and cabin hold. At night, however, we were sure to have a conference, and talk over our hopes. After nearly a month passed in this manner, without our hitting upon any plan we thought likely to succeed, he told me at last that he had determined upon everything necessary. I had a relation living in New Bedford, a Mr. Ross, at whose house I was in the habit of spending occasionally two or three weeks at a time.

The brig was to sail about the middle of June (June, 1827), and it was agreed that, a day or two before her putting to sea, my father was to receive a note, as usual, from Mr. Ross, asking me to come over and spend a fortnight with Robert and Emmet (his sons). Augustus charged himself with the editing of this note and getting it delivered. Having set out, as supposed, for New Bedford, I was then to report myself to my companion, who would contrive a hiding-place for me in the *Grampus*. This hiding-place, he assured me, would be rendered sufficiently comfort able for a residence of many days, during which I was not to make my appearance. When the brig had proceeded so far on her course as to make any turning back a matter out of question, I should then, he said, be formally installed in all the comforts of the cabin; and as to his father, he would only laugh heartily at the joke. Vessels enough would be met with by which a letter might be sent home explaining the adventure to my parents.

The middle of June at length arrived, and everything had been matured. The note was written and delivered, and on a Monday morning I left the house for the New Bedford packet, as supposed. I went, however, straight to Augustus, who was waiting for me at the corner of a street. It had been our original plan that I should keep out of the way until dark, and then slip on board the brig; but, as there was now a thick fog in our favour, it was agreed to lose no time in secreting me. Augustus led the way to the wharf, and I followed at a little distance, enveloped in a thick seaman's cloak, which he had brought with him, so that my person might not be easily recognised.

Just as we turned the second corner, after passing Mr. Edmund's well, who should appear, standing right in front of me, and looking me full in the face, but old Mr. Peterson, my grandfather. "Why, bless my soul, Gordon," said he, after a long pause, "why, why—*whose* dirty cloak is that you have on?"

"Sir!" I replied, assuming, as well as I could, in the exigency of the moment, an air of offended surprise, and talking in the gruffest of all imaginable tones—"sir! you are a sum'mat mistaken—my name, in the first place, bee'nt nothing at all like Goddin, and I'd want you for to know better, you blackguard, than to call my new obercoat a darty one!"

For my life I could hardly refrain from screaming with laughter at the odd manner in which the old gentleman received this handsome rebuke. He started back two or three steps, turned first pale and then excessively red, threw up his spectacles, then, putting them down, ran full tilt at me, with his umbrella uplifted. He stopped short, however, in his career, as if struck with a sudden recollection; and presently, turning round, hobbled off down the street, shaking all the while with rage, and muttering between his teeth, "Won't do—new glasses—thought it was Gordon—d—d good-for-nothing salt water Long Tom."

After this narrow escape we proceeded with greater caution, and arrived at our point of destination in safety. There were only one or two of the hands on board, and these were busy forward, doing something to the fore castle combings. Captain Barnard, we knew very well, was engaged at Lloyd and Vredenburg's, and would re main there until late in the evening, so we had little to apprehend on his account. Augustus went first up the vessel's side, and in a short while I followed him, with out being noticed by the men at work. We proceeded at once into the cabin, and found no person there. It was fitted up in the most comfortable style—a thing somewhat unusual in a whaling-vessel. There were four very excellent staterooms, with wide and convenient berths.

There was also a large stove, I took notice, and a remarkably thick and valuable carpet covering the floor of both the cabin and staterooms. The ceiling was full seven feet high, and, in short, everything appeared of a more roomy and agreeable nature than I had anticipated. Augustus, however, would allow me but little time for observation, insisting upon the necessity of my concealing myself as soon as possible. He led the way into his own stateroom, which was on the starboard side of the brig, and next to the bulkheads. Upon entering, he closed the door and bolted it. I thought I had never seen a nicer little room than the one in which I now found myself. It was about ten feet long, and had only one berth, which, as I said before, was wide and convenient. In that portion of the closet nearest the bulkheads there was a space of four feet square, containing a table, a chair, and a set of hanging shelves full of books, chiefly books of voyages and travels. There were many other little comforts in the room, among which I ought not to forget a kind of safe or refrigerator, in which Augustus pointed out to me a host of delicacies, both in the eating and drinking department.

He now pressed with his knuckles upon a certain spot of the carpet in one corner of the space just mentioned, letting me know that a portion of the flooring, about six teen inches square, had been neatly cut out and again adjusted. As he pressed, this portion rose up at one end sufficiently to allow the passage of his finger beneath. In this manner he raised the mouth of the trap (to which the carpet was still fastened by tacks), and I found that it led into the after hold. He next lit a small taper by means of a phosphorus match, and, placing the light in a dark lantern, descended with it through the opening, bidding me follow. I did so, and he then pulled the cover upon the hole, by means of a nail driven into the underside—the carpet, of course, resuming its original position on the floor of the stateroom, and all traces of the aperture being concealed.

The taper gave out so feeble a ray, that it was with the greatest difficulty I could grope my way through the confused mass of lumber among which I now found myself. By degrees, however, my eyes became accustomed to the gloom, and I proceeded with less trouble, holding on to the skirts of my friend's coat. He brought me, at length, after creeping and winding through innumerable narrow passages, to an iron-bound box, such as is used sometimes for packing fine earthenware. It was nearly four feet high, and full six long, but very narrow.

Two large empty oil-casks lay on the top of it, and above these, again, a vast quantity of straw matting, piled up as high as the floor of the cabin. In every other direction around was wedged as closely as possible, even up to the ceiling, a complete chaos of almost every species of ship-furniture, together with a heterogeneous medley of crates, hampers, barrels, and bales, so that it seemed a matter no less than miraculous that we had discovered any passage at all to the box. I afterward found that Augustus had purposely arranged the stowage in this hold with a view to affording me a thorough concealment, having had only one assistant in the labour, a man not going out in the brig.

My companion now showed me that one of the ends of the box could be removed at pleasure. He slipped it aside and displayed the interior, at which I was excessively amused. A mattress from one of the cabin berths covered the whole of its bottom, and it contained almost every article of mere comfort which could be crowded into so small a space, allowing me, at the same time, sufficient room for my accommodation, either in a sitting position or lying at full length. Among other things, there were some books, pen, ink, and paper, three blankets, a large jug full of water, a keg of sea-biscuit, three or four immense Bologna sausages, an enormous ham, a cold leg of roast mutton, and half a dozen bottles of cordials and liqueurs.

I proceeded immediately to take possession of my little apartment, and this with feelings of higher satisfaction, I am sure, than any monarch ever experienced upon entering a new palace. Augustus now pointed out to me the method of fastening the open end of the box, and then, holding the taper close to the deck, showed me a piece of dark whipcord lying along it. This, he said, extended from my hiding-place throughout all the necessary windings among the lumber, to a nail which was driven into the deck of the hold, immediately beneath the trapdoor leading into his stateroom. By means of this cord I should be enabled readily to trace my way out without his guidance, provided any unlooked-for accident should render such a step necessary. He now took his departure, leaving with me the lantern, together with a copious supply of tapers and phosphorus, and promising to pay me a visit as often as he could contrive to do so without observation. This was on the seventeenth of June.

I remained three days and nights (as nearly as I could guess) in my hiding-place without getting out of it at all, except twice for the purpose of stretching my limbs by standing erect between two crates just opposite the opening. During the whole period I saw nothing of Augustus; but this occasioned me little uneasiness, as I knew the brig was expected to put to sea every hour, and in the bustle he would not easily find opportunities of coming down to me. At length I heard the trap open and shut, and presently he called in a low voice, asking if all was well, and if there was anything I wanted.

"Nothing," I replied; "I am as comfortable as can be; when will the brig sail?"

"She will be under weigh in less than half an hour," he answered. "I came to let you know, and for fear you should be uneasy at my absence. I shall not have a chance of coming down again for some time—perhaps for three or four days more. All is going on right aboveboard. After I go up and close the trap, do you creep along by the whipcord to where the nail is driven in. You will find my watch there it may be useful to you, as you have no daylight to keep time by. I suppose you can't tell how long you have been, buried only three days this is the twentieth. I would bring the watch to your box, but am afraid of being missed." With this he went up.

In about an hour after he had gone I distinctly felt the brig in motion, and congratulated myself upon having at length fairly commenced a voyage. Satisfied with this idea, I determined to make my mind as easy as possible, and await the course of events until I should be permitted to exchange the box for the more roomy, al though hardly more comfortable, accommodations of the cabin. My first care was to get the watch. Leaving the taper burning, I groped along in the dark, following the cord through windings innumerable, in some of which I discovered that, after toiling a long distance, I was brought back within a foot or two of a former position.

At length I reached the nail, and, securing the object of my journey, returned with it in safety. I now looked over the books which had been so thoughtfully provided, and selected *The Expedition of Lewis and Clarke to the Mouth of the Columbia*. With this I amused myself for some time, when, growing sleepy, I extinguished the light with great care, and soon fell into a sound slumber. Upon awaking I felt strangely confused in mind, and some time elapsed before I could bring to recollection all the various circumstances of my situation. By degrees, however, I remembered all. Striking a light, I looked at the watch; but it was run down, and there were, consequently, no means of determining how long I had slept. My limbs were greatly cramped, and I was forced to relieve them by standing between the crates. Presently, feeling an almost ravenous appetite, I bethought myself of the cold mutton, some of which I had eaten just before going to sleep, and found excellent.

What was my astonishment at discovering it to be in a state of absolute putrefaction! This circumstance occasioned me great disquietude; for, connecting it with the disorder of mind I experienced upon awaking, I began to suppose that I must have slept for an inordinately long period of time. The close atmosphere of the hold might have had something to do with this, and might, in the end, be productive of the most serious results. My head ached excessively; I fancied that I drew every breath with difficulty; and, in short, I was oppressed with a multitude of gloomy feelings. Still I could not venture to make any disturbance by opening the trap or other wise, and, having wound up the watch, contented myself as well as possible.

Throughout the whole of the next tedious twenty-four hours no person came to my relief, and I could not help accusing Augustus of the grossest inattention. What alarmed me chiefly was, that the water in my jug was reduced to about half a pint, and I was suffering much from thirst, having eaten freely of the Bologna sausages after the loss of my mutton. I became very uneasy, and could no longer take any interest in my books. I was overpowered, too, with a desire to sleep, yet trembled at the thought of indulging it, lest there might exist some pernicious influence, like that of burning charcoal, in the confined air of the hold. In the meantime the roll of the brig told me that we were far in the main ocean, and a dull humming sound, which reached my ears as if from an immense distance, convinced me no ordinary gale was blowing.

I could not imagine a reason for the absence of Augustus. We were surely far enough advanced on our voyage to allow of my going up. Some accident might have happened to him—but I could think of none which would account for his suffering me to remain so long a prisoner, except, indeed, his having suddenly died or fallen overboard, and upon this idea I could not dwell with any degree of patience. It was possible that we had been baffled by head winds, and were still in the near vicinity of Nantucket. This notion, however, I was forced to abandon; for, such being the case, the brig must have frequently gone about; and I was entirely satisfied, from her continual inclination to the larboard, that she had been sailing all along with a steady breeze on her starboard quarter.

Besides, granting that we were still in the neighbourhood of the island, why should not Augustus have visited me and informed me of the circumstance? Pondering in this manner upon the difficulties of my solitary and cheerless condition, I resolved to wait yet another twenty-four hours, when, if no relief were obtained, I would make my way to the trap, and endeavour either to hold a parley with my friend, or get at least a little fresh air through the opening, and a further supply of water from his stateroom. While occupied with this thought, however, I fell, in spite of every exertion to the contrary, into a state of profound sleep, or rather stupor.

My dreams were of the most terrific description. Every species of calamity and horror befell me. Among other miseries, I was smothered to death between huge pillows, by demons of the most ghastly and ferocious aspect. Immense serpents held me in their embrace, and looked earnestly in my face with their fearfully shining eyes. Then deserts, limitless, and of the most forlorn and awe-inspiring character, spread themselves out before me. Immensely tall trunks of trees, gray and leafless, rose up in end less succession as far as the eye could reach. Their roots were concealed in wide-spreading morasses, whose dreary water lay intensely black, still, and altogether terrible, beneath. And the strange trees seemed endowed with a human vitality, and, waving to and fro their skeleton arms, were crying to the silent waters for mercy, in the shrill and piercing accents of the most acute agony and despair.

The scene changed; and I stood, naked and alone, amid the burning sand-plains of Zahara. At my feet lay crouched a fierce lion of the tropics. Suddenly his wild eyes opened and fell upon me. With a convulsive bound he sprang to his feet, and laid bare his horrible teeth. In another instant there burst from his red throat a roar like the thunder of the firmament, and I fell impetuously to the earth. Stifling in a paroxysm of terror, I at last found myself partially awake. My dream, then, was not all a dream. Now, at least, I was in possession of my senses. The paws of some huge and real monster were pressing heavily upon my bosom—his hot breath was in my ear—and his white and ghastly fangs were gleaming upon me through the gloom.

Had a thousand lives hung upon the movement of a limb or the utterance of a syllable, I could have neither stirred nor spoken. The beast, whatever it was, retained his position without attempting any immediate violence, while I lay in an utterly helpless, and, I fancied, a dying condition beneath him. I felt that my powers of body and mind were fast leaving me—in a word, that I was perishing, and perishing of sheer fright. My brain swam—I grew deadly sick—my vision failed—even the glaring eyeballs above me grew dim. Making a last strong effort, I at length breathed a faint ejaculation to God, and resigned myself to die.

The sound of my voice seemed to arouse all the latent fury of the animal. He precipitated himself at full length upon my body; but what was my astonishment, when, with a long and low whine, he commenced licking my face and hands with the greatest eagerness, and with the most extravagant demonstrations of affection and joy! I was bewildered, utterly lost in amazement—but I could not forget the peculiar whine of my Newfoundland dog Tiger, and the odd manner of his caresses I well knew. It was he. I experienced a sudden rush of blood to my temples—a giddy and overpowering sense of deliverance and reanimation. I rose hurriedly from the mattress upon which I had been lying, and, throwing myself upon the neck of my faithful follower and friend, relieved the long oppression of my bosom in a flood of the most passionate tears.

As upon a former occasion, my conceptions were in a state of the greatest indistinctness and confusion after leaving the mattress. For a long time I found it nearly impossible to connect any ideas—but, by very slow degrees, my thinking faculties returned, and I again called to memory the several incidents of my condition. For the presence of Tiger I tried in vain to account; and after busying myself with a thousand different conjectures respecting him, was forced to content myself with rejoicing that he was with me to share my dreary solitude, and render me comfort by his caresses.

Most people love their dogs—but for Tiger I had an affection far more ardent than common; and never, certainly, did any creature more truly deserve it. For seven years he had been my inseparable companion, and in a multitude of instances had given evidence of all the noble qualities for which we value the animal. I had rescued him, when a puppy, from the clutches of a malignant little villain in Nantucket, who was leading him, with a rope around his neck, to the water; and the grown dog repaid the obligation, about three years afterward, by saving me from the bludgeon of a street-robber.

Getting now hold of the watch, I found, upon applying it to my ear, that it had again run down; but at this I was not at all surprised, being convinced, from the peculiar state of my feelings, that I had slept, as before, for a very long period of time; how long, it was of course impossible to say. I was burning up with fever, and my thirst was almost intolerable. I felt about the box for my little remaining supply of water; for I had no light, the taper having burnt to the socket of the lantern, and the phosphorus-box not coming readily to hand. Upon finding the jug, however, I discovered it to be empty—Tiger, no doubt, having been tempted to drink it, as well as to devour the remnant of mutton, the bone of which lay, well picked, by the opening of the box. The spoiled meat I could well spare, but my heart sank as I thought of the water. I was feeble in the extreme—so much so that I shook all over, as with an ague, at the slightest movement or exertion.

To add to my troubles, the brig was pitching and rolling with great violence, and the oil-casks which lay upon my box were in momentary danger of falling down, so as to block up the only way of ingress or egress. I felt, also, terrible sufferings from sea-sickness. These considerations determined me to make my way, at all hazards, to the trap, and obtain immediate relief, before I should be incapacitated from doing so altogether. Having come to this resolve, I again felt about for the phosphorus-box and tapers. The former I found after some little trouble; but, not discovering the tapers as soon as I had expected (for I remembered very nearly the spot in which I had placed them), I gave up the search for the present, and bidding Tiger lie quiet, began at once my journey towards the trap.

In this attempt my great feebleness became more than ever apparent. It was with the utmost difficulty I could crawl along at all, and very frequently my limbs sank suddenly from beneath me; when, falling prostrate on my face, I would remain for some minutes in a state bordering on insensibility. Still I struggled forward by slow degrees, dreading every moment that I should swoon amid the narrow and intricate windings of the lumber, in which event I had nothing but death to expect as the result. At length, upon making a push for ward with all the energy I could command, I struck my forehead violently against the sharp corner of an iron-bound crate.

The accident only stunned me for a few moments; but I

found, to my inexpressible grief, that the quick and violent roll of the vessel had thrown the crate entirely across my path, so as effectually to block up the passage. With my utmost exertions I could not move it a single inch from its position, it being closely wedged in among the surrounding boxes and ship-furniture. It became necessary, therefore, enfeebled as I was, either to leave the guidance of the whipcord and seek out a new passage, or to climb over the obstacle, and resume the path on the other side. The former alternative presented too many difficulties and dangers to be thought of without a shudder. In my present weak state of both mind and body, I should infallibly lose my way if I attempted it, and perish miserably amid the dismal and disgusting labyrinths of the hold. I proceeded, therefore, without hesitation, to summon up all my remaining strength and fortitude, and endeavour, as I best might, to clamber over the crate.

Upon standing erect, with this end in view, I found the undertaking even a more serious task than my fears had led me to imagine. On each side of the narrow passage arose a complete wall of various heavy lumber, which the least blunder on my part might be the means of bringing down upon my head; or, if this accident did not occur, the path might be effectually blocked up against my return by the descending mass, as it was in front by the obstacle there. The crate itself was a long and unwieldy box, upon which no foothold could be obtained. In vain I attempted, by every means in my power, to reach the top, with the hope of being thus enabled to draw myself up. Had I succeeded in reaching it, it is certain that my strength would have proved utterly inadequate to the task of getting over, and it was better in every respect that I failed.

At length, in a desperate effort to force the crate from its ground, I felt a strong vibration in the side next me. I thrust my hand eagerly to the edge of the planks, and found that a very large one was loose. With my pocket-knife, which luckily I had with me, I succeeded, after great labour, in prying it entirely off; and, getting through the aperture, discovered, to my exceeding joy, that there were no boards on the opposite side—in other words, that the top was wanting, it being the bottom through which I had forced my way. I now met with no important difficulty in proceeding along the line until I finally reached the nail. With a beating heart I stood erect, and with a gentle touch pressed against the cover of the trap. It did not rise as soon as I had expected, and I pressed it with somewhat more determination, still dreading lest some other person than Augustus might be in his stateroom.

The door, however, to my astonishment, remained steady, and I became somewhat uneasy, for I knew that it had formerly required little or no effort to remove it. I pushed it strongly—it was nevertheless firm: with all my strength—it still did not give way: with rage, with fury, with despair—it set at defiance my utmost efforts; and it was evident, from the unyielding nature of the resistance, that the hole had either been discovered and effectually nailed up, or that some immense weight had been placed upon it, which it was useless to think of removing,

My sensations were those of extreme horror and dismay. In vain I attempted to reason on the probable cause of my being thus entombed. I could summon up no connected chain of reflection, and, sinking on the floor, gave way, unresistingly, to the most gloomy imaginings, in which the dreadful deaths of thirst, famine, suffocation, and premature interment, crowded upon me as the prominent disasters to be encountered.

At length there returned to me some portion of presence of mind. I arose, and felt with my fingers for the seams or cracks of the aperture. Having found them, I examined them closely to ascertain if they emitted any light from the stateroom; but none was visible. I then forced the pen-blade of my knife through them, until I met with some hard obstacle. Scraping against it, I discovered it to be a solid mass of iron, which, from its peculiar wavy feel as I passed the blade along it, I concluded to be a chain-cable. The only course now left me was to retrace my way to the box, and there either yield to my sad fate, or try so to tranquillize my mind as to admit of my arranging some plan of escape. I immediately set about the attempt, and succeeded, after innumerable difficulties, in getting back. As I sank, utterly exhausted, upon the mattress, Tiger threw himself at full length by my side, and seemed as if desirous, by his caresses, of consoling me in my troubles, and urging me to bear them with fortitude.

The singularity of his behaviour at length forcibly arrested my attention. After licking my face and hands for some minutes, he would suddenly cease doing so, and utter a low whine. Upon reaching out my hand towards him, I then invariably found him lying on his back, with his paws uplifted. This conduct, so frequently repeated, appeared strange, and I could in no manner account for it. As the dog seemed distressed, I concluded that he had received some injury; and, taking his paws in my hands, I examined them one by one, but found no sign of any hurt. I then supposed him hungry, and gave him a large piece of ham, which he devoured with avidity—afterward, however, resuming his extraordinary manoeuvres.

I now imagined that he was suffering, like myself, the torments of thirst, and was about adopting this conclusion as the true one, when the idea occurred to me that I had as yet only examined his paws, and that there might possibly be a wound upon some portion of his body or head. The latter I felt carefully over, but found nothing. On passing my hand, however, along his back, I perceived a slight erection of the hair extending completely across it. Probing this with my finger, I discovered a string, and, tracing it up, found that it encircled the whole body. Upon a closer scrutiny, I came across a small slip of what had the feeling of letter paper, through which the string had been fastened in such a manner as to bring it immediately beneath the left shoulder of the animal.

Chapter 3

The thought instantly occurred to me that the paper was a note from Augustus, and that some unaccountable accident having happened to prevent his relieving me from my dungeon, he had devised this method of acquainting me with the true state of affairs. Trembling with eagerness, I now commenced another search for my phosphorus matches and tapers. I had a confused recollection of having put them carefully away just be fore falling asleep; and, indeed, previously to my last journey to the trap, I had been able to remember the exact spot where I had deposited them. But now I endeavoured in vain to call it to mind, and busied my self for a full hour in a fruitless and vexatious search for the missing articles; never, surely, was there a more tantalizing state of anxiety and suspense. At length, while groping about, with my head close to the ballast, near the opening of the box, and outside of it, I perceived a faint glimmering of light in the direction of the steerage.

Greatly surprised, I endeavoured to make my way towards it, as it appeared to be but a few feet from my position. Scarcely had I moved with this intention, when I lost sight of the glimmer entirely, and, before I could bring it into view again, was obliged to feel along by the box until I had exactly resumed my original situation. Now, moving my head with caution to and fro, I found that, by proceeding slowly, with great care, in an opposite direction to that in which I had at first started, I was enabled to draw near the light, still keeping it in view. Presently I came directly upon it (having squeezed my way through innumerable narrow windings), and found that it proceeded from some fragments of my matches lying in an empty barrel turned upon its side.

I was wondering how they came in such a place, when my hand fell upon two or three pieces of taper-wax, which had been evidently mumbled by the dog. I concluded at once that he had devoured the whole of my supply of candles, and I felt hopeless of being ever able to read the note of Augustus. The small remnants of the wax were so mashed up among other rubbish in the barrel, that I despaired of deriving any service from them, and left them as they were. The phosphorus, of which there was only a speck or two, I gathered up as well as I could, and returned with it, after much difficulty, to my box, where Tiger had all the while remained.

What to do next I could not tell. The hold was so intensely

dark that I could not see my hand, however close I would hold it to my face. The white slip of paper could barely be discerned, and not even that when I looked at it directly; by turning the exterior portions of the retina towards it, that is to say, by survey-ing it slightly askance, I found that it became in some measure perceptible.

Thus the gloom of my prison may be imagined, and the note of my friend, if indeed it were a note from him, seemed only likely to throw me into further trouble, by disquieting to no purpose my already enfeebled and agitated mind. In vain I revolved in my brain a multitude of absurd expedients for procuring light—such expedients precisely as a man in the per-turbed sleep occasioned by opium would be apt to fall upon for a similar purpose—each and all of which appear by turns to the dreamer the most reasonable and the most preposterous of conceptions, just as the reasoning or imaginative faculties flicker, alternately, one above the other. At last an idea occurred to me which seemed rational, and which gave me cause to wonder, very justly, that I had not entertained it before.

I placed the slip of paper on the back of a book, and, col-lecting the fragments of the phosphorus matches which I had brought from the barrel, laid them together upon the paper. I then, with the palm of my hand, rubbed the whole over quickly yet steadily. A clear light diffused itself immediately throughout the whole surface; and had there been any writing upon it, I should not have experienced the least difficulty, I am sure, in reading it. Not a syllable was there, however—nothing but a dreary and unsatisfactory blank; the illumination died away in a few seconds, and my heart died away within me as it went.

I have before stated more than once that my intellect, for some period prior to this, had been in a condition nearly bor-dering on idiocy. There were, to be sure, momentary intervals of perfect sanity, and, now and then, even of energy; but these were few. It must be remembered that I had been, for many days cer-tainly, inhaling the almost pestilential atmosphere of a close hold in a whaling vessel, and a long portion of that time but scantily supplied with water. For the last fourteen or fifteen hours I had none nor had I slept during that time. Salt provisions of the most exciting kind had been my chief, and, indeed, since the loss of the mutton, my only supply of food, with the exception of the sea-biscuit; and these latter were utterly useless to me, as they were too dry and hard to be swallowed in the swollen and parched condition of my throat.

I was now in a high state of fever, and in every respect exceedingly ill. This will account for the fact that many miserable hours of despondency elapsed after my last adventure with the phosphorus, before the thought suggested itself that I had examined only one side of the paper. I shall not attempt to describe my feelings of rage (for I believe I was more angry than anything else) when the egregious oversight I had committed flashed suddenly upon my perception. The blunder itself would have been unimportant, had not my own folly and impetuosity rendered it otherwise in my disappointment at not finding some words upon the slip, I had childishly torn it in pieces and thrown it away, it was impossible to say where.

From the worst part of this dilemma I was relieved by the sagacity of Tiger. Having got, after a long search, a small piece of the note, I put it to the dog's nose, and endeavoured to make him understand that he must bring me the rest of it, To my astonishment (for I had taught him none of the usual tricks for which his breed are famous), he seemed to enter at once into my meaning, and, rummaging about for a few moments, soon found another considerable portion. Bringing me this, he paused a while, and, rubbing his nose against my hand, appeared to be waiting for my approval of what he had done. I patted him on the head, when he immediately made off again. It was now some minutes before he came back—but when he did come, he brought with him a large slip, which proved to be all the paper missing—it having been torn, it seems, only into three pieces.

Luckily, I had no trouble in finding what few fragments of the phosphorus were left—being guided by the indistinct glow one or two of the particles still emitted. My difficulties had taught me the necessity of caution, and I now took time to reflect upon what I was about to do. It was very probable, I considered, that some words were written upon that side of the paper which had not been examined—but which side was that? Fitting the pieces together gave me no clew in this respect, although it assured me that the words (if there were any) would be found all on one side, and connected in a proper manner, as written.

There was the greater necessity of ascertaining the point in question beyond a doubt, as the phosphorus remaining would be altogether insufficient for a third attempt, should I fail in the one I was now about to make. I placed the paper on a book as before, and sat for some minutes thoughtfully revolving the matter over in my mind. At last I thought it barely possible that the written side might have some unevenness on its surface, which a delicate sense of feeling might enable me to detect. I determined to make the experiment, and passed my finger very carefully over the side which first presented itself—nothing however, was perceptible, and I turned the paper, adjusting it on the book. I now again carried my forefinger cautiously along, when I was aware of an exceedingly slight, but still discernible glow, which followed as it proceeded.

This, I knew, must arise from some very minute remaining particles of the phosphorus with which I had covered the paper in my previous attempt. The other, or under side, then, was that on which lay the writing, if writing there should finally prove to be. Again I turned the note, and went to work as I had previously done. Having rubbed in the phosphorus, a brilliancy ensued as before—but this time several lines of MS. in a large hand, and apparently in red ink, became distinctly visible. The glimmer, although sufficiently bright, was but momentary. Still, had I not been too greatly excited, there would have been ample time enough for me to peruse the whole three sentences before me—for I saw there were three. In my anxiety, however, to read all at once, I succeeded only in reading the seven concluding words, which thus appeared: "*blood—your life depends upon lying close.*"

Had I been able to ascertain the entire contents of the note—the full meaning of the admonition which my friend had thus attempted to convey, that admonition, even although it should have revealed a story of disaster the most unspeakable, could not, I am firmly convinced, have imbued my mind with one tithe of the harrowing and yet indefinable horror with which I was inspired by the fragmentary warning thus received. And "*blood*" too, that word of all words—so rife at all times with mystery, and suffering, and terror how trebly full of import did it now appear—how chillily and heavily (disjointed, as it thus was, from any foregoing words to qualify or render it distinct) did its vague syllables fall, amid the deep gloom of my prison, into the inner-most recesses of my soul!

Augustus had, undoubtedly, good reasons for wishing me to remain concealed, and I formed a thousand surmises as to what they could be—but I could think of nothing affording a satisfactory solution of the mystery. Just after returning from my last journey to the trap, and before my attention had been otherwise directed by the singular conduct of Tiger, I had come to the resolution of making myself heard at all events by those on board, or, if I could not succeed in this directly, of trying to cut my way through the orlop deck. The half certainty which I felt of being able to accomplish one of these two purposes in the last emergency, had given me courage (which I should not otherwise have had) to endure the evils of my situation.

The few words I had been able to read, however, had cut me off from these final resources, and I now, for the first time, felt all the misery of my fate. In a paroxysm of despair I threw myself again upon the mattress, where, for about the period of a day and night, I lay in a kind of stupor, relieved only by momentary intervals of reason and recollection.

At length I once more arose, and busied myself in reflection upon the horrors which encompassed me. For another twen-ty-four hours it was barely possible that I might exist without water—for a longer time I could not do so. During the first portion of my imprisonment I had made free use of the cordials with which Augustus had supplied me, but they only served to excite fever, without in the least degree assuaging my thirst. I had now only about a gill left, and this was of a species of strong peach liqueur at which my stomach revolted. The sausages were entirely consumed; of the ham nothing remained but a small piece of the skin; and all the biscuit, except a few fragments of one, had been eaten by Tiger.

To add to my troubles, I found that my headache was increasing momentarily, and with it the species of delirium which had distressed me more or less since my first falling asleep. For some hours past it had been with the greatest difficulty I could breathe at all, and now each attempt at so doing was attended with the most distressing spasmodic action of the chest, But there was still another and very different source of disquietude, and one, indeed, whose harassing terrors had been the chief means of arousing me to exertion from my stupor on the mattress. It arose from the demeanour of the dog.

I first observed an alteration in his conduct while rubbing in the phosphorus on the paper in my last attempt. As I rubbed, he ran his nose against my hand with a slight snarl; but I was too greatly excited at the time to pay much attention to the circumstance. Soon afterward, it will be remembered, I threw myself on the mattress, and fell into a species of lethargy. Presently I became aware of a singular hissing sound close at my ears, and discovered it to proceed from Tiger, who was panting and wheezing in a state of the greatest apparent excitement, his eyeballs flashing fiercely through the gloom. I spoke to him, when he replied with a low growl, and then remained quiet.

Presently I relapsed into my stupor, from which I was again awakened in a similar manner. This was repeated three or four times, until finally his behaviour inspired me with so great a degree of fear that I became fully aroused. He was now lying close by the door of the box, snarling fearfully, although in a kind of under tone, and grinding his teeth as if strongly convulsed. I had no doubt whatever that the want of water or the confined atmosphere of the hold had driven him mad, and I was at a loss what course to pursue. I could not endure the thought of killing him, yet it seemed absolutely necessary for my own safety. I could distinctly perceive his eyes fastened upon me with an expression of the most deadly animosity, and I expected every instant that he would attack me.

At last I could endure my terrible situation no longer, and determined to make my way from the box at all hazards, and despatch him, if his opposition should render it necessary for me to do so. To get out, I had to pass directly over his body, and he already seemed to anticipate my design raising himself upon his forelegs (as I perceived by the altered position of his eyes), and displaying the whole of his white fangs, which were easily discernible. I took the remains of the ham-skin, and the bottle containing the liqueur, and secured them about my person, together with a large carving-knife which Augustus had left me— then, folding my cloak as closely around me as possible, I made a movement towards the mouth of the box.

No sooner did I do this than the dog sprang with a loud growl towards my throat. The whole weight of his body struck me on the right shoulder, and I fell violently to the left, while the enraged animal passed entirely over me. I had fallen upon my knees, with my head buried among the blankets, and these protected me from a second furious assault, during which I felt the sharp teeth pressing vigorously upon the woollen which enveloped my neck—yet, luckily, without being able to penetrate all the folds. I was now beneath the dog, and a few moments would place me completely in his power. Despair gave me strength, and I rose bodily up, shaking him from me by main force, and dragging with me the blankets from the mattress. These I now threw over him, and before he could extricate himself I had got through the door and closed it effectually against his pursuit.

In this struggle, however, I had been forced to drop the morsel of ham-skin, and I now found my whole stock of provisions reduced to a single gill of liqueur. As this reflection crossed my mind, I felt myself actuated by one of those fits of perverseness which might be supposed to influence a spoiled child in similar circumstances, and, raising the bottle to my lips, I drained it to the last drop, and dashed it furiously upon the floor.

Scarcely had the echo of the crash died away, when I heard my name pronounced in an eager but subdued voice, issuing from the direction of the steerage. So unexpected was anything of the kind, and so intense was the emotion excited within me by the sound, that I endeavoured in vain to reply. My powers of speech to tally failed, and, in an agony of terror lest my friend should conclude me dead, and return without attempting to reach me, I stood up between the crates near the door of the box, trembling convulsively, and gasping and struggling for utterance.

Had a thousand worlds depended upon a syllable, I could not have spoken it. There was a slight movement now audible among the lumber somewhere forward of my station. The sound presently grew less distinct, then again less so, and still less. Shall I ever forget my feelings at this moment? He was going—my friend—my companion, from whom I had a right to expect so much—he was going—he would abandon me—he was gone! He would leave me to perish miserably, to expire in the most horrible and loathsome of dungeons—and one word—one little syllable would save me—yet that single syllable I could not utter! I felt, I am sure, more than ten thousand times the agonies of death itself. My brain reeled, and I fell, deadly sick, against the end of the box.

As I fell, the carving-knife was shaken out from the waistband of my pantaloons, and dropped with a rattling sound to the floor. Never did any strain of the richest melody come so sweetly to my ears! With the intensest anxiety I listened to ascertain the effect of the noise upon Augustus—for I knew that the person who called my name could be no one but himself. All was silent for some moments. At length I again heard the word *Arthur!* repeated in a low tone, and one full of hesitation. Reviving hope loosened at once my powers of speech, and I now screamed, at the top of my voice, "*Augustus! oh Augustus!*"

"Hush—for God's sake be silent!" he replied, in a voice trembling with agitation; "I will be with you immediately—as soon as I can make my way through the hold." For a long time I heard him moving among the lumber, and every moment seemed to me an age. At length I felt his hand upon my shoulder, and he placed at the same moment a bottle of water to my lips. Those only who have been suddenly redeemed from the jaws of the tomb, or who have known the insufferable torments of thirst under circumstances as aggravated as those which encompassed me in my dreary prison, can form any idea of the unutterable transports which that one long draught of the richest of all physical luxuries afforded.

When I had in some degree satisfied my thirst, Augustus produced from his pocket three or four cold boiled potatoes, which I devoured with the greatest avidity. He had brought with him a light in a dark lantern, and the grateful rays afforded me scarcely less comfort than the food and drink. But I was impatient to learn the cause of his protracted absence, and he proceeded to recount what had happened on board during my incarceration.

CHAPTER 4

The brig put to sea, as I had supposed, in about an hour after he had left the watch. This was on the twentieth of June. It will be remembered that I had then been in the hold for three days; and, during this period, there was so constant a bustle on board, and so much running to and fro, especially in the cabin and staterooms, that he had had no chance of visiting me without the risk of having the secret of the trap discovered. When at length he did come, I had assured him that I was doing as well as possible; and, therefore, for the two next days he felt but little uneasiness on my account—still, however, watching an opportunity of going down. It was not *until the fourth day* that he found one.

Several times during this interval he had made up his mind to let his father know of the adventure, and have me come up at once; but we were still within reaching distance of Nantucket, and it was doubtful, from some expressions which had escaped

Captain Barnard, whether he would riot immediately put back if he discovered me to be on board. Besides, upon thinking the matter over, Augustus, so he told me, could not imagine that I was in immediate want, or that I would hesitate, in such case, to make myself heard at the trap. When, therefore, he considered everything, he concluded to let me stay until he could meet with an opportunity of visiting me unobserved.

This, as I said before, did not occur until the fourth day after his bringing me the watch, and the seventh since I had first entered the hold. He then went down without taking with him any water or provisions, intending in the first place merely to call my attention, and get me to come from the box to the trap—when he would go up to the stateroom and thence hand me down a supply. When he descended for this purpose he found that I was asleep, for it seems that I was snoring very loudly. From all the calculations I can make on the subject, this must have been the slumber into which I fell just after my return from the trap with the watch, and which, consequently, must have lasted *for more than three entire days and nights* at the very least.

Latterly, I have had reason, both from my own experience and the assurance of others, to be acquainted with the strong soporific effects of the stench arising from old fish-oil when closely confined; and when I think of the condition of the hold in which I was imprisoned, and the long period during which the brig had been used as a whaling vessel, I am more inclined to wonder that I awoke at all, after once falling asleep, than that I should have slept uninterruptedly for the period specified above.

Augustus called to me at first in a low voice and without closing the trap—but I made him no reply. He then shut the trap, and spoke to me in a louder, and finally in a very loud tone—still I continued to snore. He was now at a loss what to do. It would take him some time to make his way through the lumber to my box, and in the meanwhile his absence would be noticed by Captain Barnard, who had occasion for his services every minute, in arranging and copying papers connected with the business of the voyage. He determined, there fore, upon re-flection, to ascend, and await another opportunity of visiting me.

He was the more easily induced to this resolve, as my slumber appeared to be of the most tranquil nature, and he could not suppose that I had undergone any inconvenience from my incarceration. He had just made up his mind on these points when his attention was arrested by an unusual bustle, the sound of which proceeded apparently from the cabin. He sprang through the trap as quickly as possible, closed it, and threw open the door of his stateroom. No sooner had he put his foot over the threshold than a pistol flashed in his face, and he was knocked down, at the same moment, by a blow from a handspike.

A strong hand held him on the cabin floor, with a tight grasp upon his throat—still he was able to see what was going on around him. His father was tied hand and foot, and lying along the steps of the companion-way with his head down, and a deep wound in the forehead, from which the blood was flowing in a continued stream. He spoke not a word, and was apparently dying. Over him stood the first mate, eying him with an expression of fiendish derision, and deliberately searching his pockets, from which he presently drew forth a large wallet and a chronometer.

Seven of the crew (among whom was the cook, a negro) were rummaging the staterooms on the larboard for arms, where they soon equipped themselves with muskets and ammunition. Besides Augustus and Captain Barnard, there were nine men altogether in the cabin, and these among the most ruffianly of the brig's company. The villains now went upon deck, taking my friend with them, after having secured his arms behind his back. They proceeded straight to the forecastle, which was fastened down—two of the mutineers standing by it with axes—two also at the main hatch.

The mate called out in a loud voice, "Do you hear there below? tumble up with you—one by one, now, mark that—and no grumbling."

It was some minutes before anyone appeared: at last an Englishman, who had shipped as a raw hand, came up, weeping piteously. and entreating the mate in the most humble manner to spare his life. The only reply was a blow on the forehead from an axe. The poor fellow fell to the deck without a groan, and the black cook lifted him up in his arms as he would a child, and tossed him deliberately into the sea. Hearing the blow and the plunge of the body, the men below could now be induced to venture on deck neither by threats nor promises, until a proposition was made to smoke them out.

A general rush then ensued, and for a moment it seemed possible that the brig might be retaken. The mutineers, however, succeeded at last in closing the forecastle effectually before more than six of their opponents could get up. These six, finding themselves so greatly out numbered and without arms, submitted after a brief struggle. The mate gave them fair words—no doubt with a view of inducing those below to yield, for they had no difficulty in hearing all that was said on deck. The result proved his sagacity, no less than his diabolical villainy. All in the forecastle presently signified their intention of submitting, and, ascending one by one, were pinioned and thrown on their backs together with the first six—there being in all, of the crew who were not concerned in the mutiny, twenty-seven.

A scene of the most horrible butchery ensued. The bound seamen were dragged to the gangway. Here the cook stood with an axe, striking each victim on the head as he was forced over the side of the vessel by the other mutineers. In this manner twenty-two perished, and Augustus had given himself up for lost, expecting every moment his own turn to come next. But it seemed that the villains were now either weary, or in some measure disgusted with their bloody labour; for the four remaining prisoners, together with my friend, who had been thrown on the deck with the rest, were respited while the mate sent below for rum, and the whole murderous party held a drunken carouse, which lasted until sunset.

They now fell to disputing in regard to the fate of the survivors, who lay not more than four paces off, and could distinguish every word said. Upon some of the mutineers the liquor appeared to have a softening effect, for several voices were heard in favour of releasing the captives altogether, on condition of joining the mutiny and sharing the profits. The black cook, however (who in all respects was a perfect demon, and who seemed to exert as much influence, if not more, than the mate himself), would listen to no proposition of the kind, and rose repeatedly for the purpose of resuming his work at the gangway.

Fortunately, he was so far overcome by intoxication as to be easily restrained by the less blood thirsty of the party, among whom was a line-manager, who went by the name of Dirk Peters. This man was the son of an Indian squaw of the tribe of Upsarokas, who live among the fastnesses of the Black Hills near the source of the Missouri. His father was a fur-trader, I believe, or at least connected in some manner with the Indian trading-posts on Lewis River. Peters himself was one of the most purely ferocious-looking men I ever beheld. He was short in stature— not more than four feet eight inches high—but his limbs were of the most Herculean mould. His hands, especially, were so enormously thick and broad as hardly to retain a human shape. His arms, as well as legs, were *bowed* in the most singular manner, and appeared to possess no flexibility whatever.

His head was equally deformed, being of immense size, with an indentation on the crown (like that on the head of most negroes), and entirely bald. To conceal this latter deficiency, which did not proceed from old age, he usually wore a wig formed of any hair-like material which presented itself—occasionally the skin of a Spanish dog or American grizzly bear. At the time spoken of he had on a portion of one of these bearskins; and it added no little to the natural ferocity of his countenance, which betook of the Upsaroka character. The mouth extended nearly from ear to ear; the lips were thin, and seemed, like some other portions of his frame, to be devoid of natural pliancy, so that the ruling expression never varied under the influence of any emotion whatever.

This ruling expression may be conceived when it is considered that the teeth were exceedingly long and protruding, and never even partially covered, in any instance, by the lips. To pass this man with a casual glance, one might imagine him to be convulsed with laughter—but a second look would induce a shuddering acknowledgment, that if such an expression were indicative of merriment, the merriment must be that of a demon. Of this singular being many anecdotes were prevalent among the seafaring men of Nantucket. These anecdotes went to prove his prodigious strength when under excitement, and some of them had given rise to a doubt of his sanity. But on board the *Grampus*, it seems, he was regarded at the time of the mutiny with feelings more of derision than of anything else.

I have been thus particular in speaking of Dirk Peters, because, ferocious as he appeared, he proved the main instrument in preserving the life of Augustus, and because I shall have frequent occasion to mention him hereafter in the course of my narrative—a narrative, let me here say, which, in its latter portions, will be found to include incidents of a nature so entirely out of the range of human experience, and for this reason so far beyond the limits of human credulity, that I proceed in utter hopelessness of obtaining credence for all that I shall tell, yet confidently trusting in time and progressing science to verify some of the most important and most improbable of my statements.

After much indecision and two or three violent quarrels, it was determined at last that all the prisoners (with the exception of Augustus, whom Peters insisted in a jocular manner upon keeping as his clerk) should be set adrift in one of the smallest whaleboats. The mate went down into the cabin to see if Captain Barnard was still living—for, it will be remembered, he was left below when the mutineers came up. Presently the two made their appearance, the captain pale as death, but somewhat recovered from the effects of his wound. He spoke to the men in a voice hardly articulate, entreated them not to set him adrift, but to return to their duty, and promising to land them wherever they chose, and to take no steps for bringing them to justice.

He might as well have spoken to the winds. Two of the ruffians seized him by the arms and hurled him over the brig's side into the boat, which had been lowered while the mate went below. The four men who were lying on the deck were then untied and ordered to follow, which they did without attempting any resistance—Augustus being still left in his painful position, although he struggled and prayed only for the poor satisfaction of being permitted to bid his father farewell. A handful of seabiscuit and a jug of water were now handed down; but neither mast, sail, oar, nor compass. The boat was towed astern for a few minutes, during which the mutineers held another consultation—it was then finally cut adrift.

By this time night had come on—there were neither moon nor stars visible—and a short and ugly sea was running, although there was no great deal of wind. The boat was instantly out of sight, and little hope could be entertained for the unfortunate sufferers who were in it. This event happened, however, in latitude 35° 30' north, longitude 61° 20' west, and consequently at no very great distance from the Bermuda Islands. Augustus therefore endeavoured to console himself with the idea that the boat might either succeed in reaching the land, or come sufficiently near to be fallen in with by vessels off the coast.

All sail was now put upon the brig, and she continued her original course to the southwest—the mutineers being bent upon some piratical expedition, in which, from all that could be understood, a ship was to be intercepted on her way from the Cape Verd Islands to Porto Rico. No attention was paid to Augustus, who was untied and suffered to go about anywhere forward of the cabin companion-way. Dirk Peters treated him with some degree of kindness, and on one occasion saved him from the brutality of the cook. His situation was still one of the most precarious, as the men were continually intoxicated, and there was no relying upon their continued good-humour or carelessness in regard to himself.

His anxiety on my account he represented, however, as the

most distressing result of his condition; and, indeed, I had never reason to doubt the sincerity of his friendship. More than once he had resolved to acquaint the mutineers with the secret of my being on board, but was restrained from so doing, partly through recollection of the atrocities he had already beheld, and partly through a hope of being able soon to bring me relief. For the latter purpose he was constantly on the watch; but, in spite of the most constant vigilance, three days elapsed after the boat was cut adrift before any chance occurred.

At length, on the night of the third day, there came on a heavy blow from the eastward, and all hands were called up to take in sail. During the confusion which ensued, he made his way below unobserved, and into the state room. What was his grief and horror in discovering that the latter had been rendered a place of deposit for a variety of sea-stores and ship-furniture, and that several fathoms of old chain-cable, which had been stowed away beneath the companion-ladder, had been dragged thence to make room for a chest, and were now lying immediately upon the trap! To remove it without discovery was impossible, and he returned on deck as quickly as he could.

As he came up the mate seized him by the throat, and demanding what he had been doing in the cabin, was about flinging him over the larboard bulwark, when his life was again preserved through the interference of Dirk Peters. Augustus was now put in handcuffs (of which there were several pairs on board), and his feet lashed tightly together. He was then taken into the steerage, and thrown into a lower berth next to the forecastle bulkheads, with the assurance that he should never put his foot on deck again "until the brig was no longer a brig." This was the expression of the cook, who threw him into the berth—it is hardly possible to say what precise meaning was intended by the phrase. The whole affair, however, proved the ultimate means of my relief, as will presently appear.

Chapter 5

For some minutes after the cook had left the fore castle, Augustus abandoned himself to despair, never hoping to leave the berth alive. He now came to the resolution of acquainting the first of the men who should come down with my situation, thinking it better to let me take my chance with the mutineers than perish of thirst in the hold—for it had been ten days since I was first imprisoned, and my jug of water was not a plentiful supply even for four. As he was thinking on this subject, the idea came all at once into his head that it might be possible to communicate with me by the way of the main hold. In any other circumstances, the difficulty and hazard of the undertaking would have prevented him from attempting it; but now he had, at all events, little prospect of life, and consequently little to lose—he bent his whole mind, therefore, upon the task.

His handcuffs were the first consideration. At first he saw no method of removing them, and feared that he should thus be baffled in the very outset; but, upon a closer scrutiny, he discovered that the irons could be slipped off and on at pleasure with very little effort or inconvenience, merely by squeezing his hands through them—this species of manacle being altogether ineffectual in confining young persons, in whom the smaller bones readily yield to pressure. He now untied his feet, and, leaving the cord in such a manner that it could easily be readjusted in the event of any person's coming down, proceeded to examine the bulkhead where it joined the berth. The partition here was of soft pine board, an inch thick, and he saw that he should have little trouble in cutting his way through.

A voice was now heard at the forecastle companion-way, and he had just time to put his right hand into its handcuff (the left had not been removed), and to draw the rope in a slipknot around his ankle, when Dirk Peters came be low, followed by Tiger, who immediately leaped into the berth and lay down. The dog had been brought on board by Augustus, who knew my attachment to the animal, and thought it would give me pleasure to have him with me during the voyage. He went up to our house for him immediately after first taking me into the hold, but did not think of mentioning the circumstance upon his bringing the watch.

Since the mutiny, Augustus had not seen him before his appearance with Dirk Peters, and had given him up for lost, supposing him to have been thrown overboard by some of the malignant villains belonging to the mate's gang. It appeared afterward that he had crawled into a hole beneath a whaleboat, from which, not having room to turn round, he could not extricate himself. Peters at last let him out, and with a species of good feeling which my friend knew well how to appreciate, had now brought him to him in the forecastle as a companion, leaving at the same time some salt junk and potatoes, with a can of water; he then went on deck, promising to come down with something more to eat on the next day. ,

When he had gone, Augustus freed both hands from the manacles and unfastened his feet. He then turned down the head of the mattress on which he had been lying, and with his penknife (for the ruffians had not thought it worth while to search him) commenced cutting vigorously across one of the partition planks, as closely as possible to the floor of the berth. He chose to cut here, because, if suddenly interrupted, he would be able to conceal what had been done by letting the head of the mattress fall into its proper position. For the remainder of the day, however, no disturbance occurred, and by night he had completely divided the plank. It should here be observed, that none of the crew occupied the forecastle as a sleeping-place, living altogether in the cabin since the mutiny, drinking the wines, and feasting on the sea-stores of Captain Barnard, and giving no more heed than was absolutely necessary to the navigation of the brig.

These circumstances proved fortunate both for myself and Augustus; for, had matters been otherwise, he would have found it impossible to reach me. As it was, he proceeded with confidence in his design. It was near daybreak, however, before he completed the second division of the board (which was about a foot above the first cut), thus making an aperture quite large enough to admit his passage through with facility to the main orlop deck. Having got here, he made his way with but little trouble to the lower main hatch, although in so doing he had to scramble over tiers of oil-casks piled nearly as high as the upper deck, there being barely room enough left for his body. Upon reaching the hatch, he found that Tiger had followed him below, squeezing between two rows of the casks. It was now too late, however, to attempt getting to me before dawn, as the chief difficulty lay in passing through the close stowage in the lower hold. He therefore resolved to return, and wait till the next night. With this design he proceeded to loosen the hatch, so that he might have as little detention as possible when he should come again.

No sooner had he loosened it than Tiger sprang eagerly to the small opening produced, snuffed for a moment, and then uttered a long whine, scratching at the same time, as if anxious to remove the covering with his paws. There could be no doubt, from his behaviour, that he was aware of my being in the hold, and Augustus thought it possible that he would be able to get to me if he put him down. He now hit upon the expedient of sending the note, as it was especially desirable that I should make no attempt at forcing my way out, at least under existing circumstances, and there could be no certainty of his getting to me himself on the morrow as he intended.

After events proved how fortunate it was that the idea occurred to him as it did: for, had it not been for the receipt of the note, I should undoubtedly have fallen upon some plan, however desperate, of alarming the crew, and both our lives would most probably have been sacrificed in consequence.

Having concluded to write, the difficulty was now to procure the materials for so doing. An old toothpick was soon made into a pen; and this by means of feeling altogether, for the between-decks were as dark as pitch. Paper enough was obtained from the back of a letter—a duplicate of the forged letter from Mr. Ross. This had been the original draught; but the handwriting not being sufficiently well imitated, Augustus had written another, thrusting the first, by good fortune, into his coat-pocket, where it was now, most opportunely discovered. Ink alone was thus wanting, and a substitute was immediately found for this by means of a slight incision with the penknife on the back of a finger just above the nail—a copious flow of blood ensuing, as usual from wounds in that vicinity.

The note was now written, as well as it could be in the dark and under the circumstances. It briefly explained that a mutiny had taken place; that Captain Barnard was set adrift; and that I might expect immediate relief as far as provisions were concerned, but must not venture upon making any disturbance. It concluded with these words:

I have scrawled this with blood—your life depends upon lying close.

The slip of paper being tied upon the dog, he was now put down the hatchway, and Augustus made the best of his way back to the forecastle, where he found no reason to believe that any of the crew had been in his absence. To conceal the hole in the partition, he drove his knife in just above it, and hung up a pea-jacket which he found in the berth. His handcuffs were then replaced, and also the rope around his ankles.

These arrangements were scarcely completed when Dirk Peters came below, very drunk, but in excellent humour, and bringing with him my friend's allowance of provision for the day. This consisted of a dozen large Irish potatoes roasted, and a pitcher of water. He sat for some time on a chest by the berth, and talked freely about the mate, and the general concerns of the brig. His demeanour was exceedingly capricious and even grotesque. At one time Augustus was much alarmed by his odd conduct. At last, however, he went on deck, muttering a promise to bring his prisoner a good dinner on the morrow. During the day two of the crew (harpooners) came down, accompanied by the cook, all three in nearly the last stage of intoxication.

Like Peters, they made no scruple of talking unreservedly about their plans. It appeared that they were much divided among themselves as to their ultimate course, agreeing in no point except the attack on the ship from the Cape Verd Islands, with which they were in hourly expectation of meeting. As far as could be ascertained, the mutiny had not been brought about altogether for the sake of booty; a private pique of the chief mate's against Captain Barnard having been the main instigation. There now seemed to be two principal factions among the crew—one headed by the mate, the other by the cook. The former party were for seizing the first suitable vessel which should present itself, and equipping it at some of the West India Islands for a piratical cruise.

The latter division, however, which was the stronger, and included Dirk Peters among its partisans, were bent upon pursuing the course originally laid out for the brig into the South Pacific; there either to take whale, or act other wise, as circumstances should suggest. The representations of Peters, who had frequently visited these regions, had great weight, apparently, with the mutineers, wavering as they were between half-engendered notions of profit and pleasure. He dwelt on the world of novelty and amusement to be found among the innumerable islands of the Pacific, on the perfect security and freedom from all restraint to be enjoyed, but, more particularly, on the deliciousness of the climate, on the abundant means of good living, and on the voluptuous beauty of the women. As yet, nothing had been absolutely determined upon; but the pictures of the hybrid line-manager were taking strong hold upon the ardent imaginations of the seamen, and there was every probability that his intentions would be finally carried into effect.

The three men went away in about an hour, and no one else entered the forecastle all day. Augustus lay quiet until nearly night. He then freed himself from the rope and irons, and prepared for his attempt. A bottle was found in one of the berths, and this he filled with water from the pitcher left by Peters, storing his pockets at the same time with cold potatoes. To his great joy he also came across a lantern, with a small piece of tallow candle in it. This he could light at any moment, as he had in his possession a box of phosphorus matches. When it was quite dark, he got through the hole in the bulkhead, having taken the precaution to arrange the bedclothes in the berth so as to convey the idea of a person covered up.

When through, he hung up the pea-jacket on his knife, as before, to conceal the aperture—this manoeuvre being easily effected, as he did not readjust the piece of plank taken out until afterward. He was now on the main orlop deck, and proceeded to make his way, as before, between the upper deck and the oil-casks to the main hatchway. Having reached this, he lit the piece of candle, and descended, groping with extreme difficulty among the compact stowage of the hold. In a few moments he became alarmed at the insufferable stench and the closeness of the atmosphere. He could not think it possible that I had survived my confinement for so long a period breathing so oppressive an air. He called my name repeatedly, but I made him no reply, and his apprehensions seemed thus to be con firmed. The brig was rolling violently, and there was so much noise in consequence, that it was useless to listen for any weak sound, such as those of my breathing or snoring. He threw open the lantern, and held it as high as possible, whenever an opportunity occurred, in order that, by observing the light, I might, if alive, be aware that succour was approaching.

Still nothing was heard from me, and the supposition of my death began to assume the character of certainty. He determined, nevertheless, to force a passage, if possible, to the box, and at least ascertain beyond a doubt the truth of his surmises. He pushed on for some time in a most pitiable state of anxiety, until, at length, he found the pathway utterly blocked up, and that there was no possibility of making any farther way by the course in which he had set out. Overcome now by his feelings, he threw himself among the lumber in despair, and wept like a child. It was at this period that he heard the crash occasioned by the bottle which I had thrown down.

Fortunate, indeed, was it that the incident occurred—for, upon this incident, trivial as it appears, the thread of my destiny depended. Many years elapsed, however, before I was aware of this fact. A natural shame and regret for his weakness and indecision prevented Augustus from confiding to me at once what a more intimate and unreserved communion afterward induced him to reveal. Upon finding his further progress in the hold impeded by obstacles which he could not overcome, he had resolved to abandon his attempt at reaching me, and return at once to the fore castle.

Before condemning him entirely on this head, the harassing circumstances which embarrassed him should be taken into consideration. The night was fast wearing away, and his absence from the forecastle might be discovered; and, indeed, would necessarily be so, if he should fail to get back to the berth by daybreak. His candle was expiring in the socket, and there would be the greatest difficulty in retracing his way to the hatchway in the dark. It must be allowed, too, that he had every good reason to believe me dead; in which event no benefit could result to me from his reaching the box, and a world of danger would be encountered to no purpose by himself. He had repeatedly called, and I had made him no answer. I had been now eleven days and nights with no more water than that contained in the jug which he had left with me, a supply which it was not at all probable I had hoarded in the beginning of my confinement, as I had had every cause to expect a speedy release.

The atmosphere of the hold, too, must have appeared to him, coming from the comparatively open air of the steerage, of a nature absolutely poisonous, and by far more intolerable than it had seemed to me upon my first taking up my quarters in the box—the hatchways at that time having been constantly open for many months previous. Add to these considerations that of the scene of bloodshed and terror so lately witnessed by my friend; his confinement, privations, and narrow escapes from death; together with the frail and equivocal tenure by which he still existed—circumstances all so well calculated to prostrate every energy of mind—and the reader will be easily brought, as I have been, to regard his apparent falling off in friendship and in faith with sentiments rather of sorrow than of anger.

The crash of the bottle was distinctly heard, yet Augustus was not sure that it proceeded from the hold. The doubt, however, was sufficient inducement to persevere. He clambered up nearly to the orlop deck by means of the stowage, and then watching for a lull in the pitchings of the vessel, he called out to me in as loud a tone as he could command—regardless, for the moment, of the danger of being overheard by the crew. It will be remembered that on this occasion the voice reached me, but I was so entirely overcome by violent agitation as to be incapable of reply.

Confident, now, that his worst apprehensions were well founded, he descended, with a view of getting back to the forecastle without loss of time. In his haste some small boxes were thrown down, the noise occasioned by which I heard, as will be recollected. He had made considerable progress on his return when the fall of the knife again caused him to hesitate. He retraced his steps immediately, and, clambering up the stowage a second time, called out my name, loudly as before, having watched for a lull. This time I found voice to answer. Overjoyed at discovering me to be still alive, he now re solved to brave every difficulty and danger in reaching me. Having extricated himself as quickly as possible from the labyrinth of lumber by which he was hemmed in, he at length struck into an opening which promised better, and finally, after a series of struggles, arrived at the box in a state of utter exhaustion.

Chapter 6

The leading particulars of this narration were all that Augustus communicated to me while we remained near the box. It was not until afterward that he entered fully into all the details. He was apprehensive of being missed, and I was wild with impatience to leave my de tested place of confinement. We resolved to make our way at once to the hole in the bulkhead, near which I was to remain for the present, while he went through to reconnoitre. To leave Tiger in the box was what neither of us could endure to think of; yet, how to act otherwise was the question. He now seemed to be perfectly quiet, and we could not even distinguish the sound of his breathing upon applying our ears closely to the box.

I was convinced that he was dead, and determined to open the door. We found him lying at full length, apparently in a deep stupor, yet still alive. No time was to be lost, yet I could not bring myself to abandon an animal who had now been twice instrumental in saving my life, without some attempt at preserving him. We therefore dragged him along with us as well as we could, although with the greatest difficulty and fatigue; Augustus, during part of the time, being forced to clamber over the impediments in our way with the huge dog in his arms a feat to which the feebleness of my frame rendered me totally inadequate.

At length we succeeded in reaching the hole, when Augustus got through, and Tiger was pushed in afterward. All was found to be safe, and we did not fail to return sincere thanks to God for our deliverance from the imminent danger we had escaped. For the present it was agreed that I should remain near the opening, through which my companion could readily supply me with a part of his daily provision, and where I could have the advantages of breathing an atmosphere comparatively pure.

In explanation of some portions of this narrative wherein I have spoken of the stowage of the brig, and which may appear ambiguous to some of my readers who may have seen a proper or regular stowage, I must here state that the manner in which this most important duty had been performed on board the Grampus was a most shameful piece of neglect on the part of Captain Barnard, who was by no means as careful or as experienced a seaman as the hazardous nature of the service on which he was employed would seem necessarily to demand.

A proper stowage cannot be accomplished in a careless manner, and many most disastrous accidents, even within the limits of my own experience, have arisen from neglect or ignorance in this particular. Coasting vessels, in the frequent hurry and bustle attendant upon taking in or discharging cargo, are the most liable to mishap from the want of a proper attention to stowage. The great point is to allow no possibility of the cargo or ballast's shifting position even in the most violent rollings of the vessel. With this end, great attention must be paid, not only to the bulk taken in, but to the nature of the bulk, and whether there be a full or only a partial cargo. In most kinds of freight the stowage is accomplished by means of a screw.

Thus, in a load of tobacco or flour, the whole is screwed so tightly into the hold of the vessel that the barrels or hogsheads upon discharging are found to be completely flattened, and take some time to regain their original shape. This screwing, however, is resorted to principally with a view of obtaining more room in the hold; for in a full load of any such commodities as flour or tobacco, there can be no danger of any shifting whatever, at least none from which inconvenience can result. There have been in stances, indeed, where this method of screwing has resulted in the most lamentable consequences, arising from a cause altogether distinct from the danger attendant upon a shifting of cargo.

A load of cotton, for example, tightly screwed while in certain conditions, has been known, through the expansion of its bulk, to rend a vessel asunder at sea. There can be no doubt, either, that the same result would ensue in the case of tobacco, while undergoing its usual course of fermentation, were it not for the interstices consequent upon the rotundity of the hogsheads.

It is when a partial cargo is received that danger is chiefly to be apprehended from shifting, and that precautions should be always taken to guard against such misfortune. Only those who have encountered a violent gale of wind, or, rather, who have experienced the rolling of a vessel in a sudden calm after the gale, can form an idea of the tremendous force of the plunges, and of the consequent terrible impetus given to all loose articles in the vessel. It is then that the necessity of a cautious stowage, when there is a partial cargo, becomes obvious.

When lying to (especially with a small head sail), a vessel which is not properly modelled in the bows is frequently thrown upon her beam-ends; this occurring even every fifteen or twenty minutes upon an average, yet without any serious consequences resulting, provided *there be a proper stowage*. If this, however, has not been strictly attended to, in the first of these heavy lurches the whole of the cargo tumbles over to the side of the vessel which lies upon the water, and, being thus prevented from regaining her equilibrium, as she would otherwise necessarily do, she is certain to fill in a few seconds and go down. It is not too much to say that at least one half of the instances in which vessels have foundered in heavy gales at sea may be attributed to a shifting of cargo or of ballast.

When a partial cargo of any kind is taken on board, the whole, after being first stowed as compactly as may be, should be covered with a layer of stout shifting- boards, extending completely across the vessel. Upon these boards strong temporary stanchions should be erected, reaching to the timbers above, and thus securing everything in its place. In cargoes consisting of grain, or any similar matter, additional precautions are requisite. A hold filled entirely with grain upon leaving port will be found not more than three fourths full upon leaching its destination— this, too, although the freight, when measured bushel by bushel by the consignee, will overrun by a vast deal (on account of the swelling of the grain) the quantity consigned.

This result is occasioned by *settling* during the voyage, and is the more perceptible in proportion to the roughness of the weather experienced. If grain loosely thrown in a vessel, then, is ever so well secured by shifting-boards and stanchions, it will be liable to shift in a long passage so greatly as to bring about the most distressing calamities. To prevent these, every method should be employed before leaving port to *settle* the cargo as much as possible; and for this there are many contrivances, among which may be mentioned the driving of wedges into the grain.

Even after all this is done, and unusual pains taken to secure the shifting-boards, no seaman who knows what he is about will feel altogether secure in a gale of any violence with a cargo of grain on board, and, least of all, with a partial cargo. Yet there are hundreds of our coasting vessels, and, it is likely, many more from the ports of Europe, which sail daily with partial cargoes, even of the most dangerous species, and without any precautions whatever. The wonder is that no more accidents occur than do actually happen.

A lamentable instance of this heedlessness occurred to my knowledge in the case of Captain Joel Rice of the schooner *Firefly*, which sailed from Richmond, Virginia, to Madeira, with a cargo of corn, in the year 1825. The captain had gone many voyages without serious accident, al though he was in the habit of paying no attention what ever to his stowage, more than to secure it in the ordinary manner. He had never before sailed with a cargo of grain, and on this occasion had the corn thrown on board loosely, when it did not much more than half fill the vessel. For the first portion of the voyage he met with nothing more than light breezes; but when within a day's sail of Madeira there came on a strong gale from the N. N. E. which forced him to lie to. He brought the schooner to the wind under a double-reefed foresail alone, when she rode as well as any vessel could be expected to do, and shipped not a drop of water.

Towards night the gale somewhat abated, and she rolled with more unsteadiness than before, but still did very well, until a heavy lurch threw her upon her beam-ends to starboard. The corn was then heard to shift bodily, the force of the movement bursting open the main hatch way. The vessel went down like a shot. This happened within hail of a small sloop from Madeira, which picked up one of the crew (the only person saved), and which rode out the gale in perfect security, as indeed a jollyboat might have done under proper management.

The stowage on board the *Grampus* was most clumsily done, if stowage that could be called which was little better than a promiscuous huddling together of oil-casks[1] and ship furniture. I have already spoken of the condition of articles in the hold.

---

1. Whaling vessels are usually fitted with iron oil-tanks—why the *Grampus* was not I have never been able to ascertain.

On the orlop deck there was space enough for my body (as I have stated) between the oil-casks and the upper deck; a space was left open around the main hatchway; and several other large spaces were left in the stowage. Near the hole cut through the bulkhead by Augustus there was room enough for an entire cask, and in this space I found myself comfortably situated for the present.

By the time my friend had got safely into the berth, and readjusted his handcuffs and the rope, it was broad daylight. We had made a narrow escape indeed; for scarcely had he arranged all matters, when the mate came below, with Dirk Peters and the cook. They talked for some time about the vessel from the Cape Verds, and seemed to be excessively anxious for her appearance. At length the cook came to the berth in which Augustus was lying, and seated himself in it near the head. I could see and hear everything from my hiding-place, for the piece cut out had not been put back, and I was in momentary expectation that the negro would fall against the pea-jacket, which was hung up to conceal the aperture, in which case all would have been discovered, and our lives would, no doubt, have been instantly sacrificed.

Our good fortune prevailed, however; and although he frequently touched it as the vessel rolled, he never pressed against it sufficiently to bring about a discovery. The bottom of the jacket had been carefully fastened to the bulkhead, so that the hole might not be seen by its swinging to one side. All this time Tiger was lying in the foot of the berth, and appeared to have recovered in some measure his faculties, for I could see him occasionally open his eyes and draw a long breath.

After a few minutes the mate and cook went above, leaving Dirk Peters behind, who, as soon as they were gone, came and sat himself down in the place just occupied by the mate. He began to talk very sociably with Augustus, and we could now see that the greater part of his apparent intoxication, while the two others were with him, was a feint. He answered all my companion's questions with perfect freedom; told him that he had no doubt of his father's having been picked up, as there were no less than five sail in sight just before sundown on the day he was cut adrift; and used other language of a consolatory nature, which occasioned me no less surprise than pleasure.

Indeed, I began to entertain hopes, that through the instrumentality of Peters we might be finally enabled to regain possession of the brig, and this idea I mentioned to Augustus as soon as I found an opportunity. He thought the matter possible, but urged the necessity of the greatest caution in making the attempt, as the conduct of the hybrid appeared to be instigated by the most arbitrary caprice alone; and, in deed, it was difficult to say if he was at any moment of sound mind. Peters went upon deck in about an hour, and did not return again until noon, when he brought Augustus a plentiful supply of junk beef and pudding. Of this, when we were left alone, I partook heartily, without returning through the hole. No one else came down into the forecastle during the day, and at night I got into Augustus's berth, where I slept soundly and sweetly until nearly daybreak, when he awakened me upon hearing a stir upon deck, and I regained my hiding-place as quickly as possible.

When the day was fully broke, we found that Tiger had recovered his strength almost entirely, and gave no indications of hydrophobia, drinking a little water that was offered him with great apparent eagerness. During the day he regained all his former vigour and appetite. His strange conduct had been brought on, no doubt, by the deleterious quality of the air of the hold, and had no connexion with canine madness. I could not sufficiently rejoice that I had persisted in bringing him with me from the box. This day was the thirtieth of June, and the thirteenth since the *Grampus* made sail from Nantucket.

On the second of July the mate came below, drunk as usual, and in an excessively good-humour. He came to Augustus's berth, and, giving him a slap on the back, asked him if he thought he could behave himself if he let him loose, and whether he would promise not to be going into the cabin again. To this, of course, my friend answered in the affirmative, when the ruffian set him at liberty, after making him drink from a flask of rum which he drew from his coat-pocket.

Both now went on, deck, and I did not see Augustus for about three hours. He then came below with the good news that he had obtained permission to go about the brig as he pleased anywhere forward of the mainmast, and that he had been ordered to sleep, as usual, in the forecastle. He brought me, too, a good dinner, and a plentiful supply of water. The brig was still cruising for the vessel from the Cape Verds, and a sail was now in sight which was thought to be the one in question. As the events of the ensuing eight days were of little importance, and had no direct bearing upon the main incidents of my narrative, I will here throw them into the form of a journal, as I do not wish to omit them altogether.

July 3. Augustus furnished me with three blankets, with which I contrived a comfortable bed in my hiding-place. No one came below, except my companion, during the day. Tiger took his station in the berth just by the aperture, and slept heavily, as if not yet entirely recovered from the effects of his sickness. Towards night a flaw of wind struck the brig before sail could be taken in, and very nearly capsized her. The puff died away immediately, however, and no damage was done beyond the splitting of the foretopsail. Dirk Peters treated Augustus all this day with great kindness, and entered into a long conversation with him respecting the Pacific Ocean, and the islands he had visited in that region. He asked him whether he would not like to go with the mutineers on a kind of exploring and pleasure voyage in those quarters, and said that the men were gradually coming over to the mate's views. To this Augustus thought it best to reply that he would be glad to go on such an adventure, since nothing better could be done, and that anything was preferable to a piratical life.

July 4th. The vessel in sight proved to be a small brig from Liverpool, and was allowed to pass unmolested. Augustus spent most of his time on deck, with a view of obtaining all the information in his power respecting the intentions of the mutineers. They had frequent and violent quarrels among themselves, in one of which a harpooner, Jim Bonner, was thrown overboard. The party of the mate was gaining ground. Jim Bonner belonged to the cook's gang, of which Peters was a partisan.

July 5th. About daybreak there came on a stiff breeze from the west, which at noon freshened into a gale, so that the brig could carry nothing more than her trysail and foresail. In taking in the foretopsail, Simms, one of the common hands, and belonging also to the book's gang, fell overboard, being very much in liquor, and was drowned no attempt being made to save him. The whole number of persons on board was now thirteen, to wit: Dirk Peters; Seymour, the black cook; —— Jones; —— Greely; Hartman Rogers; and William Allen, of the cook's party; the mate, whose name I never learned; Absalom Hicks; —— Wilson; John Hunt; and Richard Parker, of the mate's party— besides Augustus and myself.

July 6th. The gale lasted all this day, blowing in heavy squalls, accompanied with rain. The brig took in a good deal of water through her seams, and one of the pumps was kept continually going, Augustus being forced to take his turn. Just at twilight a large ship passed close by us, without having been discovered until within hail. This ship was supposed to be the one for which the mutineers were on the look-out. The mate hailed her, but the reply was drowned in the roaring of the gale. At eleven, a sea was shipped amid-ships, which tore away a great portion of the larboard bulwarks, and did some other slight damage. Towards morning the weather moderated, and at sunrise there was very little wind.

July 7th. There was a heavy swell running all this day, during which the brig, being light, rolled excessively, and many articles broke loose in the hold, as I could hear distinctly from my hiding-place. I suffered a great deal from seasickness. Peters had a long conversation this day with Augustus, and told him that two of his gang, Greely and Allen, had gone over to the mate, and were resolved to turn pirates. He put several questions to Augustus which he did not then exactly understand. During a part of this evening the leak gained upon the vessel; and little could be done to remedy it, as it was occasioned by the brig's straining, and taking in the water through her seams. A sail was thrummed, and got under the bows, which aided us in some measure, so that we began to gain upon the leak.

July 8th. A light breeze sprung up at sunrise from the eastward, when the mate headed the brig to the southwest, with the intention of making some of the West India islands, in pursuance of his piratical designs. No opposition was made by Peters or the cook; at least none in the hearing of Augustus. All idea of taking the vessel from the Cape Verds was abandoned. The leak was now easily kept under by one pump going every three quarters of an hour. The sail was drawn from beneath the bows. Spoke two small schooners during the day.

July 9th. Fine weather. All hands employed in re pairing bulwarks. Peters had again a long conversation with Augustus, and spoke more plainly than he had done heretofore. He said nothing should induce him to come into the mate's views, and even hinted his intention of taking the brig out of his hands. He asked my friend if he could depend upon his aid in such case, to which Augustus said, "Yes," without hesitation. Peters then said he would sound the others of his party upon the subject, and went away. During the remainder of the day Augustus had no opportunity of speaking with him privately.

CHAPTER 7

July 10. Spoke a brig from Rio, bound to Norfolk, Weather hazy, with a light baffling wind from the east ward. Today Hartman Rogers died, having been attacked on the eighth with spasms after drinking a glass of grog. This man was of the cook's party, and one upon whom Peters placed his main reliance. He told Augustus that he believed the mate had poisoned him, and that he expected, if he did not be on the look-out, his own turn would come shortly. There were now only himself, Jones, and the cook belonging to his own gang—on the other side there were five. He had spoken to Jones about taking the command from the mate; but the project having been coolly received, he had been deterred from pressing the matter any further, or from saying anything to the cook.

It was well, as it happened, that he was so prudent, for in the afternoon the cook expressed his determination of siding with the mate, and went over formally to that party; while Jones took an opportunity of quarrelling with Peters, and hinted that he would let the mate know of the plan in agitation. There was now, evidently, no time to be lost, and Peters expressed his determination of attempting to take the vessel at all hazards, provided Augustus would lend him his aid. My friend at once assured him of his willingness to enter into any plan for that purpose, and, thinking the opportunity a favourable one, made known the fact of my being on board.

At this the hybrid was not more astonished than delighted, as he had no reliance whatever upon Jones, whom he already considered as belonging to the party of the mate. They went below immediately, when Augustus called to me by name, and Peters and myself were soon made acquainted. It was agreed that we should attempt to retake the vessel upon the first good opportunity, leaving Jones altogether out of our councils. In the event of success we were to run the brig into the first port that offered, and deliver her up.

The desertion of his party had frustrated Peters's design of going into the Pacific—an adventure which could not be accomplished without a crew, and he depended upon either getting acquitted upon trial on the score of insanity (which he solemnly averred had actuated him in lending his aid to the mutiny), or upon obtaining a pardon, if found guilty, through the representations of Augustus and myself. Our deliberations were interrupted for the present by the cry of "All hands take in sail," and Peters and Augustus ran up on deck.

As usual, the crew were nearly all drunk; and, before sail could be properly taken in, a violent squall laid the brig on her beam-ends. By keeping her away, however, she righted, having shipped a good deal of water. Scarcely was everything secure, when another squall took the vessel, and immediately afterward another—no damage being done. There was every appearance of a gale of wind, which, indeed, shortly came on, with great fury, from the northward and westward. All was made as snug as possible, and we laid to, as usual, under a close-reefed foresail. As night drew on, the wind increased in violence, with a remarkably heavy sea. Peters now came into the forecastle with Augustus, and we resumed our deliberations.

We agreed that no opportunity could be more favourable than the present for carrying our design into effect, as an attempt at such a moment would never be anticipated. As the brig was snugly laid to, there would be no necessity of manoeuvring her until good weather, when, if we succeeded in our attempt, we might liberate one, or perhaps two of the men, to aid us in taking her into port. The main difficulty was the great disproportion in our forces. There were only three of us, and in the cabin there were nine. All the arms on board, too, were in their possession, with the exception of a pair of small pistols which Peters had concealed about his person, and the large seaman's knife which he always wore in the waistband of his pantaloons.

From certain indications, too, such, for example, as there being no such thing as an axe or a handspike lying in their customary places, we began to fear that the mate had his suspicions, at least in regard to Peters, and that he would let slip no opportunity of getting rid of him. It was clear, indeed, that what we should determine to do could not be done too soon. Still the odds were too much against us to allow of our proceeding without the greatest caution.

Peters proposed that he should go up on deck, and enter into conversation with the watch (Allen), when he would be able to throw him into the sea without trouble, and without making any disturbance, by seizing a good opportunity; that Augustus and myself should then come up, and endeavour to provide ourselves with some kind of weapons from the deck; and that we should then make a rush together, and secure the companion-way before any opposition could be offered. I objected to this, because I could not believe that the mate (who was a cunning fellow in all matters which did not affect his superstitious preju-dices) would suffer himself to be so easily entrapped. The very fact of there being a watch on deck at all was sufficient proof that he was upon the alert—it not being usual, except in vessels where discipline is most rigidly enforced, to station a watch on deck when a vessel is lying to in a gale of wind.

As I address myself principally, if not altogether, to persons who have never been to sea, it may be as well to state the ex-act condition of a vessel under such circumstances. Lying to, or, in sea-parlance "laying to," is a measure resorted to for various purposes, and effected in various manners. In moderate weather, it is frequently done with a view of merely bringing the vessel to a stand-still, to wait for another vessel, or any similar object. If the vessel which lies to is under full sail, the manoeuvre is usually accomplished by throwing round some portion of her sails so as to let the wind take them aback, when she becomes stationary. But we are now speaking of lying to in a gale of wind. This is done when the wind is ahead, and too violent to admit of carrying sail without danger of capsizing; and sometimes even when the wind is fair, but the sea too heavy for the vessel to be put before it.

If a vessel be suffered to scud before the wind in a very heavy sea, much damage is usually done her by the shipping of wa-ter over her stern, and sometimes by the violent plunges she makes forward. This manoeuvre, then, is seldom resorted to in such case, unless through necessity. When the vessel is in a leaky condition, she is often put before the wind even in the heaviest seas; for, when lying to, her seams are sure to be greatly opened by her violent straining, and it is not so much the case when scudding. Often, too, it becomes necessary to scud a vessel, ei-ther when the blast is so exceedingly furious as to tear in pieces the sail which is employed with a view of bringing her head to the wind, or when, through the false modelling of the frame or other causes, this main object cannot be effected.

Vessels in a gale of wind are laid to in different manners, according to their peculiar construction. Some lie to best under a foresail, and this, I believe, is the sail most usually employed. Large square-rigged vessels have sails for the express purpose, called storm-staysails. But the jib is occasionally employed by itself—sometimes the jib and foresail, or a double-reefed foresail, and not unfrequently the after-sails, are made use of. Foretopsails are very often found to answer the purpose better than any other species of sail. The *Grampus* was generally laid to under a close-reefed foresail.

When a vessel is to be laid to, her head is brought up to the wind just so nearly as to fill the sail under which she lies, when hauled flat aft, that is, when brought diagonally across the vessel. This being done, the bows point within a few degrees of the direction from which the wind issues, and the windward bow of course receives the shock of the waves. In this situation a good vessel will ride out a very heavy gale of wind without shipping a drop of water, and without any farther attention being requisite on the part of the crew. The helm is usually lashed down, but this is altogether unnecessary (except on account of the noise it makes when loose), for the rudder has no effect upon the vessel when lying to. Indeed, the helm had far better be left loose than lashed very fast, for the rudder is apt to be torn off by heavy seas if there be no room for the helm to play.

As long as the sail holds, a well-modelled vessel will maintain her situation, and ride every sea, as if instinct with life and reason. If the violence of the wind, however, should tear the sail into pieces (a feat which it requires a perfect hurricane to accomplish under ordinary circumstances), there is then imminent danger. The vessel falls off from the wind, and, coming broadside to the sea, is completely at its mercy: the only resource in this case is to put her quickly before the wind, letting her scud until some other sail can be set. Some vessels will lie to under no sail whatever, but such are not to be trusted at sea.

But to return from this digression. It had never been customary with the mate to have any watch on deck when lying to in a gale of wind, and the fact that he had now one, coupled with the circumstance of the missing axes and handspikes, fully convinced us that the crew were too well on the watch to be taken by surprise in the manner Peters had suggested. Something, however, was to be done, and that with as little delay as practicable, for there could be no doubt that a suspicion having been once entertained against Peters, he would be sacrificed upon the earliest occasion, and one would certainly be either found or made upon the breaking of the gale.

Augustus now suggested that if Peters could contrive to remove, under any pretext, the piece of chain-cable which lay over the trap in the stateroom, we might possibly be able to come upon them unawares by means of the hold; but a little reflection convinced us that the vessel rolled and pitched too violently for any attempt of that nature.

By good fortune I at length hit upon the idea of working upon the superstitious terrors and guilty conscience of the mate. It will be remembered that one of the crew, Hartman Rogers, had died during the morning, having been attacked two days before with spasms after drinking some spirits and water. Peters had expressed to us his opinion that this man had been poisoned by the mate, and for this belief he had reasons, so he said, which were incontrovertible, but which he could not be prevailed upon to explain to us—this wayward refusal being only in keeping with other points of his singular character. But whether or not he had any better grounds for suspecting the mate than we had ourselves, we were easily led to fall in with his suspicion, and determined to act accordingly.

Rogers had died about eleven in the forenoon, in violent convulsions; and the corpse presented in a few minutes after death one of the most horrid and loathsome spectacles I ever remember to have seen. The stomach was swollen immensely, like that of a man who has been drowned and lain under water for many weeks. The hands were in the same condition, while the face was shrunken, shrivelled, and of a chalky whiteness, except where relieved by two or three glaring red splotches, like those occasioned by the erysipelas: one of these splotches extended diagonally across the face, completely covering up an eye as if with a band of red velvet.

In this disgusting condition the body had been brought up from the cabin at noon to be thrown overboard, when the mate getting a glimpse of it (for he now saw it for the first time), and being either touched with remorse for his crime or struck with terror at so horrible a sight, ordered the men to sew the body up in its hammock, and allow it the usual rites of sea- burial. Having given these directions he went below, as if to avoid any further sight of his victim. While preparations were making to obey his orders, the gale came on with great fury, and the design was abandoned for the present. The corpse, left to itself, was washed into the larboard scuppers, where it still lay at the time of which I speak, floundering about with the furious lurches of the brig.

Having arranged our plan, we set about putting it in execution as speedily as possible. Peters went upon deck, and, as he had anticipated, was immediately accosted by Allen, who appeared to be stationed more as a watch upon the forecastle than for any other purpose. The fate of this villain, however, was speedily and silently decided; for Peters, approaching him in a careless manner, as if about to address him, seized him by the throat, and, before he could utter a single cry, tossed him over the bulwarks. He then called to us, and we came up.

Our first precaution was to look about for something with which to arm ourselves, and in doing this we had to proceed with great care, for it was impossible to stand on deck an instant without holding fast, and violent seas broke over the vessel at every plunge forward. It was indispensable, too, that we should be quick in our operations, for every minute we expected the mate to be up to set the pumps going, as it was evident the brig must be taking in water very fast. After searching about for some time, we could find nothing more fit for our purpose than the two pump-handles, one of which Augustus took, and I the other.

Having secured these, we stripped off the shirt of the corpse and dropped the body overboard. Peters and myself then went below, leaving Augustus to watch upon deck, where he took his station just where Allen had been placed, and with his back to the cabin companion-way, so that, if any one of the mate's gang should come up, he might suppose it was the watch.

As soon as I got below I commenced disguising myself so as to represent the corpse of Rogers. The shirt which we had taken from the body aided us very much, for it was of a singular form and character, and easily recognisable—a kind of smock, which the deceased wore over his other clothing. It was a blue stocki-net, with large white stripes running across. Having put this on, I proceeded to equip myself with a false stomach, in imitation of the horrible deformity of the swollen corpse. This was soon effected by means of stuffing with some bedclothes.

I then gave the same appearance to my hands by drawing on a pair of white woollen mittens, and filling them in with any kind of rags that offered themselves. Peters then arranged my face, first rubbing it well over with white chalk, and afterward splotching it with blood, which he took from a cut in his finger. The streak across the eye was not forgotten, and presented a most shocking appearance.

Chapter 8

As I viewed myself in a fragment of looking-glass which hung up in the cabin, and by the dim light of a kind of battle-lantern, I was so impressed with a sense of vague awe at my appearance, and at the recollection of the terrific reality which I was thus representing, that I was seized with a violent tremor, and could scarcely summon resolution to go on with my part. It was necessary, however, to act with decision, and Peters and myself went upon deck.

We there found everything safe, and, keeping close to the bulwarks, the three of us crept to the cabin companion-way. It was only partially closed, precautions having been taken to prevent its being suddenly pushed to from without, by means of placing billets of wood on the upper step so as to interfere with the shutting. We found no difficulty in getting a full view of the interior of the cabin through the cracks where the hinges were placed. It now proved to have been very fortunate for us that we had not attempted to take them by surprise, for they were evidently on the alert.

Only one was asleep, and he lying just at the foot of the companion-ladder, with a musket by his side. The rest were seated on several mattresses, which had been taken from the berths and thrown on the floor. They were engaged in earnest conversation; and although they had been carousing, as appeared from two empty jugs, with some tin tumblers which lay about, they were not as much intoxicated as usual. All had knives, one or two of them pistols, and a great many muskets were lying in a berth close at hand.

We listened to their conversation for some time before we could make up our minds how to act, having as yet resolved on nothing determinate, except that we would attempt to paralyse their exertions, when we should attack them, by means of the apparition of Rogers. They were discussing their piratical plans, in which all we could hear distinctly was, that they would unite with the crew of a schooner *Hornet*, and, if possible, get the schooner herself into their possession preparatory to some attempt on a large scale, the particulars of which could not be made out by either of us.

One of the men spoke of Peters, when the mate replied to him in a low voice which could not be distinguished, and afterward added more loudly, that "he could not understand his being so much forward with the captain's brat in the forecastle, and he thought the sooner both of them were overboard the better." To this no answer was made, but we could easily perceive that the hint was well received by the whole party, and more particularly by Jones. At this period I was excessively agitated, the more so as I could see that neither Augustus nor Peters could determine how to act. I made up my mind, however, to sell my life as dearly as possible, and not to suffer myself to be overcome by any feelings of trepidation.

The tremendous noise made by the roaring of the wind in the rigging and the washing of the sea over the deck prevented us from hearing what was said except during momentary lulls. In one of these we all distinctly heard the mate tell one of the men to "go forward, and order the d—d lubbers to come into the cabin, where he could have an eye upon them, for he wanted no such secret doings on board the brig." It was well for us that the pitching of the vessel at this moment was so violent as to prevent this order from being carried into instant execution.

The cook got up from his mattress to go for us, when a tremendous lurch, which I thought would carry away the masts, threw him head long against one of the larboard stateroom doors, bursting it open, and creating a good deal of other confusion. Luckily, neither of our party was thrown from his position, and we had time to make a precipitate retreat to the forecastle, and arrange a hurried plan of action before the messenger made his appearance, or rather before he put his head out of the companion-hatch, for he did not come on deck. From this station he could not notice the absence of Allen, and he accordingly bawled out as if to him, repeating the orders of the mate. Peters cried out, "Ay, ay," in a disguised voice, and the cook immediately went below, without entertaining a suspicion that all was not right.

My two companions now proceeded boldly aft and down into the cabin, Peters closing the door after him in the same manner he had found it. The mate received them with feigned cordiality, and told Augustus that, since he had behaved himself so well of late, he might take up his quarters in the cabin, and be one of them for the future. He then poured him out a tumbler half full of rum, and made him drink it. All this I saw and heard, for I followed my friends to the cabin as soon as the door was shut, and took up my old point of observation. I had brought with me the two pump-handles, one of which I secured near the companion-way, to be ready for use when required.

I now steadied myself as well as possible so as to have a good view of all that was passing within, and endeavoured to nerve myself to the task of descending among the mutineers when Peters should make a signal to me as agreed upon. Presently he contrived to turn the conversation upon the bloody deeds of the mutiny, and, by degrees, led the men to talk of the thousand superstitions which are so universally current among seamen. I could not make out all that was said, but I could plainly see the effects of the conversation in the countenances of those present. The mate was evidently much agitated, and presently, when some one mentioned the terrific appearance of Rogers's corpse, I thought he was upon the point of swooning.

Peters now asked him if he did not think it would be better to have the body thrown overboard at once, as it was too horrible a sight to see it floundering about in the scuppers. At this the villain absolutely gasped for breath, and turned his head slowly round upon his companions, as if imploring some one to go up and perform the task. No one, however, stirred, and it was quite evident that the whole party were wound up to the highest pitch of nervous excitement. Peters now made me the signal. I immediately threw open the door of the companion-way, and, descending without uttering a syllable, stood erect in the midst of the party.

The intense effect produced by this sudden apparition is not at all to be wondered at when the various circumstances are taken into consideration. Usually, in cases of a similar nature, there is left in the mind of the spectator some glimmering of doubt as to the reality of the vision before his eyes; a degree of hope, however feeble, that he is the victim of chicanery, and that the apparition is not actually a visitant from the world of shadows. It is not too much to say that such remnants of doubt have been at the bottom of almost every such visitation, and that the appalling horror which has sometimes been brought about, is to be attributed, even in the cases most in point, and where most suffering has been experienced, more to a kind of anticipative horror, lest the apparition might *possibly be real*, than to an unwavering belief in its reality.

But, in the present instance, it will be seen immediately, that in the minds of the mutineers there was not even the shadow of a basis upon which to rest a doubt that the apparition of Rogers was indeed a re vivification of his disgusting corpse, or at least its spiritual image. The isolated situation of the brig, with its entire inaccessibility on account of the gale, confined the apparently possible means of deception within such narrow and definite limits, that they must have thought themselves enabled to survey them all at a glance. They had now been at sea twenty-four days, without holding more than a speaking communication with any vessel whatever. The whole of the crew, too, at least all whom they had the most remote reason for suspecting to be on board, were assembled in the cabin, with the exception of Allen, the watch; and his gigantic stature (he was six feet six inches high) was too familiar in their eyes to permit the notion that he was the apparition before them to enter their minds even for an instant.

Add to these considerations the awe-inspiring nature of the tempest, and that of the conversation brought about by Peters; the deep impression which the loathsomeness of the actual corpse had made in the morning upon the imaginations of the men; the excellence of the imitation in my person; and the uncertain and wavering light in which they beheld me, as the glare of the cabin lantern, swinging violently to and fro, fell dubiously and fitfully upon my figure, and there will be no reason to wonder that the deception had even more than the entire effect which we had anticipated. The mate sprang up from the mattress on which he was lying, and, without uttering a syllable, fell back, stone dead, upon the cabin floor, and was hurled to the leeward like a log by a heavy roll of the brig.

Of the remaining seven there were but three who had at first any degree of presence of mind. The four others sat for some time rooted apparently to the floor, the most pitiable objects of horror and utter despair my eyes ever encountered. The only opposition we experienced at all was from the cook, John Hunt, and Richard Parker; but they made but a feeble and irresolute defence. The two former were shot instantly by Peters, and I felled Parker with a blow on the head from the pump-handle which I had brought with me. In the meantime Augustus seized one of the muskets lying on the floor, and shot another mutineer (—— Wilson) through the breast.

There were now but three remaining; but by this time they had become aroused from their lethargy, and perhaps began to see that a deception had been practised upon them, for they fought with great resolution and fury, and, but for the immense muscular strength of Peters, might have ultimately got the better of us. These three men were —— Jones, —— Greely, and Absalom Hicks. Jones had thrown Augustus on the floor, stabbed him in several places along the right arm, and would no doubt have soon despatched him (as neither Peters nor myself could immediately get rid of our own antagonists), had it not been for the timely aid of a friend upon whose assistance we surely had never depended. This friend was no other than Tiger. With a low growl he bounded into the cabin, at a most critical moment for Augustus, and throwing himself upon Jones, pinned him to the floor in an instant.

My friend, however, was now too much injured to render us any aid whatever, and I was so encumbered with my disguise that I could do but little. The dog would not leave his hold upon the throat of Jones—Peters, nevertheless, was far more than a match for the two men who remained, and would, no doubt, have despatched them sooner, had it not been for the narrow space in which he had to act, and the tremendous lurches of the vessel. Presently he was enabled to get hold of a heavy stool, several of which lay about the floor. With this he beat out the brains of Greely as he was in the act of discharging a musket at me, and immediately afterward a roll of the brig throwing him in contact with Hicks, he seized him by the throat, and, by dint of sheer strength, strangled him instantaneously. Thus, in far less time than I have taken to tell it, we found ourselves masters of the brig.

The only person of our opponents who was left alive was

Richard Parker. This man, it will be remembered, I had knocked down with a blow from the pump-handle at the commencement of the attack. He now lay motionless by the door of the shattered stateroom; but, upon Peters touching him with his foot, he spoke, and entreated for mercy. His head was only slightly cut, and otherwise he had received no injury, having been merely stunned by the blow. He now got up, and, for the present, we secured his hands behind his back. The dog was still growling over Jones; but, upon examination, we found him completely dead, the blood issuing in a stream from a deep wound in the throat, inflicted, no doubt, by the sharp teeth of the animal.

It was now about one o'clock in the morning, and the wind was still blowing tremendously. The brig evidently laboured much more than usual, and it became absolutely necessary that something should be done with a view of easing her in some measure. At almost every roll to leeward she shipped a sea, several of which came partially down into the cabin during our scuffle, the hatchway having been left open by myself when I descended. The entire range of bulwarks to larboard had been swept away, as well as the caboose, together with the jollyboat from the counter. The creaking and working of the mainmast, too, gave indication that it was nearly sprung.

To make room for more stowage in the after hold, the heel of this mast had been stepped between decks (a very reprehensible practice, occasionally resorted to by ignorant ship-builders), so that it was in imminent danger of working from its step. But, to crown all our difficulties, we plummed the well, and found no less than seven feet water.

Leaving the bodies of the crew lying in the cabin, we got to work immediately at the pumps—Parker, of course, being set at liberty to assist us in the labour. Augustus's arm was bound up as well as we could effect it, and he did what he could, but that was not much. However, we found that we could just manage to keep the leak from gaining upon us by having one pump constantly going. As there were only four of us, this was severe labour; but we endeavoured to keep up our spirits, and looked anxiously for daybreak, when we hoped to lighten the brig by cutting away the mainmast.

In this manner we passed a night of terrible anxiety and fatigue, and, when the day at length broke, the gale had neither abated in the least, nor were there any signs of its abating. We now dragged the bodies on deck and threw them overboard. Our next care was to get rid of the mainmast. The necessary preparations having been made, Peters cut away at the mast (having found axes in the cabin), while the rest of us stood by the stays and lanyards. As the brig gave a tremendous lee-lurch, the word was given to cut away the weather-lanyards, which being done, the whole mass of wood and rigging plunged into the sea, clear of the brig, and without doing any material injury. We now found that the vessel did not labour quite as much as before, but our situation was still exceedingly precarious, and, in spite of the utmost exertions, we could not gain upon the leak without the aid of both pumps.

The little assistance which Augustus could render us was not really of any importance. To add to our distress, a heavy sea, striking the brig to windward, threw her off several points from the wind, and, before she could regain her position, another broke completely over her, and hurled her full upon her beam-ends. The ballast now shifted in a mass to leeward (the stowage had been knocking about perfectly at random for some time), and for a few moments we thought nothing could save us from capsizing. Presently, however, we partially righted; but the ballast still retaining its place to larboard, we lay so much along that it was useless to think of working the pumps, which indeed we could not have done much longer in any case, as our hands were entirely raw with the excessive labour we had undergone, and were bleeding in the most horrible manner.

Contrary to Parker's advice, we now proceeded to cut away the foremast, and at length accomplished it after much difficulty, owing to the position in which we lay. In going overboard the wreck took with it the bowsprit, and left us a complete hulk.

So far we had had reason to rejoice in the escape of our

longboat, which had received no damage from any of the huge seas which had come on board. But we had not long to congratulate ourselves; for the fore mast having gone, and, of course, the foresail with it, by which the brig had been steadied, every sea now made a complete breach over us, and in five minutes our deck was swept from stem to stern, the longboat and starboard bulwarks torn off, and even the windlass shattered into fragments. It was, indeed, hardly possible for us to be in a more pitiable condition.

At noon there seemed to be some slight appearance of the gale's abating, but in this we were sadly disappointed, for it only lulled for a few minutes to blow with redoubled fury. About four in the afternoon it was utterly impossible to stand up against the violence of the blast; and, as the night closed in upon us, I had not a shadow of hope that the vessel would hold together until morning.

By midnight we had settled very deep in the water, which was now up to the orlop deck. The rudder went soon afterward, the sea which tore it away lifting the after portion of the brig entirely from the water, against which she thumped in her descent with such a concussion as would be occasioned by going ashore. We had all calculated that the rudder would hold its own to the last, as it was unusually strong, being rigged as I have never seen one rigged either before or since. Down its main timber there ran a succession of stout iron hooks, and others in the same manner down the stern-post.

Through these hooks there extended a very thick wrought-iron rod, the rudder being thus held to the stern-post, and swinging freely on the rod. The tremendous force of the sea which tore it off may be estimated by the fact, that the hooks in the stern-post, which ran entirely through it, being clinched on the inside, were drawn every one of them completely out of the solid wood.

We had scarcely time to draw breath after the violence of this shock, when one of the most tremendous waves I had then ever known broke right on board of us, sweeping the companion-way clear off, bursting in the hatchways, and filling every inch of the vessel with water.

Chapter 9

Luckily, just before night, all four of us had lashed ourselves firmly to the fragments of the windlass, lying in this manner as flat upon the deck as possible. This precaution alone saved us from destruction. As it was, we were all more or less stunned by the immense weight of water which tumbled upon us, and which did not roll from above us until we were nearly exhausted. As soon as I could recover breath, I called aloud to my companions. Augustus alone replied, saying, "It is all over with us, and may God have mercy upon our souls." By-and-by both the others were enabled to speak, when they exhorted us to take courage, as there was still hope; it being impossible, from the nature of the cargo, that the brig could go down, and there being every chance that the gale would blow over by the morning.

These words inspired me with new life; for, strange as it may seem, although it was obvious that a vessel with a cargo of empty oil-casks would not sink, I had been hitherto so confused in mind as to have overlooked this consideration altogether; and the danger which I had for some time regarded as the most imminent was that of foundering. As hope revived within me, I made use of every opportunity to strengthen the lashings which held me to the remains of the windlass, and in this occupation I noon discovered that my companions were also busy. The night was as dark as it could possibly be, and the horrible shrieking din and confusion which surrounded us it is useless to attempt describing. Our deck lay level with the sea, or rather we were encircled with a towering ridge of foam, a portion of which swept over us every instant.

It is not too much to say that our heads were not fairly out of water more than one second in three. Although we lay close together, no one of us could see the other, or, indeed, any portion of the brig itself, upon which we were so tempestuously hurled about. At intervals we called one to the other, thus endeavouring to keep alive hope, and render consolation and encouragement to such of us as stood most in need of it. The feeble condition of Augustus made him an object of solicitude with us all; and as, from the lacerated condition of his right arm, it must have been impossible for him to secure his lashings with any degree of firmness, we were in momentary expectation of finding that he had gone overboard—yet to render him aid was a thing altogether out of the question.

Fortunately, his station was more secure than that of any of the rest of us; for the upper part of his body lying just beneath a portion of the shattered windlass, the seas, as they tumbled in upon him, were greatly broken in their violence. In any other situation than this (into which he had been accidentally thrown after having lashed himself in a very exposed spot) he must inevitably have perished before morning. Owing to the brig's lying so much along, we were all less liable to be washed off than otherwise would have been the case. The heel, as I have before stated, was to larboard, about one half of the deck being constantly under water.

The seas, therefore, which struck us to starboard were much broken by the vessel's side, only reaching us in fragments as we lay flat on our faces; while those which came from larboard, being what are called back-water seas, and obtaining little hold upon us on account of our posture, had not sufficient force to drag us from our fastenings.

In this frightful situation we lay until the day broke so as to show us more fully the horrors which surrounded us. The brig was a mere log, rolling about at the mercy of every wave; the gale was upon the increase, if anything, blowing indeed a complete hurricane, and there appeared to us no earthly prospect of deliverance. For several hours we held on in silence, expecting every moment that our lashings would either give way, that the remains of the windlass would go by the board, or that some of the huge seas, which roared in every direction around us and above us, would drive the hulk so far beneath the water that we should be drowned before it could regain the surface.

By the mercy of God, however, we were preserved from these imminent dangers, and about midday were cheered by the light of the blessed sun. Shortly afterward we could perceive a sensible diminution in the force of the wind, when, now for the first time since the latter part of the evening before, Augustus spoke, asking Peters, who lay closest to him, if he thought there was any possibility of our being saved. As no reply was at first made to this question, we all concluded that the hybrid had been drowned where he lay; but presently, to our great joy, he spoke, although very feebly, saying that he was in great pain, being so cut by the tightness of his lashings across the stomach, that he must either find means of loosening them or perish, as it was impossible that he could endure his misery much longer.

This occasioned us great distress, as it was altogether useless to think of aiding him in any manner while the sea continued washing over us as it did. We exhorted him to bear his sufferings with fortitude, and promised to seize the first opportunity which should offer itself to relieve him. He replied that it would soon be too late; that it would be all over with him before we could help him; and then, after moaning for some minutes, lay silent, when we concluded that he had perished.

As the evening drew on, the sea had fallen so much that scarcely more than one wave broke over the hulk from windward in the course of five minutes, and the wind had abated a great deal, although still blowing a severe gale. I had not heard any of my companions speak for hours, and now called to Augustus. He replied, although very feebly, so that I could not distinguish what he said. I then spoke to Peters and to Parker, neither of whom returned any answer.

Shortly after this period I fell into a state of partial insensibility, during which the most pleasing images floated in my imagination; such as green trees, waving meadows of ripe grain, processions of dancing girls, troops of cavalry, and other phantasies. I now remember that, in all which passed before my mind's eye, motion was a predominant idea. Thus, I never fancied any stationary object, such as a house, a mountain, or anything of that kind; but windmills, ships, large birds, balloons, people on horseback, carriages driving furiously, and similar moving objects, presented themselves in endless succession.

When I recovered from this state, the sun was, as near as I could guess, an hour high. I had the greatest difficulty in bringing to recollection the various circumstances connected with my situation, and for some time remained firmly convinced that I was still in the hold of the brig, near the box, and that the body of Parker was that of Tiger.

When I at length completely came to my senses, I found that the wind blew no more than a moderate breeze, and that the sea was comparatively calm; so much so that it only washed over the brig amidships. My left arm had broken loose from its lashings, and was much cut about the elbow; my right was entirely be numbed, and the hand and wrist swollen prodigiously by the pressure of the rope, which had worked from the shoulder downward. I was also in great pain from another rope which went about my waist, and had been drawn to an insufferable degree of tightness. Looking round upon my companions, I saw that Peters still lived, although a thick line was pulled so forcibly around his loins as to give him the appearance of being cut nearly in two; as I stirred, he made a feeble motion to me with his hand, pointing to the rope. Augustus gave no indication of life whatever, and was bent nearly double across a splinter of the windlass.

Parker spoke to me when he saw me moving, and asked me if I had not sufficient strength to release him from his situation; saying, that if I would summon up what spirits I could, and contrive to untie him, we might yet save our lives; but that otherwise we must all perish. I told him to take courage, and I would endeavour to free him. Feeling in my pantaloons' pocket, I got hold of my penknife, and, after several ineffectual attempts, at length succeeded in opening it. I then, with my left hand, managed to free my right from its fastenings, and afterward cut the other ropes which held me.

Upon attempting, however, to move from my position, I

found that my legs failed me altogether, and that I could not get up; neither could I move my right arm in any direction. Upon mentioning this to Parker, he advised me to lie quiet for a few minutes, holding on to the windlass with my left hand, so as to allow time for the blood to circulate. Doing this, the numbness presently began to die away, so that I could move first one of my legs, and then the other; and, shortly afterward, I regained the partial use of my right arm. I now crawled with great caution towards Parker, without getting on my legs, and soon cut loose all the lashings about him, when, after a short delay, he also re-covered the partial use of his limbs.

We now lost no time in getting loose the rope from Peters. It had cut a deep gash through the waistband of his woollen pan-taloons, and through two shirts, and made its way into his groin, from which the blood flowed out copiously as we removed the cordage. No sooner had we removed it, however, than he spoke, and seemed to experience instant relief—being able to move with much greater ease than either Parker or myself—this was no doubt owing to the discharge of blood.

We had little hope that Augustus would recover, as he evinced no signs of life; but, upon getting to him, we discovered that he had merely swooned from loss of blood, the bandages we had placed around his wounded arm having been torn off by the water; none of the ropes which held him to the windlass were drawn sufficiently tight to occasion his death. Having relieved him from the fastenings, and got him clear of the broken wood about the windlass, we secured him in a dry place to windward, with his head somewhat lower than his body, and all three of us busied ourselves in chafing his limbs. In about half an hour he came to himself, although it was not until the next morning that he gave signs of recognising any of us, or had sufficient strength to speak.

By the time we had thus got clear of our lashings it was quite dark, and it began to cloud up, so that we were again in the greatest agony lest it should come on to blow hard, in which event nothing could have saved us from perishing, exhausted as we were. By good fortune it continued very moderate during the night, the sea subsiding every minute, which gave us great hopes of ultimate preservation. A gentle breeze still blew from the N. W., but the weather was not at all cold. Augustus was lashed carefully to windward in such a manner as to prevent him from slipping overboard with the rolls of the vessel, as he was still too weak to hold on at all.

For ourselves there was no such necessity. We sat close together, supporting each other with the aid of the broken ropes about the windlass, and devising methods of escape from our frightful situation. We derived much comfort from taking off our clothes and wringing the water from them. When we put them on after this, they felt remarkably warm and pleasant, and served to invigorate us in no little degree. We helped Augustus off with his, and wrung them for him, when he experienced the same comfort.

Our chief sufferings were now those of hunger and thirst, and, when we looked forward to the means of relief in this respect, our hearts sunk within us, and we were induced to regret that we had escaped the less dreadful perils of the sea. We endeavoured, however, to console ourselves with the hope of being speedily picked up by some vessel, and encouraged each other to bear with fortitude the evils that might happen.

The morning of the fourteenth at length dawned, and the weather still continued clear and pleasant, with a steady but very light breeze from the N.W. The sea was now quite smooth, and as, from some cause which we could not determine, the brig did not lie so much along as she had done before, the deck was comparatively dry, and we could move about with freedom. We had now been better than three entire days and nights without either food or drink, and it became absolutely necessary that we should make an attempt to get up something from below.

As the brig was completely full of water, we went to this work despondingly, and with but little expectation of being able to obtain anything. We made a kind of drag by driving some nails which we broke out from the remains of the companion-hatch into two pieces of wood. Tying these across each other, and fastening them to the end of a rope, we threw them into the cabin, and dragged them to and fro, in the faint hope of being thus able to entangle some article which might be of use to us for food, or which might at least render us assistance in getting it. We spent the greater part of the morning in this labour without effect, fishing up nothing more than a few bedclothes, which were readily caught by the nails. Indeed, our contrivance was so very clumsy, that any greater success was hardly to be anticipated.

We now tried the forecastle, but equally in vain, and were upon the brink of despair, when Peters proposed that we should fasten a rope to his body, and let him make an attempt to get up something by diving into the cabin. This proposition we hailed with all the delight which reviving hope could inspire. He proceeded immediately to strip off his clothes with the exception of his pantaloons; and a strong rope was then carefully fastened around his middle, being brought up over his shoulders in such a manner that there was no possibility of its slipping. The undertaking was one of great difficulty and danger; for, as we could hardly expect to find much, if any provision in the cabin itself, it was necessary that the diver, after letting himself down, should make a turn to the right, and proceed under water a distance of ten or twelve feet, in a narrow passage, to the storeroom, and return, without drawing breath.

Everything being ready, Peters now descended into the cabin, going down the companion-ladder until the water reached his chin. He then plunged in, head first, turning to the right as he plunged, and endeavouring to make his way to the storeroom. In this first attempt, however, he was altogether unsuccessful. In less than half a minute after his going down we felt the rope jerked violently (the signal we had agreed upon when he desired to be drawn up). We accordingly drew him up instantly, but so incautiously as to bruise him badly against the ladder. He had brought nothing with him, and had been unable to penetrate more than a very little way into the passage, owing to the constant exertions he found it necessary to make in order to keep himself from floating up against the deck. Upon getting out he was very much exhausted, and had to rest full fifteen minutes before he could again venture to descend.

The second attempt met with even worse success; for he remained so long under water without giving the signal, that, becoming alarmed for his safety, we drew him out without it, and found that he was almost at the last gasp, having, as he said, repeatedly jerked at the rope without our feeling it. This was probably owing to a portion of it having become entangled in the balustrade at the foot of the ladder. This balustrade was, indeed, so much in the way, that we determined to remove it, if possible, before proceeding with our design. As we had no means of getting it away except by main force, we all descended into the water as far as we could on the ladder, and, giving a pull against it with our united strength, succeeded in breaking it down.

The third attempt was equally unsuccessful with the two first, and it now became evident that nothing could be done in this manner without the aid of some weight with which the diver might steady himself, and keep to the floor of the cabin while making his search. For a long time we looked about in vain for something which might answer this purpose; but at length, to our great joy, we discovered one of the weather-fore-chains so loose that we had not the least difficulty in wrenching it off. Having fastened this securely to one of his ankles, Peters now made his fourth descent into the cabin, and this time succeeded in making his way to the door of the steward's room.

To his inexpressible grief, however, he found it locked, and was obliged to return without effecting an entrance, as, with the greatest exertion, he could remain under water not more, at the utmost extent, than a single minute. Our affairs now looked gloomy indeed, and neither Augustus nor myself, could refrain from bursting into tears, as we thought of the host of difficulties which encompassed us, and the slight probability which existed of our finally making an escape. But this weakness was not of long duration. Throwing ourselves on our knees to God, we implored his aid in the many dangers which beset us; and arose with renewed hope and vigour to think what could yet be done by mortal means towards accomplishing our deliverance.

Shortly afterward an incident occurred which I am induced to look upon as more intensely productive of emotion, as far more replete with the extremes first of delight and then of horror, than even any of the thousand chances which afterward befell me in nine long years, crowded with events of the most startling, and, in many cases, of the most unconceived and unconceivable character. We were lying on the deck near the companionway, and debating the possibility of yet making our way into the storeroom, when, looking towards Augustus, who lay fronting myself, I perceived that he had become all at once deadly pale, and that his lips were quivering in the most singular and unaccountable manner.

Greatly alarmed, I spoke to him, but he made me no reply, and I was beginning to think that he was suddenly taken ill, when I took notice of his eyes, which were glaring apparently at some object behind me. I turned my head, and shall never forget the ecstatic joy which thrilled through every particle of my frame, when I perceived a large brig bearing down upon us, and not more than a couple of miles off. I sprung to my feet as if a musket bullet had suddenly struck me to the heart; and, stretching out my arms in the direction of the vessel, stood in this manner, motionless, and unable to articulate a syllable. Peters and Parker were equally affected, although in different ways. The former danced about the deck like a madman, uttering the most extravagant rhodomontades, intermingled with howls and imprecations, while the latter burst into tears, and continued for many minutes weeping like a child.

The vessel in sight was a large hermaphrodite brig, of a Dutch build, and painted black, with a tawdry gilt figurehead. She had evidently seen a good deal of rough weather, and, we supposed, had suffered much in the gale which had proved so disastrous to ourselves; for her fore topmast was gone, and some of her starboard bulwarks. When we first saw her, she was, as I have already said, about two miles off and to windward, bearing down upon us. The breeze was very gentle, and what astonished us chiefly was, that she had no other sails set than her foresail and mainsail, with a flying jib—of course she came down but slowly, and our impatience amounted nearly to phrensy.

The awkward manner in which she steered, too, was remarked by all of us, even excited as we were. She yawed about so considerably, that once or twice we thought it impossible she could see us, or imagined that, having seen us, and discovered no person on board, she was about to tack and make off in another direction. Upon each of these occasions we screamed and shouted at the top of our voices, when the stranger would appear to change for a moment her intention, and again hold on towards us—this singular conduct being repeated two or three times, so that at last we could think of no other manner of accounting for it than by supposing the helmsman to be in liquor.

No person was seen upon her decks until she arrived within about a quarter of a mile of us. We then saw three seamen, whom by their dress we took to be Hollanders. Two of these were lying on some old sails near the forecastle, and the third, who appeared to be looking at us with great curiosity, was leaning over the starboard bow near the bowsprit. This last was a stout and tall man, with a very dark skin. He seemed by his manner to be encouraging us to have patience, nodding to us in a cheerful although rather odd way, and smiling constantly so as to display a set of the most brilliantly white teeth. As his vessel drew nearer, we saw a red flannel cap which he had on fall from his head into the water; but of this he took little or no notice, continuing his odd smiles and gesticulations. I relate these things and circumstances minutely, and I relate them, it must be understood, precisely as they *appeared* to us.

The brig came on slowly, and now more steadily than before, and—I cannot speak calmly of this event—our hearts leaped up wildly within us, and we poured out our whole souls in shouts and thanksgiving to God for the complete, unexpected, and glorious deliverance that was so palpably at hand. Of a sudden, and all at once, there came wafted over the ocean from the strange vessel (which was now close upon us) a smell, a stench, such as the whole world has no name—for no conception—of hellish—utterly suffocating—insufferable, inconceivable. I gasped for breath, and, turning to my companions, perceived that they were paler than marble.

But we had now no time left for question or surmise—the brig was within fifty feet of us, and it seemed to be her intention to run under our counter, that we might board her without her putting out a boat. We rushed aft, when, suddenly, a wide yaw threw her off full five or six points from the course she had been running, and, as she passed under our stern at the distance of about twenty feet, we had a full view of her decks. Shall I ever forget the triple horror of that spectacle? Twenty-five or thirty human bodies, among whom were several females, lay scattered about between the counter and the galley, in the last and most loathsome state of putrefaction! We plainly saw that not a soul lived in that fated vessel!

Yet we could not help shouting to the dead for help! Yes, long and loudly did we beg, in the agony of the moment, that those silent and disgusting images would stay for us, would not abandon us to be come like them, would receive us among their goodly company! We were raving with horror and despair—thoroughly mad through the anguish of our grievous disappointment.

As our first loud yell of terror broke forth, it was replied to by something, from near the bowsprit of the stranger, so closely resembling the scream of a human voice that the nicest ear might have been startled and deceived. At this instant another sudden yaw brought the region of the forecastle for a moment into view, and we beheld at once the origin of the sound. We saw the tall stout figure still leaning on the bulwark, and still nodding his head to and fro, but his face was now turned from us so that we could not behold it. His arms were extended over the rail, and the palms of his hands fell outward. His knees were lodged upon a stout rope, tightly stretched, and reaching from the heel of the bow sprit to a cathead.

On his back, from which a portion of the shirt had been torn, leaving it bare, there sat a huge seagull, busily gorging itself with the horrible flesh, its bill and talons deep buried, and its white plumage spattered all over with blood. As the brig moved further round so as to bring us close in view, the bird, with much apparent difficulty, drew out its crimsoned head, and, after eying us for a moment as if stupefied, arose lazily from the body upon which it had been feasting, and, flying directly above our deck, hovered there a while with a portion of clotted and liver-like substance in its beak.

The horrid morsel dropped at length with a sullen splash immediately at the feet of Parker. May God forgive me, but now, for the first time, there flashed through my mind a thought, a thought which I will not mention, and I felt myself making a step towards the ensanguined spot. I looked upward, and the eyes of Augustus met my own with a degree of intense and eager meaning which immediately brought me to my senses. I sprang forward quickly, and, with a deep shudder, threw the frightful thing into the sea.

The body from which it had been taken, resting as it did upon the rope, had been easily swayed to and fro by the exertions of the carnivorous bird, and it was this motion which had at first impressed us with the belief of its being alive. As the gull relieved it of its weight, it swung round and fell partially over, so that the face was fully discovered. Never, surely, was any object so terribly full of awe! The eyes were gone, and the whole flesh around the mouth, leaving the teeth utterly naked. This, then, was the smile which had cheered us on to hope! this the—but I forbear. The brig, as I have already told, passed under our stern, and made its way slowly but steadily to leeward. With her and with her terrible crew went all our gay visions of deliverance and joy.

Deliberately as she went by, we might possibly have found

means of boarding her, had not our sudden disappointment, and the appalling nature of the discovery which accompanied it, laid entirely prostrate every active faculty of mind and body. We had seen and felt, but we could neither think nor act, until, alas, too late. How much our intellects had been weakened by this incident may be estimated by the fact, that, when the vessel had proceeded so far that we could perceive no more than the half of her hull, the proposition was seriously entertained of attempting to overtake her by swimming!

I have, since this period, vainly endeavoured to obtain some clew to the hideous uncertainty which enveloped the fate of the stranger. Her build and general appearance, as I have before stated, led us to the belief that she was a Dutch trader, and the dresses of the crew also sustained this opinion. We might have easily seen the name upon her stern, and, indeed, taken other observations which would have guided us in making out her character; but the intense excitement of the moment blinded us to everything of that nature. From the saffron-like hue of such of the corpses as were not entirely decayed, we concluded that the whole of her company had perished by the yellow fever, or some other virulent disease of the same fearful kind.

If such were the case (and I know not what else to imagine), death, to judge from the positions of the bodies, must have come upon them in a manner awfully sudden and overwhelming, in a way totally distinct from that which generally characterises even the most deadly pestilences with which mankind are acquainted. It is possible, indeed, that poison, accidentally introduced into some of their sea-stores, may have brought about the disaster; or that the eating some unknown venomous species of fish, or other marine animal, or oceanic bird, might have induced it but it is utterly useless to form conjectures where all is involved, and will, no doubt, remain for ever involved, in the most appalling and unfathomable mystery.

Chapter 11

We spent the remainder of the day in a condition of stupid lethargy, gazing after the retreating vessel until the darkness, hiding her from our sight, recalled us in some measure to our senses. The pangs of hunger and thirst then returned, absorbing all other cares and considerations. Nothing, however, could be done until the morning, and, securing ourselves as well as possible, we endeavoured to snatch a little repose. In this I succeeded beyond my expectation, sleeping until my companions, who had not been so fortunate, aroused me at daybreak to renew our attempts at getting up provision from the hull.

It was now a dead calm, with the sea as smooth as I have ever known it—the weather warm and pleasant. The brig was out of sight. We commenced our operations by wrenching off, with some trouble, another of the fore-chains; and having fastened both to Peters's feet, he again made an endeavour to reach the door of the store room, thinking it possible that he might be able to force it open, provided he could get at it in sufficient time; and this he hoped to do, as the hulk lay much more steadily than before.

He succeeded very quickly in reaching the door, when, loosening one of the chains from his ankle, he made every exertion to force a passage with it, but in vain, the framework of the room being far stronger than was anticipated. He was quite exhausted with his long stay under water, and it became absolutely necessary that some other one of us should take his place. For this service Parker immediately volunteered; but, after making three ineffectual efforts, found that he could never even succeed in getting near the door. The condition of Augustus's wounded arm rendered it useless for him to attempt going down, as he would be unable to force the room open should he reach it, and it accordingly now devolved upon me to exert myself for our common deliverance.

Peters had left one of the chains in the passage, and I found, upon plunging in, that I had not sufficient ballast to keep me firmly down. I determined, therefore, to attempt no more, in my first effort, than merely to recover the other chain. In groping along the floor of the passage for this I felt a hard substance, which I immediately grasped, not having time to ascertain what it was, but returning and ascending instantly to the surface. The prize proved to be a bottle, and our joy may be conceived when I say that it was found to be full of Port wine. Giving thanks to God for this timely and cheering assistance, we immediately drew the cork with my penknife, and, each taking a moderate sup, felt the most indescribable comfort from the warmth, strength, and spirits with which it inspired us. We then carefully recorked the bottle, and, by means of a handkerchief, swung it in such a manner that there was no possibility of its getting broken.

Having rested a while after this fortunate discovery, I again descended, and now recovered the chain, with which I instantly came up. I then fastened it on and went down for the third time, when I became fully satisfied that no exertions whatever, in that situation, would enable me to force open the door of the store-room. I therefore returned in despair.

There seemed now to be no longer any room for hope, and I could perceive in the countenances of my companions that they had made up their minds to perish. The wine had evidently produced in them a species of delirium, which, perhaps, I had been prevented from feeling by the immersion I had undergone since drinking it. They talked incoherently, and about matters unconnected with our condition, Peters repeatedly asking me questions about Nantucket. Augustus, too, I remember, approached me with a serious air, and requested me to lend him a pocket-comb, as his hair was full of fish scales, and he wished to get them out before going on shore.

Parker appeared somewhat less affected, and urged me to dive at random into the cabin, and bring up any article which might come to hand. To this I consented, and, in the first attempt, after staying under a full minute, brought up a small leather trunk belonging to Captain Barnard. This was immediately opened in the faint hope that it might contain something to eat or drink. We found nothing, however, except a box of razors and two linen shirts. I now went down again, and returned without any success. As my head came above water I heard a crash on deck, and, upon getting up, saw that my companions had ungratefully taken advantage of my absence to drink the remainder of the wine, having let the bottle fall in the endeavour to replace it before I saw them.

I remonstrated with them on the heartlessness of their conduct, when Augustus burst into tears. The other two endeavoured to laugh the matter off as a joke, but I hope never again to behold laughter of such a species: the distortion of countenance was absolutely frightful. Indeed, it was apparent that the stimulus, in the empty state of their stomachs, had taken instant and violent effect, and that they were all exceedingly intoxicated. With great difficulty I prevailed upon them to lie down, when they fell very soon into a heavy slumber, accompanied with loud stertorous breathing.

I now found myself, as it were, alone in the brig, and my reflections, to be sure, were of the most fearful and gloomy nature. No prospect offered itself to my view but a lingering death by famine, or, at the best, by being overwhelmed in the first gale which should spring up, for in our present exhausted condition we could have no hope of living through another.

The gnawing hunger which I now experienced was nearly insupportable, and I felt myself capable of going to any lengths in order to appease it. With my knife I cut off a small portion of the leather trunk, and endeavoured to eat it, but found it utterly impossible to swallow a single morsel, although I fancied that some little alleviation of my suffering was obtained by chewing small pieces of it and spitting them out.

Towards night my companions awoke, one by one, each in an indescribable state of weakness and horror, brought on by the wine, whose fumes had now evaporated. They shook as if with a violent ague, and uttered the most lamentable cries for water. Their condition affected me in the most lively degree, at the same time causing me to rejoice in the fortunate train of circumstances which had prevented me from indulging in the wine, and consequently from sharing their melancholy and most distressing sensations. Their conduct, however, gave me great uneasiness and alarm; for it was evident that, unless some favourable change took place, they could afford me no assistance in providing for our common safety.

I had not yet abandoned all idea of being able to get up something from below; but the attempt could not possibly be resumed until some one of them was sufficiently master of himself to aid me by holding the end of the rope while I went down. Parker appeared to be somewhat more in possession of his senses than the others, and I endeavoured, by every means in my power, to arouse him. Thinking that a plunge in the seawater might have a beneficial effect, I contrived to fasten the end of a rope around his body, and then, leading him to the companion-way (he remaining quite passive all the while), pushed him in, and immediately drew him out.

I had good reason to congratulate myself upon having made this experiment; for he appeared much revived and invigorated, and, upon getting out, asked me, in a rational manner, why I had so served him. Having explained my object, he expressed himself indebted to me, and said that he felt greatly better from the immersion, afterward conversing sensibly upon our situation. We then resolved to treat Augustus and Peters in the same way, which we immediately did, when they both experienced much benefit from the shock. This idea of sudden immersion had been suggested to me by reading in some medical work the good effect of the shower-bath in a case where the patient was suffering from *mania a potu*.

Finding that I could now trust my companions to hold the end of the rope, I again made three or four plunges into the cabin, although it was now quite dark, and a gentle but long swell from the northward rendered the hulk somewhat unsteady. In the course of these attempts I succeeded in bringing up two case-knives, a three-gallon jug, empty, and a blanket, but nothing which could serve us for food. I continued my efforts, after getting these articles, until I was completely exhausted, but brought up nothing else. During the night Parker and Peters occupied themselves by turns in the same manner; but nothing coming to hand, we now gave up this attempt in despair, concluding that we were exhausting ourselves in vain.

We passed the remainder of this night in a state of the most intense mental and bodily anguish that can possibly be imagined. The morning of the sixteenth at length dawned, and we looked eagerly around the horizon for relief, but to no purpose. The sea was still smooth, with only a long swell from the northward, as on yesterday. This was the sixth day since we had tasted either food or drink, with the exception of the bottle of Port wine, and it was clear that we could hold out but a very little while longer unless something could be obtained. I never saw before, nor wish to see again, human beings so utterly emaciated as Peters and Augustus.

Had I met them on shore in their present condition I should not have had the slightest suspicion that I had ever beheld them. Their countenances were totally changed in character, so that I could not bring myself to believe them really the same individuals with whom I had been in company but a few days before. Parker, although sadly reduced, and so feeble that he could not raise his head from his bosom, was not so far gone as the other two. He suffered with great patience, making no complaint, and endeavouring to inspire us with hope in every manner he could devise. For myself, although at the commencement of the voyage I had been in bad health, and was at all times of a delicate constitution, I suffered less than any of us, being much less reduced in frame, and retaining my powers of mind in a surprising degree, while the rest were completely prostrated in intellect, and seemed to be brought to a species of second childhood, generally simpering in their expressions, with idiotic smiles, and uttering the most absurd platitudes.

At intervals, however, they would appear to revive suddenly, as if inspired all at once with a consciousness of their condition, when they would spring upon their feet in a momentary flash of vigour, and speak, for a short period, of their prospects, in a manner altogether rational, although full of the most intense despair. It is possible, however, that my companions may have entertained the same opinion of their own condition as I did of mine, and that I may have unwittingly been guilty of the same extravagances and imbecilities as themselves—this is a matter which cannot be determined.

About noon Parker declared that he saw land off the larboard quarter, and it was with the utmost difficulty I could restrain him from plunging into the sea with the view of swimming towards it. Peters and Augustus took little notice of what he said, being apparently wrapped up in moody contemplation. Upon looking in the direction pointed out I could not perceive the faintest appearance of the shore—indeed, I was too well aware that we were far from any land to indulge in a hope of that nature. It was a long time, nevertheless, before I could convince Parker of his mistake. He then burst into a flood of tears, weeping like a child, with loud cries and sobs, for two or three hours, when, becoming exhausted, he fell asleep.

Peters and Augustus now made several ineffectual efforts to swallow portions of the leather. I advised them to chew it and spit it out; but they were too excessively debilitated to be able to follow my advice. I continued to chew pieces of it at intervals, and found some relief from so doing; my chief distress was for water, and I was only prevented from taking a draught from the sea by remembering the horrible consequences which thus have resulted to others who were similarly situated with ourselves.

The day wore on in this manner, when I suddenly discovered a sail to the eastward, and on our larboard bow. She appeared to be a large ship, and was coming nearly athwart us, being probably twelve or fifteen miles distant. None of my companions had as yet discovered her, and I forbore to tell them of her for the present, lest we might again be disappointed of relief. At length, upon her getting nearer, I saw distinctly that she was heading immediately for us, with her light sails filled. I could now contain myself no longer, and pointed her out to my fellow-sufferers.

They immediately sprang to their feet, again indulging in the most extravagant demonstrations of joy, weeping, laughing in an idiotic manner, jumping, stamping upon the deck, tearing their hair, and praying and cursing by turns. I was so affected by their conduct, as well as by what I now considered a sure prospect of deliverance, that I could not refrain from joining in with their madness, and gave way to the impulses of my gratitude and ecstasy by lying and rolling on the deck, clapping my hands, shouting, and other similar acts, until I was suddenly called to my recollection, and once more to the extreme of human misery and despair, by perceiving the ship all at once with her stern fully presented towards us, and steering in a direction nearly opposite to that in which I had at first perceived her.

It was some time before I could induce my poor companions to believe that this sad reverse in our prospects had actually taken place. They replied to all my assertions with a stare and a gesture implying that they were not to be deceived by such misrepresentations. The conduct of Augustus most sensibly affected me. In spite of all I could say or do to the contrary, he persisted in saying that the ship was rapidly nearing us, and in making preparations to go on board of her. Some seaweed floating by the brig, he maintained that it was the ship's boat, and endeavoured to throw himself upon it, howling and shrieking in the most heartrending manner, when I forcibly restrained him from thus casting himself into the sea.

Having become in some degree pacified, we continued to watch the ship until we finally lost sight of her, the weather becoming hazy, with a light breeze springing up. As soon as she was entirely gone, Parker turned suddenly towards me with an expression of countenance which made me shudder. There was about him an air of self-possession which I had not noticed in him until now, and before he opened his lips my heart told me what he would say. He proposed, in a few words, that one of us should die to preserve the existence of the others.

CHAPTER 12

I had, for some time past, dwelt upon the prospect of our being reduced to this last horrible extremity, and had secretly made up my mind to suffer death in any shape or under any circumstances rather than resort to such a course. Nor was this resolution in any degree weakened by the present intensity of hunger under which I laboured. The proposition had not been heard by either Peters or Augustus. I therefore took Parker aside; and mentally praying to God for power to dissuade him from the horrible purpose he entertained, I expostulated with him for a long time and in the most supplicating manner, begging him in the name of everything which he held sacred, and urging him by every species of argument which the extremity of the case suggested, to abandon the idea, and not to mention it to either of the other two.

He heard all I said without attempting to controvert any of my arguments, and I had begun to hope that he would be prevailed upon to do as I desired. But when I had ceased speaking, he said that he knew very well all I had said was true, and that to resort to such a course was the most horrible alternative which could enter into the mind of man; but that he had now held out as long as human nature could be sustained; that it was unnecessary for all to perish, when, by the death of one, it was possible, and even probable, that the rest might be finally preserved; adding that I might save myself the trouble of trying to turn him from his purpose, his mind having been thoroughly made up on the subject even before the appearance of the ship, and that only her heaving in sight had prevented him from mentioning his intention at an earlier period.

I now begged him, if he would not be prevailed upon to abandon his design, at least to defer it for another day, when some vessel might come to our relief, again reiterating every Argument I could devise, and which I thought likely to have influence with one of his rough nature. He said, in reply, that he had not spoken until the very last possible moment; that he could exist no longer without sustenance of some kind; and that therefore in another day his suggestion would be too late, as regarded himself at least.

Finding that he was not to be moved by anything I could

say in a mild tone, I now assumed a different demeanour, and told him that he must be aware I had suffered less than any of us from our calamities; that my health and strength, consequently, were at that moment far better than his own, or than that either of Peters or Augustus; in short, that I was in a condition to have my own way by force if I found it necessary; and that, if he attempted in any manner to acquaint the others with his bloody and cannibal designs, I would not hesitate to throw him into the sea.

Upon this he immediately seized me by the throat, and drawing a knife, made several ineffectual efforts to stab me in the stomach; an atrocity which his excessive debility alone prevented him from accomplishing. In the meantime, being roused to a high pitch of anger, I forced him to the vessel's side, with the full intention of throwing him overboard. He was saved from this fate, however, by the interference of Peters, who now approached and separated us, asking the cause of the disturbance. This Parker told before I could find means in any manner to prevent him.

The effect of his words was even more terrible than what I had anticipated. Both Augustus and Peters, who, it seems, had long secretly entertained the same fearful idea which Parker had been merely the first to broach, joined with him in his design, and insisted upon its being immediately carried into effect. I had calculated that one at least of the two former would be found still possessed of sufficient strength of mind to side with myself in resisting any attempt to execute so dreadful a purpose; and, with the aid of either one of them, I had no fear of being able to prevent its accomplishment.

Being disappointed in this expectation, it became absolutely necessary that I should attend to my own safety, as a further resistance on my part might possibly be considered by men in their frightful condition a sufficient excuse for refusing me fair play in the tragedy that I knew would speedily be enacted.

I now told them I was willing to submit to the proposal, merely requesting a delay of about one hour, in order that the fog which had gathered around us might have an opportunity of lifting, when it was possible that the ship we had seen might be again in sight. After great difficulty I obtained from them a promise to wait thus long; and, as I had anticipated (a breeze rapidly coming in), the fog lifted before the hour had expired, when, no vessel appearing in sight, we prepared to draw lots.

It is with extreme reluctance that I dwell upon the appalling scene which ensued; a scene which, with its minutest details, no after events have been able to efface in the slightest degree from my memory, and whose stern recollection will embitter every future moment of my existence. Let me run over this portion of my narrative with as much haste as the nature of the events to be spoken of will permit. The only method we could devise for the terrific lottery, in which we were to take each a chance, was that of drawing straws.

Small splinters of wood were made to answer our purpose, and it was agreed that I should be the holder. I retired to one end of the hulk, while my poor companions silently took up their station in the other with their backs turned towards me. The bitterest anxiety which I endured at any period of this fearful drama was while I occupied myself in the arrangement of the lots. There are few conditions into which man can possibly fall where he will not feel a deep interest in the preservation of his existence; an interest momentarily increasing with the frailness of the tenure by which that existence may be held.

But now that the silent, definite, and stern nature of the business in which I was engaged (so different from the tumultuous dangers of the storm or the gradually approaching horrors of famine) allowed me to reflect on the few chances I had of escaping the most appalling of deaths—a death for the most appalling of purposes—every particle of that energy which had so long buoyed me up departed like feathers before the wind, leaving me a helpless prey to the most abject and pitiable terror. I could not, at first, even summon up sufficient strength to tear and fit together the small splinters of wood, my fingers absolutely refusing their office, and my knees knocking violently against each other. My mind ran over rapidly a thousand absurd projects by which to avoid becoming a partner in the awful speculation.

I thought of falling on my knees to my companions, and entreating them to let me escape this necessity; of suddenly rushing upon them, and, by putting one of them to death, of rendering the decision by lot useless—in short, of everything but of going through with the matter I had in hand. At last, after wasting a long time in this imbecile conduct, I was recalled to my senses by the voice of Parker, who urged me to relieve them at once from the terrible anxiety they were enduring.

Even then I could not bring myself to arrange the splinters upon the spot, but thought over every species of finesse by which I could trick some one of my fellow-sufferers to draw the short straw, as it had been agreed that whoever drew the shortest of four splinters from my hand was to die for the preservation of the rest. Before any one condemn me for this apparent heartlessness, let him be placed in a situation precisely similar to my own.

At length delay was no longer possible, and, with a heart almost bursting from my bosom, I advanced to the region of the forecastle, where my companions were awaiting me. I held out my hand with the splinters, and Peters immediately drew. He was free—*his*, at least, was not the shortest; and there was now another chance against my escape. I summoned up all my strength, and passed the lots to Augustus. He also drew immediately, and he also was free; and now, whether I should live or die, the chances were no more than precisely even.

At this moment all the fierceness of the tiger possessed my bosom, and I felt towards my poor fellow-creature, Parker, the most intense.., the most diabolical hatred. But the feeling did not last; and, at length, with a convulsive shudder and closed eyes, I held out the two remaining splinters towards him. It was full five minutes before he could summon resolution to draw, during which period of heartrending suspense I never once opened my eyes. Presently one of the two lots was quickly drawn from my hand.

The decision was then over, yet I knew not whether it was for me or against me. No one spoke, and still I dared not satisfy myself by looking at the splinter I held. Peters at length took me by the hand, and I forced myself to look up, when I immediately saw by the countenance of Parker that I was safe, and that he it was who had been doomed to suffer. Gasping for breath, I fell senseless to the deck.

I recovered from my swoon in time to behold the consummation of the tragedy in the death of him who had been chiefly instrumental in bringing it about. He made no resistance whatever, and was stabbed in the back by Peters, when he fell instantly dead. I must not dwell upon the fearful repast which immediately ensued. Such things may be imagined, but words have no power to impress the mind with the exquisite horror of their reality. Let it suffice to say that, having in some measure appeased the raging thirst which consumed us by the blood of the victim, and having by common consent taken off the hands, feet, and head, throwing them, together with the entrails, into the sea, we devoured the rest of the body, piecemeal, during the four ever memorable days of the seventeenth eighteenth, nineteenth, and twentieth of the month.

On the nineteenth, there coming on a smart shower which lasted fifteen or twenty minutes, we contrived to catch some water by means of a sheet which had been fished up from the cabin by our drag just after the gale. The quantity we took in all did not amount to more than half a gallon; but even this scanty allowance supplied us with comparative strength and hope.

On the twenty-first we were again reduced to the last necessity. The weather still remained warm and pleas ant, with occasional fogs and light breezes, most usually from N. to W.

On the twenty-second, as we were sitting close huddled together, gloomily revolving over our lamentable condition, there flashed through my mind all at once an idea which inspired me with a bright gleam of hope. I remembered that, when the foremast had been cut away, Peters, being in the windward chains, passed one of the axes into my hand, requesting me to put it, if possible, in a place of security, and that a few minutes before the last heavy sea struck the brig and filled her I had taken this axe into the forecastle, and laid it in one of the larboard berths. I now thought it possible that, by getting at this axe, we might cut through the deck over the store room, and thus readily supply ourselves with provisions.

When I communicated this project to my companions, they uttered a feeble shout of joy, and we all proceeded forthwith to the forecastle. The difficulty of descending here was greater than that of going down in the cabin, the opening being much smaller, for it will be remembered that the whole framework about the cabin companion-hatch had been carried away, whereas the forecastle-way, being a simple hatch of only about three feet square, had remained uninjured. I did not hesitate, however, to attempt the descent; and, a rope being fastened round my body as before, I plunged boldly in, feet foremost, made my way quickly to the berth, and, at the very first attempt, brought up the axe. It was hailed with the most ecstatic joy and triumph, and the ease with which it had been obtained was regarded as an omen of our ultimate preservation.

We now commenced cutting at the deck with all the energy of rekindled hope, Peters and myself taking the axe by turns, Augustus's wounded arm not permitting him to aid us in any degree. As we were still so feeble as to be scarcely able to stand unsupported, and could consequently work but a minute or two without resting, it soon became evident that many long hours would be requisite to accomplish our task—that is, to cut an opening sufficiently large to admit of a free access to the storeroom. This consideration, however, did not discourage us; and, working all night by the light of the moon, we succeeded in effecting our purpose by daybreak on the morning of the twenty-third.

Peters now volunteered to go down; and, having made all arrangements as before, he descended, and soon returned, bringing up with him a small jar, which, to our great joy, proved to be full of olives. Having shared these among us, and devoured them with the greatest avidity, we proceeded to let him down again. This time he succeeded beyond our utmost expectations, returning instantly with a large ham and a bottle of Madeira wine. Of the latter we each took a moderate sup, having learned by experience the pernicious consequences of indulging too freely. The ham, except about two pounds near the bone, was not in a condition to be eaten, having been entirely spoiled by the salt water. The sound part was divided among us.

Peters and Augustus, not being able to restrain their appetite, swallowed theirs upon the instant; but I was more cautious, and ate but a small portion of mine, dreading the thirst which I knew would ensue. We now rested a while from our labours, which had been intolerably severe.

By noon, feeling somewhat strengthened and refreshed, we again renewed our attempt at getting up provision, Peters and myself going down alternately, and always with more or less success, until sundown. During this interval we had the good fortune to bring up, altogether, four more small jars of olives, another ham, a carboy containing nearly three gallons of excellent Cape Madeira wine, and, what gave us still more delight, a small tortoise of the Gallipago breed, several of which had been taken on board by Captain Barnard, as the Grampus was leaving port, from the schooner *Mary Pitts*, just returned from a sealing voyage in the Pacific.

In a subsequent portion of this narrative I shall have frequent occasion to mention this species of tortoise. It is found principally, as most of my readers may know, in the group of islands called the Gallipagos, which, indeed, derive their name from the animal—the Spanish word *Gallipago* meaning a fresh-water terrapin. From the peculiarity of their shape and action they have been sometimes called the elephant tortoise. They are frequently found of an enormous size. I have myself seen several which would weigh from twelve to fifteen hundred pounds, although I do not remember that any navigator speaks of having seen them weighing more than eight hundred.

Their appearance is singular, and even disgusting. Their steps are very slow, measured, and heavy, their bodies being carried about a foot from the ground. Their neck is long, and exceedingly slender; from eighteen inches to two feet is a very common length, and I killed one, where the distance from the shoulder to the extremity of the head was no less than three feet ten inches. The head has a striking resemblance to that of a serpent. They can exist without food for an almost incredible length of time, instances having been known where they have been thrown into the hold of a vessel and lain two years without nourishment of any kind—being as fat, and, in every respect, in as good order at the expiration of the time as when they were first put in.

In one particular these extraordinary animals bear a resemblance to the dromedary, or camel of the desert. In a bag at the root of the neck they carry with them a constant supply of water. In some instances, upon killing them after a full year's deprivation of all nourishment, as much as three gallons of perfectly sweet and fresh water have been found in their bags. Their food is chiefly wild parsley and celery, with purslain, sea-kelp, and prickly pears, upon which latter vegetable they thrive wonderfully, a great quantity of it being usually found on the hillsides near the shore wherever the animal itself is discovered. They are excellent and highly nutritious food, and have, no doubt, been the means of preserving the lives of thousands of seamen employed in the whale-fishery and other pursuits in the Pacific.

The one which we had the good fortune to bring up from the storeroom was not of a large size, weighing probably sixty-five or seventy pounds. It was a female, and in excellent condition, being exceedingly fat, and having more than a quart of limpid and sweet water in its bag. This was indeed a treasure; and, falling on our knees with, one accord, we returned fervent thanks to God for so seasonable a relief.

We had great difficulty in getting the animal up through the opening, as its struggles were fierce and its strength prodigious. It was upon the point of making its escape from Peters's grasp, and slipping back into the water, when Augustus, throwing a rope with a slip knot around its throat, held it up in this manner until I jumped into the hole by the side of Peters, and assisted him in lifting it out.

The water we drew carefully from the bag into the jug, which, it will be remembered, had been brought up before from the cabin. Having done this, we broke off the neck of a bottle so as to form, with the cork, a kind of glass, holding not quite half a gill. We then each drank one of these measures full, and resolved to limit ourselves to this quantity per day as long as it should hold out.

During the last two or three days, the weather having been dry and pleasant, the bedding we had obtained from the cabin, as well as our clothing, had become thoroughly dry, so that we passed this night (that of the twenty-third) in comparative comfort, enjoying a tranquil repose, after having supped plentifully on olives and ham, with a small allowance of the wine. Being afraid of losing some of our stores overboard during the night, in the event of a breeze springing up, we secured them as well as possible with cordage to the fragments of the windlass. Our tortoise, which we were anxious to preserve alive as long as we could, we threw on his back, and otherwise carefully fastened.

CHAPTER 13

July 24. This morning saw us wonderfully recruited in spirits and strength. Notwithstanding the perilous situation in which we were still placed, ignorant of our position, although certainly at a great distance from land, without more food than would last us for a fort night even with great care, almost entirely without water, and floating about at the mercy of every wind and wave, on the merest wreck in the world, still the infinitely more terrible distresses and dangers from which we had so lately and so providentially been delivered caused us to regard what we now endured as but little more than an ordinary evil—so strictly comparative is either good or ill.

At sunrise we were preparing to renew our attempts at getting up something from the storeroom, when, a smart shower coming on, with some lightning, we turned our attention to the catching of water by means of the sheet we had used before for this purpose. We had no other means of collecting the rain than by holding the sheet spread out with one of the fore-chain-plates in the middle of it. The water, thus conducted to the centre, was drained through into our jug.

We had nearly filled it in this manner, when, a heavy squall coming on from the northward, obliged us to desist, as the hulk began once more to roll so violently that we could no longer keep our feet. We now went forward, and, lashing our selves securely to the remnant of the windlass as before, awaited the event with far more calmness than could have been anticipated, or would have been imagined possible under the circumstances. At noon the wind had freshened into a two-reef breeze, and by night into a stiff gale, accompanied with a tremendously heavy swell. Experience having taught us, however, the best method of arranging our lashings, we weathered this dreary night in tolerable security, although thoroughly drenched at almost every instant by the sea, and in momentary dread of being washed off. Fortunately, the weather was so warm as to render the water rather grateful than other wise.

July 25. This morning the gale had diminished to a mere ten-knot breeze, and the sea had gone down with it so considerably that we were able to keep ourselves dry upon the deck. To our great grief, however, we found that two jars of our olives, as well as the whole of our ham, had been washed overboard, in spite of the careful manner in which they had been fastened. We determined not to kill the tortoise as yet, and contented ourselves for the present with a breakfast on a few of the olives, and a measure of water each, which latter we mixed, half and half, with wine, finding great relief and strength from the mixture, without the distressing intoxication which had ensued upon drinking the Port.

The sea was still far too rough for the renewal of our efforts at getting up provision from the storeroom. Several articles, of no importance to us in our present situation, floated up through the opening during the day, and were immediately washed overboard. We also now observed that the hulk lay more along than ever, so that we could not stand an instant without lashing ourselves. On this account we passed a gloomy and uncomfortable day. At noon the sun appeared to be nearly vertical, and we had no doubt that we had been driven down by the long succession of northward and north-westerly winds into the near vicinity of the equator. Towards evening saw several sharks, and were somewhat alarmed by the audacious manner in which an enormously large one approached us.

At one time, a lurch throwing the deck very far beneath the water, the monster actually swam in upon us, floundering for some moments just over the companion-hatch, and striking Peters violently with his tail. A heavy sea at length hurled him overboard, much to our relief. In moderate weather we might have easily captured him.

July 26. This morning, the wind having greatly abated, and the sea not being very rough, we determined to renew our exertions in the storeroom. After a great deal of hard labour during the whole day, we found that nothing further was to be expected from this quarter, the partitions of the room having been stove during the night, and its contents swept into the hold. This discovery, as may be supposed, filled us with despair.

July 27. The sea nearly smooth, with a light wind, and still from the northward and westward. The sun coming out hotly in the afternoon, we occupied our selves in drying our clothes. Found great relief from thirst, and much comfort otherwise, by bathing in the sea; in this, however, we were forced to use great caution, being afraid of sharks, several of which were seen swimming around the brig during the day.

July 28. Good weather still. The brig now began to lie along so alarmingly that we feared she would eventually roll bottom up. Prepared ourselves as well as we could for this emergency, lashing our tortoise, water-jug, and two remaining jars of olives as far as possible over to the windward, placing them outside the hull, below the main-chains. The sea very smooth all day, with little or no wind.

July 29. A continuance of the same weather. Augustus's wounded arm began to evince symptoms of mortification. He complained of drowsiness and excessive thirst, but no acute pain. Nothing could be done for his relief beyond rubbing his wounds with a little of the vinegar from the olives, and from this no benefit seemed to be experienced. We did everything in our power for his comfort, and trebled his allowance of water.

July 30. An excessively hot day, with no wind. An enormous shark kept close by the hulk during the whole of the forenoon. We made several unsuccessful attempts to capture him by means of a noose. Augustus much worse, and evidently sinking as much from want of proper nourishment as from the effect of his wounds. He constantly prayed to be released from his sufferings, wishing for nothing but death. This evening we ate the last of our olives, and found the water in our jug so putrid that we could not swallow it at all without the addition of wine. Determined to kill our tortoise in the morning.

July 31. After a night of excessive anxiety and fatigue, owing to the position of the hulk, we set about killing and cutting up our tortoise. He proved to be much smaller than we had supposed, although in good condition—the whole meat about him not amounting to more than ten pounds. With a view of preserving a portion of this as long as possible, we cut it into fine pieces, and filled with them our three remaining olive-jars and the wine-bottle (all of which had been kept), pouring in afterward the vinegar from the olives. In this manner we put away about three pounds of the tortoise, intending not to touch it until we had consumed the rest. We concluded to restrict ourselves to about four ounces of the meat per day; the whole would thus last us thirteen days.

A brisk shower, with severe thunder and lightning, came on about dusk, but lasted so short a time that we only succeeded in catching about half a pint of water. The whole of this, by common consent, was given to Augustus, who now appeared to be in the last extremity. He drank the water from the sheet as we caught it (we holding it above him as he lay so as to let it run into his mouth), for we had now nothing left capable of holding water, unless we had chosen to empty out our wine from the carboy, or the stale water from the jug. Either of these expedients would have been resorted to had the shower lasted.

The sufferer seemed to derive but little benefit from the draught. His arm was completely black from the wrist to the shoulder, and his feet were like ice. We expected every moment to see him breathe his last. He was frightfully emaciated; so much so that, although he weighed a hundred and twenty-seven pounds upon his leaving Nantucket, he now did not weigh more than *forty or fifty at the farthest.* His eyes were sunk far in his head, being scarcely perceptible, and the skin of his cheeks hung so loosely as to prevent his masticating any food, or even swallowing any liquid, without great difficulty.

August 1. A continuance of the same calm weather, with an oppressively hot sun. Suffered exceedingly from thirst, the water in the jug being absolutely putrid and swarming with vermin. We contrived, nevertheless, to swallow a portion of it by mixing it with wine—our thirst, however, was but little abated. We found more relief by bathing in the sea, but could not avail ourselves of this expedient except at long intervals, on account of the continual presence of sharks. We now saw clearly that Augustus could not be saved; that he was evidently dying. We could do nothing to relieve his sufferings, which appeared to be great.

About twelve o'clock he expired in strong convulsions, and without having spoken for several hours. His death filled us with the most gloomy forebodings, and had so great an effect upon our spirits that we sat motionless by the corpse during the whole day, and never addressed each other except in a whisper. It was not until some time after dark that we took courage to get up and throw the body overboard. It was then loathsome beyond expression, and so far decayed that, as Peters attempted to lift it, an entire leg came off in his grasp.

As the mass of putrefaction slipped over the vessel's side into the water, the glare of phosphoric light with which it was surrounded plainly discovered to us seven or eight large sharks, the clashing of whose horrible teeth, as their prey was torn to pieces among them, might have been heard at the distance of a mile. We shrunk within ourselves in the extremity of horror at the sound.

August 2. The same fearfully calm and hot weather. The dawn found us in a state of pitiable dejection as well as bodily exhaustion. The water in the jug was now absolutely useless, being a thick gelatinous mass; nothing but frightful-looking worms mingled with slime. We threw it out, and washed the jug well in the sea, afterward pouring a little vinegar in it from our bottles of pickled tortoise. Our thirst could now scarcely be endured, and we tried in vain to relieve it by wine, which seemed only to add fuel to the flame, and excited us to a high degree of intoxication. We afterward endeavoured to relieve our sufferings by mixing the wine with seawater; but this instantly brought about the most violent retchings, so that we never again attempted it.

During the whole day we anxiously sought an opportunity of bathing, but to no purpose; for the hulk was now entirely besieged on all sides with sharks—no doubt the identical monsters who had devoured our poor companion on the evening before, and who were in momentary expectation of another similar feast. This circumstance occasioned us the most bitter regret, and filled us with the most depressing and melancholy forebodings. We had experienced indescribable relief in bathing, and to have this resource cut off in so frightful a manner was more than we could bear. Nor, indeed, were we altogether free from the apprehension of immediate danger, for the least slip or false movement would have thrown us at once within reach of these voracious fish, who frequently thrust themselves directly upon us, swimming up to leeward.

No shouts or exertions on our part seemed to alarm them. Even when one of the largest was struck with an axe by Peters, and much wounded, he persisted in his attempts to push in where we were. A cloud came up at dusk, but, to our extreme anguish, passed over without discharging itself. It is quite impossible to conceive our sufferings from thirst at this period. We passed a sleepless night, both on this account and through dread of the sharks.

August 3. No prospect of relief, and the brig lying still more and more along, so that now we could not maintain a footing upon deck at all. Busied ourselves in securing our wine and tortoise-meat, so that we might not lose them in the event of our rolling over. Got out two stout spikes from the fore-chains, and, by means of the axe, drove them into the hull to windward within a couple of feet of the water; this not being very far from the keel, as we were nearly upon our beam-ends. To these spikes we now lashed our provisions, as being more secure than their former position beneath the chains. Suffered great agony from thirst during the whole day no chance of bathing on account of the sharks, which never left us for a moment. Found it impossible to sleep.

August 4. A little before daybreak we perceived that the hulk was heeling over, and aroused ourselves to pre vent being thrown off by the movement. At first the roll was slow and gradual, and we contrived to clamber over to windward very well, having taken the precaution to leave ropes hanging from the spikes we had driven in for the provision. But we had not calculated sufficiently upon the acceleration of the impetus; for presently the heel became too violent to allow of our keeping pace with it; and, before either of us knew what was to happen, we found ourselves hurled furiously into the sea, and struggling several fathoms beneath the surface, with the huge hull immediately above us.

In going under the water I had been obliged to let go my hold upon the rope; and finding that I was completely beneath the vessel, and my strength utterly exhausted, I scarcely made a struggle for life, and resigned myself, in a few seconds, to die. But here again I was deceived, not having taken into consideration the natural rebound of the hull to windward. The whirl of the water upward, which the vessel occasioned in rolling partially back, brought me to the surface still more violently than I had been plunged beneath. Upon coming up, I found myself about twenty yards from the hulk, as near as I could judge. She was lying keel up, rocking furiously from side to side, and the sea in all directions around was much agitated, and full of strong whirlpools. I could see nothing of Peters. An oil-cask was floating within a few feet of me, and various other articles from the brig were scattered about.

My principal terror was now on account of the sharks, which I knew to be in my vicinity. In order to deter these, if possible, from approaching me, I splashed the water vigorously with both hands and feet as I swam towards the hulk, creating a body of foam. I have no doubt that to this expedient, simple as it was, I was indebted for my preservation; for the sea all around the brig, just before her rolling over, was so crowded with these monsters, that I must have been, and really was, in actual contact with some of them during my progress. By great good fortune, however, I reached the side of the vessel in safety, although so utterly weakened by the violent exertion I had used that I should never have been able to get upon it but for the timely assistance of Peters, who now, to my great joy, made his appearance (having scrambled up to the keel from the opposite side of the hull), and threw me the end of a rope—one of those which had been attached to the spikes.

Having barely escaped this danger, our attention was now directed to the dreadful imminency of another; that of absolute starvation. Our whole stock of provision had been swept overboard in spite of all our care in securing it; and seeing no longer the remotest possibility of obtaining more, we gave way both of us to despair, weeping aloud like children, and neither of us attempting to offer consolation to the other.

Such weakness can scarcely be conceived, and to those who have never been similarly situated will, no doubt, appear unnatural; but it must be remembered that our intellects were so entirely disordered by the long course of privation and terror to which we had been subjected, that we could not justly be considered, at that period, in the light of rational beings. In subsequent perils, nearly as great, if not greater, I bore up with fortitude against all the evils of my situation, and Peters, it will be seen, evinced a stoical philosophy nearly as incredible as his present childlike supineness and imbecility—the mental condition made the difference.

The overturning of the brig, even with the consequent loss of the wine and turtle, would not, in fact, have rendered our situation more deplorable than before, except for the disappearance of the bedclothes by which we had been hitherto enabled to catch rainwater, and of the jug in which we had kept it when caught; for we found the whole bottom, from within two or three feet of the bends as far as the keel, together with the keel itself, *thickly covered with large barnacles, which proved to be excellent and highly nutritious food.* Thus, in two important respects, the accident we had so greatly dreaded proved a benefit rather than an injury; it had opened to us a supply of provisions, which we could not have exhausted, using it moderately, in a month; and it had greatly contributed to our comfort as regards position, we being much more at our ease, and in infinitely less danger, than before.

The difficulty, however, of now obtaining water blinded us to all the benefits of the change in our condition. That we might be ready to avail ourselves, as far as possible, of any shower which might fall, we took off our shirts, to make use of them as we had of the sheets—not hoping, of course, to get more in this way, even under the most favourable circumstances, than half a gill at a time. No signs of a cloud appeared during the day, and the agonies of our thirst were nearly intolerable At night Peters obtained about an hour's disturbed sleep, but my intense sufferings would not permit me to close my eyes for a single moment.

August 5. Today, a gentle breeze springing up carried us through a vast quantity of seaweed, among which we were so fortunate as to find eleven small crabs, which afforded us several delicious meals. Their shells being quite soft, we ate them entire, and found that they irritated our thirst far less than the barnacles. Seeing no trace of sharks among the seaweed, we also ventured to bathe, and remained in the water for four or five hours, during which we experienced a very sensible diminution of our thirst. Were greatly refreshed, and spent the night somewhat more comfortably than before, both of us snatching a little sleep.

August 6. This day we were blessed by a brisk and continual rain, lasting from about noon until after dark. Bitterly did we now regret the loss of our jug and carboy; for, in spite of the little means we had of catching the water, we might have filled one, if not both of them. As it was, we contrived to satisfy the cravings of thirst by suffering the shirts to become saturated, and then wringing them so as to let the grateful fluid trickle into our mouths. In this occupation we passed the entire day.

August 7. Just at daybreak we both at the same instant descried a sail to the eastward, and *evidently coming towards us!* We hailed the glorious sight with a long, although feeble shout of rapture; and began instantly to make every signal in our power, by flaring the shirts in the air, leaping as high as our weak condition would permit, and even by hallooing with all the strength of our lungs, although the vessel could not have been less than fifteen miles distant. However, she still continued to near our hulk, and we felt that, if she but held her present course, she must eventually come so close as to perceive us. In about an hour after we first discovered her we could clearly see the people on her decks. She was a long, low, and rakish-looking topsail schooner, with a black ball in her foretopsail, and had, apparently, a full crew.

We now became alarmed, for we could hardly imagine it possible that she did not observe us, and were apprehensive that she meant to leave us to perish as we were an act of fiendish barbarity, which, however incredible it may appear, has been repeatedly perpetrated at sea, under circumstances very nearly similar, and by beings who were regarded as be longing to the human species. (See note following).

Note:—The case of the brig *Polly*, of Boston, is one so much in point, and her fate, in many respects, so remarkably similar to our own, that I cannot forbear alluding to it here. This vessel, of one hundred and thirty tons burden, sailed from Boston, with a cargo of lumber and provisions, for Santa Croix, on the twelfth of December, 1811, under the command of Captain Casneau. There were eight souls on board besides the captain—the mate, four seamen, and the cook, together with a Mr. Hunt, and a negro girl belonging to him. On the fifteenth, having cleared the shoal of Georges, she sprung a leak in a gale of wind from the southeast, and was finally capsized; but, the mast going by the board, she afterward righted.

They remained in this situation, without fire, and with very little provision, for the period of *one hundred and ninety-one days* (from December the fifteenth to June the twentieth) when Captain Casneau and Samuel Badger, the only survivors, were taken off the wreck by the *Fame*, of Hull, Captain Featherstone, bound home from Rio Janeiro. When picked up they were in latitude 28 N., *longitude 13 W., having drifted above two thousand miles.* On the ninth of July the *Fame* fell in with the brig *Dromeo*, Captain Perkins, who landed the two sufferers in Kennebeck. The narrative from which we gather these details ends in the following words.

It is natural to inquire how they could float such a vast distance, upon the most frequented part of the Atlantic, and not be discovered all this time. *They were passed by more than a dozen sail, one of which came so nigh them that they could distinctly see the people on deck and on the rigging looking at them; but, to the inexpressible disappointment of the starving and freezing men, they stifled the dictates of compassion, hoisted sail and cruelly abandoned them to their fate.*

In this instance, however, by the mercy of God, we were

destined to be most happily deceived; for presently we were aware of a sudden commotion on the deck of the stranger, who immediately afterward run up a British flag, and, hauling her wind, bore up directly upon us. In half an hour more we found ourselves in her cabin. She proved to be the *Jane Guy*, of Liverpool, Captain Guy, bound on a sealing and trading voyage to the South Seas and Pacific.

CHAPTER 14

The *Jane Guy* was a fine-looking topsail schooner of a hundred and eighty tons burden. She was unusually sharp in the bows, and on a wind, in moderate weather, the fastest sailer I have ever seen. Her qualities, how ever, as a rough sea-boat, were not so good, and her draught of water was by far too great for the trade to which she was destined. For this peculiar service a larger vessel, and one of a light proportionate draught, is desirable—say a vessel of from three to three hundred and fifty tons. She should be barque-rigged, and in other respects of a different construction from the usual South Sea ships.

It is absolutely necessary that she should be well armed. She should have, say ten or twelve twelve pound carronades, and two or three long twelves, with brass blunderbusses, and water-tight arm-chests for each top. Her anchors and cables should be of far greater strength than is required for any other species of trade, and, above all, her crew should be numerous and efficient—not less, for such a vessel as I have described, than fifty or sixty able-bodied men. The *Jane Guy* had a crew of thirty-five, all able seamen, besides the captain and mate, but she was not altogether as well armed or otherwise equipped as a navigator acquainted with the difficulties and dangers of the trade could have desired.

Captain Guy was a gentleman of great urbanity of manner, and of considerable experience in the southern traffic, to which he had devoted a great portion of his life. He was deficient, however, in energy, and, consequently, in that spirit of enterprise which is here so absolutely requisite. He was part owner of the vessel in which he sailed, and was invested with discretionary powers to cruise in the South Seas for any cargo which might come most readily to hand. He had on board, as usual in such voyages, beads, looking-glasses, tinder-works, axes, hatchets, saws, adzes, planes, chisels, gouges, gimlets, files, spokeshaves, rasps, hammers, nails, knives, scissors, razors, needles, thread, crockery-ware, calico, trinkets, and other similar articles.

The schooner sailed from Liverpool on the tenth of July, crossed the Tropic of Cancer on the twenty-fifth, in longitude twenty degrees west, and reached Sal, one of the Cape Verd Islands, on the twenty-ninth, where she took in salt and other necessaries for the voyage. On the third of August she left the Cape Verds and steered southwest, stretching over towards the coast of Brazil so as to cross the equator between the meridians of twenty-eight and thirty degrees west longitude. This is the course usually taken by vessels bound from Europe to the Cape of Good Hope, or by that route to the East Indies.

By proceeding thus they avoid the calms and strong contrary currents which continually prevail on the coast of Guinea, while, in the end, it is found to be the shortest track, as westerly winds are never wanting afterward by which to reach the Cape. It was Captain Guy's intention to make his first stoppage at Kerguelen's Land—I hardly know for what reason. On the day we were picked up the schooner was off Cape St. Roque, in longitude 31 W.; so that, when found, we had drifted probably, from north to south, *not less than five-and-twenty degrees.*

On board the *Jane Guy* we were treated with all the kindness our distressed situation demanded. In about a fortnight, during which time we continued steering to the southeast, with gentle breezes and fine weather, both Peters and myself recovered entirely from the effects of our late privation and dreadful suffering, and we began to remember what had passed rather as a frightful dream from which we had been happily awakened, than as events which had taken place in sober and naked reality. I have since found that this species of partial oblivion is usually brought about by sudden transition, whether from joy to sorrow or from sorrow to joy—the degree of forgetfulness being proportioned to the degree of difference in the exchange.

Thus, in my own case, I now feel it impossible to realize the full extent of the misery which I endured during the days spent upon the hulk. The incidents are remembered, but not the feelings which the incidents elicited at the time of their occurrence. I only know that, when they did occur, I *then* thought human nature could sustain nothing more of agony.

We continued our voyage for some weeks without any incidents of greater moment than the occasional meeting with whaling-ships, and more frequently with the black or right whale, so called in contradistinction to the spermaceti. These, however, were chiefly found south of the twenty-fifth parallel. On the sixteenth of September, being in the vicinity of the Cape of Good Hope, the schooner encountered her first gale of any violence since leaving Liverpool.

In this neighbourhood, but more frequently to the south and east of the promontory (we were to the westward), navigators have often to contend with storms from the northward which rage with great fury. They always bring with them a heavy sea, and one of their most dangerous features is the instantaneous chopping round of the wind, an occurrence almost certain to take place during the greatest force of the gale. A perfect hurricane will be blowing at one moment from the northward or northeast, and in the next not a breath of wind will be felt in that direction, while from the southwest it will come out all at once with a violence almost inconceivable. A bright spot to the southward is the sure forerunner of the change, and vessels are thus enabled to take the proper precautions.

It was about six in the morning when the blow came on with a white squall, and, as usual, from the northward. By eight it had increased very much, and brought down upon us one of the most tremendous seas I had then ever beheld. Everything had been made as snug as possible, but the schooner laboured excessively, and gave evidence of her bad qualities as a seaboat, pitching her forecastle under at every plunge, and with the greatest difficulty struggling up from one wave before she was buried in another. Just before sunset the bright spot for which we had been on the lookout made its appearance in the southwest, and in an hour afterward we perceived the little headsail we carried flapping listlessly against the mast.

In two minutes more, in spite of every preparation, we were hurled on our beam-ends as if by magic, and a perfect wilderness of foam made a clear breach over us as we lay. The blow from the southwest, however, luckily proved to be nothing more than a squall, and we had the good fortune to right the vessel without the loss of a spar. A heavy cross sea gave us great trouble for a few hours after this, but towards morning we found ourselves in nearly as good condition as before the gale. Captain Guy considered that he had made an escape little less than miraculous.

On the thirteenth of October we came in sight of Prince Edward's Island, in latitude 46° 53' S., longitude 37° 46' E. Two days afterward we found ourselves near Possession Island, and presently passed the islands of Crozet, in latitude 42° 59' S., longitude 48° E. On the eighteenth we made Kerguelen's or Desolation Island, in the Southern Indian Ocean, and came to anchor in Christmas Harbour, having four fathoms of water.

This island, or rather group of islands, bears south-east from the Cape of Good Hope, and is distant there from nearly eight hundred leagues. It was first discovered in 1772, by the Baron de Kergulen, or Kerguelen, a Frenchman, who, thinking the land to form a portion of an extensive southern continent, carried home information to that effect, which produced much excitement at the time. The government, taking the matter up, sent the baron back in the following year for the purpose of giving his new discovery a critical examination, when the mistake was discovered.

In 1777, Captain Cook fell in with the same group, and gave to the principal one the name of Desolation Island, a title which it certainly well deserves. Upon approaching the land, however, the navigator might be induced to suppose otherwise, as the sides of most of the hills, from September to March, are clothed with very brilliant verdure. This deceitful appearance is caused by a small plant resembling saxifrage, which is abundant, growing in large patches on a species of crumbling moss. Besides this plant there is scarcely a sign of vegetation on the island, if we except some coarse rank grass near the harbour, some lichen, and a shrub which bears resemblance to a cabbage shooting into seed, and which has a bitter and acrid taste.

The face of the country is hilly, although none of the hills can be called lofty. Their tops are perpetually covered with snow. There are several harbours, of which Christmas Harbour is the most convenient. It is the first to be met with on the north-east side of the island after passing Cape François, which forms the northern shore, and, by its peculiar shape, serves to distinguish the harbour. Its projecting point terminates in a high rock, through which is a large hole, forming a natural arch.

The entrance is in latitude 48° C 40' S., longitude 69° 6' E. Passing in here, good anchorage may be found under the shelter of several small islands, which form a sufficient protection from all easterly winds. Proceeding on eastwardly from this anchorage you come to Wasp Bay, at the head of the harbour. This is a small basin, completely landlocked, into which you can go with four fathoms, and find anchorage in from ten to three, hard clay bottom. A ship might lie here with her best bower ahead all the year round with out risk. To the westward, at the head of Wasp Bay, is a small stream of excellent water, easily procured.

Some seal of the fur and hair species are still to be found on Kerguelen's Island, and sea elephants abound. The feathered tribes are discovered in great numbers. Penguins are very plenty, and of these there are four different kinds. The royal penguin, so called from its size and beautiful plumage, is the largest. The upper part of the body is usually gray, sometimes of a lilac tint; the under portion of the purest white imaginable. The head is of a glossy and most brilliant black, the feet also. The chief beauty of the plumage, however, consists in two broad stripes of a gold colour, which pass along from the head to the breast. The bill is long, and either pink or bright scarlet.

These birds walk erect, with a stately carriage. They carry their heads high, with their wings drooping like two arms, and, as their tails project from their body in a line with the legs, the resemblance to a human figure is very striking, and would be apt to deceive the spectator at a casual glance or in the gloom of the evening. The royal penguins which we met with on Kerguelen's Land were rather larger than a goose. The other kinds are the macaroni, the jackass, and the rookery penguin. These are much smaller, less beautiful in plumage, and different in other respects.

Besides the penguin many other birds are here to be found, among which may be mentioned sea-hens, blue petrels, teal, ducks, Port Egmont hens, shags, Cape pigeons, the nelly, sea-swallows, terns, seagulls, Mother Carey's chickens, Mother Carey's geese, or the great petrel, and, lastly, the albatross.

The great petrel is as large as the common albatross, and is carnivorous. It is frequently called the break-bones, or osprey petrel. They are not at all shy, and, when properly cooked, are palatable food. In flying they sometimes sail very close to the surface of the water, with the wings expanded, without appearing to move them in the least degree, or make any exertion with them whatever.

The albatross is one of the largest and fiercest of the South Sea birds. It is of the gull species, and takes its prey on the wing, never coming on land except for the purpose of breeding. Between this bird and the penguin the most singular friendship exists. Their nests are constructed with great uniformity, upon a plan concerted between the two species—that of the albatross being placed in the centre of a little square formed by the nests of four penguins. Navigators have agreed in calling an assemblage of such encampments *a rookery*. These rookeries have been often described, but, as my readers may not all have seen these descriptions, and as I shall have occasion hereafter to speak of the penguin and albatross, it will not be amiss to say something here of their mode of building and living.

When the season for incubation arrives, the birds assemble in vast numbers, and for some days appear to be deliberating upon the proper course to be pursued. At length they proceed to action. A level piece of ground is selected, of suitable extent, usually comprising three or four acres, and situated as near the sea as possible, being still beyond its reach. The spot is chosen with reference to its evenness of surface, and that is preferred which is the least encumbered with stones.

This matter being arranged, the birds proceed, with one accord, and actuated apparently by one mind, to trace out, with mathematical accuracy, either a square or other parallelogram, as may best suit the nature of the ground, and of just sufficient size to accommodate easily all the birds assembled, and no more—in this particular seeming determined upon preventing the access of future stragglers who have not participated in the labour of the encampment. One side of the place thus marked out runs parallel with the water's edge, and is left open for ingress or egress.

Having defined the limits of the rookery, the colony now begin to clear it of every species of rubbish, picking up stone by stone, and carrying them outside of the lines, and close by them, so as to form a wall on the three inland sides. Just within this wall a perfectly level and smooth walk is formed, from six to eight feet wide, and extending around the encampment—thus serving the purpose of a general promenade.

The next process is to partition out the whole area into small squares exactly equal in size. This is done by forming narrow paths, very smooth, and crossing each other at right angles throughout the entire extent of the rookery. At each intersection of these paths the nest of an albatross is constructed, and a penguin's nest in the centre of each square—thus every penguin is surrounded by four albatrosses, and each albatross by a like number of penguins. The penguin's nest consists of a hole in the earth, very shallow, being only just of sufficient depth to keep her single egg from rolling. The albatross is somewhat less simple in her arrangements, erecting a hillock about a foot high and two in diameter. This is made of earth, seaweed, and shells. On its summit she builds her nest.

The birds take especial care never to leave their nests unoccupied for an instant during the period of incubation, or, indeed, until the young progeny are sufficiently strong to take care of themselves. While the male is absent at sea in search of food, the female remains on duty, and it is only upon the return of her partner that she ventures abroad. The eggs are never left uncovered at all while one bird leaves the nest, the other nestling in by its side. This precaution is rendered necessary by the thievish propensities prevalent in the rookery, the inhabitants making no scruple to purloin each other's eggs at every good opportunity.

Although there are some rookeries in which the penguin and albatross are the sole population, yet in most of them a variety of oceanic birds are to be met with, enjoying all the privileges of citizenship, and scattering their nests here and there, wherever they can find room, never interfering, however, with the stations of the larger species. The appearance of such encampments, when seen from a distance, is exceedingly singular. The whole atmosphere just above the settlement is darkened with the immense number of the albatross (mingled with the smaller tribes) which are continually hovering over it, either going to the ocean or returning home.

At the same time a crowd of penguins are to be observed, some passing to and fro in the narrow alleys, and some marching, with the military strut so peculiar to them, around the general promenade-ground which encircles the rookery. In short, survey it as we will, no thing can be more astonishing than the spirit of reflection evinced by these feathered beings, and nothing surely can be better calculated to elicit reflection in every well-regulated human intellect.

On the morning after our arrival in Christmas Harbour the chief mate, Mr. Patterson, took the boats, and (although it was somewhat early in the season) went in search of seal, leaving the captain and a young relation of his on a point of barren land to the westward, they having some business, whose nature I could not ascertain, to transact in the interior of the island. Captain Guy took with him a bottle, in which was a sealed letter, and made his way from the point on which he was set on shore towards one of the highest peaks in the place. It is probable that his design was to leave the letter on that height for some vessel which he expected to come after him.

As soon as we lost sight of him we proceeded (Peters and myself being in the mate's boat) on our cruise around the coast, looking for seal. In this business we were occupied about three weeks, examining with great care every nook and corner, not only of Kerguelen's Land, but of the several small islands in the vicinity. Our labours, however, were not crowned with any important success. We saw a great many fur seal, but they were exceedingly shy, and, with the greatest exertions, we could only procure three hundred and fifty skins in all. Sea elephants were abundant, especially on the western coast of the main island, but of these we killed only twenty, and this with great difficulty.

On the smaller islands we discovered a good many of the hair seal, but did not molest them. We returned to the schooner on the eleventh, where we found Captain Guy and his nephew, who gave a very bad account of the interior, representing it as one of the most dreary and utterly barren countries in the world. They had remained two nights on the island, owing to some misunderstanding, on the part of the second mate, in regard to the sending a jollyboat from the schooner to take them off.

CHAPTER 15

On the twelfth we made sail from Christmas Harbour, retracing our way to the westward, and leaving Marion's Island, one of Crozet's group, on the larboard. We afterward passed Prince Edward's Island, leaving it also on our left; then, steering more to the northward, made, in fifteen days, the islands of Tristan d'Acunha, in lati tude 37° 8' S., longitude 12° 8' W.

This group, now so well known, and which consists of three circular islands, was first discovered by the Portuguese, and was visited afterward by the Dutch in 1643, and by the French in

1767. The three islands together form a triangle, and are distant from each other about ten miles, there being fine open passages between. The land in all of them is very high, especially in Tristan d'Acunha, properly so called. This is the largest of the group, being fifteen miles in circumference, and so elevated that it can be seen in clear weather at the distance of eighty or ninety miles. A part of the land to wards the north rises more than a thousand feet perpendicularly from the sea.

A tableland at this height extends back nearly to the centre of the island, and from this tableland arises a lofty cone like that of Teneriffe. The lower half of this cone is clothed with trees of good size, but the upper region is barren rock, usually hidden among the clouds, and covered with snow during the greater part of the year. There are no shoals or other dangers about the island, the shores being remark ably bold and the water deep. On the north-western coast is a bay, with a beach of black sand, where a landing with boats can be easily effected, provided there be a southerly wind. Plenty of excellent water may here be readily procured; also cod, and other fish, may be taken with hook and line.

The next island in point of size, and the most westwardly of the group, is that called the Inaccessible. Its precise situation is 37° 17' S. latitude, longitude 12° 24' W. It is seven or eight miles in circumference, and on all sides presents a forbidding and precipitous aspect. Its top is perfectly flat, and the whole region is sterile, nothing growing upon it except a few stunted shrubs.

Nightingale Island, the smallest and most southerly, is in latitude 37° 26' S., longitude 12° 12' W. Off its southern extremity is a high ledge of rocky islets; a few also of a similar appearance are seen to the north east. The ground is irregular and sterile, and a deep valley partially separates it.

The shores of these islands abound, in the proper sea son, with sea lions, sea elephants, the hair and fur seal, together with a great variety of oceanic birds. Whales are also plenty in their vicinity. Owing to the ease with which these various animals were here formerly taken, the group has been much visited since its discovery. The Dutch and French frequented it at a very early period. In 1790, Captain Patten, of the ship *Industry*, of Philadelphia, made Tristan d'Acunha, where he remained seven months (from August, 1790, to April, 1791) for the purpose of collecting sealskins. In this time he gathered no less than five thousand six hundred, and says that he would have had no difficulty in loading a large ship with oil in three weeks. Upon his arrival he found no quadrupeds, with the exception of a few wild goats—the island now abounds with all our most valuable domestic animals, which have been introduced by subsequent navigators.

I believe it was not long after Captain Patten's visit that Captain Colquhoun, of the American brig *Betsey*, touched at the largest of the islands for the purpose of refreshment. He planted onions, potatoes, cabbages, and a great many other vegetables, an abundance of all which are now to be met with.

In 1811, a Captain Heywood, in the *Nereus*, visited Tristan. He found there three Americans, who were residing upon the islands to prepare sealskins and oil. One of these men was named Jonathan Lambert, and he called himself the sovereign of the country. He had cleared and cultivated about sixty acres of land, and turned his attention to raising the coffee-plant and sugar cane, with which he had been furnished by the American minister at Rio Janeiro. This settlement, however, was finally abandoned, and in 1817 the islands were taken possession of by the British government, who sent a detachment for that purpose from the Cape of Good Hope.

They did not, however, retain them long; but, upon the evacuation of the country as a British possession, two or three English families took up their residence there in dependently of the government. On the twenty-fifth of March, 1824, the Berwick, Captain Jeffrey, from London to Van Diemen's Land, arrived at the place, where they found an Englishman of the name of Glass, formerly a corporal in the British artillery. He claimed to be supreme governor of the islands, and had under his control twenty-one men and three women. He gave a very favourable account of the salubrity of the climate and of the productiveness of the soil.

The population occupied themselves chiefly in collecting sealskins and sea elephant oil, with which they traded to the Cape of Good Hope, Glass owning a small schooner. At the period of our arrival the governor was still a resident, but his little community had multiplied, there being fifty-six persons upon Tristan, besides a smaller settlement of seven on Nightingale Island. We had no difficulty in procuring almost every kind of refreshment which we required—sheep, hogs, bullocks, rabbits, poultry, goats, fish in great variety, and vegetables were abundant. Having come to anchor close in with the large island, in eighteen fathoms, we took all we wanted on board very conveniently. Captain Guy also purchased of Glass five hundred sealskins and some ivory.

We remained here a week, during which the prevailing winds were from the northward and westward, and the weather somewhat hazy. On the fifth of November we made sail to the southward and westward, with the intention of having a thorough search for a group of islands called the Auroras, respecting whose existence a great diversity of opinion has existed.

These islands are said to have been discovered as early as 1762, by the commander of the ship Aurora. In 1790. Captain Manuel de Oyarvido, in the ship *Princess*, belonging to the Royal Philippine Company, sailed, as he asserts, directly among them. In 1794, the Spanish corvette *Atrevida* went with the determination of ascertaining their precise situation, and, in a paper published by the Royal Hydrographical Society of Madrid in the year 1809, the following language is used respecting this expedition.

The corvette *Atrevida* practised, in their immediate vicinity, from the twenty-first to the twenty-seventh of January, all the necessary observations, and measured by chronometers the difference of longitude between these islands and the port of Soledad in the Malninas. The islands are three; they are very nearly in the same meridian; the centre one is rather low, and the other two may be seen at nine leagues distance.

The observations made on board the *Atrevida* give the following results as the precise situation of each island. The most northern is in latitude 52° 37' 24" S., longitude 47° 4' 15" W.; the middle one in latitude 53° 2' 40" S., longitude 47° 55' 15" W.; and the most southern in latitude 53° 15' 22" S., longitude 47° 57' 15" W.

On the twenty-seventh of January, 1820, Captain James Weddel, of the British navy, sailed from Staten Land also in search of the Auroras. He reports that, having made the most diligent search, and passed not only immediately over the spots indicated by the commander of the *Atrevida*, but in every direction through out the vicinity of these spots, he could discover no indication of land. These conflicting statements have induced other navigators to look out for the islands; and, strange to say, while some have sailed through every inch of sea where they are supposed to lie without finding them, there have been not a few who declare positively that they have seen them, and even been close in with their shores. It was Captain Guy's intention to make every exertion within his power to settle the question so oddly in dispute.[1]

We kept on our course, between the south and west, with variable weather, until the twentieth of the month, when we found ourselves on the debated ground, being in latitude 5°3 15' S., longitude 47° 58' W. that is to say, very nearly upon the spot indicated as the situation of the most southern of the group. Not perceiving any sign of land, we continued to the westward in the parallel of fifty-three degrees south, as far as the meridian of fifty degrees west. We then stood to the north as far as the parallel of fifty-two degrees south, when we turned to the eastward, and kept our parallel by double altitudes, morning and evening, and meridian altitudes of the planets and moon. Having thus gone

---

1. Among the vessels which at various times have professed to meet with the Auroras may be mentioned the ship *San Miguel*, in 1769; the ship *Aurora*, in 1774; the brig *Pearl*, in 1779; and the ship *Dolores*, in 1790. They all agree in giving the mean latitude fifty-three degrees south.

eastwardly to the meridian of the western coast of Georgia, we kept that meridian until we were in the latitude from which we set out.

We then took diagonal courses throughout the en tire extent of sea circumscribed, keeping a lookout constantly at the masthead, and repeating our examination with the greatest care for a period of three weeks, during which the weather was remarkably pleasant and fair, with no haze whatsoever. Of course we were thoroughly satisfied that, whatever islands might have existed in this vicinity at any former period, no vestige of them remained at the present day. Since my return home I find that the same ground was traced over with equal care in 1822 by Captain Johnson, of the American schooner *Henry*, and by Captain Morrell, in the American schooner *Wasp*—in both cases with the same result as in our own.

Chapter 16

It had been Captain Guy's original intention, after satisfying himself about the Auroras, to proceed through the Strait of Magellan, and up along the western coast of Patagonia; but information received at Tristan d'Acunha induced him to steer to the southward, in the hope of falling in with some small islands said to lie about the parallel of 60° S., longitude 41° 20' W. In the event of his not discovering these lands, he designed, should the season prove favourable, to push on towards the pole. Accordingly, on the twelfth of December, we made sail in that direction. On the eighteenth we found ourselves about the station indicated by Glass, and cruised for three days in that neighbourhood without finding any traces of the islands he had mentioned.

On the twenty-first, the weather being unusually pleasant, we again made sail to the southward, with the resolution of penetrating in that course as far as possible. Before entering upon this portion of my narrative, it may be as well, for the information of those readers who have paid little attention to the progress of discovery in these regions, to give some brief account of the very few attempts at reaching the southern pole which have

139

hitherto been made.

That of Captain Cook was the first of which we have any distinct account. In 1772 he sailed to the south in the Resolution, accompanied by Lieutenant Furneaux in the *Adventure*. In December he found himself as far as the fifty-eighth parallel of south latitude, and in longitude 26° 57' E. Here he met with narrow fields of ice, about eight or ten inches thick, and running north west and southeast. This ice was in large cakes, and usually it was packed so closely that the vessels had great difficulty in forcing a passage.

At this period Captain Cook supposed, from the vast number of birds to be seen, and from other indications, that he was in the near vicinity of land. He kept on to the southward, the weather being exceedingly cold, until he reached the sixty-fourth parallel, in longitude 38° 14' E. Here he had mild weather, with gentle breezes, for five days, the thermometer being at thirty-six. In January, 1773, the vessels crossed the Antarctic circle, but did not succeed in penetrating much farther; for, upon reaching latitude 67° 15', they found all farther progress impeded by an immense body of ice, extending all along the southern horizon as far as the eye could reach. This ice was of every variety—and some large floes of it, miles in ex tent, formed a compact mass, rising eighteen or twenty feet above the water. It being late in the season, and no hope entertained of rounding these obstructions, Captain Cook now reluctantly turned to the northward.

In the November following he renewed his search in the Antarctic. In latitude 59° 40' he met with a strong current setting to the southward. In December, when the vessels were in latitude 67° 31', longitude 142° 54' W., the cold was excessive, with heavy gales and fog. Here also birds were abundant; the albatross, the penguin, and the petrel especially. In latitude 70 23' some large islands of ice were encountered, and shortly afterward, the clouds to the southward were observed to be of a snowy whiteness, indicating the vicinity of field ice. In latitude 71° 10', longitude 106° 54' W., the navigators were stopped, as before, by an immense frozen expanse, which filled the whole area of the southern horizon.

The northern edge of this expanse was ragged and broken, so firmly wedged together as to be utterly impassable, and extending about a mile to the southward. Behind it the frozen surface was comparatively smooth for some distance, until terminated in the extreme back-ground by gigantic ranges of ice mountains, the one towering above the other. Captain Cook concluded that this vast field reached the southern pole or was joined to a continent. Mr. J. N. Reynolds, whose great exertions and perseverance have at length succeeded in getting set on foot a national expedition, partly for the purpose of exploring these regions, thus speaks of the attempt of the Resolution. "We are not surprised that Captain Cook was unable to go beyond 71° 10', but we are astonished that he did attain that point on the meridian of 106° 54' west longitude.

Palmer's Land lies south of the Shetland, latitude sixty-four degrees, and tends to the southward and westward farther than any navigator has yet penetrated. Cook was standing for this land when his progress was arrested by the ice; which, we apprehend, must always be the case in that point, and so early in the season as the sixth of January—and we should not be surprised if a portion of the icy mountains described was attached to the main body of Palmer's Land, or to some other portions of land lying farther to the southward and westward."

In 1803, Captains Kreutzenstern and Lisiausky were despatched by Alexander of Russia for the purpose of circumnavigating the globe. In endeavouring to get south, they made no farther than 59° 58', in longitude 70° 15' W. They here met with strong currents setting eastwardly. Whales were abundant, but they saw no ice. In regard to this voyage, Mr. Reynolds observes that, if Kreutzenstern had arrived where he did earlier in the season, he must have encountered ice—it was March when he reached the latitude specified. The winds prevailing, as they do, from the southward and westward, had carried the floes, aided by currents, into that icy region bounded on the north by Georgia, east by Sandwich Land and the South Orkneys, and west by the South Shetland Islands.

In 1822, Captain James Weddell, of the British navy, with two very small vessels, penetrated farther to the south than any previous navigator, and this too, without encountering extraordinary difficulties. He states that although he was frequently hemmed in by ice before reaching the seventy-second parallel, yet, upon attaining it, not a particle was to be discovered, and that, upon arriving at the latitude of 74° 15', no fields, and only three islands of ice were visible. It is somewhat remarkable that, although vast flocks of birds were seen, and other usual indications of land, and although, south of the Shetlands, unknown coasts were observed from the masthead tending southwardly, Weddell discourages the idea of land existing in the polar regions of the south.

On the eleventh of January, 1823, Captain Benjamin Morrell, of the American schooner Wasp, sailed from Kerguelen's Land with a view of penetrating as far south as possible. On the first of February he found himself in latitude 64° 52' S., longitude 118 27' E. The following passage is extracted from his journal of that date.

> The wind soon freshened to an eleven-knot breeze, and we embraced this opportunity of making to the west; being however convinced that the farther we went south beyond latitude sixty-four degrees the less ice was to be apprehended, we steered a little to the south ward, until we crossed the Antarctic circle, and were in latitude 69° 15' E. In this latitude there was *no field ice,* and very few ice islands in sight.

Under the date of March fourteenth I find also this entry.

> The sea was now entirely free of field ice, and there were not more than a dozen ice islands in sight. At the same time the temperature of the air and water was at least thirteen degrees higher (more mild) than we had ever found it between the parallels of sixty and sixty-two south. We were now in latitude 70° 14' S., and the temperature of

the air was forty-seven, and that of the water forty-four. In this situation I found the variation to be 14° 27' easterly, *per azimuth* .... I have several times passed within the Antarctic circle on different meridians, and have uniformly found the temperature, both of the air and the water, to become more and more mild the farther I advanced beyond the sixty-fifth degree of south latitude, and that the variation decreases in the same proportion. While north of this latitude, say between sixty and sixty-five south, we frequently had great difficulty in finding a passage for the vessel between the immense and almost innumerable ice islands, some of which were from one to two miles in circumference, and more than five hundred feet above the surface of the water.

Being nearly destitute of fuel and water, and without proper instruments, it being also late in the season, Captain Morrell was now obliged to put back, without at tempting any farther progress to the southward, although an entirely open sea lay before him. He expresses the opinion that, had not these overruling considerations obliged him to retreat, he could have penetrated, if not to the pole itself, at least to the eighty-fifth parallel. I have given his ideas respecting these matters somewhat at length, that the reader may have an opportunity of seeing how far they were borne out by my own subsequent experience.

In 1831, Captain Briscoe, in the employ of the Messieurs Enderby, whale-ship owners of London, sailed in the brig *Lively* for the South Seas, accompanied by the cutter *Tula*. On the twenty-eighth of February, being in latitude 66° 30' S., longitude 47 31' E., he descried land, and "clearly discovered through the snow the black peaks of a range of mountains running E. S. E."

He remained in this neighbourhood during the whole of the following month, but was unable to approach the coast nearer than within ten leagues, owing to the boisterous state of the weather. Finding it impossible to make farther discovery during this season, he returned north ward to winter in Van Diemen's Land.

In the beginning of 1832 he again proceeded southwardly, and on the fourth of February land was seen to the southeast in latitude 67° 15', longitude 69° 29' W. This was soon found to be an island near the headland of the country he had first discovered. On the twenty-first of the month he succeeded in landing on the latter, and took possession of it in the name of William IV., calling it Adelaide's Island, in honour of the English queen. These particulars being made known to the Royal Geographical Society of London, the conclusion was drawn by that body "that there is a continuous tract of land extending from 47° 30' E. to 69° 29' W. longitude, running the parallel of from sixty-six to sixty-seven degrees south latitude." In respect to this conclusion Mr. Reynolds observes:

> In the correctness of it we by no means concur; nor do the discoveries of Briscoe warrant any such inference. It was within these limits that Weddell proceeded south on a meridian to the east of Georgia, Sandwich Land, and the South Orkney and Shetland Islands.

My own experience will be found to testify most directly to the falsity of the conclusion arrived at by the society.

These are the principal attempts which have been made at penetrating to a high southern latitude, and it will now be seen that there remained, previous to the voyage of the Jane, nearly three hundred degrees of longitude in which the Antarctic circle had not been crossed at all. Of course a wide field lay before us for discovery, and it was with feelings of most intense interest that I heard Captain Guy express his resolution of pushing boldly to the southward.

CHAPTER 17

We kept our course southwardly for four days after giving up the search for Glass's Islands, without meeting with any ice at all. On the twenty-sixth, at noon, we were in latitude 63° 23' S., longitude 41° 25' W. We now saw several large ice islands, and a floe of field ice, not, however, of any great extent. The winds generally blew from the southeast, or the northeast, but were very light. Whenever we had a westerly wind, which was seldom, it was invariably attended with a rain squall. Every day we had more or less snow. The thermometer, on the twenty-seventh, stood at thirty-five.

January 1, 1828. This day we found ourselves completely hemmed in by the ice, and our prospects looked cheerless indeed. A strong gale blew, during the whole forenoon, from the northeast, and drove large cakes of the drift against the rudder and counter with such violence that we all trembled for the consequences. Towards evening, the gale still blowing with fury, a large field in front separated, and we were enabled, by carrying a press of sail, to force a passage through the smaller flakes into some open water beyond. As we approached this space we took in sail by degrees, and having at length got clear, lay to under a single reefed fore sail.

January 2. We had now tolerably pleasant weather. At noon we found ourselves in latitude 69° 10' S., longitude 42° 20' W., having crossed the Antarctic circle. Very little ice was to be seen to the southward, although large fields of it lay behind us. This day we rigged some sounding gear, using a large iron pot capable of holding twenty gallons, and a line of two hundred fathoms. We found the current setting to the north, about a quarter of a mile per hour. The temperature of the air was now about thirty-three. Here we found the variation to be 14° 28' easterly, *per azimuth.*

January 5. We had still held on to the southward without any very great impediments. On this morning, however, being in latitude 73° 15' E., longitude 42° 10' W., we were again brought to a stand by an immense expanse of firm ice. We saw, nevertheless, much open water to the southward, and felt no doubt of being able to reach it eventually. Standing to the eastward along the edge of the floe, we at length came to a passage of about a mile in width, through which we warped our way by sundown. The sea in which we now were was thickly covered with ice islands, but had no field ice, and we pushed on boldly as before.

The cold did not seem to increase, although we had snow very frequently, and now and then hail squalls of great violence. Immense flocks of the albatross flew over the schooner this day, going from southeast to northwest.

January 7. The sea still remained pretty well open, so that we had no difficulty in holding on our course. To the westward we saw some icebergs of incredible size, and in the afternoon passed very near one whose summit could not have been less than four hundred fathoms from the surface of the ocean. Its girth was probably, at the base, three quarters of a league, and several streams of water were running from crevices in its sides. We remained in sight of this island two days, and then only lost it in a fog.

January 10. Early this morning we had the misfortune to lose a man overboard. He was an American, named Peter Vredenburgh, a native of New-York, and was one of the most valuable hands on board the schooner. In going over the bows his foot slipped, and he fell between two cakes of ice, never rising again. At noon of this day we were in latitude 78° 30', longitude 40° 15' W. The cold was now excessive, and we had hail squalls continually from the northward and east ward. In this direction also we saw several more immense icebergs, and the whole horizon to the eastward appeared to be blocked up with field ice, rising in tiers, one mass above the other. Some driftwood floated by during the evening, and a great quantity of birds flew over, among which were nellies, petrels, albatrosses, and a large bird of a brilliant blue plumage. The variation here, *per azimuth*, was less than it had been previously to our passing the Antarctic Circle.

January 12. Our passage to the south again looked doubtful, as nothing was to be seen in the direction of the pole but one apparently limitless floe, backed by absolute mountains of ragged ice, one precipice of which arose frowningly above the other. We stood to the westward until the fourteenth, in the hope of finding an entrance.

January 14. This morning we reached the western extremity of the field which had impeded us, and, weathering it, came to an open sea, without a particle of ice. Upon sounding with two hundred fathoms, we here found a current setting southwardly at the rate of half a mile per hour. The temperature of the air was forty-seven, that of the water thirty-four. We now sailed to the southward, without meeting any interruption of moment until the sixteenth, when, at noon, we were in latitude 81° 21', longitude 42° W. We here again sounded, and found a current setting still southwardly, and at the rate of three quarters of a mile per hour. The variation *per azimuth* had diminished, and the temperature of the air was mild and pleasant, the thermometer being as high as fifty-one. At this period not a particle of ice was to be discovered. All hands on board now felt certain of attaining the pole.

January 17. This day was full of incident. Innumerable flights of birds flew over us from the southward, and several were shot from the deck; one of them, a species of pelican, proved to be excellent eating. About midday a small floe of ice was seen from the masthead off the larboard bow, and upon it there appeared to be some large animal. As the weather was good and nearly calm, Captain Guy ordered out two of the boats to see what it was. Dirk Peters and myself accompanied the mate in the larger boat. Upon coming up with the floe, we perceived that it was in the possession of a gigantic creature of the race of the Arctic bear, but far exceeding in size the largest of these animals. Being well armed, we made no scruple of attacking it at once. Several shots were fired in quick succession, the most of which took effect, apparently, in the head and body.

Nothing discouraged, however, the monster threw himself from the ice, and swam, with open jaws, to the boat in which were Peters and myself. Owing to the confusion which ensued among us at this unexpected turn of the adventure, no person was ready immediately with a second shot, and the bear had actually succeeded in getting half his vast bulk across our gunwale, and seizing one of the men by the small of his back, before any efficient means were taken to repel him. In this extremity nothing but the promptness and agility of Peters saved us from destruction. Leaping upon the back of the huge beast, he plunged the blade of a knife behind the neck, reaching the spinal marrow at a blow. The brute tumbled into the sea lifeless, and without a struggle, rolling over Peters as he fell. The latter soon recovered himself, and a rope being thrown him, he secured the carcass before entering the boat.

We then returned in triumph to the schooner, towing our trophy behind us. This bear, upon admeasurement, proved to be full fifteen feet in his greatest length. His wool was perfectly white, and very coarse, curling tightly. The eyes were of a blood red, and larger than those of the Arctic bear—the snout also more rounded, rather resembling the snout of the bulldog. The meat was tender, but excessively rank and fishy, although the men devoured it with avidity, and declared it excellent eating.

Scarcely had we got our prize alongside, when the man at the masthead gave the joyful shout of *"land on the starboard bow!"* All hands were now upon the alert, and, a breeze springing up very opportunely from the northward and eastward, we were soon close in with the coast. It proved to be a low rocky islet, of about a league in circumference, and altogether destitute of vegetation, if we except a species of prickly pear. In approaching it from the northward, a singular ledge of rock is seen projecting into the sea, and bearing a strong resemblance to corded bales of cotton. Around this ledge to the westward is a small bay, at the bottom of which our boats effected a convenient landing.

It did not take us long to explore every portion of the island, but, with one exception, we found nothing worthy of observation. In the southern extremity, we picked up near the shore, half buried in a pile of loose stones, a piece of wood, which seemed to have formed the prow of a canoe. There had been evidently some attempt at carving upon it, and Captain Guy fancied that he made out the figure of a tortoise, but the resemblance did not strike me very forcibly. Besides this prow, if such it were, we found no other token that any living creature had ever been here before. Around the coast we discovered occasional small floes of ice—but these were very few. The exact situation of this islet (to which Captain Guy gave the name of Bennet's Islet, in honour of his partner in the ownership of the schooner) is 82° 50' S. latitude, 42° 20' W. longitude.

We had now advanced to the southward more than eight degrees farther than any previous navigators, and the sea still lay perfectly open before us. We found, too, that the variation uniformly decreased as we proceeded, and, what was still more surprising, that the temperature of the air, and latterly of the water, be came milder. The weather might even be called pleasant, and we had a steady but very gentle breeze always from some northern point of the compass. The sky was usually clear, with now and then a slight appearance of thin vapour in the southern horizon—this, how ever, was invariably of brief duration. Two difficulties alone presented themselves to our view; we were get ting short of fuel, and symptoms of scurvy had occurred among several of the crew.

These considerations began to impress upon Captain Guy the necessity of returning, and he spoke of it frequently. For my own part, confident as I was of soon arriving at land of some description upon the course we were pursuing, and having every reason to believe, from present appearances, that we should not find it the sterile soil met with in the higher Arctic latitudes, I warmly pressed upon him the expediency of persevering, at least for a few days longer, in the direction we were now holding. So tempting an opportunity of solving the great problem in regard to an Antarctic continent had never yet been afforded to man, and I confess that I felt myself bursting with indignation at the timid and ill-timed suggestions of our commander.

I believe, indeed, that what I could not refrain from saying to him on this head had the effect of inducing him to push on. While, therefore, I cannot but lament the most unfortunate and bloody events which immediately arose from my advice, I must still be allowed to feel some degree of gratification at having been instrumental, however remotely, in opening to the eye of science one of the most intensely exciting secrets which has ever engrossed its attention.

Chapter 18

January 18. This morning[1] we continued to the southward, with the same pleasant weather as before. The sea was entirely smooth, the air tolerably warm and from the northeast, the temperature of the water fifty-three. We now again got our sounding-gear in order, and, with a hundred and fifty fathoms of line, found the current setting towards the pole at the rate of a mile an hour. This constant tendency to the southward, both in the wind and current, caused some degree of speculation, and even of alarm, in different quarters of the schooner, and I saw distinctly that no little impression had been made upon the mind of Captain Guy. He was exceedingly sensitive to ridicule, however, and I finally succeeded in laughing him out of his apprehensions.

The variation was now very trivial. In the course of the day we saw several large whales of the right species, and innumerable flights of the albatross passed over the vessel. We also picked up a bush, full of red berries, like those of the hawthorn, and the carcass of a singular-looking land-animal. It was three feet in length, and but six inches in height, with four very short legs, the feet armed with long claws of a brilliant scarlet, and resembling coral in substance. The body was covered with a straight silky hair, perfectly white. The tail was peaked like that of a rat, and about a foot and a half long. The head resembled a cat's, with the exception of the ears—these were flapped like the ears of a dog. The teeth were of the same brilliant scarlet as the claws.

January 19. Today, being in latitude 83° 20', longitude 43° 5'

---

1. The terms morning and evening, which I have made use of to avoid confusion in my narrative, as far as possible, must not, of course, be taken in their ordinary sense. For a long time past we had had no night at all, the daylight being continual. The dates throughout are according to nautical time, and the bearings must be understood as per compass. I would also remark in this place, that 1 cannot, in the first portion of what is here written, pretend to strict accuracy in respect to dates, or latitudes and longitudes, having kept no regular journal until after the period of which this first portion treats. In many instances I have relied altogether upon memory.

W. (the sea being of an extraordinarily dark colour), we again saw land from the masthead, and, upon a closer scrutiny, found it to be one of a group of very large islands. The shore was precipitous, and the interior seemed to be well wooded, a circumstance which occasioned us great joy. In about four hours from our first discovering the land we came to anchor in ten fathoms, sandy bottom, a league from the coast, as a high surf, with strong ripples here and there, rendered a nearer approach of doubtful expediency. The two largest boats were now ordered out, and a party, well armed (among whom were Peters and myself), proceeded to look for an opening in the reef which appeared to encircle the island.

After searching about for some time, we discovered an inlet, which we were entering, when we saw four large canoes put off from the shore, filled with men who seemed to be well armed. We waited for them to come up, and, as they moved with great rapidity, they were soon within hail. Captain Guy now held up a white handkerchief on the blade of an oar, when the strangers made a full stop, and commenced a loud jabbering all at once, intermingled with occasional shouts, in which we could distinguish the words *Anamoo-moo!* and *Lama-Lama!* They continued this for at least half an hour, during which we had a good opportunity of observing their appearance.

In the four canoes, which might have been fifty feet long and five broad, there were a hundred and ten savages in all. They were about the ordinary stature of Europeans, but of a more muscular and brawny frame. Their complexion a jet black, with thick and long woolly hair. They were clothed in skins of an unknown black animal, shaggy and silky, and made to fit the body with some degree of skill, the hair being inside, except where turned out about the neck, wrists, and ankles. Their arms consisted principally of clubs, of a dark, and apparently very heavy wood. Some spears, however, were observed among them, headed with flint, and a few slings. The bottoms of the canoes were full of black stones about the size of a large egg.

When they had concluded their harangue (for it was clear

they intended their jabbering for such), one of them who seemed to be the chief stood up in the prow of his canoe, and made signs for us to bring our boats along side of him. This hint we pretended not to understand, thinking it the wiser plan to maintain, if possible, the interval between us, as their number more than quadrupled our own. Finding this to be the case, the chief ordered the three other canoes to hold back, while he advanced towards us with his own.

As soon as he came up with us he leaped on board the largest of our boats, and seated himself by the side of Captain Guy, pointing at the same time to the schooner, and repeating the words *Anamoo-moo!* and *Lama-Lama!* We now put back to the vessel, the four canoes following at a little distance.

Upon getting alongside the chief evinced symptoms of extreme surprise and delight, clapping his hands, slapping his thighs and breast, and laughing obstreperously. His followers behind joined in his merriment, and for some minutes the din was so excessive as to be absolutely deafening. Quiet being at length restored, Captain Guy ordered the boats to be hoisted up, as a necessary precaution, and gave the chief (whose name we soon found to be *Too-wit*) to understand that we could admit no more than twenty of his men on deck at one time. With this arrangement he appeared perfectly satisfied, and gave some directions to the canoes, when one of them approached, the rest remaining about fifty yards off. Twenty of the savages now got on board, and proceeded to ramble over every part of the deck, and scramble about among the rigging, making themselves much at home, and examining every article with great inquisitiveness.

It was quite evident that they had never before seen any of the white race—from whose complexion, indeed, they appeared to recoil. They believed the *Jane* to be a living creature, and seemed to be afraid of hurting it with the points of their spears, carefully turning them up. Our crew were much amused with the conduct of Too-wit in one instance. The cook was splitting some wood near the galley, and, by accident, struck his axe into the deck, making a gash of considerable depth. The chief immediately ran up, and pushing the cook on one side rather roughly, commenced a half whine, half howl, strongly indicative of sympathy in what he considered the sufferings of the schooner, patting and smoothing the gash with his hand, and washing it from a bucket of seawater which stood by. This was a degree of ignorance for which we were not prepared, and for my part I could not help thinking some of it affected. When the visitors had satisfied, as well as they could, their curiosity in regard to our upper works, they were admitted below, when their amazement exceeded all bounds.

Their astonishment now appeared to be far too deep for words, for they roamed about in silence, broken only by low ejaculations. The arms afforded them much food for speculation, and they were suffered to handle and examine them at leisure. I do not believe that they had the least suspicion of their actual use, but rather took them for idols, seeing the care we had of them, and the attention with which we watched their movements while handling them. At the great guns their wonder was redoubled. They approached them with every mark of the profoundest reverence and awe, but forbore to examine them minutely. There were two large mirrors in the cabin, and here was the acme of their amazement.

Too-wit was the first to approach them, and he had got in the middle of the cabin, with his face to one and his back to the other, before he fairly perceived them. Upon raising his eyes and seeing his reflected self in the glass, I thought the savage would go mad; but, upon turning short round to make a retreat, and beholding himself a second time in the opposite direction, I was afraid he would expire upon the spot. No persuasions could prevail upon him to take another look; but, throwing himself upon the floor, with his face buried in his hands, he remained thus until we were obliged to drag him upon deck.

The whole of the savages were admitted on board in this manner, twenty at a time, Too-wit being suffered to remain during the entire period. We saw no disposition to thievery among them, nor did we miss a single article after their departure. Throughout the whole of their visit they evinced the most friendly manner. There were, however, some points in their demeanour which we found it impossible to understand: for example, we could not get them to approach several very harmless objects—such as the schooner's sails, an egg, an open book, or a pan of flour. We endeavoured to ascertain if they had among them any articles which might be turned to account in the way of traffic, but found great difficulty in being comprehended.

We made out, nevertheless, what greatly astonished us, that the islands abounded in the large tortoise of the Gallipagos, one of which we saw in the canoe of Too-wit. We saw also some *biche de mer* in the hands of one of the savages, who was greedily devouring it in its natural state. These anomalies, for they were such when considered in regard to the latitude, induced Captain Guy to wish for a thorough investigation of the country, in the hope of making a profitable speculation in his discovery. For my own part, anxious as I was to know something more of these islands, I was still more earnestly bent on prosecuting the voyage to the southward without delay.

We had now fine weather, but there was no telling how long it would last; and being already in the eighty-fourth parallel, with an open sea before us, a current setting strongly to the southward, and the wind fair, I could not listen with any patience to a proposition of stopping longer than was absolutely necessary for the health of the crew and the taking on board a proper supply of fuel and fresh provisions. I represented to the captain that we might easily make this group on our return, and winter here in the event of being blocked up by the ice. He at length came into my views (for in some way, hardly known to myself, I had acquired much influence over him), and it was finally resolved that, even in the event of our finding *biche de mer*, we should only stay here a week to recruit, and then push on to the southward while we might.

Accordingly we made every necessary preparation, and, under the guidance of Too-wit, got the *Jane* through the reef in safety, coming to anchor about a mile from the shore, in an excellent bay, completely landlocked, on the south-eastern coast of the main island, and in ten fathoms of water, black sandy bottom. At the head of this bay there were three fine springs (we were told) of good water, and we saw abundance of wood in the vicinity. The four canoes followed us in, keeping, however, at a respectful distance. Too-wit himself remained on board, and, upon our dropping anchor, invited us to accompany him on shore, and visit his village in the interior.

To this Captain Guy consented; and ten savages being left on board as hostages, a party of us, twelve in all, got in readiness to attend the chief. We took care to be well armed, yet without evincing any distrust. The schooner had her guns run out, her boarding-nettings up, and every other proper precaution was taken to guard against surprise. Directions were left with the chief mate to admit no person on board during our absence, and, in the event of our not appearing in twelve hours, to send the cutter, with a swivel, round the island in search of us.

At every step we took inland the conviction forced itself upon us that we were in a country differing essentially from any hitherto visited by civilized men. We saw nothing with which we had been formerly conversant. The trees resembled no growth of either the torrid, the temperate, or the northern frigid zones, and were altogether unlike those of the lower southern latitudes we had already traversed. The very rocks were novel in their mass, their colour, and their stratification; and the streams themselves, utterly incredible as it may appear, had so little in common with those of other climates, that we were scrupulous of tasting them, and, in deed, had difficulty in bringing ourselves to believe that their qualities were purely those of nature.

At a small brook which crossed our path (the first we had reached) Too-wit and his attendants halted to drink. On account of the singular character of the water, we refused to taste it, supposing it to be polluted; and it was not until some time afterward we came to understand that such was the appearance of the streams throughout the whole group. I am at a loss to give a distinct idea of the nature of this liquid, and cannot do so without many words. Although it flowed with rapidity in all declivities where common water would do so, yet never, except when falling in a cascade, had it the customary appearance of limpidity. It was, nevertheless, in point of fact, as perfectly limpid as any limestone water in existence, the difference being only in appearance. At first sight, and especially in cases where little declivity was found, it bore resemblance, as regards consistency, to a thick infusion of gum Arabic in common water.

But this was only the least remarkable of its extraordinary qualities. It was *not* colourless, nor was it of any one uniform colour—presenting to the eye, as it flowed, every possible shade of purple, like the hues of a change able silk. This variation in shade was produced in a manner which excited as profound astonishment in the minds of our party as the mirror had done in the case of Too-wit. Upon collecting a basinful, and allowing it to settle thoroughly, we perceived that the whole mass of liquid was made up of a number of distinct veins, each of a distinct hue; that these veins did not commingle; and that their cohesion was perfect in regard to their own particles among themselves, and imperfect in regard to neighbouring veins.

Upon passing the blade of a knife athwart the veins, the water closed over it immediately, as with us, and also, in withdrawing it, all traces of the passage of the knife were instantly obliterated. If, however, the blade was passed down accurately between two veins, a perfect separation was effected, which the power of cohesion did not immediately rectify. The phenomena of this water formed the first definite link in that vast chain of apparent miracles with which I was destined to be at length encircled.

CHAPTER 19

We were nearly three hours in reaching the village, it being more than nine miles in the interior, and the path lying through a rugged country. As we passed along, the party of Too-wit (the whole hundred and ten savages of the canoes) was momentarily strengthened by smaller detachments, of from two to six or seven, which joined us, as if by accident, at different turns in the road. There appeared so much of system in this that I could not help feeling distrust, and I spoke to Captain Guy of my apprehensions. It was now too late, however, to recede, and we concluded that our best security lay in evincing a perfect confidence in the good faith of Too-wit.

We accordingly went on, keeping a wary eye upon the manoeuvres of the savages, and not permitting them to divide our numbers by pushing in between. In this way, passing through a precipitous ravine, we at length reached what we were told was the only collection of habitations upon the island. As we came in sight of them, the chief set up a shout, and frequently repeated the word *Klock-Klock*; which we supposed to be the name of the village, or perhaps the generic name for villages.

The dwellings were of the most miserable description imaginable, and, unlike those of even the lowest of the savage races with which mankind are acquainted, were of no uniform plan. Some of them (and these we found belonged to the *Wampoos* or *Yampoos*, the great men of the land) consisted of a tree cut down at about four feet from the root, with a large black skin thrown over it, and hanging in loose folds upon the ground. Under this the savage nestled. Others were formed by means of rough limbs of trees, with the withered foliage upon them, made to recline, at an angle of forty-five degrees, against a bank of clay, heaped up, without regular form, to the height of five or six feet.

Others, again, were mere holes dug in the earth perpendicularly, and covered over with similar branches, these being removed when the tenant was about to enter, and pulled on again when he had entered. A few were built among the forked limbs of trees as they stood, the upper limbs being partially cut through, so as to bend over upon the lower, thus forming thicker shelter from the weather. The greater number, however, consisted of small shallow caverns, apparently scratched in the face of a precipitous ledge of dark stone, resembling fuller's earth, with which three sides of the village was bounded.

At the door of each of these primitive caverns was a small rock, which the tenant carefully placed before the entrance upon leaving his residence, for what purpose I could not ascertain, as the stone itself was never of sufficient size to close up more than a third of the opening.

This village, if it were worthy of the name, lay in a valley of some depth, and could only be approached from the southward, the precipitous ledge of which I have already spoken cutting off all access in other directions. Through the middle of the valley ran a brawling stream of the same magical-looking water which has been described. We saw several strange animals about the dwellings, all appearing to be thoroughly domesticated. The largest of these creatures resembled our common hog in the structure of the body and snout; the tail, however, was bushy, and the legs slender as those of the antelope. Its motion was exceedingly awkward and in decisive, and we never saw it attempt to run.

We noticed also several animals very similar in appearance, but of a greater length of body, and covered with a black wool. There were a great variety of tame fowls running about, and these seemed to constitute the chief food of the natives. To our astonishment we saw black albatross among these birds in a state of entire domestication, going to sea periodically for food, but always returning to the village as a home, and using the southern shore in the vicinity as a place of incubation. There they were joined by their friends the pelicans as usual, but these latter never followed them to the dwellings of the savages.

Among the other kinds of tame fowls were ducks, differing very little from the canvass-back of our own country, black gannets, and a large bird not unlike the buzzard in appearance, but not carnivorous. Of fish there seemed to be a great abundance. We saw, during our visit, a quantity of dried salmon, rock cod, blue dolphins, mackerel, blackfish, skate, conger eels, elephant-fish, mullets, soles, parrotfish, leather-jackets, gurnards, hake, flounders, paracutas, and innumerable other varieties. We noticed, too, that most of them were similar to the fish about the group of the Lord Auckland Islands, in a latitude as low as fifty-one degrees south. The Gallipago tortoise was also very plentiful. We saw but few wild animals, and none of a large size, or of a species with which we were familiar. One or two serpents of a formidable aspect crossed our path, but the natives paid them little attention, and we concluded that they were not venomous.

As we approached the village with Too-wit and his party, a vast crowd of the people rushed out to meet us, with loud shouts, among which we could only distinguish the everlasting *Anamoo-moo!* and *Lama-Lama!* We were much surprised at perceiving that, with one or two exceptions, these new comers were entirely naked, the skins being used only by the men of the canoes. All the weapons of the country seemed also to be in the possession of the latter, for there was no appearance of any among the villagers. There were a great many women and children, the former not altogether wanting in what might be termed personal beauty.

They were straight, tall, and well formed, with a grace and freedom of carriage not to be found in civilized society. Their lips, however, like those of the men, were thick and clumsy, so that, even when laughing, the teeth were never disclosed. Their hair was of a finer texture than that of the males. Among these naked villagers there might have been ten or twelve who were clothed, like the party of Too-wit, in dresses of black skin, and armed with lances and heavy clubs. These appeared to have great influence among the rest, and were always addressed by the title *Wampoo*. These, too, were the tenants of the black skin palaces. That of Too-wit was situated in the centre of the village, and was much larger and somewhat better constructed than others of its kind.

The tree which formed its support was cut off at a distance of twelve feet or thereabout from the root, and there were several branches left just below the cut, these serving to extend the covering, and in this way prevent its flapping about the trunk. The covering, too, which consisted of four very large skins fastened together with wooden skewers, was secured at the bottom with pegs driven through it and into the ground. The floor was strewed with a quantity of dry leaves by way of carpet.

To this hut we were conducted with great solemnity, and as many of the natives crowded in after us as possible. Too-wit seated himself on the leaves, and made signs that we should follow his example. This we did, and presently found ourselves in a situation peculiarly uncomfortable, if not indeed critical. We were on the ground, twelve in number, with the savages, as many as forty, sitting on their hams so closely around us that, if any disturbance had arisen, we should have found it impossible to make use of our arms, or indeed to have risen on our feet.

The pressure was not only inside the tent, but outside, where probably was every individual on the whole island, the crowd being prevented from trampling us to death only by the incessant exertions and vociferations of Too-wit. Our chief security lay, however, in the presence of Too-wit himself among us, and we resolved to stick by him closely, as the best chance of extricating ourselves from the dilemma, sacrificing him immediately upon the first appearance of hostile design.

After some trouble a certain degree of quiet was restored, when the chief addressed us in a speech of great length, and very nearly resembling the one delivered in the canoes, with the exception that the *Anamoo-moos!* were now somewhat more strenuously insisted upon than the *Lama-Lamas!* We listened in profound silence until the conclusion of his harangue, when Captain Guy replied by assuring the chief of his eternal friendship and good will, concluding what he had to say by a present of several strings of blue beads and a knife.

At the former the monarch, much to our surprise, turned up his nose with some expression of contempt; but the knife gave him the most unlimited satisfaction, and he immediately ordered dinner. This was handed into the tent over the heads of the attendants, and consisted of the palpitating entrails of a species of unknown animal, probably one of the slim-legged hogs which we had observed in our approach to the village. Seeing us at a loss how to proceed, he began, by way of setting us an example, to devour yard after yard of the enticing food, until we could positively stand it no longer, and evinced such manifest symptoms of rebellion of stomach as inspired his majesty with a degree of astonishment only inferior to that brought about by the looking-glasses. We declined, however, partaking of the delicacies before us, and endeavoured to make him understand that we had no appetite whatever, having just finished a hearty *déejeuner*.

When the monarch had made an end of his meal, we commenced a series of cross-questioning in every ingenious manner we could devise, with a view of discovering what were the chief productions of the country, and whether any of them might be turned to profit. At length he seemed to have some idea of our meaning, and offered to accompany us to a part of the coast where he assured us the *biche de mer* (pointing to a specimen of that animal) was to be found in great abundance. We were glad at this early opportunity of escaping from the oppression of the crowd, and signified our eagerness to proceed.

We now left the tent, and, accompanied by the whole population of the village, followed the chief to the south-eastern extremity of the island, not far from the bay where our vessel lay at anchor. We waited here for about an hour, until the four canoes were brought round by some of the savages to our station. The whole of our party then getting into one of them, we were paddled along the edge of the reef before mentioned, and of another still farther out, where we saw a far greater quantity of *biche de mer* than the oldest seaman among us had ever seen in those groups of the lower latitudes most celebrated for this article of commerce.

We stayed near these reefs only long enough to satisfy ourselves that we could easily load a dozen vessels with the animal if necessary, when we were taken alongside the schooner, and parted with Too-wit after obtaining from him a promise that he would bring us, in the course of twenty-four hours, as many of the canvass-back ducks and Gallipago tortoises as his canoes would hold. In the whole of this adventure we saw nothing in the demeanour of the natives calculated to create suspicion, with the single exception of the systematic manner in which their party was strengthened during our route from the schooner to the village.

Chapter 20

The chief was as good as his word, and we were soon plentifully supplied with fresh provision. We found the tortoises as fine as we had ever seen, and the ducks surpassed our best species of wild fowl, being exceedingly tender, juicy, and well-flavoured. Besides these, the savages brought us, upon our making them comprehend our wishes, a vast quantity of brown celery and scurvy grass, with a canoe-load of fresh fish and some dried. The celery was a treat indeed, and the scurvy grass proved of incalculable benefit in restoring those of our men who had shown symptoms of disease. In a very short time we had not a single person on the sick-list. We had also plenty of other kinds of fresh provision, among which may be mentioned a species of shellfish resembling the muscle in shape, but with the taste of an oyster.

Shrimps, too, and prawns were abundant, and albatross and other birds' eggs with dark shells. We took in, too, a plentiful stock of the flesh of the hog which I have mentioned before. Most of the men found it a palatable food, but I thought it fishy and otherwise disagreeable. In return for these good things we presented the natives with blue beads, brass trinkets, nails, knives, and pieces of red cloth, they being fully delighted in the exchange. We established a regular market on shore, just under the guns of the schooner, where our barterings were carried on with every appearance of good faith, and a degree of order which their conduct at the village of *Klock-klock* had not led us to expect from the savages.

Matters went on thus very amicably for several days, during which parties of the natives were frequently on board the schooner, and parties of our men frequently on shore, making long excursions into the interior, and receiving no molestation whatever. Finding the ease with which the vessel might be loaded with *biche de mer*, owing to the friendly disposition of the islanders, and the readiness with which they would render us assistance in collecting it, Captain Guy resolved to enter into negotiation with Too-wit for the erection of suitable houses in which to cure the article, and for the services of himself and tribe in gathering as much as possible, while he himself took advantage of the fine weather to prosecute his voyage to the southward.

Upon mentioning this project to the chief he seemed very willing to enter into an agreement. A bargain was accordingly struck, perfectly satisfactory to both parties, by which it was arranged that, after making the necessary preparations, such as laying off the proper grounds, erecting a portion of the buildings, and doing some other work in which the whole of our crew would be required, the schooner should proceed on her route, leaving three of her men on the island to superintend the fulfilment of the project, and instruct the natives in drying the *biche de mer*. In regard to terms, these were made to depend upon the exertions of the savages in our absence. They were to receive a stipulated quantity of blue beads, knives, red cloth, and so forth, for every certain number of *piculs* of the *biche de mer* which should be ready on our return.

A description of the nature of this important article of commerce, and the method of preparing it, may prove of some interest to my readers, and I can find no more suitable place than this for introducing an account of it. The following comprehensive notice of the substance is taken from a modern history of a voyage to the South Seas.

It is that *mollusca* from the Indian Seas which is known in commerce by the French name *bouche de mer* (a nice morsel from the sea). If I am not much mistaken, the celebrated Cuvier calls it *gasteropeda pulmon ifera*. It is abundantly gathered in the coasts of the Pacific Islands, and gathered especially for the Chinese market, where it commands a great price, perhaps as much as their much-talked of edible bird's nests, which are probably made up of the gelatinous matter picked up by a species of swallow from the body of these *molluscae*. They have no shell, no legs, nor any prominent part, except an *absorbing* and an *excretory*, opposite organs; but, by their elastic wings, like caterpillars or worms, they creep in shallow waters, in which, when low, they can be seen by a kind of swallow, the sharp bill of which, inserted in the soft animal, draws a gummy and filamentous substance, which, by drying, can be wrought into the solid walls of their nest. Hence the name of *gasteropeda pulmonifera*.

This *mollusca* is oblong, and of different sizes, from three to eighteen inches in length; and I have seen a few that were not less than two feet long. They are nearly round, a little flattish on one side, which lies next the bottom of the sea; and they are from one to eight inches thick. They crawl up into shallow water at particular seasons of the year, probably for the purpose of gendering, as we often find them in pairs. It is when the sun has the most power on the water, rendering it tepid, that they approach the shore; and they often go up into places so shallow, that, on the tide's receding, they are left dry, exposed to the heat of the sun. But they do not bring forth their young in shallow water, as we never see any of their progeny, and the full-grown ones are always observed coming in from deep water. They feed principally on that class of zoophytes which produce the coral.

The *biche de mer* is generally taken in three or four feet water; after which they are brought on shore, and split at one end with a knife, the incision being one inch or more, according to the size of the *mollusca*. Through this opening the entrails are forced out by pressure, and they are much like those of any other small tenant of the deep. The article is then washed, and afterward boiled to a certain degree, which must not be too much or too little. They are then buried in the ground for four hours, then boiled again for a short time, after which they are dried, either by the fire or the sun. Those cured by the sun are worth the most; but where one *picul* (1331 lbs.) can be cured that way,

I can cure thirty *piculs* by the fire. When once properly cured, they can be kept in a dry place for two or three years without any risk; but they should be examined once in every few months, say four times a year, to see if any dampness is likely to affect them.

The Chinese, as before stated, consider *biche de mer* a very great luxury, believing that it wonderfully strengthens and nourishes the system, and renews the exhausted system of the immoderate voluptuary. The first quality commands a high price in Canton, being worth ninety dollars a *picul*; the second quality seventy-five dollars; the third fifty dollars; the fourth thirty dollars; the fifth twenty dollars; the sixth twelve dollars; the seventh eight dollars; and the eighth four dollars; small cargoes, however, will often bring more in Manilla, Singapore, and Batavia.

An agreement having been thus entered into, we proceeded immediately to land everything necessary for preparing the buildings and clearing the ground. A large flat space near the eastern shore of the bay was selected, where there was plenty both of wood and water, and within a convenient distance of the principal reefs on which the *biche de mer* was to be procured. We now all set to work in good earnest, and soon, to the great astonishment of the savages, had felled a sufficient number of trees for our purpose, getting them quickly in order for the framework of the houses, which in two or three days were so far under way that we could safely trust the rest of the work to the three men whom we intended to leave behind. These were John Carson, Alfred Harris, and —— Peterson (all natives of London, I believe), who volunteered their services in this respect.

By the last of the month we had everything in readiness for departure. We had agreed, however, to pay a formal visit of leaves-taking to the village, and Too-wit insisted so pertinaciously upon our keeping the promise, that we did not think it advisable to run the risk of offending him by a final refusal. I believe that not one of us had at this time the slightest suspicion of the good faith of the savages. They had uniformly behaved with the greatest decorum, aiding us with alacrity in our work, offering us their commodities frequently without price, and never, in any instance, pilfering a single article, although the high value they set upon the goods we had with us was evident by the extravagant demonstrations of joy always manifested upon our making them a present.

The women especially were most obliging in every respect, and, upon the whole, we should have been the most suspicious of human beings had we entertained a single thought of perfidy on the part of a people who treated us so well. A very short while sufficed to prove that this apparent kindness of disposition was only the result of a deeply-laid plan for our destruction, and that the islanders for whom we entertained such inordinate feelings of esteem were among the most barbarous, subtle, and bloodthirsty wretches that ever contaminated the face of the globe.

It was on the first of February that we went on shore for the purpose of visiting the village. Although, as said before, we entertained not the slightest suspicion, still no proper precaution was neglected. Six men were left in the schooner with instructions to permit none of the savages to approach the vessel during our absence, under any pretence whatever, and to remain constantly on deck. The boarding-nettings were up, the guns double-shotted with grape and canister, and the swivels loaded with canisters of musket-balls. She lay, with her anchor apeak, about a mile from the shore, and no canoe could approach her in any direction without being distinctly seen and exposed to the full fire of our swivels immediately.

The six men being left on board, our shore-party consisted of thirty-two persons in all. We were armed to the teeth, having with us muskets, pistols, and cutlasses, besides each a long kind of seaman's knife, somewhat resembling the Bowie knife now so much used throughout our western and southern country. A hundred of the black skin warriors met us at the landing for the purpose of accompanying us on our way. We noticed, however, with some surprise, that they were now entirely without arms;

and, upon questioning Too-wit in relation to this circumstance, he merely answered that *Mattee non we pa pa si*—meaning that there was no need of arms where all were brothers. We took this in good part, and proceeded.

We had passed the spring and rivulet of which I before spoke, and were now entering upon a narrow gorge leading through the chain of soapstone hills among which the village was situated. This gorge was very rocky and uneven, so much so that it was with no little difficulty we scrambled through it on our first visit to *Klock-klock*. The whole length of the ravine might have been a mile and a half, or probably two miles. It wound in every possible direction through the hills (having apparently formed, at some remote period, the bed of a torrent), in no instance proceeding more than twenty yards without an abrupt turn.

The sides of this dell would have averaged, I am sure, seventy or eighty feet in perpendicular altitude throughout the whole of their extent, and in some portions they arose to an astonishing height, overshadowing the pass so completely that but little of the light of day could penetrate. The general width was about forty feet, and occasionally it diminished so as not to allow the passage of more than five or six persons abreast, In short, there could be no place in the world better adapted for the consummation of an ambuscade, and it was no more than natural that we should look carefully to our arms as we entered upon it.

When I now think of our egregious folly, the chief subject of astonishment seems to be, that we should have ever ventured, under any circumstances, so completely into the power of unknown savages as to permit them to march both before and behind us in our progress through this ravine. Yet such was the order we blindly took up, trusting foolishly to the force of our party, the unarmed condition of Too-wit and his men, the certain efficacy of our fire arms (whose effect was yet a secret to the natives), and, more than all, to the long-sustained pretension of friendship kept up by these infamous wretches.

Five or six of them went on before, as if to lead the way, ostentatiously busying themselves in removing the larger stones and rubbish from the path. Next came our own party. We walked closely together, taking care only to prevent separation. Behind followed the main body of the savages, observing unusual order and decorum.

Dirk Peters, a man named Wilson Allen, and myself were on the right of our companions, examining, as we went along, the singular stratification of the precipice which overhung us. A fissure in the soft rock attracted our attention. It was about wide enough for one person to enter without squeezing, and extended back into the hill some eighteen or twenty feet in a straight course, sloping afterward to the left. The height of the opening, as far as we could see into it from the main gorge, was perhaps sixty or seventy feet. There were one or two stunted shrubs growing from the crevices, bearing a species of filbert, which I felt some curiosity to examine, and pushed in briskly for that purpose, gathering five or six of the nuts at a grasp, and then hastily retreating

As I turned, I found that Peters and Allen had followed me. I desired them to go back, as there was not room for two persons to pass, saying they should have some of my nuts. They accordingly turned, and were scrambling back, Allen being close to the mouth of the fissure, when I was suddenly aware of a concussion resembling nothing I had ever before experienced, and which impressed me with a vague conception, if indeed I then thought of anything, that the whole foundations of the solid globe were suddenly rent asunder, and that the day of universal dissolution was at hand.

CHAPTER 21

As soon as I could collect my scattered senses, I found myself nearly suffocated, and grovelling in utter darkness among a quantity of loose earth, which was also falling upon me heavily in every direction, threatening to bury me entirely. Horribly alarmed at this idea, I struggled to gain my feet, and at length succeeded. I then remained motionless for some moments, endeavouring to conceive what had happened to me, and where

I was. Presently I heard a deep groan just at my ear, and afterward the smothered voice of Peters calling to me for aid in the name of God. I scrambled one or two paces forward, when I fell directly over the head and shoulders of my companion, who, I soon discovered, was buried in a loose mass of earth as far as his middle, and struggling desperately to free himself from the pressure. I tore the dirt from around him with all the energy I could command, and at length succeeded in getting him out.

As soon as we sufficiently recovered from our fright and surprise to be capable of conversing rationally, we both came to the conclusion that the walls of the fissure in which we had ventured had, by some convulsion of nature, or probably from their own weight, caved in over head, and that we were consequently lost for ever, being thus entombed alive. For a long time we gave up supinely to the most intense agony and despair, such as cannot be adequately imagined by those who have never been in a similar situation. I firmly believe that no incident ever occurring in the course of human events is more adapted to inspire the supremeness of mental and bodily distress than a case like our own, of living inhumation. The blackness of darkness which envelops the victim, the terrific oppression of lungs, the stifling fumes from the damp earth, unite with the ghastly considerations that we are beyond the remotest confines of hope, and that such is the allotted portion of *the dead*, to carry into the human heart a degree of appalling awe and horror not to be tolerated—never to be conceived.

At length Peters proposed that we should endeavour to ascertain precisely the extent of our calamity, and grope about our prison; it being barely possible, he observed, that some opening might be yet left us for escape. I caught eagerly at this hope, and, arousing myself to exertion, attempted to force my way through the loose earth. Hardly had I advanced a single step before a glimmer of light became perceptible, enough to convince me that, at all events, we should not immediately perish for want of air. We now took some degree of heart, and encouraged each other to hope for the best. Having scrambled over a bank of rubbish which impeded our farther progress in the direction of the light, we found less difficulty in advancing, and also experienced some relief from the excessive oppression of lungs which had tormented us.

Presently we were enabled to obtain a glimpse of the objects around, and discovered that we were near the extremity of the straight portion of the fissure, where it made a turn to the left. A few struggles more, and we reached the bend, when, to our inexpressible joy, there appeared a long seam or crack extending upward a vast distance, generally at an angle of about forty-five degrees, although sometimes much more precipitous. We could not see through the whole extent of this opening; but, as a good deal of light came down it, we had little doubt of finding at the top of it (if we could by any means reach the top) a clear passage into the open air.

I now called to mind that three of us had entered the fissure from the main gorge, and that our companion, Allen, was still missing; we determined at once to retrace our steps and look for him. After a long search, and much danger from the farther caving in of the earth above us, Peters at length cried out to me that he had hold of our companion's foot, and that his whole body was deeply buried beneath the rubbish, beyond a possibility of extricating him. I soon found that what he said was too true, and that, of course, life had been long extinct. With sorrowful hearts, therefore, we left the corpse to its fate, and again made our way to the bend.

The breadth of the seam was barely sufficient to admit us, and, after one or two ineffectual efforts at getting up, we began once more to despair. I have before said that the chain of hills through which ran the main gorge was composed of a species of soft rock resembling soap-stone. The sides of the cleft we were now attempting to ascend were of the same material, and so excessively slippery, being wet, that we could get but little foothold upon them even in their least precipitous parts; in some places, where the ascent was nearly perpendicular, the difficulty was, of course, much aggravated; and, indeed, for some time we thought it insurmountable.

We took courage, however, from despair; and what, by dint of cutting steps in the soft stone with our Bowie knives, and swinging, at the risk of our lives, to small projecting points of a harder species of slaty rock which now and then protruded from the general mass, we at length reached a natural platform, from which was perceptible a patch of blue sky, at the extremity of a thickly-wooded ravine. Looking back now, with somewhat more leisure, at the passage through which we had thus far pro-ceeded, we clearly saw, from the appearance of its sides, that it was of late formation, and we concluded that the concussion, whatever it was, which had so unexpectedly overwhelmed us, had also, at the same moment, laid open this path for escape.

Being quite exhausted with exertion, and, indeed, so weak that we were scarcely able to stand or articulate, Peters now pro-posed that we should endeavour to bring our companions to the rescue by firing the pistols which still remained in our girdles—the muskets as well as cutlasses had been lost among the loose earth at the bottom of the chasm. Subsequent events proved that, had we fired, we should have sorely repented it; but, luckily, a half suspicion of foul play had by this time arisen in my mind, and we forbore to let the savages know of our whereabouts.

After having reposed for about an hour, we pushed on slowly up the ravine, and had gone no great way before we heard a suc-cession of tremendous yells. At length we reached what might be called the surface of the ground; for our path hitherto, since leaving the platform, had lain beneath an archway of high rock and foliage, at a vast distance overhead. With great caution we stole to a narrow opening, through which we had a clear sight of the surrounding country, when the whole dreadful secret of the concussion broke upon us in one moment and at one view.

The spot from which we looked was not far from the sum-mit of the highest peak in the range of the soapstone hills. The gorge in which our party of thirty-two had entered ran within fifty feet to the left of us. But, for at least one hundred yards, the channel or bed of this gorge was entirely filled up with the chaotic ruins of more than a million tons of earth and stone that had been artificially tumbled within it. The means by which the vast mass had been precipitated were not more simple than evident, for sure traces of the murderous work were yet remaining. In several spots along the top of the eastern side of the gorge (we were now on the western) might be seen stakes of wood driven into the earth.

In these spots the earth had not given way; but throughout the whole extent of the face of the precipice from which the mass had fallen, it was clear, from marks left in the soil resembling those made by the drill of the rock-blaster, that stakes similar to those we saw standing had been inserted, at not more than a yard apart, for the length of perhaps three hundred feet, and ranging at about ten feet back from the edge of the gulf. Strong cords of grape vine were attached to the stakes still remaining on the hill, and it was evident that such cords had also been attached to each of the other stakes. I have already spoken of the singular stratification of these soap-stone hills; and the description just given of the narrow and deep fissure through which we effected our escape from inhumation will afford a further conception of its nature.

This was such that almost every natural convulsion would be sure to split the soil into perpendicular layers or ridges running parallel with one another; and a very moderate exertion of art would be sufficient for effecting the same purpose. Of this stratification the savages had availed themselves to accomplish their treacherous ends. There can be no doubt that, by the continuous line of stakes, a partial rupture of the soil had been brought about, probably to the depth of one or two feet, when, by means of a savage pulling at the end of each of the cords (these cords being attached to the tops of the stakes, and extending back from the edge of the cliff), a vast leverage power was obtained, capable of hurling the whole face of the hill, upon a given signal, into the bosom of the abyss below. The fate of our poor companions was no longer a matter of uncertainty. We alone had escaped from the tempest of that over whelming destruction. We were the only living white men upon the island.

Our situation, as it now appeared, was scarcely less dreadful than when we had conceived ourselves entombed for ever. We saw before us no prospect but that of being put to death by the savages, or of dragging out a miserable existence in captivity among them. We might, to be sure, conceal ourselves for a time from their observation among the fastnesses of the hills, and, as a final resort, in the chasm from which we had just issued; but we must either perish in the long Polar winter through cold and famine, or be ultimately discovered in our efforts to obtain relief.

The whole country around us seemed to be swarming with savages, crowds of whom, we now perceived, had come over from the islands to the southward on flat rafts, doubtless with a view of lending their aid in the capture and plunder of the *Jane*. The vessel still lay calmly at anchor in the bay, those on board being apparently quite unconscious of any danger awaiting them. How we longed at that moment to be with them! either to aid in effecting their escape, or to perish with them in attempting a defence. We saw no chance even of warning them of their danger without bringing immediate destruction upon our own heads, with but a remote hope of benefit to them.

A pistol fired might suffice to apprize them that something wrong had occurred; but the report could not possibly inform them that their only prospect of safety lay in getting out of the harbour forthwith—it could not tell them that no principles of honour now bound them to remain, that their companions were no longer among the living. Upon hearing the discharge they could not be more thoroughly prepared to meet the foe, who were now getting ready to attack, than they already were, and always had been. No good, therefore, and infinite harm, would result from our firing, and, after mature deliberation, we forbore.

Our next thought was to attempt a rush towards the vessel,

to seize one of the four canoes which lay at the head of the bay, and endeavour to force a passage on board. But the utter impossibility of succeeding in this desperate task soon became evident. The country, as I said before, was literally swarming with the natives, skulking among the bushes and recesses of the hills, so as not to be observed from the schooner.

In our immediate vicinity especially, and blockading the sole path by which we could hope to attain the shore in the proper point, were stationed the whole party of the black skin warriors, with Too-wit at their head, and apparently only waiting for some re-enforcement to commence his onset upon the *Jane*. The canoes, too, which lay at the head of the bay were manned with savages, unarmed, it is true, but who undoubtedly had arms within reach.

We were forced, therefore, however unwillingly, to remain in our place of concealment, mere spectators of the conflict which presently ensued.

In about half an hour we saw some sixty or seventy rafts, or flatboats, with outriggers, filled with savages, and coming round the southern bight of the harbour. They appeared to have no arms except short clubs, and stones which lay in the bottom of the rafts. Immediately afterward another detachment, still larger, approached in an opposite direction, and with similar weapons. The four canoes, too, were now quickly filled with natives, starting up from the bushes at the head of the bay, and put off swiftly to join the other parties. Thus, in less time than I have taken to tell it, and as if by magic, the *Jane* saw herself surrounded by an immense multitude of *desperadoes* evidently bent upon capturing her at all hazards.

That they would succeed in so doing could not be doubted for an instant. The six men left in the vessel, however resolutely they might engage in her defence, were altogether unequal to the proper management of the guns, or in any manner to sustain a contest at such odds. I could hardly imagine that they would make resistance at all, but in this was deceived; for presently I saw them get springs upon the cable, and bring the vessel's star-

174

board broadside to bear upon the canoes, which by this time were within pistol range, the rafts being nearly a quarter of a mile to windward.

Owing to some cause unknown, but most probably to the agitation of our poor friends at seeing themselves in so hope less a situation, the discharge was an entire failure. Not a canoe was hit or a single savage injured, the shots striking short and rico- cheting over their heads. The only effect produced upon them was astonishment at the unexpected report and smoke, which was so excessive that for some moments I almost thought they would abandon their design entirely, and return to the shore. And this they would most likely have done had our men fol- lowed up their broadside by a discharge of small arms, in which, as the canoes were now so near at hand, they could not have failed in doing some execution, sufficient, at least, to deter this party from a farther advance, until they could have given the rafts also a broadside. But, in place of this, they left the canoe party to recover from their panic, and, by looking about them, to see that no injury had been sustained, while they flew to the larboard to get ready for the rafts.

The discharge to larboard produced the most terrible effect. The star and double-headed shot of the large guns cut seven or eight of the rafts completely asunder, and killed, perhaps, thirty or forty of the savages outright, while a hundred of them, at least, were thrown into the water, the most of them dreadfully wounded. The remainder, frightened out of their senses, com- menced at once a precipitate retreat, not even waiting to pick up their maimed companions, who were swimming about in every direction, screaming and yelling for aid. This great success, how- ever, came too late for the salvation of our devoted people.

The canoe party were already on board the schooner to the number of more than a hundred and fifty, the most of them hav- ing succeeded in scrambling up the chains and over the board- ing net tings even before the matches had been applied to the larboard guns. Nothing could now withstand their brute rage. Our men were borne down at once, over whelmed, trodden under foot, and absolutely torn to pieces in an instant.

Seeing this, the savages on the rafts got the better of their fears, and came up in shoals to the plunder. In five minutes the *Jane* was a pitiable scene indeed of havoc and tumultuous outrage. The decks were split open and ripped up; the cordage, sails, and everything moveable on deck demolished as if by magic; while, by dint of pushing at the stern, towing with the canoes, and hauling at the sides, as they swam in thousands around the vessel, the wretches finally forced her on shore (the cable having been slipped), and delivered her over to the good offices of Too-wit, who, during the whole of the engagement, had maintained, like a skilful general, his post of security and reconnoissance among the hills, but, now that the victory was completed to his satisfaction, condescended to scamper down with his warriors of the black skin, and become a partaker in the spoils.

Too-wit's descent left us at liberty to quit our hiding-place and reconnoitre the hill in the vicinity of the chasm. At about fifty yards from the mouth of it we saw a small spring of water, at which we slaked the burning thirst that now consumed us. Not far from the spring we discovered several of the filbert-bushes which I mentioned before. Upon tasting the nuts we found them palatable, and very nearly resembling in flavour the common English filbert. We collected our hats full immediately, deposited them within the ravine, and returned for more. While we were busily employed in gathering these, a rustling in the bushes alarmed us, and we were upon the point of stealing back to our covert, when a large black bird of the bittern species strugglingly and slowly arose above the shrubs.

I was so much startled that I could do nothing, but Peters had sufficient presence of mind to run up to it before it could make its escape, and seize it by the neck. Its struggles and screams were tremendous, and we had thoughts of letting it go, lest the noise should alarm some of the savages who might be still lurking in the neighbourhood. A stab with a Bowie knife, however, at length brought it to the ground, and we dragged it into the ravine, congratulating ourselves that, at all events, we had thus obtained a supply of food enough to last us for a week.

We now went out again to look about us, and ventured a considerable distance down the southern declivity of the hill, but met with nothing else which could serve us for food. We therefore collected a quantity of dry wood and returned, seeing one or two large parties of the natives on their way to the village, laden with the plunder of the vessel, and who, we were apprehensive, might discover us in passing beneath the hill.

Our next care was to render our place of concealment as secure as possible, and, with this object, we arranged some brushwood over the aperture which I have before spoken of as the one through which we saw the patch of blue sky, on reaching the platform from the interior of the chasm. We left only a very small opening, just wide enough to admit of our seeing the bay, without the risk of being discovered from below. Having done this, we congratulated ourselves upon the security of the position; for we were now completely excluded from observation, as long as we chose to remain within the ravine itself, and not venture out upon the hill.

We could perceive no traces of the savages having ever been within this hollow; but, indeed, when we came to reflect upon the probability that the fissure through which we attained it had been only just now created by the fall of the cliff opposite, and that no other way of attaining it could be perceived, we were not so much rejoiced at the thought of being secure from molestation as fearful lest there should be absolutely no means left us for descent. We resolved to explore the summit of the hill thoroughly, when a good opportunity should offer. In the mean time we watched the motions of the savages through our loophole.

They had already made a complete wreck of the vessel, and were now preparing to set her on fire. In a little while we saw the smoke ascending in huge volumes from her main-hatchway, and, shortly afterward, a dense mass of flame burst up from the forecastle. The rigging, masts, and what remained of the sails caught immediately, and the fire spread rapidly along the decks.

Still a great many of the savages retained their stations about her, hammering with large stones, axes, and cannon balls at the bolts and other copper and iron work. On the beach, and in canoes and rafts, there were not less, altogether, in the immediate vicinity of the schooner, than ten thousand natives, besides the shoals of them who, laden with booty, were making their way inland and over to the neighbouring islands.

We now anticipated a catastrophe, and were not disappointed. First of all there came a smart shock (which we felt distinctly where we were as if we had been slightly galvanized), but unattended with any visible signs of an explosion. The savages were evidently startled, and paused for an instant from their labours and yellings. They were upon the point of recommencing, when suddenly a mass of smoke puffed up from the decks, resembling a black and heavy thunder-cloud—then, as if from its bowels, arose a tall stream of vivid fire to the height, apparently, of a quarter of a mile—then there came a sudden circular expansion of the flame then the whole atmosphere was magically crowded, in a single instant, with a wild chaos of wood, and metal, and human limbs—and, lastly, came the concussion in its fullest fury, which hurled us impetuously from our feet, while the hills echoed and re-echoed the tumult, and a dense shower of the minutest fragments of the ruins tumbled headlong in every direction around us.

The havoc among the savages far exceeded our utmost expectation, and they had now, indeed, reaped the full and perfect fruits of their treachery. Perhaps a thousand perished by the explosion, while at least an equal number were desperately mangled. The whole surface of the bay was literally strewn with the struggling and drowning wretches, and on shore matters were even worse. They seemed utterly appalled by the suddenness and completeness of their discomfiture, and made no efforts at assisting one another. At length we observed a total change in their demeanour. From absolute stupor they appeared to be, all at once, aroused to the highest pitch of excitement, and rushed wildly about, going to and from a certain point on the beach, with the strangest expressions of mingled horror, rage, and intense curiosity depicted on their countenances, and shouting, at the top of their voices, *Tekeli-li! Tekei-li!*

Presently we saw a large body go off into the hills, whence they returned in a short time, carrying stakes of wood. These they brought to the station where the crowd was the thickest, which now separated so as to afford us a view of the object of all this excitement. We perceived something white lying on the ground, but could not immediately make out what it was. At length we saw that it was the carcass of the strange animal with the scarlet teeth and claws which the schooner had picked up at sea on the eighteenth of January. Captain Guy had had the body preserved for the purpose of stuffing the skin and taking it to England.

I remember he had given some directions about it just before our making the island, and it had been brought into the cabin and stowed away in one of the lockers. It had now been thrown on shore by the explosion; but why it had occasioned so much concern among the savages was more than we could comprehend. Although they crowded around the carcass at a little distance, none of them seemed willing to approach it closely. By-and-by the men with the stakes drove them in a circle around it, and, no sooner was this arrangement completed, than the whole of the vast assembly rushed into the interior of the island, with loud screams of *Tekeli-li! Tekeli-li!*

CHAPTER 23

During the six or seven days immediately following we remained in our hiding-place upon the hill, going out only occasionally, and then with the greatest precaution, for water and filberts. We had made a kind of penthouse on the platform, furnishing it with a bed of dry leaves, and placing in it three large flat stones, which served us for both fireplace and table. We kindled a fire without difficulty by rubbing two pieces of dry wood together, the one soft, the other hard. The bird we had taken in such good season proved excellent eating, although somewhat tough. It was not an oceanic fowl, but a species of bittern, with jet black and grizzly plumage, and diminutive wings in proportion to its bulk. We afterward saw three of the same kind in the vicinity of the ravine, apparently seeking for the one we had captured; but, as they never alighted, we had no opportunity of catching them.

As long as this fowl lasted we suffered nothing from our situation; but it was now entirely consumed, and it became absolutely necessary that we should look out for provision. The filberts would not satisfy the cravings of hunger, afflicting us, too, with severe gripings of the bowels, and, if freely indulged in, with violent headache. We had seen several large tortoises near the seashore to the eastward of the hill, and perceived they might be easily taken, if we could get at them without the observation of the natives. It was resolved, therefore, to make an attempt at descending.

We commenced by going down the southern declivity, which seemed to offer the fewest difficulties, but had not proceeded a hundred yards before (as we had anticipated from appearances on the hill-top) our progress was entirely arrested by a branch of the gorge in which our companions had perished. We now passed along the edge of this for about a quarter of a mile, when we were again stopped by a precipice of immense depth, and, not being able to make our way along the brink of it, we were forced to retrace our steps by the main ravine.

We now pushed over to the eastward, but with precisely similar fortune. After an hour's scramble, at the risk of breaking our necks, we discovered that we had merely descended into a vast pit of black granite, with fine dust at the bottom, and whence the only egress was by the rugged path in which we had come down. Toiling again up this path, we now tried the northern edge of the hill. Here we were obliged to use the greatest possible caution in our manoeuvres, as the least indiscretion would expose us to the full view of the savages in the village.

We crawled along, therefore, on our hands and knees, and, occasionally, were even forced to throw ourselves at full length, dragging our bodies along by means of the shrubbery. In this careful manner we had proceeded but a little way, when we arrived at a chasm far deeper than any we had yet seen, and leading directly into the main gorge. Thus our fears were fully confirmed, and we found ourselves cut off entirely from access to the world below. Thoroughly exhausted by our exertions, we made the best of our way back to the platform, and, throwing ourselves upon the bed of leaves, slept sweetly and soundly for some hours.

For several days after this fruitless search we were occupied in exploring every part of the summit of the hill, in order to inform ourselves of its actual resources. We found that it would afford us no food, with the exception of the unwholesome filberts, and a rank species of scurvy grass which grew in a little patch of not more than four rods square, and would be soon exhausted. On the fifteenth of February, as near as I can remember, there was not a blade of this left, and the nuts were growing scarce; our situation, therefore, could hardly be more lamentable.[1] On the sixteenth we again went round the walls of our prison, in hope of finding some avenue of escape, but to no purpose. We also descended the chasm in which we had been overwhelmed, with the faint expectation of discovering, through this channel, some opening to the main ravine. Here, too, we were disappointed, although we found and brought up with us a musket.

On the seventeenth we set out with the determination of examining more thoroughly the chasm of black granite into which we had made our way in the first search. We remembered that one of the fissures in the sides of this pit had been but partially looked into, and we were anxious to explore it, although with no expectation of discovering here any opening.

We found no great difficulty in reaching the bottom of the hollow as before, and were now sufficiently calm to survey it with some attention. It was, indeed, one of the most singular-looking places imaginable, and we could scarcely bring ourselves to believe it altogether the work of nature. The pit, from

---

1. This day was rendered remarkable by our observing in the south several huge wreaths of the grayish vapour I have before spoken of.

its eastern to its western extremity, was about five hundred yards in length, when all its windings were threaded; the distance from east to west in a straight line not being more (I should suppose, having no means of accurate examination) than forty or fifty yards. Upon first descending into the chasm, that is to say, for a hundred feet down ward from the summit of the hill, the sides of the abyss bore little resemblance to each other, and, apparently, had at no time been connected, the one surface being of the soapstone and the other of marl, granulated with some metallic matter. The average breadth, or interval between the two cliffs, was probably here sixty feet, but there seemed to be no regularity of formation. Passing down, however, beyond the limit spoken of, the interval rapidly contracted, and the sides began to run parallel, although, for some distance farther, they were still dissimilar in their material and form of surface.

Upon arriving within fifty feet of the bottom, a perfect regularity commenced. The sides were now entirely uniform in substance, in colour, and in lateral direction, the material being a very black and shining granite, and the distance between the two sides, at all points facing each other, exactly twenty yards. The precise formation of the chasm will be best understood by means of a delineation taken upon the spot; for I had luckily with me a pocketbook and pencil, which I preserved with great care through a long series of subsequent adventure, and to which I am indebted for memoranda of many subjects which would otherwise have been crowded from my remembrance.

FIGURE 1

182

This figure (see figure 1) gives the general outlines of the chasm, without the minor cavities in the sides, of which there were several, each cavity having a corresponding protuberance opposite. The bottom of the gulf was covered to the depth of three or four inches with a powder almost impalpable, beneath which we found a continuation of the black granite. To the right, at the lower extremity, will be noticed the appearance of a small opening; this is the fissure alluded to above, and to examine which more minutely than before was the object of our second visit. We now pushed into it with vigour, cutting away a quantity of brambles which impeded us, and removing a vast heap of sharp flints some what resembling arrowheads in shape.

We were encouraged to persevere, however, by perceiving some little light proceeding from the farther end. We at length squeezed our way for about thirty feet, and found that the aperture was a low and regularly-formed arch, having a bottom of the same impalpable powder as that in the main chasm. A strong light now broke upon us, and, turning a short bend, we found ourselves in another lofty chamber, similar to the one we had left in every respect but longitudinal form. Its general figure is here given. (See figure 2.)

FIGURE 2.

The total length of this chasm, commencing at the opening *a* and proceeding round the curve *b* to the extremity *d*, is five hundred and fifty yards. At *c* we discovered a small aperture similar to the one through which we had issued from the other chasm, and this was choked up in the same manner with brambles and a quantity of the white arrowhead flints. We forced our way through it, finding it about forty feet long, and emerged into a third chasm. This, too, was precisely like the first, except in its longitudinal shape, which was thus. (See figure 3.)

FIGURE 3.

FIGURE 5

We found the entire length of the third chasm three hundred and twenty yards. At the point *a* was an opening about six feet wide, and extending fifteen feet into the rock, where it terminated in a bed of marl, there being no other chasm beyond, as we had expected. We were about leaving this fissure, into which very little light was admitted, when Peters called my attention to a range of singular-looking indentures in the surface of the marl forming the termination of the *cul-de-sac*. With a very slight exertion of the imagination, the left, or most northerly of these indentures might have been taken for the intentional, although rude, representation of a human figure standing erect, with outstretched arm.

The rest of them bore also some little resemblance to alphabetical characters, and Peters was willing, at all events, to adopt the idle opinion that they were really such. I convinced him of his error, finally, by directing his attention to the floor of the fissure, where, among the powder, we picked up, piece by piece, several large flakes of the marl, which had evidently been broken off by some convulsion from the surface where the indentures were found, and which had projecting points exactly fitting the

FIGURE 4.

indentures; thus proving them to have been the work of nature. Figure 4. presents an accurate copy of the whole.

After satisfying ourselves that these singular caverns afforded us no means of escape from our prison, we made our way back, dejected and dispirited, to the summit of the hill. Nothing worth mentioning occurred during the next twenty-four hours, except that, in examining the ground to the eastward of the third chasm, we found two triangular holes of great depth, and also with black granite sides. Into these holes we did not think it worth while to attempt descending, as they had the appearance of mere natural wells, without outlet. They were each about twenty yards in circumference, and their shape, as well as relative position in regard to the third chasm, is shown in figure 5, preceding page.

CHAPTER 23

On the twentieth of the month, finding it altogether impossible to subsist any longer upon the filberts, the use of which occasioned us the most excruciating torment, we resolved to make a desperate attempt at descending the southern declivity of the hill. The face of the precipice was here of the softest species of soapstone, although nearly perpendicular throughout its whole extent (a depth of a hundred and fifty feet at the least), and in many places even overarching. After long search we discovered a narrow ledge about twenty feet below the brink of the gulf; upon this Peters contrived to leap, with what assistance I could render him by means of our pocket-handkerchiefs tied together.

With somewhat more difficulty I also got down; and we then saw the possibility of descending the whole way by the process in which we had clambered up from the chasm when we had been buried by the fall of the hill—that is, by cutting steps in the face of the soapstone with our knives. The extreme hazard of the attempt can scarcely be conceived; but, as there was no other resource, we determined to undertake it.

Upon the ledge where we stood there grew some filbert-bushes; and to one of these we made fast an end of our rope of handkerchiefs. The other end being tied round Peters's waist, I lowered him down over the edge of the precipice until the handkerchiefs were stretched tight. He now proceeded to dig a deep hole in the soapstone (as far in as eight or ten inches), sloping away the rock above to the height of a foot, or thereabout, so as to allow of his driving, with the butt of a pistol, a tolerably strong peg into the levelled surface. I then drew him up for about four feet, when he made a hole similar to the one below, driving in a peg as before, and having thus a resting-place for both feet and hands.

I now unfastened the handkerchiefs from the bush, throwing him the end, which he tied to the peg in the upper most hole, letting himself down gently to a station about three feet lower than he had yet been, that is, to the full extent of the handkerchiefs. Here he dug another hole, and drove another peg. He then drew himself up, so as to rest his feet in the hole just cut, taking hold with his hands upon the peg in the one above. It was now necessary to untie the handkerchiefs from the topmost peg, with the view of fastening them to the second; and here he found that an error had been committed in cutting the holes at so great a distance apart.

However, after one or two unsuccessful and dangerous attempts at reaching the knot (having to hold on with his left hand while he laboured to undo the fastening with his right), he at length cut the string, leaving six inches of it affixed to the peg. Tying the handkerchiefs now to the second peg, he descended to a station below the third, taking care not to go too far down.

By these means (means which I should never have conceived of myself, and for which we were indebted altogether to Peters's ingenuity and resolution) my companion finally succeeded, with the occasional aid of projections in the cliff, in reaching the bottom without accident.

It was some time before I could summon sufficient resolution to follow him; but I did at length attempt it. Peters had taken off his shirt before descending, and this, with my own, formed the rope necessary for the adventure. After throwing down the musket found in the chasm, I fastened this rope to the bushes, and let myself down rapidly, striving, by the vigour of my movements, to banish the trepidation which I could overcome in no other manner. This answered sufficiently well for the first four or five steps; but presently I found my imagination growing terribly excited by thoughts of the vast depth yet to be descended, and the precarious nature of the pegs and soapstone holes which were my only support.

It was in vain I endeavoured to banish these reflections, and to keep my eyes steadily bent upon the flat surface of the cliff before me. The more earnestly I struggled *not to think*, the more intensely vivid became my conceptions, and the more horribly distinct. At length arrived that crisis of fancy, so fearful in all similar cases, the crisis in which we begin to anticipate the feelings with which we *shall* fall—to picture to ourselves the sickness, and dizziness, and the last struggle, and the half swoon, and the final bitterness of the rushing and headlong descent. And now I found these fancies creating their own realities, and all imagined horrors crowding upon me in fact. I felt my knees strike violently together, while my fingers were gradually yet certainly relaxing their grasp.

There was a ringing in my ears, and I said, "This is my knell of death!" And now I was consumed with the irrepressible desire of looking below. I could not, I would not, confine my glances to the cliff; and, with a wild, indefinable emotion half of horror, half of a relieved oppression, I threw my vision far down into the abyss. For one moment my fingers clutched convulsively upon their hold, while, with the movement, the faintest possible idea of ultimate escape wandered, like a shadow, through my mind— in the next my whole soul was pervaded with *a longing to fall*; a desire, a yearning, a passion utterly uncontrollable. I let go at once my grasp upon the peg, and, turning half round from the precipice, remained tottering for an instant against its naked face. But now there came a spinning of the brain; a shrill-sounding and phantom voice screamed within my ears; a dusky, fiendish, and filmy figure stood immediately beneath me; and, sighing, I sunk down with a bursting heart, and plunged within its arms.

I had swooned, and Peters had caught me as I fell. He had observed my proceedings from his station at the bottom of the cliff; and, perceiving my imminent danger, had endeavoured to inspire me with courage by every suggestion he could devise; although my confusion of mind had been so great as to prevent my hearing what he said, or being conscious that he had even spoken to me at all. At length, seeing me totter, he hastened to ascend to my rescue, and arrived just in time for my preservation. Had I fallen with my full weight, the rope of linen would inevitably have snapped, and I should have been precipitated into the abyss; as it was, he contrived to let me down gently, so as to remain suspended without danger until animation returned. This was in about fifteen minutes. On recovery, my trepidation had entirely vanished; I felt a new being, and, with some little further aid from my companion, reached the bottom also in safety.

We now found ourselves not far from the ravine which had proved the tomb of our friends, and to the southward of the spot where the hill had fallen. The place was one of singular wildness, and its aspect brought to my mind the descriptions given by travellers of those dreary regions marking the site of degraded Babylon. Not to speak of the ruins of the disruptured cliff, which formed a chaotic barrier in the vista to the northward, the surface of the ground in every other direction was strewn with huge *tumuli*, apparently the wreck of some gigantic structures of art; although, in detail, no semblance of art could be detected. Scoria were abundant, and large shapeless blocks of the black granite, intermingled with others of marl,[1] and both granulated with metal. Of vegetation there were no traces whatsoever throughout the whole of the desolate area within sight. Several immense scorpions were seen, and various reptiles not elsewhere to be found in the high latitudes.

As food was our most immediate object, we resolved to make our way to the seacoast, distant not more than half a mile, with a view of catching turtle, several of which we had observed from our place of concealment on the hill. We had proceeded some hundred yards, threading our route cautiously between the huge rocks and *tumuli*, when, upon turning a corner, five savages sprung upon us from a small cavern, felling Peters to the ground with a blow from a club. As he fell the whole party rushed upon him to secure their victim, leaving me time to recover from my astonishment. I still had the musket, but the barrel had received so much injury in being thrown from the precipice that I cast it aside as useless, preferring to trust my pistols, which had been carefully preserved in order.

With these I advanced upon the assailants, firing one after the other in quick succession. Two savages fell, and one, who was in the act of thrusting a spear into Peters, sprung to his feet without accomplishing his purpose. My companion being thus released, we had no further difficulty. He had his pistols also, but prudently declined using them, confiding in his great personal strength, which far exceeded that of any person I have ever known. Seizing a club from one of the savages who had fallen, he dashed out the brains of the three who remained, killing each instantaneously with a single blow of the weapon, and leaving us completely masters of the field.

So rapidly had these events passed, that we could scarcely believe in their reality, and were standing over the bodies of the dead in a species of stupid contemplation, when we were brought to recollection by the sound of shouts in the distance.

---

1. The marl was also black; indeed, we noticed no light-coloured substances of any kind upon the island.

It was clear that the savages had been alarmed by the firing, and that we had little chance of avoiding discovery. To regain the cliff, it would be necessary to proceed in the direction of the shouts; and even should we succeed in arriving at its base, we should never be able to ascend it without being seen.

Our situation was one of the greatest peril, and we were hesitating in which path to commence a flight, when one of the savages whom I had shot, and supposed dead, sprang briskly to his feet, and attempted to make his escape. We overtook him, however, before he had advanced many paces, and were about to put him to death, when Peters suggested that we might derive some benefit from forcing him to accompany us in our attempt at escape. We therefore dragged him with us, making him understand that we would shoot him if he offered resistance. In a few minutes he was perfectly submissive, and ran by our sides as we pushed in among the rocks, making for the seashore.

So far, the irregularities of the ground we had been traversing hid the sea, except at intervals, from our sight, and, when we first had it fairly in view, it was, perhaps, two hundred yards distant. As we emerged into the open beach we saw, to our great dismay, an immense crowd of the natives pouring from the village, and from all visible quarters of the island, making towards us with gesticulations of extreme fury, and howling like wild beasts. We were upon the point of turning upon our steps, and trying to secure a retreat among the fastnesses of the rougher ground, when I discovered the bows of two canoes projecting from behind a large rock which ran out into the water.

Towards these we now ran with all speed, and, reaching them, found them unguarded, and without any other freight than three of the large Gallipago turtles and the usual supply of paddles for sixty rowers. We instantly took possession of one of them, and, forcing our captive on board, pushed out to sea with all the strength we could command.

We had not made, however, more than fifty yards from the shore before we became sufficiently calm to perceive the great oversight of which we had been guilty in leaving the other canoe in the power of the savages, who, by this time, were not more than twice as far from the beach as ourselves, and were rapidly advancing to the pursuit. No time was now to be lost. Our hope was, at best, a forlorn one, but we had none other. It was very doubtful whether, with the utmost exertion, we could get back in time to anticipate them in taking possession of the canoe; but yet there was a chance that we could. We might save ourselves if we succeeded, while not to make the attempt was to resign ourselves to inevitable butchery.

The canoe was modelled with the bow and stern alike, and, in place of turning it round, we merely changed our position in paddling. As soon as the savages perceived this they redoubled their yells, as well as their speed, and approached with inconceivable rapidity. We pulled, however, with all the energy of desperation, and arrived at the contested point before more than one of the natives had attained it. This man paid dearly for his superior agility, Peters shooting him through the head with a pistol as he approached the shore. The foremost among the rest of his party were probably some twenty or thirty paces distant as we seized upon the canoe.

We at first endeavoured to pull her into the deep water, beyond the reach of the savages, but, finding her too firmly aground, and there being no time to spare, Peters, with one or two heavy strokes from the butt of the musket, succeeded in dashing out a large portion of the bow and of one side. We then pushed off. Two of the natives by this time had got hold of our boat, obstinately refusing to let go, until we were forced to despatch them with our knives. We were now clear off, and making great way out to sea. The main body of the savages, upon reaching the broken canoe, set up the most tremendous yell of rage and disappointment conceivable. In truth, from everything I could see of these wretches, they appeared to be the most wicked, hypocritical, vindictive, bloodthirsty, and altogether fiendish race of men upon the face of the globe.

It is clear we should have had no mercy had we fallen into their hands. They made a mad attempt at following us in the fractured canoe, but, finding it useless, again vented their rage in a series of hideous vociferations, and rushed up into the hills.

We were thus relieved from immediate danger, but our situation was still sufficiently gloomy. We knew that four canoes of the kind we had were at one time in the possession of the savages, and were not aware of the fact (afterward ascertained from our captive) that two of these had been blown to pieces in the explosion of the *Jane Guy*. We calculated, therefore, upon being yet pursued, as soon as our enemies could get round to the bay (distant about three miles) where the boats were usually laid up. Fearing this, we made every exertion to leave the island behind us, and went rapidly through the water, forcing the prisoner to take a paddle. In about half an hour, when we had gained, probably, five or six miles to the southward, a large fleet of the flat-bottomed canoes or rafts was seen to emerge from the bay, evidently with the design of pursuit. Presently they put back, despairing to overtake us.

Chapter 24

We now found ourselves in the wide and desolate Antarctic Ocean, in a latitude exceeding eighty-four degrees, in a frail canoe, and with no provision but the three turtles. The long Polar winter, too, could not be considered as far distant, and it became necessary that we should deliberate well upon the course to be pursued. There were six or seven islands in sight belonging to the same group, and distant from each other about five or six leagues; but upon neither of these had we any intention to venture. In coming from the northward in the *Jane Guy* we had been gradually leaving behind us the severest regions of ice—this, however little it may be in accordance with the generally-received notions respecting the Antarctic, was a fact experience would not permit us to deny.

To attempt, therefore, getting back, would be folly—especially at so late a period of the season. Only one course seemed to be left open for hope. We resolved to steer boldly to the southward, where there was at least a probability of discovering other lands, and more than a probability of finding a still milder climate.

So far we had found the Antarctic, like the Arctic Ocean, peculiarly free from violent storms or immoderately rough water; but our canoe was, at best, of frail structure, although large, and we set busily to work with a view of rendering her as safe as the limited means in our possession would admit. The body of the boat was of no better material than bark the bark of a tree un known. The ribs were of a tough osier, well adapted to the purpose for which it was used. We had fifty feet room from stem to stern, from four to six in breadth, and in depth throughout four feet and a half—the boats thus differing vastly in shape from those of any other in habitants of the Southern Ocean with whom civilized nations are acquainted.

We never did believe them the workmanship of the ignorant islanders who owned them; and some days after this period discovered, by questioning our captive, that they were in fact made by the natives of a group to the southwest of the country where we found them, having fallen accidentally into the hands of our barbarians. What we could do for the security of our boat was very little indeed. Several wide rents were discovered near both ends, and these we contrived to patch up with pieces of woollen jacket. With the help of the superfluous paddles, of which there were a great many, we erected a kind of framework about the bow, so as to break the force of any seas which might threaten to fill us in that quarter.

We also set up two paddle-blades for masts, placing them opposite each other, one by each gunwale, thus saving the necessity of a yard. To these masts we attached a sail made of our shirts— doing this with some difficulty, as here we could get no assistance from our prisoner whatever, al though he had been willing enough to labour in all the other operations. The sight of the linen seemed to affect him in a very singular manner. He could not be prevailed upon to touch it or go near it, shuddering when we attempted to force him, and shrieking out *Tekeli-li!*

Having completed our arrangements in regard to the security of the canoe, we now set sail to the south south-east for the present, with the view of weathering the most southerly of the group in sight. This being done, we turned the bow full to the southward. The weather could by no means be considered disagreeable. We had a prevailing and very gentle wind from the northward, a smooth sea, and continual daylight. No ice whatever was to be seen; *nor did I ever see one particle of this after leaving the parallel of Bennett's Islet.*

Indeed, the temperature of the water was here far too warm for its existence in any quantity. Having killed the largest of our tortoises, and obtained from him not only food, but a copious supply of water, we continued on our course, without any incident of moment, for perhaps seven or eight days, during which period we must have proceeded a vast distance to the southward, as the wind blew constantly with us, and a very strong current set continually in the direction we were pursuing.

March 1.[1] Many unusual phenomena now indicated that we were entering upon a region of novelty and wonder. A high range of light gray vapour appeared constantly in the southern horizon, flaring up occasionally in lofty streaks, now darting from east to west, now from west to east, and again presenting a level and uniform summit—in short, having all the wild variations of the *Aurora Borealis.* The average height of this vapour, as apparent from our station, was about twenty-five degrees. The temperature of the sea seemed to be in creasing momentarily, and there was a very perceptible alteration in its colour.

March 2. Today, by repeated questioning of our captive, we came to the knowledge of many particulars in regard to the island of the massacre, its inhabitants, and customs—but with these how can I *now* detain the reader? I may say, however, that we learned there were eight islands in the group—that they were governed by a common king, named *Tsalemon* or *Psalemoun*, who resided in one of the smallest of the islands—that the black skins forming the dress of the warriors came from an

---

1. For obvious reasons I cannot pretend to strict accuracy in these dates. They are given principally with a view to perspicuity of narration, and as set down in my pencil memoranda.

animal of huge size to be found only in a valley near the court of the king—that the inhabitants of the group fabricated no other boats than the flat-bottomed rafts; the four canoes being all of the kind in their possession, and these having been obtained, by mere accident, from some large island to the southwest— that his own name was Nu-Nu—that he had no knowledge of Bennett's Islet—and that the appellation of the island we had left was *Tsalal.* The commencement of the words *Tsalemon* and *Tsalal* was given with a prolonged hissing sound, which we found it impossible to imitate, even after repeated endeavours, and which was precisely the same with the note of the black bittern we had eaten upon the summit of the hill.

March 3. The heat of the water was now truly remarkable, and its colour was undergoing a rapid change, being no longer transparent, but of a milky consistency and hue. In our immediate vicinity it was usually smooth, never so rough as to endanger the canoe—but we were frequently surprised at perceiving, to out right and left, at different distances, sudden and extensive agitations of the surface—these, we at length noticed, were always preceded by wild flickerings in the region of vapour to the southward.

March 4. Today, with the view of widening our sail, the breeze from the northward dying away perceptibly, I took from my coat-pocket a white handkerchief. Nu-Nu was seated at my elbow, and the linen accidentally flaring in his face, he became violently affected with convulsions. These were succeeded by drowsiness and stupor, and low murmurings of *Tekeli-li! Tekeli-li!*

March 5. The wind had entirely ceased, but it was evident that we were still hurrying on to the southward, under the influence of a powerful current. And now, indeed, it would seem reasonable that we should experience some alarm at the turn events were taking—but we felt none. The countenance of Peters indicated nothing of this nature, although it wore at times an expression I could not fathom. The Polar winter appeared to be coming on—but coming without its terrors. I felt a *numbness* of body and mind—a dreaminess of sensation—but this was all.

March 6. The gray vapour had now arisen many more degrees above the horizon, and was gradually losing its grayness of tint. The heat of the water was extreme, even unpleasant to the touch, and its milky hue was more evident than ever. Today a violent agitation of the water occurred very close to the canoe. It was attended, as usual, with a wild flaring up of the vapour at its summit, and a momentary division at its base. A fine white powder, resembling ashes—but certainly not such—fell over the canoe and over a large surface of the water, as the flickering died away among the vapour and the commotion subsided in the sea. Nu-Nu now threw himself on his face in the bottom of the boat, and no persuasions could induce him to arise.

March 7. This day we questioned Nu-Nu concerning the motives of his countrymen in destroying our companions; but he appeared to be too utterly overcome by terror to afford us any rational reply. He still obstinately lay in the bottom of the boat; and, upon our reiterating the questions as to the motive, made use only of idiotic gesticulations, such as raising with his forefinger the upper lip, and displaying the teeth which lay beneath it. These were black. We had never before seen the teeth of an inhabitant of Tsalal.

March 8. Today there floated by us one of the white animals whose appearance upon the beach at Tsalal had occasioned so wild a commotion among the savages. I would have picked it up, but there came over me a sudden listlessness, and I forbore. The heat of the water still increased, and the hand could no longer be endured within it. Peters spoke little, and I knew not what to think of his apathy. Nu-Nu breathed, and no more.

March 9. The white ashy material fell now continually around us, and in vast quantities. The range of vapour to the southward had arisen prodigiously in the horizon, and began to assume more distinctness of form. I can liken it to nothing but a limitless cataract, rolling silently into the sea from some immense and far-distant rampart in the heaven. The gigantic curtain ranged along the whole extent of the southern horizon. It emitted no sound.

March 21. A sullen darkness now hovered above us—but from out the milky depths of the ocean a luminous glare arose, and stole up along the bulwarks of the boat. We were nearly overwhelmed by the white ashy shower which settled upon us and upon the canoe, but melted into the water as it fell. The summit of the cataract was utterly lost in the dimness and the distance. Yet we were evidently approaching it with a hideous velocity. At intervals there were visible in it wide, yawning, but momentary rents, and from out these rents, within which was a chaos of flitting and indistinct images, there came rushing and mighty, but soundless winds, tearing up the enkindled ocean in their course.

March 22. The darkness had materially increased, relieved only by the glare of the water thrown back from the white curtain before us. Many gigantic and pallidly white birds flew continuously now from beyond the veil, and their scream was the eternal *Tekeli-li!* as they retreated from our vision. Hereupon Nu-Nu stirred in the bottom of the boat; but, upon touching him, we found his spirit departed. And now we rushed into the embraces of the cataract, where a chasm threw itself open to receive us. But there arose in our pathway a shrouded human figure, very far larger in its proportions than any dweller among men. And the hue of the skin of the figure was of the perfect whiteness of the snow.

NOTE

The circumstances connected with the late sudden and distressing death of Mr. Pym are already well known to the public through the medium of the daily press. It is feared that the few remaining chapters which were to have completed his narrative, and which were retained by him, while the above were in type, for the purpose of revision, have been irrecoverably lost through the accident by which he perished himself. This, however, may prove not to be the case, and the papers, if ultimately found, will be given to the public.

No means have been left untried to remedy the deficiency. The gentleman whose name is mentioned in the preface, and who, from the statement there made, might be supposed able to fill the vacuum, has declined the task—this for satisfactory reasons connected with the general inaccuracy of the details afforded him, and his disbelief in the entire truth of the latter portions of the narration. Peters, from whom some information might be expected, is still alive, and a resident of Illinois, but cannot be met with at present. He may hereafter be found, and will, no doubt, afford material for a conclusion of Mr. Pym's account.

The loss of the two or three final chapters (for there were but two or three) is the more deeply to be regretted, as, it cannot be doubted, they contained matter relative to the Pole itself, or at least to regions in its very near proximity; and as, too, the statements of the author in relation to these regions may shortly be verified or contradicted by means of the governmental expedition now preparing for the Southern Ocean.

On one point in the narrative some remarks may be well offered; and it would afford the writer of this appendix much pleasure if what he may here observe should have a tendency to throw credit, in any degree, upon the very singular pages now published. We allude to the chasms found in the island of Tsalal, and to the whole of the figures in chapter 3.

Mr. Pym has given the figures of the chasms without comment, and speaks decidedly of the *indentures* found at the extremity of the most easterly of these chasms as having but a fanciful resemblance to alphabetical characters, and, in short, as being positively *not such*. This assertion is made in a manner so simple, and sustained by a species of demonstration so conclusive (*viz.*, the fitting of the projections of the fragments found among the dust into the indentures upon the wall), that we are forced to believe the writer in earnest; and no reasonable reader should suppose otherwise.

But as the facts in relation to *all* the figures are most singular (especially when taken in connexion with statements made in the body of the narrative), it may be as well to say a word or two concerning them all—this, too, the more especially as the facts in question have, beyond doubt, escaped the attention of Mr. Poe.

Figure 1, then, figure 2, figure 3, and figure 5, when conjoined with one another in the precise order which the chasms themselves presented, and when deprived of the small lateral branches or arches (which, it will be remembered, served only as means of communication between the main chambers, and were of totally distinct character), constitute an Ethiopian verbal root—the root 人 ᒍ ᔕ ᒍ "To be shady"—whence all the inflections of shadow or darkness.

In regard to the "left or most northwardly" of the indentures in figure 4, it is more than probable that the opinion of Peters was correct, and that the hieroglyphical appearance was really the work of art, and intended as the representation of a human form. The delineation is before the reader, and he may, or may not, perceive the resemblance suggested; but the rest of the indentures afford strong confirmation of Peters's idea. The upper range is evidently the Arabic verbal root ᒍᐯᒪᐯᑎ "To be white," whence all the in flections of brilliancy and whiteness. The lower range is not so immediately perspicuous. The characters are somewhat broken and disjointed; nevertheless, it cannot be doubted that, in their perfect state, they formed the full Egyptian word Π ᒍᐯ ᐯᏢᏥ Ꮵ , "The region of the south." It should be observed that these interpretations confirm the opinion of Peters in regard to the "most northwardly" of the figures. The arm is outstretched towards the south.

Conclusions such as these open a wide field for speculation and exciting conjecture. They should be regarded, perhaps, in connexion with some of the most faintly-detailed incidents of the narrative; although in no visible manner is this chain of connexion complete. *Tekeli-li!* was the cry of the affrighted natives of Tsalal upon discovering the carcass of the white animal picked up at sea. This also was the shuddering exclamation of the captive Tsalalian upon encountering the *white* materials in possession of Mr. Pym. This also was the shriek of the swift-flying, *white*, and gigantic birds which is sued from the vapoury *white* curtain of the South.

Nothing *white* was to be found at Tsalal, and nothing otherwise in the subsequent voyage to the region beyond. It is not impossible that "Tsalal," the appellation of the island of the chasms, may be found, upon minute philological scrutiny, to betray either some alliance with the chasms themselves, or some reference to the Ethiopian characters so mysteriously written in their windings.

I have graven it within the hills, and my vengeance upon the dust within the rock.

William Wilson

What say of it? what says CONSCIENCE grim,
That spectre in my path?

W. Chamberlayn's *Pharonnida*.

Let me call myself, for the present, William Wilson. The fair page now lying before me need not be sullied with my real appellation. This has been already too much an object for the scorn, for the horror, for the detestation of my race. To the uttermost regions of the globe have not the indignant winds bruited its unparalleled infamy? O outcast of all outcasts most abandoned! to the earth art thou not for ever dead? to its honours, to its flowers, to its golden aspirations?—and a cloud, dense, dismal, and limitless, does it not hang eternally between thy hopes and heaven?

I would not, if I could, here or today, embody a record of my later years of unspeakable misery and unpardonable crime. This epoch—these later years—took unto themselves a sudden elevation in turpitude, whose origin alone it is my present purpose to assign. Men usually grow base by degrees. From me in an instant all virtue dropped bodily as a mantle. From comparatively trivial wickedness I passed, with the stride of a giant, into more than the enormities of an Elagabalus. What chance—what one event brought this evil thing to pass, bear with me while I relate. Death approaches, and the shadow which foreruns him has thrown a softening influence over my spirit. I long in passing through the dim valley for the sympathy, I had nearly said for the pity, of my fellow-men.

I would fain have them believe that I have been in some measure the slave of circumstances beyond human control. I would wish them to seek out for me, in the details I am about to give, some little oasis of *fatality* amid a wilderness of error. I would have them allow, what they cannot refrain from allowing, that although temptation may have erewhile existed as great, man was never *thus* at least tempted before, certainly never *thus* fell. And is it therefore that he has never thus suffered? Have I not indeed been living in a dream? And am I not now dying a victim to the horror and the mystery of the wildest of all sublunary visions?

I am the descendant of a race whose imaginative and easily excitable temperament has at all times rendered them remarkable; and in my earliest infancy I gave evidence of having fully inherited the family character. As I advanced in years it was more strongly developed, becoming for many reasons a cause of serious disquietude to my friends, and of positive injury to myself. I grew self-willed, addicted to the wildest caprices, and a prey to the most ungovernable passions. Weak-minded, and beset with constitutional infirmities akin to my own, my parents could do but little to check the evil propensities which distinguished me. Some feeble and ill-directed efforts resulted in complete failure on their part, and of course in total triumph on mine. Thenceforward my voice was a household law, and at an age when few children have abandoned their leading-strings, I was left to the guidance of my own will, and became in all but name the master of my own actions.

My earliest recollections of a school-life are connected with a large rambling Elizabethan house, in a misty-looking village of England, where were a vast number of gigantic and gnarled trees, and where all the houses were excessively ancient. In truth, it was a dream-like and spirit-soothing place that venerable old town. At this moment, in fancy, I feel the refreshing chilliness of its deeply-shadowed avenues, inhale the fragrance of its thousand shrubberies, and thrill anew with indefinable delight at the deep hollow note of the church-bell, breaking each hour with sullen and sudden roar upon the stillness of the dusky atmosphere in which the fretted Gothic steeple lay imbedded and asleep.

It gives me perhaps as much of pleasure as I can now in any manner experience to dwell upon minute recollections of the school and its concerns. Steeped in misery as I am—misery, alas! only too real—I shall be pardoned for seeking relief, however slight and temporary, in the weakness of a few rambling details. These, moreover, utterly trivial, and even ridiculous in themselves, assume to my fancy adventitious importance, as connected with a period and a locality when and where I recognise the first ambiguous monitions of the destiny which afterwards so fully overshadowed me. Let me then remember.

The house, I have said, was old and irregular. The grounds were extensive, and a high and solid brick wall, topped with a bed of mortar and broken glass, encompassed the whole. This prison-like rampart formed the limit of our domain: beyond it we saw but thrice a week, once every Saturday afternoon, when, attended by two ushers, we were permitted to take brief walks in a body through some of the neighbouring fields; and twice during Sunday, when we were paraded in the same formal manner to the morning and evening service in the one church of the village. Of this church the principal of our school was pastor. With how deep a spirit of wonder and perplexity was I wont to regard him from our remote pew in the gallery, as with step solemn and slow he ascended the pulpit! This reverend man, with countenance so demurely benign, with robes so glossy and so clerically flowing, with wig so minutely powdered, so rigid and so vast could this be he who, of late, with sour visage, and in snuffy habiliments, administered, ferule in hand, the Draconian laws of the academy? O gigantic paradox, too utterly monstrous for solution!

At an angle of the ponderous wall frowned a more ponderous gate. It was riveted and studded with iron bolts, and surmounted with jagged iron spikes. What impressions of deep awe did it inspire! It was never opened save for the three periodical egressions and ingressions already mentioned; then in every creak of its mighty hinges we found a plenitude of mystery, a world of matter for solemn remark, or for more solemn meditation.

The extensive enclosure was irregular in form, having many capacious recesses. Of these, three or four of the largest constituted the playground. It was level, and covered with fine hard gravel. I well remember it had no trees nor benches, nor anything similar within it. Of course it was in the rear of the house. In front lay a small *parterre*, planted with box and other shrubs, but through this sacred division we passed only upon rare occasions indeed, such as a first advent to school or final departure thence, or perhaps, when a parent or friend having called for us, we joyfully took our way home for the Christmas or Midsummer holidays.

But the house!—how quaint an old building was this! to me how veritably a palace of enchantment! There was really no end to its windings, to its incomprehensible sub-divisions. It was difficult, at any given time, to say with certainty upon which of its two stories one happened to be. From each room to every other there were sure to be found three or four steps either in ascent or descent. Then the lateral branches were innumerable, inconceivable, and so returning in upon themselves that our most exact ideas in regard to the whole mansion were not very far different from those with which we pondered upon infinity. During the five years of my residence here I was never able to ascertain with precision in what remote locality lay the little sleeping apartment assigned to myself and some eighteen or twenty other scholars.

The schoolroom was the largest in the house, I could not help thinking, in the world. It was very long, narrow, and dismally low, with pointed Gothic windows and a ceiling of oak. In a remote and terror-inspiring angle was a square enclosure of eight or ten feet, comprising the *sanctum*, "during hours," of our principal, the Reverend Dr. Bransby. It was a solid structure, with massy door, sooner than open which in the absence of the "*dominie*" we would all have willingly perished by the *peine forte et dure*. In other angles were two other similar boxes, far less reverenced, indeed, but still greatly matters of awe. One of these was the pulpit of the "classical" usher, one of the "English and mathematical." Interspersed about the room, crossing and recrossing in endless irregularity, were innumerable benches and desks, black, ancient, and time-worn, piled desperately with much-bethumbed books, and so beseamed with initial letters, names at full length, grotesque figures, and other multiplied efforts of the knife, as to have entirely lost what little of original form might have been their portion in days long departed. A huge bucket with water stood at one extremity of the room, and a clock of stupendous dimensions at the other.

Encompassed by the massy walls of this venerable academy, I passed, yet not in a tedium or disgust, the years of the third lustrum of my life. The teeming brain of childhood requires no external world of incident to occupy or amuse it; and the apparently dismal monotony of a school was replete with more intense excitement than my riper youth has derived from luxury, or my full manhood from crime. Yet I must believe that my first mental development had in it much of the uncommon—even much of the *outré*.. Upon mankind at large the events of very early existence rarely leave in mature age any definite impression. All is grey shadow—a weak and irregular remembrance—an indistinct regathering of feeble pleasures and phantasmagoric pains. With me this is not so. In childhood I must have felt with the energy of a man what I now find stamped upon memory in lines as vivid, as deep, and as durable as the *exergues* of the Carthaginian medals.

Yet in fact—in the fact of the world's view—how little was there to remember! The morning's awakening, the nightly summons to bed; the connings, the recitations; the periodical half-holidays, and perambulations; the playground, with its broils, its pastimes, its intrigues;—these, by a mental sorcery long forgotten, were made to involve a wilderness of sensation, a world of rich incident, a universe of varied emotion, of excitement the most passionate and spirit-stirring. "*O le bon temps, que ce siècle de fer?*"

In truth, the ardour, the enthusiasm, and the imperiousness of my disposition, soon rendered me a marked character among my schoolmates, and by slow but natural gradations gave me an ascendency over all not greatly older than myself—over all with a single exception. This exception was found in the person of a scholar, who, although no relation, bore the same Christian and surname as myself;—a circumstance, in fact, little remarkable; for notwithstanding a noble descent, mine was one of those every-day appellations which seem, by prescriptive right, to have been, time out of mind, the common property of the mob.

In this narrative I have therefore designated myself as William Wilson—a fictitious title not very dissimilar to the real. My namesake alone, of those who in school phraseology constituted "our set," presumed to compete with me in the studies of the class—in the sports and broils of the playground—to refuse implicit belief in my assertions, and submission to my will—indeed, to interfere with my arbitrary dictation in any respect whatsoever. If there is on earth a supreme and unqualified despotism, it is the despotism of a master-mind in boyhood over the less energetic spirits of its companions.

Wilson's rebellion was to me a source of the greatest embarrassment: the more so as, in spite of the bravado with which in public I made a point of treating him and his pretensions, I secretly felt that I feared him, and could not help thinking the equality which he maintained so easily with myself a proof of his true superiority, since not to be overcome cost me a perpetual struggle. Yet this superiority—even this equality—was in truth acknowledged by no one but myself; our associates, by some unaccountable blindness, seemed not even to suspect it. Indeed, his competition, his resistance, and especially his impertinent and dogged interference with my purposes, were not more pointed than private.

He appeared to be destitute alike of the ambition which urged, and of the passionate energy of mind which enabled me to excel. In his rivalry he might have been supposed actuated solely by a whimsical desire to thwart, astonish, or mortify myself; although there were times when I could not help observing, with a feeling made up of wonder, abasement, and pique, that he mingled with his injuries, his insults, or his contradictions, a certain most inappropriate, and assuredly most unwelcome *affectionateness* of manner. I could only conceive this singular behaviour to arise from a consummate self-conceit assuming the vulgar airs of patronage and protection.

Perhaps it was this latter trait in Wilson's conduct, conjoined with our identity of name, and the mere accident of our having entered the school upon the same day, which set afloat the notion that we were brothers among the senior classes in the academy. These do not usually inquire with much strictness into the affairs of their juniors. I have before said, or should have said, that Wilson was not, in the most remote degree, connected with my family. But assuredly if we *had* been brothers we must have been twins; for, after leaving Dr. Bransby's, I casually learned that my namesake was born on the nineteenth of January 1813—and this is a somewhat remarkable coincidence, for the day is precisely that of my own nativity.

It may seem strange that in spite of the continual anxiety occasioned me by the rivalry of Wilson, and his intolerable spirit of contradiction, I could not bring myself to hate him altogether. We had, to be sure, nearly every day a quarrel, in which, yielding me publicly the palm of victory, he in some manner contrived to make me feel that it was he who had deserved it, yet a sense of pride on my part and a veritable dignity on his own, kept us always upon what are called "speaking terms," while there were many points of strong congeniality in our tempers, operating to awake in me a sentiment which our position alone, perhaps, prevented from ripening into friendship.

It is difficult indeed to define or even to describe my real feelings towards him. They formed a motley and heterogeneous admixture; some petulant animosity, which was not yet hatred, some esteem, more respect, much fear, with a world of uneasy curiosity. To the moralist it will be unnecessary to say in addition that Wilson and myself were the most inseparable of companions.

It was no doubt the anomalous state of affairs existing between us which turned all my attacks upon him (and they were many, either open or covert) into the channel of banter or practical joke (giving pain while assuming the aspect of mere fun), rather than into a more serious and determined hostility. But my endeavours on this head were by no means uniformly successful, even when my plans were the most wittily concocted; for my namesake had much about him in character of that unassuming and quiet austerity which, while enjoying the poignancy of its own jokes, has no heel of Achilles in itself, and absolutely refuses to be laughed at. I could find indeed but one vulnerable point, and that lying in a personal peculiarity, arising perhaps from constitutional disease, would have been spared by any antagonist less at his wit's end than myself; my rival had a weakness in the faucial or guttural organs which precluded him from raising his voice at any time *above a very low whisper.* Of this defect I did not fail to take what poor advantage lay in my power.

Wilson's retaliations in kind were many; and there was one form of his practical wit that disturbed me beyond measure. How his sagacity first discovered at all that so petty a thing would vex me is a question I never could solve, but having discovered, he habitually practised the annoyance. I had always felt aversion to my uncourtly patronymic and its very common, ii not *plebeian prænomen.* The words were venom in my ears; and when, upon the day of my arrival, a second William Wilson came also to the academy, I felt angry with him for bearing the name, and doubly disgusted with the name because a stranger bore it, who would be the cause of its twofold repetition, who would be constantly in my presence, and whose concerns, in the ordinary routine of the school business, must inevitably, on account of the detestable coincidence, be often confounded with my own.

The feeling of vexation thus engendered grew stronger with every circumstance tending to show resemblance, moral or physical, between my rival and myself. I had not then discovered the remarkable fact that we were of the same age; but I saw that we were of the same height, and I perceived that we were even singularly alike in general contour of person and outline of feature. I was galled, too, by the rumour touching a relationship, which had grown current in the upper forms. In a word, nothing could more seriously disturb me (although I scrupulously concealed such disturbance), than any allusion to a similarity of mind, person, or condition existing between us.

But, in truth, I had no reason to believe that (with the exception of the matter of relationship, and in the case of Wilson himself) this similarity had ever been made a subject of comment or even observed at all by our schoolfellows. That *he* observed it in all its bearings, and as fixedly as I, was apparent; but that he could discover in such circumstances so fruitful a field of annoyance can only be attributed, as I said before, to his more than ordinary penetration.

His cue, which was to perfect an imitation of myself, lay both in words and in actions, and most admirably did he play his part. My dress it was an easy matter to copy my gait and general manner were without difficulty appropriated; in spite of his constitutional defect, even my voice did not escape him. My louder tones were of course unattempted, but then the key, it was identical; *and his singular whisper, it grew the very echo of my own,*

How greatly this most exquisite portraiture harassed me (for it could not justly be termed a caricature), I will not now venture to describe. I had but one consolation—in the fact that the imitation, apparently, was noticed by myself alone, and that I had to endure only the knowing and strangely sarcastic smiles of my namesake himself. Satisfied with having produced in my bosom the intended effect he seemed to chuckle in secret over the sting he had inflicted, and was characteristically disregardful of the public applause which the success of his witty endeavours might have so easily elicited.

That the school, indeed, did not feel his design, perceive its accomplishment, and participate in his sneer, was for many anxious months a riddle I could not resolve. Perhaps the *gradation* of his copy rendered it not so readily perceptible, or more possibly

I owed my security to the masterly air of the copyist, who, disdaining the letter (which in a painting is all the obtuse can see), gave but the full spirit of his original for my individual contemplation and chagrin.

I have already more than once spoken of the disgusting air of patronage which he assumed toward me, and of his frequent officious interference with my will. This interference often took the ungracious character of advice—advice not openly given but hinted or insinuated I received it with a repugnance which gained strength as I grew in years. Yet at this distant day, let me do him the simple justice to acknowledge that I can recall no occasion when the suggestions of my rival were on the side of those errors or follies so usual to his immature age and seeming inexperience; that his moral sense, at least, if not his general talents and worldly wisdom, was far keener than my own; and that I might today have been a better, and thus a happier man, had I less frequently rejected the counsels embodied in those meaning whispers which I then but too cordially hated and too bitterly despised.

As it was, I at length grew restive in the extreme under his distasteful supervision, and daily resented more and more openly what I considered his intolerable arrogance. I have said that in the first years of our connection as schoolmates, my feelings in regard to him might have been easily ripened into friendship; but, in the latter months of my residence at the academy, although the intrusion of his ordinary manner had, beyond doubt, in some measure abated, my sentiments in nearly similar proportion partook very much of positive hatred. Upon one occasion he saw this, I think, and afterwards avoided, or made a show of avoiding me.

It was about the same period, if I remember aright that, in an altercation of violence with him, in which he was more than usually thrown off his guard, and spoke and acted with an openness of demeanour rather foreign to his nature, I discovered, or fancied I discovered, in his accent, his air, and general appearance, a something which first startled, and then deeply interested me, by bringing to mind dim visions of my earliest infancy, wild, confused, and thronging memories of a time when memory herself was yet unborn. I cannot better describe the sensation which oppressed me than by saying that I could with difficulty shake off the belief of my having been acquainted with the be- ing who stood before me at some epoch very long ago, some point of the past even infinitely remote. The delusion, however, faded rapidly as it came, and I mention it at all but to define the day of the last conversation I there held with my singular namesake.

The huge old house, with its countless subdivisions, had several large chambers communicating with each other, where slept the greater number of the students. There were, however (as must necessarily happen in a building so awkwardly planned), many little nooks or recesses, the odds and ends of the structure, and these the economic ingenuity of Dr. Bransby had also fitted up as dormitories, although, being the merest closets, they were capable of accommodating but a single individual. One of these small apartments was occupied by Wilson.

One night, about the close of my fifth year at the school, and immediately after the altercation just mentioned, finding every one wrapped in sleep, I arose from bed, and, lamp in hand, stole through a wilderness of narrow passages from my own bedroom to that of my rival I had long been plotting one of those ill-na- tured pieces of practical wit at his expense in which I had hith- erto been so uniformly unsuccessful It was my intention now to put my scheme in operation, and I resolved to make him feel the whole extent of the malice with which I was imbued Having reached his closet I noiselessly entered, leaving the lamp, with a shade over it, on the outside. I advanced a step and listened to the sound of his tranquil breathing.

Assured of his being asleep, I returned, took the light, and with it again approached the bed. Close curtains were around it, which, in the prosecution of my plan, I slowly and quietly with- drew, when the bright rays fell vividly upon the sleeper, and my eyes, at the same moment, upon his countenance. I looked, and a numbness, an iciness of feeling, instantly pervaded my frame. My breast heaved, my knees tottered, my whole spirit became possessed with an objectless yet intolerable horror. Gasping for breath I lowered the lamp in still nearer proximity to the face. Were these—*these* the lineaments of William Wilson? I saw, indeed, that they were his, but I shook as if with a fit of the ague in fancying they were not. What *was* there about them to confound me in this manner? I gazed, while my brain reeled with a multitude of incoherent thoughts.

Not thus he appeared, assuredly not *thus*, in the vivacity of his waking hours. The same name, the same contour of person, the same day of arrival at the academy; and then his dogged and meaningless imitation of my gait, my voice, my habits, and my manner. Was it, in truth, within the bounds of human possibility that *what I now saw* was the result merely of the habitual practice of this sarcastic imitation. Awe-stricken, and with a creeping shudder, I extinguished the lamp, passed silently from the chamber, and left at once the halls of that old academy, never to enter them again.

After a lapse of some months, spent at home in mere idleness, I found myself a student at Eton. The brief interval had been sufficient to enfeeble my remembrance of the events at Dr. Bransby's, or at least to effect a material change in the nature of the feelings with which I remembered them. The truth, the tragedy, of the drama was no more. I could now find room to doubt the evidence of my senses, and seldom called up the subject at all but with wonder at the extent of human credulity, and a smile at the vivid force of the imagination which I hereditarily possessed. Neither was this species of scepticism likely to be diminished by the character of the life I led at Eton. The vortex of thoughtless folly into which I there so immediately and so recklessly plunged washed away all but the froth of my past hours, engulfed at once every solid or serious impression, and left to memory only the veriest levities of a former existence.

I do not wish, however, to trace the course of my miserable profligacy here—a profligacy which set at defiance the laws, while it eluded the vigilance of the institution. Three years of folly, passed without profit, had but given me rooted habits of vice, and added, in a somewhat unusual degree, to my bodily stature, when, after a week of soulless dissipation, I invited a small party of the most dissolute students to a secret carousal in my chambers. We met at a late hour of the night, for our debaucheries were to be faithfully protracted until morning.

The wine flowed freely, and there were not wanting other and perhaps more dangerous seductions, so that the grey dawn had already faintly appeared in the east, while our delirious extravagance was at its height. Madly flushed with cards and intoxication, I was in the act of insisting upon a toast of more than wonted profanity when my attention was suddenly diverted by the violent, although partial, unclosing of the door of the apartment, and by the eager voice of a servant from without. He said that some person, apparently in great haste, demanded to speak with me in the hall.

Wildly excited with wine, the unexpected interruption rather delighted than surprised me. I staggered forward at once, and a few steps brought me to the vestibule of the building. In this low and small room there hung no lamp, and now no light at all was admitted, save that of the exceedingly feeble dawn which made its way through the semi-circular window. As I put my foot over the threshold I became aware of the figure of a youth about my own height, and habited in a white kerseymere morning frock, cut in the novel fashion of the one I myself wore at the moment. This the faint light enabled me to perceive, but the features of his face I could not distinguish. Upon my entering he strode hurriedly up to me, and seizing me by the arm with a gesture of petulant impatience, whispered the words "William Wilson!" in my ear.

I grew perfectly sober in an instant.

There was that in the manner of the stranger, and in the tremulous shake of his uplifted finger, as he held it between my eyes and the light, which filled me with unqualified amazement; but it was not this which had so violently moved me. It was the pregnancy of solemn admonition in the singular, low, hissing utterance, and, above all, it was the character, the tone, *the key*, of those few, simple, and familiar, yet *whispered* syllables, which came with a thousand thronging memories of by-gone days, and struck upon my soul with the shock of a galvanic battery. Ere I could recover the use of my senses he was gone.

Although this event failed not of a vivid effect upon my disordered imagination, yet was it evanescent as vivid For some weeks, indeed, I busied myself in earnest inquiry or was wrapped in a cloud of morbid speculation. I did not pretend to disguise from my perception the identity of the singular individual who thus perseveringly interfered with my affairs, and harassed me with his insinuated counsel. But who and what was this Wilson?— and whence came he?—and what were his purposes? Upon neither of these points could I be satisfied—merely ascertaining in regard to him, that a sudden accident in his family had caused his removal from Dr. Bransby's academy on the afternoon of the day in which I myself had eloped.

But in a brief period I ceased to think upon the subject, my attention being all absorbed in a contemplated departure for Oxford. Thither I soon went, the uncalculating vanity of my parents furnishing me with an outfit and annual establishment which would enable me to indulge at will in the luxury already so dear to my heart—to vie in profuseness of expenditure with the haughtiest heirs of the wealthiest earldoms in Great Britain.

Excited by such appliances to vice, my constitutional temperament broke forth with redoubled ardour, and I spurned even the common restraints of decency in the mad infatuation of my revels. But it were absurd to pause in the detail of my extravagance. Let it suffice, that among spendthrifts I out-Heroded Herod, and that giving name to a multitude of novel follies, I added no brief appendix to the long catalogue of vices then usual in the most dissolute university of Europe.

It could hardly be credited, however, that I had, even here, so utterly fallen from the gentlemanly estate as to seek acquaintance with the vilest arts of the gambler by profession, and having become an adept in his despicable science, to practise it habitually as a means of increasing my already enormous income at the expense of the weak-minded among my fellow-collegians. Such, nevertheless, was the fact; and the very enormity of this offence against all manly and honourable sentiment proved, beyond doubt, the main, if not the sole reason of the impunity with which it was committed.

Who, indeed, among my most abandoned associates would not rather have disputed the clearest evidence of his senses than have suspected of such courses the gay, the frank, the generous William Wilson—the noblest and most liberal commoner at Oxford—him whose follies (said his parasites) were but the follies of youth and unbridled fancy—whose errors but inimitable whim—whose darkest vice but a careless and dashing extravagance?

I had been now two years successfully busied in this way when there came to the university a young *parvenu* nobleman, Glendinning—rich, said report, as Herodes Atticus—his riches, too, as easily acquired. I soon found him of weak intellect, and of course marked him as a fitting subject for my skill. I frequently engaged him in play, and contrived with the gambler's usual art to let him win considerable sums, the more effectually to entangle him in my snares. At length, my schemes being ripe, I met him (with the full intention that this meeting should be final and decisive) at the chambers of a fellow-commoner (Mr. Preston) equally intimate with both, but who, to do him justice, entertained not even a remote suspicion of my design.

To give to this a better colouring I had contrived to have assembled a party of some eight or ten, and was solicitously careful that the introduction of cards should appear accidental, and originate in the proposal of my contemplated dupe itimself. To be brief upon a vile topic, none of the low finesse was omitted, so customary upon similar occasions, that it is a just matter for wonder how any are still found so besotted as to fall its victim.

We had protracted our sitting far into the night, and I had at length effected the manoeuvre of getting Glendinning as my sole antagonist. The game, too, was my favourite *écarté*. The rest of the company, interested in the extent of our play, had abandoned their own cards, and were standing around us as spectators. The *parvenu*, who had been induced by my artifices in the early part of the evening to drink deeply, now shuffled, dealt, or played, with a wild nervousness of manner for which his intoxication I thought might partially but could not altogether account. In a very short period he had become my debtor to a large amount, when, having taken a long draught of port, he did precisely what I had been coolly anticipating—he proposed to double our already extravagant stakes.

With a well-feigned show of reluctance, and not until after my repeated refusal had seduced him into some angry words which gave a colour of *pique* to my compliance, did I finally comply. The result of course did but prove how entirely the prey was in my toils: in less than an hour he had quadrupled his debt. For some time his countenance had been losing the florid tinge lent it by the wine, but now to my astonishment I perceived that it had grown to a pallor truly fearful. I say to my astonishment. Glendinning had been represented to my eager inquiries as immeasurably wealthy; and the sums which he had as yet lost, although in themselves vast, could not, I supposed, very seriously annoy, much less so violently affect him.

That he was overcome by the wine just swallowed was the idea which most readily presented itself; and, rather with a view to the preservation of my own character in the eyes of my associates, than from any less interested motive, I was about to insist peremptorily upon a discontinuance of the play, when some expressions at my elbow from among the company, and an ejaculation evincing utter despair on the part of Glendinning, gave me to understand that I had effected his total ruin under circumstances which, rendering him an object for the pity of all, should have protected him from the ill offices even of a fiend.

What now might have been my conduct it is difficult to say. The pitiable condition of my dupe had thrown an air of embarrassed gloom over all, and for some moments a profound silence was maintained, during which I could not help feeling my cheeks tingle with the many burning glances of scorn or reproach cast upon me by the less abandoned of the party. I will even own that an intolerable weight of anxiety was a brief instant lifted from my bosom by the sudden and extraordinary interruption which ensued.

The wide heavy folding-doors of the apartment were all at once thrown open to their full extent, with a vigorous and rushing impetuosity that extinguished, as if by magic, every candle in the room. Their light, in dying, enabled us just to perceive that a stranger had entered, about my own height, and closely muffled in a cloak. The darkness, however, was now total, and we could only *feel* that he was standing in our midst. Before any one of us could recover from the extreme astonishment into which this rudeness had thrown all, we heard the voice of the intruder.

"Gentlemen," he said, in a low, distinct, and never-to-be-forgotten *whisper* which thrilled to the very marrow of my bones, "Gentlemen, I make no apology for this behaviour, because in thus behaving, I am but fulfilling my duty. You are, beyond doubt, uninformed of the true character of the person who has tonight won at *écarté* a large sum of money from Lord Glendinning. I will therefore put you upon an expeditious and decisive plan of obtaining this very necessary information. Please to examine at your leisure the inner linings of the cuff of his left sleeve, and the several little packages which may be found in the somewhat capacious pockets of his embroidered morning wrapper."

While he spoke, so profound was the stillness that one might have heard a pin drop upon the floor. In ceasing, he departed at once, and as abruptly as he had entered. Can I—shall I describe my sensations? Must I say that I felt all the horrors of the damned? Most assuredly I had little time for reflection. Many hands roughly seized me upon the spot, and lights were immediately re-procured. A search ensued. In the lining of my sleeve were found all the court cards essential in *écarté*, and in the pockets of my wrapper a number of packs, facsimiles of those used at our sittings, with the single exception that mine were of the species called, technically, *arrondées*; the honours being slightly convex at the ends, the lower cards slightly convex at the sides. In this disposition, the dupe who cuts, as customary, at the length of the pack, will invariably find that he cuts his antagonist an honour; while the gambler, cutting at the breadth, will as certainly cut nothing for his victim which may count in the records of the game.

Any burst of indignation upon this discovery Would have affected me less than the silent contempt, of the sarcastic composure, with which it was received.

"Mr. Wilson," said our host, stooping to remove from beneath his feet an exceedingly luxurious cloak of rare furs, "Mr. Wilson, this is your property." (The weather was cold; and, upon quitting my own room, I had thrown a cloak over my dressing wrapper, putting it off upon reaching the scene of play.) "I presume it is supererogatory to seek here (eyeing the folds of the garment with a bitter smile) for any further evidence of your skill. Indeed, we have had enough. You will see the necessity, I hope, of quitting Oxford—at all events, of quitting instantly my chambers."

Abased, humbled to the dust as I then was, it is probable that I should have resented this galling language by immediate personal violence, had not my whole attention been at the moment arrested by a fact of the most startling character. The cloak which I had worn was of a rare description of fur; how rare, how extravagantly costly, I shall not venture to say. Its fashion, too, was of my own fantastic invention, for I was fastidious to an absurd degree of coxcombry in matters of this frivolous nature.

When, therefore, Mr. Preston reached me that which he had picked up upon the floor, and near the folding doors of the apartment, it was with an astonishment nearly bordering upon terror, that I perceived my own already hanging on my arm (where I had no doubt unwittingly placed it), and that the one presented me was but its exact counterpart in every, in even the minutest possible particular. The singular being who had so disastrously exposed me had been muffled, I remembered, in a cloak, and none had been worn at all by any of the members of our party with the exception of myself. Retaining some presence of mind, I took the one offered me by Preston, placed it unnoticed over my own, left the apartment with a resolute scowl of defiance, and next morning, ere dawn of day, commenced a hurried journey from Oxford to the Continent in a perfect agony of horror and of shame.

I fled in vain. My evil destiny pursued me as if in exultation, and proved indeed that the exercise of its mysterious dominion had as yet only begun. Scarcely had I set foot in Paris ere I had fresh evidence of the detestable interest taken by this Wilson in my concerns. Years flew while I experienced no relief. Villain!—at Rome, with how untimely, yet with how spectral an officiousness, stepped he in between me and my ambition! At Vienna, too—at Berlin—and at Moscow! Where, in truth, had I *not* bitter cause to curse him within my heart? From his inscrutable tyranny did I at length flee, panic-stricken, as from a pestilence; and to the very ends of the earth *I fled in vain.*

And again and again, in secret communion with my own spirit, would I demand the questions "Who is he?—whence came he?—and what are his objects?" But no answer was there found. And now I scrutinised, with a minute scrutiny, the forms, and the methods, and the leading traits of his impertinent supervision. But even here there was very little upon which to base a conjecture. It was noticeable, indeed, that in no one of the multiplied instances in which he had of late crossed my path had he so crossed it except to frustrate those schemes, or to disturb those actions, which, if fully carried out, might have resulted in bitter mischief. Poor justification this, in truth, for an authority so imperiously assumed! Poor indemnity for natural rights of self-agency so pertinaciously, so insultingly denied!

I had also been forced to notice that my tormentor for a very long period of time (while scrupulously and with miraculous dexterity maintaining his whim of an identity of apparel with myself) had so contrived it, in the execution of his varied interference with my will, that I saw not at any moment the features of his face. Be Wilson what he might, *this* at least was but the veriest of affectation or of folly. Could he for an instant have supposed that in my admonisher at Eton—in the destroyer of my honour at Oxford—in him who thwarted my ambition at Rome, my revenge at Paris, my passionate love at Naples, or what he falsely termed my avarice in Egypt,—that in this, my arch-enemy and evil genius, I could fail to recognise the William Wilson of my schoolboy days,—the namesake, the companion, the rival,—the hated and dreaded rival at Dr. Bransby's? Impossible!—But let me hasten to the last eventful scene of the drama.

Thus far I had succumbed supinely to this imperious domination. The sentiment of deep awe with which I habitually regarded the elevated character, the majestic wisdom, the apparent omnipresence and omnipotence of Wilson, added to a feeling of even terror, with which certain other traits in his nature and assumptions inspired me, had operated hitherto to impress me with an idea of my own utter weakness and helplessness, and to suggest an implicit, although bitterly reluctant submission to his arbitrary will. But of late days I had given myself up entirely to wine, and its maddening influence upon my hereditary temper rendered me more and more impatient of control.

I began to murmur,—to hesitate,—to resist. And was it only fancy which induced me to believe that, with the increase of my own firmness, that of my tormentor underwent a proportional diminution? Be this as it may, I now began to feel the inspiration of a burning hope, and at length nurtured in my secret thoughts a stern and desperate resolution that I would submit no longer to be enslaved.

It was at Rome, during the Carnival of 18—, that I attended a masquerade in the *palazzo* of the Neapolitan Duke Di Broglio. I had indulged more freely than usual in the excesses of the wine-table, and now the suffocating atmosphere of the crowded rooms irritated me beyond endurance. The difficulty, too, of forcing my way through the mazes of the company contributed not a little to the ruffling of my temper; for I was anxiously seeking (let me not say with what unworthy motive) the young, the gay, the beautiful wife of the aged and doting Di Broglio. With a too unscrupulous confidence she had previously communicated to me the secret of the costume in which she would be habited, and now, having caught a glimpse of her person, I was hurrying to make my way into her presence. At this moment I felt a light hand placed upon my shoulder, and that ever-remembered, low, damnable *whisper* within my ear.

In an absolute frenzy of wrath I turned at once upon him who had thus interrupted me, and seized him violently by the collar. He was attired, as I had expected, in a costume altogether similar to my own; wearing a Spanish cloak of blue velvet, begirt about the waist with a crimson belt sustaining a rapier. A mask of black silk entirely covered his face.

"Scoundrel!" I said, in a voice husky with rage, while every syllable I uttered seemed as new fuel to my fury; "scoundrel! Impostor! accursed villain! you shall not—you *shall not* dog me unto death! Follow me, or I stab you where you stand!" and I broke my way from the ballroom into a small ante-chamber adjoining, dragging him unresistingly with me as I went.

Upon entering, I thrust him furiously from me. He staggered against the wall, while I closed the door with an oath, and commanded him to draw. He hesitated but for an instant; then, with a slight sigh, drew in silence, and put himself upon his defence.

The contest was brief indeed. I was frantic with every species of wild excitement, and felt within my single arm the energy and power of a multitude. In a few seconds I forced him by sheer strength against the wainscoting, and thus, getting him at mercy, plunged my sword, with brute ferocity, repeatedly through and through his bosom.

At that instant some person tried the latch of the door. I hastened to prevent an intrusion, and then immediately returned to my dying antagonist. But what human language can adequately portray *that* astonishment, *that* horror which possessed me at the spectacle then presented to view? The brief moment in which I averted my eyes had been sufficient to produce apparently a material change in the arrangements at the upper or farther end of the room. A large mirror—so at first it seemed to me in my confusion—now stood where none had been perceptible before; and, as I stepped up to it in extremity of terror, mine own image, but with features all pale and dabbled in blood, advanced to meet me with a feeble and tottering gait.

Thus it appeared, I say, but was not. It was my antagonist—it was Wilson who then stood before me in the agonies of his dissolution. His mask and cloak lay where he had thrown them upon the floor. Not a thread in all his raiment not a line in all the marked and singular lineaments of his face which was not, even in the most absolute identity, *mine own!*

It was Wilson; but he spoke no longer in a whisper, and I could have fancied that I myself was speaking while he said:

"You have conquered and I yield. Yet, henceforward art thou also dead—dead to the World, to Heaven, and to Hope! In me didst thou exist—and, in my death, see by this image, which is thine own l how utterly thou hast murdered thyself"

The Tell-Tale Heart

True! nervous, very, very dreadfully nervous I had been and am; but why *will* you say that I am mad? The disease had sharpened my senses, not destroyed, not dulled them. Above all was the sense of hearing acute. I heard all things in the heaven and in the earth. I heard many things in hell. How then am I mad? Hearken! and observe how healthily, how calmly, I can tell you the whole story.

It is impossible to say how first the idea entered my brain, but, once conceived, it haunted me day and night. Object there was none. Passion there was none. I loved the old man. He had never wronged me. He had never given me insult. For his gold I had no desire. I think it was his eye! Yes, it was this! One of his eyes resembled that of a vulture—a pale blue eye with a film over it. Whenever it fell upon me my blood ran cold, and so by degrees, very gradually, I made up my mind to take the life of the old man, and thus rid myself of the eye for ever.

Now this is the point. You fancy me mad. Madmen know nothing. But you should have seen *me*. You should have seen how wisely I proceeded—with what caution—with what foresight, with what dissimulation, I went to work! I was never kinder to the old man than during the whole week before I killed him. And every night about midnight I turned the latch of his door and opened it—oh, so gently! And then when I had made an opening sufficient for my head I put in a dark lantern all closed, closed so that no light shone out, and then I thrust in my head. Oh, you would have laughed to see how cunningly I thrust it in!

I moved it slowly, very, very slowly, so that I might not disturb the old man's sleep. It took me an hour to place my whole head within the opening so far that I could see him as he lay upon his bed. Ha! would a madman have been so wise as this?

And then when my head was well in the room I undid the lantern cautiously—oh, so cautiously—cautiously (for the hinges creaked), I undid it just so much that a single thin ray fell upon the vulture eye. And this I did for seven long nights, every night just at midnight, but I found the eye always closed, and so it was impossible to do the work, for it was not the old man who vexed me but his Evil Eye. And every morning, when the day broke, I went boldly into the chamber and spoke courageously to him, calling him by name in a hearty tone, and inquiring how he had passed the night. So you see he would have been a very profound old man, indeed, to suspect that every night, just at twelve, I looked in upon him while he slept.

Upon the eighth night I was more than usually cautious in opening the door. A watch's minute hand moves more quickly than did mine. Never before that night had I *felt* the extent of my own powers, of my sagacity. I could scarcely contain my feelings of triumph. To think that there I was opening the door little by little, and he not even to dream of my secret deeds or thoughts. I fairly chuckled at the idea, and perhaps he heard me, for he moved on the bed suddenly as if startled. Now you may think that I drew back—but no. His room was as black as pitch with the thick darkness (for the shutters were close fastened through fear of robbers), and so I knew that he could not see the opening of the door, and I kept pushing it on steadily, steadily.

I had my head in, and was about to open the lantern, when my thumb slipped upon the tin fastening, and the old man sprang up in the bed, crying out, "Who's there?"

I kept quite still and said nothing. For a whole hour I did not move a muscle, and in the meantime I did not hear him lie down. He was still sitting up in the bed, listening; just as I have done night after night hearkening to the death watches in the wall.

Presently I heard a slight groan, and I knew it was the groan of mortal terror. It was not a groan of pain or of grief—oh, no! it was the low stifled sound that arises from the bottom of the soul when overcharged with awe. I knew the sound well. Many a night, just at midnight, when all the world slept, it has welled up from my own bosom, deepening with its dreadful echo, the terrors that distracted me. I say I knew it well. I knew what the old man felt, and pitied him although I chuckled at heart. I knew that he had been lying awake ever since the first slight noise when he had turned in the bed. His fears had been ever since growing upon him. He had been trying to fancy them causeless, but could not. He had been saying to himself, "It is nothing but the wind in the chimney, it is only a mouse crossing the floor," or "It is merely a cricket which has made a single chirp."

Yes, he has been trying to comfort himself with these suppositions; but he had found all in vain. *All in vain*, because Death in approaching him had stalked with his black shadow before him and enveloped the victim. And it was the mournful influence of the unperceived shadow that caused him to feel, although he neither saw nor heard, to *feel* the presence of my head within the room.

When I had waited a long time very patiently without hearing him lie down, I resolved to open a little—a very very little, crevice in the lantern. So I opened it—you cannot imagine how stealthily, stealthily—until at length a single dim ray like the thread of the spider shot out from the crevice and fell upon the vulture eye.

It was open, wide, wide open, and I grew furious as I gazed upon it. I saw it with perfect distinctness—all a dull blue with a hideous veil over it that chilled the very marrow in my bones, but I could see nothing else of the old man's face or person, for I had directed the ray as if by instinct precisely upon the damned spot.

And now have I not told you that what you mistake for madness is but over-acuteness of the senses? now, I say, there came to my ears a low, dull, quick sound, such as a watch makes when enveloped in cotton. I knew *that* sound well, too. It was the beating of the old man's heart. It increased my fury, as the beating of a drum stimulates the soldier into courage.

But even yet I refrained and kept still. I scarcely breathed. I held the lantern motionless. I tried how steadily I could maintain the ray upon the eye. Meantime the hellish tattoo of the heart increased. It grew quicker and quicker, and louder and louder, every instant. The old man's terror *must* have been extreme! It grew louder, I say, louder every moment!—do you mark me well? I have told you that I am nervous: so I am. And now at the dead hour of the night, amid the dreadful silence of that old house, so strange a noise as this excited me to uncontrollable terror. Yet, for some minutes longer I refrained and stood still. But the beating grew louder, louder! I thought the heart must burst.

And now a new anxiety seized me—the sound would be heard by a neighbour! The old man's hour had come! With a loud yell, I threw open the lantern and leaped into the room. He shrieked once—once only. In an instant I dragged him to the floor, and pulled the heavy bed over him. I then smiled gaily, to find the deed so far done. But for many minutes the heart beat on with a muffled sound. This, however, did not vex me; it would not be heard through the wall. At length it ceased. The old man was dead. I removed the bed and examined the corpse. Yes, he was stone, stone dead. I placed my hand upon the heart and held it there many minutes. There was no pulsation. He was stone dead. His eye would trouble me no more.

If still you think me mad, you will think so no longer when I describe the wise precautions I took for the concealment of the body. The night waned, and I worked hastily, but in silence.

I took up three planks from the flooring of the chamber, and deposited all between the scantlings, I then replaced the boards so cleverly, so cunningly, that no human eye—not even *his*—could have detected anything wrong. There was nothing to wash out—no stain of any kind—no blood-spot whatever. I had been too wary for that.

When I had made an end of these labours, it was four o'clock—still dark as midnight. As the bell sounded the hour, there came a knocking at the street door. I went down to open it with a light heart,—for what had I *now* to fear? There entered three men, who introduced themselves, with perfect suavity, as officers of the police. A shriek had been heard by a neighbour during the night; suspicion of foul play had been aroused; information had been lodged at the police office, and they (the officers) had been deputed to search the premises.

I smiled,—for *what* had I to fear? I bade the gentlemen welcome. The shriek, I said, was my own in a dream. The old man, I mentioned, was absent in the country. I took my visitors all over the house. I bade them search—search *well*. I led them, at length, to *his* chamber. I showed them his treasures, secure, undisturbed. In the enthusiasm of my confidence, I brought chairs into the room, and desired them *here* to rest from their fatigues, while I myself, in the wild audacity of my perfect triumph, placed my own seat upon the very spot beneath which reposed the corpse of the victim.

The officers were satisfied. My *manner* had convinced them. I was singularly at ease. They sat, and while I answered cheerily, they chatted of familiar things. But, ere long, I felt myself getting pale and wished them gone. My head ached, and I fancied a ringing in my ears; but still they sat, and still chatted. The ringing became more distinct;—it continued and became more distinct: I talked more freely to get rid of the feeling: but it continued and gained definitiveness—until, at length, I found that the noise was *not* within my ears.

No doubt I now grew *very* pale;—but I talked more fluently, and with a heightened voice. Yet the sound increased and what could I do? It was *a low, dull, quick sound much such a sound as a watch makes when enveloped in cotton*. I gasped for breath—and yet the officers heard it not. I talked more quickly—more vehemently; but the noise steadily increased. I arose and argued about trifles, in a high key and with violent gesticulations; but the noise steadily increased. Why would they not be gone? I paced the floor to and fro with heavy strides, as if excited to fury by the observations of the men—but the noise steadily increased. O God! what *could* I do? I foamed—I raved—I swore! I swung the chair upon which I had been sitting, and grated it upon the boards, but the noise arose over all and continually increased. It grew louder—louder—*louder!* And still the men chatted pleasantly, and smiled. Was it possible they heard not? Almighty God!—no, no! They heard!—they suspected!—they *knew!*—they were making a mockery of my horror!—this I thought, and this I think. But anything was better than this agony! Anything was more tolerable than this derision! I could bear those hypocritical smiles no longer! I felt that I must scream or die!—and now—again!—hark! louder! louder! louder*! louder!*—

"Villains!" I shrieked, "dissemble no more! I admit the deed!—tear up the planks!—here, here!—it is the beating of his hideous heart!"

A Tale of the Ragged Mountains

During the fall of the year 1827, while residing near Charlottesville, Virginia, I casually made the acquaintance of Mr. Augustus Bedloe. This young gentleman was remarkable in every respect, and excited in me a profound interest and curiosity. I found it impossible to comprehend him either in his moral or his physical relations. Of his family I could obtain no satisfactory account. Whence he came, I never ascertained. Even about his age—although I call him a young gentleman—there was something which perplexed me in no little degree. He certainly *seemed* young—and he made a point of speaking about his youth—yet there were moments when I should have had little trouble in imagining him a hundred years of age.

But in no regard was he more peculiar than in his personal appearance. He was singularly tall and thin. He stooped much. His limbs were exceedingly long and emaciated. His forehead was broad and low. His complexion was absolutely bloodless. His mouth was large and flexible, and his teeth were more widely uneven, although sound, than I had ever before seen teeth in a human head. The expression of his smile, however, was by no means unpleasing, as might be supposed; but it had no variation whatever. It was one of profound melancholy—of a phaseless and unceasing gloom. His eyes were abnormally large, and round like those of a cat. The pupils, too, upon any accession or diminution of light, underwent contraction or dilation, just such as is observed in the feline tribe. In moments of excitement the orbs grew bright to a degree almost inconceivable; seeming to emit luminous rays, not of a reflected, but of an intrinsic lustre, as does a candle or the sun; yet their ordinary condition was so totally vapid, filmy, and dull, as to convey the idea of the eyes of a long-interred corpse.

These peculiarities of person appeared to cause him much annoyance, and he was continually alluding to them in a sort of half explanatory, half apologetic strain, which, when I first heard it, impressed me very painfully. I soon, however, grew accustomed to it, and my uneasiness wore off. It seemed to be his design rather to insinuate, than directly to assert that, physically, he had not always been what he was—that a long series of neuralgic attacks had reduced him from a condition of more than usual personal beauty, to that which I saw. For many years past he had been attended by a physician, named Templeton—an old gentleman, perhaps seventy years of age—whom he had first encountered at Saratoga, and from whose attention, while there, he either received, or fancied that he received, great benefit. The result was that Bedloe, who was wealthy, had made an arrangement with Doctor Templeton, by which the latter, in consideration of a liberal annual allowance, had consented to devote his time and medical experience exclusively to the care of the invalid.

Doctor Templeton had been a traveller in his younger days, and, at Paris, had become a convert, in great measure, to the doctrines of Mesmer. It was altogether by means of magnetic remedies that he had succeeded in alleviating the acute pains of his patient; and this success had very naturally inspired the latter with a certain degree of confidence in the opinions from which the remedies had been educed. The doctor, however like all enthusiasts, had struggled hard to make a thorough convert of his pupil, and finally so far gained his point as to induce the sufferer to submit to numerous experiments.—By a frequent repetition of these, a result had arisen, which of late days has become so common as to attract little or no attention, but which, at the period of which I write, had very rarely been known in America.

I mean to say, that between Doctor Templeton and Bedloe

there had grown up, little by little, a very distinct and strongly-marked *rapport*, or magnetic relation. I am not prepared to assert, however, that this *rapport* extended beyond the limits of the simple sleep-producing power but this power itself had attained great intensity. At the first attempt to induce the magnetic somnolency, the mesmerist entirely failed. In the fifth or sixth he succeeded very partially, and after long-continued effort. Only at the twelfth was the triumph complete. After this the will of the patient succumbed rapidly to that of the physician, so that, when I first became acquainted with the two, sleep was brought about almost instantaneously, by the mere volition of the operator, even when the invalid was unaware of his presence. It is only now, in the year 1845, when similar miracles are witnessed daily by thousands, that I dare venture to record this apparent impossibility as a matter of serious fact.

The temperament of Bedloe was, in the highest degree, sensitive, excitable, enthusiastic. His imagination was singularly vigorous and creative; and no doubt it derived additional force from the habitual use of morphine, which he swallowed in great quantity, and without which he would have found it impossible to exist. It was his practice to take a very large dose of it immediately after breakfast, each morning—or rather immediately after a cup of strong coffee, for he ate nothing in the forenoon—and then set forth alone, or attended only by a dog, upon a long ramble among the chain of wild and dreary hills that lie westward and southward of Charlottesville, and are there dignified by the title of the Ragged Mountains.

Upon a dim, warm, misty day, towards the close of November, and during the strange *interregnum* of the seasons which in America is termed the Indian Summer, Mr. Bedloe departed as usual for the hills. The day passed, and still he did not return.

About eight o'clock at night, having become seriously alarmed at his protracted absence, we were about setting out in search of him, when he unexpectedly made his appearance, in health no worse than usual, and in rather more than ordinary spirits. The account which he gave of his expedition, and of the events which had detained him, was a singular one indeed.

"You will remember," said he, "that it was about nine in the morning when I left Charlottesville. I bent my steps immediately to the mountains, and, about ten, entered a gorge which was entirely new to me. I followed the windings of this pass with much interest. The scenery which presented itself on all sides, although scarcely entitled to be called grand, had about it an indescribable, and to me, a delicious aspect of dreary desolation. The solitude seemed absolutely virgin. I could not help believing that the green sods and the grey rocks upon which I trod had never before been trodden by the foot of a human being. So entirely secluded, and in fact inaccessible, except through a series of accidents, is the entrance of the ravine, that it is by no means impossible that I was indeed the first adventurer—the very first and sole adventurer—who had ever penetrated its recesses.

"The thick and peculiar mist or smoke which distinguishes the Indian Summer, and which now hung heavily over all objects, served no doubt to deepen the vague impressions which these objects created. So dense was this pleasant fog that I could at no time see more than a dozen yards of the path before me. This path was excessively sinuous, and as the sun could not be seen, I soon lost all idea of the direction in which I journeyed. In the meantime the morphine had its customary effect—that of enduing all the external world with an intensity of interest. In the quivering of a leaf—in the hue of a blade of grass—in the shape of a trefoil—in the humming of a bee—in the gleaming of a dewdrop—in the breathing of the wind—in the faint odours that came from the forest—there came a whole universe of suggestion—a gay and motley train of rhapsodical and immethodical thought.

"Busied in this, I walked on for several hours, during which the mist deepened around me to so great an extent that at length I was reduced to an absolute groping of the way. And now an indescribable uneasiness possessed me—a species of nervous hesitation and tremor,—I feared to tread, lest I should be precipitated into some abyss. I remembered, too, strange stories told about these Ragged Hills, and of the uncouth and fierce races of men who tenanted their groves and caverns. A thousand vague fancies oppressed and disconcerted me—fancies the more distressing because vague. Very suddenly my attention was arrested by the loud beating of a drum.

"My amazement was, of course, extreme. A drum in these hills was a thing unknown. I could not have been more surprised at the sound of the trump of the Archangel. But a new and still more astounding source of interest and perplexity arose. There came a wild rattling or jingling sound, as if of a bunch of large keys—and upon the instant a dusky-visaged and half-naked man rushed past me with a shriek. He came so close to my person that I felt his hot breath upon my face. He bore in one hand an instrument composed of an assemblage of steel rings, and shook them vigorously as he ran. Scarcely had he disappeared in the mist, before, panting after him, with open mouth and glaring eyes, there darted a huge beast. I could not be mistaken in its character. It was a hyena.

"The sight of this monster rather relieved than heightened my terrors—for I now made sure that I dreamed, and endeavoured to arouse myself to waking consciousness. I stepped boldly and briskly forward. I rubbed my eyes. I called aloud. I pinched my limbs. A small spring of water presented itself to my view, and here stooping, I bathed my hands and my head and neck. This seemed to dissipate the equivocal sensations which had hitherto annoyed me. I arose, as I thought, a new man, and proceeded steadily and complacently on my unknown way.

"At length, quite overcome by exertion, and by a certain oppressive closeness of the atmosphere, I seated myself beneath a tree. Presently there came a feeble gleam of sunshine, and the shadow of the leaves of the tree fell faintly but definitely upon the grass. At this shadow I gazed wonderingly for many minutes. Its character stupefied me with astonishment. I looked upward. The tree was a palm.

"I now arose hurriedly and in a state of fearful agitation—for the fancy that I dreamed would serve me no longer. I saw—I felt that I had perfect command of my senses—and these senses now brought to my soul a world of novel and singular sensation. The heat became all at once intolerable. A strange odour loaded the breeze.—A low continuous murmur, like that arising from a full but gently-flowing river, came to my ears, intermingled with the peculiar hum of multitudinous human voices.

"While I listened in an extremity of astonishment which I need not attempt to describe, a strong and brief gust of wind bore off the incumbent fog as if by the wand of an enchanter.

"I found myself at the foot of a high mountain, and looking down into a vast plain, through which wound a majestic river. On the margin of this river stood an Eastern-looking city, such as we read of in the *Arabian Tales,* but of a character even more singular than any there described. From my position, which was far above the level of the town, I could perceive its every nook and corner, as if delineated on a map. The streets seemed innumerable, and crossed each other irregularly, in all directions, but were rather long winding alleys than streets, and absolutely swarmed with inhabitants. The houses were wildly picturesque. On every hand was a wilderness of balconies, of verandahs, of minarets, of shrines, and fantastically carved oriels. Bazaars abounded; and in these were displayed rich wares in infinite variety and profusion—silks, muslins, the most dazzling cutlery, the most magnificent jewels and gems.

"Besides these things, were seen on all sides, banners and *palanquins,* litters with stately dames close veiled, elephants gorgeously caparisoned, idols grotesquely hewn, drums, banners and gongs, spears, silver and gilded maces. And amid the crowd, and the clamour, and the general intricacy and confusion— amid the million of black and yellow men, turbaned and robed, and of flowing beard, there roamed a countless multitude of holy filleted bulls, while vast legions of the filthy but sacred ape clambered, chattering and shrieking, about the cornices of the mosques, or clung to the minarets and oriels.

"From the swarming streets to the banks of the river there descended innumerable flights of steps leading to bathing-places, while the river itself seemed to force a passage with difficulty through the vast fleets of deeply-burthened ships that far and wide encumbered its surface. Beyond the limits of the city arose, in frequent majestic groups, the palm and the cocoa, with other gigantic and weird trees of vast age; and here and there might be seen a field of rice, the thatched hut of a peasant, a tank, a stray temple, a gipsy camp, or a solitary graceful maiden taking her way, with a pitcher upon her head, to the banks of the magnificent river.

"You will say now, of course, that I dreamed; but not so. What I saw—what I heard—what I felt—what I thought—had about it nothing of the unmistakable idiosyncrasy of the dream. All was rigorously self-consistent. At first doubting that I was really awake, I entered into a series of tests which soon convinced me that I really was. Now, when one dreams, and in the dream suspects that he dreams, the suspicion *never fails to confirm itself*, and the sleeper is almost immediately aroused. Thus Novalis errs not in saying that 'we are near waking when we dream that we dream.' Had the vision occurred to me as I describe it, without my suspecting it as a dream, then a dream it might absolutely have been, but occurring as it did, and suspected and tested as it was,t I am forced to class it among other phenomena."

"In this I am not sure that you are wrong," observed Dr. Templeton, "but proceed. You arose and descended into the city."

"I arose," continued Bedloe, regarding the doctor with an air of profound astonishment, "I arose, as you say, and descended into the city. On my way, I fell in with an immense populace, crowding through every avenue, all in the same direction, and exhibiting in every action the wildest excitement. Very suddenly, and by some inconceivable impulse, I became intensely imbued with personal interest in what was going on. I seemed to feel that I had an important part to play, without exactly understanding what it was. Against the crowd which environed me, however, I experienced a deep sentiment of animosity. I shrank from amid them, and, swiftly, by a circuitous path, reached and entered the city. Here all was the wildest tumult and contention.

"A small party of men, clad in garments half Indian, half European, and officered by gentlemen in a uniform partly British, were engaged, at great odds, with the swarming rabble of the alleys. I joined the weaker party, arming myself with the weapons of a fallen officer, and fighting I knew not whom with the nervous ferocity of despair. We were soon overpowered by numbers, and driven to seek refuge in a species of kiosk. Here we barricaded ourselves, and, for the present, were secure. From a loophole near the summit of the kiosk, I perceived a vast crowd, in furious agitation, surrounding and assaulting a gay palace that overhung the river. Presently, from an upper window of this palace, there descended an effeminate-looking person, by means of a string made of the turbans of his attendants. A boat was at hand, in which he escaped to the opposite bank of the river.

"And now a new object took possession of my soul I spoke a few hurried but energetic words to my companions, and, having succeeded in gaining over a few of them to my purpose, made a frantic sally from the kiosk. We rushed amid the crowd that surrounded it. They retreated at first before us. They rallied, fought madly, and retreated again. In the meantime we were borne far from the kiosk, and became bewildered and entangled among the narrow streets of tall overhanging houses, into the recesses of which the sun had never been able to shine. The rabble pressed impetuously upon us, harassing us with their spears, and overwhelming us with flights of arrows. These latter were very remarkable, and resembled in some respects the writhing creese of the Malay. They were made to imitate the body of a creeping servant, and were long and black, with a poisoned barb. One of them struck me upon the right temple. I reeled and fell. An instantaneous and dreadful sickness seized me. I struggled—I gasped—I died. "

"You will hardly persist *now*," said I, smiling, "that the whole of your adventure was not a dream. You are not prepared to maintain that you are dead?"

When I said these words, I of course expected some lively sally from Bedloe in reply; but, to my astonishment, he hesitated, trembled, became fearfully pallid, and remained silent. I looked towards Templeton. He sat erect and rigid in his chair—his teeth chattered, and his eyes were starting from their sockets. "Proceed!" he at length said hoarsely to Bedloe.

"For many minutes," continued the latter, "my sole sentiment—my sole feeling—was that of darkness and nonentity, with the consciousness of death. At length there seemed to pass a violent and sudden shock through my soul, as if of electricity. With it came the sense of elasticity and of light. This latter I felt—not saw. In an instant I seemed to rise from the ground. But I had no bodily, no visible, audible, or palpable presence. The crowd had departed. The tumult had ceased. The city was in comparative repose. Beneath me lay my corpse, with the arrow in my temple, the whole head greatly swollen and disfigured. But all these things I felt—not saw. I took interest in nothing.

"Even the corpse seemed a matter in which I had no concern. Volition I had none, but appeared to be impelled into motion, and flitted buoyantly out of the city, retracing the circuitous path by which I had entered it. When I had attained that point of the ravine in the mountains at which I had encountered the hyena, I again experienced a shock as of a galvanic battery; the sense of weight, of volition, of substance, returned. I became my original self, and bent my steps eagerly homewards—but the past had not lost the vividness of the real—and not now, even for an instant, can I compel my understanding to regard it as a dream."

"Nor was it," said Templeton, with an air of deep solemnity, "yet it would be difficult to say how otherwise it should be termed. Let us suppose only, that the soul of the man of today is upon the verge of some stupendous psychal discoveries. Let us content ourselves with this supposition. For the rest I have some explanation to make. Here is a water-colour drawing which I should have shown you before, but which an unaccountable sentiment of horror has hitherto prevented me from showing."

We looked at the picture which he presented I saw nothing in it of an extraordinary character; but its effect upon Bedloe was prodigious. He nearly fainted as he gazed. And yet it was but a miniature portrait—a miraculously accurate one, to be sure—of his own very remarkable features. At least this was my thought as I regarded it.

"You will perceive," said Templeton, "the date of this picture—it is here, scarcely visible, in this corner—1780. In this year was the portrait taken. It is the likeness of a dead friend—a Mr. Oldeb—to whom I became much attached at Calcutta, during the administration of Warren Hastings. I was then only twenty years old. When I first saw you, Mr. Bedloe, at Saratoga, it was the miraculous similarity which existed between yourself and the painting which induced me to accost you, to seek your friendship, and to bring about those arrangements which resulted in my becoming your constant companion. In accomplishing this point I was urged partly, and perhaps principally, by a regretful memory of the deceased, but also, in part, by an uneasy and not altogether horrorless curiosity respecting yourself.

"In your detail of the vision which presented itself to you amid the hills, you have described, with the minutest accuracy, the Indian city of Benares upon the Holy River. The riots, the combats, the massacre, were the actual events of the insurrection of Cheyte Sing, which took place in 1780, when Hastings was put in imminent peril of his life. The man escaping by the string of turbans was Cheyte Sing himself. The party in the kiosk were *sepoys* and British officers headed by Hastings. Of this party I was one, and did all I could to prevent the rash and fatal sally of the officer who fell, in the crowded alleys, by the poisoned arrow of a Bengalee. That officer was my dearest friend. It was Oldeb. You will perceive by these manuscripts" (here the speaker produced a note-book in which several pages appeared to have been freshly written) "that at the very period in which you fancied these things amid the hills, I was engaged in detailing them upon paper here at home."

In about a week after this conversation, the following paragraphs appeared in a Charlottesville paper:—

We have the painful duty of announcing the death of Mr. Augustus Bedlo, a gentleman whose amiable manners and many virtues have long endeared him to the citizens of

Charlottesville.

Mr. B., for some years past, has been subject to neural-gia, which has often threatened to terminate fatally; but this can be regarded only as the mediate cause of his de-cease. The proximate cause was one of especial singularity. In an excursion to the Ragged Mountains, a few days since, a slight cold and fever were contracted, attended with great determination of blood to the head. To relieve this, Dr. Templeton resorted to topical bleeding. Leeches were applied to the temples. In a fearfully brief period the patient died, when it appeared that, in the jar contain-ing the leeches, had been introduced, by accident, one of the venomous *vermicular sangsues* which are now and then found in the neighbouring ponds. This creature fastened itself upon a small artery in the right temple. Its close re-semblance to the medicinal leech caused the mistake to be overlooked until too late.

N.B. The poisonous *sangsue* of Charlottesville may always be distinguished from the medicinal leech by its black-ness, and especially by its writhing or vermicular motions, which very nearly resemble those of a snake.

I was speaking with the editor of the paper in question, upon the topic of this remarkable accident, when it occurred to me to ask how it happened that the name of the deceased had been given as Bedlo.

"I presume," said I, "you have authority for this spelling, but I have always supposed the name to be written with an *e* at the end."

"Authority?—no," he replied. "It is a mere typographical er-ror. The name is Bedlo with an *e*, all the world over, and I never knew it to be spelt otherwise in my life."

"Then," said I mutteringly, as I turned upon my heel, "then indeed has it come to pass that one truth is stranger than any fic-tion—for Bedlo without the *e*, what is it but Oldeb conversed? And this man tells me it is a typographical error."

Bon-Bon

That Pierre Bon-Bon was a *restaurateur* of uncommon qualifications, no man who, during the reign of ———, frequented the
little *câfe* in the *cul-de-sac* Le Febre at Rouen, will, I imagine,
feel himself at liberty to dispute. That Pierre Bon-Bon was, in
an equal degree, skilled in the philosophy of that period is, I
presume, still more especially undeniable. His *patés à la fois* were
beyond doubt immaculate—but what pen can do justice to his
essays *sur la Nature*—his thoughts *sur l'Ame*—his observations
sur l'Esprit? If his *omelettes*—if his *fricandeaux* were inestimable,
what *littérateur* of that day would not have given twice as much
for an '*Idée de Bon-Bon*' as for all the trash of all the '*Idées*' of all
the rest of the savants?

Bon-Bon had ransacked libraries which no other man had
ransacked—had read more than any other would have entertained a notion of reading—had understood more than any other would have conceived the possibility of understanding; and
although, while he flourished, there were not wanting some authors at Rouen, to assert "that his *dicta* evinced neither the purity
of the academy, nor the depth of the Lyceum"— although, mark
me, his doctrines were by no means very generally comprehended, still it did not follow that they were difficult of comprehension. It was, I think, on account of their entire self-evidency
that many persons were led to consider them abstruse.

It is to Bon-Bon—but let this go no farther—it is to Bon-
Bon that Kant himself is mainly indebted for his metaphysics.
The former was not indeed a Platonist, nor strictly speaking

an Aristotelian—nor did he, like the modern Leibnitz, waste those precious hours which might be employed in the invention of a *fricassaée*, or, *facili gradu*, the analysis of a sensation, in frivolous attempts at reconciling the obstinate oils and waters of ethical discussion. Not at all. Bon-Bon was Ionic. Bon-Bon was equally Italic. He reasoned *à priori*. He reasoned also *à posteriori*. His ideas were innate—or otherwise. He believed in George of Trebizond. He believed in Bossarion. Bon-Bon was emphatically a—Bon-Bonist.

I have spoken of the philosopher in his capacity of *restaurateur*. I would not, however, have any friend of mine imagine that in fulfilling his hereditary duties in that line, our hero wanted a proper estimation of their dignity and importance. Far from it. It was impossible to say in which branch of his duplicate profession he took the greater pride. In his opinion the powers of the mind held intimate connection with the capabilities of the stomach. I am not sure, indeed, that he greatly disagreed with the Chinese, who held that the soul lies in the abdomen. The Greeks at all events were right, he thought, who employed the same word for the mind and the diaphragm, (Φρενες.). By this I do not mean to insinuate a charge of gluttony, or indeed any other serious charge to the prejudice of the metaphysician. If Pierre Bon-Bon had his failings—and what great man has not a thousand?— if Pierre Bon-Bon, I say, had his failings, they were failings of very little importance—faults indeed which in other tempers have often been looked upon rather in the light of virtues. As regards one of these foibles, I should not have mentioned it in this history but for the remarkable prominency—the extreme *alto relievo*—in which it jutted out from the plane of his general disposition. He could never let slip an opportunity of making a bargain.

Not that he was avaricious—no. It was by no means necessary to the satisfaction of the philosopher, that the bargain should be to his own proper advantage. Provided a trade could be effected—a trade of any kind, upon any terms, or under any circumstances, a triumphant smile was seen for many days thereafter to enlighten his countenance, and a knowing wink of the eye to give evidence of his sagacity.

At any epoch it would not be very wonderful if a humour so peculiar as the one I have just mentioned, should elicit attention and remark. At the epoch of our narrative, had this peculiarity *not* attracted observation, there would have been room for wonder indeed. It was soon reported that upon all occasions of the kind, the smile of Bon-Bon was wont to differ widely from the downright grin with which he would laugh at his own jokes, or welcome an acquaintance. Hints were thrown out of an exciting nature—stories were told of perilous bargains made in a hurry and repented of at leisure—and instances were adduced of unaccountable capacities, vague longings, and unnatural inclinations implanted by the author of all evil for wise purposes of his own.

The philosopher had other weaknesses—but they are scarcely worthy of our serious examination. For example, there are few men of extraordinary profundity who are found wanting in an inclination for the bottle. Whether this inclination be an exciting cause, or rather a valid proof, of such profundity, it is impossible to say. Bon-Bon, as far as I can learn, did not think the subject adapted to minute investigation—nor do I. Yet in the indulgence of a propensity so truly classical, it is not to be supposed that the restaurateur would lose sight of that intuitive discrimination which was wont to characterise, at one and the same time, his *essais* and his *omelettes*.

In his seclusions the Vin de Bourgogne had its allotted hour, and there were appropriate moments for the Côtes du Rhone. With him Sauterne was to Medoc what Catullus was to Homer. He would sport with a syllogism in sipping St. Peray, but unravel an argument over Clos de Vougeot, and upset a theory in a torrent of Chambertin. Well had it been if the same quick sense of propriety had attended him in the peddling propensity to which I have formerly alluded—but this was by no means the case. Indeed, to say the truth, *that* trait of mind in the philosophic Bon-Bon *did* begin at length to assume a character of strange intensity and mysticism, and, however singular it may seem, appeared deeply tinctured with the grotesque *diablerie* of his favourite German studies.

To enter the little *café* in the *cul-de-sac* Le Febre was, at the period of our tale, to enter the *sanctum* of a man of genius. Bon-Bon was a man of genius. There was not a *sous-cuisinier* in Rouen, who could not have told you that Bon-Bon was a man of genius. His very cat knew it, and forbore to whisk her tail in the presence of the man of genius. His large water-dog was acquainted with the fact, and upon the approach of his master, betrayed his sense of inferiority by a sanctity of deportment, a debasement of the ears, and a dropping of the lower jaw not altogether unworthy of a dog. It is, however, true that much of this habitual respect might have been attributed to the personal appearance of the metaphysician.

A distinguished exterior will, I am constrained to say, have its weight even with a beast; and I am willing to allow much in the outward man of the *restaurateur* calculated to impress the imagination of the quadruped. There is a peculiar majesty about the atmosphere of the little great—if I may be permitted so equivocal an expression—which mere physical bulk alone will be found at all times inefficient in creating. If, however, Bon-Bon was barely three feet in height, and if his head was diminutively small, still it was impossible to behold the rotundity of his stomach without a sense of magnificence nearly bordering upon the sublime. In its size both dogs and men must have seen a type of his acquirements—in its immensity a fitting habitation for his immortal soul.

I might here—if it so pleased me—dilate upon the matter of habiliment, and other mere circumstances of the external metaphysician. I might hint that the hair of our hero was worn short, combed smoothly over his forehead, and surmounted by a conical-shaped white flannel cap and tassels—that his pea-green jerkin was not after the fashion of those worn by the common class of *restaurateurs* at that day—that the sleeves were something fuller than the reigning costume permitted—that the cuffs were turned up, not as usual in that barbarous period, with cloth of the same quality and colour as the garment, but faced in a more fanciful manner with the parti-coloured velvet of Genoa—that his slippers were of a bright purple, curiously filagreed, and might have been manufactured in Japan, but for the exquisite pointing of the toes, and the brilliant tints of the binding and embroidery—that his breeches were of the yellow satin-like material called *aimable*—that his sky-blue cloak, resembling in form a dressing-wrapper, and richly bestudded all over with crimson devices, floated cavalierly upon his shoulders like a mist of the morning—and that his *tout ensemble* gave rise to the remarkable words of Benevenuta, the Improvisatrice of Florence, "that it was difficult to say whether Pierre Bon-Bon was indeed a bird of Paradise, or the rather a very Paradise of perfection."

I have said that "to enter the *café* in the *cul-de-sac* Le Febre was to enter the *sanctum* of a man of genius"—but then it was only the man of genius who could duly estimate the merits of the sanctum. A sign consisting of a vast folio swung before the entrance. On one side of the volume was painted a bottle—on the reverse a *pâté*. On the back were visible in large letters the words *Œuvres de Bon-Bon.* Thus was delicately shadowed forth the two-fold occupation of the proprietor.

Upon stepping over the threshold the whole interior of the building presented itself to view. A long, low-pitched room, of antique construction, was indeed all the accommodation afforded by the *café*. In a corner of the apartment stood the bed of the metaphysician. An array of curtains, together with a canopy *à la Gréque*, gave it an air at once classic and comfortable. In the corner diagonally opposite, appeared, in direct and friendly communion, the properties of the kitchen and the *bibliothèque*. A dish of polemics stood peacefully upon the dresser. Here lay an oven-full of the latest ethics—there a kettle of *duodecimo melanges*. Volumes of German morality were hand and glove with the gridiron—a toasting fork might be discovered by the side of Eusebius—Plato reclined at his ease in the frying pan—and contemporary manuscripts were filed away upon the spit.

In other respects the *Café de Bon-Bon* might be said to differ little from the *restaurants* of the period. A gigantic fireplace yawned opposite the door. On the right of the fire-place an open cupboard displayed a formidable array of labelled bottles.

It was here, about twelve o'clock one night, during the severe winter of ——, that Pierre Bon-Bon, after having listened for some time to the comments of his neighbours upon his singular propensity—that Pierre Bon-Bon, I say, having turned them all out of his house, locked the door upon them with a *sacre Dieu*, and betook himself in no very pacific mood to the comforts of a leather-bottomed armchair, and a fire of blazing faggots.

It was one of those terrific nights which are only met with once or twice during a century. The snow drifted down bodily in enormous masses, and the house tottered to its very centre, with the floods of wind that, rushing through the crannies in the wall, and pouring impetuously down the chimney, shook awfully the curtains of the philosopher's bed, and disorganized the economy of his *paté*-pans and papers. The huge folio sign that swung without, exposed to the fury of the tempest, creaked ominously, and gave out a moaning sound from its stanchions of solid oak.

I have said that it was in no very placid temper the metaphysician drew up his chair to its customary station by the hearth. Many circumstances of a perplexing nature had occurred during the day, to disturb the serenity of his meditations. In attempting *des oeufs à la Princesse* he had unfortunately perpetrated an *omelette à la Reine*—the discovery of a principle in ethics had been frustrated by the overturning of a stew—and last, not least, he had been thwarted in one of those admirable bargains which he at all times took such especial delight in bringing to a successful termination. But in the chafing of his mind at these unaccountable vicissitudes, there did not fail to be mingled some degree of that nervous anxiety which the fury of a boisterous night is so well calculated to produce.

Whistling to his more immediate vicinity the large black water-dog we have spoken of before, and settling himself uneasily in his chair, he could not help casting a wary and unquiet eye towards those distant recesses of the apartment whose inexorable shadows not even the red firelight itself could more than partially succeed in overcoming. Having completed a scrutiny whose exact purpose was perhaps unintelligible to himself, he drew closer to his seat a small table covered with books and papers, and soon became absorbed in the task of retouching a voluminous manuscript, intended for publication on the morrow.

"I am in no hurry, Monsieur Bon-Bon"—whispered a whining voice in the apartment.

"The devil!"—ejaculated our hero, starting to his feet, overturning the table at his side, and staring around him in astonishment.

"Very true"—calmly replied the voice.

"Very true!—what is very true?—how came you here?"—vociferated the metaphysician, as his eye fell upon something which lay stretched at full length upon the bed.

"I was saying"—said the intruder, without attending to the interrogatories—I was saying that I am not at all pushed for time— that the business upon which I took the liberty of calling is of no pressing importance—in short that I can very well wait until you have finished your Exposition."

"My Exposition!—there now!—how do *you* know—how came *you* to understand that I was writing an Exposition?—good God!"

"Hush!"—replied the figure in a shrill under tone: and, arising quickly from the bed, he made a single step towards our hero, while the iron lamp overhead swung convulsively back from his approach.

The philosopher's amazement did not prevent a narrow scrutiny of the stranger's dress and appearance. The outlines of a figure, exceedingly lean, but much above the common height, were rendered minutely distinct by means of a faded suit of black cloth which fitted tight to the skin, but was otherwise cut very much in the style of a century ago. These garments had evidently been intended for a much shorter person than their present owner. His ankles and wrists were left naked for several inches. In his shoes, however, a pair of very brilliant buckles gave the lie to the extreme poverty implied by the other portions of his dress. His head was bare, and entirely bald, with the exception of the hinder part, from which depended a *queue* of considerable length. A pair of green spectacles, with side glasses, protected his eyes from the influence of the light, and at the same time prevented our hero from ascertaining either their colour or their conformation.

About the entire person there was no evidence of a shirt; but a white cravat, of filthy appearance, was tied with extreme precision around the throat, and the ends, hanging down formally side by side, gave, (although I dare say unintentionally), the idea of an ecclesiastic. Indeed, many other points both in his appearance and demeanour might have very well sustained a conception of that nature. Over his left ear he carried, after the fashion of a modern clerk, an instrument resembling the *stylus* of the ancients. In a breast-pocket of his coat appeared conspicuously a small black volume fastened with clasps of steel. This book, whether accidentally or not, was so turned outwardly from the person as to discover the words "*Rituel Catholique*" in white letters upon the back.

His entire physiognomy was interestingly saturnine—even cadaverously pale. The forehead was lofty, and deeply furrowed with the ridges of contemplation. The corners of the mouth were drawn down into an expression of the most submissive humility. There was also a clasping of the hands, as he stepped towards our hero—a deep sigh—and altogether a look of such utter sanctity as could not have failed to be unequivocally prepossessing. Every shadow of anger faded from the countenance of the metaphysician, as, having completed a satisfactory survey of his visitor's person, he shook him cordially by the hand, and conducted him to a seat.

There would however be a radical error in attributing this instantaneous transition of feeling in the philosopher to any one of those causes which might naturally be supposed to have had an influence. Indeed Pierre Bon-Bon, from what I have been able to understand of his disposition, was of all men the least likely to be imposed upon by any speciousness of exterior deportment. It was impossible that so accurate an observer of men and things should have failed to discover, upon the moment, the real character of the personage who had thus intruded upon his hospitality.

To say no more, the conformation of his visitor's feet was sufficiently remarkable—there was a tremulous swelling in the hinder part of his breeches—and the vibration of his coat tail was a palpable fact. Judge then with what feelings of satisfaction our hero found himself thrown thus at once into the society of a—of a person for whom he had at all times entertained such unqualified respect. He was, however, too much of the diplomatist to let escape him any intimation of his suspicions, or rather—I should say—his certainty in regard to the true state of affairs. It was not his cue to appear at all conscious of the high honour he thus unexpectedly enjoyed, but by leading his guest into conversation, to elicit some important ethical ideas which might, in obtaining a place in his contemplated publication, enlighten the human race, and at the same time immortalize himself—ideas which, I should have added, his visitor's great age, and well known proficiency in the science of morals, might very well have enabled him to afford.

Actuated by these enlightened views our hero bade the gentleman sit down, while he himself took occasion to throw some faggots upon the fire, and place upon the now re-established table some bottles of *Mousseux*. Having quickly completed these operations, he drew his chair *vis-à-vis* to his companion's, and waited until he should open the conversation. But plans even the most skilfully matured are often thwarted in the outset of their application, and the *restaurateur* found himself entirely *nonplussed* by the very first words of his visitor's speech.

"I see you know me, Bon-Bon,"—said he:—"ha! ha! ha!—he! he! he!—hi! hi! hi!—ho! ho! ho!—hu! hu! hu!"—and the devil, dropping at once the sanctity of his demeanour, opened to its fullest extent a mouth from ear to ear, so as to display a set of jagged and fang-like teeth, and throwing back his head, laughed long, loud, wickedly, and uproariously, while the black dog, crouching down upon his haunches, joined lustily in the chorus, and the tabby cat, flying off at a tangent, stood up on end and shrieked in the farthest corner of the apartment.

Not so the philosopher: he was too much a man of the world either to laugh like the dog, or by shrieks to betray the indecorous trepidation of the cat. It must be confessed, however, that he felt a little astonishment to see the white letters which formed the words "*Rituel Catholique*" on the book in his guest's pocket, momently changing both their colour and their import, and in a few seconds in place of the original title, the words "*Régitre des Condamnés*" blaze forth in characters of red. This startling circumstance, when Bon-Bon replied to his visitor's remark, imparted to his manner an air of embarrassment which might not probably have otherwise been observable.

"Why, sir,"—said the philosopher—"why, sir, to speak sincerely—I believe you are—upon my word—the d—dest—that is to say I think—I imagine—I *have* some faint—some *very* faint idea—of the remarkable honour—"

"Oh!—ah!—yes!—very well!"—interrupted his majesty— "say no more—I see how it is." And hereupon, taking off his green spectacles, he wiped the glasses carefully with the sleeve of his coat, and deposited them in his pocket.

If Bon-Bon had been astonished at the incident of the book, his amazement was now much increased by the spectacle which here presented itself to view. In raising his eyes, with a strong feeling of curiosity to ascertain the colour of his guest's, he found them by no means black, as he had anticipated—nor gray, as might have been imagined—nor yet hazel nor blue—nor indeed yellow, nor red—nor purple—nor white—nor green—nor any other colour in the heavens above, or in the earth beneath, or in the waters under the earth.

In short, Pierre Bon-Bon not only saw plainly that His Majesty had no eyes whatsoever, but could discover no indications of their having existed at any previous period—for the space where eyes should naturally have been, was, I am constrained to say, simply a dead level of flesh.

It was not in the nature of the metaphysician to forbear making some inquiry into the sources of so strange a phenomenon, and to his surprise the reply of His Majesty was at once prompt, dignified, and satisfactory.

"Eyes!—my dear Bon-Bon, eyes! did you say?—oh! ah! I perceive. The ridiculous prints, eh? which are in circulation, have given you a false idea of my personal appearance. Eyes!!—true. Eyes, Pierre Bon- Bon, are very well in their proper place—*that*, you would say, is the head—right—the head of a worm. To *you* likewise these optics are indispensable—yet I will convince you that my vision is more penetrating than your own. There is a cat, I see, in the corner—a pretty cat!—look at her!—observe her well. Now, Bon-Bon, do you behold the thoughts—the thoughts, I say—the ideas—the reflections—engendering in her pericranium? There it is now!—you do not. She is thinking we admire the profundity of her mind. She has just concluded that I am the most distinguished of ecclesiastics, and that you are the most superfluous of metaphysicians. Thus you see I am not altogether blind: but to one of my profession the eyes you speak of would be merely an encumbrance, liable at any time to be put out by a toasting iron or a pitchfork. To you, I allow, these optics are indispensable. Endeavour, Bon-Bon, to use them well—*my* vision is the soul."

Hereupon the guest helped himself to the wine upon the table, and pouring out a bumper for Bon-Bon, requested him to drink it without scruple, and make himself perfectly at home.

"A clever book that of yours, Pierre"—resumed his majesty, tapping our friend knowingly upon the shoulder, as the latter put down his glass after a thorough compliance with his visitor's injunction. "A clever book that of yours, upon my honour. It's a work after my own heart. Your arrangement of matter, I think, however, might be improved, and many of your notions remind me of Aristotle. That philosopher was one of my most intimate acquaintances. I liked him as much for his terrible ill temper, as for his happy knack at making a blunder. There is only one solid truth in all that he has written, and for that I gave him the hint out of pure compassion for his absurdity. I suppose, Pierre Bon-Bon, you very well know to what divine moral truth I am alluding."

"Cannot say that I—"

"Indeed!—why I told Aristotle that by sneezing men expelled superfluous ideas through the proboscis."

"Which is—hiccup!—undoubtedly the case"—said the metaphysician, while he poured out for himself another bumper of *Mousseux*, and offered his snuff-box to the fingers of his visitor.

"There was Plato, too"—continued his majesty, modestly declining the snuff-box and the compliment—"there was Plato, too, for whom I, at one time, felt all the affection of a friend. You knew, Plato, Bon-Bon?—ah! no, I beg a thousand pardons. He met me at Athens, one day, in the Parthenon, and told me he was distressed for an idea. I bade him write down that ὁ νοῦς ἐστιν αὐλος.

He said that he would do so, and went home, while I stepped over to the Pyramids. But my conscience smote me for the lie, and hastening back to Athens, I arrived behind the philosopher's chair as he was inditing the ' αὐλος. ' Giving the gamma a fillip with my finger I turned it upside down.

So the sentence now reads ' ὁ νοῦς ἐστιν   αὐλος, ,' and is, you perceive, the fundamental doctrine of his metaphysics."

"Were you ever at Rome?"—asked the *restaurateur* as he finished his second bottle of Mousseux, and drew from the closet a larger supply of Vin de Chambertin.

"But once, Monsieur Bon-Bon—but once. There was a time"—said the devil, as if reciting some passage from a book— "there was a time when occurred an anarchy of five years during which the republic, bereft of all its officers, had no magistracy besides the tribunes of the people, and these were not legally vested with any degree of executive power'—at that time, Monsieur Bon-Bon—at that time *only* I was in Rome, and I have no earthly acquaintance, consequently, with any of its philosophy."[1]

"What do you think of Epicurus?—what do you think of—(hiccup!)—Epicurus?"

"What do I think of *whom?*"—said the devil in astonishment—"you cannot surely mean to find any fault with Epicurus! What do I think of Epicurus! Do you mean me, sir?—I am Epicurus. I am the same philosopher who wrote each of the three hundred treatises commemorated by Diogenes Laertes."

"That's a lie!"—said the metaphysician, for the wine had gotten a little into his head.

"Very well!—very well, sir!—very well indeed, sir"—said His Majesty.

"That's a lie!"—repeated the *restaurateur* dogmatically—"that's a—(hiccup!)—lie!"

"Well, well! have it your own way"—said the devil pacifically: and Bon-Bon, having beaten his majesty at an argument, thought it his duty to conclude a second bottle of Chambertin.

"As I was saying"—resumed the visitor—"as I was observing a little while ago, there are some very *outre* notions in that book of yours, Monsieur Bon-Bon. What, for instance, do you mean by all that humbug about the soul? Pray, sir, what is the soul?"

"The—(hiccup!)—soul"—replied the metaphysician, referring to his MS.—"is undoubtedly—"

"No, sir!"

"Indubitably—"

"No, sir!"

"Indisputably—"

"No, sir!"

"Evidently—"

"No, sir!"

"Incontrovertibly—"

"No, sir!"

"Hiccup!—"

---

1. *Ils ecrivaient sur la Philosophie (Cicero, Lucretius, Seneca) mais c'etait la Philosophie Grecque.*—Condorcet.

"No, sir!"

"And beyond all question a—"

"No, sir! the soul is no such thing." (Here the philosopher finished his third bottle of Chambertin.)

"Then—(hic-cup!)—pray—sir—what—what is it?"

"That is neither here nor there, Monsieur BonBon," replied His Majesty, musingly. "I have tasted—that is to say I have known some very bad souls, and some too—pretty good ones." Here the devil licked his lips, and, having unconsciously let fall his hand upon the volume in his pocket, was seized with a violent fit of sneezing.

His majesty continued.

"There was the soul of Cratinus—passable:—Aristophanes—racy:—Plato—exquisite:—not *your* Plato, but Plato the comic poet: your Plato would have turned the stomach of Cerberus—faugh! Then let me see! there were Noevius, and Andronicus, and Plautus, and Terentius. Then there were Lucilius, and Catullus, and Naso, and Quintius Flaccus—dear Quinty! as I called him when he sung a *seculare* for my amusement, while I toasted him in pure good humour on a fork. But they want *flavour* these Romans. One fat Greek is worth a dozen of them, and besides will *keep*, which cannot be said of a Quirite. Let us taste your Sauterne."

Bon-Bon had by this time made up his mind to the *nil admirari*, and endeavoured to hand down the bottles in question. He was, however, conscious of a strange sound in the room like the wagging of a tail. Of this, although extremely indecent in His Majesty, the philosopher took no notice—simply kicking the black water-dog and requesting him to be quiet. The visitor continued.

"I found that Horace tasted very much like Aristotle—you know I am fond of variety. Terentius I could not have told from Menander. Naso, to my astonishment, was Nicander in disguise. Virgilius had a strong twang of Theocritus. Martial put me much in mind of Archilochus—and Titus Livy was positively Polybius and none other."

"Hic—cup!"—here replied Bon-Bon, and his majesty proceeded.

"But if I *have* a *penchant*, Monsieur Bon-Bon,—if I *have* a *penchant*, it is for a philosopher. Yet, let me tell you, sir, it is not every dev—I mean it is not every gentleman who knows how to *choose* a philosopher. Long ones are *not* good; and the best, if not carefully shelled, are apt to be a little rancid on account of the gall."

"Shelled!!"

"I mean taken out of the carcass."

"What do you think of a—(hiccup!)—physician?"

"*Don't* mention them!—ugh! ugh!" (Here his majesty retched violently.) "I never tasted but one—that rascal Hippocrates!—smelt of *asafoetida*—ugh! ugh! ugh!—caught a wretched cold washing him in the Styx—and after all he gave me the *cholera-morbus*."

"The—(hiccup!)—wretch!"—ejaculated BonBon—"the—(hic-cup!)—abortion of a pill-box!"—and the philosopher dropped a tear.

"After all"—continued the visitor—"after all, if a dev—if a gentleman wishes to *live* he must have more talents than one or two; and with us a fat face is an evidence of diplomacy."

"How so?"

"Why we are sometimes exceedingly pushed for provisions. You must know that in a climate so sultry as mine, it is frequently impossible to keep a spirit alive for more than two or three hours; and after death, unless pickled immediately, (and a pickled spirit is *not* good,) they will—smell—you understand, eh? Putrefaction is always to be apprehended when the spirits are consigned to us in the usual way."

"(Hiccup!—hiccup!)—good God! how *do* you manage?"

Here the iron lamp commenced swinging with redoubled violence, and the devil half started from his seat—however, with a slight sigh, he recovered his composure, merely saying to our hero in a low tone, "I tell you what, Pierre Bon-Bon, we *must* have no more swearing."

Bon-Bon swallowed another bumper, and his visitor continued.

"Why there are *several* ways of managing. The most of us starve: some put up with the pickle. For my part I purchase my spirits *vivente corpore,* in which case I find they keep very well."

"But the body!—(hiccup!)—the body!!!"—vociferated the philosopher, as he finished a bottle of Sauterne.

"The body, the body—well, what of the body?—oh! ah! I perceive. Why, sir, the body is not *at all* affected by the transaction. I have made innumerable purchases of the kind in my day, and the parties never experienced any inconvenience. There were Cain, and Nimrod, and Nero, and Caligula, and Dionysius, and Pisistratus, and—and a thousand others, who never knew what it was to have a soul during the latter part of their lives; yet, sir, these men adorned society. Why is'nt there A——, now, whom you know as well as I? Is *he* not in possession of all his faculties, mental and corporeal? Who writes a keener epigram? Who reasons more wittily? Who—but, stay! I have his agreement in my pocket-book."

Thus saying, he produced a red leather wallet, and took from it a number of papers. Upon some of these Bon-Bon caught a glimpse of the letters *Machi—Maza—Robesp*—with the words *Caligul, George, Elizabeth.* His majesty selected a narrow slip of parchment, and from it read aloud the following words:

"In consideration of certain mental endowments which it is unnecessary to specify, and in farther consideration of one thousand *louis d'or,* I, being aged one year and one month, do hereby make over to the bearer of this agreement all my right, title, and appurtenance in the shadow called my soul. (Signed) A——."[2] (Here his majesty repeated a name which I do not feel myself justifiable in indicating more unequivocally.)

"A clever fellow that."—resumed he; "but like you, Monsieur Bon-Bon, he was mistaken about the soul. The soul a shadow truly!—no such nonsense, Monsieur Bon-Bon. The soul a shadow!! ha! ha! ha!—he! he! he!—hu! hu! hu! Only think of a

2. Quere-Aroue?

fricasséed shadow!"

"*Only* think—(hiccup!)—of a *fricasséed* shadow!!" echoed our hero, whose faculties were becoming gloriously illuminated by the profundity of His Majesty's discourse.

"Only think of a—(hiccup!)—*fricasséed* shadow!!! Now, damme!—(hiccup!)—humph!—if *I* would have been such a—(hiccup!)—nincompoop. My soul, Mr.—humph!"

"*Your* soul, Monsieur Bon-Bon?"

"Yes, sir—(hiccup!)—*my* soul is—"

"What, sir?"

"*No* shadow, damme!"

"Did not mean to say—"

"Yes, sir, *my* soul is—(hiccup!)—humph!—yes, sir."

"Did not intend to assert—"

"*My* soul is—(hiccup!)—peculiarly qualified for—(hiccup!)—a—"

"What, sir?"

"Stew."

"Ha!"

"*Souflée.*"

"Eh?"

"*Fricassée.*"

"Indeed!"

"*Ragout* or *fricandeau*—and see here!—I'll let you have it—(hiccup!)—a bargain." Here the philosopher slapped His majesty upon the back.

"Could'nt think of such a thing," said the latter calmly, at the same time arising from his seat. The metaphysician stared.

"Am supplied at present," said His Majesty.

"(Hiccup!)—e-h?"—said the philosopher.

"Have no funds on hand."

"What?"

"Besides, very unhandsome in me—"

"Sir!"

"To take advantage of—"

"(Hiccup!)"

"Your present disgusting and ungentlemanly situation."

Here the visitor bowed and withdrew—in what manner could not precisely be ascertained—but in a well-concerted effort to discharge a bottle at "the villain," the slender chain was severed that depended from the ceiling, and the metaphysician prostrated by the downfall of the lamp.

Eleonora

Sub conservatione formae specificae salva anima.
—Raymond Lully.

I am come of a race noted for vigour of fancy and ardour of passion. Men have called me mad; but the question is not yet settled, whether madness is or is not the loftiest intelligence— whether much that is glorious—whether all that is profound— does not spring from disease of thought—from *moods* of mind exalted at the expense of the general intellect. They who dream by day are cognizant of many things which escape those who dream only by night. In their gray visions they obtain glimpses of eternity, and thrill, in awakening, to find that they have been upon the verge of the great secret. In snatches, they learn something of the wisdom which is of good, and more of the mere knowledge which is of evil. They penetrate, however, rudderless or compassless into the vast ocean of the "light ineffable," and again, like the adventures of the Nubian geographer, "*agressi sunt mare tenebrarum, quid in eo esset exploraturi.*"

We will say, then, that I am mad. I grant, at least, that there are two distinct conditions of my mental existence—the condition of a lucid reason, not to be disputed, and belonging to the memory of events forming the first epoch of my life—and a condition of shadow and doubt, appertaining to the present, and to the recollection of what constitutes the second great era of my being. Therefore, what I shall tell of the earlier period, believe; and to what I may relate of the later time, give only such credit as may seem due, or doubt it altogether, or, if doubt it ye cannot, then play unto its riddle the Œdipus.

She whom I loved in youth, and of whom I now pen calmly and distinctly these remembrances, was the sole daughter of the only sister of my mother long departed. Eleonora was the name of my cousin. We had always dwelled together, beneath a tropical sun, in the Valley of the Many-Coloured Grass. No unguided footstep ever came upon that vale; for it lay away up among a range of giant hills that hung beetling around about it, shutting out the sunlight from its sweetest recesses. No path was trodden in its vicinity; and, to reach our happy home, there was need of putting back, with force, the foliage of many thousands of forest trees, and of crushing to death the glories of many millions of fragrant flowers. Thus it was that we lived all alone, knowing nothing of the world without the valley—I, and my cousin, and her mother.

From the dim regions beyond the mountains at the upper end of our encircled domain, there crept out a narrow and deep river, brighter than all save the eyes of Eleonora; and, winding stealthily about in mazy courses, it passed away, at length, through a shadowy gorge, among hills still dimmer than those whence it had issued. We called it the "River of Silence"; for there seemed to be a hushing influence in its flow. No murmur arose from its bed, and so gently it wandered along, that the pearly pebbles upon which we loved to gaze, far down within its bosom, stirred not at all, but lay in a motionless content, each in its own old station, shining on gloriously forever.

The margin of the river, and of the many dazzling rivulets that glided through devious ways into its channel, as well as the spaces that extended from the margins away down into the depths of the streams until they reached the bed of pebbles at the bottom,—these spots, not less than the whole surface of the valley, from the river to the mountains that girdled it in, were carpeted all by a soft green grass, thick, short, perfectly even, and vanilla-perfumed, but so besprinkled throughout with the yellow buttercup, the white daisy, the purple violet, and the ruby-red asphodel, that its exceeding beauty spoke to our hearts in loud tones, of the love and of the glory of God.

And, here and there, in groves about this grass, like wilder-nesses of dreams, sprang up fantastic trees, whose tall slender stems stood not upright, but slanted gracefully toward the light that peered at noon-day into the centre of the valley. Their mark was speckled with the vivid alternate splendour of ebony and silver, and was smoother than all save the cheeks of Eleonora; so that, but for the brilliant green of the huge leaves that spread from their summits in long, tremulous lines, dallying with the Zephyrs, one might have fancied them giant serpents of Syria doing homage to their sovereign the Sun.

Hand in hand about this valley, for fifteen years, roamed I with Eleonora before Love entered within our hearts. It was one evening at the close of the third lustrum of her life, and of the fourth of my own, that we sat, locked in each other's embrace, beneath the serpent-like trees, and looked down within the wa-ter of the River of Silence at our images therein. We spoke no words during the rest of that sweet day, and our words even upon the morrow were tremulous and few. We had drawn the God Eros from that wave, and now we felt that he had enkindled within us the fiery souls of our forefathers.

The passions which had for centuries distinguished our race, came thronging with the fancies for which they had been equal-ly noted, and together breathed a delirious bliss over the Val-ley of the Many-Coloured Grass. A change fell upon all things. Strange, brilliant flowers, star-shaped, burn out upon the trees where no flowers had been known before. The tints of the green carpet deepened; and when, one by one, the white daisies shrank away, there sprang up in place of them, ten by ten of the ruby-red asphodel. And life arose in our paths; for the tall flamingo, hitherto unseen, with all gay glowing birds, flaunted his scarlet plumage before us. The golden and silver fish haunted the river, out of the bosom of which issued, little by little, a murmur that swelled, at length, into a lulling melody more divine than that of the harp of Æolus-sweeter than all save the voice of Eleonora.

And now, too, a voluminous cloud, which we had long

watched in the regions of Hesper, floated out thence, all gorgeous in crimson and gold, and settling in peace above us, sank, day by day, lower and lower, until its edges rested upon the tops of the mountains, turning all their dimness into magnificence, and shutting us up, as if forever, within a magic prison-house of grandeur and of glory.

The loveliness of Eleonora was that of the Seraphim; but she was a maiden artless and innocent as the brief life she had led among the flowers. No guile disguised the fervour of love which animated her heart, and she examined with me its inmost recesses as we walked together in the Valley of the Many-Coloured Grass, and discoursed of the mighty changes which had lately taken place therein.

At length, having spoken one day, in tears, of the last sad change which must befall Humanity, she thenceforward dwelt only upon this one sorrowful theme, interweaving it into all our converse, as, in the songs of the bard of Schiraz, the same images are found occurring, again and again, in every impressive variation of phrase.

She had seen that the finger of Death was upon her bosom—that, like the ephemeron, she had been made perfect in loveliness only to die; but the terrors of the grave to her lay solely in a consideration which she revealed to me, one evening at twilight, by the banks of the River of Silence. She grieved to think that, having entombed her in the Valley of the Many-Coloured Grass, I would quit forever its happy recesses, transferring the love which now was so passionately her own to some maiden of the outer and everyday world. And, then and there, I threw myself hurriedly at the feet of Eleonora, and offered up a vow, to herself and to Heaven, that I would never bind myself in marriage to any daughter of Earth—that I would in no manner prove recreant to her dear memory, or to the memory of the devout affection with which she had blessed me.

And I called the Mighty Ruler of the Universe to witness the pious solemnity of my vow. And the curse which I invoked of *Him* and of her, a saint in Helusion should I prove traitorous to that promise, involved a penalty the exceeding great horror of which will not permit me to make record of it here. And the bright eyes of Eleonora grew brighter at my words; and she sighed as if a deadly burthen had been taken from her breast; and she trembled and very bitterly wept; but she made acceptance of the vow, (for what was she but a child?) and it made easy to her the bed of her death. And she said to me, not many days afterward, tranquilly dying, that, because of what I had done for the comfort of her spirit she would watch over me in that spirit when departed, and, if so it were permitted her return to me visibly in the watches of the night; but, if this thing were, indeed, beyond the power of the souls in Paradise, that she would, at least, give me frequent indications of her presence, sighing upon me in the evening winds, or filling the air which I breathed with perfume from the censers of the angels. And, with these words upon her lips, she yielded up her innocent life, putting an end to the first epoch of my own.

Thus far I have faithfully said. But as I pass the barrier in Time's path, formed by the death of my beloved, and proceed with the second era of my existence, I feel that a shadow gathers over my brain, and I mistrust the perfect sanity of the record. But let me on.—Years dragged themselves along heavily, and still I dwelled within the Valley of the Many-Coloured Grass; but a second change had come upon all things. The star-shaped flowers shrank into the stems of the trees, and appeared no more. The tints of the green carpet faded; and, one by one, the ruby-red asphodels withered away; and there sprang up, in place of them, ten by ten, dark, eye-like violets, that writhed uneasily and were ever encumbered with dew.

And Life departed from our paths; for the tall flamingo flaunted no longer his scarlet plumage before us, but flew sadly from the vale into the hills, with all the gay glowing birds that had arrived in his company. And the golden and silver fish swam down through the gorge at the lower end of our domain and be-decked the sweet river never again. And the lulling melody that had been softer than the wind-harp of Æolus, and more divine than all save the voice of Eleonora, it died little by little away, in murmurs growing lower and lower, until the stream returned, at length, utterly, into the solemnity of its original silence. And then, lastly, the voluminous cloud uprose, and, abandoning the tops of the mountains to the dimness of old, fell back into the regions of Hesper, and took away all its manifold golden and gorgeous glories from the Valley of the Many-Coloured Grass.

Yet the promises of Eleonora were not forgotten; for I heard the sounds of the swinging of the censers of the angels; and streams of a holy perfume floated ever and ever about the valley; and at lone hours, when my heart beat heavily, the winds that bathed my brow came unto me laden with soft sighs; and indistinct murmurs filled often the night air, and once—oh, but once only! I was awakened from a slumber, like the slumber of death, by the pressing of spiritual lips upon my own.

But the void within my heart refused, even thus, to be filled. I longed for the love which had before filled it to overflowing. At length the valley pained me through its memories of Eleonora, and I left it for ever for the vanities and the turbulent triumphs of the world.

I found myself within a strange city, where all things might have served to blot from recollection the sweet dreams I had dreamed so long in the Valley of the Many-Coloured Grass. The pomps and pageantries of a stately court, and the mad clangour of arms, and the radiant loveliness of women, bewildered and intoxicated my brain. But as yet my soul had proved true to its vows, and the indications of the presence of Eleonora were still given me in the silent hours of the night. Suddenly these manifestations they ceased, and the world grew dark before mine eyes, and I stood aghast at the burning thoughts which possessed, at the terrible temptations which beset me; for there came from some far, far distant and unknown land, into the gay court of the king I served, a maiden to whose beauty my whole recreant heart yielded at once—at whose footstool I bowed down without a struggle, in the most ardent, in the most abject worship of love.

What, indeed, was my passion for the young girl of the valley in comparison with the fervour, and the delirium, and the spirit-lifting ecstasy of adoration with which I poured out my whole soul in tears at the feet of the ethereal Ermengarde?—Oh, bright was the seraph Ermengarde! and in that knowledge I had room for none other.—Oh, divine was the angel Ermengarde! and as I looked down into the depths of her memorial eyes, I thought only of them—and of her.

I wedded;—nor dreaded the curse I had invoked; and its bitterness was not visited upon me. And once—but once again in the silence of the night; there came through my lattice the soft sighs which had forsaken me; and they modelled themselves into familiar and sweet voice, saying:

Sleep in peace!—for the Spirit of Love reigneth and ruleth, and, in taking to thy passionate heart her who is Ermengarde, thou art absolved, for reasons which shall be made known to thee in Heaven, of thy vows unto Eleonora.

Four Beasts in One—The Homo-Cameleopard

Chacun a ses vertus.
—Crebillon's Xerxes.

Antiochus Epiphanes is very generally looked upon as the Gog of the prophet Ezekiel. This honour is, however, more properly attributable to Cambyses, the son of Cyrus. And, indeed, the character of the Syrian monarch does by no means stand in need of any adventitious embellishment. His accession to the throne, or rather his usurpation of the sovereignty, a hundred and seventy-one years before the coming of Christ; his attempt to plunder the temple of Diana at Ephesus; his implacable hostility to the Jews; his pollution of the Holy of Holies; and his miserable death at Taba, after a tumultuous reign of eleven years, are circumstances of a prominent kind, and therefore more generally noticed by the historians of his time than the impious, dastardly, cruel, silly, and whimsical achievements which make up the sum total of his private life and reputation.

✶✶✶✶✶✶

Let us suppose, gentle reader, that it is now the year of the world three thousand eight hundred and thirty, and let us, for a few minutes, imagine ourselves at that most grotesque habitation of man, the remarkable city of Antioch. To be sure there were, in Syria and other countries, sixteen cities of that appellation, besides the one to which I more particularly allude. But *ours* is that which went by the name of Antiochia Epidaphne, from its vicinity to the little village of Daphne, where stood a temple to that divinity. It was built (although about this matter there is some dispute) by Seleucus Nicanor, the first king of the country after Alexander the Great, in memory of his father Antiochus, and became immediately the residence of the Syrian monarchy. In the flourishing times of the Roman Empire, it was the ordinary station of the prefect of the eastern provinces; and many of the emperors of the queen city (among whom may be mentioned, especially, Verus and Valens) spent here the greater part of their time. But I perceive we have arrived at the city itself. Let us ascend this battlement, and throw our eyes upon the town and neighbouring country.

"What broad and rapid river is that which forces its way, with innumerable falls, through the mountainous wilderness, and finally through the wilderness of buildings?"

That is the Orontes, and it is the only water in sight, with the exception of the Mediterranean, which stretches, like a broad mirror, about twelve miles off to the southward. Every one has seen the Mediterranean; but let me tell you, there are few who have had a peep at Antioch. By few, I mean, few who, like you and me, have had, at the same time, the advantages of a modern education. Therefore cease to regard that sea, and give your whole attention to the mass of houses that lie beneath us. You will remember that it is now the year of the world three thousand eight hundred and thirty. Were it later—for example, were it the year of our Lord eighteen hundred and forty-five, we should be deprived of this extraordinary spectacle.

In the nineteenth century Antioch is—that is to say, Antioch *will be*—in a lamentable state of decay. It will have been, by that time, totally destroyed, at three different periods, by three successive earthquakes. Indeed, to say the truth, what little of its former self may then remain, will be found in so desolate and ruinous a state that the patriarch shall have removed his residence to Damascus. This is well. I see you profit by my advice, and are making the most of your time in inspecting the premises—in

—satisfying your eyes

266

With the memorials and the things of fame
That most renown this city.—

I beg pardon; I had forgotten that Shakespeare will not flourish for seventeen hundred and fifty years to come. But does not the appearance of Epidaphne justify me in calling it *grotesque?*

"It is well fortified; and in this respect is as much indebted to nature as to art."

Very true.

"There are a prodigious number of stately palaces."

There are.

"And the numerous temples, sumptuous and magnificent, may bear comparison with the most lauded of antiquity."

All this I must acknowledge. Still there is an infinity of mud huts, and abominable hovels. We cannot help perceiving abundance of filth in every kennel, and, were it not for the over-powering fumes of idolatrous incense, I have no doubt we should find a most intolerable stench. Did you ever behold streets so insufferably narrow, or houses so miraculously tall? What gloom their shadows cast upon the ground! It is well the swinging lamps in those endless colonnades are kept burning throughout the day; we should otherwise have the darkness of Egypt in the time of her desolation.

"It is certainly a strange place! What is the meaning of yonder singular building? See! it towers above all others, and lies to the eastward of what I take to be the royal palace."

That is the new Temple of the Sun, who is adored in Syria under the title of Elah Gabalah. Hereafter a very notorious Roman Emperor will institute this worship in Rome, and thence derive a cognomen, Heliogabalus. I dare say you would like to take a peep at the divinity of the temple. You need not look up at the heavens; his Sunship is not there—at least not the Sunship adored by the Syrians. *That* deity will be found in the interior of yonder building. He is worshipped under the figure of a large stone pillar terminating at the summit in a cone or *pyramid*, whereby is denoted Fire.

"Hark—behold!—who *can* those ridiculous beings be, half

267

naked, with their faces painted, shouting and gesticulating to the rabble?"

Some few are mountebanks. Others more particularly belong to the race of philosophers. The greatest portion, however—those especially who belabour the populace with clubs—are the principal courtiers of the palace, executing as in duty bound, some laudable comicality of the king's.

"But what have we here? Heavens! the town is swarming with wild beasts! How terrible a spectacle!—how dangerous a peculiarity!"

Terrible, if you please; but not in the least degree dangerous. Each animal if you will take the pains to observe, is following, very quietly, in the wake of its master. Some few, to be sure, are led with a rope about the neck, but these are chiefly the lesser or timid species. The lion, the tiger, and the leopard are entirely without restraint. They have been trained without difficulty to their present profession, and attend upon their respective owners in the capacity of *valets-de-chambre*. It is true, there are occasions when Nature asserts her violated dominions;—but then the devouring of a man-at-arms, or the throttling of a consecrated bull, is a circumstance of too little moment to be more than hinted at in Epidaphne.

"But what extraordinary tumult do I hear? Surely this is a loud noise even for Antioch! It argues some commotion of unusual interest."

Yes—undoubtedly. The king has ordered some novel spectacle—some gladiatorial exhibition at the hippodrome—or perhaps the massacre of the Scythian prisoners—or the conflagration of his new palace—or the tearing down of a handsome temple—or, indeed, a bonfire of a few Jews. The uproar increases. Shouts of laughter ascend the skies. The air becomes dissonant with wind instruments, and horrible with clamour of a million throats. Let us descend, for the love of fun, and see what is going on! This way—be careful! Here we are in the principal street, which is called the street of Timarchus. The sea of people is coming this way, and we shall find a difficulty in stemming the tide. They are pouring through the alley of Heraclides, which leads directly from the palace;—therefore the king is most probably among the rioters.

Yes;—I hear the shouts of the herald proclaiming his approach in the pompous phraseology of the East. We shall have a glimpse of his person as he passes by the temple of Ashimah. Let us ensconce ourselves in the vestibule of the sanctuary; he will be here *anon*. In the meantime let us survey this image. What is it? Oh! it is the god Ashimah in proper person. You perceive, however, that he is neither a lamb, nor a goat, nor a satyr, neither has he much resemblance to the Pan of the Arcadians. Yet all these appearances have been given—I beg pardon—*will* be given—by the learned of future ages, to the Ashimah of the Syrians. Put on your spectacles, and tell me what it is. What is it?

"Bless me! it is an ape!"

True—a baboon; but by no means the less a deity. His name is a derivation of the Greek *Simia*—what great fools are antiquarians! But see!—see!—yonder scampers a ragged little urchin. Where is he going? What is he bawling about? What does he say? Oh! he says the king is coming in triumph; that he is dressed in state; that he has just finished putting to death, with his own hand, a thousand chained Israelitish prisoners! For this exploit the ragamuffin is lauding him to the skies. Hark! here comes a troop of a similar description. They have made a Latin hymn upon the valor of the king, and are singing it as they go:

Mille, mille, mille,
Mille, mille, mille,
Decollavimus, unus homo!
Mille, mille, mille, mille, decollavimus!
Mille, mille, mille,
Vivat qui mille mille occidit!
Tantum vini habet nemo
Quantum sanguinis effudit![1]

---

1. Flavius Vospicus says, that the hymn here introduced was sung by the rabble upon the occasion of Aurelian, in the Sarmatic war, having slain, with his own hand, nine hundred and fifty of the enemy.

Which may be thus paraphrased:

A thousand, a thousand, a thousand,
A thousand, a thousand, a thousand,
We, with one warrior, have slain!
A thousand, a thousand, a thousand, a thousand.
Sing a thousand over again!
Soho!—let us sing
Long life to our king,
Who knocked over a thousand so fine!
Soho!—let us roar,
He has given us more
Red gallons of gore
Than all Syria can furnish of wine!

"Do you hear that flourish of trumpets?"

Yes: the king is coming! See! the people are aghast with admiration, and lift up their eyes to the heavens in reverence. He comes;—he is coming;—there he is!

"Who?—where?—the king?—do not behold him—cannot say that I perceive him."

Then you must be blind.

"Very possible. Still I see nothing but a tumultuous mob of idiots and madmen, who are busy in prostrating themselves before a gigantic cameleopard, and endeavouring to obtain a kiss of the animal's hoofs. See! the beast has very justly kicked one of the rabble over—and another—and another—and another. Indeed, I cannot help admiring the animal for the excellent use he is making of his feet."

Rabble, indeed!—why these are the noble and free citizens of Epidaphne! Beasts, did you say?—take care that you are not overheard. Do you not perceive that the animal has the visage of a man? Why, my dear sir, that cameleopard is no other than Antiochus Epiphanes, Antiochus the Illustrious, King of Syria, and the most potent of all the autocrats of the East! It is true, that he is entitled, at times, Antiochus Epimanes—Antiochus the madman—but that is because all people have not the capacity to appreciate his merits. It is also certain that he is at present ensconced in the hide of a beast, and is doing his best to play the part of a cameleopard; but this is done for the better sustaining his dignity as king. Besides, the monarch is of gigantic stature, and the dress is therefore neither unbecoming nor over large.

We may, however, presume he would not have adopted it but for some occasion of especial state. Such, you will allow, is the massacre of a thousand Jews. With how superior a dignity the monarch perambulates on all fours! His tail, you perceive, is held aloft by his two principal concubines, Elline and Argelais; and his whole appearance would be infinitely prepossessing, were it not for the protuberance of his eyes, which will certainly start out of his head, and the queer colour of his face, which has become nondescript from the quantity of wine he has swallowed. Let us follow him to the hippodrome, whither he is proceeding, and listen to the song of triumph which he is commencing:

Who is king but Epiphanes?
Say—do you know?
Who is king but Epiphanes?
Bravo!—bravo!
There is none but Epiphanes,
No—there is none:
So tear down the temples,
And put out the sun!

Well and strenuously sung! The populace are hailing him 'Prince of Poets,' as well as 'Glory of the East,' 'Delight of the Universe,' and 'Most Remarkable of Cameleopards.' They have *encored* his effusion, and do you hear?—he is singing it over again. When he arrives at the hippodrome, he will be crowned with the poetic wreath, in anticipation of his victory at the approaching Olympics.

"But, good Jupiter! what is the matter in the crowd behind us?"

Behind us, did you say?—oh! ah!—I perceive. My friend, it is well that you spoke in time. Let us get into a place of safety as soon as possible. Here!—let us conceal ourselves in the arch of this aqueduct, and I will inform you presently of the origin of the commotion. It has turned out as I have been anticipating. The singular appearance of the cameleopard and the head of a man, has, it seems, given offence to the notions of propriety entertained, in general, by the wild animals domesticated in the city.

A mutiny has been the result; and, as is usual upon such occasions, all human efforts will be of no avail in quelling the mob. Several of the Syrians have already been devoured; but the general voice of the four-footed patriots seems to be for eating up the cameleopard. 'The Prince of Poets,' therefore, is upon his hinder legs, running for his life. His courtiers have left him in the lurch, and his concubines have followed so excellent an example. 'Delight of the Universe,' thou art in a sad predicament! 'Glory of the East,' thou art in danger of mastication!

Therefore never regard so piteously thy tail; it will undoubtedly be draggled in the mud, and for this there is no help. Look not behind thee, then, at its unavoidable degradation; but take courage, ply thy legs with vigour, and scud for the hippodrome! Remember that thou art Antiochus Epiphanes. Antiochus the Illustrious!—also 'Prince of Poets,' 'Glory of the East,' 'Delight of the Universe,' and 'Most Remarkable of Cameleopards!' Heavens! what a power of speed thou art displaying! What a capacity for leg-bail thou art developing! Run, Prince!—Bravo, Epiphanes! Well done, Cameleopard!—Glorious Antiochus!—He runs!— he leaps!—he flies! Like an arrow from a catapult he approaches the hippodrome! He leaps!—he shrieks!—he is there!

This is well; for hadst thou, 'Glory of the East,' been half a second longer in reaching the gates of the Amphitheatre, there is not a bear's cub in Epidaphne that would not have had a nibble at thy carcase. Let us be off—let us take our departure!—for we shall find our delicate modern ears unable to endure the vast uproar which is about to commence in celebration of the king's escape! Listen! it has already commenced. See!—the whole town is topsy-turvy.

"Surely this is the most populous city of the East! What a wilderness of people! what a jumble of all ranks and ages! what a multiplicity of sects and nations! what a variety of costumes! what a Babel of languages! what a screaming of beasts! what a tinkling of instruments! what a parcel of philosophers!"

Come let us be off.

"Stay a moment! I see a vast hubbub in the hippodrome; what is the meaning of it, I beseech you?"

That?—oh, nothing! The noble and free citizens of Epidaphne being, as they declare, well satisfied of the faith, valour, wisdom, and divinity of their king, and having, moreover, been eye-witnesses of his late superhuman agility, do think it no more than their duty to invest his brows (in addition to the poetic crown) with the wreath of victory in the footrace—a wreath which it is evident he must obtain at the celebration of the next Olympiad, and which, therefore, they now give him in advance.

Hop-Frog

A.k.a. *The Eight Chained Orang-utans*

I never knew anyone so keenly alive to a joke as the king was. He seemed to live only for joking. To tell a good story of the joke kind, and to tell it well, was the surest road to his favour. Thus it happened that his seven ministers were all noted for their accomplishments as jokers. They all took after the king, too, in being large, corpulent, oily men, as well as inimitable jokers. Whether people grow fat by joking, or whether there is something in fat itself which predisposes to a joke, I have never been quite able to determine; but certain it is that a lean joker is a *rara avis in terris.*

About the refinements, or, as he called them, the 'ghost' of wit, the king troubled himself very little. He had an especial admiration for *breadth* in a jest, and would often put up with *length*, for the sake of it. Over-niceties wearied him. He would have preferred Rabelais' 'Gargantua' to the 'Zadig' of Voltaire: and, upon the whole, practical jokes suited his taste far better than verbal ones.

At the date of my narrative, professing jesters had not altogether gone out of fashion at court. Several of the great continental 'powers' still retain their 'fools,' who wore motley, with caps and bells, and who were expected to be always ready with sharp witticisms, at a moment's notice, in consideration of the crumbs that fell from the royal table.

Our king, as a matter of course, retained his 'fool.' The fact is, he *required* something in the way of folly—if only to counterbalance the heavy wisdom of the seven wise men who were his ministers—not to mention himself.

His fool, or professional jester, was not *only* a fool, however. His value was trebled in the eyes of the king, by the fact of his being also a dwarf and a cripple. Dwarfs were as common at court, in those days, as fools; and many monarchs would have found it difficult to get through their days (days are rather longer at court than elsewhere) without both a jester to laugh *with*, and a dwarf to laugh *at*. But, as I have already observed, your jesters, in ninety-nine cases out of a hundred, are fat, round, and unwieldy—so that it was no small source of self-gratulation with our king that, in Hop-Frog (this was the fool's name), he possessed a triplicate treasure in one person.

I believe the name 'Hop-Frog' was *not* that given to the dwarf by his sponsors at baptism, but it was conferred upon him, by general consent of the several ministers, on account of his inability to walk as other men do. In fact, Hop-Frog could only get along by a sort of interjectional gait—something between a leap and a wriggle—a movement that afforded illimitable amusement, and of course consolation, to the king, for (notwithstanding the protuberance of his stomach and a constitutional swelling of the head) the king, by his whole court, was accounted a capital figure.

But although Hop-Frog, through the distortion of his legs, could move only with great pain and difficulty along a road or floor, the prodigious muscular power which nature seemed to have bestowed upon his arms, by way of compensation for deficiency in the lower limbs, enabled him to perform many feats of wonderful dexterity, where trees or ropes were in question, or any thing else to climb. At such exercises he certainly much more resembled a squirrel, or a small monkey, than a frog.

I am not able to say, with precision, from what country Hop-Frog originally came. It was from some barbarous region, however, that no person ever heard of—a vast distance from the court of our king. Hop-Frog, and a young girl very little less dwarfish than himself (although of exquisite proportions, and a marvellous dancer), had been forcibly carried off from their respective homes in adjoining provinces, and sent as presents to the king, by one of his ever-victorious generals.

Under these circumstances, it is not to be wondered at that a close intimacy arose between the two little captives. Indeed, they soon became sworn friends. Hop-Frog, who, although he made a great deal of sport, was by no means popular, had it not in his power to render Trippetta many services; but *she*, on account of her grace and exquisite beauty (although a dwarf), was universally admired and petted; so she possessed much influence; and never failed to use it, whenever she could, for the benefit of Hop-Frog.

On some grand state occasion—I forgot what—the king determined to have a masquerade, and whenever a masquerade or any thing of that kind, occurred at our court, then the talents, both of Hop-Frog and Trippetta were sure to be called into play. Hop-Frog, in especial, was so inventive in the way of getting up pageants, suggesting novel characters, and arranging costumes, for masked balls, that nothing could be done, it seems, without his assistance.

The night appointed for the *fête* had arrived. A gorgeous hall had been fitted up, under Trippetta's eye, with every kind of device which could possibly give *éclat* to a masquerade. The whole court was in a fever of expectation. As for costumes and characters, it might well be supposed that everybody had come to a decision on such points. Many had made up their minds (as to what *rôles* they should assume) a week, or even a month, in advance; and, in fact, there was not a particle of indecision anywhere—except in the case of the king and his seven minsters. Why *they* hesitated I never could tell, unless they did it by way of a joke. More probably, they found it difficult, on account of being so fat, to make up their minds. At all events, time flew; and, as a last resort they sent for Trippetta and Hop-Frog.

When the two little friends obeyed the summons of the king they found him sitting at his wine with the seven members of his cabinet council; but the monarch appeared to be in a very ill humour. He knew that Hop-Frog was not fond of wine, for it excited the poor cripple almost to madness; and madness is no comfortable feeling. But the king loved his practical jokes, and took pleasure in forcing Hop-Frog to drink and (as the king called it) 'to be merry.'

"Come here, Hop-Frog," said he, as the jester and his friend entered the room; "swallow this bumper to the health of your absent friends, (here Hop-Frog sighed,) and then let us have the benefit of your invention. We want characters—*characters*, man—something novel—out of the way. We are wearied with this everlasting sameness. Come, drink! the wine will brighten your wits."

Hop-Frog endeavoured, as usual, to get up a jest in reply to these advances from the king; but the effort was too much. It happened to be the poor dwarf's birthday, and the command to drink to his 'absent friends' forced the tears to his eyes. Many large, bitter drops fell into the goblet as he took it, humbly, from the hand of the tyrant.

"Ah! ha! ha!" roared the latter, as the dwarf reluctantly drained the beaker.—"See what a glass of good wine can do! Why, your eyes are shining already!"

Poor fellow! his large eyes *gleamed*, rather than shone; for the effect of wine on his excitable brain was not more powerful than instantaneous. He placed the goblet nervously on the table, and looked round upon the company with a half—insane stare. They all seemed highly amused at the success of the king's '*joke*.'

"And now to business," said the prime minister, a *very* fat man.

"Yes," said the king; "Come lend us your assistance. Characters, my fine fellow; we stand in need of characters—all of us—ha! ha! ha!" and as this was seriously meant for a joke, his laugh was chorused by the seven.

Hop-Frog also laughed although feebly and somewhat vacantly.

"Come, come," said the king, impatiently, "have you nothing to suggest?"

"I am endeavouring to think of something *novel*," replied the dwarf, abstractedly, for he was quite bewildered by the wine.

"Endeavouring!" cried the tyrant, fiercely; "what do you mean by *that*? Ah, I perceive. You are Sulky, and want more wine. Here, drink this!" and he poured out another goblet full and offered it to the cripple, who merely gazed at it, gasping for breath.

"Drink, I say!" shouted the monster, "or by the fiends—"

The dwarf hesitated. The king grew purple with rage. The courtiers smirked. Trippetta, pale as a corpse, advanced to the monarch's seat, and, falling on her knees before him, implored him to spare her friend.

The tyrant regarded her, for some moments, in evident wonder at her audacity. He seemed quite at a loss what to do or say—how most becomingly to express his indignation. At last, without uttering a syllable, he pushed her violently from him, and threw the contents of the brimming goblet in her face.

The poor girl got up the best she could, and, not daring even to sigh, resumed her position at the foot of the table.

There was a dead silence for about half a minute, during which the falling of a leaf, or of a feather, might have been heard. It was interrupted by a low, but harsh and protracted *grating* sound which seemed to come at once from every corner of the room.

"What—what—*what* are you making that noise for?" demanded the king, turning furiously to the dwarf.

The latter seemed to have recovered, in great measure, from his intoxication, and looking fixedly but quietly into the tyrant's face, merely ejaculated:

"I—I? How could it have been me?"

"The sound appeared to come from without," observed one of the courtiers. "I fancy it was the parrot at the window, whetting his bill upon his cage-wires."

"True," replied the monarch, as if much relieved by the suggestion; "but, on the honour of a knight, I could have sworn that it was the gritting of this vagabond's teeth."

Hereupon the dwarf laughed (the king was too confirmed

a joker to object to any one's laughing), and displayed a set of large, powerful, and very repulsive teeth. Moreover, he avowed his perfect willingness to swallow as much wine as desired. The monarch was pacified; and having drained another bumper with no very perceptible ill effect, Hop-Frog entered at once, and with spirit, into the plans for the masquerade.

"I cannot tell what was the association of idea," observed he, very tranquilly, and as if he had never tasted wine in his life, "but *just after* your majesty, had struck the girl and thrown the wine in her face—*just after* your majesty had done this, and while the parrot was making that odd noise outside the window, there came into my mind a capital diversion—one of my own country frolics—often enacted among us, at our masquerades: but here it will be new altogether. Unfortunately, however, it requires a company of eight persons and-"

"Here we *are!*" cried the king, laughing at his acute discovery of the coincidence; "eight to a fraction—I and my seven ministers. Come! what is the diversion?"

"We call it," replied the cripple, "the Eight Chained Orang-utans, and it really is excellent sport if well enacted."

"*We* will enact it," remarked the king, drawing himself up, and lowering his eyelids.

"The beauty of the game," continued Hop-Frog, "lies in the fright it occasions among the women."

"Capital!" roared in chorus the monarch and his ministry.

"I will equip you as orang-utans," proceeded the dwarf; "leave all that to me. The resemblance shall be so striking, that the company of masquerades will take you for real beasts—and of course, they will be as much terrified as astonished."

"Oh, this is exquisite!" exclaimed the king. "Hop-Frog! I will make a man of you."

"The chains are for the purpose of increasing the confusion by their jangling. You are supposed to have escaped, *en masse*, from your keepers. Your majesty cannot conceive the effect produced, at a masquerade, by eight chained orang-utans, imagined to be real ones by most of the company; and rushing in with savage cries, among the crowd of delicately and gorgeously habited men and women. The *contrast* is inimitable!"

"It *must* be," said the king: and the council arose hurriedly (as it was growing late), to put in execution the scheme of Hop-Frog.

His mode of equipping the party as orang-utans was very simple, but effective enough for his purposes. The animals in question had, at the epoch of my story, very rarely been seen in any part of the civilized world; and as the imitations made by the dwarf were sufficiently beast-like and more than sufficiently hideous, their truthfulness to nature was thus thought to be secured.

The king and his ministers were first encased in tight-fitting stockinet shirts and drawers. They were then saturated with tar. At this stage of the process, some one of the party suggested feathers; but the suggestion was at once overruled by the dwarf, who soon convinced the eight, by ocular demonstration, that the hair of such a brute as the orang-utan was much more efficiently represented by *flax*.. A thick coating of the latter was accordingly plastered upon the coating of tar. A long chain was now procured. First, it was passed about the waist of the king, *and tied*, then about another of the party, and also tied; then about all successively, in the same manner. When this chaining arrangement was complete, and the party stood as far apart from each other as possible, they formed a circle; and to make all things appear natural, Hop-Frog passed the residue of the chain in two diameters, at right angles, across the circle, after the fashion adopted, at the present day, by those who capture Chimpanzees, or other large apes, in Borneo.

The grand saloon in which the masquerade was to take place, was a circular room, very lofty, and receiving the light of the sun only through a single window at top. At night (the season for which the apartment was especially designed) it was illuminated principally by a large chandelier, depending by a chain from the centre of the sky-light, and lowered, or elevated, by means of a counter-balance as usual; but (in order not to look unsightly) this latter passed outside the cupola and over the roof.

The arrangements of the room had been left to Trippetta's superintendence; but, in some particulars, it seems, she had been guided by the calmer judgment of her friend the dwarf. At his suggestion it was that, on this occasion, the chandelier was removed. Its waxen drippings (which, in weather so warm, it was quite impossible to prevent) would have been seriously detrimental to the rich dresses of the guests, who, on account of the crowded state of the saloon, could not *all* be expected to keep from out its centre; that is to say, from under the chandelier. Additional sconces were set in various parts of the hall, out of the war, and a *flambeau*, emitting sweet odour, was placed in the right hand of each of the Caryatides that stood against the wall—some fifty or sixty altogether.

The eight orang-utans, taking Hop-Frog's advice, waited patiently until midnight (when the room was thoroughly filled with masqueraders) before making their appearance. No sooner had the clock ceased striking, however, than they rushed, or rather rolled in, all together—for the impediments of their chains caused most of the party to fall, and all to stumble as they entered.

The excitement among the masqueraders was prodigious, and filled the heart of the king with glee. As had been anticipated, there were not a few of the guests who supposed the ferocious-looking creatures to be beasts of some kind in reality, if not precisely orang-utans. Many of the women swooned with affright; and had not the king taken the precaution to exclude all weapons from the saloon, his party might soon have expiated their frolic in their blood. As it was, a general rush was made for the doors; but the king had ordered them to be locked immediately upon his entrance; and, at the dwarf's suggestion, the keys had been deposited with *him*.

While the tumult was at its height, and each masquerader attentive only to his own safety (for, in fact, there was much *real* danger from the pressure of the excited crowd), the chain by which the chandelier ordinarily hung, and which had been drawn up on its removal, might have been seen very gradually to descend, until its hooked extremity came within three feet of the floor.

Soon after this, the king and his seven friends having reeled about the hall in all directions, found themselves, at length, in its centre, and, of course, in immediate contact with the chain. While they were thus situated, the dwarf, who had followed noiselessly at their heels, inciting them to keep up the commotion, took hold of their own chain at the intersection of the two portions which crossed the circle diametrically and at right angles. Here, with the rapidity of thought, he inserted the hook from which the chandelier had been wont to depend; and, in an instant, by *some* unseen agency, the chandelier-chain was drawn so far upward as to take the hook out of reach, and, as an inevitable consequence, to drag the orang-utans together in close connection, and face to face.

The masqueraders, by this time, had recovered, in some measure, from their alarm; and, beginning to regard the whole matter as a well-contrived pleasantry, set up a loud shout of laughter at the predicament of the apes.

"Leave them to *me!*" now screamed Hop-Frog, his shrill voice making itself easily heard through all the din. "Leave them to *me*. I fancy *I* know them. If I can only get a good look at them, *I* can soon tell who they are."

Here, scrambling over the heads of the crowd, he managed to get to the wall; when, seizing a *flambeau* from one of the Caryatides, he returned, as he went, to the centre of the room-leaping, with the agility of a monkey, upon the kings head, and thence clambered a few feet up the chain; holding down the torch to examine the group of orang-utans, and still screaming: "*I* shall soon find out who they are!"

And now, while the whole assembly (the apes included) were convulsed with laughter, the jester suddenly uttered a shrill whistle; when the chain flew violently up for about thirty feet—dragging with it the dismayed and struggling orang-utans, and leaving them suspended in mid-air between the sky-light and the floor. Hop-Frog, clinging to the chain as it rose, still maintained his relative position in respect to the eight maskers, and still (as if nothing were the matter) continued to thrust his torch down toward them, as though endeavouring to discover who they were.

So thoroughly astonished was the whole company at this ascent, that a dead silence, of about a minute's duration, ensued. It was broken by just such a low, harsh, *grating* sound, as had before attracted the attention of the king and his councillors when the former threw the wine in the face of Trippetta. But, on the present occasion, there could be no question as to *whence* the sound issued. It came from the fang—like teeth of the dwarf, who ground them and gnashed them as he foamed at the mouth, and glared, with an expression of maniacal rage, into the upturned countenances of the king and his seven companions.

"Ah, ha!" said at length the infuriated jester. "Ah, ha! I begin to see who these people *are,* now!" Here, pretending to scrutinize the king more closely, he held the flambeau to the flaxen coat which enveloped him, and which instantly burst into a sheet of vivid flame. In less than half a minute the whole eight orang-utans were blazing fiercely, amid the shrieks of the multitude who gazed at them from below, horror-stricken, and without the power to render them the slightest assistance.

At length the flames, suddenly increasing in virulence, forced the jester to climb higher up the chain, to be out of their reach; and, as he made this movement, the crowd again sank, for a brief instant, into silence. The dwarf seized his opportunity, and once more spoke:

"I now see *distinctly*." he said, "what manner of people these maskers are. They are a great king and his seven privy-councillors,—a king who does not scruple to strike a defence-less girl and his seven councillors who abet him in the outrage. As for myself, I am simply Hop-Frog, the jester—and *this is my last jest*."

Owing to the high combustibility of both the flax and the tar to which it adhered, the dwarf had scarcely made an end of his brief speech before the work of vengeance was complete. The eight corpses swung in their chains, a fetid, blackened, hideous, and indistinguishable mass. The cripple hurled his torch at them, clambered leisurely to the ceiling, and disappeared through the sky-light.

It is supposed that Trippetta, stationed on the roof of the saloon, had been the accomplice of her friend in his fiery revenge, and that, together, they effected their escape to their own country: for neither was seen again.

King Pest

A Tale Containing an Allegory.

The gods do bear and will allow in kings
The things which they abhor in rascal routes.
>—Buckhurst's *Tragedy of Ferrex and Porrex.*

About twelve o'clock, one night in the month of October, and during the chivalrous reign of the third Edward, two seamen belonging to the crew of the *Free and Easy*, a trading schooner plying between Sluys and the Thames, and then at anchor in that river, were much astonished to find themselves seated in the tap-room of an ale-house in the parish of St. Andrews, London—which ale-house bore for sign the portraiture of a "Jolly Tar."

The room, although ill-contrived, smoke-blackened, low-pitched, and in every other respect agreeing with the general character of such places at the period—was, nevertheless, in the opinion of the grotesque groups scattered here and there within it, sufficiently well adapted to its purpose.

Of these groups our two seamen formed, I think, the most interesting, if not the most conspicuous.

The one who appeared to be the elder, and whom his companion addressed by the characteristic appellation of "Legs," was at the same time much the taller of the two. He might have measured six feet and a half, and an habitual stoop in the shoulders seemed to have been the necessary consequence of an altitude so enormous.—Superfluities in height were, however, more than accounted for by deficiencies in other respects. He was exceedingly thin; and might, as his associates asserted, have answered, when drunk, for a pennant at the mast-head, or, when sober, have served for a jib-boom. But these jests, and others of a similar nature, had evidently produced, at no time, any effect upon the cachinnatory muscles of the tar. With high cheek-bones, a large hawk-nose, retreating chin, fallen under-jaw, and huge protruding white eyes, the expression of his countenance, although tinged with a species of dogged indifference to matters and things in general, was not the less utterly solemn and serious beyond all attempts at imitation or description.

The younger seaman was, in all outward appearance, the converse of his companion. His stature could not have exceeded four feet. A pair of stumpy bow-legs supported his squat, unwieldy figure, while his unusually short and thick arms, with no ordinary fists at their extremities, swung off dangling from his sides like the fins of a sea-turtle. Small eyes, of no particular colour, twinkled far back in his head. His nose remained buried in the mass of flesh which enveloped his round, full, and purple face; and his thick upper-lip rested upon the still thicker one beneath with an air of complacent self-satisfaction, much heightened by the owner's habit of licking them at intervals. He evidently regarded his tall shipmate with a feeling half-wondrous, half-quizzical; and stared up occasionally in his face as the red setting sun stares up at the crags of Ben Nevis.

Various and eventful, however, had been the peregrinations of the worthy couple in and about the different tap-houses of the neighbourhood during the earlier hours of the night. Funds even the most ample, are not always everlasting: and it was with empty pockets our friends had ventured upon the present hostelry.

At the precise period, then, when this history properly commences, Legs, and his fellow Hugh Tarpaulin, sat, each with both elbows resting upon the large oaken table in the middle of the floor, and with a hand upon either cheek. They were eyeing, from behind a huge flagon of unpaid-for "humming-stuff," the portentous words, "No Chalk," which to their indignation and astonishment were scored over the doorway by means of that very mineral whose presence they purported to deny. Not that the gift of deciphering written characters—a gift among the commonalty of that day considered little less cabalistical than the art of inditing—could, in strict justice, have been laid to the charge of either disciple of the sea; but there was, to say the truth, a certain twist in the formation of the letters—an indescribable lee-lurch about the whole—-which foreboded, in the opinion of both seamen, a long run of dirty weather; and determined them at once, in the allegorical words of Legs himself, to "pump ship, clew up all sail, and scud before the wind."

Having accordingly disposed of what remained of the ale, and looped up the points of their short doublets, they finally made a bolt for the street. Although Tarpaulin rolled twice into the fire-place, mistaking it for the door, yet their escape was at length happily effected—and half after twelve o'clock found our heroes ripe for mischief, and running for life down a dark alley in the direction of St. Andrew's Stair, hotly pursued by the landlady of the "Jolly Tar."

At the epoch of this eventful tale, and periodically, for many years before and after, all England, but more especially the metropolis, resounded with the fearful cry of "Plague!" The city was in a great measure depopulated—and in those horrible regions, in the vicinity of the Thames, where amid the dark, narrow, and filthy lanes and alleys, the Demon of Disease was supposed to have had his nativity, Awe, Terror, and Superstition were alone to be found stalking abroad.

By authority of the king such districts were placed *under ban*, and all persons forbidden, under pain of death, to intrude upon their dismal solitude. Yet neither the mandate of the monarch, nor the huge barriers erected at the entrances of the streets, nor the prospect of that loathsome death which, with almost absolute certainty, overwhelmed the wretch whom no peril could deter from the adventure, prevented the unfurnished and un-tenanted dwellings from being stripped, by the hand of nightly rapine, of every article, such as iron, brass, or lead-work, which could in any manner be turned to a profitable account.

Above all, it was usually found, upon the annual winter opening of the barriers, that locks, bolts, and secret cellars, had proved but slender protection to those rich stores of wines and liquors which, in consideration of the risk and trouble of removal, many of the numerous dealers having shops in the neighbourhood had consented to trust, during the period of exile, to so insufficient a security.

But there were very few of the terror-stricken people who attributed these doings to the agency of human hands. Pest-spirits, plague-goblins, and fever-demons, were the popular imps of mischief; and tales so blood-chilling were hourly told, that the whole mass of forbidden buildings was, at length, enveloped in terror as in a shroud, and the plunderer himself was often scared away by the horrors his own depreciations had created; leaving the entire vast circuit of prohibited district to gloom, silence, pestilence, and death.

It was by one of the terrific barriers already mentioned, and which indicated the region beyond to be under the Pest-ban, that, in scrambling down an alley, Legs and the worthy Hugh Tarpaulin found their progress suddenly impeded. To return was out of the question, and no time was to be lost, as their pursuers were close upon their heels. With thorough-bred seamen to clamber up the roughly fashioned plank-work was a trifle; and, maddened with the twofold excitement of exercise and liquor, they leaped unhesitatingly down within the enclosure, and holding on their drunken course with shouts and yellings, were soon bewildered in its noisome and intricate recesses.

Had they not, indeed, been intoxicated beyond moral sense, their reeling footsteps must have been palsied by the horrors of their situation. The air was cold and misty. The paving-stones, loosened from their beds, lay in wild disorder amid the tall, rank grass, which sprang up around the feet and ankles. Fallen houses choked up the streets. The most fetid and poisonous smells everywhere prevailed;—and by the aid of that ghastly light which, even at midnight, never fails to emanate from a vapory and pestilential at atmosphere, might be discerned lying in the by-paths and alleys, or rotting in the windowless habitations, the carcass of many a nocturnal plunderer arrested by the hand of the plague in the very perpetration of his robbery.

—But it lay not in the power of images, or sensations, or impediments such as these, to stay the course of men who, naturally brave, and at that time especially, brimful of courage and of "humming-stuff!" would have reeled, as straight as their condition might have permitted, undauntedly into the very jaws of Death. Onward—still onward stalked the grim Legs, making the desolate solemnity echo and re-echo with yells like the terrific war-whoop of the Indian: and onward, still onward rolled the dumpy Tarpaulin, hanging on to the doublet of his more active companion, and far surpassing the latter's most strenuous exertions in the way of vocal music, by bull-roarings *in basso,* from the profundity of his stentorian lungs.

They had now evidently reached the strong hold of the pestilence. Their way at every step or plunge grew more noisome and more horrible—the paths more narrow and more intricate. Huge stones and beams falling momently from the decaying roofs above them, gave evidence, by their sullen and heavy descent, of the vast height of the surrounding houses; and while actual exertion became necessary to force a passage through frequent heaps of rubbish, it was by no means seldom that the hand fell upon a skeleton or rested upon a more fleshly corpse.

Suddenly, as the seamen stumbled against the entrance of a tall and ghastly-looking building, a yell more than usually shrill from the throat of the excited Legs, was replied to from within, in a rapid succession of wild, laughter-like, and fiendish shrieks. Nothing daunted at sounds which, of such a nature, at such a time, and in such a place, might have curdled the very blood in hearts less irrevocably on fire, the drunken couple rushed headlong against the door, burst it open, and staggered into the midst of things with a volley of curses.

The room within which they found themselves proved to be the shop of an undertaker; but an open trap-door, in a corner of the floor near the entrance, looked down upon a long range of wine-cellars, whose depths the occasional sound of bursting bottles proclaimed to be well stored with their appropriate contents. In the middle of the room stood a table—in the centre of which again arose a huge tub of what appeared to be punch. Bottles of various wines and cordials, together with jugs, pitchers, and flagons of every shape and quality, were scattered profusely upon the board. Around it, upon coffin-trestles, was seated a company of six. This company I will endeavour to delineate one by one.

Fronting the entrance, and elevated a little above his companions, sat a personage who appeared to be the president of the table. His stature was gaunt and tall, and Legs was confounded to behold in him a figure more emaciated than himself. His face was as yellow as saffron—but no feature excepting one alone, was sufficiently marked to merit a particular description. This one consisted in a forehead so unusually and hideously lofty, as to have the appearance of a bonnet or crown of flesh superadded upon the natural head. His mouth was puckered and dimpled into an expression of ghastly affability, and his eyes, as indeed the eyes of all at table, were glazed over with the fumes of intoxication. This gentleman was clothed from head to foot in a richly-embroidered black silk-velvet pall, wrapped negligently around his form after the fashion of a Spanish cloak.—His head was stuck full of sable hearse-plumes, which he nodded to and fro with a jaunty and knowing air; and, in his right hand, he held a huge human thigh-bone, with which he appeared to have been just knocking down some member of the company for a song.

Opposite him, and with her back to the door, was a lady of no whit the less extraordinary character. Although quite as tall as the person just described, she had no right to complain of his unnatural emaciation. She was evidently in the last stage of a dropsy; and her figure resembled nearly that of the huge puncheon of October beer which stood, with the head driven in, close by her side, in a corner of the chamber. Her face was exceedingly round, red, and full; and the same peculiarity, or rather want of peculiarity, attached itself to her countenance, which I before mentioned in the case of the president—that is to say, only one feature of her face was sufficiently distinguished to need a separate characterisation: indeed the acute Tarpaulin immediately observed that the same remark might have applied to each individual person of the party; every one of whom seemed to possess a monopoly of some particular portion of physiognomy. With the lady in question this portion proved to be the mouth. Commencing at the right ear, it swept with a terrific chasm to the left—the short pendants which she wore in either auricle continually bobbing into the aperture. She made, however, every exertion to keep her mouth closed and look dignified, in a dress consisting of a newly starched and ironed shroud coming up close under her chin, with a crimpled ruffle of cambric muslin.

At her right hand sat a diminutive young lady whom she appeared to patronise. This delicate little creature, in the trembling of her wasted fingers, in the livid hue of her lips, and in the slight hectic spot which tinged her otherwise leaden complexion, gave evident indications of a galloping consumption. An air of gave extreme *haut ton*, however, pervaded her whole appearance; she wore in a graceful and *degagé* manner, a large and beautiful winding-sheet of the finest India lawn; her hair hung in ringlets over her neck; a soft smile played about her mouth; but her nose, extremely long, thin, sinuous, flexible and pimpled, hung down far below her under lip, and in spite of the delicate manner in which she now and then moved it to one side or the other with her tongue, gave to her countenance a somewhat equivocal expression.

Over against her, and upon the left of the dropsical lady, was seated a little puffy, wheezing, and gouty old man, whose cheeks reposed upon the shoulders of their owner, like two huge bladders of Oporto wine. With his arms folded, and with one bandaged leg deposited upon the table, he seemed to think himself entitled to some consideration. He evidently prided himself much upon every inch of his personal appearance, but took more especial delight in calling attention to his gaudy-coloured *surtout*. This, to say the truth, must have cost him no little money, and was made to fit him exceedingly well—being fashioned from one of the curiously embroidered silken covers appertaining to those glorious escutcheons which, in England and elsewhere, are customarily hung up, in some conspicuous place, upon the dwellings of departed aristocracy.

Next to him, and at the right hand of the president, was a gentleman in long white hose and cotton drawers. His frame shook, in a ridiculous manner, with a fit of what Tarpaulin called "the horrors." His jaws, which had been newly shaved, were tightly tied up by a bandage of muslin; and his arms being fastened in a similar way at the wrists, prevented him from helping himself too freely to the liquors upon the table; a precaution rendered necessary, in the opinion of Legs, by the peculiarly sottish and wine-bibbing cast of his visage. A pair of prodigious ears, nevertheless, which it was no doubt found impossible to confine, towered away into the atmosphere of the apartment, and were occasionally pricked up in a spasm, at the sound of the drawing of a cork.

Fronting him, sixthly and lastly, was situated a singularly stiff-looking personage, who, being afflicted with paralysis, must, to speak seriously, have felt very ill at ease in his unaccommodating habiliments. He was habited, somewhat uniquely, in a new and handsome mahogany coffin. Its top or head-piece pressed upon the skull of the wearer, and extended over it in the fashion of a hood, giving to the entire face an air of indescribable interest. Arm-holes had been cut in the sides, for the sake not more of elegance than of convenience; but the dress, nevertheless, prevented its proprietor from sitting as erect as his associates; and as he lay reclining against his trestle, at an angle of forty-five degrees, a pair of huge goggle eyes rolled up their awful whites towards the ceiling in absolute amazement at their own enormity.

Before each of the party lay a portion of a skull, which was used as a drinking cup. Overhead was suspended a human skeleton, by means of a rope tied round one of the legs and fastened to a ring in the ceiling. The other limb, confined by no such fetter, stuck off from the body at right angles, causing the whole loose and rattling frame to dangle and twirl about at the caprice of every occasional puff of wind which found its way into the apartment. In the cranium of this hideous thing lay quantity of ignited charcoal, which threw a fitful but vivid light over the entire scene; while coffins, and other wares appertaining to the shop of an undertaker, were piled high up around the room, and against the windows, preventing any ray from escaping into the street.

At sight of this extraordinary assembly, and of their still more extraordinary paraphernalia, our two seamen did not conduct themselves with that degree of decorum which might have been expected. Legs, leaning against the wall near which he happened to be standing, dropped his lower jaw still lower than usual, and spread open his eyes to their fullest extent: while Hugh Tarpaulin, stooping down so as to bring his nose upon a level with the table, and spreading out a palm upon either knee, burst into a long, loud, and obstreperous roar of very ill-timed and immoderate laughter.

Without, however, taking offence at behaviour so excessively rude, the tall president smiled very graciously upon the intruders—nodded to them in a dignified manner with his head of sable plumes—and, arising, took each by an arm, and led him to a seat which some others of the company had placed in the meantime for his accommodation. Legs to all this offered not the slightest resistance, but sat down as he was directed; while the gallant Hugh, removing his coffin trestle from its station near the head of the table, to the vicinity of the little consumptive lady in the winding sheet, plumped down by her side in high glee, and pouring out a skull of red wine, quaffed it to their better acquaintance. But at this presumption the stiff gentleman in the coffin seemed exceedingly nettled; and serious consequences might have ensued, had not the president, rapping upon the table with his truncheon, diverted the attention of all present to the following speech:

"It becomes our duty upon the present happy occasion"—

"Avast there!" interrupted Legs, looking very serious, "avast there a bit, I say, and tell us who the devil ye all are, and what business ye have here, rigged off like the foul fiends, and swilling the snug blue ruin stowed away for the winter by my honest shipmate, Will Wimble the undertaker!"

At this unpardonable piece of ill-breeding, all the original company half started to their feet, and uttered the same rapid succession of wild fiendish shrieks which had before caught the attention of the seamen. The president, however, was the first to recover his composure, and at length, turning to Legs with great dignity, recommenced:

"Most willingly will we gratify any reasonable curiosity on the part of guests so illustrious, unbidden though they be. Know then that in these dominions I am monarch, and here rule with undivided empire under the title of 'King Pest the First.'

"This apartment, which you no doubt profanely suppose to be the shop of Will Wimble the undertaker—a man whom we know not, and whose plebeian appellation has never before this night thwarted our royal ears—this apartment, I say, is the Dais-Chamber of our Palace, devoted to the councils of our kingdom, and to other sacred and lofty purposes.

"The noble lady who sits opposite is Queen Pest, our Serene Consort. The other exalted personages whom you behold are all of our family, and wear the insignia of the blood royal under the respective titles of 'His Grace the Arch Duke Pest-Iferous'—'His Grace the Duke Pest-Ilential'—'His Grace the Duke Tem-Pest'—and 'Her Serene Highness the Arch Duchess Ana-Pest.'

"As regards," continued he, "your demand of the business upon which we sit here in council, we might be pardoned for replying that it concerns, and concerns *alone*, our own private and regal interest, and is in no manner important to any other than ourself. But in consideration of those rights to which as guests and strangers you may feel yourselves entitled, we will furthermore explain that we are here this night, prepared by deep research and accurate investigation, to examine, analyse, and thoroughly determine the indefinable spirit—the incomprehensible qualities and nature—of those inestimable treasures of the palate, the wines, ales, and liqueurs of this goodly metropolis: by so doing to advance not more our own designs than the true welfare of that unearthly sovereign whose reign is over us all, whose dominions are unlimited, and whose name is 'Death.'

"Whose name is Davy Jones!" ejaculated Tarpaulin, helping the lady by his side to a skull of liqueur, and pouring out a second for himself.

"Profane varlet!" said the president, now turning his attention to the worthy Hugh, "profane and execrable wretch!—we have said, that in consideration of those rights which, even in thy filthy person, we feel no inclination to violate, we have condescended to make reply to thy rude and unseasonable inquiries. We nevertheless, for your unhallowed intrusion upon our councils, believe it our duty to mulct thee and thy companion in each a gallon of Black Strap—having imbibed which to the prosperity of our kingdom—at a single draught—and upon your bended knees—ye shall be forthwith free either to proceed upon your way, or remain and be admitted to the privileges of our table, according to your respective and individual pleasures."

"It would be a matter of utter impossibility," replied Legs, whom the assumptions and dignity of King Pest the First had evidently inspired some feelings of respect, and who arose and steadied himself by the table as he spoke—"It would, please your majesty, be a matter of utter impossibility to stow away in my hold even one-fourth part of the same liquor which your majesty has just mentioned. To say nothing of the stuffs placed on board in the forenoon by way of ballast, and not to mention the various ales and liqueurs shipped this evening at different sea-ports, I have, at present, a full cargo of 'humming stuff' taken in and duly paid for at the sign of the 'Jolly Tar.' You will, therefore, please your majesty, be so good as to take the will for the deed—for by no manner of means either can I or will I swallow another drop—least of all a drop of that villainous bilge-water that answers to the hall of 'Black Strap.'"

"Belay that!" interrupted Tarpaulin, astonished not more at

the length of his companion's speech than at the nature of his refusal—"Belay that you tubber!—and I say, Legs, none of your palaver! *My* hull is still light, although I confess you yourself seem to be a little top-heavy; and as for the matter of your share of the cargo, why rather than raise a squall I would find stowage-room for it myself, but"—

"This proceeding," interposed the president, "is by no means in accordance with the terms of the mulct or sentence, which is in its nature Median, and not to be altered or recalled. The conditions we have imposed must be fulfilled to the letter, and that without a moment's hesitation—in failure of which fulfilment we decree that you do here be tied neck and heels together, and duly drowned as rebels in yon hogshead of October beer!"

"A sentence!—a sentence!—a righteous and just sentence!—a glorious decree!—a most worthy and upright, and holy condemnation!" shouted the Pest family altogether. The king elevated his forehead into innumerable wrinkles; the gouty little old man puffed like a pair of bellows; the lady of the winding sheet waved her nose to and fro; the gentleman in the cotton drawers pricked up his ears; she of the shroud gasped like a dying fish; and he of the coffin looked stiff and rolled up his eyes.

"Ugh! ugh! ugh!" chuckled Tarpaulin without heeding the general excitement, "ugh! ugh! ugh!—ugh! ugh! ugh!—ugh! ugh! ugh!—I was saying," said he, "I was saying when Mr. King Pest poked in his marlin-spike, that as for the matter of two or three gallons more or less of Black Strap, it was a trifle to a tight sea-boat like myself not overstowed—but when it comes to drinking the health of the Devil (whom God assoilzie) and going down upon my marrow bones to his ill-favoured majesty there, whom I know, as well as I know myself to be a sinner, to be nobody in the whole world, but Tim Hurlygurly the stage-player—why! it's quite another guess sort of a thing, and utterly and altogether past my comprehension."

He was not allowed to finish this speech in tranquillity. At the name Tim Hurlygurly the whole assembly leaped from their name seats.

"Treason!" shouted His Majesty King Pest the First.

"Treason!" said the little man with the gout.

"Treason!" screamed the Arch Duchess Ana-Pest.

"Treason!" muttered the gentleman with his jaws tied up.

"Treason!" growled he of the coffin.

"Treason! treason!" shrieked her majesty of the mouth; and, seizing by the hinder part of his breeches the unfortunate Tarpaulin, who had just commenced pouring out for himself a skull of liqueur, she lifted him high into the air, and let him fall without ceremony into the huge open puncheon of his beloved ale. Bobbing up and down, for a few seconds, like an apple in a bowl of toddy, he, at length, finally disappeared amid the whirlpool of foam which, in the already effervescent liquor, his struggles easily succeeded in creating.

Not tamely, however, did the tall seaman behold the discomfiture of his companion. Jostling King Pest through the open trap, the valiant Legs slammed the door down upon him with an oath, and strode towards the centre of the room. Here tearing down the skeleton which swung over the table, he laid it about him with so much energy and good will, that, as the last glimpses of light died away within the apartment, he succeeded in knocking out the brains of the little gentleman with the gout. Rushing then with all his force against the fatal hogshead full of October ale and Hugh Tarpaulin, he rolled it over and over in an instant. Out burst a deluge of liquor so fierce—so impetuous—so overwhelming—that the room was flooded from wall to wall—the loaded table was overturned—the trestles were thrown upon their backs—the tub of punch into the fire-place—and the ladies into hysterics.

Piles of death-furniture floundered about. Jugs, pitchers, and carboys mingled promiscuously in the *mêlée*, and wicker flagons encountered desperately with bottles of junk. The man with the horrors was drowned upon the spot—the little stiff gentleman floated off in his coffin—and the victorious Legs, seizing by the waist the fat lady in the shroud, rushed out with her into the street, and made a bee-line for the *Free and Easy*, followed under easy sail by the redoubtable Hugh Tarpaulin, who, having sneezed three or four times, panted and puffed after him with the Arch Duchess Ana-Pest.

Loss of Breath

O Breathe not, etc. —Moore's Melodies

The most notorious ill-fortune must in the end yield to the untiring courage of philosophy—as the most stubborn city to the ceaseless vigilance of an enemy. Salmanezer, as we have it in holy writings, lay three years before Samaria; yet it fell. Sardanapalus—see Diodorus—maintained himself seven in Nineveh; but to no purpose. Troy expired at the close of the second lustrum; and Azoth, as Aristaeus declares upon his honour as a gentleman, opened at last her gates to Psammitticus, after having barred them for the fifth part of a century. . . .

"Thou wretch!—thou vixen!—thou shrew!" said I to my wife on the morning after our wedding; "thou witch!—thou hag!—thou whippersnapper—thou sink of iniquity!—thou fiery-faced quintessence of all that is abominable!—thou—thou—" here standing upon tiptoe, seizing her by the throat, and placing my mouth close to her ear, I was preparing to launch forth a new and more decided epithet of opprobrium, which should not fail, if ejaculated, to convince her of her insignificance, when to my extreme horror and astonishment I discovered that *I had lost my breath*.

The phrases "I am out of breath," "I have lost my breath," etc., are often enough repeated in common conversation; but it had never occurred to me that the terrible accident of which I speak could *bona fide* and actually happen! Imagine—that is if you have a fanciful turn—imagine, I say, my wonder—my consternation—my despair!

There is a good genius, however, which has never entirely deserted me. In my most ungovernable moods I still retain a sense of propriety, *et le chémin des passions me conduit*—as Lord Edouard in the *Julie* says it did him—*à la philosophie veritable.*

Although I could not at first precisely ascertain to what degree the occurrence had affected me, I determined at all events to conceal the matter from my wife, until further experience should discover to me the extent of this my unheard of calamity. Altering my countenance, therefore, in a moment, from its bepuffed and distorted appearance, to an expression of arch and *coquettish* benignity, I gave my lady a pat on the one cheek, and a kiss on the other, and without saying one syllable (Furies! I could not), left her astonished at my drollery, as I pirouetted out of the room in a *pas de zephyr.*

Behold me then safely ensconced in my private *boudoir*, a fearful instance of the ill consequences attending upon irascibility—alive, with the qualifications of the dead—dead, with the propensities of the living—an anomaly on the face of the earth—being very calm, yet breathless.

Yes! breathless. I am serious in asserting that my breath was entirely gone. I could not have stirred with it a feather if my life had been at issue, or sullied even the delicacy of a mirror. Hard fate!—yet there was some alleviation to the first overwhelming paroxysm of my sorrow. I found, upon trial, that the powers of utterance which, upon my inability to proceed in the conversation with my wife, I then concluded to be totally destroyed, were in fact only partially impeded, and I discovered that had I, at that interesting crisis, dropped my voice to a singularly deep guttural, I might still have continued to her the communication of my sentiments; this pitch of voice (the guttural) depending, I find, not upon the current of the breath, but upon a certain spasmodic action of the muscles of the throat.

Throwing myself upon a chair, I remained for some time absorbed in meditation. My reflections, be sure, were of no consolatory kind. A thousand vague and lachrymatory fancies took possession of my soul—and even the idea of suicide flitted across my brain; but it is a trait in the perversity of human nature to re-ject the obvious and the ready, for the far-distant and equivocal. Thus I shuddered at self-murder as the most decided of atroci-ties while the tabby cat purred strenuously upon the rug, and the very water dog wheezed assiduously under the table, each taking to itself much merit for the strength of its lungs, and all obviously done in derision of my own pulmonary incapacity.

Oppressed with a tumult of vague hopes and fears, I at length heard the footsteps of my wife descending the staircase. Being now assured of her absence, I returned with a palpitating heart to the scene of my disaster.

Carefully locking the door on the inside, I commenced a vigorous search. It was possible, I thought, that, concealed in some obscure corner, or lurking in some closet or drawer, might be found the lost object of my inquiry. It might have a vapory—it might even have a tangible form. Most philosophers, upon many points of philosophy, are still very unphilosophical. Wil-liam Godwin, however, says in his *Mandeville*, that "invisible things are the only realities," and this, all will allow, is a case in point. I would have the judicious reader pause before accusing such asseverations of an undue quantum of absurdity. Anaxago-ras, it will be remembered, maintained that snow is black, and this I have since found to be the case.

Long and earnestly did I continue the investigation: but the contemptible reward of my industry and perseverance proved to be only a set of false teeth, two pair of hips, an eye, and a bundle of *billets-doux* from Mr. Windenough to my wife. I might as well here observe that this confirmation of my lady's partiality for Mr. W. occasioned me little uneasiness. That Mrs. Lackobreath should admire anything so dissimilar to myself was a natural and necessary evil. I am, it is well known, of a robust and cor-pulent appearance, and at the same time somewhat diminutive in stature. What wonder, then, that the lath-like tenuity of my acquaintance, and his altitude, which has grown into a proverb, should have met with all due estimation in the eyes of Mrs. Lackobreath. But to return.

My exertions, as I have before said, proved fruitless. Closet after closet—drawer after drawer—corner after corner—were scrutinized to no purpose. At one time, however, I thought myself sure of my prize, having, in rummaging a dressing-case, accidentally demolished a bottle of Grandjean's Oil of Archangels—which, as an agreeable perfume, I here take the liberty of recommending.

With a heavy heart I returned to my *boudoir*—there to ponder upon some method of eluding my wife's penetration, until I could make arrangements prior to my leaving the country, for to this I had already made up my mind. In a foreign climate, being unknown, I might, with some probability of success, endeavour to conceal my unhappy calamity—a calamity calculated, even more than beggary, to estrange the affections of the multitude, and to draw down upon the wretch the well-merited indignation of the virtuous and the happy. I was not long in hesitation. Being naturally quick, I committed to memory the entire tragedy of *Metamora*. I had the good fortune to recollect that in the accentuation of this drama, or at least of such portion of it as is allotted to the hero, the tones of voice in which I found myself deficient were altogether unnecessary, and the deep guttural was expected to reign monotonously throughout.

I practised for some time by the borders of a well frequented marsh;—herein, however, having no reference to a similar proceeding of Demosthenes, but from a design peculiarly and conscientiously my own. Thus armed at all points, I determined to make my wife believe that I was suddenly smitten with a passion for the stage. In this, I succeeded to a miracle; and to every question or suggestion found myself at liberty to reply in my most frog-like and sepulchral tones with some passage from the tragedy—any portion of which, as I soon took great pleasure in observing, would apply equally well to any particular subject. It is not to be supposed, however, that in the delivery of such passages I was found at all deficient in the looking asquint—the showing my teeth—the working my knees—the shuffling my feet—or in any of those unmentionable graces which are now justly considered the characteristics of a popular performer. To be sure they spoke of confining me in a strait-jacket—but, good God! they never suspected me of having lost my breath.

Having at length put my affairs in order, I took my seat very early one morning in the mail stage for ———, giving it to be understood, among my acquaintances, that business of the last importance required my immediate personal attendance in that city.

The coach was crammed to repletion; but in the uncertain twilight the features of my companions could not be distinguished. Without making any effectual resistance, I suffered myself to be placed between two gentlemen of colossal dimensions; while a third, of a size larger, requesting pardon for the liberty he was about to take, threw himself upon my body at full length, and falling asleep in an instant, drowned all my guttural ejaculations for relief, in a snore which would have put to blush the roarings of the bull of Phalaris. Happily the state of my respiratory faculties rendered suffocation an accident entirely out of the question.

As, however, the day broke more distinctly in our approach to the outskirts of the city, my tormentor, arising and adjusting his shirt-collar, thanked me in a very friendly manner for my civility. Seeing that I remained motionless (all my limbs were dislocated and my head twisted on one side), his apprehensions began to be excited; and arousing the rest of the passengers, he communicated, in a very decided manner, his opinion that a dead man had been palmed upon them during the night for a living and responsible fellow-traveller; here giving me a thump on the right eye, by way of demonstrating the truth of his suggestion.

Hereupon all, one after another (there were nine in company), believed it their duty to pull me by the ear. A young practising physician, too, having applied a pocket-mirror to my mouth, and found me without breath, the assertion of my persecutor was pronounced a true bill; and the whole party expressed a determination to endure tamely no such impositions for the future, and to proceed no farther with any such carcasses for the present.

I was here, accordingly, thrown out at the sign of the "Crow" (by which tavern the coach happened to be passing), without meeting with any farther accident than the breaking of both my arms, under the left hind wheel of the vehicle. I must besides do the driver the justice to state that he did not forget to throw after me the largest of my trunks, which, unfortunately falling on my head, fractured my skull in a manner at once interesting and extraordinary.

The landlord of the "Crow," who is a hospitable man, finding that my trunk contained sufficient to indemnify him for any little trouble he might take in my behalf, sent forthwith for a surgeon of his acquaintance, and delivered me to his care with a bill and receipt for ten dollars.

The purchaser took me to his apartments and commenced operations immediately. Having cut off my ears, however, he discovered signs of animation. He now rang the bell, and sent for a neighbouring apothecary with whom to consult in the emergency. In case of his suspicions with regard to my existence proving ultimately correct, he, in the meantime, made an incision in my stomach, and removed several of my viscera for private dissection.

The apothecary had an idea that I was actually dead. This idea I endeavoured to confute, kicking and plunging with all my might, and making the most furious contortions—for the operations of the surgeon had, in a measure, restored me to the possession of my faculties. All, however, was attributed to the effects of a new galvanic battery, wherewith the apothecary, who is really a man of information, performed several curious experiments, in which, from my personal share in their fulfilment, I could not help feeling deeply interested. It was a course of mortification to me, nevertheless, that although I made several attempts at conversation, my powers of speech were so entirely in abeyance, that I could not even open my mouth; much less, then, make reply to some ingenious but fanciful theories of which, under other circumstances, my minute acquaintance with the Hippocratian pathology would have afforded me a ready confutation.

Not being able to arrive at a conclusion, the practitioners remanded me for farther examination. I was taken up into a garret; and the surgeon's lady having accommodated me with drawers and stockings, the surgeon himself fastened my hands, and tied up my jaws with a pocket-handkerchief—then bolted the door on the outside as he hurried to his dinner, leaving me alone to silence and to meditation.

I now discovered to my extreme delight that I could have spoken had not my mouth been tied up with the pocket-handkerchief. Consoling myself with this reflection, I was mentally repeating some passages of the *Omnipresence of the Deity*, as is my custom before resigning myself to sleep, when two cats, of a greedy and vituperative turn, entering at a hole in the wall, leaped up with a flourish *à la Catalani*, and alighting opposite one another on my visage, betook themselves to indecorous contention for the paltry consideration of my nose.

But, as the loss of his ears proved the means of elevating to the throne of Cyrus, the Magian or Mige-Gush of Persia, and as the cutting off his nose gave Zopyrus possession of Babylon, so the loss of a few ounces of my countenance proved the salvation of my body. Aroused by the pain, and burning with indignation, I burst, at a single effort, the fastenings and the bandage. Stalking across the room I cast a glance of contempt at the belligerents, and throwing open the sash to their extreme horror and disappointment, precipitated myself, very dexterously, from the window.

The mail-robber W——, to whom I bore a singular resemblance, was at this moment passing from the city jail to the scaffold erected for his execution in the suburbs. His extreme infirmity and long continued ill health had obtained him the privilege of remaining unmanacled; and habited in his gallows costume—one very similar to my own,—he lay at full length in the bottom of the hangman's cart (which happened to be under the windows of the surgeon at the moment of my precipitation) without any other guard than the driver, who was asleep, and two recruits of the sixth infantry, who were drunk.

As ill-luck would have it, I alit upon my feet within the vehicle. W——, who was an acute fellow, perceived his opportunity. Leaping up immediately, he bolted out behind, and turning down an alley, was out of sight in the twinkling of an eye. The recruits, aroused by the bustle, could not exactly comprehend the merits of the transaction. Seeing, however, a man, the precise counterpart of the felon, standing upright in the cart before their eyes, they were of the opinion that the rascal (meaning W——) was after making his escape, (so they expressed themselves,) and, having communicated this opinion to one another, they took each a dram, and then knocked me down with the butt-ends of their muskets.

It was not long ere we arrived at the place of destination. Of course nothing could be said in my defence. Hanging was my inevitable fate. I resigned myself thereto with a feeling half stupid, half acrimonious. Being little of a cynic, I had all the sentiments of a dog. The hangman, however, adjusted the noose about my neck. The drop fell.

I forbear to depict my sensations upon the gallows; although here, undoubtedly, I could speak to the point, and it is a topic upon which nothing has been well said. In fact, to write upon such a theme it is necessary to have been hanged. Every author should confine himself to matters of experience. Thus Mark Antony composed a treatise upon getting drunk.

I may just mention, however, that die I did not. My body *was*, but I had no breath *to be,* suspended; and but for the knot under my left ear (which had the feel of a military stock) I dare say that I should have experienced very little inconvenience. As for the jerk given to my neck upon the falling of the drop, it merely proved a corrective to the twist afforded me by the fat gentleman in the coach.

For good reasons, however, I did my best to give the crowd the worth of their trouble. My convulsions were said to be extraordinary. My spasms it would have been difficult to beat. The populace *encored*. Several gentlemen swooned; and a multitude of ladies were carried home in hysterics. Pinxit availed himself of the opportunity to retouch, from a sketch taken upon the spot, his admirable painting of the "Marsyas flayed alive."

When I had afforded sufficient amusement, it was thought proper to remove my body from the gallows;—this the more especially as the real culprit had in the meantime been retaken and recognised, a fact which I was so unlucky as not to know.

Much sympathy was, of course, exercised in my behalf, and as no one made claim to my corpse, it was ordered that I should be interred in a public vault.

Here, after due interval, I was deposited. The sexton departed, and I was left alone. A line of Marston's *Malcontent*—

Death's a good fellow and keeps open house—

—struck me at that moment as a palpable lie.

I knocked off, however, the lid of my coffin, and stepped out. The place was dreadfully dreary and damp, and I became troubled with *ennui*. By way of amusement, I felt my way among the numerous coffins ranged in order around. I lifted them down, one by one, and breaking open their lids, busied myself in speculations about the mortality within.

"This," I soliloquized, tumbling over a carcass, puffy, bloated, and rotund—"this has been, no doubt, in every sense of the word, an unhappy—an unfortunate man. It has been his terrible lot not to walk but to waddle—to pass through life not like a human being, but like an elephant—not like a man, but like a rhinoceros.

"His attempts at getting on have been mere abortions, and his circumgyratory proceedings a palpable failure. Taking a step forward, it has been his misfortune to take two toward the right, and three toward the left. His studies have been confined to the poetry of Crabbe. He can have no idea of the wonder of a *pirouette*. To him a *pas de papillon* has been an abstract conception. He has never ascended the summit of a hill. He has never viewed from any steeple the glories of a metropolis. Heat has been his mortal enemy. In the dog-days his days have been the days of a dog. Therein, he has dreamed of flames and suffocation—of mountains upon mountains—of Pelion upon Ossa. He was short of breath—to say all in a word, he was short of breath. He thought it extravagant to play upon wind instruments. He was the inventor of self-moving fans, wind-sails, and ventilators. He patronized Du Pont the bellows-maker, and he died miserably in attempting to smoke a cigar. His was a case in which I feel a deep interest—a lot in which I sincerely sympathise.

"But here,"—said I—"here"—and I dragged spitefully from its receptacle a gaunt, tall and peculiar-looking form, whose remarkable appearance struck me with a sense of unwelcome familiarity—"here is a wretch entitled to no earthly commiseration." Thus saying, in order to obtain a more distinct view of my subject, I applied my thumb and forefinger to its nose, and causing it to assume a sitting position upon the ground, held it thus, at the length of my arm, while I continued my soliloquy.

"Entitled," I repeated, "to no earthly commiseration. Who indeed would think of compassioning a shadow? Besides, has he not had his full share of the blessings of mortality? He was the originator of tall monuments—shot-towers—lightning-rods—Lombardy poplars. His treatise upon *Shades and Shadows* has immortalized him. He edited with distinguished ability the last edition of *South on the Bones*. He went early to college and studied pneumatics. He then came home, talked eternally, and played upon the French-horn. He patronised the bagpipes. Captain Barclay, who walked against Time, would not walk against *him*. Windham and Allbreath were his favourite writers,—his favourite artist, Phiz. He died gloriously while inhaling gas—*levique flatu corrupitur*, like the *fama pudicitae* in Hieronymus.[1] He was indubitably a——"

"How *can* you?—how—*can*—you?"—interrupted the object of my animadversions, gasping for breath, and tearing off, with a desperate exertion, the bandage around its jaws—"how *can* you,

---

1. *Tenera res infeminis fama pudicitiæ, et quari pulcherrimus, citoad levem marcescit auram levigue flatu corrupitur, maxime, etc.*—*Hieronymus ad Salviniam.*

Mr. Lackobreath, be so infernally cruel as to pinch me in that manner by the nose? Did you not see how they had fastened up my mouth—and you *must* know—if you know any thing—how vast a superfluity of breath I have to dispose of! If you do *not* know, however, sit down and you shall see. In my situation it is really a great relief to be able to open ones mouth—to be able to expatiate—to be able to communicate with a person like yourself, who do not think yourself called upon at every period to interrupt the thread of a gentleman's discourse.

"Interruptions are annoying and should undoubtedly be abolished—don't you think so?—no reply, I beg you,—one person is enough to be speaking at a time.—I shall be done by and by, and then you may begin.—How the devil sir, did you get into this place?—not a word I beseech you—been here some time myself—terrible accident!—heard of it, I suppose?—awful calamity!—walking under your windows—some short while ago—about the time you were stage-struck—horrible occurrence!—heard of *catching one's breath*, eh?—hold your tongue I tell you!—I caught somebody elses!—had always too much of my own—met Blab at the corner of the street—wouldn't give me a chance for a word—couldn't get in a syllable edgeways—attacked, consequently, with epilepsies—Blab made his escape—damn all fools!—they took me up for dead, and put me in this place—pretty doings all of them!—heard all you said about me—every word a lie—horrible!—wonderful—outrageous!—hideous!—incomprehensible!—*et cetera—et cetera—et cetera—et cetera—*"

It is impossible to conceive my astonishment at so unexpected a discourse, or the joy with which I became gradually convinced that the breath so fortunately caught by the gentleman (whom I soon recognised as my neighbour Windenough) was, in fact, the identical expiration mislaid by myself in the conversation with my wife. Time, place, and circumstances rendered it a matter beyond question. I did not, however, immediately release my hold upon Mr. W's proboscis—not at least during the long period in which the inventor of Lombardy poplars continued to favour me with his explanations.

In this respect I was actuated by that habitual prudence which has ever been my predominating trait. I reflected that many difficulties might still lie in the path of my preservation which only extreme exertion on my part would be able to surmount. Many persons, I considered, are prone to estimate commodities in their possession—however valueless to the then proprietor—however troublesome, or distressing—in direct ratio with the advantages to be derived by others from their attainment, or by themselves from their abandonment. Might not this be the case with Mr. Windenough? In displaying anxiety for the breath of which he was at present so willing to get rid, might I not lay myself open to the exactions of his avarice? There are scoundrels in this world, I remembered with a sigh, who will not scruple to take unfair opportunities with even a next door neighbour, and (this remark is from Epictetus) it is precisely at that time when men are most anxious to throw off the burden of their own calamities that they feel the least desirous of relieving them in others.

Upon considerations similar to these, and still retaining my grasp upon the nose of Mr. W., I accordingly thought proper to model my reply.

"Monster!" I began in a tone of the deepest indignation—"monster and double-winded idiot!—dost *thou*, whom for thine iniquities it has pleased heaven to accurse with a two-fold respiration—dost *thou*, I say, presume to address me in the familiar language of an old acquaintance?—'I lie,' forsooth! and 'hold my tongue,' to be sure!—pretty conversation indeed, to a gentleman with a single breath!—all this, too, when I have it in my power to relieve the calamity under which thou dost so justly suffer—to curtail the superfluities of thine unhappy respiration."

Like Brutus, I paused for a reply—with which, like a tornado, Mr. Windenough immediately overwhelmed me. Protestation followed upon protestation, and apology upon apology. There were no terms with which he was unwilling to comply, and there were none of which I failed to take the fullest advantage.

Preliminaries being at length arranged, my acquaintance delivered me the respiration; for which (having carefully examined it) I gave him afterward a receipt.

I am aware that by many I shall be held to blame for speaking in a manner so cursory, of a transaction so impalpable. It will be thought that I should have entered more minutely, into the details of an occurrence by which—and this is very true—much new light might be thrown upon a highly interesting branch of physical philosophy.

To all this I am sorry that I cannot reply. A hint is the only answer which I am permitted to make. There were *circumstances*—but I think it much safer upon consideration to say as little as possible about an affair so delicate—*so delicate*, I repeat, and at the time involving the interests of a third party whose sulphurous resentment I have not the least desire, at this moment, of incurring.

We were not long after this necessary arrangement in effecting an escape from the dungeons of the sepulchre. The united strength of our resuscitated voices was soon sufficiently apparent. Scissors, the *Whig* editor, republished a treatise upon "the nature and origin of subterranean noises." A reply—rejoinder—confutation—and justification—followed in the columns of a *Democratic Gazette*. It was not until the opening of the vault to decide the controversy, that the appearance of Mr. Windenough and myself proved both parties to have been decidedly in the wrong.

I cannot conclude these details of some very singular passages in a life at all times sufficiently eventful, without again recalling to the attention of the reader the merits of that indiscriminate philosophy which is a sure and ready shield against those shafts of calamity which can neither be seen, felt nor fully understood. It was in the spirit of this wisdom that, among the ancient Hebrews, it was believed the gates of Heaven would be inevitably opened to that sinner, or saint, who, with good lungs and implicit confidence, should vociferate the word "*Amen!*" It was in the spirit of this wisdom that, when a great plague raged at Athens, and every means had been in vain attempted for its removal, Epimenides, as Laërtius relates, in his second book, of that philosopher, advised the erection of a shrine and temple "to the proper God."

Lyttleton Barry.

Mesmeric Revelation

Whatever doubt may still envelop the rationale of mesmerism, its startling *facts* are now almost universally admitted. Of these latter, those who doubt, are your mere doubters by profession—an unprofitable and disreputable tribe. There can be no more absolute waste of time than the attempt to *prove*, at the present day, that man, by mere exercise of will, can so impress his fellow, as to cast him into an abnormal condition, of which the phenomena resemble very closely those of *death*, or at least resemble them more nearly than they do the phenomena of any other normal condition within our cognizance; that, while in this state, the person so impressed employs only with effort, and then feebly, the external organs of sense, yet perceives, with keenly refined perception, and through channels supposed unknown, matters beyond the scope of the physical organs; that, moreover, his intellectual faculties are wonderfully exalted and invigorated; that his sympathies with the person so impressing him are profound; and, finally, that his susceptibility to the impression increases with its frequency, while, in the same proportion, the peculiar phenomena elicited are more extended and more *pronounced*.

I say that these—which are the laws of mesmerism in its general features—it would be supererogation to demonstrate; nor shall I inflict upon my readers so needless a demonstration; today. My purpose at present is a very different one indeed. I am impelled, even in the teeth of a world of prejudice, to detail without comment the very remarkable substance of a colloquy, occurring between a sleep-waker and myself.

I had been long in the habit of mesmerizing the person in question, (Mr. Vankirk,) and the usual acute susceptibility and exaltation of the mesmeric perception had supervened. For many months he had been labouring under confirmed phthisis, the more distressing effects of which had been relieved by my manipulations; and on the night of Wednesday, the fifteenth instant, I was summoned to his bedside.

The invalid was suffering with acute pain in the region of the heart, and breathed with great difficulty, having all the ordinary symptoms of asthma. In spasms such as these he had usually found relief from the application of mustard to the nervous centres, but tonight this had been attempted in vain.

As I entered his room he greeted me with a cheerful smile, and although evidently in much bodily pain, appeared to be, mentally, quite at ease.

"I sent for you tonight," he said, "not so much to administer to my bodily ailment, as to satisfy me concerning certain psychal impressions which, of late, have occasioned me much anxiety and surprise. I need not tell you how sceptical I have hitherto been on the topic of the soul's immortality. I cannot deny that there has always existed, as if in that very soul which I have been denying, a vague half-sentiment of its own existence. But this half-sentiment at no time amounted to conviction. With it my reason had nothing to do. All attempts at logical inquiry resulted, indeed, in leaving me more sceptical than before. I had been advised to study Cousin. I studied him in his own works as well as in those of his European and American echoes.

"The *Charles Elwood* of Mr. Brownson, for example, was placed in my hands. I read it with profound attention. Throughout I found it logical, but the portions which were not *merely* logical were unhappily the initial arguments of the disbelieving hero of the book. In his summing up it seemed evident to me that the reasoner had not even succeeded in convincing himself. His end had plainly forgotten his beginning, like the government of Trinculo. In short, I was not long in perceiving that if man is to be intellectually convinced of his own immortality, he will never be so convinced by the mere abstractions which have been so long the fashion of the moralists of England, of France, and of Germany. Abstractions may amuse and exercise, but take no hold on the mind. Here upon earth, at least, philosophy, I am persuaded, will always in vain call upon us to look upon qualities as things. The will may assent—the soul—the intellect, never.

"I repeat, then, that I only half felt, and never intellectually believed. But latterly there has been a certain deepening of the feeling, until it has come so nearly to resemble the acquiescence of reason, that I find it difficult to distinguish between the two. I am enabled, too, plainly to trace this effect to the mesmeric influence. I cannot better explain my meaning than by the hypothesis that the mesmeric exaltation enables me to perceive a train of ratiocination which, in my abnormal existence, convinces, but which, in full accordance with the mesmeric phenomena, does not extend, except through its *effect*, into my normal condition. In sleep-waking, the reasoning and its conclusion—the cause and its effect—are present together. In my natural state, the cause vanishing, the effect only, and perhaps only partially, remains.

"These considerations have led me to think that some good results might ensue from a series of well-directed questions propounded to me while mesmerised. You have often observed the profound self-cognizance evinced by the sleep-waker—the extensive knowledge he displays upon all points relating to the mesmeric condition itself; and from this self-cognisance may be deduced hints for the proper conduct of a catechism."

I consented of course to make this experiment. A few passes threw Mr. Vankirk into the mesmeric sleep. His breathing became immediately more easy, and he seemed to suffer no physical uneasiness. The following conversation then ensued:—V. in the dialogue representing the patient, and P. myself.

P. Are you asleep?

V. Yes—no I would rather sleep more soundly.

P. (*After a few more passes.*) Do you sleep now?

V. Yes.

315

P. How do you think your present illness will result?

V. (*After a long hesitation and speaking as if with effort.*) I must die.

P. Does the idea of death afflict you?

V. (*Very quickly.*) No—no!

P. Are you pleased with the prospect?

V. If I were awake I should like to die, but now it is no matter. The mesmeric condition is so near death as to content me.

P. I wish you would explain yourself, Mr. Vankirk.

V. I am willing to do so, but it requires more effort than I feel able to make. You do not question me properly.

P. What then shall I ask?

V. You must begin at the beginning.

P. The beginning! but where is the beginning?

V. You know that the beginning is GOD. (*This was said in a low, fluctuating tone, and with every sign of the most profound veneration.*)

P. What then is God?

V. (*Hesitating for many minutes.*) I cannot tell.

P. Is not God spirit?

V. While I was awake I knew what you meant by "spirit," but now it seems only a word—such for instance as truth, beauty—a quality, I mean.

P. Is not God immaterial?

V. There is no immateriality—it is a mere word. That which is not matter, is not at all—unless qualities are things.

P. Is God, then, material?

V. No. (*This reply startled me very much.*)

P. What then is he?

V. (*After a long pause, and mutteringly.*) I see—but it is a thing difficult to tell. (*Another long pause.*) He is not spirit, for he exists. Nor is he matter, as *you understand it.* But there are *gradations* of matter of which man knows nothing; the grosser impelling the finer, the finer pervading the grosser. The atmosphere, for example, impels the electric principle, while the electric principle permeates the atmosphere. These gradations of matter increase in rarity or fineness, until we arrive at a matter *unparticled*—without particles—indivisible—*one* and here the law of impulsion and permeation is modified. The ultimate, or unparticled matter, not only permeates all things but impels all things—and thus *is* all things within itself. This matter is God. What men attempt to embody in the word "thought," is this matter in motion.

P. The metaphysicians maintain that all action is reducible to motion and thinking, and that the latter is the origin of the former.

V. Yes; and I now see the confusion of idea. Motion is the action of *mind*—not of *thinking*. The unparticled matter, or God, in quiescence, is (as nearly as we can conceive it) what men call mind. And the power of self-movement (equivalent in effect to human volition) is, in the unparticled matter, the result of its unity and omniprevalence; *how* I know not, and now clearly see that I shall never know. But the unparticled matter, set in motion by a law, or quality, existing within itself, is thinking.

P. Can you give me no more precise idea of what you term the unparticled matter?

V. The matters of which man is cognizant, escape the senses in gradation. We have, for example, a metal, a piece of wood, a drop of water, the atmosphere, a gas, caloric, electricity, the luminiferous ether. Now we call all these things matter, and embrace all matter in one general definition; but in spite of this, there can be no two ideas more essentially distinct than that which we attach to a metal, and that which we attach to the luminiferous ether. When we reach the latter, we feel an almost irresistible inclination to class it with spirit, or with nihility. The only consideration which restrains us is our conception of its atomic constitution; and here, even, we have to seek aid from our notion of an atom, as something possessing in infinite minuteness, solidity, palpability, weight.

Destroy the idea of the atomic constitution and we should no longer be able to regard the ether as an entity, or at least as matter. For want of a better word we might term it spirit. Take, now, a step beyond the luminiferous ether—conceive a matter as much more rare than the ether, as this ether is more rare than the metal, and we arrive at once (in spite of all the school dogmas) at a unique mass—an unparticled matter. For although we may admit infinite littleness in the atoms themselves, the infinitude of littleness in the spaces between them is an absurdity. There will be a point—there will be a degree of rarity, at which, if the atoms are sufficiently numerous, the interspaces must vanish, and the mass absolutely coalesce.

But the consideration of the atomic constitution being now taken away, the nature of the mass inevitably glides into what we conceive of spirit. It is clear, however, that it is as fully matter as before. The truth is, it is impossible to conceive spirit, since it is impossible to imagine what is not. When we flatter ourselves that we have formed its conception, we have merely deceived our understanding by the consideration of infinitely rarified matter.

P. There seems to me an insurmountable objection to the idea of absolute coalescence;—and that is the very slight resistance experienced by the heavenly bodies in their revolutions through space—a resistance now ascertained, it is true, to exist in *some* degree, but which is, nevertheless, so slight as to have been quite overlooked by the sagacity even of Newton. We know that the resistance of bodies is, chiefly, in proportion to their density. Absolute coalescence is absolute density. Where there are no interspaces, there can be no yielding. An ether, absolutely dense, would put an infinitely more effectual stop to the progress of a star than would an ether of adamant or of iron.

V. Your objection is answered with an ease which is nearly in the ratio of its apparent unanswerability.—As regards the progress of the star, it can make no difference whether the star passes through the ether *or the ether through it.* There is no astronomical error more unaccountable than that which reconciles the known retardation of the comets with the idea of their passage through an ether: for, however rare this ether be supposed, it would put a stop to all sidereal revolution in a very far briefer period than has been admitted by those astronomers who have endeavored to slur over a point which they found it impossible to comprehend. The retardation actually experienced is, on the other hand, about that which might be expected from the *friction* of the ether in the instantaneous passage through the orb. In the one case, the retarding force is momentary and complete within itself—in the other it is endlessly accumulative.

P. But in all this—in this identification of mere matter with God—is there nothing of irreverence? (*I was forced to repeat this question before the sleep-waker fully comprehended my meaning.*)

V. Can you say *why* matter should be less reverenced than mind? But you forget that the matter of which I speak is, in all respects, the very "mind" or "spirit" of the schools, so far as regards its high capacities, and is, moreover, the "matter" of these schools at the same time. God, with all the powers attributed to spirit, is but the perfection of matter.

P. You assert, then, that the unparticled matter, in motion, is thought?

V. In general, this motion is the universal thought of the universal mind. This thought creates. All created things are but the thoughts of God.

P. You say, "in general."

V. Yes. The universal mind is God. For new individualities, *matter* is necessary.

P. But you now speak of "mind" and "matter" as do the metaphysicians.

V. Yes—to avoid confusion. When I say "mind," I mean the unparticled or ultimate matter; by "matter," I intend all else.

P. You were saying that "for new individualities matter is necessary."

V. Yes; for mind, existing unincorporate, is merely God. To create individual, thinking beings, it was necessary to incarnate portions of the divine mind. Thus man is individualized. Divested of corporate investiture, he were God. Now, the particular motion of the incarnated portions of the unparticled matter is the thought of man; as the motion of the whole is that of God.

P. You say that divested of the body man will be God?

V. (After much hesitation.) I could not have said this; it is an absurdity.

P. (Referring to my notes.) You *did* say that "divested of corporate investiture man were God."

V. And this is true. Man thus divested *would be* God—would be unindividualised. But he can never be thus divested—at least never *will be*—else we must imagine an action of God returning upon itself—a purposeless and futile action. Man is a creature. Creatures are thoughts of God. It is the nature of thought to be irrevocable.

P. I do not comprehend. You say that man will never put off the body?

V. I say that he will never be bodiless.

P. Explain.

V. There are two bodies—the rudimental and the complete; corresponding with the two conditions of the worm and the butterfly. What we call "death," is but the painful metamorphosis. Our present incarnation is progressive, preparatory, temporary. Our future is perfected, ultimate, immortal. The ultimate life is the full design.

P. But of the worm's metamorphosis we are palpably cognizant.

V. We, certainly—but not the worm. The matter of which our rudimental body is composed, is within the ken of the organs of that body; or, more distinctly, our rudimental organs are adapted to the matter of which is formed the rudimental body; but not to that of which the ultimate is composed. The ultimate body thus escapes our rudimental senses, and we perceive only the shell which falls, in decaying, from the inner form; not that inner form itself; but this inner form, as well as the shell, is appreciable by those who have already acquired the ultimate life.

P. You have often said that the mesmeric state very nearly resembles death. How is this?

V. When I say that it resembles death, I mean that it resembles the ultimate life; for when I am entranced the senses of my rudimental life are in abeyance, and I perceive external things directly, without organs, through a medium which I shall employ in the ultimate, unorganised life.

P. Unorganised?

V. Yes; organs are contrivances by which the individual is brought into sensible relation with particular classes and forms of matter, to the exclusion of other classes and forms. The organs of man are adapted to his rudimental condition, and to that only; his ultimate condition, being unorganized, is of unlimited comprehension in all points but one—the nature of the volition of God—that is to say, the motion of the unparticled matter. You will have a distinct idea of the ultimate body by conceiving it to be entire brain. This it is *not*; but a conception of this nature will bring you near a comprehension of what it *is*.

A luminous body imparts vibration to the luminiferous ether. The vibrations generate similar ones within the retina; these again communicate similar ones to the optic nerve. The nerve conveys similar ones to the brain; the brain, also, similar ones to the unparticled matter which permeates it. The motion of this latter is thought, of which perception is the first undulation. This is the mode by which the mind of the rudimental life communicates with the external world; and this external world is, to the rudimental life, limited, through the idiosyncrasy of its organs.

But in the ultimate, unorganised life, the external world reaches the whole body, (which is of a substance having affinity to brain, as I have said,) with no other intervention than that of an infinitely rarer ether than even the luminiferous; and to this ether—in unison with it—the whole body vibrates, setting in motion the unparticled matter which permeates it. It is to the absence of idiosyncratic organs, therefore, that we must attribute the nearly unlimited perception of the ultimate life. To rudimental beings, organs are the cages necessary to confine them until fledged.

P. You speak of rudimental "beings." Are there other rudimental thinking beings than man?

V. The multitudinous conglomeration of rare matter into

nebulæ, planets, suns, and other bodies which are neither neb-ulæ, suns, nor planets, is for the sole purpose of supplying *pabulum* for the idiosyncrasy of the organs of an infinity of rudimental beings. But for the necessity of the rudimental, prior to the ultimate life, there would have been no bodies such as these. Each of these is tenanted by a distinct variety of organic, rudimental, thinking creatures. In all, the organs vary with the features of the place tenanted. At death, or metamorphosis, these creatures, enjoying the ultimate life—immortality—and cognizant of all secrets but *the one*, act all things and pass everywhere by mere volition:—indwelling, not the stars, which to us seem the sole palpabilities, and for the accommodation of which we blindly deem space created—but that *space* itself—that infinity of which the truly substantive vastness swallows up the star-shadows—blotting them out as nonentities from the perception of the angels.

P. You say that "but for the *necessity* of the rudimental life" there would have been no stars. But why this necessity?

V. In the inorganic life, as well as in the inorganic matter generally, there is nothing to impede the action of one simple *unique* law—the Divine Volition. With the view of producing impediment, the organic life and matter, (complex, substantial, and law-encumbered,) were contrived.

P. But again—why need this impediment have been produced?

V. The result of law inviolate is perfection—right—negative happiness. The result of law violate is imperfection, wrong, positive pain. Through the impediments afforded by the number, complexity, and substantiality of the laws of organic life and matter, the violation of law is rendered, to a certain extent, practicable. Thus pain, which in the inorganic life is impossible, is possible in the organic.

P. But to what good end is pain thus rendered possible?

V. All things are either good or bad by comparison. A sufficient analysis will show that pleasure, in all cases, is but the contrast of pain. *Positive* pleasure is a mere idea. To be happy at any one point we must have suffered at the same. Never to suffer would have been never to have been blessed. But it has been shown that, in the inorganic life, pain cannot be thus the necessity for the organic. The pain of the primitive life of Earth, is the sole basis of the bliss of the ultimate life in Heaven.

P. Still, there is one of your expressions which I find it impossible to comprehend—"the truly *substantive* vastness of infinity."

V. This, probably, is because you have no sufficiently generic conception of the term "*substance*" itself. We must not regard it as a quality, but as a sentiment:—it is the perception, in thinking beings, of the adaptation of matter to their organization. There are many things on the Earth, which would be nihility to the inhabitants of Venus—many things visible and tangible in Venus, which we could not be brought to appreciate as existing at all. But to the inorganic beings—to the angels—the whole of the unparticled matter is substance—that is to say, the whole of what we term "space" is to them the truest substantiality;—the stars, meantime, through what we consider their materiality, escaping the angelic sense, just in proportion as the unparticled matter, through what we consider its immateriality, eludes the organic.

As the sleep-waker pronounced these latter words, in a feeble tone, I observed on his countenance a singular expression, which somewhat alarmed me, and induced me to awake him at once. No sooner had I done this, than, with a bright smile irradiating all his features, he fell back upon his pillow and expired. I noticed that in less than a minute afterward his corpse had all the stern rigidity of stone. His brow was of the coldness of ice. Thus, ordinarily, should it have appeared, only after long pressure from Azrael's hand. Had the sleep-waker, indeed, during the latter portion of his discourse, been addressing me from out the region of the shadows?

The Spectacles

Many years ago, it was the fashion to ridicule the idea of "love at first sight;" but those who think, not less than those who feel deeply, have always advocated its existence. Modern discoveries, indeed, in what may be termed ethical magnetism or magnetoesthetics, render it probable that the most natural, and, consequently, the truest and most intense of the human affections are those which arise in the heart as if by electric sympathy—in a word, that the brightest and most enduring of the psychal fetters are those which are riveted by a glance. The confession I am about to make will add another to the already almost innumerable instances of the truth of the position.

My story requires that I should be somewhat minute. I am still a very young man—not yet twenty-two years of age. My name, at present, is a very usual and rather plebeian one—Simpson. I say "at present;" for it is only lately that I have been so called—having legislatively adopted this surname within the last year in order to receive a large inheritance left me by a distant male relative, Adolphus Simpson, Esq. The bequest was conditioned upon my taking the name of the testator,—the family, not the Christian name; my Christian name is Napoleon Bonaparte—or, more properly, these are my first and middle appellations.

I assumed the name, Simpson, with some reluctance, as in my true patronym, Froissart, I felt a very pardonable pride—believing that I could trace a descent from the immortal author of the *Chronicles*. While on the subject of names, by the bye, I may mention a singular coincidence of sound attending the names of some of my immediate predecessors. My father was a Monsieur Froissart, of Paris. His wife—my mother, whom he married at fifteen—was a Mademoiselle Croissart, eldest daughter of Croissart the banker, whose wife, again, being only sixteen when married, was the eldest daughter of one Victor Voissart. Monsieur Voissart, very singularly, had married a lady of similar name—a Mademoiselle Moissart. She, too, was quite a child when married; and her mother, also, Madame Moissart, was only fourteen when led to the altar. These early marriages are usual in France. Here, however, are Moissart, Voissart, Croissart, and Froissart, all in the direct line of descent. My own name, though, as I say, became Simpson, by act of Legislature, and with so much repugnance on my part, that, at one period, I actually hesitated about accepting the legacy with the useless and annoying *proviso* attached.

As to personal endowments, I am by no means deficient. On the contrary, I believe that I am well made, and possess what nine tenths of the world would call a handsome face. In height I am five feet eleven. My hair is black and curling. My nose is sufficiently good. My eyes are large and gray; and although, in fact they are weak a very inconvenient degree, still no defect in this regard would be suspected from their appearance. The weakness itself, however, has always much annoyed me, and I have resorted to every remedy—short of wearing glasses. Being youthful and good-looking, I naturally dislike these, and have resolutely refused to employ them.

I know nothing, indeed, which so disfigures the countenance of a young person, or so impresses every feature with an air of demureness, if not altogether of sanctimoniousness and of age. An eyeglass, on the other hand, has a savour of downright foppery and affectation. I have hitherto managed as well as I could without either. But something too much of these merely personal details, which, after all, are of little importance. I will content myself with saying, in addition, that my temperament is sanguine, rash, ardent, enthusiastic—and that all my life I have been a devoted admirer of the women.

One night last winter I entered a box at the P—— Theatre, in company with a friend, Mr. Talbot. It was an opera night, and the bills presented a very rare attraction, so that the house was excessively crowded. We were in time, however, to obtain the front seats which had been reserved for us, and into which, with some little difficulty, we elbowed our way.

For two hours my companion, who was a musical *fanatico*, gave his undivided attention to the stage; and, in the meantime, I amused myself by observing the audience, which consisted, in chief part, of the very *élite* of the city. Having satisfied myself upon this point, I was about turning my eyes to the *prima donna*, when they were arrested and riveted by a figure in one of the private boxes which had escaped my observation.

If I live a thousand years, I can never forget the intense emotion with which I regarded this figure. It was that of a female, the most exquisite I had ever beheld. The face was so far turned toward the stage that, for some minutes, I could not obtain a view of it—but the form was divine; no other word can sufficiently express its magnificent proportion—and even the term *divine* seems ridiculously feeble as I write it.

The magic of a lovely form in woman—the necromancy of female gracefulness—was always a power which I had found it impossible to resist, but here was grace personified, incarnate, the *beau ideal* of my wildest and most enthusiastic visions. The figure, almost all of which the construction of the box permitted to be seen, was somewhat above the medium height, and nearly approached, without positively reaching, the majestic. Its perfect fullness and *tournure* were delicious. The head of which only the back was visible, rivalled in outline that of the Greek Psyche, and was rather displayed than concealed by an elegant cap of *gaze aérienne*, which put me in mind of the *ventum textilem* of Apuleius.

The right arm hung over the balustrade of the box, and thrilled every nerve of my frame with its exquisite symmetry. Its upper portion was draperied by one of the loose open sleeves now in fashion. This extended but little below the elbow. Beneath it was worn an under one of some frail material, close-fitting, and terminated by a cuff of rich lace, which fell gracefully over the top of the hand, revealing only the delicate fingers, upon one of which sparkled a diamond ring, which I at once saw was of extraordinary value. The admirable roundness of the wrist was well set off by a bracelet which encircled it, and which also was ornamented and clasped by a magnificent *aigrette* of jewels-telling, in words that could not be mistaken, at once of the wealth and fastidious taste of the wearer.

I gazed at this queenly apparition for at least half an hour, as if I had been suddenly converted to stone; and, during this period, I felt the full force and truth of all that has been said or sung concerning "love at first sight." My feelings were totally different from any which I had hitherto experienced, in the presence of even the most celebrated specimens of female loveliness. An unaccountable, and what I am compelled to consider a *magnetic*, sympathy of soul for soul, seemed to rivet, not only my vision, but my whole powers of thought and feeling, upon the admirable object before me. I saw—I felt—I knew that I was deeply, madly, irrevocably in love—and this even before seeing the face of the person beloved. So intense, indeed, was the passion that consumed me, that I really believe it would have received little if any abatement had the features, yet unseen, proved of merely ordinary character, so anomalous is the nature of the only true love—of the love at first sight—and so little really dependent is it upon the external conditions which only seem to create and control it.

While I was thus wrapped in admiration of this lovely vision, a sudden disturbance among the audience caused her to turn her head partially toward me, so that I beheld the entire profile of the face. Its beauty even exceeded my anticipations—and yet there was something about it which disappointed me without my being able to tell exactly what it was. I said "disappointed," but this is not altogether the word. My sentiments were at once quieted and exalted. They partook less of transport and more of calm enthusiasm of enthusiastic repose. This state of feeling arose, perhaps, from the Madonna-like and matronly air of the face; and yet I at once understood that it could not have arisen entirely from this.

There was something else—some mystery which I could not develop—some expression about the countenance which slightly disturbed me while it greatly heightened my interest. In fact, I was just in that condition of mind which prepares a young and susceptible man for any act of extravagance. Had the lady been alone, I should undoubtedly have entered her box and accosted her at all hazards; but, fortunately, she was attended by two companions—a gentleman, and a strikingly beautiful woman, to all appearance a few years younger than herself.

I revolved in my mind a thousand schemes by which I might obtain, hereafter, an introduction to the elder lady, or, for the present, at all events, a more distinct view of her beauty. I would have removed my position to one nearer her own, but the crowded state of the theatre rendered this impossible; and the stern decrees of fashion had, of late, imperatively prohibited the use of the opera-glass in a case such as this, even had I been so fortunate as to have one with me—but I had not—and was thus in despair.

At length I bethought me of applying to my companion.

"Talbot," I said, "*you* have an opera-glass. Let me have it."

"An opera—glass!—no!—what do you suppose *I* would be doing with an opera-glass?" Here he turned impatiently toward the stage.

"But, Talbot," I continued, pulling him by the shoulder, "listen to me will you? Do you see the stage—box?—there!—no, the next.—did you ever behold as lovely a woman?"

"She is very beautiful, no doubt," he said.

"I wonder who she can be?"

"Why, in the name of all that is angelic, don't you *know* who she is? '*Not to know her argues yourself unknown.*' She is the celebrated Madame Lalande—the beauty of the day *par excellence*, and the talk of the whole town. Immensely wealthy too—a widow, and a great match—has just arrived from Paris."

"Do you know her?"

"Yes; I have the honour."

"Will you introduce me?"

"Assuredly, with the greatest pleasure; when shall it be?"

"Tomorrow, at one, I will call upon you at B—'s."

"Very good; and now *do* hold your tongue, *if* you can."

In this latter respect I was forced to take Talbot's advice; for he remained obstinately deaf to every further question or suggestion, and occupied himself exclusively for the rest of the evening with what was transacting upon the stage.

In the meantime I kept my eyes riveted on Madame Lalande, and at length had the good fortune to obtain a full front view of her face. It was exquisitely lovely—this, of course, my heart had told me before, even had not Talbot fully satisfied me upon the point—but still the unintelligible something disturbed me. I finally concluded that my senses were impressed by a certain air of gravity, sadness, or, still more properly, of weariness, which took something from the youth and freshness of the countenance, only to endow it with a seraphic tenderness and majesty, and thus, of course, to my enthusiastic and romantic temperament, with an interest tenfold.

While I thus feasted my eyes, I perceived, at last, to my great trepidation, by an almost imperceptible start on the part of the lady, that she had become suddenly aware of the intensity of my gaze. Still, I was absolutely fascinated, and could not withdraw it, even for an instant. She turned aside her face, and again I saw only the chiselled contour of the back portion of the head. After some minutes, as if urged by curiosity to see if I was still looking, she gradually brought her face again around and again encountered my burning gaze. Her large dark eyes fell instantly, and a deep blush mantled her cheek. But what was my astonishment at perceiving that she not only did not a second time avert her head, but that she actually took from her girdle a double eyeglass—elevated it—adjusted it—and then regarded me through it, intently and deliberately, for the space of several minutes.

Had a thunderbolt fallen at my feet I could not have been

more thoroughly astounded—astounded *only*—not offended or disgusted in the slightest degree; although an action so bold in any other woman would have been likely to offend or disgust. But the whole thing was done with so much quietude—so much *nonchalance*—so much repose—with so evident an air of the highest breeding, in short—that nothing of mere effrontery was perceptible, and my sole sentiments were those of admiration and surprise.

I observed that, upon her first elevation of the glass, she had seemed satisfied with a momentary inspection of my person, and was withdrawing the instrument, when, as if struck by a second thought, she resumed it, and so continued to regard me with fixed attention for the space of several minutes—for five minutes, at the very least, I am sure.

This action, so remarkable in an American theatre, attracted very general observation, and gave rise to an indefinite movement, or *buzz*, among the audience, which for a moment filled me with confusion, but produced no visible effect upon the countenance of Madame Lalande.

Having satisfied her curiosity—if such it was—she dropped the glass, and quietly gave her attention again to the stage; her profile now being turned toward myself, as before. I continued to watch her unremittingly, although I was fully conscious of my rudeness in so doing. Presently I saw the head slowly and slightly change its position; and soon I became convinced that the lady, while pretending to look at the stage was, in fact, attentively regarding myself. It is needless to say what effect this conduct, on the part of so fascinating a woman, had upon my excitable mind.

Having thus scrutinised me for perhaps a quarter of an hour, the fair object of my passion addressed the gentleman who attended her, and while she spoke, I saw distinctly, by the glances of both, that the conversation had reference to myself.

Upon its conclusion, Madame Lalande again turned toward the stage, and, for a few minutes, seemed absorbed in the performance. At the expiration of this period, however, I was thrown into an extremity of agitation by seeing her unfold, for the second time, the eye-glass which hung at her side, fully confront me as before, and, disregarding the renewed buzz of the audience, survey me, from head to foot, with the same miraculous composure which had previously so delighted and confounded my soul.

This extraordinary behaviour, by throwing me into a perfect fever of excitement—into an absolute delirium of love-served rather to embolden than to disconcert me. In the mad intensity of my devotion, I forgot everything but the presence and the majestic loveliness of the vision which confronted my gaze. Watching my opportunity, when I thought the audience were fully engaged with the opera, I at length caught the eyes of Madame Lalande, and, upon the instant, made a slight but unmistakable bow.

She blushed very deeply—then averted her eyes—then slowly and cautiously looked around, apparently to see if my rash action had been noticed—then leaned over toward the gentleman who sat by her side.

I now felt a burning sense of the impropriety I had committed, and expected nothing less than instant exposure; while a vision of pistols upon the morrow floated rapidly and uncomfortably through my brain. I was greatly and immediately relieved, however, when I saw the lady merely hand the gentleman a play-bill, without speaking, but the reader may form some feeble conception of my astonishment—of my *profound* amazement—my delirious bewilderment of heart and soul—when, instantly afterward, having again glanced furtively around, she allowed her bright eyes to set fully and steadily upon my own, and then, with a faint smile, disclosing a bright line of her pearly teeth, made two distinct, pointed, and unequivocal affirmative inclinations of the head.

It is useless, of course, to dwell upon my joy—upon my transport—upon my illimitable ecstasy of heart. If ever man was mad with excess of happiness, it was myself at that moment. I loved. This was my *first* love—so I felt it to be. It was love supreme-indescribable. It was "love at first sight;" and at first sight, too, it had been appreciated and *returned*.

Yes, returned. How and why should I doubt it for an instant. What other construction could I possibly put upon such conduct, on the part of a lady so beautiful—so wealthy—evidently so accomplished—of so high breeding—of so lofty a position in society—in every regard so entirely respectable as I felt assured was Madame Lalande? Yes, she loved me—she returned the enthusiasm of my love, with an enthusiasm as blind—as uncompromising—as uncalculating—as abandoned—and as utterly unbounded as my own! These delicious fancies and reflections, however, were now interrupted by the falling of the drop-curtain.

The audience arose; and the usual tumult immediately supervened. Quitting Talbot abruptly, I made every effort to force my way into closer proximity with Madame Lalande. Having failed in this, on account of the crowd, I at length gave up the chase, and bent my steps homeward; consoling myself for my disappointment in not having been able to touch even the hem of her robe, by the reflection that I should be introduced by Talbot, in due form, upon the morrow.

This morrow at last came, that is to say, a day finally dawned upon a long and weary night of impatience; and then the hours until "one" were snail-paced, dreary, and innumerable. But even Stamboul, it is said, shall have an end, and there came an end to this long delay. The clock struck. As the last echo ceased, I stepped into B——'s and inquired for Talbot.

"Out," said the footman—Talbot's own.

"Out!" I replied, staggering back half a dozen paces—"let me tell you, my fine fellow, that this thing is thoroughly impossible and impracticable; Mr. Talbot is *not* out. What do you mean?"

"Nothing, sir; only Mr. Talbot is not in, that's all. He rode over to S——, immediately after breakfast, and left word that he would not be in town again for a week."

I stood petrified with horror and rage. I endeavoured to reply, but my tongue refused its office. At length I turned on my heel, livid with wrath, and inwardly consigning the whole tribe of the Talbots to the innermost regions of Erebus. It was evident that my considerate friend, *il fanatico*, had quite forgotten his appointment with myself—had forgotten it as soon as it was made. At no time was he a very scrupulous man of his word. There was no help for it; so smothering my vexation as well as I could, I strolled moodily up the street, propounding futile inquiries about Madame Lalande to every male acquaintance I met. By report she was known, I found, to all—to many by sight—but she had been in town only a few weeks, and there were very few, therefore, who claimed her personal acquaintance. These few, being still comparatively strangers, could not, or would not, take the liberty of introducing me through the formality of a morning call. While I stood thus in despair, conversing with a trio of friends upon the all absorbing subject of my heart, it so happened that the subject itself passed by.

"As I live, there she is!" cried one.

"Surprisingly beautiful!" exclaimed a second.

"An angel upon earth!" ejaculated a third.

I looked; and in an open carriage which approached us, passing slowly down the street, sat the enchanting vision of the opera, accompanied by the younger lady who had occupied a portion of her box.

"Her companion also wears remarkably well," said the one of my trio who had spoken first.

"Astonishingly," said the second; "still quite a brilliant air, but art will do wonders. Upon my word, she looks better than she did at Paris five years ago. A beautiful woman still;—don't you think so, Froissart?—Simpson, I mean."

"*Still!*" said I, "and why shouldn't she be? But compared with her friend she is as a rush—light to the evening star—a glow—worm to Antares.

"Ha! ha! ha!—why, Simpson, you have an astonishing tact at making discoveries—original ones, I mean." And here we separated, while one of the trio began humming a gay *vaudeville*, of which I caught only the lines—

Ninon, Ninon, Ninon à bas—
À bas Ninon de l'Enclos!

During this little scene, however, one thing had served greatly to console me, although it fed the passion by which I was consumed. As the carriage of Madame Lalande rolled by our group, I had observed that she recognised me; and more than this, she had blessed me, by the most seraphic of all imaginable smiles, with no equivocal mark of the recognition.

As for an introduction, I was obliged to abandon all hope of it until such time as Talbot should think proper to return from the country. In the meantime I perseveringly frequented every reputable place of public amusement; and, at length, at the theatre, where I first saw her, I had the supreme bliss of meeting her, and of exchanging glances with her once again. This did not occur, however, until the lapse of a fortnight. Every day, in the *interim*, I had inquired for Talbot at his hotel, and every day had been thrown into a spasm of wrath by the everlasting "Not come home yet" of his footman.

Upon the evening in question, therefore, I was in a condition little short of madness. Madame Lalande, I had been told, was a Parisian—had lately arrived from Paris—might she not suddenly return?—return before Talbot came back—and might she not be thus lost to me forever? The thought was too terrible to bear. Since my future happiness was at issue, I resolved to act with a manly decision. In a word, upon the breaking up of the play, I traced the lady to her residence, noted the address, and the next morning sent her a full and elaborate letter, in which I poured out my whole heart.

I spoke boldly, freely—in a word, I spoke with passion. I concealed nothing—nothing even of my weakness. I alluded to the romantic circumstances of our first meeting—even to the glances which had passed between us. I went so far as to say that I felt assured of her love; while I offered this assurance, and my own intensity of devotion, as two excuses for my otherwise unpardonable conduct. As a third, I spoke of my fear that she might quit the city before I could have the opportunity of

a formal introduction. I concluded the most wildly enthusiastic epistle ever penned, with a frank declaration of my worldly
circumstances—of my affluence—and with an offer of my heart
and of my hand.

In an agony of expectation I awaited the reply. After what
seemed the lapse of a century it came.

Yes, *actually came*. Romantic as all this may appear, I really received a letter from Madame Lalande—the beautiful, the wealthy,
the idolized Madame Lalande. Her eyes—her magnificent eyes,
had not belied her noble heart. Like a true Frenchwoman as she
was she had obeyed the frank dictates of her reason—the generous impulses of her nature—despising the conventional pru-
deries of the world. She had *not* scorned my proposals. She had
not sheltered herself in silence. She had *not* returned my letter
unopened. She had even sent me, in reply, one penned by her
own exquisite fingers. It ran thus:

> Monsieur Simpson vill *pardonne* me for not compose de
> butefulle tong of his *contrée* so vell as might. It is only de
> late dat I am arrive, and not yet ave do *opportunité* for to—
> *l'étudier.*
> *Vid dis apologie for the manière, I vill now say dat, hélas!—*
> *Monsieur Simpson ave guess but de too true. Need I say de*
> *more? Hélas! am I not ready speak de too moshe?*
> Eugénie Laland.

This noble—spirited note I kissed a million times, and committed, no doubt, on its account, a thousand other extravagances
that have now escaped my memory. Still Talbot *would* not return. Alas! could he have formed even the vaguest idea of the
suffering his absence had occasioned his friend, would not his
sympathizing nature have flown immediately to my relief? Still,
however, he came *not*. I wrote. He replied. He was detained by
urgent business—but would shortly return. He begged me not
to be impatient—to moderate my transports—to read soothing
books—to drink nothing stronger than Hock—and to bring the
consolations of philosophy to my aid. The fool! if he could not

come himself, why, in the name of every thing rational, could he not have enclosed me a letter of presentation? I wrote him again, entreating him to forward one forthwith. My letter was returned by *that* footman, with the following endorsement in pencil. The scoundrel had joined his master in the country:

Left S— yesterday, for parts unknown—did not say where—or when be back—so thought best to return letter, knowing your handwriting, and as how you is always, more or less, in a hurry.

Yours sincerely,

Stubbs.

After this, it is needless to say, that I devoted to the infernal deities both master and valet:—but there was little use in anger, and no consolation at all in complaint.

But I had yet a resource left, in my constitutional audacity. Hitherto it had served me well, and I now resolved to make it avail me to the end. Besides, after the correspondence which had passed between us, what act of mere informality *could* I commit, within bounds, that ought to be regarded as indecorous by Madame Lalande? Since the affair of the letter, I had been in the habit of watching her house, and thus discovered that, about twilight, it was her custom to promenade, attended only by a negro in livery, in a public square overlooked by her windows. Here, amid the luxuriant and shadowing groves, in the gray gloom of a sweet midsummer evening, I observed my opportunity and accosted her.

The better to deceive the servant in attendance, I did this with the assured air of an old and familiar acquaintance. With a presence of mind truly Parisian, she took the cue at once, and, to greet me, held out the most bewitchingly little of hands. The valet at once fell into the rear, and now, with hearts full to overflowing, we discoursed long and unreservedly of our love.

As Madame Lalande spoke English even less fluently than she wrote it, our conversation was necessarily in French. In this sweet tongue, so adapted to passion, I gave loose to the impetuous enthusiasm of my nature, and, with all the eloquence I could command, besought her to consent to an immediate marriage.

At this impatience she smiled. She urged the old story of decorum—that bug-bear which deters so many from bliss until the opportunity for bliss has forever gone by. I had most imprudently made it known among my friends, she observed, that I desired her acquaintance—thus that I did not possess it—thus, again, there was no possibility of concealing the date of our first knowledge of each other. And then she adverted, with a blush, to the extreme recency of this date. To wed immediately would be improper—would be indecorous—would be *outré*. All this she said with a charming air of *naïveté* which enraptured while it grieved and convinced me.

She went even so far as to accuse me, laughingly, of rashness—of imprudence. She bade me remember that I really even know not who she was—what were her prospects, her connections, her standing in society. She begged me, but with a sigh, to reconsider my proposal, and termed my love an infatuation—a will o' the wisp—a fancy or fantasy of the moment—a baseless and unstable creation rather of the imagination than of the heart. These things she uttered as the shadows of the sweet twilight gathered darkly and more darkly around us—and then, with a gentle pressure of her fairy-like hand, overthrew, in a single sweet instant, all the argumentative fabric she had reared.

I replied as best I could—as only a true lover can. I spoke at length, and perseveringly of my devotion, of my passion—of her exceeding beauty, and of my own enthusiastic admiration. In conclusion, I dwelt, with a convincing energy, upon the perils that encompass the course of love—that course of true love that never did run smooth—and thus deduced the manifest danger of rendering that course unnecessarily long.

This latter argument seemed finally to soften the rigor of her determination. She relented; but there was yet an obstacle, she said, which she felt assured I had not properly considered. This was a delicate point—for a woman to urge, especially so; in mentioning it, she saw that she must make a sacrifice of her feelings; still, for *me*, every sacrifice should be made. She alluded to the topic of *age*. Was I aware—was I fully aware of the discrepancy between us? That the age of the husband, should surpass by a few years—even by fifteen or twenty—the age of the wife, was regarded by the world as admissible, and, indeed, as even proper, but she had always entertained the belief that the years of the wife should never exceed in number those of the husband. A discrepancy of this unnatural kind gave rise, too frequently, alas! to a life of unhappiness. Now she was aware that my own age did not exceed two and twenty; and I, on the contrary, perhaps, was *not* aware that the years of my Eugénie extended very considerably beyond that sum.

About all this there was a nobility of soul—a dignity of candour—which delighted—which enchanted me—which eternally riveted my chains. I could scarcely restrain the excessive transport which possessed me.

"My sweetest Eugénie," I cried, "what is all this about which you are discoursing? Your years surpass in some measure my own. But what then? The customs of the world are so many conventional follies. To those who love as ourselves, in what respect differs a year from an hour? I am twenty-two, you say, granted: indeed, you may as well call me, at once, twenty-three. Now you yourself, my dearest Eugénie, can have numbered no more than—can have numbered no more than—no more than—than—than—than—"

Here I paused for an instant, in the expectation that Madame Lalande would interrupt me by supplying her true age. But a Frenchwoman is seldom direct, and has always, by way of answer to an embarrassing query, some little practical reply of her own. In the present instance, Eugénie, who for a few moments past had seemed to be searching for something in her bosom, at length let fall upon the grass a miniature, which I immediately picked up and presented to her.

"Keep it!" she said, with one of her most ravishing smiles. "Keep it for my sake—for the sake of her whom it too flatteringly represents. Besides, upon the back of the trinket you may discover, perhaps, the very information you seem to desire. It is now, to be sure, growing rather dark—but you can examine it at your leisure in the morning. In the meantime, you shall be my escort home tonight. My friends are about holding a little musical *levée*. I can promise you, too, some good singing. We French are not nearly so punctilious as you Americans, and I shall have no difficulty in smuggling you in, in the character of an old acquaintance."

With this, she took my arm, and I attended her home. The mansion was quite a fine one, and, I believe, furnished in good taste. Of this latter point, however, I am scarcely qualified to judge; for it was just dark as we arrived; and in American mansions of the better sort lights seldom, during the heat of summer, make their appearance at this, the most pleasant period of the day. In about an hour after my arrival, to be sure, a single shaded solar lamp was lit in the principal drawing-room; and this apartment, I could thus see, was arranged with unusual good taste and even splendour; but two other rooms of the suite, and in which the company chiefly assembled, remained, during the whole evening, in a very agreeable shadow. This is a well-conceived custom, giving the party at least a choice of light or shade, and one which our friends over the water could not do better than immediately adopt.

The evening thus spent was unquestionably the most delicious of my life. Madame Lalande had not overrated the musical abilities of her friends; and the singing I here heard I had never heard excelled in any private circle out of Vienna. The instrumental performers were many and of superior talents. The vocalists were chiefly ladies, and no individual sang less than well. At length, upon a peremptory call for "Madame Lalande," she arose at once, without affectation or demur, from the *chaise longue* upon which she had sat by my side, and, accompanied by one or two gentlemen and her female friend of the opera, repaired to the piano in the main drawing-room. I would have escorted her myself, but felt that, under the circumstances of my introduction to the house, I had better remain unobserved where I was. I was thus deprived of the pleasure of seeing, although not of hearing, her sing.

The impression she produced upon the company seemed electrical but the effect upon myself was something even more. I know not how adequately to describe it. It arose in part, no doubt, from the sentiment of love with which I was imbued; but chiefly from my conviction of the extreme sensibility of the singer. It is beyond the reach of art to endow either air or recitative with more impassioned *expression* than was hers. Her utterance of the romance in Otello—the tone with which she gave the words "*Sul mio sasso*," in the Capuletti—is ringing in my memory yet. Her lower tones were absolutely miraculous. Her voice embraced three complete octaves, extending from the *contralto* D to the D upper *soprano*, and, though sufficiently powerful to have filled the San Carlos, executed, with the minutest precision, every difficulty of vocal composition-ascending and descending scales, cadences, or *fiorituri*. In the final of the Somnambula, she brought about a most remarkable effect at the words:

> *Ah! non guinge uman pensiero*
> *Al contento ond 'io son piena.*

Here, in imitation of Malibran, she modified the original phrase of Bellini, so as to let her voice descend to the tenor G, when, by a rapid transition, she struck the G above the treble stave, springing over an interval of two octaves.

Upon rising from the piano after these miracles of vocal execution, she resumed her seat by my side; when I expressed to her, in terms of the deepest enthusiasm, my delight at her performance. Of my surprise I said nothing, and yet was I most unfeignedly surprised; for a certain feebleness, or rather a certain tremulous indecision of voice in ordinary conversation, had prepared me to anticipate that, in singing, she would not acquit herself with any remarkable ability.

Our conversation was now long, earnest, uninterrupted, and totally unreserved. She made me relate many of the earlier passages of my life, and listened with breathless attention to every word of the narrative. I concealed nothing—felt that I had a right to conceal nothing—from her confiding affection. Encouraged by her candour upon the delicate point of her age, I entered, with perfect frankness, not only into a detail of my many minor vices, but made full confession of those moral and even of those physical infirmities, the disclosure of which, in demanding so much higher a degree of courage, is so much surer an evidence of love. I touched upon my college indiscretions—upon my extravagances—upon my carousals—upon my debts—upon my flirtations. I even went so far as to speak of a slightly hectic cough with which, at one time, I had been troubled—of a chronic rheumatism—of a twinge of hereditary gout—and, in conclusion, of the disagreeable and inconvenient, but hitherto carefully concealed, weakness of my eyes.

"Upon this latter point," said Madame Lalande, laughingly, "you have been surely injudicious in coming to confession; for, without the confession, I take it for granted that no one would have accused you of the crime. By the by," she continued, "have you any recollection-" and here I fancied that a blush, even through the gloom of the apartment, became distinctly visible upon her cheek—"have you any recollection, *mon cher ami* of this little ocular assistant, which now depends from my neck?"

As she spoke she twirled in her fingers the identical double eye-glass which had so overwhelmed me with confusion at the opera.

"Full well—alas! do I remember it," I exclaimed, pressing passionately the delicate hand which offered the glasses for my inspection. They formed a complex and magnificent toy, richly chased and filigreed, and gleaming with jewels, which, even in the deficient light, I could not help perceiving were of high value.

"*Eh bien! mon ami*" she resumed with a certain *empressment* of manner that rather surprised me—"*Eh bien! mon ami*, you have earnestly besought of me a favour which you have been pleased to denominate priceless. You have demanded of me my hand upon the morrow. Should I yield to your entreaties—and, I may add, to the pleadings of my own bosom—would I not be entitled to demand of you a very—a very little boon in return?"

"Name it!" I exclaimed with an energy that had nearly drawn upon us the observation of the company, and restrained by their presence alone from throwing myself impetuously at her feet. "Name it, my beloved, my Eugenie, my own!—name it!—but, alas! it is already yielded ere named."

"You shall conquer, then, *mon ami*," said she, "for the sake of the Eugénie whom you love, this little weakness which you have at last confessed—this weakness more moral than physical—and which, let me assure you, is so unbecoming the nobility of your real nature—so inconsistent with the candour of your usual character—and which, if permitted further control, will assuredly involve you, sooner or later, in some very disagreeable scrape. You shall conquer, for my sake, this affectation which leads you, as you yourself acknowledge, to the tacit or implied denial of your infirmity of vision.

"For, this infirmity you virtually deny, in refusing to employ the customary means for its relief. You will understand me to say, then, that I wish you to wear spectacles;—ah, hush!—you have already consented to wear them, *for my sake*. You shall accept the little toy which I now hold in my hand, and which, though admirable as an aid to vision, is really of no very immense value as a gem. You perceive that, by a trifling modification thus—or thus—it can be adapted to the eyes in the form of spectacles, or worn in the waistcoat pocket as an eye-glass. It is in the former mode, however, and habitually, that you have already consented to wear it *for my sake*."

This request—must I confess it?—confused me in no little degree. But the condition with which it was coupled rendered hesitation, of course, a matter altogether out of the question.

"It is done!" I cried, with all the enthusiasm that I could muster at the moment. "It is done—it is most cheerfully agreed. I sacrifice every feeling for your sake. Tonight I wear this dear eye-glass, *as* an eye-glass, and upon my heart; but with the earliest dawn of that morning which gives me the pleasure of calling you wife, I will place it upon my—upon my nose,—and there wear it ever afterward, in the less romantic, and less fashionable, but certainly in the more serviceable, form which you desire."

Our conversation now turned upon the details of our arrangements for the morrow. Talbot, I learned from my betrothed, had just arrived in town. I was to see him at once, and procure a carriage. The *soirée* would scarcely break up before two; and by this hour the vehicle was to be at the door, when, in the confusion occasioned by the departure of the company, Madame L. could easily enter it unobserved. We were then to call at the house of a clergyman who would be in waiting; there be married, drop Talbot, and proceed on a short tour to the East, leaving the fashionable world at home to make whatever comments upon the matter it thought best.

Having planned all this, I immediately took leave, and went in search of Talbot, but, on the way, I could not refrain from stepping into a hotel, for the purpose of inspecting the miniature; and this I did by the powerful aid of the glasses. The countenance was a surpassingly beautiful one! Those large luminous eyes!—that proud Grecian nose!—those dark luxuriant curls!—"Ah!" said I, exultingly to myself, "this is indeed the speaking image of my beloved!" I turned the reverse, and discovered the words—"Eugénie Lalande—aged twenty-seven years and seven months."

I found Talbot at home, and proceeded at once to acquaint him with my good fortune. He professed excessive astonishment, of course, but congratulated me most cordially, and proffered every assistance in his power. In a word, we carried out our arrangement to the letter, and, at two in the morning, just ten minutes after the ceremony, I found myself in a close carriage with Madame Lalande—with Mrs. Simpson, I should say—and driving at a great rate out of town, in a direction Northeast by North, half-North.

It had been determined for us by Talbot, that, as we were to be up all night, we should make our first stop at C—, a village about twenty miles from the city, and there get an early breakfast and some repose, before proceeding upon our route. At four precisely, therefore, the carriage drew up at the door of the principal inn. I handed my adored wife out, and ordered breakfast forthwith. In the meantime we were shown into a small parlour, and sat down.

It was now nearly if not altogether daylight; and, as I gazed, enraptured, at the angel by my side, the singular idea came, all at once, into my head, that this was really the very first moment since my acquaintance with the celebrated loveliness of Madame Lalande, that I had enjoyed a near inspection of that loveliness by daylight at all.

"And now, *mon ami*," said she, taking my hand, and so interrupting this train of reflection, "and now, *mon cher ami*, since we are indissolubly one—since I have yielded to your passionate entreaties, and performed my portion of our agreement—I presume you have not forgotten that you also have a little favour to bestow—a little promise which it is your intention to keep. Ah! let me see! Let me remember! Yes; full easily do I call to mind the precise words of the dear promise you made to Eugénie last night. Listen! You spoke thus:

'It is done!—it is most cheerfully agreed! I sacrifice every feeling for your sake. Tonight I wear this dear eye-glass as an eye-glass, and upon my heart; but with the earliest dawn of that morning which gives me the privilege of calling you wife, I will place it upon my—upon my nose,—and there wear it ever afterward, in the less romantic, and less fashionable, but certainly in the more serviceable, form which you desire.'

These were the exact words, my beloved husband, were they not?"

"They were," I said; "you have an excellent memory; and assuredly, my beautiful Eugénie, there is no disposition on my part to evade the performance of the trivial promise they imply. See! Behold! they are becoming—rather—are they not?" And here, having arranged the glasses in the ordinary form of spectacles, I applied them gingerly in their proper position; while Madame

Simpson, adjusting her cap, and folding her arms, sat bolt upright in her chair, in a somewhat stiff and prim, and indeed, in a somewhat undignified position.

"Goodness gracious me!" I exclaimed, almost at the very instant that the rim of the spectacles had settled upon my nose— "*My!* goodness gracious me!—why, what can be the matter with these glasses?" and taking them quickly off, I wiped them carefully with a silk handkerchief, and adjusted them again.

But if, in the first instance, there had occurred something which occasioned me surprise, in the second, this surprise became elevated into astonishment; and this astonishment was profound—was extreme—indeed I may say it was horrific. What, in the name of everything hideous, did this mean? Could I believe my eyes?—*could* I?—that was the question. Was that—was that—was that *rouge?* And were those—and were those—were those *wrinkles*, upon the visage of Eugénie Lalande? And oh! Jupiter, and every one of the gods and goddesses, little and big! what—what—what—*what* had become of her teeth? I dashed the spectacles violently to the ground, and, leaping to my feet, stood erect in the middle of the floor, confronting Mrs. Simpson, with my arms set *akimbo*, and grinning and foaming, but, at the same time, utterly speechless with terror and with rage.

Now I have already said that Madame Eugénie Lalande— that is to say, Simpson—spoke the English language but very little better than she wrote it, and for this reason she very properly never attempted to speak it upon ordinary occasions. But rage will carry a lady to any extreme; and in the present care it carried Mrs. Simpson to the very extraordinary extreme of attempting to hold a conversation in a tongue that she did not altogether understand.

"Vell, *Monsieur*," said she, after surveying me, in great apparent astonishment, for some moments—"Vell, *Monsieur?*—and vat den?—vat *de* matter now? Is it *de* dance of *de* Saint itusse dat you ave? If not like me, vat for vy buy *de* pig in the poke?"

"You wretch!" said I, catching my breath—"you—you—you villainous old hag!"

"Ag?—ole?—me not so ver ole, after all! Me not one single day more dan de eighty-doo."

"Eighty-two!" I ejaculated, staggering to the wall—"eighty-two hundred thousand baboons! The miniature said twenty-seven years and seven months!"

"To be sure!—*dat* is so!—*ver* true! but *den de portraite* has been take for dese fifty-five year. Ven I go marry my segonde usbande, Monsieur Lalande, at *dat* time I had *de portraite* take for my daughter by my first usbande, Monsieur Moissart!"

"Moissart!" said I.

"Yes, Moissart," said she, mimicking my pronunciation, which, to speak the truth, was none of the best,—"and vat *den*? Vat you know about *de* Moissart?"

"Nothing, you old fright!—I know nothing about him at all; only I had an ancestor of that name, once upon a time."

"*Dat* name! and vat you ave for say to *dat* name? 'Tis *ver goot* name; and so is Voissart—*dat* is *ver goot* name too. My daughter, Mademoiselle Moissart, she marry von Monsieur Voissart,—and *de* name is both *ver* respectaable name."

"Moissart?" I exclaimed, "and Voissart! Why, what is it you mean?"

"Vat I mean?—I mean Moissart and Voissart; and for *de* matter of *dat*, I mean Croissart and Froisart, too, if I only tink proper to mean it. My daughter's daughter, Mademoiselle Voissart, she marry von Monsieur Croissart, and den again, my daughter's grande daughter, Mademoiselle Croissart, she marry von Monsieur Froissart; and I suppose you say *dat dat* is not von *ver* respectaable name."

"Froissart!" said I, beginning to faint, "why, surely you don't say Moissart, and Voissart, and Croissart, and Froissart?"

"Yes," she replied, leaning fully back in her chair, and stretching out her lower limbs at great length; "yes, Moissart, and Voissart, and Croissart, and Froissart. But Monsieur Froissart, he vas von *ver* big vat you call fool—he vas von *ver* great big donce like yourself—for he lef *la belle* France for come to *dis stupide* Amerique—and ven he get here he went and ave *von* ver *stupide*, von ver, ver *stupide* sonn, so I hear, dough I not yet av ad *de plaisir* to meet vid him—neither me nor my companion, de Madame Stephanie Lalande. He is name de Napoleon Bonaparte Froissart, and I suppose you say *dat dat*, too, is not von ver respectable name."

Either the length or the nature of this speech, had the effect of working up Mrs. Simpson into a very extraordinary passion indeed; and as she made an end of it, with great labour, she lumped up from her chair like somebody bewitched, dropping upon the floor an entire universe of bustle as she lumped. Once upon her feet, she gnashed her gums, brandished her arms, rolled up her sleeves, shook her fist in my face, and concluded the performance by tearing the cap from her head, and with it an immense wig of the most valuable and beautiful black hair, the whole of which she dashed upon the ground with a yell, and there trampled and danced a *fandango* upon it, in an absolute ecstasy and agony of rage.

Meantime I sank aghast into the chair which she had vacated. "Moissart and Voissart!" I repeated, thoughtfully, as she cut one of her pigeon-wings, and "Croissart and Froissart!" as she completed another—"Moissart and Voissart and Croissart and Napoleon Bonaparte Froissart!—why, you ineffable old serpent, that's *me*—that's me—d'ye hear? that's *me*"—here I screamed at the top of my voice—"that's *me-e-e!* I am Napoleon Bonaparte Froissart! and if I havn't married my great, great, grandmother, I wish I may be everlastingly confounded!"

Madame Eugénie Lalande, *quasi* Simpson—formerly Moissart—was, in sober fact, my great, great, grandmother. In her youth she had been beautiful, and even at eighty-two, retained the majestic height, the sculptural contour of head, the fine eyes and the Grecian nose of her girlhood. By the aid of these, of pearl-powder, of rouge, of false hair, false teeth, and false *tournure*, as well as of the most skilful *modistes* of Paris, she contrived to hold a respectable footing among the beauties *en peu passées* of the French metropolis. In this respect, indeed, she might have been regarded as little less than the equal of the celebrated Ninon de l'Enclos.

She was immensely wealthy, and being left, for the second time, a widow without children, she bethought herself of my existence in America, and for the purpose of making me her heir, paid a visit to the United States, in company with a distant and exceedingly lovely relative of her second husband's—a Madame Stephanie Lalande.

At the opera, my great, great, grandmother's attention was arrested by my notice; and, upon surveying me through her eyeglass, she was struck with a certain family resemblance to herself. Thus interested, and knowing that the heir she sought was actually in the city, she made inquiries of her party respecting me. The gentleman who attended her knew my person, and told her who I was. The information thus obtained induced her to renew her scrutiny; and this scrutiny it was which so emboldened me that I behaved in the absurd manner already detailed. She returned my bow, however, under the impression that, by some odd accident, I had discovered her identity. When, deceived by my weakness of vision, and the arts of the toilet, in respect to the age and charms of the strange lady, I demanded so enthusiastically of Talbot who she was, he concluded that I meant the younger beauty, as a matter of course, and so informed me, with perfect truth, that she was "the celebrated widow, Madame Lalande."

In the street, next morning, my great, great, grandmother encountered Talbot, an old Parisian acquaintance; and the conversation, very naturally turned upon myself. My deficiencies of vision were then explained; for these were notorious, although I was entirely ignorant of their notoriety, and my good old relative discovered, much to her chagrin, that she had been deceived in supposing me aware of her identity, and that I had been merely making a fool of myself in making open love, in a theatre, to an old woman unknown. By way of punishing me for this imprudence, she concocted with Talbot a plot. He purposely kept out of my way to avoid giving me the introduction.

My street inquiries about "the lovely widow, Madame Lalande," were supposed to refer to the younger lady, of course, and thus the conversation with the three gentlemen whom I encountered shortly after leaving Talbot's hotel will be easily explained, as also their allusion to Ninon de l'Enclos. I had no opportunity of seeing Madame Lalande closely during daylight; and, at her musical *soirée*, my silly weakness in refusing the aid of glasses effectually prevented me from making a discovery of her age. When "Madame Lalande" was called upon to sing, the younger lady was intended; and it was she who arose to obey the call; my great, great, grandmother, to further the deception, arising at the same moment and accompanying her to the piano in the main drawing-room.

Had I decided upon escorting her thither, it had been her design to suggest the propriety of my remaining where I was; but my own prudential views rendered this unnecessary. The songs which I so much admired, and which so confirmed my impression of the youth of my mistress, were executed by Madame Stephanie Lalande. The eyeglass was presented by way of adding a reproof to the hoax—a sting to the epigram of the deception. Its presentation afforded an opportunity for the lecture upon affectation with which I was so especially edified. It is almost superfluous to add that the glasses of the instrument, as worn by the old lady, had been exchanged by her for a pair better adapted to my years. They suited me, in fact, to a T.

The clergyman, who merely pretended to tie the fatal knot, was a boon companion of Talbot's, and no priest. He was an excellent "whip," however; and having doffed his cassock to put on a great-coat, he drove the hack which conveyed the "happy couple" out of town. Talbot took a seat at his side. The two scoundrels were thus "in at the death," and through a half-open window of the back parlour of the inn, amused themselves in grinning at the *dénouement* of the drama. I believe I shall be forced to call them both out.

Nevertheless, I am *not* the husband of my great, great, grandmother; and this is a reflection which affords me infinite relief,— but I *am* the husband of Madame Lalande—of Madame Stephanie Lalande—with whom my good old relative, besides making me her sole heir when she dies—if she ever does—has been at the trouble of concocting me a match. In conclusion: I am done forever with *billets doux* and am never to be met without *spectacles*.

The Black Cat

For the most wild, yet most homely narrative which I am about to pen, I neither expect nor solicit belief. Mad indeed would I be to expect it, in a case where my very senses reject their own evidence. Yet, mad am I not—and very surely do I not dream. But tomorrow I die, and today I would unburthen my soul. My immediate purpose is to place before the world, plainly, succinctly, and without comment, a series of mere household events. In their consequences, these events have terrified—have tortured—have destroyed me. Yet I will not attempt to expound them. To me, they have presented little but Horror—to many they will seem less terrible than *barroques*. Hereafter, perhaps, some intellect may be found which will reduce my phantasm to the common-place—some intellect more calm, more logical, and far less excitable than my own, which will perceive, in the circumstances I detail with awe, nothing more than an ordinary succession of very natural causes and effects.

From my infancy I was noted for the docility and humanity of my disposition. My tenderness of heart was even so conspicuous as to make me the jest of my companions. I was especially fond of animals, and was indulged by my parents with a great variety of pets. With these I spent most of my time, and never was so happy as when feeding and caressing them. This peculiarity of character grew with my growth, and in my manhood, I derived from it one of my principal sources of pleasure. To those who have cherished an affection for a faithful and sagacious dog, I need hardly be at the trouble of explaining the nature or the intensity of the gratification thus derivable. There is something in the unselfish and self-sacrificing love of a brute, which goes directly to the heart of him who has had frequent occasion to test the paltry friendship and gossamer fidelity of mere *Man*.

I married early, and was happy to find in my wife a disposition not uncongenial with my own. Observing my partiality for domestic pets, she lost no opportunity of procuring those of the most agreeable kind. We had birds, gold-fish, a fine dog, rabbits, a small monkey, and a *cat*.

This latter was a remarkably large and beautiful animal, entirely black, and sagacious to an astonishing degree. In speaking of his intelligence, my wife, who at heart was not a little tinctured with superstition, made frequent allusion to the ancient popular notion, which regarded all black cats as witches in disguise. Not that she was ever *serious* upon this point—and I mention the matter at all for no better reason than that it happens, just now, to be remembered.

Pluto—this was the cat's name—was my favorite pet and playmate. I alone fed him, and he attended me wherever I went about the house. It was even with difficulty that I could prevent him from following me through the streets.

Our friendship lasted, in this manner, for several years, during which my general temperament and character—through the instrumentality of the Fiend Intemperance—had (I blush to confess it) experienced a radical alteration for the worse. I grew, day by day, more moody, more irritable, more regardless of the feelings of others. I suffered myself to use intemperate language to my wife. At length, I even offered her personal violence. My pets, of course, were made to feel the change in my disposition. I not only neglected, but ill-used them. For Pluto, however, I still retained sufficient regard to restrain me from maltreating him, as I made no scruple of maltreating the rabbits, the monkey, or even the dog, when by accident, or through affection, they came in my way. But my disease grew upon me—for what disease is like alcohol!—and at length even Pluto, who was now becoming old, and consequently somewhat peevish—even Pluto began to experience the effects of my ill temper.

One night, returning home, much intoxicated, from one of my haunts about town, I fancied that the cat avoided my presence. I seized him; when, in his fright at my violence, he inflicted a slight wound upon my hand with his teeth. The fury of a demon instantly possessed me. I knew myself no longer. My original soul seemed, at once, to take its flight from my body and a more than fiendish malevolence, gin-nurtured, thrilled every fibre of my frame. I took from my waistcoat-pocket a pen-knife, opened it, grasped the poor beast by the throat, and deliberately cut one of its eyes from the socket! I blush, I burn, I shudder, while I pen the damnable atrocity.

When reason returned with the morning—when I had slept off the fumes of the night's debauch—I experienced a sentiment half of horror, half of remorse, for the crime of which I had been guilty; but it was, at best, a feeble and equivocal feeling, and the soul remained untouched. I again plunged into excess, and soon drowned in wine all memory of the deed.

In the meantime the cat slowly recovered. The socket of the lost eye presented, it is true, a frightful appearance, but he no longer appeared to suffer any pain. He went about the house as usual, but, as might be expected, fled in extreme terror at my approach. I had so much of my old heart left, as to be at first grieved by this evident dislike on the part of a creature which had once so loved me. But this feeling soon gave place to irritation. And then came, as if to my final and irrevocable overthrow, the spirit of *perverseness*. Of this spirit philosophy takes no account.

Yet I am not more sure that my soul lives, than I am that perverseness is one of the primitive impulses of the human heart—one of the indivisible primary faculties, or sentiments, which give direction to the character of Man. Who has not, a hundred times, found himself committing a vile or a silly action, for no other reason than because he knows he should *not?* Have we not a perpetual inclination, in the teeth of our best judgment, to violate that which is *law*, merely because we understand it to be such? This spirit of perverseness, I say, came to my final overthrow. It was this unfathomable longing of the soul *to vex itself*—to offer violence to its own nature—to do wrong for the wrong's sake only—that urged me to continue and finally to consummate the injury I had inflicted upon the unoffending brute.

One morning, in cool blood, I slipped a noose about its neck and hung it to the limb of a tree;—hung it with the tears streaming from my eyes, and with the bitterest remorse at my heart;—hung it *because* I knew that it had loved me, and *because* I felt it had given me no reason of offence;—hung it *because* I knew that in so doing I was committing a sin—a deadly sin that would so jeopardize my immortal soul as to place it—if such a thing wore possible—even beyond the reach of the infinite mercy of the Most Merciful and Most Terrible God.

On the night of the day on which this cruel deed was done, I was aroused from sleep by the cry of fire. The curtains of my bed were in flames. The whole house was blazing. It was with great difficulty that my wife, a servant, and myself, made our escape from the conflagration. The destruction was complete. My entire worldly wealth was swallowed up, and I resigned myself thenceforward to despair.

I am above the weakness of seeking to establish a sequence of cause and effect, between the disaster and the atrocity. But I am detailing a chain of facts—and wish not to leave even a possible link imperfect. On the day succeeding the fire, I visited the ruins. The walls, with one exception, had fallen in. This exception was found in a compartment wall, not very thick, which stood about the middle of the house, and against which had rested the head of my bed. The plastering had here, in great measure, resisted the action of the fire—a fact which I attributed to its having been recently spread. About this wall a dense crowd were collected, and many persons seemed to be examining a particular portion of it with very minute and eager attention. The words "strange!" "singular!" and other similar expressions, excited my curiosity. I approached and saw, as if graven in *bas relief* upon the white surface, the figure of a gigantic *cat*. The impression was given with an accuracy truly marvellous. There was a rope about the animal's neck.

When I first beheld this apparition—for I could scarcely re-gard it as less—my wonder and my terror were extreme. But at length reflection came to my aid. The cat, I remembered, had been hung in a garden adjacent to the house. Upon the alarm of fire, this garden had been immediately filled by the crowd—by someone of whom the animal must have been cut from the tree and thrown, through an open window, into my chamber. This had probably been done with the view of arousing me from sleep. The falling of other walls had compressed the victim of my cruelty into the substance of the freshly-spread plaster; the lime of which, with the flames, and the *ammonia* from the carcass, had then accomplished the portraiture as I saw it.

Although I thus readily accounted to my reason, if not al-together to my conscience, for the startling fact just detailed, it did not the less fail to make a deep impression upon my fancy. For months I could not rid myself of the phantasm of the cat; and, during this period, there came back into my spirit a half-sentiment that seemed, but was not, remorse. I went so far as to regret the loss of the animal, and to look about me, among the vile haunts which I now habitually frequented, for another pet of the same species, and of somewhat similar appearance, with which to supply its place.

One night as I sat, half stupefied, in a den of more than infamy, my attention was suddenly drawn to some black object, reposing upon the head of one of the immense hogsheads of Gin, or of Rum, which constituted the chief furniture of the apartment. I had been looking steadily at the top of this hogshead for some minutes, and what now caused me surprise was the fact that I had not sooner perceived the object thereupon. I approached it, and touched it with my hand. It was a black cat—a very large one—fully as large as Pluto, and closely resembling him in every respect but one. Pluto had not a white hair upon any portion of his body; but this cat had a large, although indefinite splotch of white, covering nearly the whole region of the breast. Upon my touching him, he immediately arose, purred loudly, rubbed against my hand, and appeared delighted with my notice. This, then, was the very creature of which I was in search. I at once offered to purchase it of the landlord; but this person made no claim to it—knew nothing of it—had never seen it before.

I continued my caresses, and, when I prepared to go home, the animal evinced a disposition to accompany me. I permitted it to do so; occasionally stooping and patting it as I proceeded. When it reached the house it domesticated itself at once, and became immediately a great favorite with my wife.

For my own part, I soon found a dislike to it arising within me. This was just the reverse of what I had anticipated; but—I know not how or why it was—its evident fondness for myself rather disgusted and annoyed. By slow degrees, these feelings of disgust and annoyance rose into the bitterness of hatred. I avoided the creature; a certain sense of shame, and the remembrance of my former deed of cruelty, preventing me from physically abusing it. I did not, for some weeks, strike, or otherwise violently ill use it; but gradually—very gradually—I came to look upon it with unutterable loathing, and to flee silently from its odious presence, as from the breath of a pestilence.

What added, no doubt, to my hatred of the beast, was the discovery, on the morning after I brought it home, that, like Pluto, it also had been deprived of one of its eyes. This circumstance, however, only endeared it to my wife, who, as I have already said, possessed, in a high degree, that humanity of feeling which had once been my distinguishing trait, and the source of many of my simplest and purest pleasures.

With my aversion to this cat, however, its partiality for myself seemed to increase. It followed my footsteps with a pertinacity which it would be difficult to make the reader comprehend. Whenever I sat, it would crouch beneath my chair, or spring upon my knees, covering me with its loathsome caresses. If I arose to walk it would get between my feet and thus nearly throw me down, or, fastening its long and sharp claws in my dress, clamber, in this manner, to my breast. At such times, although I longed to destroy it with a blow, I was yet withheld from so doing, partly by a memory of my former crime, but chiefly—let me confess it at once—by absolute *dread* of the beast.

This dread was not exactly a dread of physical evil—and yet I should be at a loss how otherwise to define it. I am almost ashamed to own—yes, even in this felon's cell, I am almost ashamed to own—that the terror and horror with which the animal inspired me, had been heightened by one of the merest chimaeras it would be possible to conceive. My wife had called my attention, more than once, to the character of the mark of white hair, of which I have spoken, and which constituted the sole visible difference between the strange beast and the one I had destroyed.

The reader will remember that this mark, although large, had been originally very indefinite; but, by slow degrees—degrees nearly imperceptible, and which for a long time my reason struggled to reject as fanciful—it had, at length, assumed a rigorous distinctness of outline. It was now the representation of an object that I shudder to name—and for this, above all, I loathed, and dreaded, and would have rid myself of the monster *had I dared*—it was now, I say, the image of a hideous—of a ghastly thing—of the *gallows!*—oh, mournful and terrible engine of Horror and of Crime—of Agony and of Death!

And now was I indeed wretched beyond the wretchedness of mere Humanity. And *a brute beast* —whose fellow I had contemptuously destroyed—*a brute beast* to work out for *me*—for me a man, fashioned in the image of the High God—so much of insufferable woe! Alas! neither by day nor by night knew I the blessing of rest any more! During the former the creature left me no moment alone; and, in the latter, I started, hourly, from dreams of unutterable fear, to find the hot breath of *the thing* upon my face, and its vast weight—an incarnate nightmare that I had no power to shake off—incumbent eternally upon my *heart!*

Beneath the pressure of torments such as these, the feeble

remnant of the good within me succumbed. Evil thoughts became my sole intimates—the darkest and most evil of thoughts. The moodiness of my usual temper increased to hatred of all things and of all mankind; while, from the sudden, frequent, and ungovernable outbursts of a fury to which I now blindly abandoned myself, my uncomplaining wife, alas! was the most usual and the most patient of sufferers.

One day she accompanied me, upon some household errand, into the cellar of the old building which our poverty compelled us to inhabit. The cat followed me down the steep stairs, and, nearly throwing me headlong, exasperated me to madness. Uplifting an axe, and forgetting, in my wrath, the childish dread which had hitherto stayed my hand, I aimed a blow at the animal which, of course, would have proved instantly fatal had it descended as I wished. But this blow was arrested by the hand of my wife. Goaded, by the interference, into a rage more than demoniacal, I withdrew my arm from her grasp and buried the axe in her brain. She fell dead upon the spot, without a groan.

This hideous murder accomplished, I set myself forthwith, and with entire deliberation, to the task of concealing the body. I knew that I could not remove it from the house, either by day or by night, without the risk of being observed by the neighbors. Many projects entered my mind. At one period I thought of cutting the corpse into minute fragments, and destroying them by fire. At another, I resolved to dig a grave for it in the floor of the cellar. Again, I deliberated about casting it in the well in the yard—about packing it in a box, as if merchandize, with the usual arrangements, and so getting a porter to take it from the house. Finally I hit upon what I considered a far better expedient than either of these. I determined to wall it up in the cellar—as the monks of the middle ages are recorded to have walled up their victims.

For a purpose such as this the cellar was well adapted. Its walls were loosely constructed, and had lately been plastered throughout with a rough plaster, which the dampness of the atmosphere had prevented from hardening. Moreover, in one of the walls was a projection, caused by a false chimney, or fireplace, that had been filled up, and made to resemble the red of the cellar. I made no doubt that I could readily displace the bricks at this point, insert the corpse, and wall the whole up as before, so that no eye could detect any thing suspicious. And in this calculation I was not deceived.

By means of a crow-bar I easily dislodged the bricks, and, having carefully deposited the body against the inner wall, I propped it in that position, while, with little trouble, I re-laid the whole structure as it originally stood. Having procured mortar, sand, and hair, with every possible precaution, I prepared a plaster which could not be distinguished from the old, and with this I very carefully went over the new brickwork. When I had finished, I felt satisfied that all was right. The wall did not present the slightest appearance of having been disturbed. The rubbish on the floor was picked up with the minutest care. I looked around triumphantly, and said to myself—"Here at least, then, my labor has not been in vain."

My next step was to look for the beast which had been the cause of so much wretchedness; for I had, at length, firmly resolved to put it to death. Had I been able to meet with it, at the moment, there could have been no doubt of its fate; but it appeared that the crafty animal had been alarmed at the violence of my previous anger, and forbore to present itself in my present mood. It is impossible to describe, or to imagine, the deep, the blissful sense of relief which the absence of the detested creature occasioned in my bosom. It did not make its appearance during the night—and thus for one night at least, since its introduction into the house, I soundly and tranquilly slept; aye, *slept* even with the burden of murder upon my soul!

The second and the third day passed, and still my tormentor came not. Once again I breathed as a freeman. The monster, in terror, had fled the premises forever! I should behold it no more! My happiness was supreme! The guilt of my dark deed disturbed me but little. Some few inquiries had been made, but these had been readily answered. Even a search had been instituted—but of course nothing was to be discovered. I looked upon my future felicity as secured.

Upon the fourth day of the assassination, a party of the police came, very unexpectedly, into the house, and proceeded again to make rigorous investigation of the premises. Secure, however, in the inscrutability of my place of concealment, I felt no embarrassment whatever. The officers bade me accompany them in their search. They left no nook or corner unexplored. At length, for the third or fourth time, they descended into the cellar. I quivered not in a muscle. My heart beat calmly as that of one who slumbers in innocence. I walked the cellar from end to end. I folded my arms upon my bosom, and roamed easily to and fro. The police were thoroughly satisfied and prepared to depart. The glee at my heart was too strong to be restrained. I burned to say if but one word, by way of triumph, and to render doubly sure their assurance of my guiltlessness.

"Gentlemen," I said at last, as the party ascended the steps, "I delight to have allayed your suspicions. I wish you all health, and a little more courtesy. By the bye, gentlemen, this—this is a very well constructed house." (In the rabid desire to say something easily, I scarcely knew what I uttered at all.)—"I may say an *excellently* well constructed house. These walls—are you going, gentlemen?—these walls are solidly put together;" and here, through the mere phrenzy of bravado, I rapped heavily, with a cane which I held in my hand, upon that very portion of the brick-work behind which stood the corpse of the wife of my bosom.

But may God shield and deliver me from the fangs of the Arch-Fiend! No sooner had the reverberation of my blows sunk into silence, than I was answered by a voice from within the tomb!—by a cry, at first muffled and broken, like the sobbing of a child, and then quickly swelling into one long, loud, and continuous scream, utterly anomalous and inhuman—a howl—a wailing shriek, half of horror and half of triumph, such as might have arisen only out of hell, conjointly from the throats of the dammed in their agony and of the demons that exult in the damnation.

Of my own thoughts it is folly to speak. Swooning, I staggered to the opposite wall. For one instant the party upon the stairs remained motionless, through extremity of terror and of awe. In the next, a dozen stout arms were toiling at the wall. It fell bodily. The corpse, already greatly decayed and clotted with gore, stood erect before the eyes of the spectators. Upon its head, with red extended mouth and solitary eye of fire, sat the hideous beast whose craft had seduced me into murder, and whose informing voice had consigned me to the hangman. I had walled the monster up within the tomb!

Some Words With a Mummy

The *symposium* of the preceding evening had been a little too much for my nerves. I had a wretched headache, and was desperately drowsy. Instead of going out therefore to spend the evening as I had proposed, it occurred to me that I could not do a wiser thing than just eat a mouthful of supper and go immediately to bed.

A *light* supper of course. I am exceedingly fond of Welsh rabbit. More than a pound at once, however, may not at all times be advisable. Still, there can be no material objection to two. And really between two and three, there is merely a single unit of difference. I ventured, perhaps, upon four. My wife will have it five;—but, clearly, she has confounded two very distinct affairs. The abstract number, five, I am willing to admit; but, concretely, it has reference to bottles of Brown Stout, without which, in the way of condiment, Welsh rabbit is to be eschewed.

Having thus concluded a frugal meal, and donned my night-cap, with the serene hope of enjoying it till noon the next day, I placed my head upon the pillow, and, through the aid of a capital conscience, fell into a profound slumber forthwith.

But when were the hopes of humanity fulfilled? I could not have completed my third snore when there came a furious ringing at the street-door bell, and then an impatient thumping at the knocker, which awakened me at once. In a minute afterward, and while I was still rubbing my eyes, my wife thrust in my face a note, from my old friend, Doctor Ponnonner. It ran thus:

Come to me, by all means, my dear good friend, as soon

as you receive this. Come and help us to rejoice. At last, by long persevering diplomacy, I have gained the assent of the Directors of the City Museum, to my examination of the Mummy—you know the one I mean. I have permission to unswathe it and open it, if desirable. A few friends only will be present—you, of course. The Mummy is now at my house, and we shall begin to unroll it at eleven tonight.

Yours, ever,

Ponnonner.

By the time I had reached the "Ponnonner," it struck me that I was as wide awake as a man need be. I leaped out of bed in an ecstasy, overthrowing all in my way; dressed myself with a rapidity truly marvellous; and set off, at the top of my speed, for the doctor's.

There I found a very eager company assembled. They had been awaiting me with much impatience; the Mummy was extended upon the dining-table; and the moment I entered its examination was commenced.

It was one of a pair brought, several years previously, by Captain Arthur Sabretash, a cousin of Ponnonner's from a tomb near Eleithias, in the Lybian mountains, a considerable distance above Thebes on the Nile. The grottoes at this point, although less magnificent than the Theban sepulchres, are of higher interest, on account of affording more numerous illustrations of the private life of the Egyptians. The chamber from which our specimen was taken, was said to be very rich in such illustrations; the walls being completely covered with fresco paintings and bas-reliefs, while statues, vases, and Mosaic work of rich patterns, indicated the vast wealth of the deceased.

The treasure had been deposited in the Museum precisely in the same condition in which Captain Sabretash had found it;—that is to say, the coffin had not been disturbed. For eight years it had thus stood, subject only externally to public inspection. We had now, therefore, the complete Mummy at our disposal; and to those who are aware how very rarely the unransacked antique reaches our shores, it will be evident, at once that we had great reason to congratulate ourselves upon our good fortune.

Approaching the table, I saw on it a large box, or case, nearly seven feet long, and perhaps three feet wide, by two feet and a half deep. It was oblong—not coffin-shaped. The material was at first supposed to be the wood of the sycamore (*platanus*), but, upon cutting into it, we found it to be pasteboard, or, more properly, *papier maché*, composed of papyrus. It was thickly ornamented with paintings, representing funeral scenes, and other mournful subjects—interspersed among which, in every variety of position, were certain series of hieroglyphical characters, intended, no doubt, for the name of the departed. By good luck, Mr. Gliddon formed one of our party; and he had no difficulty in translating the letters, which were simply phonetic, and represented the word *Allamistakeo*.

We had some difficulty in getting this case open without injury; but having at length accomplished the task, we came to a second, coffin-shaped, and very considerably less in size than the exterior one, but resembling it precisely in every other respect. The interval between the two was filled with resin, which had, in some degree, defaced the colours of the interior box.

Upon opening this latter (which we did quite easily), we arrived at a third case, also coffin-shaped, and varying from the second one in no particular, except in that of its material, which was cedar, and still emitted the peculiar and highly aromatic odour of that wood. Between the second and the third case there was no interval—the one fitting accurately within the other.

Removing the third case, we discovered and took out the body itself. We had expected to find it, as usual, enveloped in frequent rolls, or bandages, of linen; but, in place of these, we found a sort of sheath, made of papyrus, and coated with a layer of plaster, thickly gilt and painted. The paintings represented subjects connected with the various supposed duties of the soul, and its presentation to different divinities, with numerous identical human figures, intended, very probably, as portraits of the persons embalmed. Extending from head to foot was a columnar, or perpendicular, inscription, in phonetic hieroglyphics, giving again his name and titles, and the names and titles of his relations.

Around the neck thus ensheathed, was a collar of cylindrical glass beads, diverse in colour, and so arranged as to form images of deities, of the *scarabaeus*, etc, with the winged globe. Around the small of the waist was a similar collar or belt.

Stripping off the *papyrus*, we found the flesh in excellent preservation, with no perceptible odour. The colour was reddish. The skin was hard, smooth, and glossy. The teeth and hair were in good condition. The eyes (it seemed) had been removed, and glass ones substituted, which were very beautiful and wonderfully life-like, with the exception of somewhat too determined a stare. The fingers and the nails were brilliantly gilded.

Mr. Gliddon was of opinion, from the redness of the epidermis, that the embalmment had been effected altogether by *asphaltum*; but, on scraping the surface with a steel instrument, and throwing into the fire some of the powder thus obtained, the flavour of camphor and other sweet-scented gums became apparent.

We searched the corpse very carefully for the usual openings through which the entrails are extracted, but, to our surprise, we could discover none. No member of the party was at that period aware that entire or unopened mummies are not infrequently met. The brain it was customary to withdraw through the nose; the intestines through an incision in the side; the body was then shaved, washed, and salted; then laid aside for several weeks, when the operation of embalming, properly so called, began.

As no trace of an opening could be found, Doctor Ponnonner was preparing his instruments for dissection, when I observed that it was then past two o'clock. Hereupon it was agreed to postpone the internal examination until the next evening; and we were about to separate for the present, when some one suggested an experiment or two with the Voltaic pile.

The application of electricity to a mummy three or four thousand years old at the least, was an idea, if not very sage, still sufficiently original, and we all caught it at once. About one-tenth in earnest and nine-tenths in jest, we arranged a battery in the doctor's study, and conveyed thither the Egyptian.

It was only after much trouble that we succeeded in laying bare some portions of the temporal muscle which appeared of less stony rigidity than other parts of the frame, but which, as we had anticipated, of course, gave no indication of galvanic susceptibility when brought in contact with the wire. This, the first trial, indeed, seemed decisive, and, with a hearty laugh at our own absurdity, we were bidding each other goodnight, when my eyes, happening to fall upon those of the Mummy, were there immediately riveted in amazement. My brief glance, in fact, had sufficed to assure me that the orbs which we had all supposed to be glass, and which were originally noticeable for a certain wild stare, were now so far covered by the lids, that only a small portion of the *tunica albuginea* remained visible.

With a shout I called attention to the fact, and it became immediately obvious to all.

I cannot say that I was *alarmed* at the phenomenon, because "alarmed" is, in my case, not exactly the word. It is possible, however, that, but for the Brown Stout, I might have been a little nervous. As for the rest of the company, they really made no attempt at concealing the downright fright which possessed them. Doctor Ponnonner was a man to be pitied. Mr. Gliddon, by some peculiar process, rendered himself invisible. Mr. Silk Buckingham, I fancy, will scarcely be so bold as to deny that he made his way, upon all fours, under the table.

After the first shock of astonishment, however, we resolved, as a matter of course, upon further experiment forthwith. Our operations were now directed against the great toe of the right foot. We made an incision over the outside of the exterior *os sesamoideum pollicis pedis,* and thus got at the root of the *abductor* muscle. Readjusting the battery, we now applied the fluid to the bisected nerves—when, with a movement of exceeding life-likeness, the Mummy first drew up its right knee so as to bring it nearly in contact with the abdomen, and then, straightening the limb with inconceivable force, bestowed a kick upon Doctor

Ponnonner, which had the effect of discharging that gentleman, like an arrow from a catapult, through a window into the street below.

We rushed out *en masse* to bring in the mangled remains of the victim, but had the happiness to meet him upon the staircase, coming up in an unaccountable hurry, brimful of the most ardent philosophy, and more than ever impressed with the necessity of prosecuting our experiment with vigour and with zeal.

It was by his advice, accordingly, that we made, upon the spot, a profound incision into the tip of the subject's nose, while the doctor himself, laying violent hands upon it, pulled it into vehement contact with the wire.

Morally and physically—figuratively and literally—was the effect electric. In the first place, the corpse opened its eyes and winked very rapidly for several minutes, as does Mr. Barnes in the pantomime, in the second place, it sneezed; in the third, it sat upon end; in the fourth, it shook its fist in Doctor Ponnonner's face; in the fifth, turning to Messieurs Gliddon and Buckingham, it addressed them, in very capital Egyptian, thus:

"I must say, gentlemen, that I am as much surprised as I am mortified at your behaviour. Of Doctor Ponnonner nothing better was to be expected. He is a poor little fat fool who *knows* no better. I pity and forgive him. But you, Mr. Gliddon—and you, Silk—who have travelled and resided in Egypt until one might imagine you to the manner born—you, I say who have been so much among us that you speak Egyptian fully as well, I think, as you write your mother tongue—you, whom I have always been led to regard as the firm friend of the mummies—I really did anticipate more gentlemanly conduct from *you*. What am I to think of your standing quietly by and seeing me thus unhandsomely used? What am I to suppose by your permitting Tom, Dick, and Harry to strip me of my coffins, and my clothes, in this wretchedly cold climate? In what light (to come to the point) am I to regard your aiding and abetting that miserable little villain, Doctor Ponnonner, in pulling me by the nose?"

It will be taken for granted, no doubt, that upon hearing this speech under the circumstances, we all either made for the door, or fell into violent hysterics, or went off in a general swoon. One of these three things was, I say, to be expected. Indeed each and all of these lines of conduct might have been very plausibly pursued. And, upon my word, I am at a loss to know how or why it was that we pursued neither the one nor the other. But, perhaps, the true reason is to be sought in the spirit of the age, which proceeds by the rule of contraries altogether, and is now usually admitted as the solution of every thing in the way of paradox and impossibility. Or, perhaps, after all, it was only the Mummy's exceedingly natural and matter-of-course air that divested his words of the terrible. However this may be, the facts are clear, and no member of our party betrayed any very particular trepidation, or seemed to consider that anything had gone very especially wrong.

For my part I was convinced it was all right, and merely stepped aside, out of the range of the Egyptian's fist. Doctor Ponnonner thrust his hands into his breeches' pockets, looked hard at the Mummy, and grew excessively red in the face. Mr. Glidden stroked his whiskers and drew up the collar of his shirt. Mr. Buckingham hung down his head, and put his right thumb into the left corner of his mouth.

The Egyptian regarded him with a severe countenance for some minutes and at length, with a sneer, said:

"Why don't you speak, Mr. Buckingham? Did you hear what I asked you, or not? Do take your thumb out of your mouth!"

Mr. Buckingham, hereupon, gave a slight start, took his right thumb out of the left corner of his mouth, and, by way of indemnification inserted his left thumb in the right corner of the aperture above-mentioned.

Not being able to get an answer from Mr. B., the figure turned peevishly to Mr. Gliddon, and, in a peremptory tone, demanded in general terms what we all meant.

Mr. Gliddon replied at great length, in phonetics; and but for the deficiency of American printing-offices in hieroglyphical type, it would afford me much pleasure to record here, in the original, the whole of his very excellent speech.

I may as well take this occasion to remark, that all the subsequent conversation in which the Mummy took a part, was carried on in primitive Egyptian, through the medium (so far as concerned myself and other untraveled members of the company)—through the medium, I say, of Messieurs Gliddon and Buckingham, as interpreters. These gentlemen spoke the mother tongue of the Mummy with inimitable fluency and grace; but I could not help observing that (owing, no doubt, to the introduction of images entirely modern, and, of course, entirely novel to the stranger) the two travellers were reduced, occasionally, to the employment of sensible forms for the purpose of conveying a particular meaning.

Mr. Gliddon, at one period, for example, could not make the Egyptian comprehend the term "politics," until he sketched upon the wall, with a bit of charcoal a little carbuncle-nosed gentleman, out at elbows, standing upon a stump, with his left leg drawn back, right arm thrown forward, with his fist shut, the eyes rolled up toward Heaven, and the mouth open at an angle of ninety degrees. Just in the same way Mr. Buckingham failed to convey the absolutely modern idea "wig," until (at Doctor Ponnonner's suggestion) he grew very pale in the face, and consented to take off his own.

It will be readily understood that Mr. Gliddon's discourse turned chiefly upon the vast benefits accruing to science from the unrolling and disembowelling of mummies; apologizing, upon this score, for any disturbance that might have been occasioned *him*, in particular, the individual Mummy called Allamistakeo; and concluding with a mere hint (for it could scarcely be considered more) that, as these little matters were now explained, it might be as well to proceed with the investigation intended. Here Doctor Ponnonner made ready his instruments.

In regard to the latter suggestions of the orator, it appears that Allamistakeo had certain scruples of conscience, the nature of which I did not distinctly learn; but he expressed himself satisfied with the apologies tendered, and, getting down from the table, shook hands with the company all round.

When this ceremony was at an end, we immediately busied ourselves in repairing the damages which our subject had sustained from the scalpel. We sewed up the wound in his temple, bandaged his foot, and applied a square inch of black plaster to the tip of his nose.

It was now observed that the count (this was the title, it seems, of Allamistakeo) had a slight fit of shivering—no doubt from the cold. The doctor immediately repaired to his wardrobe, and soon returned with a black dress coat, made in Jennings' best manner, a pair of sky-blue plaid pantaloons with straps, a pink gingham *chemise*, a flapped vest of brocade, a white sack overcoat, a walking cane with a hook, a hat with no brim, patent-leather boots, straw-coloured kid gloves, an eye-glass, a pair of whiskers, and a waterfall cravat. Owing to the disparity of size between the count and the doctor (the proportion being as two to one), there was some little difficulty in adjusting these *habiliments* upon the person of the Egyptian; but when all was arranged, he might have been said to be dressed. Mr. Gliddon, therefore, gave him his arm, and led him to a comfortable chair by the fire, while the doctor rang the bell upon the spot and ordered a supply of cigars and wine.

The conversation soon grew animated. Much curiosity was, of course, expressed in regard to the somewhat remarkable fact of Allamistakeo's still remaining alive.

"I should have thought," observed Mr. Buckingham, "that it is high time you were dead."

"Why," replied the count, very much astonished, "I am little more than seven hundred years old! My father lived a thousand, and was by no means in his dotage when he died."

Here ensued a brisk series of questions and computations, by means of which it became evident that the antiquity of the Mummy had been grossly misjudged. It had been five thousand and fifty years and some months since he had been consigned to the catacombs at Eleithias.

"But my remark," resumed Mr. Buckingham, "had no reference to your age at the period of interment (I am willing to grant, in fact, that you are still a young man), and my illusion was to the immensity of time during which, by your own showing, you must have been done up in *asphaltum*."

"In what?" said the count.

"In *asphaltum*," persisted Mr. B.

"Ah, yes; I have some faint notion of what you mean; it might be made to answer, no doubt—but in my time we employed scarcely any thing else than the Bichloride of Mercury."

"But what we are especially at a loss to understand," said Doctor Ponnonner, "is how it happens that, having been dead and buried in Egypt five thousand years ago, you are here to-day all alive and looking so delightfully well."

"Had I been, as you say, *dead*," replied the count, "it is more than probable that dead, I should still be; for I perceive you are yet in the infancy of Calvanism, and cannot accomplish with it what was a common thing among us in the old days. But the fact is, I fell into catalepsy, and it was considered by my best friends that I was either dead or should be; they accordingly embalmed me at once—I presume you are aware of the chief principle of the embalming process?"

"Why not altogether."

"Why, I perceive—a deplorable condition of ignorance! Well I cannot enter into details just now: but it is necessary to explain that to embalm (properly speaking), in Egypt, was to arrest indefinitely *all* the animal functions subjected to the process. I use the word 'animal' in its widest sense, as including the physical not more than the moral and *vital* being. I repeat that the leading principle of embalmment consisted, with us, in the immediately arresting, and holding in perpetual *abeyance*, *all* the animal functions subjected to the process. To be brief, in whatever condition the individual was, at the period of embalmment, in that condition he remained. Now, as it is my good fortune to be of the blood of the Scarabaeus, I was embalmed *alive*, as you see me at present."

"The blood of the Scarabaeus!" exclaimed Doctor Ponnonner.

"Yes. The Scarabaeus was the *insignium* or the 'arms,' of a very distinguished and very rare patrician family. To be 'of the blood of the Scarabaeus,' is merely to be one of that family of which the Scarabaeus is the *insignium*. I speak figuratively."

"But what has this to do with you being alive?"

"Why, it is the general custom in Egypt to deprive a corpse, before embalmment, of its bowels and brains; the race of the Scarabaei alone did not coincide with the custom. Had I not been a Scarabeus, therefore, I should have been without bowels and brains; and without either it is inconvenient to live."

"I perceive that," said Mr. Buckingham, "and I presume that all the *entire* mummies that come to hand are of the race of Scarabaei."

"Beyond doubt."

"I thought," said Mr. Gliddon, very meekly, "that the Scarabaeus was one of the Egyptian gods."

"One of the Egyptian *what?*" exclaimed the Mummy, starting to its feet.

"Gods!" repeated the traveller.

"Mr. Gliddon, I really am astonished to hear you talk in this style," said the count, resuming his chair. "No nation upon the face of the earth has ever acknowledged more than *one god*. The Scarabaeus, the Ibis, etc., were with us (as similar creatures have been with others) the symbols, or *media*, through which we offered worship to the Creator too august to be more directly approached."

There was here a pause. At length the colloquy was renewed by Doctor Ponnonner.

"It is not improbable, then, from what you have explained," said he, "that among the catacombs near the Nile there may exist other mummies of the Scarabaeus tribe, in a condition of vitality?"

"There can be no question of it," replied the count; "all the Scarabaei embalmed accidentally while alive, are alive now. Even some of those *purposely* so embalmed, may have been overlooked by their executors, and still remain in the tomb."

"Will you be kind enough to explain," I said, "what you mean by 'purposely so embalmed'?"

"With great pleasure!" answered the Mummy, after surveying me leisurely through his eye-glass—for it was the first time I had ventured to address him a direct question.

"With great pleasure," he said. "The usual duration of man's life, in my time, was about eight hundred years. Few men died, unless by most extraordinary accident, before the age of six hundred; few lived longer than a decade of centuries; but eight were considered the natural term. After the discovery of the embalming principle, as I have already described it to you, it occurred to our philosophers that a laudable curiosity might be gratified, and, at the same time, the interests of science much advanced, by living this natural term in instalments. In the case of history, indeed, experience demonstrated that something of this kind was indispensable. An historian, for example, having attained the age of five hundred, would write a book with great labour and then get himself carefully embalmed; leaving instructions to his executors *pro tem.*, that they should cause him to be revivified after the lapse of a certain period—say five or six hundred years.

"Resuming existence at the expiration of this time, he would invariably find his great work converted into a species of haphazard note-book—that is to say, into a kind of literary arena for the conflicting guesses, riddles, and personal squabbles of whole herds of exasperated commentators. These guesses, etc., which passed under the name of annotations, or emendations, were found so completely to have enveloped, distorted, and overwhelmed the text, that the author had to go about with a lantern to discover his own book. When discovered, it was never worth the trouble of the search.

"After re-writing it throughout, it was regarded as the bounden duty of the historian to set himself to work immediately in correcting, from his own private knowledge and experience, the traditions of the day concerning the epoch at which he had originally lived. Now this process of rescription and personal rectification, pursued by various individual sages from time to time, had the effect of preventing our history from degenerating into absolute fable."

"I beg your pardon," said Doctor Ponnonner at this point, laying his hand gently upon the arm of the Egyptian—"I beg your pardon, sir, but may I presume to interrupt you for one moment?"

"By all means, sir," replied the count, drawing up.

"I merely wished to ask you a question," said the doctor. "You mentioned the historian's personal correction of *traditions* respecting his own epoch. Pray, sir, upon an average what proportion of these *Kabbala* were usually found to be right?"

"The *Kabbala*, as you properly term them, sir, were generally discovered to be precisely on a par with the facts recorded in the unrewritten histories themselves;—that is to say, not one individual iota of either was ever known, under any circumstances, to be not totally and radically wrong."

"But since it is quite clear," resumed the doctor, "that at least five thousand years have elapsed since your entombment, I take it for granted that your histories at that period, if not your traditions were sufficiently explicit on that one topic of universal interest, the Creation, which took place, as I presume you are aware, only about ten centuries before."

"Sir!" said the Count Allamistakeo.

The doctor repeated his remarks, but it was only after much additional explanation that the foreigner could be made to comprehend them. The latter at length said, hesitatingly:

"The ideas you have suggested are to me, I confess, utterly novel. During my time I never knew anyone to entertain so singular a fancy as that the universe (or this world if you will have it so) ever had a beginning at all. I remember once, and once only, hearing something remotely hinted, by a man of many speculations, concerning the origin *of the human race;* and by this individual, the very word *Adam* (or Red Earth), which you make use of, was employed. He employed it, however, in a generical sense, with reference to the spontaneous germination from rank soil (just as a thousand of the lower *genera* of creatures are germinated)—the spontaneous germination, I say, of five vast hordes of men, simultaneously upspringing in five distinct and nearly equal divisions of the globe."

Here, in general, the company shrugged their shoulders, and one or two of us touched our foreheads with a very significant air. Mr. Silk Buckingham, first glancing slightly at the *occiput* and then at the *sinciput* of Allamistakeo, spoke as follows:

"The long duration of human life in your time, together with the occasional practice of passing it, as you have explained, in instalments, must have had, indeed, a strong tendency to the general development and conglomeration of knowledge. I presume, therefore, that we are to attribute the marked inferiority of the old Egyptians in all particulars of science, when compared with the moderns, and more especially with the Yankees, altogether to the superior solidity of the Egyptian skull."

"I confess again," replied the count, with much suavity, "that I am somewhat at a loss to comprehend you; pray, to what particulars of science do you allude?"

Here our whole party, joining voices, detailed, at great length, the assumptions of phrenology and the marvels of animal magnetism.

Having heard us to an end, the count proceeded to relate a few anecdotes, which rendered it evident that prototypes of Gall and Spurzheim had flourished and faded in Egypt so long ago as to have been nearly forgotten, and that the manoeuvres of Mesmer were really very contemptible tricks when put in collation with the positive miracles of the Theban *savans*, who created lice and a great many other similar things.

I here asked the count if his people were able to calculate eclipses. He smiled rather contemptuously, and said they were.

This put me a little out, but I began to make other inquiries in regard to his astronomical knowledge, when a member of the company, who had never as yet opened his mouth, whispered in my ear, that for information on this head, I had better consult Ptolemy (whoever Ptolemy is), as well as one Plutarch *de facie lunae.*

I then questioned the Mummy about burning-glasses and lenses, and, in general, about the manufacture of glass; but I had not made an end of my queries before the silent member again touched me quietly on the elbow, and begged me for God's sake to take a peep at Diodorus Siculus. As for the count, he merely asked me, in the way of reply, if we moderns possessed any such microscopes as would enable us to cut cameos in the style of the Egyptians. While I was thinking how I should answer this question, little Doctor Ponnonner committed himself in a very extraordinary way.

"Look at our architecture!" he exclaimed, greatly to the indignation of both the travellers, who pinched him black and blue to no purpose.

"Look," he cried with enthusiasm, "at the Bowling-Green Fountain in New York! or if this be too vast a contemplation, regard for a moment the Capitol at Washington, D. C.!"—and the good little medical man went on to detail very minutely, the proportions of the fabric to which he referred. He explained that the *portico* alone was adorned with no less than four and twenty columns, five feet in diameter, and ten feet apart.

The count said that he regretted not being able to remember, just at that moment, the precise dimensions of any one of the principal buildings of the city of Aznac, whose foundations were laid in the night of Time, but the ruins of which were still standing, at the epoch of his entombment, in a vast plain of sand to the westward of Thebes. He recollected, however, (talking of the *porticoes*,) that one affixed to an inferior palace in a kind of suburb called Carnac, consisted of a hundred and forty-four columns, thirty-seven feet in circumference, and twenty-five feet apart. The approach to this *portico*, from the Nile, was through an avenue two miles long, composed of sphynxes, statues, and obelisks, twenty, sixty, and a hundred feet in height.

The palace itself (as well as he could remember) was, in one direction, two miles long, and might have been altogether about seven in circuit. Its walls were richly painted all over, within and without, with hieroglyphics. He would not pretend to *assert* that even fifty or sixty of the doctor's Capitols might have been built within these walls, but he was by no means sure that two or three hundred of them might not have been squeezed in with some trouble. That palace at Carnac was an insignificant little building after all. He (the count), however, could not conscientiously refuse to admit the ingenuity, magnificence, and superiority of the Fountain at the Bowling Green, as described by the doctor. Nothing like it, he was forced to allow, had ever been seen in Egypt or elsewhere.

I here asked the count what he had to say to our railroads.

"Nothing," he replied, "in particular." They were rather slight, rather ill-conceived, and clumsily put together. They could not be compared, of course, with the vast, level, direct, iron-grooved causeways upon which the Egyptians conveyed entire temples and solid obelisks of a hundred and fifty feet in altitude.

I spoke of our gigantic mechanical forces.

He agreed that we knew something in that way, but inquired how I should have gone to work in getting up the imposts on the lintels of even the little palace at Carnac.

This question I concluded not to hear, and demanded if he had any idea of Artesian wells; but he simply raised his eyebrows; while Mr. Gliddon winked at me very hard and said, in a low tone, that one had been recently discovered by the engineers employed to bore for water in the Great Oasis.

I then mentioned our steel; but the foreigner elevated his nose, and asked me if our steel could have executed the sharp carved work seen on the obelisks, and which was wrought altogether by edge-tools of copper.

This disconcerted us so greatly that we thought it advisable to vary the attack to Metaphysics. We sent for a copy of a book called the *Dial*, and read out of it a chapter or two about something that is not very clear, but which the Bostonians call the Great Movement of Progress.

The count merely said that Great Movements were awfully common things in his day, and as for Progress, it was at one time quite a nuisance, but it never progressed.

We then spoke of the great beauty and importance of democracy, and were at much trouble in impressing the count with a due sense of the advantages we enjoyed in living where there was suffrage *ad libitum*, and no king.

He listened with marked interest, and in fact seemed not a little amused. When we had done, he said that, a great while ago, there had occurred something of a very similar sort. Thirteen Egyptian provinces determined all at once to be free, and to set a magnificent example to the rest of mankind. They assembled their wise men, and concocted the most ingenious constitution it is possible to conceive. For a while they managed remarkably well; only their habit of bragging was prodigious. The thing ended, however, in the consolidation of the thirteen states, with some fifteen or twenty others, in the most odious and insupportable despotism that was ever heard of upon the face of the Earth.

I asked what was the name of the usurping tyrant.

As well as the count could recollect, it was Mob.

Not knowing what to say to this, I raised my voice, and deplored the Egyptian ignorance of steam.

The count looked at me with much astonishment, but made no answer. The silent gentleman, however, gave me a violent nudge in the ribs with his elbows—told me I had sufficiently exposed myself for once—and demanded if I was really such a fool as not to know that the modern steam-engine is derived from the invention of Hero, through Solomon de Caus.

We were now in imminent danger of being discomfited; but, as good luck would have it, Doctor Ponnonner, having rallied, returned to our rescue, and inquired if the people of Egypt would seriously pretend to rival the moderns in the all—important particular of dress.

The count, at this, glanced downward to the straps of his pantaloons, and then taking hold of the end of one of his coat-tails, held it up close to his eyes for some minutes. Letting it fall, at last, his mouth extended itself very gradually from ear to ear; but

I do not remember that he said any thing in the way of reply.

Hereupon we recovered our spirits, and the doctor, approaching the Mummy with great dignity, desired it to say candidly, upon its honour as a gentleman, if the Egyptians had comprehended, at *any* period, the manufacture of either Ponnonner's lozenges or Brandreth's pills.

We looked, with profound anxiety, for an answer—but in vain. It was not forthcoming. The Egyptian blushed and hung down his head. Never was triumph more consummate; never was defeat borne with so ill a grace. Indeed, I could not endure the spectacle of the poor Mummy's mortification. I reached my hat, bowed to him stiffly, and took leave.

Upon getting home I found it past four o'clock, and went immediately to bed. It is now ten a.m. I have been up since seven, penning these memoranda for the benefit of my family and of mankind. The former I shall behold no more. My wife is a shrew. The truth is, I am heartily sick of this life and of the nineteenth century in general. I am convinced that everything is going wrong. Besides, I am anxious to know who will be President in 2045. As soon, therefore, as I shave and swallow a cup of coffee, I shall just step over to Ponnonner's and get embalmed for a couple of hundred years.

The Masque of the Red Death

The "Red Death" had long devastated the country. No pestilence had ever been so fatal, or so hideous. Blood was its avatar
and its seal—the redness and the horror of blood. There were
sharp pains, and sudden dizziness, and then profuse bleeding at
the pores, with dissolution. The scarlet stains upon the body and
especially upon the face of the victim, were the pest ban which
shut him out from the aid and from the sympathy of his fellow-
men. And the whole seizure, progress and termination of the
disease, were the incidents of half an hour.

But the Prince Prospero was happy and dauntless and sagacious. When his dominions were half depopulated, he summoned to his presence a thousand hale and light-hearted friends
from among the knights and dames of his court, and with these
retired to the deep seclusion of one of his castellated abbeys. This
was an extensive and magnificent structure, the creation of the
prince's own eccentric yet august taste. A strong and lofty wall
girdled it in. This wall had gates of iron. The courtiers, having
entered, brought furnaces and massy hammers and welded the
bolts. They resolved to leave means neither of ingress or egress
to the sudden impulses of despair or of frenzy from within.

The abbey was amply provisioned. With such precautions the
courtiers might bid defiance to contagion. The external world
could take care of itself. In the meantime it was folly to grieve,
or to think. The prince had provided all the appliances of pleasure. There were buffoons, there were *improvisatori*, there were
ballet-dancers, there were musicians, there was beauty, there was

wine. All these and security were within. Without was the "Red Death."

It was toward the close of the fifth or sixth month of his seclusion, and while the pestilence raged most furiously abroad, that the Prince Prospero entertained his thousand friends at a masked ball of the most unusual magnificence.

It was a voluptuous scene, that masquerade. But first let me tell of the rooms in which it was held. There were seven—an imperial suite. In many palaces, however, such suites form a long and straight *vista*, while the folding doors slide back nearly to the walls on either hand, so that the view of the whole extent is scarcely impeded. Here the case was very different; as might have been expected from the duke's love of the *bizarre*. The apartments were so irregularly disposed that the vision embraced but little more than one at a time. There was a sharp turn at every twenty or thirty yards, and at each turn a novel effect.

To the right and left, in the middle of each wall, a tall and narrow Gothic window looked out upon a closed corridor which pursued the windings of the suite. These windows were of stained glass whose colour varied in accordance with the pre-vailing hue of the decorations of the chamber into which it opened. That at the eastern extremity was hung, for example, in blue—and vividly blue were its windows. The second chamber was purple in its ornaments and tapestries, and here the panes were purple. The third was green throughout, and so were the casements. The fourth was furnished and lighted with orange—the fifth with white—the sixth with violet. The seventh apart-ment was closely shrouded in black velvet tapestries that hung all over the ceiling and down the walls, falling in heavy folds upon a carpet of the same material and hue. But in this chamber only, the colour of the windows failed to correspond with the decorations. The panes here were scarlet—a deep blood colour.

Now in no one of the seven apartments was there any lamp or candelabrum, amid the profusion of golden ornaments that lay scattered to and fro or depended from the roof. There was no light of any kind emanating from lamp or candle within the suite of chambers. But in the corridors that followed the suite, there stood, opposite to each window, a heavy tripod, bearing a brazier of fire that projected its rays through the tinted glass and so glaringly illumined the room. And thus were produced a multitude of gaudy and fantastic appearances. But in the western or black chamber the effect of the fire-light that streamed upon the dark hangings through the blood-tinted panes, was ghastly in the extreme, and produced so wild a look upon the countenances of those who entered, that there were few of the company bold enough to set foot within its precincts at all.

It was in this apartment, also, that there stood against the western wall, a gigantic clock of ebony. Its pendulum swung to and fro with a dull, heavy, monotonous clang; and when the minute-hand made the circuit of the face, and the hour was to be stricken, there came from the brazen lungs of the clock a sound which was clear and loud and deep and exceedingly musical, but of so peculiar a note and emphasis that, at each lapse of an hour, the musicians of the orchestra were constrained to pause, momentarily, in their performance, to hearken to the sound; and thus the waltzers perforce ceased their evolutions; and there was a brief disconcert of the whole gay company; and, while the chimes of the clock yet rang, it was observed that the giddiest grew pale, and the more aged and sedate passed their hands over their brows as if in confused reverie or meditation.

But when the echoes had fully ceased, a light laughter at once pervaded the assembly; the musicians looked at each other and smiled as if at their own nervousness and folly, and made whispering vows, each to the other, that the next chiming of the clock should produce in them no similar emotion; and then, after the lapse of sixty minutes, (which embrace three thousand and six hundred seconds of the Time that flies,) there came yet another chiming of the clock, and then were the same disconcert and tremulousness and meditation as before.

But, in spite of these things, it was a gay and magnificent revel. The tastes of the duke were peculiar. He had a fine eye for colours and effects. He disregarded the *decora* of mere fashion.

His plans were bold and fiery, and his conceptions glowed with barbaric lustre. There are some who would have thought him mad. His followers felt that he was not. It was necessary to hear and see and touch him to be sure that he was not.

He had directed, in great part, the moveable embellishments of the seven chambers, upon occasion of this great *fête*; and it was his own guiding taste which had given character to the masqueraders. Be sure they were grotesque. There were much glare and glitter and piquancy and phantasm—much of what has been since seen in *Hernani*. There were arabesque figures with unsuited limbs and appointments. There were delirious fancies such as the madman fashions. There was much of the beautiful, much of the wanton, much of the *bizarre*, something of the terrible, and not a little of that which might have excited disgust. To and fro in the seven chambers there stalked, in fact, a multitude of dreams. And these—the dreams—writhed in and about, taking hue from the rooms, and causing the wild music of the orchestra to seem as the echo of their steps.

And, *anon*, there strikes the ebony clock which stands in the hall of the velvet. And then, for a moment, all is still, and all is silent save the voice of the clock. The dreams are stiff-frozen as they stand. But the echoes of the chime die away—they have endured but an instant—and a light, half-subdued laughter floats after them as they depart. And now again the music swells, and the dreams live, and writhe to and fro more merrily than ever, taking hue from the many-tinted windows through which stream the rays from the tripods. But to the chamber which lies most westwardly of the seven, there are now none of the maskers who venture; for the night is waning away; and there flows a ruddier light through the blood-coloured panes; and the blackness of the sable drapery appals; and to him whose foot falls upon the sable carpet, there comes from the near clock of ebony a muffled peal more solemnly emphatic than any which reaches *their* ears who indulge in the more remote gaieties of the other apartments.

But these other apartments were densely crowded, and in

them beat feverishly the heart of life. And the revel went whirlingly on, until at length there commenced the sounding of midnight upon the clock. And then the music ceased, as I have told; and the evolutions of the waltzers were quieted; and there was an uneasy cessation of all things as before. But now there were twelve strokes to be sounded by the bell of the clock; and thus it happened, perhaps, that more of thought crept, with more of time, into the meditations of the thoughtful among those who revelled. And thus, too, it happened, perhaps, that before the last echoes of the last chime had utterly sunk into silence, there were many individuals in the crowd who had found leisure to become aware of the presence of a masked figure which had arrested the attention of no single individual before. And the rumour of this new presence having spread itself whisperingly around, there arose at length from the whole company a buzz, or murmur, expressive of disapprobation and surprise—then, finally, of terror, of horror, and of disgust.

In an assembly of phantasms such as I have painted, it may well be supposed that no ordinary appearance could have excited such sensation. In truth the masquerade license of the night was nearly unlimited; but the figure in question had out-Heroded Herod, and gone beyond the bounds of even the prince's indefinite decorum. There are chords in the hearts of the most reckless which cannot be touched without emotion. Even with the utterly lost, to whom life and death are equally jests, there are matters of which no jest can be made. The whole company, indeed, seemed now deeply to feel that in the costume and bearing of the stranger neither wit nor propriety existed.

The figure was tall and gaunt, and shrouded from head to foot in the habiliments of the grave. The mask which concealed the visage was made so nearly to resemble the countenance of a stiffened corpse that the closest scrutiny must have had difficulty in detecting the cheat. And yet all this might have been endured, if not approved, by the mad revellers around. But the mummer had gone so far as to assume the type of the Red Death. His vesture was dabbled in *blood*—and his broad brow, with all the features of the face, was besprinkled with the scarlet horror.

When the eyes of Prince Prospero fell upon this spectral image (which with a slow and solemn movement, as if more fully to sustain its *rôle*, stalked to and fro among the waltzers) he was seen to be convulsed, in the first moment with a strong shudder either of terror or distaste; but, in the next, his brow reddened with rage.

"Who dares?" he demanded hoarsely of the courtiers who stood near him—"who dares insult us with this blasphemous mockery? Seize him and unmask him—that we may know whom we have to hang at sunrise, from the battlements!"

It was in the eastern or blue chamber in which stood the Prince Prospero as he uttered these words. They rang throughout the seven rooms loudly and clearly—for the prince was a bold and robust man, and the music had become hushed at the waving of his hand.

It was in the blue room where stood the prince, with a group of pale courtiers by his side. At first, as he spoke, there was a slight rushing movement of this group in the direction of the intruder, who at the moment was also near at hand, and now, with deliberate and stately step, made closer approach to the speaker. But from a certain nameless awe with which the mad assumptions of the mummer had inspired the whole party, there were found none who put forth hand to seize him; so that, unimpeded, he passed within a yard of the prince's person; and, while the vast assembly, as if with one impulse, shrank from the centres of the rooms to the walls, he made his way uninterruptedly, but with the same solemn and measured step which had distinguished him from the first, through the blue chamber to the purple—through the purple to the green—through the green to the orange—through this again to the white—and even thence to the violet, ere a decided movement had been made to arrest him.

It was then, however, that the Prince Prospero, maddening with rage and the shame of his own momentary cowardice, rushed hurriedly through the six chambers, while none followed him on account of a deadly terror that had seized upon all. He bore aloft a drawn dagger, and had approached, in rapid impetuosity, to within three or four feet of the retreating figure, when the latter, having attained the extremity of the velvet apartment, turned suddenly and confronted his pursuer. There was a sharp cry—and the dagger dropped gleaming upon the sable carpet, upon which, instantly afterwards, fell prostrate in death the Prince Prospero. Then, summoning the wild courage of despair, a throng of the revellers at once threw themselves into the black apartment, and, seizing the mummer, whose tall figure stood erect and motionless within the shadow of the ebony clock, gasped in unutterable horror at finding the grave-cerements and corpse-like mask which they handled with so violent a rudeness, untenanted by any tangible form.

And now was acknowledged the presence of the Red Death. He had come like a thief in the night. And one by one dropped the revellers in the blood-bedewed halls of their revel, and died each in the despairing posture of his fall. And the life of the ebony clock went out with that of the last of the gay. And the flames of the tripods expired. And Darkness and Decay and the Red Death held illimitable dominion over all.

The Sphinx

During the dread reign of the cholera in New York, I had accepted the invitation of a relative to spend a fortnight with him in the retirement of his *cottage ornée* on the banks of the Hudson. We had here around us all the ordinary means of summer amusement; and what with rambling in the woods, sketching, boating, fishing, bathing, music, and books, we should have passed the time pleasantly enough, but for the fearful intelligence which reached us every morning from the populous city. Not a day elapsed which did not bring us news of the decease of some acquaintance. Then as the fatality increased, we learned to expect daily the loss of some friend.

At length we trembled at the approach of every messenger. The very air from the South seemed to us redolent with death. That palsying thought, indeed, took entire possession of my soul. I could neither speak, think, nor dream of any thing else. My host was of a less excitable temperament, and, although greatly depressed in spirits, exerted himself to sustain my own. His richly philosophical intellect was not at any time affected by unrealities. To the substances of terror he was sufficiently alive, but of its shadows he had no apprehension.

His endeavours to arouse me from the condition of abnormal gloom into which I had fallen, were frustrated, in great measure, by certain volumes which I had found in his library. These were of a character to force into germination whatever seeds of hereditary superstition lay latent in my bosom. I had been reading these books without his knowledge, and thus he was often at a loss to account for the forcible impressions which had been made upon my fancy.

A favourite topic with me was the popular belief in omens—a belief which, at this one epoch of my life, I was almost seriously disposed to defend. On this subject we had long and animated discussions—he maintaining the utter groundlessness of faith in such matters,—I contending that a popular sentiment arising with absolute spontaneity—that is to say, without apparent traces of suggestion—had in itself the unmistakable elements of truth, and was entitled to as much respect as that intuition which is the idiosyncrasy of the individual man of genius.

The fact is, that soon after my arrival at the cottage there had occurred to myself an incident so entirely inexplicable, and which had in it so much of the portentous character, that I might well have been excused for regarding it as an omen. It appalled, and at the same time so confounded and bewildered me, that many days elapsed before I could make up my mind to communicate the circumstances to my friend.

Near the close of exceedingly warm day, I was sitting, book in hand, at an open window, commanding, through a long *vista* of the river banks, a view of a distant hill, the face of which nearest my position had been denuded by what is termed a landslide, of the principal portion of its trees. My thoughts had been long wandering from the volume before me to the gloom and desolation of the neighbouring city. Uplifting my eyes from the page, they fell upon the naked face of the bill, and upon an object—upon some living monster of hideous conformation, which very rapidly made its way from the summit to the bottom, disappearing finally in the dense forest below. As this creature first came in sight, I doubted my own sanity—or at least the evidence of my own eyes; and many minutes passed before I succeeded in convincing myself that I was neither mad nor in a dream. Yet when I described the monster (which I distinctly saw, and calmly surveyed through the whole period of its progress), my readers, I fear, will feel more difficulty in being convinced of these points than even I did myself.

Estimating the size of the creature by comparison with the diameter of the large trees near which it passed—the few giants of the forest which had escaped the fury of the land-slide—I concluded it to be far larger than any ship of the line in existence. I say ship of the line, because the shape of the monster suggested the idea—the hull of one of our seventy-four might convey a very tolerable conception of the general outline. The mouth of the animal was situated at the extremity of a proboscis some sixty or seventy feet in length, and about as thick as the body of an ordinary elephant. Near the root of this trunk was an immense quantity of black shaggy hair—more than could have been supplied by the coats of a score of buffaloes; and projecting from this hair downwardly and laterally, sprang two gleaming tusks not unlike those of the wild boar, but of infinitely greater dimensions.

Extending forward, parallel with the proboscis, and on each side of it, was a gigantic staff, thirty or forty feet in length, formed seemingly of pure crystal and in shape a perfect prism,—it reflected in the most gorgeous manner the rays of the declining sun. The trunk was fashioned like a wedge with the apex to the earth. From it there were outspread two pairs of wings—each wing nearly one hundred yards in length—one pair being placed above the other, and all thickly covered with metal scales; each scale apparently some ten or twelve feet in diameter. I observed that the upper and lower tiers of wings were connected by a strong chain. But the chief peculiarity of this horrible thing was the representation of a *Death's Head*, which covered nearly the whole surface of its breast, and which was as accurately traced in glaring white, upon the dark ground of the body, as if it had been there carefully designed by an artist.

While I regarded the terrific animal, and more especially the appearance on its breast, with a feeling or horror and awe—with a sentiment of forthcoming evil, which I found it impossible to quell by any effort of the reason, I perceived the huge jaws at the extremity of the proboscis suddenly expand themselves, and from them there proceeded a sound so loud and so expressive of woe, that it struck upon my nerves like a knell and as the monster disappeared at the foot of the hill, I fell at once, fainting, to the floor.

Upon recovering, my first impulse, of course, was to inform my friend of what I had seen and heard—and I can scarcely explain what feeling of repugnance it was which, in the end, operated to prevent me.

At length, one evening, some three or four days after the occurrence, we were sitting together in the room in which I had seen the apparition—I occupying the same seat at the same window, and he lounging on a sofa near at hand. The association of the place and time impelled me to give him an account of the phenomenon. He heard me to the end—at first laughed heartily—and then lapsed into an excessively grave demeanour, as if my insanity was a thing beyond suspicion. At this instant I again had a distinct view of the monster—to which, with a shout of absolute terror, I now directed his attention. He looked eagerly—but maintained that he saw nothing—although I designated minutely the course of the creature, as it made its way down the naked face of the hill.

I was now immeasurably alarmed, for I considered the vision either as an omen of my death, or, worse, as the fore-runner of an attack of mania. I threw myself passionately back in my chair, and for some moments buried my face in my hands. When I uncovered my eyes, the apparition was no longer apparent.

My host, however, had in some degree resumed the calmness of his demeanour, and questioned me very rigorously in respect to the conformation of the visionary creature. When I had fully satisfied him on this head, he sighed deeply, as if relieved of some intolerable burden, and went on to talk, with what I thought a cruel calmness, of various points of speculative philosophy, which had heretofore formed subject of discussion between us. I remember his insisting very especially (among other things) upon the idea that the principle source of error in all human investigations lay in the liability of the understanding to under-rate or to over-value the importance of an object, through mere mis-admeasurement of its propinquity. "To estimate properly, for example," he said, "the influence to be exercised on mankind at large by the thorough diffusion of Democracy, the distance of the epoch at which such diffusion may possibly be accomplished should not fail to form an item in the estimate. Yet can you tell me one writer on the subject of government who has ever thought this particular branch of the subject worthy of discussion at all?"

He here paused for a moment, stepped to a book-case, and brought forth one of the ordinary synopses of *Natural History*. Requesting me then to exchange seats with him, that he might the better distinguish the fine print of the volume, he took my armchair at the window, and, opening the book, resumed his discourse very much in the same tone as before.

"But for your exceeding minuteness," he said, "in describing the monster, I might never have had it in my power to demonstrate to you what it was. In the first place, let me read to you a schoolboy account of the genus *Sphinx*, of the family *Crepuscularia* of the order *Lepidoptera*, of the class of *Insecta*—or insects. The account runs thus:

"'Four membranous wings covered with little coloured scales of metallic appearance; mouth forming a rolled proboscis, produced by an elongation of the jaws, upon the sides of which are found the rudiments of mandibles and downy *palpi*; the inferior wings retained to the superior by a stiff hair; antennae in the form of an elongated club, prismatic; abdomen pointed, The Death's—headed Sphinx has occasioned much terror among the vulgar, at times, by the melancholy kind of cry which it utters, and the insignia of death which it wears upon its corselet.'"

He here closed the book and leaned forward in the chair, placing himself accurately in the position which I had occupied at the moment of beholding "the monster."

"Ah, here it is," he presently exclaimed—"it is reascending the face of the hill, and a very remarkable looking creature I admit it to be. Still, it is by no means so large or so distant as you imagined it,—for the fact is that, as it wriggles its way up this thread, which some spider has wrought along the window-sash, I find it to be about the sixteenth of an inch in its extreme length, and also about the sixteenth of an inch distant from the pupil of my eye."

Never Bet the Devil Your Head

A Tale With a Moral.

"*Con tal que las costumbres de un autor,*" says Don Thomas de las Torres, in the preface to his *Amatory Poems* "*sean puras y castas, importo muy poco que no sean igualmente severas sus obras*"— meaning, in plain English, that, provided the morals of an author are pure personally, it signifies nothing what are the morals of his books. We presume that Don Thomas is now in Purgatory for the assertion. It would be a clever thing, too, in the way of poetical justice, to keep him there until his *Amatory Poems* get out of print, or are laid definitely upon the shelf through lack of readers. Every fiction *should have* a moral; and, what is more to the purpose, the critics have discovered that every fiction *has*. Philip Melanchthon, some time ago, wrote a commentary upon the *Batrachomyomachia*, and proved that the poet's object was to excite a distaste for sedition.

Pierre la Seine, going a step farther, shows that the intention was to recommend to young men temperance in eating and drinking. Just so, too, Jacobus Hugo has satisfied himself that, by Euenis, Homer meant to insinuate John Calvin; by Antinous, Martin Luther; by the Lotophagi, Protestants in general; and, by the Harpies, the Dutch. Our more modern Scholiasts are equally acute. These fellows demonstrate a hidden meaning in *The Antediluv*ians, a parable in Powhatan, "new views in Cock Robin," and transcendentalism in *Hop O' My Thumb*.

In short, it has been shown that no man can sit down to write without a very profound design. Thus to authors in general much trouble is spared. A novelist, for example, need have no care of his moral. It is there—that is to say, it is somewhere—and the moral and the critics can take care of themselves. When the proper time arrives, all that the gentleman intended, and all that he did not intend, will be brought to light, in the *Dial*, or the *Down-Easter*, together with all that he ought to have intended, and the rest that he clearly meant to intend:—so that it will all come very straight in the end.

There is no just ground, therefore, for the charge brought against me by certain ignoramuses—that I have never written a moral tale, or, in more precise words, a tale with a moral. They are not the critics predestined to bring me out, and *develop* my morals:—that is the secret. By and by the *North American Quarterly Humdrum* will make them ashamed of their stupidity. In the meantime, by way of staying execution—by way of mitigating the accusations against me—I offer the sad history appended,—a history about whose obvious moral there can be no question whatever, since he who runs may read it in the large capitals which form the title of the tale. I should have credit for this arrangement—a far wiser one than that of La Fontaine and others, who reserve the impression to be conveyed until the last moment, and thus sneak it in at the fag end of their fables.

Defuncti injuria ne afficiantur was a law of the twelve tables, and *De mortuis nil nisi bonum* is an excellent injunction—even if the dead in question be nothing but dead small beer. It is not my design, therefore, to vituperate my deceased friend, Toby Dammit. He was a sad dog, it is true, and a dog's death it was that he died; but he himself was not to blame for his vices. They grew out of a personal defect in his mother. She did her best in the way of flogging him while an infant—for duties to her well—regulated mind were always pleasures, and babies, like tough steaks, or the modern Greek olive trees, are invariably the better for beating—but, poor woman! she had the misfortune to be left-handed, and a child flogged left-handedly had better be left unflogged. The world revolves from right to left.

It will not do to whip a baby from left to right. If each blow in the proper direction drives an evil propensity out, it follows that every thump in an opposite one knocks its quota of wickedness in. I was often present at Toby's chastisements, and, even by the way in which he kicked, I could perceive that he was getting worse and worse every day. At last I saw, through the tears in my eyes, that there was no hope of the villain at all, and one day when he had been cuffed until he grew so black in the face that one might have mistaken him for a little African, and no effect had been produced beyond that of making him wriggle himself into a fit, I could stand it no longer, but went down upon my knees forthwith, and, uplifting my voice, made prophecy of his ruin.

The fact is that his precocity in vice was awful. At five months of age he used to get into such passions that he was unable to articulate. At six months, I caught him gnawing a pack of cards. At seven months he was in the constant habit of catching and kissing the female babies. At eight months he peremptorily refused to put his signature to the Temperance pledge. Thus he went on increasing in iniquity, month after month, until, at the close of the first year, he not only insisted upon wearing *moustaches*, but had contracted a propensity for cursing and swearing, and for backing his assertions by bets.

Through this latter most ungentlemanly practice, the ruin which I had predicted to Toby Dammit overtook him at last. The fashion had "grown with his growth and strengthened with his strength," so that, when he came to be a man, he could scarcely utter a sentence without interlarding it with a proposition to gamble. Not that he actually *laid* wagers—no. I will do my friend the justice to say that he would as soon have laid eggs. With him the thing was a mere formula—nothing more. His expressions on this head had no meaning attached to them whatever. They were simple if not altogether innocent expletives—imaginative phrases wherewith to round off a sentence. When he said "I'll bet you so and so," nobody ever thought of taking him up; but still I could not help thinking it my duty to put him down.

The habit was an immoral one, and so I told him. It was a vulgar one—this I begged him to believe. It was discountenanced by society—here I said nothing but the truth. It was forbidden by act of Congress—here I had not the slightest intention of telling a lie. I remonstrated—but to no purpose. I demonstrated—in vain. I entreated—he smiled. I implored—he laughed. I preached—he sneered. I threatened—he swore. I kicked him—he called for the police. I pulled his nose—he blew it, and offered to bet the Devil his head that I would not venture to try that experiment again.

Poverty was another vice which the peculiar physical deficiency of Dammit's mother had entailed upon her son. He was detestably poor, and this was the reason, no doubt, that his expletive expressions about betting, seldom took a pecuniary turn. I will not be bound to say that I ever heard him make use of such a figure of speech as "I'll bet you a dollar." It was usually "I'll bet you what you please," or "I'll bet you what you dare," or "I'll bet you a trifle," or else, more significantly still, "*I'll bet the Devil my head.*"

This latter form seemed to please him best;—perhaps because it involved the least risk; for Dammit had become excessively parsimonious. Had any one taken him up, his head was small, and thus his loss would have been small too. But these are my own reflections and I am by no means sure that I am right in attributing them to him. At all events the phrase in question grew daily in favor, notwithstanding the gross impropriety of a man betting his brains like bank-notes:—but this was a point which my friend's perversity of disposition would not permit him to comprehend. In the end, he abandoned all other forms of wager, and gave himself up to "*I'll bet the Devil my head,*" with a pertinacity and exclusiveness of devotion that displeased not less than it surprised me.

I am always displeased by circumstances for which I cannot account. Mysteries force a man to think, and so injure his health. The truth is, there was something in *the air* with which Mr. Dammit was wont to give utterance to his offensive expression—something in his *manner* of enunciation—which at first interested, and afterwards made me very uneasy—something which, for want of a more definite term at present, I must be permitted to call queer; but which Mr. Coleridge would have called mystical, Mr. Kant pantheistical, Mr. Carlyle twistical, and Mr. Emerson hyperquizzitistical. I began not to like it at all. Mr. Dammits soul was in a perilous state. I resolved to bring all my eloquence into play to save it. I vowed to serve him as St. Patrick, in the Irish chronicle, is said to have served the toad,—that is to say, "awaken him to a sense of his situation." I addressed myself to the task forthwith. Once more I betook myself to remonstrance. Again I collected my energies for a final attempt at expostulation.

When I had made an end of my lecture, Mr. Dammit indulged himself in some very equivocal behaviour. For some moments he remained silent, merely looking me inquisitively in the face. But presently he threw his head to one side, and elevated his eyebrows to a great extent. Then he spread out the palms of his hands and shrugged up his shoulders. Then he winked with the right eye. Then he repeated the operation with the left. Then he shut them both up very tight. Then he opened them both so very wide that I became seriously alarmed for the consequences. Then, applying his thumb to his nose, he thought proper to make an indescribable movement with the rest of his fingers. Finally, setting his arms *akimbo*, he condescended to reply.

I can call to mind only the beads of his discourse. He would be obliged to me if I would hold my tongue. He wished none of my advice. He despised all my insinuations. He was old enough to take care of himself. Did I still think him baby Dammit? Did I mean to say any thing against his character? Did I intend to insult him? Was I a fool? Was my maternal parent aware, in a word, of my absence from the domiciliary residence? He would put this latter question to me as to a man of veracity, and he would bind himself to abide by my reply. Once more he would demand explicitly if my mother knew that I was out. My confusion, he said, betrayed me, and he would be willing to bet the

Devil his head that she did not.

Mr. Dammit did not pause for my rejoinder. Turning upon his heel, he left my presence with undignified precipitation. It was well for him that he did so. My feelings had been wounded. Even my anger had been aroused. For once I would have taken him up upon his insulting wager. I would have won for the Arch-Enemy Mr. Dammit's little head—for the fact is, my mamma was very well aware of my merely temporary absence from home.

But *Khoda shefa midêhed*—Heaven gives relief—as the Mussulmans say when you tread upon their toes. It was in pursuance of my duty that I had been insulted, and I bore the insult like a man. It now seemed to me, however, that I had done all that could be required of me, in the case of this miserable individual, and I resolved to trouble him no longer with my counsel, but to leave him to his conscience and himself. But although I forbore to intrude with my advice, I could not bring myself to give up his society altogether. I even went so far as to humour some of his less reprehensible propensities; and there were times when I found myself lauding his wicked jokes, as epicures do mustard, with tears in my eyes:—so profoundly did it grieve me to hear his evil talk.

One fine day, having strolled out together, arm in arm, our route led us in the direction of a river. There was a bridge, and we resolved to cross it. It was roofed over, by way of protection from the weather, and the archway, having but few windows, was thus very uncomfortably dark. As we entered the passage, the contrast between the external glare and the interior gloom struck heavily upon my spirits. Not so upon those of the unhappy Dammit, who offered to bet the Devil his head that I was hipped. He seemed to be in an unusual good humor. He was excessively lively—so much so that I entertained I know not what of uneasy suspicion. It is not impossible that he was affected with the transcendentals. I am not well enough versed, however, in the diagnosis of this disease to speak with decision upon the point; and unhappily there were none of my friends of the *Dial* present.

I suggest the idea, nevertheless, because of a certain species of austere Merry-Andrewism which seemed to beset my poor friend, and caused him to make quite a Tom-Fool of himself. Nothing would serve him but wriggling and skipping about under and over everything that came in his way; now shouting out, and now lisping out, all manner of odd little and big words, yet preserving the gravest face in the world all the time. I really could not make up my mind whether to kick or to pity him. At length, having passed nearly across the bridge, we approached the termination of the footway, when our progress was impeded by a turnstile of some height.

Through this I made my way quietly, pushing it around as usual. But this turn would not serve the turn of Mr. Dammit. He insisted upon leaping the stile, and said he could cut a pigeon-wing over it in the air. Now this, conscientiously speaking, I did not think he could do. The best pigeon-winger over all kinds of style was my friend Mr. Carlyle, and as I knew *he* could not do it, I would not believe that it could be done by Toby Dammit. I therefore told him, in so many words, that he was a *braggadocio*, and could not do what he said. For this I had reason to be sorry afterward;—for he straightway offered to *bet the Devil his head* that he could.

I was about to reply, notwithstanding my previous resolutions, with some remonstrance against his impiety, when I heard, close at my elbow, a slight cough, which sounded very much like the ejaculation "*ahem!*" I started, and looked about me in surprise. My glance at length fell into a nook of the frame—work of the bridge, and upon the figure of a little lame old gentleman of venerable aspect. Nothing could be more reverend than his whole appearance; for he not only had on a full suit of black, but his shirt was perfectly clean and the collar turned very neatly down over a white cravat, while his hair was parted in front like a girl's. His hands were clasped pensively together over his stomach, and his two eyes were carefully rolled up into the top of his head.

Upon observing him more closely, I perceived that he wore a black silk apron over his small-clothes; and this was a thing which I thought very odd. Before I had time to make any remark, however, upon so singular a circumstance, he interrupted me with a second "*ahem!*"

To this observation I was not immediately prepared to reply. The fact is, remarks of this laconic nature are nearly unanswerable. I have known a *Quarterly Review nonplussed* by the word "*Fudge!*" I am not ashamed to say, therefore, that I turned to Mr. Dammit for assistance.

"Dammit," said I, "what are you about? don't you hear?—the gentleman says '*ahem!*'" I looked sternly at my friend while I thus addressed him; for, to say the truth, I felt particularly puzzled, and when a man is particularly puzzled he must knit his brows and look savage, or else he is pretty sure to look like a fool.

"Dammit," observed I—although this sounded very much like an oath, than which nothing was further from my thoughts—"Dammit," I suggested—"the gentleman says '*ahem!*'"

I do not attempt to defend my remark on the score of profundity; I did not think it profound myself; but I have noticed that the effect of our speeches is not always proportionate with their importance in our own eyes; and if I had shot Mr. D. through and through with a Paixhan bomb, or knocked him in the head with the *Poets and Poetry of America*, he could hardly have been more discomfited than when I addressed him with those simple words: "Dammit, what are you about?—don't you hear?—the gentleman says '*ahem!*'"

"You don't say so?" gasped he at length, after turning more colours than a pirate runs up, one after the other, when chased by a man-of-war. "Are you quite sure he said *that?* Well, at all events I am in for it now, and may as well put a bold face upon the matter. Here goes, then—*ahem!*"

At this the little old gentleman seemed pleased—God only knows why. He left his station at the nook of the bridge, limped forward with a gracious air, took Dammit by the hand and shook it cordially, looking all the while straight up in his face with an air of the most unadulterated benignity which it is possible for the mind of man to imagine.

"I am quite sure you will win it, Dammit," said he, with the frankest of all smiles, "but we are obliged to have a trial, you know, for the sake of mere form."

"Ahem!" replied my friend, taking off his coat, with a deep sigh, tying a pocket-handkerchief around his waist, and producing an unaccountable alteration in his countenance by twisting up his eyes and bringing down the corners of his mouth—"ahem!" And "ahem!" said he again, after a pause; and not another word more than "ahem!" did I ever know him to say after that. "Aha!" thought I, without expressing myself aloud—"this is quite a remarkable silence on the part of Toby Dammit, and is no doubt a consequence of his verbosity upon a previous occasion. One extreme induces another. I wonder if he has forgotten the many unanswerable questions which he propounded to me so fluently on the day when I gave him my last lecture? At all events, he is cured of the transcendentals."

"Ahem!" here replied Toby, just as if he had been reading my thoughts, and looking like a very old sheep in a reverie.

The old gentleman now took him by the arm, and led him more into the shade of the bridge—a few paces back from the turnstile. "My good fellow," said he, "I make it a point of conscience to allow you this much run. Wait here, till I take my place by the stile, so that I may see whether you go over it handsomely, and transcendentally, and don't omit any flourishes of the pigeon-wing. A mere form, you know. I will say 'one, two, three, and away.' Mind you, start at the word 'away'" Here he took his position by the stile, paused a moment as if in profound reflection, then *looked up* and, I thought, smiled very slightly, then tightened the strings of his apron, then took a long look at Dammit, and finally gave the word as agreed upon-

One—two—three—and—away!

Punctually at the word "away," my poor friend set off in a strong gallop. The stile was not very high, like Mr. Lord's—nor yet very low, like that of Mr. Lord's reviewers, but upon the whole I made sure that he would clear it. And then what if he did not?—ah, that was the question—what if he did not? "What right," said I, "had the old gentleman to make any other gentleman jump? The little old dot-and-carry-one! who is *he?* If he asks *me* to jump, I won't do it, that's flat, and I don't care who *the devil he is.*" The bridge, as I say, was arched and covered in, in a very ridiculous manner, and there was a most uncomfortable echo about it at all times—an echo which I never before so particularly observed as when I uttered the four last words of my remark.

But what I said, or what I thought, or what I heard, occupied only an instant. In less than five seconds from his starting, my poor Toby had taken the leap. I saw him run nimbly, and spring grandly from the floor of the bridge, cutting the most awful flourishes with his legs as he went up. I saw him high in the air, pigeon-winging it to admiration just over the top of the stile; and of course I thought it an unusually singular thing that he did not *continue* to go over. But the whole leap was the affair of a moment, and, before I had a chance to make any profound reflections, down came Mr. Dammit on the flat of his back, on the same side of the stile from which he had started.

At the same instant I saw the old gentleman limping off at the top of his speed, having caught and wrapt up in his apron something that fell heavily into it from the darkness of the arch just over the turnstile. At all this I was much astonished; but I had no leisure to think, for Dammit lay particularly still, and I concluded that his feelings had been hurt, and that he stood in need of my assistance. I hurried up to him and found that he had received what might be termed a serious injury. The truth is, he had been deprived of his head, which after a close search I could not find anywhere; so I determined to take him home and send for the homoeopathists. In the meantime a thought struck me, and I threw open an adjacent window of the bridge, when the sad truth flashed upon me at once.

About five feet just above the top of the turnstile, and crossing the arch of the foot-path so as to constitute a brace, there extended a flat iron bar, lying with its breadth horizontally, and forming one of a series that served to strengthen the structure throughout its extent. With the edge of this brace it appeared evident that the neck of my unfortunate friend had come precisely in contact.

He did not long survive his terrible loss. The homoeopathists did not give him little enough physic, and what little they did give him he hesitated to take. So in the end he grew worse, and at length died, a lesson to all riotous livers. I bedewed his grave with my tears, worked a *bar* sinister on his family escutcheon, and, for the general expenses of his funeral, sent in my very moderate bill to the transcendentalists. The scoundrels refused to pay it, so I had Mr. Dammit dug up at once, and sold him for dog's meat.

The Unparalleled Adventures of One Hans Pfaal

With a heart of furious fancies,
Whereof I am commander,
With a burning spear and a horse of air,
To the Wilderness I wander.

—Tom O'Bedlam's Song

By late accounts from Rotterdam, that city seems to be in a high state of philosophical excitement. Indeed, phenomena have there occurred of a nature so completely unexpected—so entirely novel—so utterly at variance with preconceived opinions—as to leave no doubt on my mind that long ere this all Europe is in an uproar, all physics in a ferment, all reason and astronomy together by the ears.

It appears that on the —— day of —— (I am not positive about the date), a vast crowd of people, for purposes not specifically mentioned, were assembled in the great square of the Exchange in the well-conditioned city of Rotterdam. The day was warm—unusually so for the season—there was hardly a breath of air stirring; and the multitude were in no bad humour at being now and then besprinkled with friendly showers of momentary duration, that fell from large white masses of cloud which chequered in a fitful manner the blue vault of the firmament.

Nevertheless, about noon, a slight but remarkable agitation became apparent in the assembly: the clattering of ten thousand tongues succeeded; and, in an instant afterward, ten thousand faces were upturned toward the heavens, ten thousand pipes descended simultaneously from the corners of ten thousand mouths, and a shout, which could be compared to nothing but the roaring of Niagara, resounded long, loudly, and furiously, through all the environs of Rotterdam.

The origin of this hubbub soon became sufficiently evident. From behind the huge bulk of one of those sharply-defined masses of cloud already mentioned, was seen slowly to emerge into an open area of blue space, a queer, heterogeneous, but apparently solid substance, so oddly shaped, so whimsically put together, as not to be in any manner comprehended, and never to be sufficiently admired, by the host of sturdy *burghers* who stood open-mouthed below. What could it be? In the name of all devils in Rotterdam, what could it possibly portend? No one knew, no one could imagine; no one—not even the *burgomaster* Mynheer Superbus Von Underduk—had the slightest clew by which to unravel the mystery; so, as nothing more reasonable could be done, every one to a man replaced his pipe carefully in the corner of his mouth, and cocking up his right eye towards the phenomenon, puffed, paused, waddled about, and grunted significantly—then waddled back, grunted, paused, and finally—puffed again.

In the meantime, however, lower and still lower toward the goodly city, came the object of so much curiosity, and the cause of so much smoke. In a very few minutes it arrived near enough to be accurately discerned. It appeared to be—yes! it *was* undoubtedly a species of balloon; but surely no *such* balloon had ever been seen in Rotterdam before. For who, let me ask, ever heard of a balloon manufactured entirely of dirty newspapers? No man in Holland certainly; yet here, under the very noses of the people, or rather at some distance *above* their noses was the identical thing in question, and composed, I have it on the best authority, of the precise material which no one had ever before known to be used for a similar purpose. It was an egregious insult to the good sense of the *burghers* of Rotterdam.

As to the shape of the phenomenon, it was even still more reprehensible. Being little or nothing better than a huge foolscap turned upside down. And this similitude was regarded as by no means lessened when, upon nearer inspection, there was perceived a large tassel depending from its apex, and, around the upper rim or base of the cone, a circle of little instruments, resembling sheep-bells, which kept up a continual tinkling to the tune of Betty Martin.

But still worse. Suspended by blue ribbons to the end of this fantastic machine, there hung, by way of car, an enormous drab beaver hat, with a brim superlatively broad, and a hemispherical crown with a black band and a silver buckle. It is, however, somewhat remarkable that many citizens of Rotterdam swore to having seen the same hat repeatedly before; and indeed the whole assembly seemed to regard it with eyes of familiarity; while the *vrow* Grettel Pfaall, upon sight of it, uttered an exclamation of joyful surprise, and declared it to be the identical hat of her good man himself.

Now this was a circumstance the more to be observed, as Pfaall, with three companions, had actually disappeared from Rotterdam about five years before, in a very sudden and unaccountable manner, and up to the date of this narrative all attempts had failed of obtaining any intelligence concerning them whatsoever. To be sure, some bones which were thought to be human, mixed up with a quantity of odd-looking rubbish, had been lately discovered in a retired situation to the east of Rotterdam, and some people went so far as to imagine that in this spot a foul murder had been committed, and that the sufferers were in all probability Hans Pfaall and his associates. But to return.

The balloon (for such no doubt it was) had now descended to within a hundred feet of the earth, allowing the crowd below a sufficiently distinct view of the person of its occupant. This was in truth a very droll little somebody. He could not have been more than two feet in height; but this altitude, little as it was, would have been sufficient to destroy his *equilibrium*, and tilt him over the edge of his tiny car, but for the intervention of a circular rim reaching as high as the breast, and rigged on to the cords of the balloon. The body of the little man was more than proportionately broad, giving to his entire figure a rotundity highly absurd.

His feet, of course, could not be seen at all, although a horny substance of suspicious nature was occasionally protruded through a rent in the bottom of the car, or to speak more properly, in the top of the hat. His hands were enormously large. His hair was extremely gray, and collected in a *queue* behind. His nose was prodigiously long, crooked, and inflammatory; his eyes full, brilliant, and acute; his chin and cheeks, although wrinkled with age, were broad, puffy, and double; but of ears of any kind or character there was not a semblance to be discovered upon any portion of his head. This odd little gentleman was dressed in a loose *surtout* of sky-blue satin, with tight breeches to match, fastened with silver buckles at the knees. His vest was of some bright yellow material; a white taffety cap was set jauntily on one side of his head; and, to complete his equipment, a blood-red silk handkerchief enveloped his throat, and fell down, in a dainty manner, upon his bosom, in a fantastic bow-knot of super-eminent dimensions.

Having descended, as I said before, to about one hundred feet from the surface of the earth, the little old gentleman was suddenly seized with a fit of trepidation, and appeared disinclined to make any nearer approach to *terra firma*. Throwing out, therefore, a quantity of sand from a canvas bag, which, he lifted with great difficulty, he became stationary in an instant. He then proceeded, in a hurried and agitated manner, to extract from a side-pocket in his *surtout* a large morocco pocket-book. This he poised suspiciously in his hand, then eyed it with an air of extreme surprise, and was evidently astonished at its weight.

He at length opened it, and drawing there from a huge letter sealed with red sealing-wax and tied carefully with red tape, let it fall precisely at the feet of the *burgomaster*, Superbus Von Underduk. His Excellency stooped to take it up. But the aeronaut, still greatly discomposed, and having apparently no farther business to detain him in Rotterdam, began at this moment to make busy preparations for departure; and it being necessary to discharge a portion of ballast to enable him to reascend, the half dozen bags which he threw out, one after another, without taking the trouble to empty their contents, tumbled, every one of them, most unfortunately upon the back of the *burgomaster*, and rolled him over and over no less than one-and-twenty times, in the face of every man in Rotterdam.

It is not to be supposed, however, that the great Underduk suffered this impertinence on the part of the little old man to pass off with impunity. It is said, on the contrary, that during each of his half-dozen circumvolutions he emitted no less than half a dozen distinct and furious whiffs from his pipe, to which he held fast the whole time with all his might, and to which he intends holding fast(God willing) until the day of his decease.

In the meantime the balloon arose like a lark, and, soaring far away above the city, at length drifted quietly behind a cloud similar to that from which it had so oddly emerged, and was thus lost forever to the wondering eyes of the good citizens of Rotterdam. All attention was now directed to the letter, the descent of which, and the consequences attending thereupon, had proved so fatally subversive of both person and personal dignity to his Excellency, Von Underduk. That functionary, however, had not failed, during his circumgyratory movements, to bestow a thought upon the important subject of securing the packet in question, which was seen, upon inspection, to have fallen into the most proper hands, being actually addressed to himself and Professor Rubadub, in their official capacities of President and Vice-President of the Rotterdam College of Astronomy. It was accordingly opened by those dignitaries upon the spot, and found to contain the following extraordinary, and indeed very serious, communications.

To their Excellencies Von Underduk and Rubadub, President and Vice-President of the States' College of Astronomers, in the city of Rotterdam.

Your Excellencies may perhaps be able to remember an

humble artisan, by name Hans Pfaall, and by occupation a mender of bellows, who, with three others, disappeared from Rotterdam, about five years ago, in a manner which must have been considered by all parties at once sudden, and extremely unaccountable. If, however, it so please your Excellencies, I, the writer of this communication, am the identical Hans Pfaall himself. It is well known to most of my fellow citizens, that for the period of forty years I continued to occupy the little square brick building, at the head of the alley called Sauerkraut, in which I resided at the time of my disappearance.

My ancestors have also resided therein time out of mind—they, as well as myself, steadily following the respectable and indeed lucrative profession of mending of bellows. For, to speak the truth, until of late years, that the heads of all the people have been set agog with politics, no better business than my own could an honest citizen of Rotterdam either desire or deserve. Credit was good, employment was never wanting, and on all hands there was no lack of either money or goodwill. But, as I was saying, we soon began to feel the effects of liberty and long speeches, and radicalism, and all that sort of thing. People who were formerly, the very best customers in the world, had now not a moment of time to think of us at all. They had, so they said, as much as they could do to read about the revolutions, and keep up with the march of intellect and the spirit of the age.

If a fire wanted fanning, it could readily be fanned with a newspaper, and as the government grew weaker, I have no doubt that leather and iron acquired durability in proportion—for, in a very short time, there was not a pair of bellows in all Rotterdam that ever stood in need of a stitch or required the assistance of a hammer. This was a state of things not to be endured. I soon grew as poor as a rat, and, having a wife and children to provide for, my burdens at length became intolerable, and I spent hour after hour in reflecting upon the most convenient method of putting an end to my life. Duns, in the meantime, left me little leisure for contemplation.

My house was literally besieged from morning till night, so that I began to rave, and foam, and fret like a caged tiger against the bars of his enclosure. There were three fellows in particular who worried me beyond endurance, keeping watch continually about my door, and threatening me with the law. Upon these three I internally vowed the bitterest revenge, if ever I should be so happy as to get them within my clutches; and I believe nothing in the world but the pleasure of this anticipation prevented me from putting my plan of suicide into immediate execution, by blowing my brains out with a blunderbuss. I thought it best, however, to dissemble my wrath, and to treat them with promises and fair words, until, by some good turn of fate, an opportunity of vengeance should be afforded me.

One day, having given my creditors the slip, and feeling more than usually dejected, I continued for a long time to wander about the most obscure streets without object whatever, until at length I chanced to stumble against the corner of a bookseller's stall. Seeing a chair close at hand, for the use of customers, I threw myself doggedly into it, and, hardly knowing why, opened the pages of the first volume which came within my reach. It proved to be a small pamphlet treatise on *Speculative Astronomy*, written either by Professor Encke of Berlin or by a Frenchman of somewhat similar name.

I had some little tincture of information on matters of this nature, and soon became more and more absorbed in the contents of the book— reading it actually through twice before I awoke to a recollection of what was passing around me. By this time it began to grow dark, and I directed my steps toward home. But the treatise (in conjunction with a discovery in pneumatics, lately communicated to me as an important secret, by a cousin from Nantz) had made an indelible impression on my mind, and, as I sauntered along the dusky streets, I revolved carefully over in my memory the wild and sometimes unintelligible reasonings of the writer. There are some particular passages which affected my imagination in a powerful and extraordinary manner. The longer I meditated upon these the more intense grew the interest which had been excited within me. The limited nature of my education in general, and more especially my ignorance on subjects connected with natural philosophy, so far from rendering me diffident of my own ability to comprehend what I had read, or inducing me to mistrust the many vague notions which had arisen in consequence, merely served as a farther stimulus to imagination; and I was vain enough, or perhaps reasonable enough, to doubt whether those crude ideas which, arising in ill-regulated minds, have all the appearance, may not often in effect possess all the force, the reality, and other inherent properties, of instinct or intuition.

It was late when I reached home, and I went immediately to bed. My mind, however, was too much occupied to sleep, and I lay the whole night buried in meditation. Arising early in the morning, and contriving again to escape the vigilance of my creditors, I repaired eagerly to the bookseller's stall, and laid out what little ready money I possessed, in the purchase of some volumes of *Mechanics and Practical Astronomy*. Having arrived at home safely with these, I devoted every spare moment to their perusal, and soon made such proficiency in studies of this nature as I thought sufficient for the execution of a certain design with which either the Devil or my better genius had inspired me. In the intervals of this period, I made every endeavour to conciliate the three creditors who had given me so much annoyance.

In this I finally succeeded—partly by selling enough of my household furniture to satisfy a moiety of their claim, and partly by a promise of paying the balance upon completion of a little project which I told them I had in view, and for assistance in which I solicited their services. By these means—for they were ignorant men—I found little difficulty in gaining them over to my purpose.

Matters being thus arranged, I contrived, by the aid of my wife and with the greatest secrecy and caution, to dispose of what property I had remaining, and to borrow, in small sums, under various pretences, and without giving any attention (I am ashamed to say) to my future means of repayment, no inconsiderable quantity of ready money. With the means thus accruing I proceeded to procure at intervals, cambric muslin, very fine, in pieces of twelve yards each; twine; a lot of the varnish of *caoutchouc*; a large and deep basket of wicker-work, made to order; and several other articles necessary in the construction and equipment of a balloon of extraordinary dimensions.

This I directed my wife to make up as soon as possible, and gave her all requisite information as to the particular method of proceeding. In the meantime I worked up the twine into net-work of sufficient dimensions; rigged it with a hoop and the necessary cords; and made purchase of numerous instruments and materials for experiment in the upper regions of the upper atmosphere. I then took opportunities of conveying by night, to a retired situation east of Rotterdam, five iron-bound casks, to contain about fifty gallons each, and one of a larger size; six tin tubes, three inches in diameter, properly shaped, and ten feet in length; a quantity of a *particular metallic substance, or semi-metal*, which I shall not name, and a dozen demijohns of *a very common acid*. The gas to be formed from these latter materials is a gas never yet generated by any other person than myself—or at least never applied to any similar purpose.

I can only venture to say here, that it is a *constituent of azote*, so long considered irreducible, and that its density is about 37.4 times *less than that of hydrogen*. It is tasteless, but not odourless; burns, when pure, with a greenish flame; and is instantaneously fatal to animal life. Its full secret I would make no difficulty in disclosing, but that it of right belongs (as I have before hinted) to a citizen of Nantz, in France, by whom it was conditionally communicated to myself. The same individual submitted to me, without being at all aware of my intentions, a method of constructing balloons from the membrane of a certain animal, through which substance any escape of gas was nearly an impossibility.

I found it however altogether too expensive, and was not sure, upon the whole, whether cambric muslin with a coating of gum *caoutchouc*, was not equally as good. I mention this circumstance, because I think it probable that hereafter the individual in question may attempt a balloon ascension with the novel gas and material I have spoken of, and I do not wish to deprive him of the honour of a very singular invention.

On the spot which I intended each of the smaller casks to occupy respectively during the inflation of the balloon, I privately dug a small hole; the holes forming in this manner a circle twenty-five feet in diameter. In the centre of this circle, being the station designed for the large cask, I also dug a hole of greater depth. In each of the five smaller holes, I deposited a canister containing fifty pounds, and in the larger one a keg holding one hundred and fifty pounds, of cannon powder. These—the keg and canisters—I connected in a proper manner with covered trains; and having let into one of the canisters the end of about four feet of slow-match, I covered up the hole, and placed the cask over it, leaving the other end of the match protruding about an inch, and barely visible beyond the cask. I then filled up the remaining holes, and placed the barrels over them in their destined situation!

Besides the articles above enumerated, I conveyed to the *dépôt*, and there secreted, one of M. Grimm's improvements upon the apparatus for condensation of the atmospheric air. I found this machine, however, to require considerable alteration before it could be adapted to the purposes to which I intended making it applicable. But, with severe labour and unremitting perseverance, I at length met with entire success in all my preparations. My balloon was soon completed. It would contain more than forty thousand cubic feet of gas; would take me up easily, I calculated, with all my implements, and, if I managed rightly, with one hundred and seventy-five pounds of ballast into the bargain. It had received three coats of varnish, and I found the cambric muslin to answer all the purposes of silk itself, being quite as strong and a good deal less expensive.

Everything being now ready, I exacted from my wife an oath of secrecy in relation to all my actions from the day of my first visit to the bookseller's stall; and promising, on my part, to return as soon as circumstances would permit, I gave her what little money I had left, and bade her farewell. Indeed I had no fear on her account. She was what people call a notable woman, and could manage matters in the world without my assistance. I believe, to tell the truth, she always looked upon me as an idle body—a mere make-weight—good for nothing but building castles in the air,—and was rather glad to get rid of me.

It was a dark night when I bade her goodbye, and taking with me, as *aides-de-camp*, the three creditors who had given me so much trouble, we carried the balloon, with the car and accoutrements, by a roundabout way, to the station where the other articles were deposited. We there found them all unmolested, and I proceeded immediately to business.

It was the first of April. The night, as I said before, was dark; there was not a star to be seen; and a drizzling rain, falling at intervals, rendered us very uncomfortable. But my chief anxiety was concerning the balloon, which, in spite of the varnish with which it was defended, began to grow rather heavy with the moisture; the powder also was liable to damage. I therefore kept my three duns working with great diligence, pounding down ice around the central cask, and stirring the acid in the others. They did not cease, however, importuning me with questions as to what I intended to do with all this apparatus, and expressed much dissatisfaction at the terrible labour I made them undergo. They could not perceive (so they said) what good was likely to result from their getting wet to the skin, merely to take a part in such horrible incantations.

I began to get uneasy, and worked away with all my might, for I verily believe the idiots supposed that I had entered into a compact with the Devil, and that, in short, what I was now doing was nothing better than it should be. I was, therefore, in great fear of their leaving me altogether. I contrived, however, to pacify them by promises of payment of all scores in full, as soon as I could bring the present business to a termination. To these speeches they gave, of course, their own interpretation; fancying, no doubt, that at all events I should come into possession of vast quantities of ready money; and provided I paid them all I owed, and a trifle more, in consideration of their services, I dare say they cared very little what became of either my soul or my carcass.

In about four hours and a half I found the balloon sufficiently inflated. I attached the car, therefore, and put all my implements in it: a telescope; a barometer, with some important modifications; a thermometer; an electrometer; a compass; a magnetic needle; a seconds watch; a bell; a speaking-trumpet, etc., etc., etc.; also a globe of glass, exhausted of air, and carefully closed with a stopper,—not forgetting the condensing apparatus, some unslacked lime, a stick of sealing-wax, a copious supply of water, and a large quantity of provisions, such as pemmican, in which much nutriment is contained in comparatively little bulk. I also secured in the car a pair of pigeons and a cat.

It was now nearly daybreak, and I thought it high time

to take my departure. Dropping a lighted cigar on the ground, as if by accident, I took the opportunity, in stooping to pick it up, of igniting privately the piece of slow-match, the end of which, as I said before, protruded a little beyond the lower rim of one of the smaller casks. This manoeuvre was totally unperceived on the part of the three duns; and, jumping into the car, I immediately cut the single cord which held me to the earth, and was pleased to find that I shot upward with inconceivable rapidity, carrying with all ease one hundred and seventy-five pounds of leaden ballast, and able to have carried up as many more. As I left the earth, the barometer stood at thirty inches, and the centigrade thermometer at 19°.

Scarcely, however, had I attained the height of fifty yards, when, roaring and rumbling up after me in the most tumultuous and terrible manner, came so dense a hurricane of fire, and gravel, and burning wood, and blazing metal, and mangled limbs, that my very heart sunk within me, and I fell down in the bottom of the car, trembling with terror. Indeed, I now perceived that I had entirely overdone the business, and that the main consequences of the shock were yet to be experienced. Accordingly, in less than a second, I felt all the blood in my body rushing to my temples, and immediately thereupon, a concussion, which I shall never forget, burst abruptly through the night, and seemed to rip the very firmament asunder.

When I afterward had time for reflection, I did not fail to attribute the extreme violence of the explosion, as regarded myself, to its proper cause—my situation directly above it, and in the line of its greatest power. But at the time, I thought only of preserving my life. The balloon at first collapsed, then furiously expanded, then whirled round and round with sickening velocity, and finally, reeling and staggering like a drunken man, hurled me over the rim of the car, and left me dangling, at a terrific height, with my head downward, and my face outward, by a piece of

slender cord about three feet in length, which hung accidentally through a crevice near the bottom of the wicker-
work, and in which, as I fell, my left foot became most
providentially entangled. It is impossible—utterly impossible—to form any adequate idea of the horror of my situation. I gasped convulsively for breath—a shudder resembling a fit of the ague agitated every nerve and muscle in
my frame—I felt my eyes starting from their sockets—a
horrible nausea overwhelmed me—and at length I lost all
consciousness in a swoon.

How long I remained in this state it is impossible to say.
It must, however, have been no inconsiderable time, for
when I partially recovered the sense of existence, I found
the day breaking, the balloon at a prodigious height over
a wilderness of ocean, and not a trace of land to be discovered far and wide within the limits of the vast horizon.
My sensations, however, upon thus recovering, were by no
means so replete with agony as might have been anticipated. Indeed, there was much of madness in the calm survey
which I began to take of my situation. I drew up to my
eyes each of my hands, one after the other, and wondered
what occurrence could have given rise to the swelling of
the veins, and the horrible blackness of the finger-nails.

I afterward carefully examined my head, shaking it repeatedly, and feeling it with minute attention, until I succeeded in satisfying myself that it was not, as I had more than
half suspected, larger than my balloon. Then, in a knowing
manner, I felt in both my breeches pockets, and, missing
therefrom a set of tablets and a tooth-pick case, endeavoured to account for their disappearance, and not being
able to do so, felt inexpressibly chagrined. It now occurred
to me that I suffered great uneasiness in the joint of my
left ankle, and a dim consciousness of my situation began
to glimmer through my mind,

But, strange to say! I was neither astonished nor horror-
stricken. If I felt any emotion at all, it was a kind of chuck-

ling satisfaction at the cleverness I was about to display in extricating myself from this dilemma; and never, for a moment, did I look upon my ultimate safety as a question susceptible of doubt. For a few minutes I remained wrapped in the profoundest meditation. I have a distinct recollection of frequently compressing my lips, putting my fore-finger to the side of my nose, and making use of other gesticulations and grimaces common to men who, at ease in their armchairs, meditate upon matters of intricacy or importance.

Having, as I thought, sufficiently collected my ideas, I now, with great caution and deliberation, put my hands behind my back, and unfastened the large iron buckle which belonged to the waistband of my pantaloons. This buckle had three teeth, which, being somewhat rusty, turned with great difficulty on their axis. I brought them, however, after some trouble, at right angles to the body of the buckle, and was glad to find them remain firm in that position. Holding within my teeth the instrument thus obtained, I now proceeded to untie the knot of my cravat. I had to rest several times before I could accomplish this manoeuvre; but it was at length accomplished. To one end of the cravat I then made fast the buckle, and the other end I tied, for greater security, tightly around my wrist. Drawing now my body upward, with a prodigious exertion of muscular force, I succeeded, at the very first trial, in throwing the buckle over the car, and entangling it, as I had anticipated, in the circular rim of the wickerwork.

My body was now inclined toward the side of the car, at an angle of about forty-five degrees; but it must not be understood that I was therefore only forty-five degrees below the perpendicular. So far from it, I still lay nearly level with the plane of the horizon; for the change of situation which I had acquired, had forced the bottom of the car considerably outward from my position, which was accordingly one of the most imminent peril. It should be remembered, however, that when I fell, in the first instance, from the car, if I had fallen with my face turned toward the balloon, instead of turned outwardly from it, as it actually was; or if, in the second place, the cord by which I was suspended had chanced to hang over the upper edge, instead of through a crevice near the bottom of the car,—I say it may readily be conceived that, in either of these supposed cases, I should have been unable to accomplish even as much as I had now accomplished, and the disclosures now made would have been utterly lost to posterity.

I had therefore every reason to be grateful; although, in point of fact, I was still too stupid to be anything at all, and hung for, perhaps, a quarter of an hour, in that extraordinary manner, without making the slightest farther exertion, and in a singularly tranquil state of idiotic enjoyment. But this feeling did not fail to die rapidly away, and thereunto succeeded horror, and dismay, and a sense of utter helplessness and ruin. In fact, the blood so long accumulating in the vessels of my head and throat, and which had hitherto buoyed up my spirits with delirium, had now begun to retire within their proper channels, and the distinctness which was thus added to my perception of the danger, merely served to deprive me of the self-possession and courage to encounter it.

But this weakness was, luckily for me, of no very long duration. In good time came to my rescue the spirit of despair, and, with frantic cries and struggles, I jerked my way bodily upward, till at length, clutching with a vise-like grip the long-desired rim, I writhed my person over it, and fell headlong and shuddering within the car.

It was not until some time afterward that I recovered myself sufficiently to attend to the ordinary cares of the balloon. I then, however, examined it with attention, and found it, to my great relief, uninjured. My implements were all safe, and, fortunately, I had lost neither ballast nor provisions.

Indeed, I had so well secured them in their places, that such an accident was entirely out of the question. Looking at my watch, I found it six o'clock. I was still rapidly ascending, and the barometer gave a present altitude of three and three-quarter miles. Immediately beneath me in the ocean, lay a small black object, slightly oblong in shape, seemingly about the size of a domino, and in every respect bearing a great resemblance to one of those toys.

Bringing my telescope to bear upon it, I plainly discerned it to be a British ninety-four-gun ship, close-hauled, and pitching heavily in the sea with her head to the W. S. W. Besides this ship, I saw nothing but the ocean and the sky, and the sun, which had long arisen.

It is now high time that I should explain to your Excellencies the object of my voyage. Your Excellencies will bear in mind that distressed circumstances in Rotterdam had at length driven me to the resolution of committing suicide. It was not, however, that to life itself I had any positive disgust, but that I was harassed beyond endurance by the adventitious miseries attending my situation. In this state of mind, wishing to live, yet wearied with life, the treatise at the stall of the bookseller, backed by the opportune discovery of my cousin of Nantz, opened a resource to my imagination.

I then finally made up my mind. I determined to depart, yet live—to leave the world, yet continue to exist—in short, to drop enigmas, I resolved, let what would ensue, to force a passage, if I could, *to the moon*. Now, lest I should be supposed more of a madman than I actually am, I will detail, as well as I am able, the considerations which led me to believe that an achievement of this nature, although without doubt difficult, and full of danger, was not absolutely, to a bold spirit, beyond the confines of the possible.

The moon's actual distance from the earth was the first thing to be attended to. Now, the mean or average interval between the *centres* of the two planets is 59.9643 of the earth's equatorial *radii*, or only about 237,000 miles. I say the mean or average interval; but it must be borne in mind that the form of the moon's orbit being an ellipse of eccentricity amounting to no less than 0.05484 of the major semi-axis of the ellipse itself, and the earth's centre being situated in its focus, if I could, in any manner, contrive to meet the moon in its perigee, the above-mentioned distance would be materially diminished.

But, to say nothing at present of this possibility, it was very certain that, at all events, from the 237,000 miles I would have to deduct the *radius* of the earth, say 4,000, and the radius of the moon, say 1,080, in all 5,080, leaving an actual interval to be traversed, under average circumstances, of 231,920 miles. Now this, I reflected, was no very extraordinary distance. Travelling on the land has been repeatedly accomplished at the rate of sixty miles per hour; and indeed a much greater speed may be anticipated. But even at this velocity, it would take me no more than 161 days to reach the surface of the moon. There were, however, many particulars inducing me to believe that my average rate of travelling might possibly very much exceed that of sixty miles per hour, and, as these considerations did not fail to make a deep impression upon my mind, I will mention them more fully hereafter.

The next point to be regarded was one of far greater importance. From indications afforded by the barometer, we find that, in ascensions from the surface of the earth we have, at the height of 1,000 feet, left below us about one thirtieth of the entire mass of atmospheric air; that at 10,600 we have ascended through nearly one third; and that at 18,000, which is not far from the elevation of Cotopaxi, we have surmounted one half the material, or, at all events, one half the *ponderable*, body of air incumbent upon our globe.

It is also calculated that at an altitude not exceeding the hundredth part of the earth's diameter—that is, not exceeding eighty miles—the rarefaction would be so excessive that animal life could in no manner be sustained, and, moreover, that the most delicate means we possess of ascertaining the presence of the atmosphere would be inadequate to assure us of its existence. But I did not fail to perceive that these latter calculations are founded altogether on our experimental knowledge of the properties of air, and the mechanical laws regulating its dilation and compression, in what may be called, comparatively speaking, *the immediate vicinity* of the earth itself; and, at the same time, it is taken for granted that animal life is and must be essentially *incapable of modification* at any given unattainable distance from the surface.

Now, all such reasoning and from such *data* must, of course, be simply analogical. The greatest height ever reached by man was that of 25,000 feet, attained in the aeronautic expedition of Messieurs Gay-Lussac and Biot. This is a moderate altitude, even when compared with the eighty miles in question; and I could not help thinking that the subject admitted room for doubt and great latitude for speculation.

But, in point of fact, an ascension being made to any given altitude, the ponderable quantity of air surmounted in any *farther* ascension is by no means in proportion to the additional height ascended (as may be plainly seen from what has been stated before), but in a *ratio* constantly decreasing. It is therefore evident that, ascend as high as we may, we cannot, literally speaking, arrive at a limit beyond which no atmosphere is to be found. It *must exist*, I argued; although it may exist in a state of infinite rarefaction.

On the other hand, I was aware that arguments have not been wanting to prove the existence of a real and definite limit to the atmosphere, beyond which there is absolutely no air whatsoever. But a circumstance which has been left out of view by those who contend for such a limit, seemed to me, although no positive refutation of their creed, still a point worthy very serious investigation. On comparing the intervals between the successive arrivals of Encke's comet at its perihelion, after giving credit, in the most exact manner, for all the disturbances due to the attractions of the planets, it appears that the periods are gradually diminishing; that is to say, the major axis of the comet's ellipse is growing shorter, in a slow but perfectly regular decrease.

Now, this is precisely what ought to be the case, if we suppose a resistance experienced from the comet from an extremely *rare ethereal medium* pervading the regions of its orbit. For it is evident that such a medium must, in retarding the comet's velocity, increase its centripetal, by weakening its centrifugal, force. In other words, the sun's attraction would be constantly attaining greater power, and the comet would be drawn nearer at every revolution. Indeed, there is no other way of accounting for the variation in question. But again:—The real diameter of the same comet's nebulosity is observed to contract rapidly as it approaches the sun, and dilate with equal rapidity in its departure toward its aphelion.

Was I not justifiable in supposing, with M. Valz, that this apparent condensation of volume has its origin in the compression of the same ethereal medium I have spoken of before, and which is dense in proportion to its vicinity to the sun? The lenticular-shaped phenomenon, also called the zodiacal light, was a matter worthy of attention. This radiance, so apparent in the tropics, and which cannot be mistaken for any meteoric lustre, extends from the horizon obliquely upward, and follows generally the direction of the sun's equator. It appeared to me evidently in the nature of a rare atmosphere extending from the sun outward, beyond the orbit of Venus at least, and I believed indefinitely farther.[1]

1. The zodiacal light is probably what the ancients called Trabes. *Emicant Trabes quos docos vocant.*—Pliny lib. 2, p. 26.

Indeed, this medium I could not suppose confined to the path of the comet's ellipse, or to the immediate neighbourhood of the sun. It was easy, on the contrary, to imagine it pervading the entire regions of our planetary system, condensed into what we call atmosphere at the planets themselves, and perhaps at some of them modified by considerations purely geological; that is to say, modified, or varied in its proportions (or absolute nature) by matters volatilized from the respective orbs.

Having adopted this view of the subject, I had little farther hesitation. Granting that on my passage I should meet with atmosphere *essentially* the same as at the surface of the earth, I conceived that, by means of the very ingenious apparatus of M. Grimm, I should readily be enabled to condense it in sufficient quantity for the purposes of respiration. This would remove the chief obstacle in a journey to the moon. I had indeed spent some money and great labour in adapting the apparatus to the object intended, and confidently looked forward to its successful application, if I could manage to complete the voyage within any reasonable period. This brings me back to the *rate* at which it would be possible to travel.

It is true that balloons, in the first stage of their ascensions from the earth, are known to rise with a velocity comparatively moderate. Now, the power of elevation lies altogether in the superior gravity of the atmospheric air compared with the gas in the balloon; and, at first sight, it does not appear probable that, as the balloon acquires altitude, and consequently arrives successively in atmospheric *strata* of densities rapidly diminishing—I say, it does not appear at all reasonable that, in this its progress upward, the original velocity should be accelerated.

On the other hand, I was not aware that, in any recorded ascension, a *diminution* had been proved to be apparent in the absolute rate of ascent; although such should have been the case, if on account of nothing else, on account of the escape of gas through balloons ill-constructed, and varnished with no better material than the ordinary varnish. It seemed, therefore, that the effect of such escape was only sufficient to counterbalance the effect of the acceleration attained in the diminishing of the balloon's distance from the gravitating centre.

I now considered that, provided in my passage I found the *medium* I had imagined, and provided that it should prove to be *essentially* what we denominate atmospheric air, it could make comparatively little difference at what extreme state of rarefaction I should discover it—that is to say, in regard to my power of ascending—for the gas in the balloon would not only be itself subject to similar rarefaction (in proportion to the occurrence of which, I could suffer an escape of so much as would be requisite to prevent explosion), but, *being what it was*, would, at all events, continue specifically lighter than any compound whatever of mere nitrogen and oxygen.

Thus there was a chance—in fact there was a strong probability—that, *at no epoch of my ascent, I should reach a point where the united weights of my immense balloon, the inconceivably rare gas within it, the car, and its contents, should equal the weight of the mass of the surrounding atmosphere displaced;* and this will be readily understood as the sole condition upon which my upward flight would be arrested. But, if this point were even attained, I could dispense with ballast and other weight to the amount of nearly three hundred pounds. In the meantime, the force of gravitation would be constantly diminishing, in proportion to the squares of the distances, and so, with a velocity prodigiously accelerating, I should at length arrive in those distant regions where the force of the earth's attraction would be superseded by that of the moon.

There was another difficulty, however, which occasioned me some little disquietude. It has been observed, that, in balloon ascensions to any considerable height, besides the pain attending respiration, great uneasiness is experienced about the head and body, often accompanied with bleeding at the nose, and other symptoms of an alarming kind, and growing more and more inconvenient in proportion to the altitude attained.[2] This was a reflection of a nature somewhat startling.

Was it not probable that these symptoms would increase until terminated by death itself? I finally thought not. Their origin was to be looked for in the progressive removal of the *customary* atmospheric pressure upon the surface of the body, and consequent distention of the superficial blood-vessels—not in any positive disorganization of the animal system, as in the case of difficulty in breathing, where the atmospheric density is *chemically insufficient* for the due renovation of blood in a ventricle of the heart.

Unless for default of this renovation, I could see no reason, therefore, why life could not be sustained even in a *vacuum*; for the expansion and compression of chest, commonly called breathing, is action purely muscular, and the cause, not the *effect*, of respiration. In a word, I conceived that, as the body should become habituated to the want of atmospheric pressure, the sensations of pain would gradually diminish—and to endure them while they continued, I relied with confidence upon the iron hardihood of my constitution.

Thus, may it please your Excellencies, I have detailed some, though by no means all, the considerations which led me to form the project of a lunar voyage. I shall now proceed to lay before you the result of an attempt so apparently audacious in conception, and, at all events, so utterly unparalleled in the annals of mankind.

Having attained the altitude before mentioned—that is to say three miles and three quarters—I threw out from the

2. Since the original publication of Hans Pfaall, I find that Mr. Green, of Nassau-balloon notoriety, and other late aeronauts, deny the assertions of Humboldt, in this respect, and speak of a *decreasing* inconvenience,—precisely in accordance with the theory here urged.

car a quantity of feathers, and found that I still ascended with sufficient rapidity; there was, therefore, no necessity for discharging any ballast. I was glad of this, for I wished to retain with me as much weight as I could carry, for the obvious reason that I could not be positive either about the gravitation or the atmospheric density of the moon. I as yet suffered no bodily inconvenience, breathing with great freedom, and feeling no pain whatever in the head. The cat was lying very demurely upon my coat, which I had taken off, and eyeing the pigeons with an air of nonchalance. These latter being tied by the leg, to prevent their escape, were busily employed in picking up some grains of rice scattered for them in the bottom of the car. At twenty minutes past six o'clock, the barometer showed an elevation of 26,400 feet, or five miles to a fraction. The prospect seemed unbounded. Indeed, it is very easily calculated by means of spherical geometry, how great an extent of the earth's area I beheld. The convex surface of any segment of a sphere is, to the entire surface of the sphere itself, as the versed sine of the segment to the diameter of the sphere. Now, in my case, the versed sine—that is to say, the thickness of the segment beneath me—was about equal to my elevation, or the elevation of the point of sight above the surface. 'As five miles, then, to eight thousand,' would express the proportion of the earth's area seen by me.

In other words, I beheld as much as a sixteen-hundredth part of the whole surface of the globe. The sea appeared unruffled as a mirror, although, by means of the telescope, I could perceive it to be in a state of violent agitation. The ship was no longer visible, having drifted away, apparently to the eastward. I now began to experience, at intervals, severe pain in the head, especially about the ears—still, however, breathing with tolerable freedom. The cat and pigeons seemed to suffer no inconvenience whatsoever.

At twenty minutes before seven, the balloon entered a

long series of dense cloud, which put me to great trouble, by damaging my condensing apparatus, and wetting me to the skin; this was, to be sure, a singular rencontre, for I had not believed it possible that a cloud of this nature could be sustained at so great an elevation. I thought it best, however, to throw out two five-pound pieces of ballast, reserving still a weight of one hundred and sixty-five pounds. Upon so doing, I soon rose above the difficulty, and perceived immediately, that I had obtained a great increase in my rate of ascent.

In a few seconds after my leaving the cloud, a flash of vivid lightning shot from one end of it to the other, and caused it to kindle up, throughout its vast extent, like a mass of ignited charcoal. This, it must be remembered, was in the broad light of day. No fancy may picture the sublimity which might have been exhibited by a similar phenomenon taking place amid the darkness of the night. Hell itself might have been found a fitting image. Even as it was, my hair stood on end, while I gazed afar down within the yawning abysses, letting imagination descend, and stalk about in the strange vaulted halls, and ruddy gulfs, and red ghastly chasms of the hideous and unfathomable fire. I had indeed made a narrow escape.

Had the balloon remained a very short while longer within the cloud—that is to say, had not the inconvenience of getting wet, determined me to discharge the ballast—my destruction might, and probably would, have been the consequence. Such perils, although little considered, are perhaps the greatest which must be encountered in balloons. I had by this time, however, attained too great an elevation to be any longer uneasy on this head.

I was now rising rapidly, and by seven o'clock the barometer indicated an altitude of no less than nine miles and a half. I began to find great difficulty in drawing my breath. My head, too, was excessively painful; and, having felt for some time a moisture about my cheeks, I at length discovered it to be blood, which was oozing quite fast from the drums of my ears. My eyes, also, gave me great uneasiness. Upon passing the hand over them they seemed to have protruded from their sockets in no inconsiderable degree; and all objects in the car, and even the balloon itself, appeared distorted to my vision. These symptoms were more than I had expected, and occasioned me some alarm.

At this juncture, very imprudently, and without consideration, I threw out from the car three five-pound pieces of ballast. The accelerated rate of ascent thus obtained, carried me too rapidly, and without sufficient gradation, into a highly rarefied *stratum* of the atmosphere, and the result had nearly proved fatal to my expedition and to myself. I was suddenly seized with a spasm which lasted for more than five minutes, and even when this, in a measure, ceased, I could catch my breath only at long intervals, and in a gasping manner,—bleeding all the while copiously at the nose and ears, and even slightly at the eyes. The pigeons appeared distressed in the extreme, and struggled to escape; while the cat mewed piteously, and, with her tongue hanging out of her mouth, staggered to and fro in the car as if under the influence of poison.

I now too late discovered the great rashness of which I had been guilty in discharging the ballast, and my agitation was excessive. I anticipated nothing less than death, and death in a few minutes. The physical suffering I underwent contributed also to render me nearly incapable of making any exertion for the preservation of my life. I had, indeed, little power of reflection left, and the violence of the pain in my head seemed to be greatly on the increase.

Thus I found that my senses would shortly give way altogether, and I had already clutched one of the valve ropes with the view of attempting a descent, when the recollection of the trick I had played the three creditors, and the possible consequences to myself, should I return, operated to deter me for the moment. I lay down in the bottom of the car, and endeavoured to collect my faculties. In this I so far succeeded as to determine upon the experiment of losing blood.

Having no lancet, however, I was constrained to perform the operation in the best manner I was able, and finally succeeded in opening a vein in my left arm, with the blade of my penknife. The blood had hardly commenced flowing when I experienced a sensible relief, and by the time I had lost about half a moderate basin-full, most of the worst symptoms had abandoned me entirely. I nevertheless did not think it expedient to attempt getting on my feet immediately; but, having tied up my arm as well as I could, I lay still for about a quarter of an hour. At the end of this time I arose, and found myself freer from absolute pain of any kind than I had been during the last hour and a quarter of my ascension.

The difficulty of breathing, however, was diminished in a very slight degree, and I found that it would soon be positively necessary to make use of my condenser. In the meantime, looking toward the cat, who was again snugly stowed away upon my coat, I discovered to my infinite surprise, that she had taken the opportunity of my indisposition to bring into light a litter of three little kittens. This was an addition to the number of passengers on my part altogether unexpected; but I was pleased at the occurrence. It would afford me a chance of bringing to a kind of test the truth of a surmise, which, more than any thing else, had influenced me in attempting this ascension.

I had imagined that the habitual endurance of the atmospheric pressure at the surface of the earth was the cause, or nearly so, of the pain attending animal existence at a distance above the surface. Should the kittens be found to suffer uneasiness in an equal degree with their mother, I must consider my theory in fault, but a failure to do so I should look upon as a strong confirmation of my idea.

By eight o'clock I had actually attained an elevation of

seventeen miles above the surface of the earth. Thus it seemed to me evident that my rate of ascent was not only on the increase, but that the progression would have been apparent in a slight degree even had I not discharged the ballast which I did. The pains in my head and ears returned, at intervals, with violence, and I still continued to bleed occasionally at the nose; but, upon the whole, I suffered much less than might have been expected. I breathed, however, at every moment, with more and more difficulty, and each inhalation was attended with a troublesome spasmodic action of the chest. I now unpacked the condensing apparatus, and got it ready for immediate use.

The view of the earth, at this period of my ascension, was beautiful indeed. To the westward, the northward, and the southward, as far as I could see, lay a boundless sheet of apparently unruffled ocean, which every moment gained a deeper and deeper tint of blue. At a vast distance to the eastward, although perfectly discernible, extended the islands of Great Britain, the entire Atlantic coasts of France and Spain, with a small portion of the northern part of the continent of Africa. Of individual edifices not a trace could be discovered, and the proudest cities of mankind had utterly faded away from the face of the earth.

What mainly astonished me, in the appearance of things below, was the seeming concavity of the surface of the globe. I had, thoughtlessly enough, expected to see its real convexity become evident as I ascended; but a very little reflection sufficed to explain the discrepancy. A line, dropped from my position perpendicularly to the earth, would have formed the perpendicular of a right-angled triangle, of which the base would have extended from the right-angle to the horizon, and the hypotenuse from the horizon to my position.

But my height was little or nothing in comparison with my prospect. In other words, the base and hypotenuse of the supposed triangle would, in my case, have been so long, when compared to the perpendicular, that the two former might have been regarded as nearly parallel. In this manner the horizon of the aeronaut appears always to be upon a level with the car. But as the point immediately beneath him seems, and is, at a great distance below him, it seems, of course, also at a great distance below the horizon. Hence the impression of concavity; and this impression must remain, until the elevation shall bear so great a proportion to the prospect, that the apparent parallelism of the base and hypotenuse disappears.

The pigeons about this time seeming to undergo much suffering, I determined upon giving them their liberty. I first untied one of them, a beautiful gray-mottled pigeon, and placed him upon the rim of the wicker-work. He appeared extremely uneasy, looking anxiously around him, fluttering his wings, and making a loud cooing noise, but could not be persuaded to trust himself from the car. I took him up at last, and threw him to about half a dozen yards from the balloon. He made, however, no attempt to descend as I had expected, but struggled with great vehemence to get back, uttering at the same time very shrill and piercing cries. He at length succeeded in regaining his former station on the rim, but had hardly done so when his head dropped upon his breast, and he fell dead within the car. The other one did not prove so unfortunate.

To prevent his following the example of his companion, and accomplishing a return, I threw him downward with all my force, and was pleased to find him continue his descent, with great velocity, making use of his wings with ease, and in a perfectly natural manner. In a very short time he was out of sight, and I have no doubt he reached home in safety. Puss, who seemed in a great measure recovered from her illness, now made a hearty meal of the dead bird, and then went to sleep with much apparent satisfaction. Her kittens were quite lively, and so far evinced not the slightest sign of any uneasiness.

At a quarter past eight, being able no longer to draw breath without the most intolerable pain, I proceeded forthwith to adjust around the car the apparatus belonging to the condenser. This apparatus will require some little explanation, and your Excellencies will please to bear in mind that my object, in the first place, was to surround myself and car entirely with a barricade against the highly rarefied atmosphere in which I was existing, with the intention of introducing within this barricade, by means of my condenser, a quantity of this same atmosphere sufficiently condensed for the purposes of respiration. With this object in view I had prepared a very strong, perfectly air-tight, but flexible gum-elastic bag. In this bag, which was of sufficient dimensions, the entire car was in a manner placed. That is to say, it (the bag) was drawn over the whole bottom of the car, up its sides, and so on, along the outside of the ropes, to the upper rim or hoop where the net-work is attached. Having pulled the bag up in this way, and formed a complete enclosure on all sides, and at bottom, it was now necessary to fasten up its top or mouth, by passing its material over the hoop of the net-work,—in other words, between the net-work and the hoop. But if the net-work were separated from the hoop to admit this passage, what was to sustain the car in the meantime? Now the net-work was not permanently fastened to the hoop, but attached by a series of running loops or nooses.

I therefore undid only a few of these loops at one time, leaving the car suspended by the remainder. Having thus inserted a portion of the cloth forming the upper part of the bag, I refastened the loops—not to the hoop, for that would have been impossible, since the cloth now intervened,—but to a series of large buttons, affixed to the cloth itself, about three feet below the mouth of the bag; the intervals between the buttons having been made to correspond to the intervals between the loops. This done, a few more of the loops were unfastened from the rim, a farther portion of the cloth introduced, and the disengaged loops then connected with their proper buttons.

In this way it was possible to insert the whole upper part of the bag between the net-work and the hoop. It is evident that the hoop would now drop down within the car, while the whole weight of the car itself, with all its contents, would be held up merely by the strength of the buttons. This, at first sight, would seem an inadequate dependence; but it was by no means so, for the buttons were not only very strong in themselves, but so close together that a very slight portion of the whole weight was supported by any one of them.

Indeed, had the car and contents been three times heavier than they were, I should not have been at all uneasy. I now raised up the hoop again within the covering of gum-elastic, and propped it at nearly its former height by means of three light poles prepared for the occasion. This was done, of course, to keep the bag distended at the top, and to preserve the lower part of the net-work in its proper situation. All that now remained was to fasten up the mouth of the enclosure; and this was readily accomplished by gathering the folds of the material together, and twisting them up very tightly on the inside by means of a kind of stationary tourniquet.

In the sides of the covering thus adjusted round the car, had been inserted three circular panes of thick but clear glass, through which I could see without difficulty around me in every horizontal direction. In that portion of the cloth forming the bottom, was likewise a fourth window, of the same kind, and corresponding with a small aperture in the floor of the car itself. This enabled me to see perpendicularly down, but having found it impossible to place any similar contrivance overhead, on account of the peculiar manner of closing up the opening there, and the consequent wrinkles in the cloth, I could expect to see no objects situated directly in my zenith. This, of course, was a matter of little consequence; for, had I even been able to place a window at top, the balloon itself would have prevented my making any use of it.

About a foot below one of the side windows was a circular opening, three inches in diameter, and fitted with a brass rim adapted in its inner edge to the windings of a screw. In this rim was screwed the large tube of the condenser, the body of the machine being, of course, within the chamber of gum-elastic. Through this tube a quantity of the rare atmosphere circumjacent being drawn by means of a vacuum created in the body of the machine, was thence discharged, in a state of condensation, to mingle with the thin air already in the chamber.

This operation being repeated several times, at length filled the chamber with atmosphere proper for all the purposes of respiration; but in so confined a space it would, in a short time, necessarily become foul, and unfit for use from frequent contact with the lungs. It was then ejected by a small valve at the bottom of the car;—the dense air readily sinking into the thinner atmosphere below. To avoid the inconvenience of making a total vacuum at any moment within the chamber, this purification was never accomplished all at once, but in a gradual manner,—the valve being opened only for a few seconds, then closed again, until one or two strokes from the pump of the condenser had supplied the place of the atmosphere ejected.

For the sake of experiment I had put the cat and kittens in a small basket, and suspended it outside the car to a button at the bottom, close by the valve, through which I could feed them at any moment when necessary. I did this at some little risk, and before closing the mouth of the chamber, by reaching under the car with one of the poles before mentioned to which a hook had been attached. As soon as dense air was admitted in the chamber, the hoop and poles became unnecessary; the expansion of the enclosed atmosphere powerfully distending the gum-elastic. By the time I had fully completed these arrangements and filled the chamber as explained, it wanted only ten minutes of nine o'clock. During the whole period of my being thus employed, I endured the most terrible distress from difficulty of respiration, and bitterly did I repent the negligence or rather fool-hardiness, of which I had been guilty, of putting off to the last moment a matter of so much importance. But having at length accomplished it, I soon began to reap the benefit of my invention.

Once again I breathed with perfect freedom and ease— and indeed why should I not? I was also agreeably surprised to find myself, in a great measure, relieved from the violent pains which had hitherto tormented me. A slight headache, accompanied with a sensation of fullness or distension about the wrists, the ankles, and the throat, was nearly all of which I had now to complain. Thus it seemed evident that a greater part of the uneasiness attending the removal of atmospheric pressure had actually worn off, as I had expected, and that much of the pain endured for the last two hours should have been attributed altogether to the effects of a deficient respiration.

At twenty minutes before nine o'clock—that is to say, a short time prior to my closing up the mouth of the chamber, the mercury attained its limit, or ran down, in the barometer, which, as I mentioned before, was one of an extended construction. It then indicated an altitude on my part of 132,000 feet, or five-and-twenty miles, and I consequently surveyed at that time an extent of the earth's area amounting to no less than the three-hundred-and-twentieth part of its entire surperficies.

At nine o'clock I had again lost sight of land to the eastward, but not before I became aware that the balloon was drifting rapidly to the N. N. W. The ocean beneath me still retained its apparent concavity, although my view was often interrupted by the masses of cloud which floated to and fro.

At half past nine I tried the experiment of throwing out a handful of feathers through the valve. They did not float as I had expected; but dropped down perpendicularly, like a bullet, *en masse*, and with the greatest velocity,—being out of sight in a very few seconds. I did not at first know what to make of this extraordinary phenomenon; not being able to believe that my rate of ascent had, of a sudden, met with so prodigious an acceleration. But it soon occurred to me that the atmosphere was now far too rare to sustain even the feathers; that they actually fell, as they appeared to do, with great rapidity; and that I had been surprised by the united velocities of their descent and my own elevation.

By ten o'clock I found that I had very little to occupy my immediate attention. Affairs went on swimmingly, and I believed the balloon to be going upward with a speed increasing momently although I had no longer any means of ascertaining the progression of the increase. I suffered no pain or uneasiness of any kind, and enjoyed better spirits than I had at any period since my departure from Rotterdam; busying myself now in examining the state of my various apparatus, and now in regenerating the atmosphere within the chamber. This latter point I determined to attend to at regular intervals of forty minutes, more on account of the preservation of my health, than from so frequent a renovation being absolutely necessary. In the meanwhile I could not help making anticipations.

Fancy revelled in the wild and dreamy regions of the moon. Imagination, feeling herself for once unshackled, roamed at will among the ever-changing wonders of a shadowy and unstable land. Now there were hoary and time-honoured forests, and craggy precipices, and waterfalls tumbling with a loud noise into abysses without a bottom. Then I came suddenly into still noonday solitudes, where no wind of heaven ever intruded, and where vast meadows of poppies, and slender, lily-looking flowers spread themselves out a weary distance, all silent and motionless for ever. Then again I journeyed far down away into another country where it was all one dim and vague lake, with a boundary line of clouds.

But fancies such as these were not the sole possessors of my brain. Horrors of a nature most stern and most appalling would too frequently obtrude themselves upon my mind, and shake the innermost depths of my soul with the bare supposition of their possibility. Yet I would not suffer my thoughts for any length of time to dwell upon these latter speculations, rightly judging the real and palpable dangers of the voyage sufficient for my undivided attention.

At five o'clock, p. m., being engaged in regenerating the atmosphere within the chamber, I took that opportunity of observing the cat and kittens through the valve. The cat herself appeared to suffer again very much, and I had no hesitation in attributing her uneasiness chiefly to a difficulty in breathing; but my experiment with the kittens had resulted very strangely. I had expected, of course, to see them betray a sense of pain, although in a less degree than their mother; and this would have been sufficient to confirm my opinion concerning the habitual endurance of atmospheric pressure. But I was not prepared to find them, upon close examination, evidently enjoying a high degree of health, breathing with the greatest ease and perfect regularity, and evincing not the slightest sign of any uneasiness.

I could only account for all this by extending my theory, and supposing that the highly rarefied atmosphere around might perhaps not be, as I had taken for granted, chemically insufficient for the purposes of life, and that a person born in such a *medium* might, possibly, be unaware of any inconvenience attending its inhalation, while, upon removal to the denser *strata* near the earth, he might endure tortures of a similar nature to those I had so lately experienced. It has since been to me a matter of deep regret that an awkward accident, at this time, occasioned me the loss of my little family of cats, and deprived me of the insight into this matter which a continued experiment might have afforded. In passing my hand through the valve, with a cup of water for the old puss, the sleeve of my shirt became entangled in the loop which sustained the basket, and thus, in a moment, loosened it from the button.

Had the whole actually vanished into air, it could not have shot from my sight in a more abrupt and instantaneous manner. Positively, there could not have intervened the tenth part of a second between the disengagement of the basket and its absolute disappearance with all that it contained. My good wishes followed it to the earth, but of course, I had no hope that either cat or kittens would ever live to tell the tale of their misfortune.

At six o'clock, I perceived a great portion of the earth's visible area to the eastward involved in thick shadow, which continued to advance with great rapidity, until, at five minutes before seven, the whole surface in view was enveloped in the darkness of night. It was not, however, until long after this time that the rays of the setting sun ceased to illumine the balloon; and this circumstance, although of course fully anticipated, did not fail to give me an infinite deal of pleasure.

It was evident that, in the morning, I should behold the rising luminary many hours at least before the citizens of Rotterdam, in spite of their situation so much farther to the eastward, and thus, day after day, in proportion to the height ascended, would I enjoy the light of the sun for a longer and a longer period. I now determined to keep a journal of my passage, reckoning the days from one to twenty-four hours continuously, without taking into consideration the intervals of darkness.

At ten o'clock, feeling sleepy, I determined to lie down for the rest of the night; but here a difficulty presented itself, which, obvious as it may appear, had escaped my attention up to the very moment of which I am now speaking. If I went to sleep as I proposed, how could the atmosphere in the chamber be regenerated in the *interim?* To breathe it for more than an hour, at the farthest, would be a matter of impossibility; or, if even this term could be extended to an hour and a quarter, the most ruinous consequences might ensue.

The consideration of this dilemma gave me no little disquietude; and it will hardly be believed, that, after the dangers I had undergone, I should look upon this business in so serious a light, as to give up all hope of accomplishing my ultimate design, and finally make up my mind to the necessity of a descent. But this hesitation was only momentary. I reflected that man is the veriest slave of custom, and that many points in the routine of his existence are deemed *essentially* important, which are only so *at all* by his having rendered them habitual. It was very certain that I could not do without sleep; but I might easily bring myself to feel no inconvenience from being awakened at intervals of an hour during the whole period of my repose. It would require but five minutes at most to regenerate the atmosphere in the fullest manner—and the only real difficulty was to contrive a method of arousing myself at the proper moment for so doing.

But this was a question which, I am willing to confess, occasioned me no little trouble in its solution. To be sure, I had heard of the student who, to prevent his falling asleep over his books, held in one hand a ball of copper, the din of whose descent into a basin of the same metal on the floor beside his chair, served effectually to startle him up, if, at any moment, he should be overcome with drowsiness. My own case, however, was very different indeed, and left me no room for any similar idea; for I did not wish to keep awake, but to be aroused from slumber at regular intervals of time. I at length hit upon the following expedient, which, simple as it may seem, was hailed by me, at the moment of discovery, as an invention fully equal to that of the telescope, the steam-engine, or the art of printing itself.

It is necessary to premise, that the balloon, at the elevation now attained, continued its course upward with an even and undeviating ascent, and the car consequently followed with a steadiness so perfect that it would have been impossible to detect in it the slightest vacillation. This circumstance favoured me greatly in the project I now determined to adopt. My supply of water had been put on board in kegs containing five gallons each, and ranged very securely around the interior of the car. I unfastened one of these, and taking two ropes, tied them tightly across the rim of the wicker-work from one side to the other; placing them about a foot apart and parallel, so as to form a kind of shelf, upon which I placed the keg, and steadied it in a horizontal position.

About eight inches immediately below these ropes, and four feet from the bottom of the car I fastened another shelf—but made of thin plank, being the only similar piece of wood I had. Upon this latter shelf, and exactly beneath one of the rims of the keg, a small earthen pitcher was deposited. I now bored a hole in the end of the keg over the pitcher, and fitted in a plug of soft wood, cut in a tapering or conical shape. This plug I pushed in or pulled out, as might happen, until, after a few experiments, it arrived at that exact degree of tightness, at which the water, oozing from the hole, and falling into the pitcher below, would fill the latter to the brim in the period of sixty minutes.

This, of course, was a matter briefly and easily ascertained, by noticing the proportion of the pitcher filled in any given time. Having arranged all this, the rest of the plan is obvious. My bed was so contrived upon the floor of the car, as to bring my head, in lying down, immediately below the mouth of the pitcher. It was evident, that, at the expiration of an hour, the pitcher, getting full, would be forced to run over, and to run over at the mouth, which was somewhat lower than the rim. It was also evident, that the water thus falling from a height of more than four feet, could not do otherwise than fall upon my face, and that the sure consequence would be, to waken me up instantaneously, even from the soundest slumber in the world.

It was fully eleven by the time I had completed these arrangements, and I immediately betook myself to bed, with full confidence in the efficiency of my invention. Nor in this matter was I disappointed. Punctually every sixty minutes was I aroused by my trusty chronometer, when, having emptied the pitcher into the bung-hole of the keg, and performed the duties of the condenser, I retired again to bed. These regular interruptions to my slumber caused me even less discomfort than I had anticipated; and when I finally arose for the day, it was seven o'clock, and the sun had attained many degrees above the line of my horizon.

April 3rd. I found the balloon at an immense height indeed, and the earth's convexity had now become strikingly manifest. Below me in the ocean lay a cluster of black specks, which undoubtedly were islands. Overhead, the sky was of a jetty black, and the stars were brilliantly visible; indeed they had been so constantly since the first day of ascent. Far away to the northward I perceived a thin, white, and exceedingly brilliant line, or streak, on the edge of the horizon, and I had no hesitation in supposing it to be the southern disc of the ices of the Polar Sea. My curiosity was greatly excited, for I had hopes of passing on much farther to the north, and might possibly, at some period, find myself placed directly above the Pole itself. I now lamented that my great elevation would, in this case, prevent my taking as accurate a survey as I could wish. Much, however, might be ascertained.

Nothing else of an extraordinary nature occurred during the day. My apparatus all continued in good order, and the balloon still ascended without any perceptible vacillation. The cold was intense, and obliged me to wrap up closely in an overcoat. When darkness came over the earth, I betook myself to bed, although it was for many hours afterward broad daylight all around my immediate situation. The water-clock was punctual in its duty, and I slept until next morning soundly, with the exception of the periodical interruption.

April 4th. Arose in good health and spirits, and was astonished at the singular change which had taken place in the appearance of the sea. It had lost, in a great measure, the deep tint of blue it had hitherto worn, being now of a grayish-white, and of a lustre dazzling to the eye. The convexity of the ocean had become so evident, that the entire mass of the distant water seemed to be tumbling headlong over the abyss of the horizon, and I found myself listening on tiptoe for the echoes of the mighty cataract. The islands were no longer visible; whether they had passed down the horizon to the southeast, or whether my increasing elevation had left them out of sight, it is impossible to say. I was inclined, however, to the latter opinion. The rim of ice to the northward was growing more and more apparent. Cold by no means so intense. Nothing of importance occurred, and I passed the day in reading, having taken care to supply myself with books.

April 5th. Beheld the singular phenomenon of the sun rising while nearly the whole visible surface of the earth continued to be involved in darkness. In time, however, the light spread itself over all, and I again saw the line of ice to the northward. It was now very distinct, and appeared of a much darker hue than the waters of the ocean. I was evidently approaching it, and with great rapidity. Fancied I could again distinguish a strip of land to the eastward, and one also to the westward, but could not be certain. Weather moderate. Nothing of any consequence happened during the day. Went early to bed.

April 6th. Was surprised at finding the rim of ice at a very moderate distance, and an immense field of the same material stretching away off to the horizon in the north. It was evident that if the balloon held its present course, it would soon arrive above the frozen ocean, and I had now little doubt of ultimately seeing the Pole. During the whole of the day I continued to near the ice. Toward night the limits of my horizon very suddenly and materially increased, owing undoubtedly to the earth's form being that of an oblate spheroid, and my arriving above the flattened regions in the vicinity of the Arctic circle. When darkness at length overtook me, I went to bed in great anxiety, fearing to pass over the object of so much curiosity when I should have no opportunity of observing it.

April 7th. Arose early, and, to my great joy, at length beheld what there could be no hesitation in supposing the northern Pole itself. It was there, beyond a doubt, and immediately beneath my feet; but, alas! I had now ascended to so vast a distance, that nothing could with accuracy be discerned. Indeed, to judge from the progression of the numbers indicating my various altitudes, respectively, at different periods, between six a.m. on the second of April, and twenty minutes before nine a.m. of the same day (at which time the barometer ran down), it might be fairly inferred that the balloon had now, at four o'clock in the morning of April the seventh, reached a height of *not less*, certainly, than 7254 miles above the surface of the sea. This elevation may appear immense, but the estimate upon which it is calculated gave a result in all probability far inferior to the truth,

At all events I undoubtedly beheld the whole of the earth's major diameter; the entire northern hemisphere lay beneath me like a chart orthographically projected: and the great circle of the equator itself formed the boundary line of my horizon. Your Excellencies may, however, readily imagine that the confined regions hitherto unexplored within the limits of the Arctic circle, although situated directly beneath me, and therefore seen without any appearance of being foreshortened, were still, in themselves, comparatively too diminutive, and at too great a distance from the point of sight, to admit of any very accurate examination.

Nevertheless, what could be seen was of a nature singular and exciting. Northwardly from that huge rim before mentioned, and which, with slight qualification, may be called the limit of human discovery in these regions, one unbroken, or nearly unbroken, sheet of ice continues to extend. In the first few degrees of this its progress, its surface is very sensibly flattened, farther on depressed into a plane, and finally, becoming *not a little concave*, it terminates, at the Pole itself, in a circular centre, sharply defined, whose apparent diameter subtended at the balloon an angle of about sixty-five seconds, and whose dusky hue, varying in intensity, was, at all times, darker than any other spot upon the visible hemisphere, and occasionally deepened into the most absolute blackness.

Farther than this, little could be ascertained. By twelve o'clock the circular centre had materially decreased in circumference, and by seven p.m. I lost sight of it entirely; the balloon passing over the western limb of the ice, and floating away rapidly in the direction of the equator.

April 8th. Found a sensible diminution in the earth's apparent diameter, besides a material alteration in its general colour and appearance. The whole visible area partook in different degrees of a tint of pale yellow, and in some portions had acquired a brilliancy even painful to the eye. My view downward was also considerably impeded by the dense atmosphere in the vicinity of the surface being loaded with clouds, between whose masses I could only now and then obtain a glimpse of the earth itself. This difficulty of direct vision had troubled me more or less for the last forty-eight hours; but my present enormous elevation brought closer together, as it were, the floating bodies of vapour, and the inconvenience became, of course, more and more palpable in proportion to my ascent.

Nevertheless, I could easily perceive that the balloon now hovered above the range of great lakes in the continent of North America, and was holding a course, due south, which would soon bring me to the tropics. This circumstance did not fail to give me the most heartfelt satisfaction, and I hailed it as a happy omen of ultimate success. Indeed, the direction I had hitherto taken, had filled me with uneasiness; for it was evident that, had I continued it much longer, there would have been no possibility of my arriving at the moon at all, whose orbit is inclined to the ecliptic at only .the small angle of 5° 8' 48". Strange as it may seem, it was only at this late period that I began to understand the great error I had committed, in not taking my departure from earth at some point *in the plane of the lunar ellipse.*

April 9th. Today the earth's diameter was greatly diminished, and the colour of the surface assumed hourly a deeper tint of yellow. The balloon kept steadily on her course to the southward, and arrived, at nine p.m., over the northern edge of the Mexican Gulf.

April 10th. I was suddenly aroused from slumber, about five o'clock this morning, by a loud, crackling, and terrific sound, for which I could in no manner account. It was of very brief duration, but, while it lasted, resembled nothing in the world of which I had any previous experience. It is needless to say that I became excessively alarmed, having, in the first instance, attributed the noise to the bursting of the balloon. I examined all my apparatus, however, with great attention, and could discover nothing out of order. Spent a great part of the day in meditating upon an occurrence so extraordinary, but could find no means whatever of accounting for it. Went to bed dissatisfied, and in a state of great anxiety and agitation.

April 11th. Found a startling diminution in the apparent diameter of the earth, and a considerable increase, now observable for the first time, in that of the moon itself, which wanted only a few days of being full. It now required long and excessive labour to condense within the chamber sufficient atmospheric air for the sustenance of life.

April 12th. A singular alteration took place in regard to the direction of the balloon, and although fully anticipated, afforded me the most unequivocal delight. Having reached, in its former course, about the twentieth parallel of southern latitude, it turned off suddenly, at an acute angle, to the eastward, and thus proceeded throughout the day, keeping nearly, if not altogether, *in the exact plane of the lunar ellipse.* What was worthy of remark, a very perceptible vacillation in the car was a consequence of this change of route,—a vacillation which prevailed, in a more or less degree, for a period of many hours.

April 13th. Was again very much alarmed by a repetition of the loud crackling noise which terrified me on the tenth. Thought long upon the subject, but was unable to form any satisfactory conclusion. Great decrease in the earth's apparent diameter, which now subtended from the balloon an angle of very little more than twenty-five degrees. The moon could not be seen at all, being nearly in my zenith. I still continued in the plane of the ellipse, but made little progress to the eastward.

April 14th. Extremely rapid decrease in the diameter of the earth. Today I became strongly impressed with the idea, that the balloon was now actually running up the line of apsides to the point of perigee,—in other words, holding the direct course which would bring it immediately to the moon in that part of its orbit the nearest to the earth. The moon itself was directly overhead, and consequently hidden from my view. Great and long-continued labour necessary for the condensation of the atmosphere.

April 15th. Not even the outlines of continents and seas could now be traced upon the earth with distinctness. About twelve o'clock I became aware, for the third time, of that appalling sound which had so astonished me before. It now, however, continued for some moments, and gathered intensity as it continued. At length, while, stupefied and terror-stricken, I stood in expectation of I knew not what hideous destruction, the car vibrated with excessive violence, and a gigantic and flaming mass of some material which I could not distinguish, came with a voice of a thousand thunders, roaring and booming by the balloon. When my fears and astonishment had in some degree subsided, I had little difficulty in supposing it to be some mighty volcanic fragment ejected from that world to which I was so rapidly approaching, and, in all probability, one of that singular class of substances occasionally picked up on the earth, and termed meteoric stones for want of a better appellation.

April 16th. Today, looking upward as well as could, through each of the side windows alternately, I beheld, to my great delight, a very small portion of the moon's disk protruding, as it were, on all sides beyond the huge circumference of the balloon. My agitation was extreme; for I had now little doubt of soon reaching the end of my perilous voyage. Indeed, the labour now required by the condenser, had increased to a most oppressive degree, and allowed me scarcely any respite from exertion. Sleep was a matter nearly out of the question. I became quite ill, and my frame trembled with exhaustion. It was impossible that human nature could endure this state of intense suffering much longer. During the now brief interval of darkness a meteoric stone again passed in my vicinity, and the frequency of these phenomena began to occasion me much apprehension.

April 17th. This morning proved an epoch in my voyage. It will be remembered that, on the thirteenth, the earth subtended an angular breadth of twenty-five degrees. On the fourteenth this had greatly diminished; on the fifteenth a still more remarkable decrease was observable; and, on retiring on the night of the sixteenth, I had noticed an angle of no more than about seven degrees and fifteen minutes. What, therefore, must have been my amazement, on awakening from a brief and disturbed slumber, on the morning of this day, the seventeenth, at finding the surface beneath me so suddenly and wonderfully *augmented* in volume, as to subtend no less than thirty-nine degrees in apparent angular diameter! I was thunderstruck!

No words can give any adequate idea of the extreme, the absolute horror and astonishment, with which I was seized, possessed, and altogether overwhelmed. My knees tottered beneath me—my teeth chattered—my hair started up on end. 'The balloon, then, had actually burst!' These were the first tumultuous ideas that hurried through my mind: 'The balloon had positively burst!—I was falling—falling with the most impetuous, the most unparalleled velocity! To judge by the immense distance already so quickly passed over, it could not be more than ten minutes, at the farthest, before I should reach the surface of the earth, and be hurled into annihilation!'

But at length reflection came to my relief. I paused; I considered; and I began to doubt. The matter was impossible. I could not in any reason have so rapidly come down. Besides, although I was evidently approaching the surface below me, it was with a speed by no means commensurate with the velocity I had at first conceived. This consideration served to calm the perturbation of my mind, and I finally succeeded in regarding the phenomenon in its proper point of view. In fact, amazement must have fairly deprived me of my senses, when I could not see the vast difference, in appearance, between the surface below me, and the surface of my mother earth. The latter was indeed over my head, and completely hidden by the balloon, while the moon—the moon itself in all its glory—lay beneath me, and at my feet.

The stupor and surprise produced in my mind by this extraordinary change in the posture of affairs, was, perhaps, after all, that part of the adventure least susceptible of explanation. For the *bouleversement* in itself was not only natural and inevitable, but had been long actually anticipated as a circumstance to be expected whenever I should arrive at that exact point of my voyage where the attraction of the planet should be superseded by the attraction of the satellite—or, more precisely, where the gravitation of the balloon toward the earth should be less powerful than its gravitation toward the moon.

To be sure I arose from a sound slumber, with all my senses in confusion, to the contemplation of a very startling phenomenon, and one which, although expected, was not expected at the moment. The revolution itself must, of course, have taken place in an easy and gradual manner, and it is by no means clear that, had I even been awake at the time of the occurrence, I should have been made aware of it by any *internal* evidence of an inversion,—that is to say, by any inconvenience or disarrangement, either about my person or about my apparatus.

It is almost needless to say that, upon coming to a due sense of my situation, and emerging from the terror which had absorbed every faculty of my soul, my attention was, in the first place, wholly directed to the contemplation of the general physical appearance of the moon. It lay beneath me like a chart—and although I judged it to be still at no inconsiderable distance, the indentures of its surface were defined to my vision with a most striking and altogether unaccountable distinctness. The entire absence of ocean or sea, and indeed of any lake or river, or body of water whatsoever, struck me, at first glance, as the most extraordinary feature in its geological condition.

Yet, strange to say, I beheld vast level regions of a character decidedly alluvial, although by far the greater portion of the hemisphere in sight was covered with innumerable volcanic mountains, conical in shape, and having more the appearance of artificial than of natural protuberances. The highest among them does not exceed three and three-quarter miles in perpendicular elevation; but a map of the volcanic districts of the Campi Phlegraei would afford to your Excellencies a better idea of their general surface than any unworthy description I might think proper to attempt. The greater part of them were in a state of evident eruption, and gave me fearfully to understand their fury and their power, by the repeated thunders of the miscalled meteoric stones, which now rushed upward by the balloon with a frequency more and more appalling.

April 18th. Today I found an enormous increase in the moon's apparent bulk—and the evidently accelerated velocity of my descent began to fill me with alarm. It will be remembered, that, in the earliest stage of my speculations upon the possibility of a passage to the moon, the existence, in its vicinity, of an atmosphere, dense in proportion to the bulk of the planet, had entered largely into my calculations; this too in spite of many theories to the contrary, and, it may be added, in spite of a general disbelief in the existence of any lunar atmosphere at all.

But, in addition to what I have already urged in regard to Encke's comet and the zodiacal light, I had been strengthened in my opinion by certain observations of Mr. Schroeter, of Lilienthal. He observed the moon when two days and a half old, in the evening soon after sunset, before the dark part was visible, and continued to watch it until it became visible. The two cusps appeared tapering in a very sharp faint prolongation, each exhibiting its farthest extremity faintly illuminated by the solar rays, before any part of the dark hemisphere was visible. Soon afterward, the whole dark limb became illuminated. This prolongation of the cusps beyond the semicircle, I thought, must have arisen from the refraction of the sun's rays by the moon's atmosphere.

I computed, also, the height of the atmosphere (which could refract light enough into its dark hemisphere to produce a twilight more luminous than the light reflected from the earth when the moon is about 32° from the new) to be 1356 Paris feet; in this view, I supposed the greatest height capable of refracting the solar ray, to be 5376 feet. My ideas on this topic had also received confirmation by a passage in the eighty-second volume of the Philosophical Transactions, in which it is stated, that, at an occupation of Jupiter's satellites, the third disappeared after having been about 1" or 2" of time indistinct, and the fourth became indiscernible near the limb.[3]

Upon the resistance or, more properly, upon the support of an atmosphere, existing in the state of density imagined, I had, of course, entirely depended for the safety of my ultimate descent. Should I then, after all, prove to have been mistaken, I had in consequence nothing better to expect, as a *finale* to my adventure, than being dashed into atoms against the rugged surface of the satellite. And, indeed, I

3. Hevelius writes that he has several times found, in skies perfectly clear, when even stars of the sixth and seventh magnitude were conspicuous, that, at the same altitude of the moon, at the same elongation from the earth, and with one and the same excellent telescope, the moon and its maculae did not appear equally lucid at all times. From the circumstances of the observation, it is evident that the cause of this phenomenon is not either in our air, in the tube, in the moon, or in the eye of the spectator, but must be looked for in something (an atmosphere?) existing about the moon.

Cassini frequently observed Saturn, Jupiter, and the fixed stars, when approaching the moon to occultation, to have their circular figure changed into an oval one; and, in other occultations, he found no alteration of figure at all. Hence it might be supposed, that at some times, and not at others, there is a dense matter encompassing the moon wherein the rays of the stars are refracted.

had now every reason to be terrified. My distance from the moon was comparatively trifling, while the labour required by the condenser was diminished not at all, and I could discover no indication whatever of a decreasing rarity in the air.

April 19th. This morning, to my great joy, about nine o'clock, the surface of the moon being frightfully near, and my apprehensions excited to the utmost, the pump of my condenser at length gave evident tokens of an alteration in the atmosphere. By ten, I had reason to believe its density considerably increased. By eleven, very little labour was necessary at the apparatus; and at twelve o'clock, with some hesitation, I ventured to unscrew the *tourniquet*, when, finding no inconvenience from having done so, I finally threw open the gum-elastic chamber, and unrigged it from around the car.

As might have been expected, spasms and violent headache were the immediate consequences of an experiment so precipitate and full of danger. But these and other difficulties attending respiration, as they were by no means so great as to put me in peril of my life, I determined to endure as I best could, in consideration of my leaving them behind me momently in my approach to the denser *strata* near the moon. This approach, however, was still impetuous in the extreme; and it soon became alarmingly certain that, although I had probably not been deceived in the expectation of an atmosphere dense in proportion to the mass of the satellite, still I had been wrong in supposing this density, even at the surface, at all adequate to the support of the great weight contained in the car of my balloon.

Yet this *should* have been the case, and in an equal degree as at the surface of the earth, the actual gravity of bodies at either planet supposed in the ratio of the atmospheric condensation. That it *was not* the case, however, my precipitous downfall gave testimony enough; *why* it was not so, can only be explained by a reference to those possible geological disturbances to which I have formerly alluded. At all events I was now close upon the planet, and coming down with the most terrible impetuosity. I lost not a moment, accordingly, in throwing overboard first my ballast, then my water-kegs, then my condensing apparatus and gum-elastic chamber, and finally every article within the car.

But it was all to no purpose. I still fell with horrible rapidity, and was now not more than half a mile from the surface. As a last resource, therefore, having got rid of my coat, hat, and boots, I cut loose from the balloon *the car itself*, which was of no inconsiderable weight, and thus, clinging with both hands to the net-work, I had barely time to observe that the whole country, as far as the eye could reach, was thickly interspersed with diminutive habitations, ere I tumbled headlong into the very heart of a fantastical-looking city, and into the middle of a vast crowd of ugly little people, who none of them uttered a single syllable, or gave themselves the least trouble to render me assistance, but stood, like a parcel of idiots, grinning in a ludicrous manner, and eyeing me and my balloon askant, with their arms set *akimbo*.

I turned from them in contempt, and, gazing upward at the earth so lately left, and left perhaps for ever, beheld it like a huge, dull, copper shield, about two degrees in diameter, fixed immovably in the heavens overhead, and tipped on one of its edges with a crescent border of the most brilliant gold. No traces of land or water could be discovered, and the whole was clouded with variable spots, and belted with tropical and equatorial zones.

Thus, may it please your Excellencies, after a series of great anxieties, unheard-of dangers, and unparalleled escapes, I had, at length, on the nineteenth day of my departure from Rotterdam, arrived in safety at the conclusion of a voyage undoubtedly the most extraordinary, and the most momentous, ever accomplished, undertaken, or conceived by any denizen of earth. But my adventures yet remain to be related. And indeed your Excellencies may well imagine that, after a residence of five years upon a planet not only deeply interesting in its own peculiar character, but rendered doubly so by its intimate connection, in capacity of satellite, with the world inhabited by man, I may have intelligence for the private ear of the States' College of Astronomers of far more importance than the details, however wonderful, of the mere *voyage* which so happily concluded.

This is, in fact, the case. I have much—very much which it would give me the greatest pleasure to communicate. I have much to say of the climate of the planet; of its wonderful alternations of heat and cold; of unmitigated and burning sunshine for one fortnight, and more than polar frigidity for the next; of a constant transfer of moisture, by distillation like that *in vacuo*, from the point beneath the sun to the point the farthest from it; of a variable zone of running water; of the people themselves; of their manners, customs, and political institutions; of their peculiar physical construction; of their ugliness; of their want of ears, those useless appendages in an atmosphere so peculiarly modified; of their consequent ignorance of the use and properties of speech; of their substitute for speech in a singular method of inter-communication; of the incomprehensible connection between each particular individual in the moon with some particular individual on the earth—a connection analogous with, and depending upon, that of the orbs of the planet and the satellite, and by means of which the lives and destinies of the inhabitants of the one are interwoven with the lives and destinies of the inhabitants of the other; and above all, if it so please your Excellencies—above all, of those dark and hideous mysteries which lie in the outer regions of the moon,—regions which, owing to the almost miraculous accordance of the satellite's rotation on its own axis with its sidereal revolution about the earth, have never yet been turned, and, by God's mercy, never shall be turned, to the scrutiny of the telescopes of man.

All this, and more—much more—would I most willingly detail. But, to be brief, I must have my reward. I am pining for a return to my family and to my home; and as the price of any farther communication on my part—in consideration of the light which I have it in my power to throw upon many very important branches of physical and metaphysical science—I must solicit, through the influence of your honourable body, a pardon for the crime of which I have been guilty in the death of the creditors upon my departure from Rotterdam. This, then, is the object of the present paper. Its bearer, an inhabitant of the moon, whom I have prevailed upon, and properly instructed, to be my messenger to the earth, will await your Excellencies' pleasure, and return to me with the pardon in question, if it can, in any manner, be obtained.

I have the honour to be, etc., your Excellencies' very humble servant,

Hans Pfaall.

Upon finishing the perusal of this very extraordinary document, Professor Rubadub, it is said, dropped his pipe upon the ground in the extremity of his surprise, and Mynheer Superbus Von Underduk having taken off his spectacles, wiped them, and deposited them in his pocket, so far forgot both himself and his dignity, as to turn round three times upon his heel in the quintessence of astonishment and admiration. There was no doubt about the matter—the pardon should be obtained. So at least swore, with a round oath, Professor Rubadub, and so finally thought the illustrious Von Underduk, as he took the arm of his brother in science, and without saying a word, began to make the best of his way home to deliberate upon the measures to be adopted.

Having reached the door, however, of the *burgomaster's* dwelling, the professor ventured to suggest that as the messenger had thought proper to disappear—no doubt frightened to death by the savage appearance of the *burghers* of Rotterdam—the pardon would be of little use, as no one but a man of the moon would undertake a voyage to so vast a distance. To the truth of this observation the *burgomaster* assented, and the matter was therefore at an end. Not so, however, rumours and speculations. The letter, having been published, gave rise to a variety of gossip and opinion. Some of the over-wise even made themselves ridiculous by decrying the whole business as nothing better than a hoax. But hoax, with these sort of people, is, I believe, a general term for all matters above their comprehension. For my part, I cannot conceive upon what data they have founded such an accusation. Let us see what they say:

Imprimis. That certain wags in Rotterdam have certain especial antipathies to certain *burgomasters* and astronomers.

Secondly. That an odd little dwarf and bottle conjurer, both of whose ears, for some misdemeanour, have been cut off close to his head, has been missing for several days from the neighbouring city of Bruges.

Thirdly. That the newspapers which were stuck all over the little balloon were newspapers of Holland, and therefore could not have been made in the moon. They were dirty papers—very dirty—and Gluck, the printer, would take his bible oath to their having been printed in Rotterdam.

Fourthly. That Hans Pfaall himself, the drunken villain, and the three very idle gentlemen styled his creditors, were all seen, no longer than two or three days ago, in a tippling house in the suburbs, having just returned, with money in their pockets, from a trip beyond the sea.

Lastly. That it is an opinion very generally received, or which ought to be generally received, that the College of Astronomers in the city of Rotterdam, as well as all other colleges in all other parts of the world,—not to mention colleges and astronomers in general,—are, to say the least of the matter, not a whit better, nor greater, nor wiser than they ought to be.

Note.—Strictly speaking, there is but little similarity between the above sketchy trifle and the celebrated *Moon-Story* of Mr. Locke; but as both have the character of hoaxes, (although the one is in a tone of banter, the other of downright earnest,) and as both hoaxes are on the same subject, the moon,—moreover, as both attempt to give plausibility by scientific detail,—the author of *Hans Pfaall* thinks it necessary to say, *in self-defence*, that his own *jeu d'esprit* was published, in the *Southern Literary Messenger*, about three weeks before the commencement of Mr. L's in the *New York Sun*. Fancying a likeness which, perhaps, does not exist, some of the New York papers copied *Hans Pfaall*, and collated it with the *Moon-Hoax,* by way of detecting the writer of the one in the writer of the other.

As many more persons were actually gulled by the *Moon-Hoax* than would be willing to acknowledge the fact, it may here afford some little amusement to show why no one should have been deceived—to point out those particulars of the story which should have been sufficient to establish its real character. Indeed, however rich the imagination displayed in this ingenious fiction, it wanted much of the force which might have been given it by a more scrupulous attention to facts and to general analogy. That the public were misled, even for an instant, merely proves the gross ignorance which is so generally prevalent upon subjects of an astronomical nature.

The moon's distance from the earth is, in round numbers, 240,000 miles. If we desire to ascertain how near, apparently, a lens would bring the satellite (or any distant object), we, of course, have but to divide the distance by the magnifying or, more strictly, by the space-penetrating power of the glass. Mr. L. makes his lens have a power of 42,000 times. By this divide 240,000 (the moon's real distance), and we have five miles and five sevenths, as the apparent distance. No animal at all could be seen so far; much less the minute points particularized in the story.

Mr. L. speaks about Sir John Herschel's perceiving flowers (the Papaver rheas, etc.), and even detecting the colour and the shape of the eyes of small birds. Shortly before, too, he has himself observed that the lens would not render perceptible objects of less than eighteen inches in diameter; but even this, as I have said, is giving the glass by far too great power. It may be observed, in passing, that this prodigious glass is said to have been moulded at the glass-house of Messrs. Hartley and Grant, in Dumbarton; but Messrs. H. and G's establishment had ceased operations for many years previous to the publication of the hoax.

On page 13, pamphlet edition, speaking of "a hairy veil" over the eyes of a species of bison, the author says: "It immediately occurred to the acute mind of Dr. Herschel that this was a providential contrivance to protect the eyes of the animal from the great extremes of light and darkness to which all the inhabitants of our side of the moon are periodically subjected." But this cannot be thought a very "acute" observation of the doctor's. The inhabitants of our side of the moon have, evidently, no darkness at all, so there can be nothing of the "extremes" mentioned. In the absence of the sun they have a light from the earth equal to that of thirteen full unclouded moons.

The topography throughout, even when professing to accord with Blunt's Lunar Chart, is entirely at variance with that or any other lunar chart, and even grossly at variance with itself. The points of the compass, too, are in inextricable confusion; the writer appearing to be ignorant that, on a lunar map, these are not in accordance with terrestrial points; the east being to the left, etc.

Deceived, perhaps, by the vague titles, *Mare Nubium, Mare Tranquillitatis, Mare Fæcunditatis* , etc., given to the dark spots by former astronomers, Mr. L. has entered into details regarding oceans and other large bodies of water in the moon; whereas there is no astronomical point more positively ascertained than that no such bodies exist there. In examining the boundary between light and darkness (in the crescent or gibbous moon) where this boundary crosses any of the dark places, the line of division is found to be rough and jagged; but, were these dark places liquid, it would evidently be even.

The description of the wings of the man-bat, on page 21, is but a literal copy of Peter Wilkins' account of the wings of his flying islanders. This simple fact should have induced suspicion, at least, it might be thought.

On page 23, we have the following: "What a prodigious influence must our thirteen times larger globe have exercised upon this satellite when an embryo in the womb of time, the passive subject of chemical affinity!" This is very fine; but it should be observed that no astronomer would have made such remark, especially to any journal of science; for the earth, in the sense intended, is not only thirteen, but forty-nine times *larger* than the moon. A similar objection applies to the whole of the concluding pages, where, by way of introduction to some discoveries in Saturn, the philosophical correspondent enters into a minute school-boy account of that planet:—this to the *Edinburgh Journal of Science!*

But there is one point, in particular, which should have betrayed the fiction. Let us imagine the power actually possessed of seeing animals upon the moon's surface;—what would *first* arrest the attention of an observer from the earth? Certainly neither their shape, size, nor any other such peculiarity, so soon as their remarkable *situation.* They would appear to be walking, with heels up and head down, in the manner of flies on a ceiling. The *real* observer would have uttered an instant ejaculation of surprise (however prepared by previous knowledge) at the singularity of their position; the *fictitious* observer has not even mentioned the subject, but speaks of seeing the entire bodies of such creatures, when it is demonstrable that he could have seen only the diameter of their heads!

It might as well be remarked, in conclusion, that the size, and particularly the powers of the man-bats (for example, their ability to fly in so rare an atmosphere—if, indeed, the moon have any), with most of the other fancies in regard to animal and vegetable existence, are at variance, generally, with all analogical reasoning on these themes; and that analogy here will often amount to conclusive demonstration. It is, perhaps, scarcely necessary to add, that all the suggestions attributed to Brewster and Herschel, in the beginning of the article, about "a transfusion of artificial light through the focal object of vision," etc., etc., belong to that species of figurative writing which comes, most properly, under the denomination of rigmarole.

There is a real and very definite limit to optical discovery among the stars—a limit whose nature need only be stated to be understood. If, indeed, the casting of large lenses were all that is required, man's ingenuity would ultimately prove equal to the task, and we might have them of any size demanded. But, unhappily, in proportion to the increase of size in the lens, and consequently, of space-penetrating power, is the diminution of light from the object, by diffusion of its rays.

And for this evil there is no remedy within human ability; for an object is seen by means of that light alone which proceeds from itself, whether direct or reflected. Thus the only "*artificial*" light which could avail Mr. Locke, would be some artificial light which he should be able to throw—not upon the "focal object of vision," but upon the real object to be viewed—to wit: *upon the moon*. It has been easily calculated that, when the light pro-ceeding from a star becomes so diffused as to be as weak as the natural light proceeding from the whole of the stars, in a clear and moonless night, then the star is no longer visible for any practical purpose.

The Earl of Ross telescope, lately constructed in England, has a *speculum* with a reflecting surface of 4071 square inches; the Herschel telescope having one of only 181 1, The metal of the Earl of Ross' is 6 feet diameter; it is 5 1 inches thick at the edges, and 5 at the centre. The weight is 3 tons. The focal length is 50 feet.

I have lately read a singular and somewhat ingenious little book, whose title-page runs thus:—"*L'Homme dans la lune, ou le Voyage Chimerique fait au Monde de la Lune, nouuellement decouuert par Dominique Gonzales, Aduanturier Espagnol, autremèt dit le Cou-rier volant. Mis en notre langve par J. B. D.A. Paris, chez Francois Piot, pres la Fontaine de Saint Benoist. Et chez J. Goignard, au premier pilier*

de la grand' salle du Palais, proche les Consultations, MDCXLVII."
Pp. 176.

The writer professes to have translated his work from the English of one Mr. D' Avisson (Davidson?) although there is a terrible ambiguity in the statement. "*L'en ai eu,*" says he, "*l'original de Monsieur D'Avisson, medecin des mieux versez qui soient aujourd'huy dans la cônoissance des Belles Lettres, et sur tout de la Philosophic Naturelle. Je lui ai cette obligation entre les autres, de m' auoir non seulement mis en main ce livre en anglois, mais encore le Manuscrit du Sieur Thomas D'Anan, gentilhomme Eccossois, recommandable pour sa vertu, sur la version duquel j' advoue que j' ay tiré le plan de la mienne.*"

After some irrelevant adventures, much in the manner of Gil Blas, and which occupy the first thirty pages, the author relates that, being ill during a sea voyage, the crew abandoned him, together with a negro servant, on the island of St. Helena. To increase the chances of obtaining food, the two separate, and live as far apart as possible. This brings about a training of birds, to serve the purpose of carrier-pigeons between them. By and by these are taught to carry parcels of some weight—and this weight is gradually increased. At length the idea is entertained of uniting the force of a great number of the birds, with a view to raising the author himself. A machine is contrived for the purpose, and we have a minute description of it, which is materially helped out by a steel engraving. Here we perceive the Signor Gonzales, with point ruffles and a huge periwig, seated astride something which resembles very closely a broomstick, and borne aloft by a multitude of wild swans (*ganzas*) who had strings reaching from their tails to the machine.

The main event detailed in the Signor's narrative depends upon a very important fact, of which the reader is kept in ignorance until near the end of the book. The *ganzas*, with whom he had become so familiar, were not really denizens of St. Helena, but of the moon. Thence it had been their custom, time out of mind, to migrate annually to some portion of the earth. In proper season, of course, they would return home; and the author, happening, one day, to require their services for a short voyage, is unexpectedly carried straight up, and in a very brief period arrives at the satellite. Here he finds, among other odd things, that the people enjoy extreme happiness; that they have no *law*; that they die without pain; that they are from ten to thirty feet in height; that they live five thousand years; that they have an emperor called Irdonozur; and that they can jump sixty feet high, when, being out of the gravitating influence, they fly about with fans.

I cannot forbear giving a specimen of the general *philosophy* of the volume.

"I must now declare to you," says the Signor Gonzales, "the nature of the place in which I found myself. All the clouds were beneath my feet, or, if you please, spread between me and the earth. As to the stars, *since there was no night where I was, they always had the same appearance; not brilliant, as usual, but pale, and very nearly like the moon of a morning.* But few of them were visible, and these ten times larger (as well as I could judge), than they seem to the inhabitants of the earth. The moon which wanted two days of being full, was of a terrible bigness.

"I must not forget here, that the stars appeared only on that side of the globe turned toward the moon, and that the closer they were to it the larger they seemed. I have also to inform you that, whether it was calm weather or stormy, I found myself *always immediately between the moon and the earth.* I was convinced of this for two reasons—because my birds always flew in a straight line; and because whenever we attempted to rest, *we were carried insensibly around the globe of the earth.* For I admit the opinion of Copernicus, who maintains that it never ceases to revolve *from the east to the west,* not upon the poles of the Equinoctial, commonly called the poles of the world, but upon those of the Zodiac, a question of which I propose to speak more at length hereafter, when I shall have leisure to refresh my memory in regard to the astrology which I learned at Salamanca when young, and have since forgotten."

Notwithstanding the blunders italicized, the book is not

without some claim to attention, as affording a naive specimen of the current astronomical notions of the time. One of these assumed, that the "gravitating power" extended but a short distance from the earth's surface, and, accordingly, we find our voyager "carried insensibly around the globe," etc.

There have been other "voyages to the moon," but none of higher merit than the one just mentioned. That of Bergerac is utterly meaningless. In the third volume of the American *Quarterly Review* will be found quite an elaborate criticism upon a certain "Journey" of the kind in question;—a criticism in which it is difficult to say whether the critic most exposes the stupidity of the book, or his own absurd ignorance of astronomy. I forget the title of the work; but the means of the voyage are more deplorably ill conceived than are even the *ganzas* of our friend the Signor Gonzales.

The adventurer, in digging the earth, happens to discover a peculiar metal for which the moon has a strong attraction, and straightway constructs of it a box, which, when cast loose from its terrestrial fastenings, flies with him, forthwith, to the satellite. The *Flight of Thomas O'Rourke*, is a *jeu d'esprit* not altogether contemptible, and has been translated into German. Thomas, the hero, was, in fact, the game-keeper of an Irish peer, whose eccentricities gave rise to the tale. The "flight" is made on an eagle's back, from Hungry Hill, a lofty mountain at the end of Bantry Bay.

In these various *brochures* the aim is always satirical; the theme being a description of Lunarian customs as compared with ours. In none, is there any effort at *plausibility* in the details of the voyage itself. The writers seem, in each instance, to be utterly uninformed in respect to astronomy. In *Hans Pfaall* the design is original, inasmuch as regards an attempt at *verisimilitude,* in the application of scientific principles (so far as the whimsical nature of the subject would permit), to the actual passage between the earth and the moon.

MS. Found in a Bottle

Qui n'a plus qu'un moment à vivre
N'a plus rien à dissimuler.

Quinault—Atys.

Of my country and of my family I have little to say. Ill-usage and length of years have driven me from the one, and estranged me from the other. Hereditary wealth afforded me an education of no common order and a contemplative turn of mind enabled me to methodise the stores which early study very diligently garnered up. Beyond all things, the works of the German moralists gave me great delight; not from any ill-advised admiration of their eloquent madness, but from the ease with which my habits of rigid thought enabled me to detect their falsities. I have often been reproached with the aridity of my genius; a deficiency of imagination has been imputed to me as a crime; and the Pyrrhonism of my opinions has at all times rendered me notorious.

Indeed, a strong relish for physical philosophy has, I fear, tinctured my mind with a very common error of this age—I mean the habit of referring occurrences, even the least susceptible of such reference, to the principles of that science. Upon the whole, no person could be less liable than myself to be led away from the severe precincts of truth by the *ignes fatui* of superstition. I have thought proper to premise thus much, lest the incredible tale I have to tell should be considered rather the raving of a crude imagination than the positive experience of a mind to which the reveries of fancy have been a dead letter and a nullity.

After many years spent in foreign travel, I sailed in the year 18—, from the port of Batavia, in the rich and populous island of Java, on a voyage to the Archipelago of the Sunda Islands. I went as passenger—having no other inducement than a kind of nervous restlessness which haunted me as a fiend.

Our vessel was a beautiful ship of about four hundred tons, copper-fastened, and built at Bombay of Malabar teak. She was freighted with cotton-wool and oil, from the Lachadive Islands. We had also on board *coir, jaggeree, ghee*, cocoa-nuts, and a few cases of opium. The stowage was clumsily done, and the vessel consequently crank.

We got under way with a mere breath of wind, and for many days stood along the eastern coast of Java, without any other incident to beguile the monotony of our course than the occasional meeting with some of the small grabs of the Archipelago to which we were bound.

One evening, leaning over the taffrail, I observed a very singular isolated cloud to the N.W. It was remarkable, as well for its colour as from its being the first we had seen since our departure from Batavia. I watched it attentively until sunset, when it spread all at once to the eastward and westward, girting in the horizon with a narrow strip of vapour, and looking like a long line of low beach. My notice was soon afterwards attracted by the dusky-red appearance of the moon, and the peculiar character of the sea. The latter was undergoing a rapid change, and the water seemed more than usually transparent. Although I could distinctly see the bottom, yet heaving the lead, I found the ship in fifteen fathoms. The air now became intolerably hot, and was loaded with spiral exhalations similar to those arising from heated iron.

As night came on, every breath of wind died away, and a more entire calm it is impossible to conceive. The flame of a candle burned upon the poop without the least perceptible motion, and a long hair, held between the finger and thumb, hung without the possibility of detecting a vibration. However, as the captain said he could perceive no indication of danger, and as we were drifting in bodily to shore, he ordered the sails to be furled, and the anchor let go. No watch was set, and the crew, consisting principally of Malays, stretched themselves deliberately upon deck. I went below not without a full presentiment of evil. Indeed, every appearance warranted me in apprehending a *simoom*. I told the captain my fears; but he paid no attention to what I said, and left me without deigning to give a reply.

My uneasiness, however, prevented me from sleeping, and about midnight I went upon deck. As I placed my foot upon the upper step of the companion-ladder, I was startled by a loud, humming noise like that occasioned by the rapid revolution of a mill-wheel, and before I could ascertain its meaning, I found the ship quivering to its centre. In the next instant, a wilderness of foam hurled us upon our beam-ends, and, rushing over us fore and aft, swept the entire decks from stem to stern.

The extreme fury of the blast proved, in a great measure, the salvation of the ship. Although completely water-logged, yet, as her masts had gone by the board, she rose, after a minute, heavily from the sea, and, staggering awhile beneath the immense pressure of the tempest, finally righted.

By what miracle I escaped destruction it is impossible to say. Stunned by the shock of the water, I found myself, upon recovery, jammed in between the sternpost and rudder. With great difficulty I gained my feet, and, looking dizzily around, was at first struck with the idea of our being among breakers; so terrific, beyond the wildest imagination, was the whirlpool of mountainous and foaming ocean within which we were engulfed. After a while, I heard the voice of an old Swede, who had shipped with us at the moment of our leaving port. I hallooed to him with all my strength, and presently he came reeling aft. We soon discovered that we were the sole survivors of the accident. All on deck, with the exception of ourselves, had been swept overboard; the captain and mates must have perished as they slept, for the cabins were deluged with water.

Without assistance, we could expect to do little for the security of the ship, and our exertions were at first paralysed by the momentary expectation of going down. Our cable had, of course, parted like packthread at the first breath of the hurricane, or we should have been instantaneously overwhelmed. We scudded with frightful velocity before the sea, and the water made clear breaches over us. The framework of our stern was shattered excessively, and in almost every respect we had received considerable injury; but to our extreme joy we found the pumps unchoked, and that we had made no great shifting of our ballast.

The main fury of the blast had already blown over, and we apprehended little danger from the violence of the wind; but we looked forward to its total cessation with dismay; well believing, that in our shattered condition, we should inevitably perish in the tremendous swell which would ensue. But this very just apprehension seemed by no means likely to be soon verified. For five entire days and nights—during which our only subsistence was a small quantity of *jaggeree*, procured with great difficulty from the forecastle—the hulk flew at a rate defying computation, before rapidly succeeding flaws of wind, which, without equalling the first violence of the simoom, were still more terrific than any tempest I had before encountered.

Our course for the first four days was, with trifling variations, S.E. and by S.; and we must have run down the coast of New Holland. On the fifth day the cold became extreme, although the wind had hauled round a point more to the northward. The sun arose with a sickly yellow lustre, and clambered a very few degrees above the horizon—emitting no decisive light. There were no clouds apparent, yet the wind was upon the increase, and blew with a fitful and unsteady fury. About noon, as nearly as we could guess, our attention was again arrested by the appearance of the sun. It gave out no light, properly so called, but a dull and sullen glow without reflection, as if all its rays were polarised.

Just before sinking within the turgid sea, its central fires suddenly went out, as if hurriedly extinguished by some unaccountable power. It was a dim, silver-like rim, alone, as it rushed down the unfathomable ocean.

We waited in vain for the arrival of the sixth day—that day to me has not arrived—to the Swede never did arrive. Thenceforward we were enshrouded in pitchy darkness, so that we could not have seen an object at twenty paces from the ship. Eternal night continued to envelope us, all unrelieved by the phosphoric sea-brilliancy to which we had been accustomed in the tropics. We observed, too, that although the tempest continued to rage with unabated violence, there was no longer to be discovered the usual appearance of surf, or foam, which had hitherto attended us. All around were horror, and thick gloom, and a black sweltering desert of ebony.

Superstitious terror crept by degrees into the spirit of the old Swede, and my own soul was wrapped up in silent wonder. We neglected all care of the ship as worse than useless, and securing ourselves, as well as possible, to the stump of the mizenmast, looked out bitterly into the world of ocean. We had no means of calculating time, nor could we form any guess of our situation. We were, however, well aware of having made farther to the southward than any previous navigators, and felt great amazement at not meeting with the usual impediments of ice. In the meantime every moment threatened to be our last—every mountainous billow hurried to overwhelm us. The swell surpassed anything I had imagined possible, and that we were not instantly buried is a miracle. My companion spoke of the lightness of our cargo, and reminded me of the excellent qualities of our ship; but I could not help feeling the utter hopelessness of hope itself, and prepared myself gloomily for that death which I thought nothing could defer beyond an hour, as, with every knot of way the ship made, the swelling of the black stupendous seas became more dismally appalling.

At times we gasped for breath at an elevation beyond the albatross—at times became dizzy with the velocity of our descent into some watery hell, where the air grew stagnant, and no sound disturbed the slumbers of the *kraken*.

We were at the bottom of one of the abysses, when a quick scream from my companion broke fearfully upon the night. "See! see!" cried he, shrieking in my ears, "Almighty God! see! see!" As he spoke, I became aware of a dull, sullen glare of red light which streamed down the sides of the vast chasm where we lay, and threw a fitful brilliancy upon our deck. Casting my eyes upwards, I beheld a spectacle which froze the current of my blood. At a terrific height directly above us, and upon the very verge of the precipitous descent, hovered a gigantic ship, of perhaps four thousand tons. Although upreared upon the summit of a wave more than a hundred times her own altitude, her apparent size still exceeded that of any ship of the line or East Indiaman in existence. Her huge hull was of a deep dingy black, unrelieved by any of the customary carvings of a ship.

A single row of brass cannon protruded from her open ports, and dashed from their polished surfaces the fires of innumerable battle-lanterns, which swung to and fro about her rigging. But what mainly inspired us with horror and astonishment was, that she bore up under a press of sail in the very teeth of that supernatural sea, and of that ungovernable hurricane. When we first discovered her, her bows were alone to be seen, as she rose slowly from the dim and horrible gulf beyond her. For a moment of intense terror she paused upon the giddy pinnacle, as if in contemplation of her own sublimity, then trembled and tottered, and—came down.

At this instant, I know not what sudden self-possession came over my spirit. Staggering as far aft as I could, I awaited fearlessly the ruin that was to overwhelm. Our own vessel was at length ceasing from her struggles, and sinking with her head to the sea. The shock of the descending mass struck her, consequently, in that portion of her frame which was already under water, and the inevitable result was to hurl me, with irresistible violence, upon the rigging of the stranger.

As I fell, the ship hove in stays, and went about; and to the confusion ensuing I attributed my escape from the notice of the crew. With little difficulty I made my way unperceived, to the main hatchway, which was partially open, and soon found an opportunity of secreting myself in the hold. Why I did so I can hardly tell. An indefinite sense of awe, which at first sight of the navigators of the ship had taken hold of my mind, was perhaps the principle of my concealment. I was unwilling to trust myself with a race of people who had offered, to the cursory glance I had taken, so many points of vague novelty, doubt, and apprehension. I therefore thought proper to contrive a hiding-place in the hold. This I did by removing a small portion of the shifting-boards, in such a manner as to afford me a convenient retreat between the huge timbers of the ship.

I had scarcely completed my work, when a footstep in the hold forced me to make use of it. A man passed by my place of concealment with a feeble and unsteady gait. I could not see his face, but had an opportunity of observing his general appearance. There was about it an evidence of great age and infirmity. His knees tottered beneath a load of years, and his entire frame quivered under the burden. He muttered to himself in a low broken tone, some words of a language which I could not understand, and groped in a corner among a pile of singular-looking instruments, and decayed charts of navigation. His manner was a wild mixture of the peevishness of second childhood and the solemn dignity of a God. He at length went on deck, and I saw him no more.

★★★★★★

A feeling, for which I have no name, has taken possession of my soul—a sensation which will admit of no analysis, to which the lessons of bygone time are inadequate, and for which I fear futurity itself will offer me no key. To a mind constituted like my own, the latter consideration is an evil. I shall never—I know that I shall never—be satisfied with regard to the nature of my conceptions. Yet it is not wonderful that these conceptions are indefinite, since they have their origin in sources so utterly novel. A new sense—a new entity is added to my soul.

★★★★★★

It is long since I first trod the deck of this terrible ship, and the rays of my destiny are, I think, gathering to a focus. Incomprehensible men! Wrapped up in meditations of a kind which I cannot divine, they pass me by unnoticed. Concealment is utter folly on my part, for the people *will not* see. It was but just now that I passed directly before the eyes of the mate; it was no long while ago that I ventured into the captain's own private cabin and took thence the materials with which I write, and have written. I shall from time to time continue this journal. It is true that I may not find an opportunity of transmitting it to the world, but I will not fail to make the endeavour. At the last moment I will enclose the MS. in a bottle and cast it within the sea.

★★★★★★

An incident has occurred which has given me new room for meditation. Are such things the operation of ungoverned chance? I had ventured upon deck and thrown myself down, without attracting any notice, among a pile of ratline-stuff and old sails, in the bottom of the yawl. While musing upon the singularity of my fate, I unwittingly daubed with a tar-brush the edges of a neatly-folded studding-sail which lay near me on a barrel. The studding-sail is now bent upon the ship, and the thoughtless touches of the brush are spread out into the word *Discovery*.

I have made many observations lately upon the structure of the vessel. Although well armed, she is not, I think, a ship of war. Her rigging, build, and general equipment all negative a supposition of this kind. What she *is not*, I can easily perceive; what she *is*, I fear it is impossible to say. I know not how it is, but in scrutinising her strange model and singular cast of spars, her huge size and overgrown suits of canvas, her severely simple bow and antiquated stern, there will occasionally flash across my mind a sensation of familiar things, and there is always mixed up with such indistinct shadows of recollection an unaccountable memory of old foreign chronicles and ages long ago.

★★★★★★

I have been looking at the timbers of the ship. She is built of a material to which I am a stranger. There is a peculiar character about the wood which strikes me as rendering it unfit for the purpose to which it has been applied, I mean its extreme *porousness*, considered independently of the worm-eaten condition which is a consequence of navigation in these seas, and apart from the rottenness attendant upon age. It will appear perhaps an observation somewhat over-curious, but this wood would have every characteristic of Spanish oak, if Spanish oak were distended by any unnatural means.

In reading the above sentence, a curious apothegm of an old weather-beaten Dutch navigator comes full upon my recollection. "It is as sure," he was wont to say, when any doubt was entertained of his veracity, "as sure as there is a sea where the ship itself will grow in bulk like the living body of the seaman."

★★★★★★

About an hour ago, I made bold to thrust myself among a group of the crew. They paid me no manner of attention, and, although I stood in the very midst of them all, seemed utterly unconscious of my presence. Like the one I had first seen in the hold, they all bore about them the marks of a hoary old age. Their knees trembled with infirmity; their shoulders were bent double with decrepitude; their shrivelled skins rattled in the wind; their voices were low, tremulous, and broken; their eyes glistened with the rheum of years; and their grey hairs streamed terribly in the tempest. Around them, on every part of the deck, lay scattered mathematical instruments of the most quaint and obsolete construction.

★★★★★★

I mentioned some time ago the bending of a studdingsail. From that period, the ship, being thrown dead off the wind, has continued her terrific course due south, with every rag of canvas packed upon her, from her trucks to her lower studding-sail booms, and rolling every moment her top-gallant yard-arms into the most appalling hell of water which it can enter into the mind of man to imagine. I have just left the deck, where I find it impossible to maintain a footing, although the crew seem to experience little inconvenience. It appears to me a miracle of miracles that our enormous bulk is not swallowed up at once and for ever. We are surely doomed to hover continually upon the brink of eternity, without taking a final plunge into the abyss.

From billows a thousand times more stupendous than any I have ever seen, we glide away with the facility of the arrowy sea-gull; and the colossal waters rear their heads above us like demons of the deep, but like demons confined to simple threats, and forbidden to destroy. I am led to attribute these frequent escapes to the only natural cause which can account for such effect. I must suppose the ship to be within the influence of some strong current, or impetuous under-tow.

★★★★★★

I have seen the captain face to face, and in his own cabin but, as I expected, he paid me no attention. Although in his appearance there is, to a casual observer, nothing which might bespeak him more or less than man, still a feeling of irrepressible reverence and awe mingled with the sensation of wonder with which I regarded him. In stature, he is nearly my own height; that is, about five feet eight inches. He is of a well-knit and compact frame of body, neither robust nor remarkable otherwise. But it is the singularity of the expression which reigns upon the face—it is the intense, the wonderful, the thrilling evidence of old age, so utter, so extreme, which excites within my spirit a sense—a sentiment ineffable. His forehead although little wrinkled, seems to bear upon it the stamp of a myriad of years. His grey hairs are records of the past, and his greyer eyes are sibyls of the future.

The cabin floor was thickly strewn with strange, iron-clasped folios, and mouldering instruments of science, and obsolete long-forgotten charts. His head was bowed down upon his hands, and he pored with a fiery unquiet eye over a paper which I took to be a commission, and which, at all events, bore the signature of a monarch. He muttered to himself—as did the first seaman whom I saw in the hold—some low peevish syllables of a foreign tongue; and although the speaker was close at my elbow, his voice seemed to reach my ears from the distance of a mile.

★★★★★★

The ship and all in it are imbued with the spirit of Eld. The crew glide to and fro like the ghosts of buried centuries; their eyes have an eager and uneasy meaning; and when their figures fall athwart my path in the wild glare of the battle-lanterns, I feel as I have never felt before, although I have been all my life a dealer in antiquities, and have imbibed the shadows of fallen columns at Balbec, and Tadmor, and Persepolis, until my very soul has become a ruin.

★★★★★★

When I look around me I feel ashamed of my former apprehensions. If I trembled at the blast which has hitherto attended us, shall I not stand aghast at a warring of wind and ocean, to convey any idea of which the words tornado and simoom are trivial and ineffective? All in the immediate vicinity of the ship is the blackness of eternal night, and a chaos of foamless water; but, about a league on either side of us, may be seen, indistinctly and at intervals, stupendous ramparts of ice towering away into the desolate sky, and looking like the walls of the universe.

★★★★★★

As I imagined, the ship proves to be in a current—if that appellation can properly be given to a tide which, howling and shrieking by the white ice, thunders on to the southward with a velocity like the headlong dashing of a cataract.

★★★★★★

To conceive the horror of my sensations is, I presume, utterly impossible; yet a curiosity to penetrate the mysteries of these awful regions predominates even over my despair, and will reconcile me to the most hideous aspect of death. It is evident that we are hurrying onwards to some exciting knowledge—some never-to-be-imparted secret, whose attainment is destruction. Perhaps this current leads us to the southern pole itself. It must be confessed that a supposition apparently so wild has every probability in its favour.

★★★★★★

The crew pace the deck with unquiet and tremulous step; but there is upon their countenances an expression more of the eagerness of hope than of the apathy of despair.

In the meantime the wind is still in our poop, and as we carry a crowd of canvas the ship is at times lifted bodily from out the sea! Oh, horror upon horror!—the ice opens suddenly to the right, and to the left, and we are whirling dizzily, in immense concentric circles, round and round the borders of a gigantic amphitheatre, the summit of whose walls is lost in the darkness and the distance But little time will be left me to ponder upon my destiny! The circles rapidly grow small—we are plunging madly within the grasp of the whirlpool—and amid a roaring, and bellowing, and thundering of ocean and of tempest, the ship is quivering—Oh God!—and going down!

> Note. The *MS. Found in a Bottle* was originally published in 1831, and it was not until many years afterwards that I became acquainted with the maps of Mercator, in which the ocean is represented as rushing, by four mouths, into the (northern) Polar Gulf, to be absorbed into the bowels of the earth; the Pole itself being represented by a black rock towering to a prodigious height.

Three Sundays in a Week

"You hard-headed, dunder-headed, obstinate, rusty, crusty, musty, fusty, old savage!" said I, in fancy, one afternoon, to my grand uncle Rumgudgeon—shaking my fist at him in imagination.

Only in imagination. The fact is, some trivial discrepancy *did* exist, just then, between what I said and what I had not the courage to say—between what I did and what I had half a mind to do.

The old porpoise, as I opened the drawing-room door, was sitting with his feet upon the mantel-piece, and a bumper of port in his paw, making strenuous efforts to accomplish the ditty.

Remplis ton verre vide!
Vide ton verre plein!

"My *dear* uncle," said I, closing the door gently, and approaching him with the blandest of smiles, "you are always so *very* kind and considerate, and have evinced your benevolence in so many—so *very* many ways—that—that I feel I have only to suggest this little point to you once more to make sure of your full acquiescence."

"Hem!" said he, "good boy! go on!"

"I am sure, my dearest uncle (you confounded old rascal!), that you have no design really, seriously, to oppose my union with Kate. This is merely a joke of yours, I know—ha! ha! ha!—how *very* pleasant you are at times."

"Ha! ha! ha!" said he, "curse you! yes!"

"To be sure—of course! I *knew* you were jesting. Now, uncle, all that Kate and myself wish at present, is that you would oblige us with your advice as—as regards the *time*—*you* know, uncle—in short, when will it be most convenient for yourself, that the wedding shall—shall come off, you know?"

"Come off, you scoundrel!—what do you mean by that?—Better wait till it goes on."

"Ha! ha! ha!—he! he! he!—hi! hi! hi!—ho! ho! ho!—hu! hu! hu!—that's good!—oh that's capital—such a wit! But all we want just *now*, you know, uncle, is that you would indicate the time precisely."

"Ah!—precisely?"

"Yes, uncle—that is, if it would be quite agreeable to your-self."

"Wouldn't it answer, Bobby, if I were to leave it at random—some time within a year or so, for example?—*must* I say precisely?"

"*If* you please, uncle—precisely."

"Well, then, Bobby, my boy—you're a fine fellow, aren't you?—since you *will* have the exact time I'll—why I'll oblige you for once:"

"Dear uncle!"

"Hush, sir!" (drowning my voice)—"I'll oblige you for once. You shall have my consent—and the *plum*, we mus'n't forget the plum—let me see! when shall it be? Today's Sunday—isn't it? Well, then, you shall be married precisely—*precisely*, now mind!—*when three Sundays come together in a week!* Do you hear me, sir! *What* are you gaping at? I say, you shall have Kate and her plum when three Sundays come together in a week—but not *till* then—you young scapegrace—not *till* then, if I die for it. You know me—*I'm a man of my word*—now be off!" Here he swallowed his bumper of port, while I rushed from the room in despair.

A very "fine old English gentleman," was my grand-uncle Rumgudgeon, but unlike him of the song, he had his weak points. He was a little, pursy, pompous, passionate semicircular somebody, with a red nose, a thick scull, (sic) a long purse, and a strong sense of his own consequence. With the best heart in the world, he contrived, through a predominant whim of *contradiction*, to earn for himself, among those who only knew him superficially, the character of a curmudgeon. Like many excellent people, he seemed possessed with a spirit of *tantalisation*, which might easily, at a casual glance, have been mistaken for malevolence. To every request, a positive "No!" was his immediate answer, but in the end—in the long, long end—there were exceedingly few requests which he refused. Against all attacks upon his purse he made the most sturdy defence; but the amount extorted from him, at last, was generally in direct ratio with the length of the siege and the stubbornness of the resistance. In charity no one gave more liberally or with a worse grace.

For the fine arts, and especially for the belles-lettres, he entertained a profound contempt. With this he had been inspired by Casimir Perier, whose pert little query "*A quoi un poete est il bon?*" he was in the habit of quoting, with a very droll pronunciation, as the *ne plus ultra* of logical wit. Thus my own inkling for the Muses had excited his entire displeasure. He assured me one day, when I asked him for a new copy of Horace, that the translation of *Poeta nascitur non fit* was "a nasty poet for nothing fit"—a remark which I took in high dudgeon.

His repugnance to "the humanities" had, also, much increased of late, by an accidental bias in favour of what he supposed to be natural science. Somebody had accosted him in the street, mistaking him for no less a personage than Doctor Dubble L. Dee, the lecturer upon quack physics. This set him off at a tangent; and just at the epoch of this story—for story it is getting to be after all—my grand-uncle Rumgudgeon was accessible and pacific only upon points which happened to chime in with the caprioles of the hobby he was riding. For the rest, he laughed with his arms and legs, and his politics were stubborn and easily understood. He thought, with Horsley, that "the people have nothing to do with the laws but to obey them."

I had lived with the old gentleman all my life. My parents, in dying, had bequeathed me to him as a rich legacy. I believe the old villain loved me as his own child—nearly if not quite as well as he loved Kate—but it was a dog's existence that he led me, after all. From my first year until my fifth, he obliged me with very regular floggings. From five to fifteen, he threatened me, hourly, with the House of Correction. From fifteen to twenty, not a day passed in which he did not promise to cut me off with a shilling. I was a sad dog, it is true—but then it was a part of my nature—a point of my faith. In Kate, however, I had a firm friend, and I knew it. She was a good girl, and told me very sweetly that I might have her (plum and all) whenever I could badger my grand-uncle Rumgudgeon, into the necessary consent.

Poor girl!—she was barely fifteen, and without this consent, her little amount in the funds was not come-at-able until five immeasurable summers had "dragged their slow length along." What, then, to do? At fifteen, or even at twenty-one (for I had now passed my fifth Olympiad) five years in prospect are very much the same as five hundred. In vain we besieged the old gentleman with importunities. Here was a *piece de resistance* (as Messieurs Ude and Careme would say) which suited his perverse fancy to a T. It would have stiffed the indignation of Job himself, to see how much like an old mouser he behaved to us two poor wretched little mice.

In his heart he wished for nothing more ardently than our union. He had made up his mind to this all along. In fact, he would have given ten thousand pounds from his own pocket (Kate's plum was *her own*) if he could have invented anything like an excuse for complying with our very natural wishes. But then we had been so imprudent as to broach the subject *ourselves*. Not to oppose it under such circumstances, I sincerely believe, was not in his power.

I have said already that he had his weak points; but in speaking of these, I must not be understood as referring to his obstinacy: which was one of his strong points—"*assurement ce n'etait pas sa foible.*" When I mention his weakness I have allusion to a bizarre old-womanish superstition which beset him. He was great in dreams, portents, *et id genus omne* of rigmarole. He was excessively punctilious, too, upon small points of honour, and, after his own fashion, was a man of his word, beyond doubt. This was, in fact, one of his hobbies. The *spirit* of his vows he made no scruple of setting at naught, but the *letter* was a bond inviolable. Now it was this latter peculiarity in his disposition, of which Kate's ingenuity enabled us one fine day, not long after our interview in the dining-room, to take a very unexpected advantage, and, having thus, in the fashion of all modern bards and orators, exhausted in *prolegomena*, all the time at my command, and nearly all the room at my disposal, I will sum up in a few words what constitutes the whole pith of the story.

It happened then—so the Fates ordered it—that among the naval acquaintances of my betrothed, were two gentlemen who had just set foot upon the shores of England, after a year's absence, each, in foreign travel. In company with these gentlemen, my cousin and I, preconcertedly paid uncle Rumgudgeon a visit on the afternoon of Sunday, October the tenth,—just three weeks after the memorable decision which had so cruelly defeated our hopes. For about half an hour the conversation ran upon ordinary topics, but at last, we contrived, quite naturally, to give it the following turn:

Capt. Pratt. "Well I have been absent just one year.—Just one year today, as I live—let me see! yes!—this is October the tenth. You remember, Mr. Rumgudgeon, I called, this day year to bid you goodbye. And by the way, it *does* seem something like a coincidence, does it not—that our friend, Captain Smitherton, here, has been absent exactly a year also—a year today!"

Smitherton. "Yes! just one year to a fraction. You will remember, Mr. Rumgudgeon, that I called with Capt. Pratol on this very day, last year, to pay my parting respects."

Uncle. "Yes, yes, yes—I remember it very well—very queer indeed! Both of you gone just one year. A very strange coincidence, indeed! Just what Doctor Dubble L. Dee would denominate an extraordinary concurrence of events. Doctor Dub-"

Kate. (Interrupting.) "To be sure, papa, it *is* something strange; but then Captain Pratt and Captain Smitherton didn't go altogether the same route, and that makes a difference, you know."

Uncle. "I don't know any such thing, you hussy! How should I? I think it only makes the matter more remarkable, Doctor Dubble L. Dee—"

Kate. "Why, papa, Captain Pratt went round Cape Horn, and Captain Smitherton doubled the Cape of Good Hope."

Uncle. "Precisely!—the one went east and the other went west, you jade, and they both have gone quite round the world. By the by, Doctor Dubble L. Dee—"

Myself. (*Hurriedly.*) "Captain Pratt, you must come and spend the evening with us tomorrow—you and Smitherton—you can tell us all about your voyage, and well have a game of whist and—"

Pratt. "Whist, my dear fellow—you forget. Tomorrow will be Sunday. Some other evening—"

Kate. "Oh, no, fie!—Robert's not *quite* so bad as that. Today's Sunday."

Pratt. "I beg both your pardons—but I can't be so much mistaken. I know tomorrow's Sunday, because—"

Smitherton. (*Much surprised.*) "What *are* you all thinking about? Wasn't *yesterday*, Sunday, I should like to know?"

All. "Yesterday indeed! you *are* out!"

Uncle. "Today's Sunday, I say—don't *I* know?"

Pratt. "Oh no!—tomorrow's Sunday."

Smitherton. "You are *all* mad—every one of you. I am as positive that yesterday was Sunday as I am that I sit upon this chair."

Kate. (*jumping up eagerly.*) "I see it—I see it all. Papa, this is a judgment upon you, about—about you know what. Let me alone, and I'll explain it all in a minute. It's a very simple thing, indeed. Captain Smitherton says that yesterday was Sunday: so it was; he is right. Cousin Bobby, and uncle and I say that today is Sunday: so it is; we are right. Captain Pratt maintains that tomorrow will be Sunday: so it will; he is right, too. The fact is, we are all right, and thus *three Sundays have come together in a week.*"

Smitherton. (*After a pause.*) "By the by, Pratt, Kate has us completely. What fools we two are! Mr. Rumgudgeon, the matter stands thus: the earth, you know, is twenty-four thousand miles in circumference. Now this globe of the earth turns upon its own axis—revolves—spins round—these twenty-four thousand miles of extent, going from west to east, in precisely twenty-four hours. Do you understand Mr. Rumgudgeon?—"

Uncle. "To be sure—to be sure—Doctor Dub—"

Smitherton. (*Drowning his voice.*) "Well, sir; that is at the rate of one thousand miles per hour. Now, suppose that I sail from this position a thousand miles east. Of course I anticipate the rising of the sun here at London by just one hour. I see the sun rise one hour before you do. Proceeding, in the same direction, yet another thousand miles, I anticipate the rising by two hours— another thousand, and I anticipate it by three hours, and so on, until I go entirely round the globe, and back to this spot, when, having gone twenty-four thousand miles east, I anticipate the rising of the London sun by no less than twenty-four hours; that is to say, I am a day *in advance* of your time. Understand, eh?"

Uncle. "But Double L. Dee—"

Smitherton. (*Speaking very loud.*) "Captain Pratt, on the contrary, when he had sailed a thousand miles west of this position, was an hour, and when he had sailed twenty-four thousand miles west, was twenty-four hours, or one day, *behind* the time at London. Thus, with me, yesterday was Sunday—thus, with you, today is Sunday—and thus, with Pratt, tomorrow will be Sunday. And what is more, Mr. Rumgudgeon, it is positively clear that we are *all right*; for there can be no philosophical reason assigned why the idea of one of us should have preference over that of the other."

Uncle. "My eyes!—well, Kate—well, Bobby!—this *is* a judgment upon me, as you say. But I am a man of my word—*mark that!* you shall have her, boy, (plum and all), when you please. Done up, by Jove! Three Sundays all in a row! I'll go, and take Dubble L. Dee's opinion upon *that*."

The Thousand-and-Second Tale of Scheherazade

Truth is stranger than fiction.—*Old Saying.*

Having had occasion, lately, in the course of some Oriental investigations, to consult the Tellmenow Isitsoornot, a work which (like the Zohar of Simeon Jochaides) is scarcely known at all, even in Europe; and which has never been quoted, to my knowledge, by any American—if we except, perhaps, the author of the *Curiosities of American Literature*;—having had occasion, I say, to turn over some pages of the first-mentioned very remarkable work, I was not a little astonished to discover that the literary world has hitherto been strangely in error respecting the fate of the *vizier's* daughter, Scheherazade, as that fate is depicted in the *Arabian Nights*; and that the *dénouement* there given, if not altogether inaccurate, as far as it goes, is at least to blame in not having gone very much farther.

For full information on this interesting topic, I must refer the inquisitive reader to the "Isitsoornot" itself, but in the meantime, I shall be pardoned for giving a summary of what I there discovered.

It will be remembered, that, in the usual version of the tales, a certain monarch having good cause to be jealous of his queen, not only puts her to death, but makes a vow, by his beard and the prophet, to espouse each night the most beautiful maiden in his dominions, and the next morning to deliver her up to the executioner.

Having fulfilled this vow for many years to the letter, and with a religious punctuality and method that conferred great credit upon him as a man of devout feeling and excellent sense, he was interrupted one afternoon (no doubt at his prayers) by a visit from his grand *vizier*, to whose daughter, it appears, there had occurred an idea.

Her name was Scheherazade, and her idea was, that she would either redeem the land from the depopulating tax upon its beauty, or perish, after the approved fashion of all heroines, in the attempt.

Accordingly, and although we do not find it to be leap-year (which makes the sacrifice more meritorious), she deputes her father, the grand *vizier*, to make an offer to the king of her hand. This hand the king eagerly accepts—(he had intended to take it at all events, and had put off the matter from day to day, only through fear of the *vizier*),—but, in accepting it now, he gives all parties very distinctly to understand, that, grand *vizier* or no grand vizier, he has not the slightest design of giving up one iota of his vow or of his privileges.

When, therefore, the fair Scheherazade insisted upon marrying the king, and did actually marry him despite her father's excellent advice not to do anything of the kind—when she would and did marry him, I say, will I, nill I, it was with her beautiful black eyes as thoroughly open as the nature of the case would allow.

It seems, however, that this politic damsel (who had been reading Machiavelli, beyond doubt), had a very ingenious little plot in her mind. On the night of the wedding, she contrived, upon I forget what specious pretence, to have her sister occupy a couch sufficiently near that of the royal pair to admit of easy conversation from bed to bed; and, a little before cock-crowing, she took care to awaken the good monarch, her husband (who bore her none the worse will because he intended to wring her neck on the morrow),—she managed to awaken him, I say, (although on account of a capital conscience and an easy digestion, he slept well) by the profound interest of a story (about a rat and a black cat, I think) which she was narrating (all in an undertone, of course) to her sister.

When the day broke, it so happened that this history was not altogether finished, and that Scheherazade, in the nature of things could not finish it just then, since it was high time for her to get up and be bowstrung—a thing very little more pleasant than hanging, only a trifle more genteel.

The king's curiosity, however, prevailing, I am sorry to say, even over his sound religious principles, induced him for this once to postpone the fulfilment of his vow until next morning, for the purpose and with the hope of hearing that night how it fared in the end with the black cat (a black cat, I think it was) and the rat.

The night having arrived, however, the lady Scheherazade not only put the finishing stroke to the black cat and the rat (the rat was blue) but before she well knew what she was about, found herself deep in the intricacies of a narration, having reference (if I am not altogether mistaken) to a pink horse (with green wings) that went, in a violent manner, by clockwork, and was wound up with an indigo key. With this history the king was even more profoundly interested than with the other—and, as the day broke before its conclusion (notwithstanding all the queen's endeavours to get through with it in time for the bowstringing), there was again no resource but to postpone that ceremony as before, for twenty-four hours.

The next night there happened a similar accident with a similar result; and then the next—and then again the next; so that, in the end, the good monarch, having been unavoidably deprived of all opportunity to keep his vow during a period of no less than one thousand and one nights, either forgets it altogether by the expiration of this time, or gets himself absolved of it in the regular way, or (what is more probable) breaks it outright, as well as the head of his father confessor. At all events, Scheherazade, who, being lineally descended from Eve, fell heir, perhaps, to the whole seven baskets of talk, which the latter lady, we all know, picked up from under the trees in the garden of Eden—Scheherazade, I say, finally triumphed, and the tariff upon beauty was repealed.

Now, this conclusion (which is that of the story as we have it upon record) is, no doubt, excessively proper and pleasant—but alas! like a great many pleasant things, is more pleasant than true, and I am indebted altogether to the "Isitsoornot" for the means of correcting the error. "*Le mieux,*" says a French proverb, "*est l'ennemi du bien,*" and, in mentioning that Scheherazade had inherited the seven baskets of talk, I should have added that she put them out at compound interest until they amounted to seventy-seven.

"My dear sister," said she, on the thousand-and-second night, (I quote the language of the "Isitsoornot" at this point, *verbatim*) "my dear sister," said she, "now that all this little difficulty about the bowstring has blown over, and that this odious tax is so happily repealed, I feel that I have been guilty of great indiscretion in withholding from you and the king (who I am sorry to say, snores—a thing no gentleman would do) the full conclusion of Sinbad the sailor. This person went through numerous other and more interesting adventures than those which I related; but the truth is, I felt sleepy on the particular night of their narration, and so was seduced into cutting them short—a grievous piece of misconduct, for which I only trust that *Allah* will forgive me. But even yet it is not too late to remedy my great neglect—and as soon as I have given the king a pinch or two in order to wake him up so far that he may stop making that horrible noise, I will forthwith entertain you (and him if he pleases) with the sequel of this very remarkable story."

Hereupon the sister of Scheherazade, as I have it from the "Isitsoornot," expressed no very particular intensity of gratification; but the king, having been sufficiently pinched, at length ceased snoring, and finally said, "*hum!*" and then "*hoo!*" when the queen, understanding these words (which are no doubt Arabic) to signify that he was all attention, and would do his best not to snore any more—the queen, I say, having arranged these matters to her satisfaction, re-entered thus, at once, into the history of

Sinbad the sailor:

"'At length, in my old age,' (these are the words of Sinbad himself, as retailed by Scheherazade)—'at length, in my old age, and after enjoying many years of tranquillity at home, I became once more possessed of a desire of visiting foreign countries; and one day, without acquainting any of my family with my design, I packed up some bundles of such merchandise as was most precious and least bulky, and, engaged a porter to carry them, went with him down to the sea-shore, to await the arrival of any chance vessel that might convey me out of the kingdom into some region which I had not as yet explored.

"'Having deposited the packages upon the sands, we sat down beneath some trees, and looked out into the ocean in the hope of perceiving a ship, but during several hours we saw none whatever. At length I fancied that I could hear a singular buzzing or humming sound; and the porter, after listening awhile, declared that he also could distinguish it. Presently it grew louder, and then still louder, so that we could have no doubt that the object which caused it was approaching us. At length, on the edge of the horizon, we discovered a black speck, which rapidly increased in size until we made it out to be a vast monster, swimming with a great part of its body above the surface of the sea. It came toward us with inconceivable swiftness, throwing up huge waves of foam around its breast, and illuminating all that part of the sea through which it passed, with a long line of fire that extended far off into the distance.

"'As the thing drew near we saw it very distinctly. Its length was equal to that of three of the loftiest trees that grow, and it was as wide as the great hall of audience in your palace, O most sublime and munificent of the Caliphs. Its body, which was unlike that of ordinary fishes, was as solid as a rock, and of a jetty blackness throughout all that portion of it which floated above the water, with the exception of a narrow blood-red streak that completely begirdled it. The belly, which floated beneath the surface, and of which we could get only a glimpse now and then as the monster rose and fell with the billows, was entirely covered with metallic scales, of a colour like that of the moon in misty weather. The back was flat and nearly white, and from it there extended upwards of six spines, about half the length of the whole body.

"'The horrible creature had no mouth that we could perceive, but, as if to make up for this deficiency, it was provided with at least four score of eyes, that protruded from their sockets like those of the green dragon-fly, and were arranged all around the body in two rows, one above the other, and parallel to the blood-red streak, which seemed to answer the purpose of an eyebrow. Two or three of these dreadful eyes were much larger than the others, and had the appearance of solid gold.

"'Although this beast approached us, as I have before said, with the greatest rapidity, it must have been moved altogether by necromancy—for it had neither fins like a fish nor web-feet like a duck, nor wings like the seashell which is blown along in the manner of a vessel; nor yet did it writhe itself forward as do the eels. Its head and its tail were shaped precisely alike, only, not far from the latter, were two small holes that served for nostrils, and through which the monster puffed out its thick breath with prodigious violence, and with a shrieking, disagreeable noise.

"'Our terror at beholding this hideous thing was very great, but it was even surpassed by our astonishment, when upon getting a nearer look, we perceived upon the creature's back a vast number of animals about the size and shape of men, and altogether much resembling them, except that they wore no garments (as men do), being supplied (by nature, no doubt) with an ugly uncomfortable covering, a good deal like cloth, but fitting so tight to the skin, as to render the poor wretches laughably awkward, and put them apparently to severe pain. On the very tips of their heads were certain square-looking boxes, which, at first sight, I thought might have been intended to answer as turbans, but I soon discovered that they were excessively heavy and solid, and I therefore concluded they were contrivances designed, by their great weight, to keep the heads of the animals steady and safe upon their shoulders.

"'Around the necks of the creatures were fastened black collars, (badges of servitude, no doubt,) such as we keep on our dogs, only much wider and infinitely stiffer, so that it was quite impossible for these poor victims to move their heads in any direction without moving the body at the same time; and thus they were doomed to perpetual contemplation of their noses—a view puggish and snubby in a wonderful, if not positively in an awful degree.

"'When the monster had nearly reached the shore where we stood, it suddenly pushed out one of its eyes to a great extent, and emitted from it a terrible flash of fire, accompanied by a dense cloud of smoke, and a noise that I can compare to nothing but thunder. As the smoke cleared away, we saw one of the odd man-animals standing near the head of the large beast with a trumpet in his hand, through which (putting it to his mouth) he presently addressed us in loud, harsh, and disagreeable accents, that, perhaps, we should have mistaken for language, had they not come altogether through the nose.

"'Being thus evidently spoken to, I was at a loss how to reply, as I could in no manner understand what was said; and in this difficulty I turned to the porter, who was near swooning through affright, and demanded of him his opinion as to what species of monster it was, what it wanted, and what kind of creatures those were that so swarmed upon its back. To this the porter replied, as well as he could for trepidation, that he had once before heard of this sea-beast; that it was a cruel demon, with bowels of sulphur and blood of fire, created by evil *genii* as the means of inflicting misery upon mankind; that the things upon its back were vermin, such as sometimes infest cats and dogs, only a little larger and more savage; and that these vermin had their uses, however evil—for, through the torture they caused the beast by their nibbling and stingings, it was goaded into that degree of wrath which was requisite to make it roar and commit ill, and so fulfil the vengeful and malicious designs of the wicked *genii*.

"This account determined me to take to my heels, and, without once even looking behind me, I ran at full speed up into the hills, while the porter ran equally fast, although nearly in an opposite direction, so that, by these means, he finally made his escape with my bundles, of which I have no doubt he took excellent care—although this is a point I cannot determine, as I do not remember that I ever beheld him again.

"'For myself, I was so hotly pursued by a swarm of the men-vermin (who had come to the shore in boats) that I was very soon overtaken, bound hand and foot, and conveyed to the beast, which immediately swam out again into the middle of the sea.

"'I now bitterly repented my folly in quitting a comfortable home to peril my life in such adventures as this; but regret being useless, I made the best of my condition, and exerted myself to secure the goodwill of the man-animal that owned the trumpet, and who appeared to exercise authority over his fellows. I suc-ceeded so well in this endeavour that, in a few days, the creature bestowed upon me various tokens of his favour, and in the end even went to the trouble of teaching me the rudiments of what it was vain enough to denominate its language; so that, at length, I was enabled to converse with it readily, and came to make it comprehend the ardent desire I had of seeing the world.

"'*Washish squashish squeak, Sinbad, hey-diddle diddle, grunt unt grumble, hiss, fiss, whiss,*' said he to me, one day after dinner—but I beg a thousand pardons, I had forgotten that your majesty is not conversant with the dialect of the Cock-neighs (so the man-animals were called; I presume because their language formed the connecting link between that of the horse and that of the rooster). With your permission, I will translate. '*Washish squash-ish,*' and so forth:—that is to say, 'I am happy to find, my dear Sinbad, that you are really a very excellent fellow; we are now about doing a thing which is called circumnavigating the globe; and since you are so desirous of seeing the world, I will strain a point and give you a free passage upon back of the beast.'"

When the Lady Scheherazade had proceeded thus far, relates the "Isitsoornot," the king turned over from his left side to his right, and said:

"It is, in fact, *very* surprising, my dear queen, that you omit-ted, hitherto, these latter adventures of Sinbad. Do you know I think them exceedingly entertaining and strange?"

The king having thus expressed himself, we are told, the fair Scheherazade resumed her history in the following words:

"Sinbad went on in this manner with his narrative to the *caliph*—'I thanked the man-animal for its kindness, and soon found myself very much at home on the beast, which swam at a prodigious rate through the ocean; although the surface of the latter is, in that part of the world, by no means flat, but round like a pomegranate, so that we went—so to say—either up hill or down hill all the time.'

"That I think, was very singular," interrupted the king.

"Nevertheless, it is quite true," replied Scheherazade.

"I have my doubts," rejoined the king; "but, pray, be so good as to go on with the story."

"I will," said the queen. "'The beast,' continued Sinbad to the *caliph*, 'swam, as I have related, up hill and down hill until, at length, we arrived at an island, many hundreds of miles in circumference, but which, nevertheless, had been built in the middle of the sea by a colony of little things like caterpillars'"[1]

"*Hum!*" said the king.

"'Leaving this island,' said Sinbad—(for Scheherazade, it must be understood, took no notice of her husband's ill-mannered ejaculation) 'leaving this island, we came to another where the forests were of solid stone, and so hard that they shivered to pieces the finest-tempered axes with which we endeavoured to cut them down.'"[2]

---

1. The corallites.
2. "One of the most remarkable natural curiosities in Texas is a petrified forest, near the head of Pasigno River. It consists of several hundred trees, in an erect position, all turned to stone. Some trees, now growing, are partly petrified. This is a startling fact for natural philosophers, and must cause them to modify the existing theory of petrification.—*Kennedy*. This account, at first discredited, has since been corroborated by the discovery of a completely petrified forest, near the headwaters of the Cheyenne, or Chienne River, which has its source in the Black Hills of the rocky chain. There is scarcely, perhaps, a spectacle on the surface of the globe more remarkable, either in a geological or picturesque point of view than that presented by the petrified forest, near Cairo. The traveller, having passed the tombs of the *caliphs*, just beyond the gates of the city, proceeds to the southward, nearly at right angles to the road across the desert to Suez, (continued next page),

"*Hum!*" said the king, again; but Scheherazade, paying him no attention, continued in the language of Sinbad.

"'Passing beyond this last island, we reached a country where there was a cave that ran to the distance of thirty or forty miles within the bowels of the earth, and that contained a greater number of far more spacious and more magnificent palaces than are to be found in all Damascus and Bagdad. From the roofs of these palaces there hung myriads of gems, like diamonds, but larger than men; and in among the streets of towers and pyramids and temples, there flowed immense rivers as black as ebony, and swarming with fish that had no eyes.'"[3]

"Hum!" said the king. "'We then swam into a region of the sea where we found a lofty mountain, down whose sides there streamed torrents of melted metal, some of which were twelve miles wide and sixty miles long [4]; while from an abyss on the summit, issued so vast a quantity of ashes that the sun was entirely blotted out from the heavens, and it became darker than the darkest midnight; so that when we were even at the distance of a hundred and fifty miles from the mountain, it was impossible to see the whitest object, however close we held it to our

---

and after having travelled some ten miles up a low barren valley, covered with sand, gravel, and sea shells, fresh as if the tide had retired but yesterday, crosses a low range of sandhills, which has for some distance run parallel to his path. The scene now presented to him is beyond conception singular and desolate. A mass of fragments of trees, all converted into stone, and when struck by his horse's hoof ringing like cast iron, is seen to extend itself for miles and miles around him, in the form of a decayed and prostrate forest. The wood is of a dark brown hue, but retains its form in perfection, the pieces being from one to fifteen feet in length, and from half a foot to three feet in thickness, strewed so closely together, as far as the eye can reach, that an Egyptian donkey can scarcely thread its way through amongst them, and so natural that, were it in Scotland or Ireland, it might pass without remark for some enormous drained bog, on which the exhumed trees lay rotting in the sun. The roots and rudiments of the branches are, in many cases, nearly perfect, and in some the worm-holes eaten under the bark are readily recognizable. The most delicate of the sap vessels, and all the finer portions of the centre of the wood, are perfectly entire, and bear to be examined with the strongest magnifiers. The whole are so thoroughly silicified as to scratch glass and are capable of receiving the highest polish.— *Asiatic Magazine*.

3. The Mammoth Cave of Kentucky.

4. In Iceland, 1783.

eyes.'" [5]

"*Hum!*" said the king.

"'After quitting this coast, the beast continued his voyage until we met with a land in which the nature of things seemed reversed—for we here saw a great lake, at the bottom of which, more than a hundred feet beneath the surface of the water, there flourished in full leaf a forest of tall and luxuriant trees.'" [6]

"*Hoo!*" said the king.

"Some hundred miles farther on brought us to a climate where the atmosphere was so dense as to sustain iron or steel, just as our own does feather.'" [7]

"Fiddle de dee," said the king.

"Proceeding still in the same direction, we presently arrived at the most magnificent region in the whole world. Through it there meandered a glorious river for several thousands of miles. This river was of unspeakable depth, and of a transparency richer than that of amber. It was from three to six miles in width; and its banks which arose on either side to twelve hundred feet in perpendicular height, were crowned with ever-blossoming trees and perpetual sweet-scented flowers, that made the whole territory one gorgeous garden; but the name of this luxuriant land was the Kingdom of Horror, and to enter it was inevitable death'"[8]

---

5. "During the eruption of Hecla, in 1766, clouds of this kind produced such a degree of darkness that, at Glaumba, which is more than fifty leagues from the mountain, people could only find their way by groping. During the eruption of Vesuvius, in 1794, at Caserta, four leagues distant, people could only walk by the light of torches. On the first of May, 1812, a cloud of volcanic ashes and sand, coming from a volcano in the island of St. Vincent, covered the whole of Barbadoes, spreading over it so intense a darkness that, at mid-day, in the open air, one could not perceive the trees or other objects near him, or even a white handkerchief placed at the distance of six inches from the eye. "—*Murray, p. 215, Phil. edit.*

6. In the year 1790, in the Caraccas during an earthquake a portion of the granite soil sank and left a lake eight hundred yards in diameter, and from eighty to a hundred feet deep. It was a part of the forest of Aripao which sank, and the trees remained green for several months under the water."—*Murray.*

7. The hardest steel ever manufactured may, under the action of a blowpipe, be reduced to an impalpable powder, which will float readily in the atmospheric air.

8. The region of the Niger. See Simmona's *Colonial Magazine.*

"*Humph!*" said the king.

"'We left this kingdom in great haste, and, after some days, came to another, where we were astonished to perceive myriads of monstrous animals with horns resembling scythes upon their heads. These hideous beasts dig for themselves vast caverns in the soil, of a funnel shape, and line the sides of them with rocks, so disposed one upon the other that they fall instantly, when trodden upon by other animals, thus precipitating them into the monster's dens, where their blood is immediately sucked, and their carcasses afterwards hurled contemptuously out to an immense distance from "the caverns of death."'" [9]

"Pooh!" said the king.

"'Continuing our progress, we perceived a district with vegetables that grew not upon any soil but in the air. [10] There were others that sprang from the substance of other vegetables; [11] others that derived their substance from the bodies of living animals; [12] and then again, there were others that glowed all over with intense fire; [13] others that moved from place to place at pleasure, [14] and what was still more wonderful, we discovered flowers that lived and breathed and moved their limbs at will

9. The *Myrmeleon*-lion-ant. The term "monster" is equally applicable to small abnormal things and to great, while such epithets as "vast" are merely comparative. The cavern of the myrmeleon is *vast* in comparison with the hole of the common red ant. A grain of silex is also a "rock."

10. The *Epidendron, Flos Aeris,* of the family of the *Orchideae,* grows with merely the surface of its roots attached to a tree or other object, from which it derives no nutriment—subsisting altogether upon air.

11. The *Parasites,* such as the wonderful *Rafflesia Arnaldii.*

12. *Schouw* advocates a class of plants that grow upon living animals—the *Plantae Epizoae.* Of this class are the *Fuci* and *Algae.* Mr. J. B. Williams, of Salem, Mass., presented the "National Institute" with an insect from New Zealand, with the following description: "'*The Hotte,* a decided caterpillar, or worm, is found gnawing at the root of the *Rota* tree, with a plant growing out of its head. This most peculiar and extraordinary insect travels up both the *Rota* and *Ferriri* trees, and entering into the top, eats its way, perforating the trunk of the trees until it reaches the root, and dies, or remains dormant, and the plant propagates out of its head; the body remains perfect and entire, of a harder substance than when alive. From this insect the natives make a colouring for tattooing.

13. In mines and natural caves we find a species of cryptogamous *fungus* that emits an intense phosphorescence.

14. The orchis, scabius and valisneria.

and had, moreover, the detestable passion of mankind for enslaving other creatures, and confining them in horrid and solitary prisons until the fulfillment of appointed tasks.'" [15]

"Pshaw!" said the king.

"'Quitting this land, we soon arrived at another in which the bees and the birds are mathematicians of such genius and erudition, that they give daily instructions in the science of geometry to the wise men of the empire. The king of the place having offered a reward for the solution of two very difficult problems, they were solved upon the spot—the one by the bees, and the other by the birds; but the king keeping their solution a secret, it was only after the most profound researches and labour, and the writing of an infinity of big books, during a long series of years, that the men-mathematicians at length arrived at the identical solutions which had been given upon the spot by the bees and by the birds.'" [16]

---

15. The corolla of this flower (*Aristolochia Clematitis*), which is tubular, but terminating upwards in a ligulate limb, is inflated into a globular figure at the base. The tubular part is internally beset with stiff hairs, pointing downwards. The globular part contains the pistil, which consists merely of a germen and stigma, together with the surrounding stamens. But the stamens, being shorter than the germen, cannot discharge the pollen so as to throw it upon the stigma, as the flower stands always upright till after impregnation. And hence, without some additional and peculiar aid, the pollen must necessarily fan down to the bottom of the flower. Now, the aid that nature has furnished in this case, is that of the *Tiputa Pennicornis*, a small insect, which entering the tube of the corrolla in quest of honey, descends to the bottom, and rummages about till it becomes quite covered with pollen; but not being able to force its way out again, owing to the downward position of the hairs, which converge to a point like the wires of a mouse-trap, and being somewhat impatient of its confinement it brushes backwards and forwards, trying every corner, till, after repeatedly traversing the stigma, it covers it with pollen sufficient for its impregnation, in consequence of which the flower soon begins to droop, and the hairs to shrink to the sides of the tube, effecting an easy passage for the escape of the insect."—*Rev. P. Keith-System of Physiological Botany.*

16. The bees—ever since bees were—have been constructing their cells with just such sides, in just such number, and at just such inclinations, as it has been demonstrated (in a problem involving the profoundest mathematical principles) are the very sides, in the very number, and at the very angles, which will afford the creatures the most room that is compatible with the greatest stability of structure. During the latter part of the last century, the question arose among mathematicians—"to determine the best form that can be given to the sails of a windmill, according to their varying distances from the revolving vanes, and (continued next page),

"Oh my!" said the king.

"'We had scarcely lost sight of this empire when we found ourselves close upon another, from whose shores there flew over our heads a flock of fowls a mile in breadth, and two hundred and forty miles long; so that, although they flew a mile during every minute, it required no less than four hours for the whole flock to pass over us—in which there were several millions of millions of fowl.'" [17]

"Oh fy!" said the king.

"'No sooner had we got rid of these birds, which occasioned us great annoyance, than we were terrified by the appearance of a fowl of another kind, and infinitely larger than even the rocs which I met in my former voyages; for it was bigger than the biggest of the domes on your *seraglio*, oh, most Munificent of Caliphs. This terrible fowl had no head that we could perceive, but was fashioned entirely of belly, which was of a prodigious fatness and roundness, of a soft-looking substance, smooth, shining and striped with various colours. In its talons, the monster was bearing away to his eyrie in the heavens, a house from which it had knocked off the roof, and in the interior of which we distinctly saw human beings, who, beyond doubt, were in a state of frightful despair at the horrible fate which awaited them. We shouted with all our might, in the hope of frightening the bird into letting go of its prey, but it merely gave a snort or puff, as if of rage and then let fall upon our heads a heavy sack which proved to be filled with sand!'"

"Stuff!" said the king.

---

likewise from the centres of the revolution." This is an excessively complex problem, for it is, in other words, to find the best possible position at an infinity of varied distances and at an infinity of points on the arm. There were a thousand futile attempts to answer the query on the part of the most illustrious mathematicians, and when at length, an undeniable solution was discovered, men found that the wings of a bird had given it with absolute precision ever since the first bird had traversed the air.

17. He observed a flock of pigeons passing betwixt Frankfort and the Indian territory, one mile at least in breadth; it took up four hours in passing, which, at the rate of one mile per minute, gives a length of 240 miles; and, supposing three pigeons to each square yard, gives 2,230,272,000 Pigeons.—*Travels in Canada and the United States, by Lieut. F. Hall.*

"'It was just after this adventure that we encountered a continent of immense extent and prodigious solidity, but which, nevertheless, was supported entirely upon the back of a sky-blue cow that had no fewer than four hundred horns.'" [18]

"That, now, I believe," said the king, "because I have read something of the kind before, in a book."

"'We passed immediately beneath this continent, (swimming in between the legs of the cow), and, after some hours, found ourselves in a wonderful country indeed, which, I was informed by the man-animal, was his own native land, inhabited by things of his own species. This elevated the man-animal very much in my esteem, and in fact, I now began to feel ashamed of the contemptuous familiarity with which I had treated him; for I found that the man-animals in general were a nation of the most powerful magicians, who lived with worms in their brain, [19] which, no doubt, served to stimulate them by their painful writhings and wrigglings to the most miraculous efforts of imagination!'"

"Nonsense!" said the king.

"'Among the magicians, were domesticated several animals of very singular kinds; for example, there was a huge horse whose bones were iron and whose blood was boiling water. In place of corn, he had black stones for his usual food; and yet, in spite of so hard a diet, he was so strong and swift that he would drag a load more weighty than the grandest temple in this city, at a rate surpassing that of the flight of most birds.'" [20]

"Twattle!" said the king.

"'I saw, also, among these people a hen without feathers, but bigger than a camel; instead of flesh and bone she had iron and brick; her blood, like that of the horse, (to whom, in fact, she was nearly related,) was boiling water; and like him she ate

---

18. The earth is upheld by a cow of a blue colour, having horns four hundred in number."—*Sale's Koran*.

19. "The *Entozoa*, or intestinal worms, have repeatedly been observed in the muscles, and in the cerebral substance of men."—See *Wyatt's Physiology*.

20. On the Great Western Railway, between London and Exeter, a speed of 71 miles per hour has been attained. A train weighing 90 tons was whirled from Paddington to Didcot (53 miles) in 51 minutes.

nothing but wood or black stones. This hen brought forth very frequently, a hundred chickens in the day; and, after birth, they took up their residence for several weeks within the stomach of their mother.'" [21]

"Fa! lal!" said the king.

"'One of this nation of mighty conjurors created a man out of brass and wood, and leather, and endowed him with such ingenuity that he would have beaten at chess, all the race of mankind with the exception of the great *caliph*, Haroun Alraschid. [22] Another of these *magi* constructed (of like material) a creature that put to shame even the genius of him who made it; for so great were its reasoning powers that, in a second, it performed calculations of so vast an extent that they would have required the united labour of fifty thousand fleshy men for a year. [23] But a still more wonderful conjuror fashioned for himself a mighty thing that was neither man nor beast, but which had brains of lead, intermixed with a black matter like pitch, and fingers that it employed with such incredible speed and dexterity that it would have had no trouble in writing out twenty thousand copies of the *Koran* in an hour, and this with so exquisite a precision, that in all the copies there should not be found one to vary from another by the breadth of the finest hair. This thing was of prodigious strength, so that it erected or overthrew the mightiest empires at a breath; but its powers were exercised equally for evil and for good.'"

"Ridiculous!" said the king.

"'Among this nation of necromancers there was also one who had in his veins the blood of the salamanders; for he made no scruple of sitting down to smoke his *chibouc* in a red-hot oven until his dinner was thoroughly roasted upon its floor.[24] Another had the faculty of converting the common metals into gold, without even looking at them during the process. [25] Another had such a delicacy of touch that he made a wire so fine as to

---

21. The *Eccalobeion*.
22. Maelzel's Automaton Chess-player.
23. Babbage's Calculating Machine.
24. *Chabert*, and since him, a hundred others.
25. The Electrotype.

be invisible. [26] Another had such quickness of perception that he counted all the separate motions of an elastic body, while it was springing backward and forward at the rate of nine hundred millions of times in a second."' [27]

"Absurd!" said the king.

"'Another of these magicians, by means of a fluid that no-body ever yet saw, could make the corpses of his friends brandish their arms, kick out their legs, fight, or even get up and dance at his will. [28] Another had cultivated his voice to so great an extent that he could have made himself heard from one end of the world to the other. [29] Another had so long an arm that he could sit down in Damascus and indite a letter at Bagdad—or indeed at any distance whatsoever. [30] Another commanded the lightning to come down to him out of the heavens, and it came at his call; and served him for a plaything when it came. Another took two loud sounds and out of them made a silence. Another constructed a deep darkness out of two brilliant lights. [31] Another made ice in a red-hot furnace. [32] Another directed the sun to

26. *Wollaston* made of platinum for the field of views in a telescope a wire one eighteen-thousandth part of an inch in thickness. It could be seen only by means of the microscope.

27. Newton demonstrated that the retina beneath the influence of the violet ray of the spectrum, vibrated 900,000,000 of times in a second.

28. Voltaic pile.

29. The Electro Telegraph Printing Apparatus.

30. The Electro telegraph transmits intelligence instantaneously—at least at so far as regards any distance upon the earth.

31. Common experiments in Natural Philosophy. If two red rays from two lumi-nous points be admitted into a dark chamber so as to fall on a white surface, and differ in their length by 0.0000258 of an inch, their intensity is doubled. So also if the difference in length be any whole-number multiple of that fraction. A multiple by 2¼, 3¼, &c., gives an intensity equal to one ray only; but a multiple by 2½, 3½, &c., gives the result of total darkness. In violet rays similar effects arise when the difference in length is 0.000157 of an inch; and with all other rays the results are the same—the difference varying with a uniform increase from the violet to the red. "Analogous experiments in respect to sound produce analogous results."

32. Place a platina crucible over a spirit lamp, and keep it a red heat; pour in some sulphuric acid, which, though the most volatile of bodies at a common temperature, will be found to become completely fixed in a hot crucible, and not a drop evapo-rates—being surrounded by an atmosphere of its own, it does not, in fact, touch the sides. A few drops of water are now introduced, when the acid, immediately coming in contact with the heated sides of the crucible, flies off in (continued next page),

paint his portrait, and the sun did. [33] Another took this luminary with the moon and the planets, and having first weighed them with scrupulous accuracy, probed into their depths and found out the solidity of the substance of which they were made. But the whole nation is, indeed, of so surprising a necromantic ability, that not even their infants, nor their commonest cats and dogs have any difficulty in seeing objects that do not exist at all, or that for twenty millions of years before the birth of the nation itself had been blotted out from the face of creation."' [34]

"Preposterous!" said the king.

"'The wives and daughters of these incomparably great and wise *magi*,'" continued Scheherazade, without being in any manner disturbed by these frequent and most ungentlemanly interruptions on the part of her husband—"'the wives and daughters of these eminent conjurers are everything that is accomplished and refined; and would be everything that is interesting and beautiful, but for an unhappy fatality that besets them, and from which not even the miraculous powers of their husbands and fathers has, hitherto, been adequate to save. Some fatalities come in certain shapes, and some in others—but this of which I speak has come in the shape of a crotchet.'"

"A what?" said the king.

"'A crotchet'" said Scheherazade. "'One of the evil *genii*, who are perpetually upon the watch to inflict ill, has put it into the heads of these accomplished ladies that the thing which we describe as personal beauty consists altogether in the protuberance of the region which lies not very far below the small of

sulphurous acid vapour, and so rapid is its progress, that the caloric of the water passes off with it, which falls a lump of ice to the bottom; by taking advantage of the moment before it is allowed to remelt, it may be turned out a lump of ice from a red-hot vessel.

33. The Daguerreotype.

34. Although light travels 167,000 miles in a second, the distance of 61 Cygni (the only star whose distance is ascertained) is so inconceivably great, that its rays would require more than ten years to reach the earth. For stars beyond this, 20—or even 1000 years—would be a moderate estimate. Thus, if they had been annihilated 20, or 1000 years ago, we might still see them today by the light which started from their surfaces 20 or 1000 years in the past time. That many which we see daily are really extinct, is not impossible—not even improbable.

the back. Perfection of loveliness, they say, is in the direct ratio of the extent of this lump. Having been long possessed of this idea, and bolsters being cheap in that country, the days have long gone by since it was possible to distinguish a woman from a dromedary—'"

"Stop!" said the king—"I can't stand that, and I won't. You have already given me a dreadful headache with your lies. The day, too, I perceive, is beginning to break. How long have we been married?—my conscience is getting to be troublesome again. And then that dromedary touch—do you take me for a fool? Upon the whole, you might as well get up and be throttled."

These words, as I learn from the "Isitsoornot," both grieved and astonished Scheherazade; but, as she knew the king to be a man of scrupulous integrity, and quite unlikely to forfeit his word, she submitted to her fate with a good grace. She derived, however, great consolation, (during the tightening of the bowstring,) from the reflection that much of the history remained still untold, and that the petulance of her brute of a husband had reaped for him a most righteous reward, in depriving him of many inconceivable adventures.

A Predicament
A.k.a. *The Scythe of Time*

What chance, good lady, hath bereft you thus?
—Comus.

It was a quiet and still afternoon when I strolled forth in the goodly city of Edina. The confusion and bustle in the streets were terrible. Men were talking. Women were screaming. Children were choking. Pigs were whistling. Carts they rattled. Bulls they bellowed. Cows they lowed. Horses they neighed. Cats they caterwauled. Dogs they danced. *Danced!* Could it then be possible? *Danced!* Alas, thought I, *my* dancing days are over! Thus it is ever. What a host of gloomy recollections will ever and *anon* be awakened in the mind of genius and imaginative contemplation, especially of a genius doomed to the everlasting and eternal, and continual, and, as one might say, the—*continued*—yes, the *continued and continuous*, bitter, harassing, disturbing, and, if I may be allowed the expression, the *very* disturbing influence of the serene, and godlike, and heavenly, and exalted, and elevated, and purifying effect of what may be rightly termed the most enviable, the most *truly* enviable—nay! the most benignly beautiful, the most deliciously ethereal, and, as it were, the most *pretty* (if I may use so bold an expression) *thing* (pardon me, gentle reader!) in the world—but I am always led away by my feelings.

In *such* a mind, I repeat, what a host of recollections are stirred up by a trifle! The dogs danced! *I*—I *could* not! They frisked—I wept. They capered—I sobbed aloud. Touching circumstances! which cannot fail to bring to the recollection of the classical reader that exquisite passage in relation to the fitness of things, which is to be found in the commencement of the third volume of that admirable and venerable Chinese novel the *Jo-Go-Slow*.

In my solitary walk through, the city I had two humble but faithful companions. Diana, my poodle! sweetest of creatures! She had a quantity of hair over her one eye, and a blue ribband tied fashionably around her neck. Diana was not more than five inches in height, but her head was somewhat bigger than her body, and her tail being cut off exceedingly close, gave an air of injured innocence to the interesting animal which rendered her a favourite with all.

And Pompey, my negro!—sweet Pompey! how shall I ever forget thee? I had taken Pompey's arm. He was three feet in height (I like to be particular) and about seventy, or perhaps eighty, years of age. He had bow-legs and was corpulent. His mouth should not be called small, nor his ears short. His teeth, however, were like pearl, and his large full eyes were deliciously white. Nature had endowed him with no neck, and had placed his ankles (as usual with that race) in the middle of the upper portion of the feet. He was clad with a striking simplicity. His sole garments were a stock of nine inches in height, and a near-ly—new drab overcoat which had formerly been in the service of the tall, stately, and illustrious Dr. Moneypenny. It was a good overcoat. It was well cut. It was well made. The coat was nearly new. Pompey held it up out of the dirt with both hands.

There were three persons in our party, and two of them have already been the subject of remark. There was a third—that person was myself. I am the Signora Psyche Zenobia. I am *not* Suky Snobbs. My appearance is commanding. On the memorable occasion of which I speak I was habited in a crimson satin dress, with a sky-blue Arabian *mantelet*. And the dress had trimmings of green *agraffas*, and seven graceful flounces of the orange-coloured *auricula*. I thus formed the third of the party. There was the poodle. There was Pompey. There was myself. We were *three*. Thus it is said there were originally but three Furies—Melty, Nimmy, and Hetty—Meditation, Memory, and Fiddling.

Leaning upon the arm of the gallant Pompey, and attended at a respectable distance by Diana, I proceeded down one of the populous and very pleasant streets of the now deserted Edina. On a sudden, there presented itself to view a church—a Gothic cathedral—vast, venerable, and with a tall steeple, which towered into the sky. What madness now possessed me? Why did I rush upon my fate? I was seized with an uncontrollable desire to ascend the giddy pinnacle, and then survey the immense extent of the city. The door of the cathedral stood invitingly open. My destiny prevailed. I entered the ominous archway.

Where then was my guardian angel?—if indeed such angels there be. *If!* Distressing monosyllable! what world of mystery, and meaning, and doubt, and uncertainty is there involved in thy two letters! I entered the ominous archway! I entered; and, without injury to my orange-coloured *auriculas*, I passed beneath the portal, and emerged within the vestibule. Thus it is said the immense river Alfred passed, unscathed, and unwetted, beneath the sea.

I thought the staircase would never have an end. *Round!* Yes, they went round and up, and round and up and round and up, until I could not help surmising, with the sagacious Pompey, upon whose supporting arm I leaned in all the confidence of early affection—I *could* not help surmising that the upper end of the continuous spiral ladder had been accidentally, or perhaps designedly, removed. I paused for breath; and, in the meantime, an accident occurred of too momentous a nature in a moral, and also in a metaphysical point of view, to be passed over without notice. It appeared to me—indeed I was quite confident of the fact—I could not be mistaken—no! I had, for some moments, carefully and anxiously observed the motions of my Diana—I say that I *could not be* mistaken—Diana *smelt a rat!*

At once I called Pompey's attention to the subject, and he— he agreed with me. There was then no longer any reasonable room for doubt. The rat had been smelled—and by Diana. Heavens! shall I ever forget the intense excitement of the moment? Alas! what is the boasted intellect of man? The rat!—it was there—that is to say, it was somewhere. Diana smelled the rat. I—*I could* not! Thus it is said the Prussian Isis has, for some persons, a sweet and very powerful perfume, while to others it is perfectly scentless.

The staircase had been surmounted, and there were now only three or four more upward steps intervening between us and the summit. We still ascended, and now only one step remained. One step! One little, little step! Upon one such little step in the great staircase of human life how vast a sum of human happiness or misery depends! I thought of myself, then of Pompey, and then of the mysterious and inexplicable destiny which surrounded us. I thought of Pompey!—alas, I thought of love! I thought of my many false *steps* which have been taken, and may be taken again. I resolved to be more cautious, more reserved. I abandoned the arm of Pompey, and, without his assistance, surmounted the one remaining step, and gained the chamber of the belfry. I was followed immediately afterward by my poodle.

Pompey alone remained behind. I stood at the head of the staircase, and encouraged him to ascend. He stretched forth to me his hand, and unfortunately in so doing was forced to abandon his firm hold upon the overcoat. Will the gods never cease their persecution? The overcoat is dropped, and, with one of his feet, Pompey stepped upon the long and trailing skirt of the overcoat. He stumbled and fell—this consequence was inevitable. He fell forward, and, with his accursed head, striking me full in the—in the breast, precipitated me headlong, together with himself, upon the hard, filthy, and detestable floor of the belfry. But my revenge was sure, sudden, and complete. Seizing him furiously by the wool with both hands, I tore out a vast quantity of black, and crisp, and curling material, and tossed it from me with every manifestation of disdain. It fell among the ropes of the belfry and remained.

Pompey arose, and said no word. But he regarded me piteously with his large eyes and—sighed. Ye Gods—that sigh! It sunk into my heart. And the hair—the wool! Could I have reached that wool I would have bathed it with my tears, in testimony of regret. But alas! it was now far beyond my grasp. As it dangled among the cordage of the bell, I fancied it alive. I fancied that it stood on end with indignation. Thus the *happydandy Flos Aeris* of Java bears, it is said, a beautiful flower, which will live when pulled up by the roots. The natives suspend it by a cord from the ceiling and enjoy its fragrance for years.

Our quarrel was now made up, and we looked about the room for an aperture through which to survey the city of Edina. Windows there were none. The sole light admitted into the gloomy chamber proceeded from a square opening, about a foot in diameter, at a height of about seven feet from the floor. Yet what will the energy of true genius not effect? I resolved to clamber up to this hole. A vast quantity of wheels, pinions, and other cabalistic—looking machinery stood opposite the hole, close to it; and through the hole there passed an iron rod from the machinery. Between the wheels and the wall where the hole lay there was barely room for my body—yet I was desperate, and determined to persevere. I called Pompey to my side.

"You perceive that aperture, Pompey. I wish to look through it. You will stand here just beneath the hole—so. Now, hold out one of your hands, Pompey, and let me step upon it—thus. Now, the other hand, Pompey, and with its aid I will get upon your shoulders."

He did every thing I wished, and I found, upon getting up, that I could easily pass my head and neck through the aperture. The prospect was sublime. Nothing could be more magnificent. I merely paused a moment to bid Diana behave herself, and assure Pompey that I would be considerate and bear as lightly as possible upon his shoulders. I told him I would be tender of his feelings—*ossi tender que beefsteak*. Having done this justice to my faithful friend, I gave myself up with great zest and enthusiasm to the enjoyment of the scene which so obligingly spread itself out before my eyes.

Upon this subject, however, I shall forbear to dilate. I will not describe the city of Edinburgh. Every one has been to the city of Edinburgh. Every one has been to Edinburgh—the classic Edina. I will confine myself to the momentous details of my own lamentable adventure. Having, in some measure, satisfied my curiosity in regard to the extent, situation, and general appearance of the city, I had leisure to survey the church in which I was, and the delicate architecture of the steeple. I observed that the aperture through which I had thrust my head was an opening in the dial-plate of a gigantic clock, and must have appeared, from the street, as a large key-hole, such as we see in the face of the French watches. No doubt the true object was to admit the arm of an attendant, to adjust, when necessary, the hands of the clock from within.

I observed also, with surprise, the immense size of these hands, the longest of which could not have been less than ten feet in length, and, where broadest, eight or nine inches in breadth. They were of solid steel apparently, and their edges appeared to be sharp. Having noticed these particulars, and some others, I again turned my eyes upon the glorious prospect below, and soon became absorbed in contemplation.

From this, after some minutes, I was aroused by the voice of Pompey, who declared that he could stand it no longer, and requested that I would be so kind as to come down. This was unreasonable, and I told him so in a speech of some length. He replied, but with an evident misunderstanding of my ideas upon the subject. I accordingly grew angry, and told him in plain words, that he was a fool, that he had committed an *ignoramus e-clench-eye*, that his notions were mere *insommary Bovis,* and his words little better than *an ennemywerrybor'em*. With this he appeared satisfied, and I resumed my contemplations.

It might have been half an hour after this altercation when, as I was deeply absorbed in the heavenly scenery beneath me, I was startled by something very cold which pressed with a gentle pressure on the back of my neck. It is needless to say that I felt inexpressibly alarmed. I knew that Pompey was beneath my feet, and that Diana was sitting, according to my explicit directions, upon her hind legs, in the farthest corner of the room. What could it be? Alas! I but too soon discovered. Turning my head gently to one side, I perceived, to my extreme horror, that the huge, glittering, scimitar-like minute-hand of the clock had, in the course of its hourly revolution, *descended upon my neck.* There was, I knew, not a second to be lost.

I pulled back at once—but it was too late. There was no chance of forcing my head through the mouth of that terrible trap in which it was so fairly caught, and which grew narrower and narrower with a rapidity too horrible to be conceived. The agony of that moment is not to be imagined. I threw up my hands and endeavoured, with all my strength, to force upward the ponderous iron bar. I might as well have tried to lift the cathedral itself. Down, down, down it came, closer and yet closer. I screamed to Pompey for aid; but he said that I had hurt his feelings by calling him 'an ignorant old squint-eye:' I yelled to Diana; but she only said 'bow-wow-wow,' and that I had told her 'on no account to stir from the corner.' Thus I had no relief to expect from my associates.

Meantime the ponderous and terrific *Scythe of Time* (for I now discovered the literal import of that classical phrase) had not stopped, nor was it likely to stop, in its career. Down and still down, it came. It had already buried its sharp edge a full inch in my flesh, and my sensations grew indistinct and confused. At one time I fancied myself in Philadelphia with the stately Dr. Moneypenny, at another in the back parlour of Mr. Blackwood receiving his invaluable instructions. And then again the sweet recollection of better and earlier times came over me, and I thought of that happy period when the world was not all a desert, and Pompey not altogether cruel.

The ticking of the machinery amused me. *Amused me*, I say, for my sensations now bordered upon perfect happiness, and the most trifling circumstances afforded me pleasure. The eternal *click-clak, click-clak, click-clak* of the clock was the most melodious of music in my ears, and occasionally even put me in mind of the graceful sermonic harangues of Dr. Ollapod. Then there were the great figures upon the dial-plate—how intelligent how intellectual, they all looked! And presently they took to dancing the Mazurka, and I think it was the figure V. who performed the most to my satisfaction. She was evidently a lady of breeding. None of your swaggerers, and nothing at all indelicate in her motions. She did the pirouette to admiration—whirling round upon her apex. I made an endeavour to hand her a chair, for I saw that she appeared fatigued with her exertions—and it was not until then that I fully perceived my lamentable situation. Lamentable indeed! The bar had buried itself two inches in my neck. I was aroused to a sense of exquisite pain. I prayed for death, and, in the agony of the moment, could not help repeating those exquisite verses of the poet Miguel De Cervantes:

Vanny Buren, tan escondida
Query no te senty venny
Pork and pleasure, delly morry
Nommy, torny, darry, widdy!

But now a new horror presented itself, and one indeed sufficient to startle the strongest nerves. My eyes, from the cruel pressure of the machine, were absolutely starting from their sockets. While I was thinking how I should possibly manage without them, one actually tumbled out of my head, and, rolling down the steep side of the steeple, lodged in the rain gutter which ran along the eaves of the main building. The loss of the eye was not so much as the insolent air of independence and contempt with which it regarded me after it was out. There it lay in the gutter just under my nose, and the airs it gave itself would have been ridiculous had they not been disgusting. Such a winking and blinking were never before seen.

This behaviour on the part of my eye in the gutter was not only irritating on account of its manifest insolence and shameful ingratitude, but was also exceedingly inconvenient on account of the sympathy which always exists between two eyes of the same head, however far apart. I was forced, in a manner, to wink and to blink, whether I would or not, in exact concert with the scoundrelly thing that lay just under my nose. I was presently relieved, however, by the dropping out of the other eye. In fall-

510

ing it took the same direction (possibly a concerted plot) as its fellow. Both rolled out of the gutter together, and in truth I was very glad to get rid of them.

The bar was now four inches and a half deep in my neck, and there was only a little bit of skin to cut through. My sensations were those of entire happiness, for I felt that in a few minutes, at farthest, I should be relieved from my disagreeable situation. And in this expectation I was not at all deceived. At twenty-five minutes past five in the afternoon, precisely, the huge minute-hand had proceeded sufficiently far on its terrible revolution to sever the small remainder of my neck. I was not sorry to see the head which had occasioned me so much embarrassment at length make a final separation from my body. It first rolled down the side of the steeple, then lodge, for a few seconds, in the gutter, and then made its way, with a plunge, into the middle of the street.

I will candidly confess that my feelings were now of the most singular—nay, of the most mysterious, the most perplexing and incomprehensible character. My senses were here and there at one and the same moment. With my head I imagined, at one time, that I, the head, was the real Signora Psyche Zenobia—at another I felt convinced that myself, the body, was the proper identity. To clear my ideas on this topic I felt in my pocket for my snuff-box, but, upon getting it, and endeavouring to apply a pinch of its grateful contents in the ordinary manner, I became immediately aware of my peculiar deficiency, and threw the box at once down to my head. It took a pinch with great satisfaction, and smiled me an acknowledgement in return. Shortly afterward it made me a speech, which I could hear but indistinctly without ears. I gathered enough, however, to know that it was astonished at my wishing to remain alive under such circumstances. In the concluding sentences it quoted the noble words of Ariosto—

Il pover hommy che non sera corty
And have a combat tenty erry morty;

Thus comparing me to the hero who, in the heat of the combat, not perceiving that he was dead, continued to contest the battle with inextinguishable valour. There was nothing now to prevent my getting down from my elevation, and I did so. What it was that Pompey saw so very peculiar in my appearance I have never yet been able to find out. The fellow opened his mouth from ear to ear, and shut his two eyes as if he were endeavouring to crack nuts between the lids. Finally, throwing off his overcoat, he made one spring for the staircase and disappeared. I hurled after the scoundrel these vehement words of Demosthenes—

Andrew O'Phlegethon, you really make haste to fly,

And then turned to the darling of my heart, to the one-eyed! the shaggy-haired Diana. Alas! what a horrible vision affronted my eyes? *Was* that a rat I saw skulking into his hole? *Are* these the picked bones of the little angel who has been cruelly devoured by the monster? Ye gods! and what *do* I behold—*is* that the departed spirit, the shade, the ghost, of my beloved puppy, which I perceive sitting with a grace so melancholy, in the corner? Hearken! for she speaks, and, heavens! it is in the German of Schiller—

Unt stubby duk, so stubby dun
Duk she! duk she!

Alas! and are not her words too true?

And if I died, at least I died
For thee—for thee.

Sweet creature! she *too* has sacrificed herself in my behalf. Dogless, niggerless, headless, what *now* remains for the unhappy Signora Psyche Zenobia? Alas—*nothing!* I have done.

Von Kempelen and His Discovery

After the very minute and elaborate paper by Arago, to say nothing of the summary in *Silliman's Journal*, with the detailed statement just published by Lieutenant Maury, it will not be supposed, of course, that in offering a few hurried remarks in reference to Von Kempelen's discovery, I have any design to look at the subject in a *scientific* point of view. My object is simply, in the first place, to say a few words of Von Kempelen himself (with whom, some years ago, I had the honor of a slight personal acquaintance), since every thing which concerns him must necessarily, at this moment, be of interest; and, in the second place, to look in a general way, and speculatively, at the *results* of the discovery.

It may be as well, however, to premise the cursory observations which I have to offer, by denying, very decidedly, what seems to be a general impression (gleaned, as usual in a case of this kind, from the newspapers), *viz.*: that this discovery, astounding as it unquestionably is, is *unanticipated*.'

By reference to the *Diary of Sir Humphrey Davy*, it will be seen that this illustrious chemist had not only conceived the idea now in question, but had actually made *no inconsiderable progress, experimentally,* in the very *identical analysis* now so triumphantly brought to an issue by Von Kempelen, who although he makes not the slightest allusion to it, is, *without doubt* (I say it unhesitatingly, and can prove it, if required), indebted to the *Diary* for at least the first hint of his own undertaking.

The paragraph from the *Courier and Enquirer*, which is now

going the rounds of the press, and which purports to claim the invention for a Mr. Kissam, of Brunswick, Maine, appears to me, I confess, a little apocryphal, for several reasons; although there is nothing either impossible or very improbable in the statement made. I need not go into details. My opinion of the paragraph is founded principally upon its *manner*. It does not *look* true. Persons who are narrating *facts*, are seldom so particular as Mr. Kissam seems to be, about day and date and precise location. Besides, if Mr. Kissam actually did come upon the discovery he says he did, at the period designated—nearly eight years ago—how happens it that he took no steps, *on the instant*, to reap the immense benefits which the merest bumpkin must have known would have resulted to him individually, if not to the world at large, from the discovery?

It seems to me quite incredible that any man of common understanding could have discovered what Mr. Kissam says he did, and yet have subsequently acted so like a baby—so like an owl—as Mr. Kissam *admits* that he did. By-the-way, who *is* Mr. Kissam? and is not the whole paragraph in the *Courier and Enquirer* a fabrication got up to 'make a talk'? It must be confessed that it has an amazingly moon-hoaxy-air. Very little dependence is to be placed upon it, in my humble opinion; and if I were not well aware, from experience, how very easily men of science are mystified, on points out of their usual range of inquiry, I should be profoundly astonished at finding so eminent a chemist as Professor Draper, discussing Mr. Kissam's (or is it Mr. Quizzem's?) pretensions to the discovery, in so serious a tone.

But to return to the *Diary* of Sir Humphrey Davy. This pamphlet was *not* designed for the public eye, even upon the decease of the writer, as any person at all conversant with authorship may satisfy himself at once by the slightest inspection of the style. At page 13, for example, near the middle, we read, in reference to his researches about the protoxide of azote: 'In less than half a minute the *respiration* being continued, (these feelings) diminished gradually and were succeeded by (a sensation) analogous to gentle pressure on all the muscles.'

A hundred similar instances go to show that the MS. so inconsiderately published, was merely *a rough note-book*, meant only for the writer's own eye, but an inspection of the pamphlet will convince almost any thinking person of the truth of my suggestion. The fact is, Sir Humphrey Davy was about the last man in the world to *commit himself* on scientific topics. Not only had he a more than ordinary dislike to quackery, but he was morbidly afraid of *appearing* empirical; so that, however fully he might have been convinced that he was on the right track in the matter now in question, he would never have spoken out, until he had every thing ready for the most practical demonstration. I verily believe that his last moments would have been rendered wretched, could he have suspected that his wishes in regard to burning this *Diary* (full of crude speculations) would have been unattended to; as, it seems, they were.

I say 'his wishes,' for that he meant to include this note-book among the miscellaneous papers directed 'to be burnt,' I think there can be no manner of doubt. Whether it escaped the flames by good fortune or by bad, yet remains to be seen. That the passages quoted above, with the other similar ones referred to, gave Von Kempelen *the hint*, I do not in the slightest degree question; but I repeat, it yet remains to be seen whether this momentous discovery itself (*momentous* under any circumstances) will be of service or disservice to mankind at large. That Von Kempelen and his immediate friends will reap a rich harvest, it would be folly to doubt for a moment. They will scarcely be so weak as not to '*realise*,' in time, by large purchases of houses and land, with other property of *intrinsic* value.

In the brief account of Von Kempelen which appeared in the *Home Journal*, and has since been extensively copied, several misapprehensions of the German original seem to have been made by the translator, who professes to have taken the passage from a late number of the Presburg *Schnellpost*. *Viele* has evidently been misconceived (as it often is), and what the translator renders by 'sorrows,' is probably *lieden*, which, in its true version, 'sufferings,' would give a totally different complexion to the whole account;

but, of course, much of this is merely guess, on my part.

Von Kempelen, however, is by no means 'a misanthrope,' in appearance, at least, whatever he may be in fact. My acquaintance with him was casual altogether; and I am scarcely warranted in saying that I know him at all; but to have seen and conversed with a man of so *prodigious* a notoriety as he has attained, or *will* attain in a few days, is not a small matter, as times go.

The Literary World speaks of him, confidently, as a *native* of Presburg (misled, perhaps, by the account in *The Home Journal*) but I am pleased in being able to state *positively*, since I have it from his own lips, that he was born in Utica, in the State of New York, although both his parents, I believe, are of Presburg descent. The family is connected, in some way, with Mäelzel, of Automaton-chess-player memory. (*If we are not mistaken, the name of the inventor of the chess-player was either Kempelen, Von kempelen, or something like it.*) In person, he is short and stout, with large, *fat*, blue eyes, sandy hair and whiskers, a wide but pleasing mouth, fine teeth, and I think a Roman nose. There is some defect in one of his feet. His address is frank, and his whole manner noticeable for *bonhomie*.

Altogether, he looks, speaks, and acts as little like 'a misanthrope' as any man I ever saw. We were fellow-sojourners for a week about six years ago, at Earl's Hotel, in Providence, Rhode Island; and I presume that I conversed with him, at various times, for some three or four hours altogether. His principal topics were those of the day, and nothing that fell from him led me to suspect his scientific attainments. He left the hotel before me, intending to go to New York, and thence to Bremen; it was in the latter city that his great discovery was first made public; or, rather, it was there that he was first suspected of having made it. This is about all that I personally know of the now immortal Von Kempelen; but I have thought that even these few details would have interest for the public.

There can be little question that most of the marvellous rumours afloat about this affair are pure inventions, entitled to about as much credit as the story of Aladdin's lamp; and yet, in a case of this kind, as in the case of the discoveries in California, it is clear that the truth *may be* stranger than fiction. The following anecdote, at least, is so well authenticated, that we may receive it implicitly.

Von Kempelen had never been even tolerably well off during his residence at Bremen; and often, it was well known, he had been put to extreme shifts in order to raise trifling sums. When the great excitement occurred about the forgery on the house of Gutsmuth & Co., suspicion was directed toward Von Kempelen, on account of his having purchased a considerable property in Gasperitch Lane, and his refusing, when questioned, to explain how he became possessed of the purchase money. He was at length arrested, but nothing decisive appearing against him, was in the end set at liberty.

The police, however, kept a strict watch upon his movements, and thus discovered that he left home frequently, taking always the same road, and invariably giving his watchers the slip in the neighborhood of that labyrinth of narrow and crooked passages known by the flash name of the 'Dondergat.' Finally, by dint of great perseverance, they traced him to a garret in an old house of seven stories, in an alley called Flatzplatz,—and, coming upon him suddenly, found him, as they imagined, in the midst of his counterfeiting operations. His agitation is represented as so excessive that the officers had not the slightest doubt of his guilt. After hand-cuffing him, they searched his room, or rather rooms, for it appears he occupied all the *mansarde*.

Opening into the garret where they caught him, was a closet, ten feet by eight, fitted up with some chemical apparatus, of which the object has not yet been ascertained. In one corner of the closet was a very small furnace, with a glowing fire in it, and on the fire a kind of duplicate crucible—two crucibles connected by a tube. One of these crucibles was nearly full of *lead* in a state of fusion, but not reaching up to the aperture of the tube, which was close to the brim. The other crucible had some liquid in it, which, as the officers entered, seemed to be furiously dissipating in vapor. They relate that, on finding himself taken,

Kempelen seized the crucibles with both hands (which were encased in gloves that afterwards turned out to be asbestic), and threw the contents on the tiled floor.

It was now that they hand-cuffed him; and before proceeding to ransack the premises they searched his person, but nothing unusual was found about him, excepting a paper parcel, in his coat-pocket, containing what was afterward ascertained to be a mixture of antimony and some unknown substance, in nearly, but not quite, equal proportions. All attempts at analyzing the *unknown substance* have, so far, failed, but that it will ultimately be analyzed, is not to be doubted.

Passing out of the closet with their prisoner, the officers went through a sort of ante-chamber, in which nothing material was found, to the chemist's sleeping-room. They here rummaged some drawers and boxes, but discovered only a few papers, of no importance, and some good coin, silver and gold. At length, looking under the bed, they saw *a large, common hair trunk, without hinges, hasp, or lock,* and with the top lying carelessly across the bottom portion. Upon attempting to draw this trunk out from under the bed, they found that, with their united strength (there were three of them, all powerful men), they 'could not stir it one inch.' Much astonished at this, one of them crawled under the bed, and looking into the trunk, said:

'No wonder we couldn't move it—why it's full to the brim of old bits of brass!'

Putting his feet, now, against the wall so as to get a good purchase, and pushing with all his force, while his companions pulled with all theirs, the trunk, with much difficulty, was slid out from under the bed, and its contents examined. The supposed brass with which it was filled was all in small, smooth pieces, varying from the size of a pea to that of a dollar; but the pieces were irregular in shape, although more or less flat-looking, upon the whole, 'very much as lead looks when thrown upon the ground in a molten state, and there suffered to grow cool.' Now, not one of these officers for a moment suspected this metal to be anything *but* brass.

The idea of its being *gold* never entered their brains, of course; how *could* such a wild fancy have entered it? And their astonishment may be well conceived, when the next day it became known, all over Bremen, that the 'lot of brass' which they had carted so contemptuously to the police office, without putting themselves to the trouble of pocketing the smallest scrap, was not only gold—real gold—but gold far finer than any employed in coinage-gold, in fact, absolutely pure, virgin, without the slightest appreciable alloy.

I need not go over the details of Von Kempelen's confession (as far as it went) and release, for these are familiar to the public. That he has actually realized, in spirit and in effect, if not to the letter, the old *chimaera* of the philosopher's stone, no sane person is at liberty to doubt. The opinions of Arago are, of course, entitled to the greatest consideration; but he is by no means infallible; and what he says of *bismuth*, in his report to the Academy, must be taken *cum grano salis*. The simple truth is, that up to this period all analysis has failed; and until Von Kempelen chooses to let us have the key to his own published enigma, it is more than probable that the matter will remain, for years, *in statu quo*. All that as yet can fairly be said to be known is, that '*Pure gold can be made at will, and very readily from lead in connection with certain other substances, in kind and in proportions, unknown.*'

Speculation, of course, is busy as to the immediate and ultimate results of this discovery—a discovery which few thinking persons will hesitate in referring to an increased interest in the matter of gold generally, by the late developments in California; and this reflection brings us inevitably to another—the exceeding *inopportuneness* of Von Kempelen's analysis. If many were prevented from adventuring to California, by the mere apprehension that gold would so materially diminish in value, on account of its plentifulness in the mines there, as to render the speculation of going so far in search of it a doubtful one—what impression will be wrought *now*, upon the minds of those about to emigrate, and especially upon the minds of those actually in the mineral region, by the announcement of this astounding discovery of Von Kempelen? a discovery which declares, in so many words, that beyond its intrinsic worth for manufacturing purposes (whatever that worth may be), gold now is, or at least soon will be (for it cannot be supposed that Von Kempelen can *long* retain his secret), of no greater *value* than lead, and of far inferior value to silver.

It is, indeed, exceedingly difficult to speculate prospectively upon the consequences of the discovery, but one thing may be positively maintained—that the announcement of the discovery six months ago would have had material influence in regard to the settlement of California.

In Europe, as yet, the most noticeable results have been a rise of two hundred *per cent.* in the price of lead, and nearly twenty-five *per cent.* that of silver.

The Oblong Box

Some years ago, I engaged passage from Charleston, S. C, to the city of New York, in the fine packet-ship *Independence*, Captain Hardy. We were to sail on the fifteenth of the month (June), weather permitting; and on the fourteenth, I went on board to arrange some matters in my state-room.

I found that we were to have a great many passengers, including a more than usual number of ladies. On the list were several of my acquaintances, and among other names, I was rejoiced to see that of Mr. Cornelius Wyatt, a young artist, for whom I entertained feelings of warm friendship. He had been with me a fellow-student at C— University, where we were very much together. He had the ordinary temperament of genius, and was a compound of misanthropy, sensibility, and enthusiasm. To these qualities he united the warmest and truest heart which ever beat in a human bosom.

I observed that his name was carded upon *three* state-rooms; and, upon again referring to the list of passengers, I found that he had engaged passage for himself, wife, and two sisters—his own. The state-rooms were sufficiently roomy, and each had two berths, one above the other. These berths, to be sure, were so exceedingly narrow as to be insufficient for more than one person; still, I could not comprehend why there were *three* state-rooms for these four persons. I was, just at that epoch, in one of those moody frames of mind which make a man abnormally inquisitive about trifles: and I confess, with shame, that I busied myself in a variety of ill-bred and preposterous conjectures about this

521

matter of the supernumerary state-room. It was no business of mine, to be sure, but with none the less pertinacity did I occupy myself in attempts to resolve the enigma.

At last I reached a conclusion which wrought in me great wonder why I had not arrived at it before. "It is a servant of course," I said; "what a fool I am, not sooner to have thought of so obvious a solution!" And then I again repaired to the list—but here I saw distinctly that *no* servant was to come with the party, although, in fact, it had been the original design to bring one—for the words "and servant" had been first written and then overscored. "Oh, extra baggage, to be sure," I now said to myself—"something he wishes not to be put in the hold—something to be kept under his own eye—ah, I have it—a painting or so—and this is what he has been bargaining about with Nicolino, the Italian Jew." This idea satisfied me, and I dismissed my curiosity for the nonce.

Wyatt's two sisters I knew very well, and most amiable and clever girls they were. His wife he had newly married, and I had never yet seen her. He had often talked about her in my presence, however, and in his usual style of enthusiasm. He described her as of surpassing beauty, wit, and accomplishment. I was, therefore, quite anxious to make her acquaintance.

On the day in which I visited the ship (the fourteenth), Wyatt and party were also to visit it—so the captain informed me—and I waited on board an hour longer than I had designed, in hope of being presented to the bride, but then an apology came. "Mrs. W. was a little indisposed, and would decline coming on board until to-morrow, at the hour of sailing."

The morrow having arrived, I was going from my hotel to the wharf, when Captain Hardy met me and said that, "owing to circumstances" (a stupid but convenient phrase), "he rather thought the *Independence* would not sail for a day or two, and that when all was ready, he would send up and let me know." This I thought strange, for there was a stiff southerly breeze; but as "the circumstances" were not forthcoming, although I pumped for them with much perseverance, I had nothing to do but to return home and digest my impatience at leisure.

I did not receive the expected message from the captain for nearly a week. It came at length, however, and I immediately went on board. The ship was crowded with passengers, and everything was in the bustle attendant upon making sail. Wyatt's party arrived in about ten minutes after myself. There were the two sisters, the bride, and the artist—the latter in one of his customary fits of moody misanthropy. I was too well used to these, however, to pay them any special attention. He did not even introduce me to his wife—this courtesy devolving, per force, upon his sister Marian—a very sweet and intelligent girl, who, in a few hurried words, made us acquainted.

Mrs. Wyatt had been closely veiled; and when she raised her veil, in acknowledging my bow, I confess that I was very profoundly astonished. I should have been much more so, however, had not long experience advised me not to trust, with too implicit a reliance, the enthusiastic descriptions of my friend, the artist, when indulging in comments upon the loveliness of woman. When beauty was the theme, I well knew with what facility he soared into the regions of the purely ideal.

The truth is, I could not help regarding Mrs. Wyatt as a decidedly plain-looking woman. If not positively ugly, she was not, I think, very far from it. She was dressed, however, in exquisite taste—and then I had no doubt that she had captivated my friend's heart by the more enduring graces of the intellect and soul. She said very few words, and passed at once into her stateroom with Mr. W.

My old inquisitiveness now returned. There was *no* servant— *that* was a settled point. I looked, therefore, for the extra baggage. After some delay, a cart arrived at the wharf, with an oblong pine box, which was every thing that seemed to be expected. Immediately upon its arrival we made sail, and in a short time were safely over the bar and standing out to sea.

The box in question was, as I say, oblong. It was about six feet in length by two and a half in breadth; I observed it attentively, and like to be precise. Now this shape was *peculiar*; and no sooner had I seen it, than I took credit to myself for the accuracy of my guessing. I had reached the conclusion, it will be remembered, that the extra baggage of my friend, the artist, would prove to be pictures, or at least a picture; for I knew he had been for several weeks in conference with Nicolino:—and now here was a box, which, from its shape, *could* possibly contain nothing in the world but a copy of Leonardo's "Last Supper;" and a copy of this very "Last Supper," done by Rubini the younger, at Florence, I had known, for some time, to be in the possession of Nicolino. This point, therefore, I considered as sufficiently settled. I chuckled excessively when I thought of my acumen. It was the first time I had ever known Wyatt to keep from me any of his artistical secrets; but here he evidently intended to steal a march upon me, and smuggle a fine picture to New York, under my very nose; expecting me to know nothing of the matter. I resolved to quiz him *well*, now and hereafter.

One thing, however, annoyed me not a little. The box did *not* go into the extra state-room. It was deposited in Wyatt's own; and there, too, it remained, occupying very nearly the whole of the floor—no doubt to the exceeding discomfort of the artist and his wife;—this the more especially as the tar or paint with which it was lettered in sprawling capitals, emitted a strong, disagreeable, and, to *my* fancy, a peculiarly disgusting odour. On the lid were painted the words—

Mrs. Adelaide Curtis, Albany, New York. Charge of Cornelius Wyatt, Esq. This side up. To be handled with care.

Now, I was aware that Mrs. Adelaide Curtis, of Albany, was the artist's wife's mother,—but then I looked upon the whole address as a mystification, intended especially for myself. I made up my mind, of course, that the box and contents would never get farther north than the studio of my misanthropic friend, in Chambers Street, New York.

For the first three or four days we had fine weather, although the wind was dead ahead; having chopped round to the northward, immediately upon our losing sight of the coast. The passengers were, consequently, in high spirits and disposed to be social. I *must* except, however, Wyatt and his sisters, who behaved stiffly, and, I could not help thinking, uncourteously to the rest of the party. *Wyatt's* conduct I did not so much regard. He was gloomy, even beyond his usual habit—in fact he was *morose*—but in him I was prepared for eccentricity. For the sisters, however, I could make no excuse. They secluded themselves in their staterooms during the greater part of the passage, and absolutely refused, although I repeatedly urged them, to hold communication with any person on board.

Mrs. Wyatt herself was far more agreeable. That is to say, she was *chatty*; and to be chatty is no slight recommendation at sea. She became *excessively* intimate with most of the ladies; and, to my profound astonishment, evinced no equivocal disposition to coquet with the men. She amused us all very much. I say "*amused*"—and scarcely know how to explain myself. The truth is, I soon found that Mrs. W. was far oftener laughed *at* than *with*. The gentlemen said little about her; but the ladies, in a little while, pronounced her "a good-hearted thing, rather indifferent looking, totally uneducated, and decidedly vulgar." The great wonder was, how Wyatt had been entrapped into such a match. Wealth was the general solution—but this I knew to be no solution at all; for Wyatt had told me that she neither brought him a dollar nor had any expectations from any source whatever.

"He had married," he said, "for love, and for love only; and his bride was far more than worthy of his love." When I thought of these expressions, on the part of my friend, I confess that I felt indescribably puzzled. Could it be possible that he was taking leave of his senses? What else could I think? *He*, so refined, so intellectual, so fastidious, with so exquisite a perception of the faulty, and so keen an appreciation of the beautiful! To be sure, the lady seemed especially fond of *him*—particularly so in his absence—when she made herself ridiculous by frequent quotations of what had been said by her "beloved husband, Mr. Wyatt."

The word "husband" seemed forever—to use one of her own

delicate expressions—forever "on the tip of her tongue." In the meantime, it was observed by all on board, that he avoided *her* in the most pointed manner, and, for the most part, shut himself up alone in his state-room, where, in fact, he might have been said to live altogether, leaving his wife at full liberty to amuse herself as she thought best, in the public society of the main cabin.

My conclusion, from what I saw and heard, was, that, the artist, by some unaccountable freak of fate, or perhaps in some fit of enthusiastic and fanciful passion, had been induced to unite himself with a person altogether beneath him, and that the natural result, entire and speedy disgust, had ensued. I pitied him from the bottom of my heart—but could not, for that reason, quite forgive his incommunicativeness in the matter of the "Last Supper." For this I resolved to have my revenge.

One day he came upon deck, and, taking his arm as had been my wont, I sauntered with him backward and forward. His gloom, however (which I considered quite natural under the circumstances), seemed entirely unabated. He said little, and that moodily, and with evident effort. I ventured a jest or two, and he made a sickening attempt at a smile. Poor fellow!—as I thought of *his wife*, I wondered that he could have heart to put on even the semblance of mirth. I determined to commence a series of covert insinuations, or innuendoes, about the oblong box—just to let him perceive, gradually, that I was *not* altogether the butt, or victim, of his little bit of pleasant mystification. My first observation was by way of opening a masked battery. I said something about the "peculiar shape of *that* box;" and, as I spoke the words, I smiled knowingly, winked, and touched him gently with my forefinger in the ribs.

The manner in which Wyatt received this harmless pleasantry convinced me, at once, that he was mad. At first he stared at me as if he found it impossible to comprehend the witticism of my remark; but as its point seemed slowly to make its way into his brain, his eyes, in the same proportion, seemed protruding from their sockets. Then he grew very red—then hideously pale— then, as if highly amused with what I had insinuated, he began a loud and boisterous laugh, which, to my astonishment, he kept up, with gradually increasing vigour, for ten minutes or more. In conclusion, he fell flat and heavily upon the deck. When I ran to uplift him, to all appearance he was *dead*.

I called assistance, and, with much difficulty, we brought him to himself. Upon reviving he spoke incoherently for some time. At length we bled him and put him to bed. The next morning he was quite recovered, so far as regarded his mere bodily health. Of his mind I say nothing, of course. I avoided him during the rest of the passage, by advice of the captain, who seemed to co-incide with me altogether in my views of his insanity, but cautioned me to say nothing on this head to any person on board.

Several circumstances occurred immediately after this fit of Wyatt which contributed to heighten the curiosity with which I was already possessed. Among other things, this: I had been nervous—drank too much strong green tea, and slept ill at night—in fact, for two nights I could not be properly said to sleep at all. Now, my state-room opened into the main cabin, or dining-room, as did those of all the single men on board. Wyatt's three rooms were in the after-cabin, which was separated from the main one by a slight sliding door, never locked even at night.

As we were almost constantly on a wind, and the breeze was not a little stiff, the ship heeled to leeward very considerably; and whenever her starboard side was to leeward, the sliding door between the cabins slid open, and so remained, nobody taking the trouble to get up and shut it. But my berth was in such a po-sition, that when my own state-room door was open, as well as the sliding door in question (and my own door was *always* open on account of the heat,) I could see into the after-cabin quite distinctly, and just at that portion of it, too, where were situated the state-rooms of Mr. Wyatt. Well, during two nights (*not* con-secutive) while I lay awake, I clearly saw Mrs. W., about eleven o'clock upon each night, steal cautiously from the state-room of Mr. W., and enter the extra room, where she remained until daybreak, when she was called by her husband and went back.

That they were virtually separated was clear. They had separate apartments—no doubt in contemplation of a more permanent divorce; and here, after all I thought was the mystery of the extra state-room.

There was another circumstance, too, which interested me much. During the two wakeful nights in question, and immediately after the disappearance of Mrs. Wyatt into the extra state-room, I was attracted by certain singular cautious, subdued noises in that of her husband. After listening to them for some time, with thoughtful attention, I at length succeeded perfectly in translating their import. They were sounds occasioned by the artist in prying open the oblong box, by means of a chisel and mallet—the latter being apparently muffled, or deadened, by some soft woollen or cotton substance in which its head was enveloped.

In this manner I fancied I could distinguish the precise moment when he fairly disengaged the lid—also, that I could determine when he removed it altogether, and when he deposited it upon the lower berth in his room; this latter point I knew, for example, by certain slight taps which the lid made in striking against the wooden edges of the berth, as he endeavoured to lay it down *very* gently—there being no room for it on the floor. After this there was a dead stillness, and I heard nothing more, upon either occasion, until nearly daybreak; unless, perhaps, I may mention a low sobbing, or murmuring sound, so very much suppressed as to be nearly inaudible—if, indeed, the whole of this latter noise were not rather produced by my own imagination.

I say it seemed to *resemble* sobbing or sighing—but, of course, it could not have been either. I rather think it was a ringing in my own ears. Mr. Wyatt, no doubt, according to custom, was merely giving the rein to one of his hobbies—indulging in one of his fits of artistic enthusiasm. He had opened his oblong box, in order to feast his eyes on the pictorial treasure within. There was nothing in this, however, to make him *sob*. I repeat, therefore, that it must have been simply a freak of my own fancy, distempered by good Captain Hardy's green tea. Just before dawn, on each of the two nights of which I speak, I distinctly heard Mr. Wyatt replace the lid upon the oblong box, and force the nails into their old places by means of the muffled mallet. Having done this, he issued from his state-room, fully dressed, and proceeded to call Mrs. W. from hers.

We had been at sea seven days, and were now off Cape Hatteras, when there came a tremendously heavy blow from the southwest. We were, in a measure, prepared for it, however, as the weather had been holding out threats for some time. Every thing was made snug, alow and aloft; and as the wind steadily freshened, we lay to, at length, under spanker and foretopsail, both double-reefed.

In this trim we rode safely enough for forty-eight hours— the ship proving herself an excellent sea-boat in many respects, and shipping no water of any consequence. At the end of this period, however, the gale had freshened into a hurricane, and our after—sail split into ribbons, bringing us so much in the trough of the water that we shipped several prodigious seas, one immediately after the other. By this accident we lost three men overboard with the caboose, and nearly the whole of the larboard bulwarks. Scarcely had we recovered our senses, before the foretopsail went into shreds, when we got up a storm stay—sail and with this did pretty well for some hours, the ship heading the sea much more steadily than before.

The gale still held on, however, and we saw no signs of its abating. The rigging was found to be ill-fitted, and greatly strained; and on the third day of the blow, about five in the afternoon, our mizzen-mast, in a heavy lurch to windward, went by the board. For an hour or more, we tried in vain to get rid of it, on account of the prodigious rolling of the ship; and, before we had succeeded, the carpenter came aft and announced four feet of water in the hold. To add to our dilemma, we found the pumps choked and nearly useless.

All was now confusion and despair—but an effort was made to lighten the ship by throwing overboard as much of her cargo as could be reached, and by cutting away the two masts that remained. This we at last accomplished—but we were still unable to do any thing at the pumps; and, in the meantime, the leak gained on us very fast.

At sundown, the gale had sensibly diminished in violence, and as the sea went down with it, we still entertained faint hopes of saving ourselves in the boats. At eight p. m., the clouds broke away to windward, and we had the advantage of a full moon—a piece of good fortune which served wonderfully to cheer our drooping spirits.

After incredible labour we succeeded, at length, in getting the longboat over the side without material accident, and into this we crowded the whole of the crew and most of the passengers. This party made off immediately, and, after undergoing much suffering, finally arrived, in safety, at Ocracoke Inlet, on the third day after the wreck.

Fourteen passengers, with the captain, remained on board, resolving to trust their fortunes to the jolly-boat at the stern. We lowered it without difficulty, although it was only by a miracle that we prevented it from swamping as it touched the water. It contained, when afloat, the captain and his wife, Mr. Wyatt and party, a Mexican officer, wife, four children, and myself, with a negro valet.

We had no room, of course, for anything except a few positively necessary instruments, some provisions, and the clothes upon our backs. No one had thought of even attempting to save anything more. What must have been the astonishment of all, then, when having proceeded a few fathoms from the ship, Mr. Wyatt stood up in the stern-sheets, and coolly demanded of Captain Hardy that the boat should be put back for the purpose of taking in his oblong box!

"Sit down, Mr. Wyatt," replied the captain, somewhat sternly, "you will capsize us if you do not sit quite still. Our gunwhale is almost in the water now."

"The box!" vociferated Mr. Wyatt, still standing—"the box, I say! Captain Hardy, you cannot, you *will* not refuse me. Its weight will be but a trifle—it is nothing—mere nothing. By the mother who bore you—for the love of Heaven—by your hope of salvation, I *implore* you to put back for the box!"

The captain, for a moment, seemed touched by the earnest appeal of the artist, but he regained his stern composure, and merely said:

"Mr. Wyatt, you are *mad*. I cannot listen to you. Sit down, I say, or you will swamp the boat. Stay—hold him—seize him!—he is about to spring overboard! There—I knew it—he is over!"

As the captain said this, Mr. Wyatt, in fact, sprang from the boat, and, as we were yet in the lee of the wreck, succeeded, by almost superhuman exertion, in getting hold of a rope which hung from the fore-chains. In another moment he was on board, and rushing frantically down into the cabin.

In the meantime, we had been swept astern of the ship, and being quite out of her lee, were at the mercy of the tremendous sea which was still running. We made a determined effort to put back, but our little boat was like a feather in the breath of the tempest. We saw at a glance that the doom of the unfortunate artist was sealed.

As our distance from the wreck rapidly increased, the madman (for as such only could we regard him) was seen to emerge from the companion—way, up which by dint of strength that appeared gigantic, he dragged, bodily, the oblong box. While we gazed in the extremity of astonishment, he passed, rapidly, several turns of a three-inch rope, first around the box and then around his body. In another instant both body and box were in the sea—disappearing suddenly, at once and forever.

We lingered awhile sadly upon our oars, with our eyes riveted upon the spot. At length we pulled away. The silence remained unbroken for an hour. Finally, I hazarded a remark.

"Did you observe, captain, how suddenly they sank? Was not that an exceedingly singular thing? I confess that I entertained some feeble hope of his final deliverance, when I saw him lash himself to the box, and commit himself to the sea."

"They sank as a matter of course," replied the captain, "and that like a shot. They will soon rise again, however—*but not till the salt melts.*"

"The salt!" I ejaculated.

"Hush!" said the captain, pointing to the wife and sisters of the deceased. "We must talk of these things at some more appropriate time."

We suffered much, and made a narrow escape, but fortune befriended *us*, as well as our mates in the long-boat. We landed, in fine, more dead than alive, after four days of intense distress, upon the beach opposite Roanoke Island. We remained here a week, were not ill-treated by the wreckers, and at length obtained a passage to New York.

About a month after the loss of the *Independence*, I happened to meet Captain Hardy in Broadway. Our conversation turned, naturally, upon the disaster, and especially upon the sad fate of poor Wyatt. I thus learned the following particulars.

The artist had engaged passage for himself, wife, two sisters and a servant. His wife was, indeed, as she had been represented, a most lovely, and most accomplished woman. On the morning of the fourteenth of June (the day in which I first visited the ship), the lady suddenly sickened and died. The young husband was frantic with grief—but circumstances imperatively forbade the deferring his voyage to New York. It was necessary to take to her mother the corpse of his adored wife, and, on the other hand, the universal prejudice which would prevent his doing so openly was well known. Nine-tenths of the passengers would have abandoned the ship rather than take passage with a dead body.

In this dilemma, Captain Hardy arranged that the corpse, being first partially embalmed, and packed, with a large quantity of salt, in a box of suitable dimensions, should be conveyed on board as merchandise. Nothing was to be said of the lady's decease; and, as it was well understood that Mr. Wyatt had engaged passage for his wife, it became necessary that some person should personate her during the voyage. This the deceased lady's-maid was easily prevailed on to do. The extra state-room, originally engaged for this girl during her mistress' life, was now merely retained. In this state-room the pseudo-wife, slept, of course, every night. In the daytime she performed, to the best of her ability, the part of her mistress—whose person, it had been carefully ascertained, was unknown to any of the passengers on board.

My own mistake arose, naturally enough, through too careless, too inquisitive, and too impulsive a temperament. But of late, it is a rare thing that I sleep soundly at night. There is a countenance which haunts me, turn as I will. There is an hysterical laugh which will forever ring within my ears.

The Pit and the Pendulum

*Impia tortorum longas hic turba furores
Sanguinis innocui, non satiata, aluit.
Sospite nunc patria, fracto nunc funeris antro,
Mors ubi dira fuit vita salusque patent.*
(Quatrain composed for the gates of a market to be erected upon the site of the Jacobin Club House at Paris.)

I was sick, sick unto death, with that long agony, and when they at length unbound me, and I was permitted to sit, I felt that my senses were leaving me. The sentence, the dread sentence of death, was the last of distinct accentuation which reached my ears. After that, the sound of the inquisitorial voices seemed merged in one dreamy intermediate hum. It conveyed to my soul the idea of *revolution*, perhaps from its association in fancy with the burr of a mill-wheel. This only for a brief period, for presently I heard no more. Yet, for a while, I saw, but with how terrible an exaggeration! I saw the lips of the black-robed judges. They appeared to me white—whiter than the sheet upon which I trace these words—and thin even to grotesqueness; thin with the intensity of their expression of firmness, of immovable resolution, of stern contempt of human torture.

I saw that the decrees of what to me was fate were still issuing from those lips. I saw them writhe with a deadly locution. I saw them fashion the syllables of my name, and I shuddered, because no sound succeeded. I saw, too, for a few moments of delirious horror, the soft and nearly imperceptible waving of the sable draperies which enwrapped the walls of the apartment; and then my vision fell upon the seven tall candles upon the table. At first they wore the aspect of charity, and seemed white slender angels who would save me; but then all at once there came a most deadly nausea over my spirit, and I felt every fibre in my frame thrill, as if I had touched the wire of a galvanic battery, while the angel forms became meaningless spectres, with heads of flame, and I saw that from them there would be no help. And then there stole into my fancy, like a rich musical note, the thought of what sweet rest there must be in the grave.

The thought came gently and stealthily, and it seemed long before it attained full appreciation; but just as my spirit came at length properly to feel and entertain it, the figures of the judges vanished, as if magically, from before me; the tall candles sank into nothingness; their flames went out utterly; the blackness of darkness supervened; all sensations appeared swallowed up in a mad rushing descent as of the soul into Hades. Then silence, and stillness, and night were the universe.

I had swooned; but still will not say that all of consciousness was lost. What of it there remained I will not attempt to define, or even to describe; yet all was not lost. In the deepest slumber no!—In delirium—no! In a swoon—no! In death—no! Even in the grave all *is not* lost. Else there is no immortality for man. Arousing from the most profound of slumbers, we break the gossamer web of *some* dream. Yet in a second afterwards (so frail may that web have been) we remember not that we have dreamed. In the return to life from the swoon there are two stages; first, that of the sense of mental or spiritual; secondly, that of the sense of physical existence. It seems probable that if, upon reaching the second stage, we could recall the impressions of the first, we should find these impressions eloquent in memories of the gulf beyond. And that gulf is—what? How at least shall we distinguish its shadows from those of the tomb?

But if the impressions of what I have termed the first stage are not at will recalled, yet, after long interval, do they not come unbidden, while we marvel whence they come? He who has never swooned is not he who finds strange palaces and wildly familiar faces in coals that glow; is not he who beholds floating in mid-air the sad visions that the many may not view; is not he who ponders over the perfume of some novel flower; is not he whose brain grows bewildered with the meaning of some musical cadence which has never before arrested his attention.

Amid frequent and thoughtful endeavours to remember, amid earnest struggles to regather some token of the state of seeming nothingness into which my soul had lapsed, there have been moments when I have dreamed of success; there have been brief, very brief periods when I have conjured up remembrances which the lucid reason of a later epoch assures me could have had reference only to that condition of seeming unconsciousness. These shadows of memory tell indistinctly of tall figures that lifted and bore me in silence down—down—still down—till a hideous dizziness oppressed me at the mere idea of the interminableness of the descent. They tell also of a vague horror at my heart on account of that heart's unnatural stillness. Then comes a sense of sudden motionlessness throughout all things; as if those who bore me (a ghastly train!) had outrun, in their descent, the limits of the limitless, and paused from the wearisomeness of their toil. After this I call to mind flatness and dampness; and then all is madness—the madness of a memory which busies itself among forbidden things.

Very suddenly there came back to my soul motion and sound the tumultuous motion of the heart, and in my ears the sound of its beating. Then a pause in which all is blank. Then again sound, and motion, and touch, a tingling sensation pervading my frame. Then the mere consciousness of existence, without though— a condition which lasted long. Then, very suddenly, *thought*, and shuddering terror, and earnest endeavour to comprehend my true state. Then a strong desire to lapse into insensibility. Then a rushing revival of soul and a successful effort to move. And now a full memory of the trial, of the judges, of the sable draperies, of the sentence, of the sickness, of the swoon. Then entire forgetfulness of all that followed; of all that a later day and much earnestness of endeavour have enabled me vaguely to recall.

So far I had not opened my eyes. I felt that I lay upon my back unbound. I reached out my hand, and it fell heavily upon something damp and hard. There I suffered it to remain for many minutes, while I strove to imagine where and *what* I could be. I longed, yet dared not, to employ my vision. I dreaded the first glance at objects around me. It was not that I feared to look upon things horrible, but that I grew aghast lest there should be *nothing* to see. At length, with a wild desperation at heart, I quickly unclosed my eyes. My worst thoughts, then, were confirmed. The blackness of eternal night encompassed me. I struggled for breath. The intensity of the darkness seemed to oppress and stifle me. The atmosphere was intolerably close. I still lay quietly, and made effort to exercise my reason.

I brought to mind the inquisitorial proceedings, and attempted from that point to deduce my real condition. The sentence had passed, and it appeared to me that a very long interval of time had since elapsed. Yet not for a moment did I suppose myself actually dead. Such a supposition, notwithstanding what we read in fiction, is altogether inconsistent with real existence;—but where and in what state was I? The condemned to death, I knew, perished usually at the *autos-da-fé,* and one of these had been held on the very night of the day of my trial. Had I been remanded to my dungeon, to await the next sacrifice, which would not take place for many months? This I at once saw could not be. Victims had been in immediate demand. Moreover my dungeon, as well as all the condemned cells at Toledo, had stone floors, and light was not altogether excluded.

A fearful idea now suddenly drove the blood in torrents upon my heart, and for a brief period I once more relapsed into insensibility. Upon recovering, I at once started to my feet, trembling convulsively in every fibre. I thrust my arms wildly above and around me in all directions. I felt nothing; yet dreaded to move a step, lest I should be impeded by the walls of a *tomb*. Perspiration burst from every pore, and stood in cold big beads upon my forehead. The agony of suspense grew at length intolerable, and I cautiously moved forward, with my arms extended, and my eyes straining from their sockets, in the hope of catching some faint ray of light. I proceeded for many paces, but still all was blackness and vacancy. I breathed more freely. It seemed evident that mine was not, at least, the most hideous of fates.

And now, as I still continued to step cautiously onward, there came thronging upon my recollection a thousand vague rumours of the horrors of Toledo. Of the dungeons there had been strange things narrated—fables I had always deemed them—but yet strange, and too ghastly to repeat, save in a whisper. Was I left to perish of starvation in this subterranean world of darkness; or what fate perhaps even more fearful awaited me? That the result would be death, and a death of more than customary bitterness, I knew too well the character of my judges to doubt. The mode and the hour were all that occupied or distracted me.

My outstretched hands at length encountered some solid obstruction. It was a wall, seemingly of stone masonry—very smooth, slimy, and cold. I followed it up; stepping with all the careful distrust with which certain antique narratives had inspired me. This process, however, afforded me no means of ascertaining the dimensions of my dungeon; as I might make its circuit, and return to the point whence I set out, without being aware of the fact, so perfectly uniform seemed the wall I therefore sought the knife which had been in my pocket when led into the inquisitorial chamber, but it was gone; my clothes had been exchanged for a wrapper of coarse serge. I had thought of forcing the blade in some minute crevice of the masonry, so as to identify my point of departure.

The difficulty, nevertheless, was but trivial, although, in the disorder of my fancy, it seemed at first insuperable. I tore a part of the hem from the robe, and placed the fragment at full length, and at right angles to the wall. In groping my way around the prison, I could not fail to encounter this rag upon completing the circuit. So, at least, I thought, but I had not counted upon the extent of the dungeon or upon my own weakness. The ground was moist and slippery. I staggered onward for some time, when I stumbled and fell. My excessive fatigue induced me to remain prostrate, and sleep soon overtook me as I lay.

Upon awaking, and stretching forth an arm, I found beside me a loaf and a pitcher with water. I was too much exhausted to reflect upon this circumstance, but ate and drank with avidity. Shortly afterwards I resumed my tour around the prison, and with much toil came at last upon the fragment of the serge. Up to the period when I fell I had counted fifty-two paces, and upon resuming my walk I had counted forty-eight more, when I arrived at the rag. There were in all, then, a hundred paces; and, admitting two paces to the yard, I presumed the dungeon to be fifty yards in circuit. I had met, however, with many angles in the wall, and thus I could form no guess at the shape of the vault, for vault I could not help supposing it to be.

I had little object—certainly no hope—in these researches, but a vague curiosity prompted me to continue them. Quitting the wall, I resolved to cross the area of the enclosure. At first I proceeded with extreme caution, for the floor, although seemingly of solid material, was treacherous with slime. At length, however, I took courage and did not hesitate to step firmly—endeavouring to cross in as direct a line as possible. I had advanced some ten or twelve paces in this manner, when the remnant of the torn hem of my robe became entangled between my legs. I stepped on it, and fell violently on my face.

In the confusion attending my fall, I did not immediately apprehend a somewhat startling circumstance, which yet, in a few seconds afterward, and while I still lay prostrate, arrested my attention. It was this: my chin rested upon the floor of the prison, but my lips, and the upper portion of my head, although seemingly at a less elevation than the chin, touched nothing. At the same time, my forehead seemed bathed in a clammy vapour, and the peculiar smell of decayed fungus arose to my nostrils. I put forward my arm, and shuddered to find that I had fallen at the very brink of a circular pit, whose extent of course I had no means of ascertaining at the moment. Groping about the masonry just below the margin, I succeeded in dislodging a small fragment, and let it fall into the abyss. For many seconds I hearkened to its reverberations as it dashed against the sides of the chasm in its descent; at length there was a sullen plunge into water, succeeded by loud echoes. At the same moment there came a sound resembling the quick opening, and as rapid closing, of a door overhead, while a faint gleam of light flashed suddenly through the gloom, and as suddenly faded away.

I saw clearly the doom which had been prepared for me, and congratulated myself upon the timely accident by which I had escaped. Another step before my fall, and the world had seen me no more; and the death just avoided was of that very character which I had regarded as fabulous and frivolous in the tales respecting the Inquisition. To the victims of its tyranny, there was the choice of death with its direst physical agonies, or death with its most hideous moral horrors. I had been reserved for the latter. By long suffering my nerves had been unstrung, until I trembled at the sound of my own voice, and had become in every respect a fitting subject for the species of torture which awaited me.

Shaking in every limb, I groped my way back to the wall—resolving there to perish rather than risk the terrors of the wells, of which my imagination now pictured many in various positions about the dungeon. In other conditions of mind I might have had courage to end my misery at once by a plunge into one of these abysses; but now I was the veriest of cowards. Neither could I forget what I had read of these pits—that the *sudden* extinction of life formed no part of their most horrible plan.

Agitation of spirit kept me awake for many long hours; but at length I again slumbered. Upon arousing, I found by my side, as before, a loaf and a pitcher of water. A burning thirst consumed me, and I emptied the vessel at a draught. It must have been drugged, for scarcely had I drunk before I became irresistibly drowsy. A deep sleep fell upon me—a sleep like that of death. How long it lasted of course I know not; but when once again I unclosed my eyes the objects around me were visible. By a wild sulphurous lustre, the origin of which I could not at first determine, I was enabled to see the extent and aspect of the prison.

In its size I had been greatly mistaken. The whole circuit of its walls did not exceed twenty-five yards. For some minutes this fact occasioned me a world of vain trouble; vain indeed—for what could be of less importance, under the terrible circumstances which environed me, than the mere dimensions of my dungeon? But my soul took a wild interest in trifles, and I busied myself in endeavours to account for the error I had committed in my measurement.

The truth at length flashed upon me. In my first attempt at exploration I had counted fifty-two paces up to the period when I fell; I must then have been within a pace or two of the fragment of serge; in fact I had nearly performed the circuit of the vault. I then slept, and upon awaking, I must have returned upon my steps, thus supposing the circuit nearly double what it actually was. My confusion of mind prevented me from observing that I began my tour with the wall to the left, and ended it with the wall to the right.

I had been deceived, too, in respect to the shape of the enclosure. In feeling my way I had found many angles, and thus deduced an idea of great irregularity, so potent is the effect of total darkness upon one arousing from lethargy or sleep! The angles were simply those of a few slight depressions or niches at odd intervals. The general shape of the prison was square. What I had taken for masonry seemed now to be iron, or some other metal, in huge plates, whose sutures or joints occasioned the depression. The entire surface of this metallic enclosure was rudely daubed in all the hideous and repulsive devices to which the charnel superstition of the monks has given rise. The figures of fiends in aspects of menace, with skeleton forms and other more really fearful images, overspread and disfigured the walls. I observed that the outlines of these monstrosities were sufficiently distinct, but that the colours seemed faded and blurred, as if from the effects of a damp atmosphere. I now noticed the floor, too, which was of stone. In the centre yawned the circular pit from whose jaws I had escaped; but it was the only one in the dungeon.

All this I saw indistinctly and by much effort, for my personal condition had been greatly changed during slumber. I now lay upon my back, and at full length, on a species of low framework of wood. To this I was securely bound by a long strap resembling a surcingle. It passed in many convolutions about my limbs and body, leaving at liberty only my head, and my left arm to such extent that I could by dint of much exertion supply myself with food from an earthen dish which lay by my side on the floor. I saw to my horror that the pitcher had been removed. I say to my horror, for I was consumed with intolerable thirst. This thirst it appeared to be the design of my persecutors to stimulate, for the food in the dish was meat pungently seasoned.

Looking upward, I surveyed the ceiling of my prison. It was some thirty or forty feet overhead, and constructed much as the side walls. In one of its panels a very singular figure riveted my whole attention. It was the painted figure of Time as he is commonly represented, save that in lieu of a scythe he held what at a casual glance I supposed to be the pictured image of a huge pendulum, such as we see on antique clocks. There was something, however, in the appearance of this machine which caused me to regard it more attentively. While I gazed directly upward at it (for its position was immediately over my own), I fancied that I saw it in motion. In an instant afterward the fancy was confirmed. Its sweep was brief, and of course slow. I watched it for some minutes, somewhat in fear but more in wonder. Wearied at length with observing its dull movement, I turned my eyes upon the other objects in the cell.

A slight noise attracted my notice, and looking to the floor, I saw several enormous rats traversing it. They had issued from the well which lay just within view to my right. Even then while I gazed, they came up in troops, hurriedly, with ravenous eyes, allured by the scent of the meat. From this it required much effort and attention to scare them away.

It might have been half-an-hour, perhaps even an hour (for I could take but imperfect note of time), before I against cast my eyes upward. What I then saw confounded and amazed me. The sweep of the pendulum had increased in extent by nearly a yard.

As a natural consequence, its velocity was also much greater. But what mainly disturbed me was the idea that it had perceptibly *descended*. I now observed, with what horror it is needless to say, that its nether extremity was formed of a crescent of glittering steel, about a foot in length from horn to horn; the horns upward, and the under edge evidently as keen as that of a razor. Like a razor also it seemed massy and heavy, tapering from the edge into a solid and broad structure above. It was appended to a weighty rod of brass, and the whole *hissed* as it swung through the air.

I could no longer doubt the doom prepared for me by monkish ingenuity in torture. My cognisance of the pit had become known to the inquisitorial agents—*the pit*, whose horrors had been destined for so bold a recusant as myself, *the pit*, typical of hell, and regarded by rumour as the Ultima Thule of all their punishments. The plunge into this pit I had avoided by the merest of accidents, and I knew that surprise or entrapment into torment formed an important portion of all the *grotesquerie* of these dungeon deaths. Having failed to fall, it was no part of the demon plan to hurl me into the abyss, and thus (there being no alternative) a different and a milder destruction awaited me. Milder! I half smiled in my agony as I thought of such application of such a term.

What boots it to tell of the long, long hours of horror more than mortal, during which I counted the rushing oscillations of the steel! Inch by inch—line by line—with a descent only appreciable at intervals that seemed ages—down and still down it came! Days passed—it might have been that many days passed—ere it swept so closely over me as to fan me with its acrid breath. The odour of the sharp steel forced itself into my nostrils. I prayed—I wearied heaven with my prayer for its more speedy descent. I grew frantically mad, and struggled to force myself upward against the sweep of the fearful scimitar. And then I fell suddenly calm and lay smiling at the glittering death as a child at some rare bauble.

There was another interval of utter insensibility; it was brief, for upon again lapsing into life there had been no perceptible descent in the pendulum. But it might have been long—for I knew there were demons who took note of my swoon, and who could have arrested the vibration at pleasure. Upon my recovery, too, I felt very—oh! inexpressibly—sick and weak, as if through long inanition. Even amid the agonies of that period the human nature craved food. With painful effort I outstretched my left arm as far as my bonds permitted, and took possession of the small remnant which had been spared me by the rats.

As I put a portion of it within my lips there rushed to my mind a half-formed thought of joy—of hope. Yet what business had *I* with hope? It was, as I say, a half-formed thought—man has many such, which are never completed. I felt that it was of joy—of hope; but I felt also that it had perished in its formation. In vain I struggled to perfect—to regain it. Long suffering had nearly annihilated all my ordinary powers of mind. I was an imbecile—an idiot

The vibration of the pendulum was at right angles to my length. I saw that the crescent was designed to cross the region of the heart. It would fray the serge of my robe; it would return and repeat its operations—again—and again. Notwithstanding its terrifically wide sweep (some thirty feet or more) and the hissing vigour of its descent, sufficient to sunder these very walls of iron, still the fraying of my robe would be all that, for several minutes, it would accomplish; and at this thought I paused. I dared not go farther than this reflection. I dwelt upon it with a pertinacity of attention—as if, in so dwelling, I could arrest *here* the descent of the steel. I forced myself to ponder upon the sound of the crescent as it should pass across the garment upon the peculiar thrilling sensation which the friction of cloth produces on the nerves. I pondered upon all this frivolity until my teeth were on edge.

Down—steadily down it crept. I took a frenzied pleasure in contrasting its downward with its lateral velocity. To the right— to the left—far and wide—with the shriek of a damned spirit! to my heart with the stealthy pace of the tiger! I alternately laughed and howled, as the one or the other idea grew pre-dominant.

Down—certainly, relentlessly, down! It vibrated within three inches of my bosom! I struggled violently—furiously—to free my left arm. This was free only from the elbow to the hand. I could reach the latter, from the platter beside me, to my mouth with great effort, but no farther. Could I have broken the fas-tenings above the elbow, I would have seized and attempted to arrest the pendulum. I might as well have attempted to arrest an avalanche!

Down—still unceasingly—still inevitably down! I gasped and struggled at each vibration. I shrunk convulsively at its every sweep. My eyes followed its outward or upward whirls with the eagerness of the most unmeaning despair; they closed themselves spasmodically at the descent, although death would have been a relief, O, how unspeakable! Still I quivered in every nerve to think how slight a sinking of the machinery would precipitate that keen glistening axe upon my bosom. It was *hope* that prompted the nerve to quiver—the frame to shrink. It was *hope*—the hope that triumphs on the rack—that whispers to the death-condemned even in the dungeons of the Inquisition.

I saw that some ten or twelve vibrations would bring the steel in actual contact with my robe, and with this observation there suddenly came over my spirit all the keen, collected calmness of despair. For the first time during many hours, or perhaps days, I *thought*. It now occurred to me that the bandage or surcingle which enveloped me was unique. I was tied by no separate cord. The first stroke of the razor-like crescent athwart any portion of the band would so detach it that it might be unwound from my person by means of my left hand. But how fearful, in that case, the proximity of the steel! The result of the slightest strug-gle, how deadly! Was it likely, moreover, that the minions of the torturer had not foreseen and provided for this possibility? Was it probable that the bandage crossed my bosom in the track of the pendulum? Dreading to find my faint, and, as it seemed, my last hope frustrated, I so far elevated my head as to obtain a distinct view of my breast. The surcingle enveloped my limbs and body close in all directions *save in the path of the destroying crescent.*

Scarcely had I dropped my head back into its original position when there flashed upon my mind what I cannot better describe than as the unformed half of that idea of deliverance to which I have previously alluded, and of which a moiety only floated indeterminately through my brain when I raised food to my burning lips. The whole thought was now present—feeble, scarcely sane, scarcely definite, but still entire. I proceeded at once, with the nervous energy of despair, to attempt its execution.

For many hours the immediate vicinity of the low framework upon which I lay had been literally swarming with rats. They were wild, bold, ravenous, their red eyes glaring upon me as if they waited but for motionlessness on my part to make me their prey. "To what food," I thought, "have they been accustomed in the well?"

They had devoured, in spite of all my efforts to prevent them, all but a small remnant of the contents of the dish. I had fallen into an habitual see-saw or wave of the hand about the platter; and at length the unconscious uniformity of the movement deprived it of effect. In their voracity the vermin frequently fastened their sharp fangs in my fingers. With the particles of the oily and spicy viand which now remained, I thoroughly rubbed the bandage wherever I could reach it; then, raising my hand from the floor, I lay breathlessly still.

At first the ravenous animals were startled and terrified at the change—at the cessation of movement. They shrank alarmedly back; many sought the well. But this was only for a moment. I had not counted in vain upon their voracity. Observing that I remained without motion, one or two of the boldest leaped upon the frame-work and smelt at the surcingle. This seemed the signal for a general rush. Forth from the well they hurried in fresh troops. They clung to the wood, they overran it, and leaped in hundreds upon my person. The measured movement of the pendulum disturbed them not at all. Avoiding its strokes, they busied themselves with the anointed bandage. They pressed, they swarmed upon me in ever accumulating heaps. They writhed upon my throat; their cold lips sought my own; I was half stifled by their thronging pressure; disgust, for which the world has no name, swelled my bosom, and chilled with heavy clamminess my heart. Yet one minute and I felt that the struggle would be over. Plainly I perceived the loosening of the bandage. I knew that in more than one place it must be already severed. With a more than human resolution I lay *still*.

Nor had I erred in my calculations, nor had I endured in vain. I at length felt that I was *free*. The surcingle hung in ribands from my body. But the stroke of the pendulum already pressed upon my bosom. It had divided the serge of the robe. It had cut through the linen beneath. Twice again it swung, and a sharp sense of pain shot through every nerve. But the moment of escape had arrived. At a wave of my hand my deliverers hurried tumultuously away. With a steady movement, cautious, sidelong, shrinking, and slow, I slid from the embrace of the bandage and beyond the reach of the scimitar. For the moment, at least, *I was free*.

Free!—and in the grasp of the Inquisition! I had scarcely stepped from my wooden bed of horror upon the stone floor of the prison, when the motion of the hellish machine ceased, and I beheld it drawn up by some invisible force through the ceiling. This was a lesson which I took desperately to heart. My every motion was undoubtedly watched. Free!—I had but escaped death in one form of agony to be delivered unto worse than death in some other. With that thought I rolled my eyes nervously around on the barriers of iron that hemmed me in. Something unusual—some change which at first I could not appreciate distinctly—it was obvious had taken place in the apartment. For many minutes of a dreamy and trembling abstraction I busied myself in vain, unconnected conjecture. During this period I became aware, for the first time, of the origin of the sulphurous light which illumined the cell. It proceeded from a fissure about half-an-inch in width extending entirely around the prison at the base of the walls which thus appeared, and were completely separated from the floor. I endeavoured, but of course in vain, to look through the aperture.

As I arose from the attempt the mystery of the alteration in the chamber broke at once upon my understanding. I have observed that although the outlines of the figures upon the walls were sufficiently distinct, yet the colours seemed blurred and indefinite. These colours had now assumed, and were momentarily assuming, a startling and most intense brilliancy, that gave to the spectral and fiendish portraitures an aspect that might have thrilled even firmer nerves than my own. Demon eyes, of a wild and ghastly vivacity, glared upon me in a thousand directions where none had been visible before, and gleamed with the lurid lustre of a fire that I could not force my imagination to regard as unreal.

Unreal!—Even while I breathed there came to my nostrils the breath of the vapour of heated iron! A suffocating odour pervaded the prison! A deeper glow settled each moment in the eyes that glared at my agonies! A richer tint of crimson diffused itself over the pictured horrors of blood. I panted I I gasped for breath! There could be no doubt of the design of my tormentors—oh, most unrelenting! oh, most demoniac of men I I shrank from the glowing metal to the centre of the cell. Amid the thought of the fiery destruction that impended, the idea of the coolness of the well came over my soul like balm. I rushed to its deadly brink. I threw my straining vision below. The glare from the enkindled roof illumined its inmost recesses. Yet, for a wild moment, did my spirit refuse to comprehend the meaning of what I saw. At length it forced—it wrestled its way into my soul—it burned itself in upon my shuddering reason. for a voice to speak!—oh, horror!—oh, any horror but this! With a shriek I rushed from the margin and buried my face in my hands—weeping bitterly.

The heat rapidly increased, and once again I looked up, shuddering as with a fit of the ague. There had been a second change in the cell and now the change was obviously in the *form*. As before, it was in vain that I at first endeavoured to appreciate or understand what was taking place. But not long was I left in doubt. The Inquisitorial vengeance had been hurried by my two-fold escape, and there was to be no more dallying with the King of Terrors. The room had been square. I saw that two of its iron angles were now acute—two, consequently, obtuse. The fearful difference quickly increased with a low rumbling or moaning sound. In an instant the apartment had shifted its form into that of a lozenge.

But the alteration stopped not here—I neither hoped nor desired it to stop. I could have clasped the red walls to my bosom as a garment of eternal peace. "Death," I said, "any death but that of the pit!" Fool! might I not have known that *into the pit* it was the object of the burning iron to urge me? Could I resist its glow? or if even that, could I withstand its pressure? And now, flatter and flatter grew the lozenge, with a rapidity that left me no time for contemplation. Its centre, and, of course, its great-est width, came just over the yawning gulf. I shrank back—but the closing walls pressed me resistlessly onward. At length for my seared and writhing body there was no longer an inch of foothold on the firm floor of the prison. I struggled no more, but the agony of my soul found vent in one loud, long, and final scream of despair. I felt that I tottered upon the brink—I averted my eyes—

There was a discordant hum of human voices! There was a loud blast as of many trumpets! There was a harsh grating as of a thousand thunders! The fiery walls rushed back! An outstretched arm caught my own as I fell fainting into the abyss. It was that of General Lasalle. The French Army had entered Toledo. The Inquisition was in the hands of its enemies.

A Tale of Jerusalem

Intensos rigidarn in frontern ascendere canos
Passus erat——
　　　—Lucan—De Catone
　　——a bristly bore.
　　　　　Translation

"Let us hurry to the walls," said Abel-Phittim to Buzi-Ben-Levi and Simeon the Pharisee, on the tenth day of the month Thammuz, in the year of the world three thousand nine hundred and forty-one—"let us hasten to the ramparts adjoining the gate of Benjamin, which is in the city of David, and overlooking the camp of the uncircumcised; for it is the last hour of the fourth watch, being sunrise; and the idolaters, in fulfilment of the promise of Pompey, should be awaiting us with the lambs for the sacrifices."

Simeon, Abel-Phittim, and Buzi-Ben-Levi were the Gizbarim, or sub-collectors of the offering, in the holy city of Jerusalem.

"Verily," replied the Pharisee; "let us hasten: for this generosity in the heathen is unwonted; and fickle-mindedness has ever been an attribute of the worshippers of Baal."

"'That they are fickle-minded and treacherous is as true as the Pentateuch," said Buzi-Ben-Levi, "but that is only toward the people of Adonai. When was it ever known that the Ammonites proved wanting to their own interests? Methinks it is no great stretch of generosity to allow us lambs for the altar of the Lord, receiving in lieu thereof thirty silver *shekels* per head!"

"Thou forgettest, however, Ben-Levi," replied Abel-Phittim, "that the Roman Pompey, who is now impiously besieging the city of the Most High, has no assurity that we apply not the lambs thus purchased for the altar, to the sustenance of the body, rather than of the spirit."

"Now, by the five corners of my beard!" shouted the Phari-see, who belonged to the sect called The Dashers (that little knot of saints whose manner of *dashing* and lacerating the feet against the pavement was long a thorn and a reproach to less zealous devotees—a stumbling-block to less gifted perambulators)—"by the five corners of that beard which, as a priest, I am forbidden to shave!-have we lived to see the day when a blaspheming and idolatrous upstart of Rome shall accuse us of appropriating to the appetites of the flesh the most holy and consecrated ele-ments? Have we lived to see the day when—"

"Let us not question the motives of the Philistine," inter-rupted Abel-Phittim' "for today we profit for the first time by his avarice or by his generosity; but rather let us hurry to the ramparts, lest offerings should be wanting for that altar whose fire the rains of heaven can not extinguish, and whose pillars of smoke no tempest can turn aside."

That part of the city to which our worthy Gizbarim now hastened, and which bore the name of its architect, King David, was esteemed the most strongly fortified district of Jerusalem; being situated upon the steep and lofty hill of Zion. Here, a broad, deep, circumvolutory trench, hewn from the solid rock, was defended by a wall of great strength erected upon its inner edge. This wall was adorned, at regular interspaces, by square towers of white marble; the lowest sixty, and the highest one hundred and twenty cubits in height. But, in the vicinity of the gate of Benjamin, the wall arose by no means from the margin of the fosse. On the contrary, between the level of the ditch and the basement of the rampart sprang up a perpendicular cliff of two hundred and fifty cubits, forming part of the precipitous Mount Moriah. So that when Simeon and his associates arrived on the summit of the tower called Adoni-Bezek—the loftiest of all the turrets around about Jerusalem, and the usual place of conference with the besieging army—they looked down upon the camp of the enemy from an eminence excelling by many feet that of the Pyramid of Cheops, and, by several, that of the temple of Belus.

"Verily," sighed the Pharisee, as he peered dizzily over the precipice, "the uncircumcised are as the sands by the seashore-as the locusts in the wilderness! The valley of the King hath become the valley of Adommin."

"And yet," added Ben-Levi, "thou canst not point me out a Philistine—no, not one—from Aleph to Tau-from the wilderness to the battlements—who seemeth any bigger than the letter Jod!"

"Lower away the basket with the *shekels* of silver!" here shouted a Roman soldier in a hoarse, rough voice, which appeared to issue from the regions of Pluto—"lower away the basket with the accursed coin which it has broken the jaw of a noble Roman to pronounce! Is it thus you evince your gratitude to our master Pompeius, who, in his condescension, has thought fit to listen to your idolatrous importunities? The god Phoebus, who is a true god, has been charioted for an hour-and were you not to be on the ramparts by sunrise? Ædepol! do you think that we, the conquerors of the world, have nothing better to do than stand waiting by the walls of every kennel, to traffic with the dogs of the earth? Lower away! I say—and see that your trumpery be bright in color and just in weight!"

"El Elohim!" ejaculated the Pharisee, as the discordant tones of the centurion rattled up the crags of the precipice, and fainted away against the temple—"El Elohim!—*who* is the god Phoebus?—*whom* doth the blasphemer invoke? Thou, Buzi-Ben-Levi! who art read in the laws of the Gentiles, and hast sojourned among them who dabble with the Teraphim!—is it Nergal of whom the idolater speaketh?—-or Ashimah?—or Nibhaz,—or Tartak?—or Adramalech?—or Anamalech?—or Succoth-Benith?—or Dagon?—or Belial?—or Baal-Perith?—or Baal-Peor?—or Baal-Zebub?"

"Verily it is neither-but beware how thou lettest the rope slip too rapidly through thy fingers; for should the wicker-work chance to hang on the projection of Yonder crag, there will be a woeful outpouring of the holy things of the sanctuary."

By the assistance of some rudely constructed machinery, the heavily laden basket was now carefully lowered down among the multitude; and, from the giddy pinnacle, the Romans were seen gathering confusedly round it; but owing to the vast height and the prevalence of a fog, no distinct view of their operations could be obtained.

Half an hour had already elapsed.

"We shall be too late!" sighed the Pharisee, as at the expiration of this period he looked over into the abyss—"we shall be too late! we shall be turned out of office by the Katholim."

"No more," responded Abel-Phittim—"no more shall we feast upon the fat of the land-no longer shall our beards be odorous with frankincense—our loins girded up with fine linen from the Temple."

"Racal" swore Ben-Levi, "Racal do they mean to defraud us of the purchase money? or, Holy Moses! are they weighing the *shekels* of the tabernacle?"

"They have given the signal at last!" cried the Pharisee— "they have given the signal at last! pull away, Abel-Phittim!— and thou, Buzi-Ben-Levi, pull away!—for verily the Philistines have either still hold upon the basket, or the Lord hath softened their hearts to place therein a beast of good weight!" And the Gizbarim pulled away, while their burden swung heavily upward through the still increasing mist.

★★★★★★

"*Booshoh he!*"—as, at the conclusion of an hour, some object at the extremity of the rope became indistinctly visible— "*Booshoh he!*" was the exclamation which burst from the lips of Ben-Levi.

"*Booshoh he!*—for shame!—it is a ram from the thickets of Engedi, and as rugged as the valley of Jehoshaphat!"

"It is a firstling of the flock," said Abel-Phittim, "I know him by the bleating of his lips, and the innocent folding of his limbs. His eyes are more beautiful than the jewels of the Pectoral, and his flesh is like the honey of Hebron."

"It is a fatted calf from the pastures of Bashan," said the Pharisee, "the heathen have dealt wonderfully with us——let us raise up our voices in a psalm—let us give thanks on the shawm and on the psaltery-on the harp and on the huggab-on the cythern and on the sackbut!"

It was not until the basket had arrived within a few feet of the Gizbarim that a low grunt betrayed to their perception a *hog* of no common size.

"Now El Emanu!" slowly and with upturned eyes ejaculated the trio, as, letting go their hold, the emancipated porker tumbled headlong among the Philistines, "El Emanu!—God be with us—it is *the unutterable flesh!*"